SIX NOVELS

The Vagabond   Chéri   The Last of Chéri
The Ripening Seed   The Cat   Gigi

Colette

SECKER & WARBURG
LONDON

This selection first published in England 1988 by
Martin Secker & Warburg Limited
Michelin House, 81 Fulham Road
London SW3 6RB

LA VAGABONDE par Colette Willy, Paris, P. Ollendorff, 1911.
English translation from the *Fleuron* edition, Vol. IV, oeuvres
complètes de Colette de l'Académie Goncourt (1949), first
published in the Uniform Edition (1954) by Martin Secker &
Warburg Ltd. Reprinted 1954, 1974.

CHÉRI, Paris, A. Fayard, 1920.
English translation published by Gollancz, 1930.
Translated from the *Fleuron* edition, oeuvres complètes de
Colette de l'Académie Goncourt (1949), and published in the
Uniform Edition (1951) by Martin Secker & Warburg Ltd.
Reprinted 1951, 1961, 1968, 1972, 1974.

LA FIN DE CHÉRI, Paris, E. Flammarion, 1926.
English translation published by Gollancz, 1933.
Translated from the *Fleuron* edition, oeuvres complètes de
Colette de l'Académie Goncourt (1949) and first published
(1951) by Martin Secker & Warburg Ltd. Reprinted 1951, new
edition 1954, reprinted 1961, 1969, 1973.

LE BLÉ EN HERBE
Translated from the *Fleuron* edition, oeuvres complètes de
Colette de l'Académie Goncourt (1949) and first published
(1955) by Martin Secker & Warburg Ltd. New edition 1969.

LA CHATTE, Paris, 1933, Bernard Grasset
GIGI, Lausanne, 1944, La Guilde du Livre
English translation from the *Fleuron* edition, oeuvres complètes
de Colette de l'Académie Goncourt (1949) and first published
(1953) by Martin Secker & Warburg Ltd. Reprinted 1957,
reissued 1971.

British Library Cataloguing in Publication Data

Colette
   Six novels.
   I. Title
   843'.912[F]   PQ2605.028
ISBN 0–436–10522–5

Printed in Great Britain by
Mackays of Chatham Ltd, Chatham, Kent

CONTENTS

THE VAGABOND

Translated by
Enid McLeod

PART ONE

ONE

TEN thirty. . . . Once again I'm ready too soon. My friend Brague, who helped me when I first began miming, often takes me to task for this in that salty language of his:

"You poor boob of an amateur! You've always got ants in your pants. If we listened to you we'd be putting on our make-up base at half-past seven in the middle of bolting the *hors-d'œuvre!*"

After three years of music-hall and theatre I'm still the same: always ready too soon.

Ten thirty-five. . . . I'd better open that book lying on the make-up shelf, even though I've read it over and over again, or the copy of *Paris-Sport* the dresser was marking just now with my eyebrow pencil; otherwise I'll find myself all alone, face to face with that painted mentor who gazes at me from the other side of the looking-glass, with deep-set eyes under lids smeared with purplish grease-paint. Her cheek-bones are as brightly coloured as garden phlox and her blackish-red lips gleam as though they were varnished. She gazes at me for a long time and I know she is going to speak to me. She is going to say:

"Is that you there? All alone, there in that cage where idle, impatient, imprisoned hands have scored the white walls with interlaced initials and embellished them with crude, indecent shapes? On those plaster walls reddened

nails, like yours, have unconsciously inscribed the appeal
of the forsaken. Behind you a feminine hand has carved
Marie, and the name ends in a passionate mounting
flourish, like a cry to heaven. Is it you there, all alone
under that ceiling booming and vibrating beneath the
feet of the dancers, like the floor of a mill in action? Why
are you there, all alone? And why not somewhere else?"

Yes, this is the dangerous, lucid hour. Who will knock
at the door of my dressing-room, what face will come
between me and the painted mentor peering at me from
the other side of the looking-glass? Chance, my master
and my friend, will, I feel sure, deign once again to send
me the spirits of his unruly kingdom. All my trust is
now in him—and in myself. But above all in him, for
when I go under he always fishes me out, seizing and
shaking me like a life-saving dog whose teeth tear my
skin a little every time. So now, whenever I despair, I
no longer expect my end, but some bit of luck, some
commonplace little miracle which, like a glittering link,
will mend again the necklace of my days.

Faith, that is what it is, genuine faith, as blind as it
sometimes pretends to be, with all the dissembling
renunciations of faith, and that obstinacy which makes
it continue to hope even at the moment of crying. "I am
utterly forsaken!" There is no doubt that, if ever my
heart were to call my master Chance by another name, I
should make an excellent Catholic.

How the floor vibrates this evening! It's obvious that
it's a cold night: the Russian dancers are warming themselves up! When they all shout "Yoo!" in chorus, in
voices as shrill and hoarse as those of young pigs, it will
be ten past eleven. My clock is infallible, it does not vary
by so much as five minutes in a month. Ten o'clock: I
arrive; Mme Cavalier is singing her three songs, *The*

Little Guttersnipes, The Farewell Kiss, and *The Little You-know-what.* Ten ten: Antonieff and his dogs. Ten twenty-two: shots, barks, end of dog-act. The iron staircase creaks and someone coughs: Jadin is coming down. She swears in the middle of her coughing because she's treading on the hem of her frock; it happens every time. Ten thirty-five: Whimsical Bouty. Ten forty-seven: the Russian dancers, and, finally, eleven ten: me!

Me. As that word came into my head, I involuntarily looked in the mirror. There's no getting away from it, it really is me there behind that mask of purplish rouge, my eyes ringed with a halo of blue grease-paint beginning to melt. Can the rest of my face be going to melt also? What if nothing were to remain from my whole reflection but a streak of dyed colour stuck to the glass like a long, muddy tear?

It's absolutely freezing in here! I rub my hands together, grey with cold under the wet white which is beginning to crack. Good Lord! the radiator pipes are icy; it is Saturday and on Saturdays here they rely on the high-spirited popular audience, rowdy and slightly drunk, to warm the auditorium. No one has given a thought to the artistes' dressing-rooms.

The door shudders under a blow from a fist, which makes my very ears quiver. I open it to my pal Brague, dressed as a swarthy Roumanian bandit, and conscientious as ever.

"You know it's our turn next?"

"Yes I know. And about time too! I'm frozen to death!"

At the top of the iron staircase leading to the stage, the good, dry, dusty warmth wraps me round like a comfortable dirty cloak. While the ever-meticulous Brague keeps an eye on the setting of the scene and sees to the raising of the stage lights—for a sunset effect—I mechanically glue my eye to the luminous peephole in the drop curtain.

There's a grand Saturday house in this favourite local *café-concert*. The auditorium is dark, as the projectors are not strong enough to illuminate it, and you might bet a shilling you would not find a collar from the tenth row of the stalls to the second gallery! A pall of reddish smoke floats over it all, full of the horrible smell of stale tobacco and twopenny cigars smoked too far down. The stage-boxes, on the other hand, look like four flower-stands. It is indeed a fine Saturday house but, as little Jadin vigorously puts it: "To hell with the house, I don't get a rake-off on the takings!"

As soon as the first bars of our overture strike up, I feel soothed and ready for anything, grown all of a sudden gay and irresponsible. With my elbows propped on the canvas balcony, I calmly consider the layer of powdered dirt—composed of mud from shoes, dust, hairs of dogs and crushed gum—covering the boards where soon my bare knees will be crawling, and sniff an artificial red geranium. From that moment I no longer belong to myself, and all is well. I know that I shall not fall when I dance, that my heel will not catch in the hem of my skirt, and that when Brague handles me roughly I shall collapse without grazing my elbows or flattening my nose. I shall keep a straight face when I vaguely hear the little scene-shifter making noises like farts behind the wings at the most dramatic moments to make us laugh. The harsh light sustains me, the music governs my gestures, a mysterious discipline controls and protects me . . . all is well.

All is indeed well! Our dun-coloured Saturday public has rewarded us with an uproar compounded of bravos, catcalls, shrieks and well-meant ribaldries, and I received, plumb on a corner of my mouth, a little bunch of cheap carnations, those anaemic white carnations which the street flower-sellers dip in carmine-tinted water to dye them. I take it home, pinned to the lapel of my jacket; it smells of pepper and wet dog.

I take home also a letter which has just been handed to me:

"Madame, I was in the first row of the stalls. Your gifts as a mime incline me to think that you must possess others, more special and still more captivating. Give me the pleasure of supping this evening with me."

It is signed "Marquis de Fontanges"—yes, it really is— and written from the Café du Delta. What a number of descendants of noble families which one had thought extinct long ago have taken up residence at the Café du Delta! Unlikely as it seems, I can't help suspecting a close relationship between this Marquis de Fontanges and a Comte de Lavallière who, last week, offered me a "five o'clock" in his bachelors' chambers. Commonplace impostures though these are, one can divine in them that romantic admiration for high life, that respect for a title, which lurks in this tough neighbourhood under more than one battered cap.

TWO

As always, I give a great sigh when I close the door of my ground-floor flat behind me. Is it a sigh of weariness, or relaxation, or relief? Or does it spring from the bitterness of solitude? Better not think of it, far better not!

But what on earth is the matter with me tonight? It must be this icy December fog, like particles of frost hanging in the air, quivering in an iridescent halo round the gas lamps and melting on one's lips with a taste of creosote. And besides, this new quarter where I live, looming up all white behind Les Ternes, is enough to discourage both one's eyes and one's spirit.

My street, under the greenish gas at this hour, is a morass of toffee-like, creamy mud—coffee-coloured, maroon and caramel yellow—a sort of crumbling, slushy trifle in which the floating bits of meringue are lumps of concrete. Even my house, the only one in the street, has a sort of "it can't be true" look. But its new walls and thin partitions offer, at a modest rent, a shelter sufficiently comfortable for "ladies on their own" like me.

When you are a "lady on your own", in other words the landlords' abomination, outcast and terror all rolled into one, you take what you find, lodge where you may and put up with newly plastered walls.

The house where I live compassionately shelters quite a colony of "ladies on their own". On the mezzanine floor we have the acknowledged mistress of Young, of Young-Automobiles; above, the girl-friend, very much "kept", of the Comte de Bravailles; higher up are two fair-haired sisters, both of whom are visited every day by the same man, a very-correct-gentleman-in-industry; higher still a terrible little tart makes as much of a racket night and day as an unleashed fox-terrier, screaming, playing the piano, singing and throwing empty bottles out of the window.

"She's a disgrace to the house," Madame Young-Automobiles said one day.

Finally, on the ground floor, there is myself who neither screams, nor plays the piano, nor ever receives gentlemen and still less ladies. The little tart on the fourth floor makes too much noise and I not enough, as the concierge does not fail to remark to me. "It's funny, one never knows whether Madame is there because one doesn't hear her. One would never think she was an artiste!"

What an ugly December night it is! The radiator smells of iodoform, Blandine has forgotten to put my hot-water bottle in my bed, and even my dog is in a bad mood. Grumpy and shivering, she merely casts one black and white glance at me, without leaving her basket. I must say! I don't expect triumphal arches and illuminations, but all the same . . .

No need to search the place, to peer in the corners or look under the bed, there is no one here, no one but myself. What I see in the big looking-glass in my bed-room is no longer the painted image of an itinerant music-hall artiste. It reflects only—myself.

Behold me then, just as I am! This evening I shall not be able to escape the meeting in the long mirror, the soliloquy which I have a hundred times avoided, accepted, fled from, taken up again and broken off. I feel in advance, alas, the uselessness of trying to change the subject. This

evening I shall not feel sleepy, and the spell of a book—
even a brand-new book with that smell of printers' ink
and paper fresh from the press that makes you think of
coal and trains and departures!—even that spell will not
be able to distract me from myself.

Behold me then, just as I am! Alone, alone, and for the
rest of my life, no doubt. Already alone; it's early for
that. When I turned thirty I did not feel cast down
because mine is a face that depends on the expression
which animates it, the colour of my eyes, and the defiant
smile that plays over it—what Marinetti calls my *gaiezza
volpina*. But if I look like a fox, it's a fox without guile,
which a hen could catch! And a fox without rapacity, one
that remembers only the trap and the cage. A gay-looking
fox, if you like, but only because the corners of its mouth
and eyes look as if they were smiling. A captive fox, tired
of dancing to the sound of music.

It is true enough that I do look like a fox. But a slender,
pretty fox is not an ugly thing, is it? Brague says too that
I look like a rat when I purse my lips and blink my
eyelids so as to see better. I see nothing to mind in that.

But how I dislike seeing myself with that drooping
mouth and those slack shoulders, the weight of my whole
sad body slumped on one leg! My hair hangs dank and
lank and in a little while I shall have to brush it for a long
time to give it back its shining beaver brown. My eyes
are still faintly ringed with blue eye-shadow and there's a
wavering trace of red on my nails. It will take me at
least fifty good minutes of bathing and grooming to get
rid of all that.

It is one o'clock already. What am I waiting for? A
smart little lash with the whip to make the obstinate
creature go on again. But no one will give it me because
. . . because I am alone. How clearly one sees, in that long

frame which holds my reflection, that I'm used already to living alone!

No matter what visitor, for a mere tradesman, or even for my charwoman Blandine, I should raise this drooping neck, straighten that slouching hip and clasp those empty hands. But tonight I am so alone.

Alone! Really one might think I was pitying myself for it!

"If you live all alone," said Brague, "it's because you really want to, isn't it?"

Certainly I "really" want to, and in fact I *want* to, quite simply. Only, well . . . there are days when solitude, for someone of my age, is a heady wine which intoxicates you with freedom, others when it is a bitter tonic, and still others when it is a poison which makes you beat your head against the wall.

This evening I would much prefer not to say which it is; all I want is to remain undecided, and not to be able to say whether the shiver which will seize me when I slip between the cold sheets comes from fear or contentment.

Alone . . . and for a long time past. The proof is that I am giving way to the habit of talking to myself and of holding conversations with my dog, and the fire, and my own reflection. It is an idiosyncracy which recluses and old prisoners fall into; but I'm not like them, I'm free. And if I talk to myself it is because I have a writer's need to express my thoughts in rhythmical language.

Facing me from the other side of the looking-glass, in that mysterious reflected room, is the image of "a woman of letters who has turned out badly". They also say of me that I'm "on the stage", but they never call me an actress. Why? The nuance is subtle, but there is certainly a polite refusal, on the part both of the public and my friends themselves, to accord me any standing in this career which I have nevertheless adopted. A woman of letters who has turned out badly: that is what I must remain for everyone, I who no longer write, who deny myself the pleasure, the luxury of writing.

To write, to be able to write, what does it mean? It means spending long hours dreaming before a white page, scribbling unconsciously, letting your pen play round a blot of ink and nibble at a half-formed word, scratching it, making it bristle with darts and adorning it with antennae and paws until it loses all resemblance to a legible word and turns into a fantastic insect or a fluttering creature half butterfly, half fairy.

To write is to sit and stare, hypnotised, at the reflection of the window in the silver ink-stand, to feel the divine fever mounting to one's cheeks and forehead while the hand that writes grows blissfully numb upon the paper. It also means idle hours curled up in the hollow of the divan, and then the orgy of inspiration from which one emerges stupefied and aching all over, but already recompensed and laden with treasures that one unloads slowly on to the virgin page in the little round pool of light under the lamp.

To write is to pour one's innermost self passionately upon the tempting paper, at such frantic speed that sometimes one's hand struggles and rebels, overdriven by the impatient god who guides it—and to find, next day, in place of the golden bough that bloomed miraculously in that dazzling hour, a withered bramble and a stunted flower.

To write is the joy and torment of the idle. Oh to write! From time to time I feel a need, sharp as thirst in summer, to note and to describe. And then I take up my

pen again and attempt the perilous and elusive task of
seizing and pinning down, under its flexible double-
pointed nib, the many-hued, fugitive, thrilling adjec-
tive. . . . The attack does not last long; it is but the
itching of an old scar.

It takes up too much time to write. And the trouble is,
I am no Balzac! The fragile story I am constructing
crumbles away when the tradesman rings, or the shoe-
maker sends in his bill, when the solicitor, or one's
counsel, telephones, or when the theatrical agent summons me to his office for "a social engagement at the
house of some people of very good position but not in
the habit of paying large fees".

The problem is, since I have been living alone, that I
have had first to live, then to divorce, and then to go on
living. To do all that demands incredible activity and
persistence. And to get where? Is there, for me, no other
haven than this commonplace room done up in gimcrack
Louis XVI? Must I stay for ever before this impenetrable
mirror where I come up against myself, face to face?

Tomorrow is Sunday: that means afternoon and evening performances at the *Empyrée-Clichy*. Two o'clock
already! High time for a woman of letters who has
turned out badly to go to sleep.

THREE

"Look alive, for Heaven's sake, look alive! Jadin's not here!"

"How d'you mean, not here? Is she ill?"

"Ill? I'll say! On the spree, more like. The result's the same for us: we go on twenty minutes sooner!"

The mime Brague has just emerged from his dressing-room as I pass, a frightening sight under his khaki-coloured make-up base, and I rush to my dressing-room, full of dismay at the thought that, for the first time in my life, I may be late.

Jadin's not here! I hurry, trembling with nerves, for you can't trifle with our local public, especially at a Sunday matinée. If, as our wild-beast tamer of a stage-manager says, we let it "get hungry" for five minutes between two acts, hootings and cigarette ends and orange peel automatically begin to fly.

Jadin not here! We might have known it would happen one of these days.

Jadin is a little singer, so new to the *café-concert* that she has not yet had time to peroxide her light brown hair; she came straight to the stage from the outer boule-vards, flabbergasted at being able to earn two hundred and ten francs a month by singing. She is eighteen. Luck—should one call it?—immediately got her in its grip, and everything about her, the elbows with which she defends herself and her whole obstinate person bent for-ward like a gargoyle, looks as if it were warding off the blows of a brutal and fraudulent fate.

She sings like a little sempstress or a street singer, and

it never occurs to her that there is any other way of singing. In her artless way she forces her harsh, seductive contralto which goes so well with her face, the face of a pink and sulky young apache. The public adores her just as she is, with her dress that is too long and bought goodness knows where, her light brown hair not even waved, her hunched shoulder which looks as if it were still lugging along the laundry basket, and the down on her upper lip all white with cheap powder. The manageress promises her, for next season, her name in lights twice over, and as for a raise—well we'll see, after that. When she is on the stage Jadin is radiant and exultant. Every evening she recognises, among the public of the upper galleries, some pal of a childish escapade, and she can never resist interrupting her sentimental ditty to greet him with a joyful shout, a shrill schoolgirl laugh or even a resounding slap on her thigh.

And this is the girl who is missing from today's programme. In half an hour they will be rampaging in the house, calling "Jadin! Jadin!", stamping their boots and rattling their mazagran spoons against their glasses.

It was bound to happen. Jadin, they say, is not ill, and our stage-manager grumbles:

"'Flu, my foot! She's come a cropper into a bed, that's what she's done! And someone's using his wallet as a compress to keep her there! Otherwise she'd have let us know."

Jadin has found a fancier who does not belong to this district. A girl must live. But she was living already, with Tom, Dick and Harry. Shall I ever again see her little gargoyle silhouette, with one of those "modish" forage caps she used to fabricate herself, coming right down to her eyebrows? Only last night she thrust her badly-powdered little mug into my dressing-room to show me her latest creation: an "imitation white fox" toque of rabbit fur, so tight fitting that it pressed her little pink ears down on each side.

"You look the dead spit of Attila," Brague told her, with never a smile.

And now she's gone. The long corridor, perforated with little square dressing-rooms, buzzes with derisive laughter: it seems that everyone except me suspected this flight. Bouty, the little funny-man who sings the songs that Dranem made famous, walks up and down outside my dressing-room, made up like an ape, with a glass of milk in his hand, and I hear him prophesying: "It was a cert! But I couldn't help thinking Jadin would hold out another five or six days, or even a month! The boss must be livid! But it'll take more than that to make her decide to raise the screw of us artistes who make the reputation of her house for her. Just you mark my words: we'll be seeing Jadin back again; it's only a jaunt, that's all. She's a girl who knows where she belongs, she'll never be able to keep a fancy chap."

I open my door to speak to Bouty while I am putting the wet white on my hands: "Didn't she tell you she was going away, Bouty?"

He shrugs his shoulders, turning towards me his red gorilla mask, with its white-rimmed eyes: "Not likely! I'm not her mother." Whereupon he starts gulping his glass of milk, as blue as starch, in little sips.

Poor little Bouty, trailing about with him everywhere his chronic enteritis and his bottle of tested milk! When he removes that white and vermilion mask he reveals a gentle, sickly face, delicate and intelligent, with beautiful tender eyes, and the heart of an ownerless dog ready to devote itself to anyone who will adopt it. His illness and his exacting profession are killing him, he lives on milk

and boiled macaroni, and has just enough strength to
sing and dance negro dances for twenty minutes. When
he leaves the set he falls exhausted in the wings, unable
immediately to go down to his dressing-room. Sometimes his slender body, stretched out there as if dead,
bars my way, and I have to harden myself not to stoop
and pick him up and call for help. His fellow actors and
the old stage-setter content themselves with shaking their
heads with an important air as they pass him, and saying:
"Bouty's an artist who 'tires' quickly."

"Come on now, we must get a move on, full speed
ahead! The house didn't yell for Jadin as much as they
might. That's a bit of luck for us!"

Brague hustles me up the iron staircase: the combina-
tion of dusty heat and stage-lighting makes me dizzy;
this matinée has been like one of those dreams full of
incident, half the day has melted away I don't know how,
leaving me with nothing but the kind of nervous chill
and contraction of the stomach which follow awakenings
and rapid risings in the middle of the night. In an hour
it will be time for dinner, then a taxi, and it starts all over
again.

And that's how it will be for a month! The present
show is quite a success and anyhow we must keep it
going until the *Revue* begins.

"We're in clover here," says Brague. "Forty days with
nothing to think about!"

With nothing to think about. . . . If only I could do
as he does! I've got forty days, the whole year, a lifetime
for thinking in. How long am I going to spend trailing
round, from music-hall to theatre, and from theatre to
casino, "gifts" that everyone politely agrees to consider
interesting? They admit in addition that my mimicry is

"exact", my diction "clear", and my figure "impeccable". It's very kind of them. It goes even beyond what is necessary. But . . . where does it lead?

It's no good, I can see I'm in for a bad fit of the blues. I await it calmly, with a heart that is used to it, knowing I shall recognise its normal phases and get the better of it once again. No one will know anything about it. This evening Brague gives me a quizzical look with his penetrating little eyes, but merely says: "Wool-gathering, aren't you?"

Back in my dressing-room I wash my hands, stained red-currant colour to simulate blood, in front of the looking-glass where my painted mentor and I gravely take stock of each other like well-matched adversaries.

I know there's no escaping what's coming: suffering, regrets, and the insomnia and solitary musings that make the deepest hours of the night longer still. So I go to meet it with a kind of grim gaiety, and with all the serenity of a creature still young and resistant, who has been through it before. Two habits have taught me how to keep back my tears: the habit of concealing my thoughts, and that of darkening my lashes with mascara. . . .

"Come in!"

Someone has just knocked and I answered mechanically, my thoughts elsewhere.

It is neither Brague nor the old dresser, but an unknown person, tall, gaunt and dark, who bows his bare head announces, without pausing for breath: "Every night this week, Madame, I have come here to applaud you in *The Pursuit*. If my visit appears to you somewhat . . . out of place I hope you will forgive it, but I feel that my admiration for your talent and . . . your

figure . . . is sufficient excuse for my presenting myself
so . . . unconventionally and that . . ."

I do not answer this imbecile. Damp with sweat and
still out of breath, with my dress half undone, I look at
him, while I wipe my hands, with such evident ferocity
that his fine phrases falter and die suddenly on his lips.

Ought I to slap his face and leave on both cheeks the
marks of my fingers still wet with carmine-tinted water?
Ought I to raise my voice and hurl at that angular, bony
face, barred with a black moustache, the words I have
learnt behind the scenes and in the street?

He has the eyes of a sad coal-miner, this intruder. I
have no idea how he interprets my look and my silence,
but all of a sudden his expression changes.

"Oh my goodness, Madame, what a clumsy creature I
am, nothing but a noodle and I've only just realised it.
Turn me out, do, I've richly deserved it, but not before
I've laid my respectful compliments at your feet."

He bows once more, like a man who is just about to
go—and does not go. With that somewhat harlot-like
artfulness that men have, he waits for half a second to
see if his changed approach may have brought him any
reward and—after all I'm not so terrible—it has.

"Well then, Monsieur, I will say to you politely what a
moment ago I would have said harshly: please go!"

As I show him the door I laugh in a jolly way. But he
does not laugh. He remains where he is, craning forward,
his free hand hanging down with the fist clenched. In this
attitude he looks awkward and almost menacing, with the
slightly clumsy air of a wood-cutter on his best behaviour.
The ceiling light is reflected in his sleek, almost lacquered-
looking black hair brushed back at the sides; but his eyes
are so deep set I cannot see their expression.

The reason why he does not laugh is because he desires

me. He does not want my well-being, this man, he merely wants me. He is not in a mood for jests, even smutty ones. In the end this makes me uncomfortable and I would prefer him to be unashamedly lustful, like a man who has dined well and thoroughly enjoyed an eyeful in the front row of the stalls.

He is as hampered by his ardent desire for me as if it were a weapon getting in his way.

"Well, Monsieur, aren't you going?"

His answer bursts out as if I had awakened him: "Of course, of course, Madame! Certainly I'm going. I beg you to accept my excuses and . . ."

". . . and believe me to be your humble servant!" I could not help ending.

It is not very funny, but he laughs, at last he laughs, and changes that obstinate expression which I had found so disconcerting.

"It's kind of you to help me out, Madame! There's another thing too I wanted to ask you . . ."

"Oh no, you don't, you're going right away this minute. I've been amazingly long-suffering with you already, and if I don't soon take off this dress, after sweating in it like three furniture-removers, I shall get bronchitis!"

I push him out with the tip of my first finger, for as soon as I spoke of taking off my dress his face went dark and set again. Even after the door is shut and bolted, I can hear his muffled voice begging: "Madame! Madame! I wanted to know if you like flowers, and if so which ones?"

"Monsieur! Monsieur! leave me in peace! I don't ask you which are your favourite poets or if you prefer the sea to the mountains. Go away!"

"I'm going, Madame! Good evening, Madame!"

Ouf! This great noodle of a man has driven away my black mood; that is something at any rate.

For the last three years my amorous conquests have all been like this. The gentleman in the eleventh stall, the gentleman in the fourth box, the gigolo in the upper circle. A letter, two letters, a bouquet, another letter . . . and that's the end of it. Silence soon discourages them and I have to admit to myself that they are not over-persistent.

Fate, by way of sparing my energies for the future, seems to keep away from me those obstinate lovers, those hunters who pursue a woman until she physically does not know which way to turn. Those whom I attract do not write me love letters. Their letters are urgent, brutal and awkward, betraying their desires, not their thoughts. The one exception was a wretched youth who covered twelves pages with his abashed and garrulous love. He must have been very young. He used to dream of himself as a Prince Charming, poor lad, rich and powerful too: "I am writing you all this at the table in a pub where I'm having my lunch, and every time I raise my head I see my ugly mug in the looking-glass opposite."

At least that little admirer with the "ugly mug", lost in his azure palaces and enchanted forests, could dream of someone. But there is no one waiting for me on the road I follow, a road leading neither to glory nor riches nor love. Not that anything, as I well know, leads to love. It is love who throws himself across your path. And then he either blocks it for ever or, if he abandons it, leaves it in rack and ruin.

What remains of my life reminds me of the pieces of a jigsaw puzzle. Have I got to try and reconstruct, piece by piece, the original scene of it: a quiet house in the middle of a wood? No, no, I can't, someone has jumbled together all the outlines of that sweet landscape; I should never even be able to find again the bits of the blue roof patterned with yellow lichen, nor the virginia creeper, nor the deep forest without birds. . . .

Eight years of marriage and three of separation: that accounts for a third of my whole existence.

My ex-husband? You all knew him, Adolphe Taillandy, the pastellist. He has been doing the same portrait of a woman for the last twenty years. She is always in evening dress, posed against a misty gold background borrowed from Lévy-Dhurmer, and her hair, like floss silk, forms a halo round the velvety bloom of her face. The flesh on her temples, in the shadow of her neck, and between the swelling curves of her breasts, glows with the same impalpable bloom, the dusky blue of luscious grapes which tempt one's lips.

"Even Potel and Chabot can't improve on it!" said Forain one day before a pastel of my husband's.

Apart from his famous "bloom" I do not think that Adolphe Taillandy has any talent. But I freely admit that his portraits are irresistible, especially to women. To begin with, he resolutely sees everything in a rosy light. He has even found—goodness knows where—some red and golden glints to beautify the hair of that withered and superannuated brunette, Madame de Guimont-Fautru. These flecks of light, scattered over her lustreless face and Greek nose turn her into a voluptuous Venetian courtesan.

Once upon a time Taillandy did my portrait too. No one now remembers that I was the model for his picture of the little bacchante with the shiny nose, where a splash of sunlight, falling full on her face, makes it look like a mask of mother-of-pearl. I still remember my surprise at finding myself so blonde. I remember, too, the success of this pastel and of those which followed it. There were the portraits of Mme de Guimont-Fautru, of Baroness Avelot, of Mme de Chalis, of Mme Robert-Durand, and of the singer Jane Doré. Then we come to those which were less illustrious because of the anonymity of the sitters: the portraits of Mlle J.R., of Mlle S.S., of Mme U., of Mme Van O., and of Mrs F.W.

That was the period when Adolphe Taillandy used to declare, with that typical effrontery of the handsome man which became him so well: "I want no models but my mistresses, and no mistresses but my models!"

As far as I am concerned, the only genius he had was for lying. No woman, none of his women, could possibly have appraised and admired, feared and cursed his passion for lying as much as I did. Adolphe Taillandy used to lie feverishly, voluptuously, untiringly, almost involuntarily. For him, adultery was merely a type of falsehood, and by no means the most delectable.

He luxuriated in lies, with a strength and prodigality that was undiminished by the passing years. And while he was busy elaborating some ingenious piece of perfidy, designed with infinite care and embellished with all the studied refinements at the command of this arch-deceiver, I would see him squandering his passion for cunning in crude and vulgar deceptions that were quite unnecessary, and stories that were childish to the point of imbecility.

I met him, married him, lived with him for eight years . . . and what do I know of him? That he paints pastels and has mistresses. I know, too, that he achieves daily the disconcerting feat of being, for one person, a "plodder" who thinks of nothing but his art: for one woman a seductive and unscrupulous ruffian; for another a fatherly lover who seasons a passing infatuation with a piquant flavour of incest; for still another the tired, disillusioned and aging artist seeking to adorn his autumn with a delicate idyll. There is even the woman ʾfor whom he is, quite simply, an unchartered libertine, still vigorous and as lecherous as could be desired; and finally there is the silly little goose, well brought up and deeply enamoured, whom Adolphe Taillandy taunts, torments, spurns and takes back again with all the literary cruelty of an "artist" in a society novel.

This same Taillandy slips without transition into the no less conventional but more old-fashioned "artist" who, in order to overcome the last resistance of the little woman who is married and the mother of two children, throws down his chalks, tears up his sketch, weeps real tears which wet his Kaiser-like moustache and, seizing his broad-brimmed felt, rushes off to the waters of the Seine.

There are still many more Taillandys whom I shall never know, not to mention one of the most shocking: Taillandy in his business dealings, the shady juggler in money matters who is brazen and brutal, or smooth and shifty as occasion demands.

Among all those men which is the real one? I humbly declare that I have no idea. I believe there is no *real* Taillandy. There came a day when this prolific genius of a liar suddenly lost the power to make me despair and even ceased to interest me. Time was when he had been for me a sort of terrifying Machiavelli; perhaps after all he was only Fregoli.

In any case he still continues as before. There are times when I think of his second wife with a faint compassion. Is she still in love and blissfully savouring what she calls her victory over me? No, by this time, terrified and helpless, she must be beginning to find out what manner of man she has married.

Sometimes I sigh: "Heavens, how young I was and how I loved that man! And how I suffered!" But when I do, it is not at all a cry of pain or vengeful lamentation. It is rather as though I were saying: "If you knew how ill I was four years ago!" And when I admit: "I've been jealous to the point of wanting to kill, and die", I do it in the same way as those people who tell you: "I ate rats in '70!" They remember they did, but the memory of it is all they have. They know they ate rats, but they can no longer conjure up in themselves the shiver of horror, nor the anguish of famine.

After the first betrayals, the revolts and submissions of a youthful love determined to hope and to endure, I settled down to suffering with an unyielding pride and obstinacy, and to producing literature.

Just for the pleasure of taking refuge in a still recent past, I wrote *The Ivy on the Wall*, a cheerful little provincial novel, as clear and unruffled as the pools in my part of the world, a chaste little novel of love and marriage, slightly insipid and very agreeable, which had an unexpected and extravagant success. I found my photo in all the illustrated papers, *Life Today* awarded me its annual prize, and Adolphe and I became "the most interesting couple in Paris", the couple one invites to dinner and points out to distinguished foreigners. "You don't know the Taillandys? Renée Taillandy is extremely gifted." "Really? And what about him?" "He? Oh, he's irresistible!"

My second book, *Next Door to Love*, did not sell nearly as well. Yet in giving birth to it I had savoured the voluptuous pleasure of writing, the patient struggling with a phrase until it becomes supple and finally settles down, curled up like a tamed animal, the motionless lying in wait for a word by which in the end one *ensnares* it. Yes, my second volume sold very little. But it managed to win me the—what is the expression one uses? oh yes, of course—"the esteem of the literary world". As for the third, *The Forest Without Birds*, it fell flat and never picked up again. Yet this one is my favourite, my private "unrecognised masterpiece". It was considered diffuse and muddled, incomprehensible and long. Even now, whenever I open it, I love it and wholeheartedly admire myself in it. Incomprehensible? Perhaps it is for you. But for me its warm obscurity is clear as day; for me a single word is enough to create again the smell and colour of hours I have lived through. It is as sonorous and full of mystery as a shell in which the sea sings, and I should love it less, I think, if you loved it too. But rest assured, I shall not write another like that, I never could.

At present other tasks and cares fill my time, especially that of earning my living, bartering my gestures, my dances and the sound of my voice for hard cash. I have got very quickly into the way of that and enjoy it, having a characteristically feminine fondness for money. And earn my living I certainly do. On my good days I joyfully say over and over again to myself that I earn my living. The music-hall where I became mime, dancer and even on occasion, actress, turned me also, despite my astonishment at finding myself reckoning, haggling and bargaining, into a tough but honest little business woman. The least gifted of women soon learns how to be that when her life and liberty depend upon it.

No one could understand our separation at all. But would anyone in the least have understood my patience and my utter complacency, so cowardly and long-lasting, before it came to that? It is, alas, only the first forgiveness which is difficult. Adolphe soon learnt that I

belonged to the true, the best breed of females: in other
words, that I was the kind of woman who, having for-
given on the first occasion, can gradually and cleverly be
let to become one who submits and then finally accepts.
What an expert master I had in him! How skilfully he
alternated between indulgence and exigence! When I
showed myself too intractable he even went so far as to
beat me, though I believe he never really wanted to do
that. A man who has lost his temper does not beat as
well as he did, and he only struck me from time to time
to keep up his prestige. At the time of our divorce the
world was almost ready to lay all the blame on me, in
order to exculpate "that good-looking Taillandy", whose
only fault was that he was attractive and faithless. I was
within an inch of giving in and letting myself be intimidated and reduced to my habitual submissiveness by the
turmoil which the whole thing created around us.

"D'you mean to say that he's been deceiving her for
eight years and it's only now that she's thought of
complaining?"

I received visits from domineering friends, superior
persons who know "what life is"; and others from aged
relations whose most serious argument was: "What do
you expect, my dear child!"

What did I expect? At bottom I knew very well. I had
had enough of it. What did I want? To die, rather than
prolong that humiliating life of a woman "who has everything to make her happy"; to die, yes, and risk misery
before suicide, but never again to see Adolphe Taillandy,
the Adolphe Taillandy who only showed himself in
domestic privacy, the one who, without raising his voice,
thrusting that formidable adjutant's chin of his towards
me, knew so well how to warn me: "Tomorrow I'm
beginning the portrait of Mme Mothier. You'll be good

enough, I am sure, to take that expression off your face in future when you're looking at her."

To die, risking utter ruin first, but never again to surprise the sudden gesture which conceals a crumpled letter, nor the falsely commonplace conversation on the telephone, nor the glance of the servant who is in the know, and never again to hear myself told in a casual tone: "Oughtn't you to go and stay with your mother for a couple of days this week?"

To go away, but never again to lower myself to taking one of my husband's mistresses out for a walk all day, while he, reassured and protected by me, was embracing another. To go away, and die, but no longer to pretend ignorance, no longer to endure the nightly waiting, the vigil when one's feet grow cold in the too-big bed, no longer to think out those plans for vengeance which, born in the dark and inflated by the beatings of a lacerated heart, poisoned by jealousy, collapse at the rattle of a key in the lock and feebly let themselves be mollified when a familiar voice cries: "What? Not asleep yet?"

I had had enough.

You can get used to not eating, to having toothache or a pain in your stomach, you can even get used to the absence of a beloved person; but you cannot get used to jealousy. And so there happened what Adolphe Taillandy, who thinks of everything, had not foreseen: one day when without courtesy he had shown me *my own* door, so that he might better entertain Mme Mothier on the big divan in the studio, I did not return.

I returned neither that night, nor the next, nor on any night thereafter. And that is where my story ends—or begins.

I will not dwell on a short and gloomy period of

transition during which I received, with the same peevish humour, blame, advice, sympathy and even congratulations.

I discouraged the few persistent friends who came and rang at the door of a tiny flat I had chanced to rent. I felt so outraged to think that, in order to see me, anyone should appear to be defying that sacrosanct, all-powerful and vile thing, public opinion, that I severed, with a furious gesture, the last remaining links that still bound me to my past.

And what followed? Isolation? Yes, isolation, except for three or four friends, obstinate, burr-like creatures who had resolved to put up with all my rebuffs. How ill I received them, but how I loved them, and how frightened I was, when I watched them go, that they might not come again.

Isolation indeed. I was scared of it, as of a remedy which may kill. And then I discovered that all I was doing was to go on living alone. My training in that had begun long ago, in my childhood, and the first years of my marriage had barely interrupted it. Then it had started anew, severe this time and harsh enough to draw tears; and that is the most ordinary part of my story. What numbers of women have experienced that retreat into themselves, that patient withdrawal which follows their rebellious tears! I will do them this justice, which flatters me too: it is only in pain that a woman is capable of rising above mediocrity. Her resistance to pain is infinite; one can use and abuse it without any fear that she will die, as long as some childish physical cowardice or some religious hope keeps her from the suicide that offers a way out.

"She is dying of grief. . . . She has died of grief. . . ." When you hear those clichés you can shake your head, more in disbelief than compassion: a woman can never

die of grief. She is such a solid creature, so hard to kill!
You think that grief eats into her? Not at all. Very often,
though born weak and sickly, she gains from grief indestructible nerves, an inflexible pride, a capacity for waiting
and dissimulating which increases her stature, and a contempt for those who are happy. She grows supple in the
practice of suffering and dissimulation, as if they were
daily exercises full of risks. For she is always on the
verge of that keenest and sweetest and most seductive of
all temptations, the temptation of revenge.

Sometimes, if she is too weak or too loving, she kills.
And when that happens she will be able to astonish the
whole world with an example of that disconcerting
feminine resistance. Like a cunning animal leading on
inexperienced dogs, she will wear out her judges in the
course of interminable sessions and finally leave them
exhausted. You can be certain that long patience, and
griefs jealously hidden have tempered and sharpened and
toughened this woman till everyone cries "She's made of
steel!" No, she is merely made "of woman"—and that is
enough.

Solitude, freedom, my pleasant and painful work as
mime and dancer, tired and happy muscles, and, by way
of a change from all that, the new anxiety about earning
my meals, my clothes, and my rent—such, all of a sudden,
was my lot. But with it too went a savage defiance, a disgust for the milieu where I had lived and suffered, a
stupid fear of man, of men, and of women too. I felt a
morbid need to ignore what was happening round me,
to have near me none but rudimentary creatures who
would hardly think at all. Very quickly, too, there came
to me that odd sensation that only on the stage was I
really alone and safe from my fellow-creatures, protected
from the whole world by the barrier of light.

FOUR

SUNDAY again! But now the murky cold has given place to a bright cold, so we have taken our exercise, my dog and I, in the Bois between eleven and twelve. There is a matinée after lunch. The creature is ruining me. If it were not for her I could get to the Bois in the Metro, but she gives me pleasure in return for my three francs on the taxi. Black as a truffle, polished with a brush and a flannel rag, she gleams in the sun; the whole wood is hers and she takes possession of it, grunting like a pig and barking as she scatters the dry leaves.

How lovely it is, the Bois de Boulogne on a fine Sunday! For Fossette and me, city tramps who hardly know the country now, it is our forest and our park. Fossette runs faster than I do, but I walk faster than she does, and when she is not playing at "inner circle" with mad bulging eyes and her tongue hanging out, she bounds along after me in short rushes of little trotting gallops which make everyone laugh.

One can gaze full at the tarnished sun because its light is filtered by a fine rosy mist. A quivering, silvery incense, smelling faintly of mushrooms, rises from the open stretches of grass. My veil clings to my nose as I rush along, my whole body glowing with running and tingling with the cold. Am I in truth any different from what I was at twenty? On such a winter morning as this, surely even in the full flower of adolescence I was neither more firm nor more supple nor more sensually happy?

I can believe it as long as I am running through the Bois, but when I return home my fatigue undeceives me.

It is no longer the *same* fatigue. When I was twenty I should have enjoyed my temporary lassitude, sunk in a half-dream without any mental reserves. But nowadays I begin to find fatigue irksome, like a sort of bodily distress.

Fossette is a born luxury-dog and play-actress: the *boards* thrill her and she has a craze for jumping into every elegant car she sees. Yet it was Stephen-the-Dancer who sold her to me, and at no time did Fossette ever belong to a successful actress. Stephen-the-Dancer is one of my comrades working at the moment in the same "dump", the *Empyrée-Clichy*. A prey to tuberculosis which year by year is eating him up, this fair Gaul witnesses the gradual dissolution of his biceps, his rosy thighs gleaming with golden down, and the beautiful chest muscles of which he is so justly proud. Already he has had to give up boxing for dancing and roller-skating. He *rinks* here on the sloping stage; in addition he has set up as a dancing teacher, and on the side he also breeds domestic bull-dogs. This winter he is coughing a great deal. Often in the evenings he comes to my dressing-room, coughs, sits down and suggests that I should buy "a brindled, grey, bulldog bitch, a perfect beauty, who missed the first prize this year because of some jealousy".

It so happens that I arrive today in the underground corridor, honey-combed with square cells, which leads to my dressing-room, just at the moment when Stephen-the-Dancer is leaving the stage. With his slender waist, broad shoulders, tight-fitting Polish dolman of myrtle-green edged with imitation chinchilla, and fur cap over one ear, the young man still draws the eyes of the women, with his blue eyes and slightly rouged cheeks. But he is getting slowly thinner and thinner and his successes with women hasten his disease.

"Hullo!"

"Hullo, Stephen! Good house?"

"I'll say! But I can't think why the buzzards muck around here when it's so lovely in the country. By the way you don't happen to need a schipperke bitch who weighs just over a pound—a bargain I could get hold of through an acquaintance . . ."

"Just over a pound! Thanks, my flat's too small!"

He immediately laughs and does not insist. I know them well, those schipperke bitches, weighing just over a pound, that Stephen sells. They weigh round about six pounds. It is not dishonesty, it is business.

What will Stephen-the-Dancer do when he's down to his last lung, when he can't dance any more or sleep any longer with kind-hearted little women who buy him cigars, ties and drinks? What hospital, what institution will take in his beautiful hollow carcass? How far from funny all that is! And indeed what a lot of people there are whose misery doesn't bear thinking of!

"Hullo, Bouty! Hullo, Brague! Any news of Jadin?"

Brague shrugs his shoulders without answering, so intent is he on the tricky job of making up his eyebrows; he paints them dark violet because "that gives a fiercer look". He has a particular blue for wrinkles, a particular orangy-red for the inside of lips, a particular ochre for make-up base, a particular syrupy carmine for dripping blood, and above all a particular white for Pierrot masks, "the recipe for which", he avers, "I wouldn't give to my own brother!" There's no denying that he makes a very skilful use of this multi-coloured mania of his, and it is the only absurdity I know of in this intelligent, almost over-conscientious mime.

Bouty, looking skinnier than ever in his loose checked

garment, makes a mysterious sign to me. "I say, I've seen that kid Jadin. I saw her on the boulevard, with a bloke. She had feathers like that! And a muff like that! And a look as though she was bored to death at the rate of a pound a minute!"

"Well, if she's getting a pound a minute she's got nothing to complain of," interrupts Brague, always logical.

"I didn't say she was, old chap. But she won't stay on the boulevard; she's a girl who has no idea of money. I've kept my eye on Jadin for a long time, I have; she and her mother used to live in my court. . . ."

From my open dressing-room, opposite that of Brague, I can see little Bouty, who has suddenly fallen silent in the middle of his sentence. He has put his half-litre of tested milk to warm on the hot-water pipe which runs through the dressing-rooms just above floor level. You can't make out much of his real face behind the brick-red and chalk-white mask of his make-up; but I can't help thinking that, since Jadin's departure, poor little Bouty is more wretched than ever.

When I get to the stage of whitening and powdering my shoulders, and my knees which are a mass of bruises —for Brague is not exactly gentle when he throws me to the ground—I close the door, feeling sure in any case that Bouty will say no more. Like the rest of them, and myself too, he hardly ever speaks of his private life. It was this silence, this obstinate modesty, which gave me the wrong impression of his comrades during my early days at the music-hall. The most expansive and the vainest of them talk of their successes and their artistic ambitions with the emphasis and gravity that their code demands; the most malicious go as far as running down the "dump" and their pals; the most talkative are always repeating old stage and green-room jokes; but only one in ten feels the need to say: "I've got a wife—I've got two kids—my mother's ill—I'm awfully worried about my girl friend. . . ."

This silence about their private lives seems like a polite way of saying: "The rest is no concern of yours!" As soon as they have removed their grease-paint and put on their hats and scarves, they separate and disappear with a promptitude which I like to think comes as much from pride as discretion. Proud they nearly all are, and poor: the pal who is always "on the cadge" is an exception in the music-hall. My silent sympathy, which has been making discoveries and learning during these last three years, goes out to all of them without any preferences.

How unrecognised they are, these *café-concert artistes*, how disparaged and how little understood! Fanciful, proud, and full of an absurd and outmoded faith in Art, they are the only people left who still dare to assert with passionate belief "An *artiste* must not . . . an *artiste* cannot accept . . . an *artiste* will not consent . . ." Proud they certainly are, for though they often exclaim: "Lousy job, ours!" or "What a dog's life!", I have never heard one of them sigh "How unhappy I am!"

Proud, and resigned to existing for only one hour in the twenty-four since, even when it applauds them, the unjust public forgets them afterwards. A newspaper may enquire with discreet solicitude into the way Mlle X. of the *Comédie Française* spends her time, and beguile the leisure hours of the whole world with her opinions on fashion, politics, cooking and love; but who will condescend to wonder what you do, poor intelligent, sensitive little Bouty, and what you think and do not say when darkness has swallowed you up and you are hurrying, towards midnight, along the Boulevard Rochechouart,

so thin you are almost transparent in your long "English
style" overcoat, which comes from the Samaritaine?

For the twentieth time I ponder, all alone to myself, on
these things that are so far from cheerful. And while I do
so my fingers briskly and unconsciously perform their
accustomed task: white grease, pink grease, powder, dry
rose, blue, brown, red, black. . . . I have barely finished
when a hard claw scratches the bottom of my door. I
open at once because it is the begging paw of a little
Brabançon terrier who "has a part" in the first half of
the show.

"Hullo, Nelle!"

In she comes, confident and as grave as a trusted
employee, and lets me pat her little flanks, hot with
exercise, while her teeth, slightly yellowed with age,
crumble a biscuit. Nelle has a gleaming sandy coat, with
a face like a black marmoset's, in which shine beautiful
squirrel's eyes.

"Want another biscuit, Nelle?"

Well brought up, she accepts without a smile. Behind
her, in the corridor, her family is waiting for her. Her
family consists of a tall, lean man, silent and impenetrable,
who speaks to no one, and two courteous white collies
who look very much like their master. Where does he
come from? What paths have led him and his collies here,
like three disinherited princes? His gestures, his way of
raising his hat, his long hatchet face—everything about
him suggests a man of the world. It was perhaps some
gift of divination which made my comrades christen
him "the Archduke".

He waits in the corridor till Nelle has finished her biscuit. Nothing could be sadder, more dignified or more
disdainful than this man and his three creatures, proudly
resigned to their wandering lot.

"Goodbye, Nelle."

I close the door and the tinklings of the little dog's bell grow faint. Shall I see her again? A fortnight's pro- gramme comes to an end this evening and perhaps it is the end of an engagement for "Antonieff and his dogs". Where will they go next? Where will Nelle's beautiful brown eyes be shining, those eyes which say to me so clearly: "Yes, I know, you fondle me, you love me, you keep a box of biscuits for me. But tomorrow, or the day after, we shall leave. So don't expect any more of me than the civility of a nice little dog who knows how to walk on her front paws and perform a risky jump. Ten- derness, like rest and security, is for us an inaccessible luxury."

FIVE

In bright weather my ground floor, between its two cliffs of new houses, enjoys a shaft of sunshine from eight in the morning until two in the afternoon. First a glittering pencil touches my bed, then it spreads out there like a square cloth of light and the coverlet throws a pink reflection up to the ceiling.

I wait, lazily, until the sunlight reaches my face, dazzling me through my closed eyelids, and the shadow of each pedestrian passes swiftly over me like a dark blue wing. Or perhaps, roused to action, I jump out of bed and begin some feverish scouring: Fossette's ears undergo a delicate probing and her coat gleams under the hard brush. Or perhaps I take advantage of the brilliant, pitiless light to inspect what is already showing signs of age in me: the delicate silk of my eyelids, the corner of my mouth where my smile has already begun to engrave a sad line, and round my throat that triple necklace of Venus which an invisible hand presses a little more deeply into my flesh every day.

Today this severe examination is interrupted by the visit of my comrade Brague, brisk, sober and on the spot as usual. I receive him as I do in my dressing-room, with nothing on but a crêpe kimono on which Fossette's paws, one rainy day, printed some little grey, four-petalled flowers.

No need to powder my nose for Brague, nor to lengthen my eyelids with blue pencil. Brague never looks at me except at rehearsals, to say "Don't do that: it's ugly. Don't open your mouth vertically: you look like a fish. Don't blink your eyes: you look like a white rat.

Don't wobble your behind when you walk: you look like a mare."

It was Brague who guided, if not my first steps, at least my first gestures on the stage; and if I still show him the trust of a pupil, he for his part often continues to treat me as an "intelligent amateur", by which I mean that he is slightly impatient of discussion and considers that his opinion ought to prevail.

As he comes in this morning he plasters his hair against his neck as though he were pulling down a wig; and since that alert but sober expression, so characteristic of his clean-shaven, Catalan face, remains unchanged, I begin to wonder whether it is good news he is bringing, or bad. He eyes my ray of sunshine as though it were some precious object and looks at the two windows.

"What d'you pay for this ground floor of yours?"

"I've told you already: seventeen hundred."

"And you've got the lift too! Topping sunshine, might think you were in Nice! But that's not what I've come about: we've got an evening engagement."

"When?"

"When? Why, tonight."

"Oh!"

"Why 'Oh'? Is it awkward for you?"

"No. Do we take our act?"

"No, not the act, it's too important for that. Your dances. And I shall do my *Neurotic Pierrot* for them."

I jump up, really scared.

"My dances! But I can't! And besides, I lost my music at Aix! And then the girl who accompanies me has changed her address. If we'd at least had two days' notice. . . ."

"Out of the question," says Brague, unmoved. "They had Badet on the programme and she's ill."

"So that's it, a stop-gap! If that isn't the limit! Do your *Pierrot* if you like, I'm not going to dance!"

Brague lights a cigarette and lets fall these two words: "Five hundred."

"For the two of us?"

"For you. And the same for me."

Five hundred! A quarter of my rent. Brague goes on smoking without looking at me: he knows I shall accept.

"Well of course, five hundred. What time do they want us?"

"Midnight, of course. You'll get busy about your music and everything, won't you? So long then, till this evening. Oh, by the way, Jadin's come back!"

He was closing the door, but I pull it open again: "She hasn't! When?"

"Yesterday, at midnight, you'd just gone. She looked awful! You'll see her; she's singing at our dump again. ... Seventeen hundred, did you say? It's amazing. And women on every floor!"

And off he goes, grave and ribald.

An evening reception. . . . A social engagement. Those three words are quite enough to demoralise me. I don't dare say so to Brague, but I admit it to myself as I look at my funereal face in the glass, while a little shiver of cowardice grips the skin of my back.

To see *them* again . . . them whom I left so abruptly, those who once upon a time called me "Madame Renée", because it was their affectation never to give me my husband's name. Those men—and the women! The women who betrayed me with my husband, and the men who knew I was betrayed.

The time is past now when I used to see in every

woman one of Adolphe's mistresses, actual or probable, and to such an adoring wife as I was, men were never much of a menace. But I have retained an idiotic and superstitious terror of those drawing-rooms where I might meet witnesses or accomplices of my past unhappiness.

This social engagement begins by spoiling my tête-à-téte lunch with my faithful old friend Hamond, a painter already old-fashioned and in poor health, who comes from time to time to eat his boiled macaroni with me. We don't talk much. He leans his head, like that of a sick Don Quixote, against the back of an armchair, and after lunch we play at making each other miserable. He talks to me about Adolphe Taillandy, not to hurt me, but to recall a time when he himself was happy. And I discuss with him his cruel young wife whom he foolishly married, and who went off four months later with I don't know whom.

These afternoons of melancholy in which we indulge leave us worn out, with faces so aged and bitter, and mouths so dry from having said all over again so many distressing things, that we swear never to do it again. But the next Saturday finds us reunited at my table, glad to see each other again and quite impenitent: Hamond has discovered an unknown anecdote about Adolphe Taillandy and, in order to enjoy the sight of my best friend sniffing back his tears, I have dug out of a drawer an amateur snapshot in which I am holding the arm of a little, fair-haired aggressive Madame Hamond, as upright as a serpent on its tail.

But this morning our lunch isn't going well. Although Hamond, numb with cold but gay, has brought me some beautiful December grapes, blue as plums, every grape a little skinful of sweet, tasteless water—this accursed evening engagement casts its shadow over my whole day.

At a quarter to twelve Brague and I arrive in the Avenue du Bois. It's a splendid house, they must be most sumptuously bored in it. The imposing footman who leads us to the "sitting-room reserved for the artistes" offers to help me off with my fur coat. I refuse tartly: does he suppose I am going to await the good pleasure of these ladies and gentlemen, dressed in four blue necklaces, a winged scarab and a few yards of gauze?

Much better brought up than I, the imposing footman does not insist and leaves us alone. Brague, looking so thin as to be almost insubstantial in his loose Pierrot's smock, under his white mask, stands stretching in front of a looking-glass. He likes this social engagement no better than I do. Not that he misses the "barrier of light" between himself and *them* as much as I do, but he has a poor opinion of what he calls drawing-room "clients", and treats the fashionable audience with something of the malicious indifference which he shows us.

"D'you suppose it's ever entered these people's heads to try to write my name properly?" says he, holding out a little card to me. "They call me Brag*n*e on their programmes!"

Very much hurt, at heart, he disappears, pursing up his thin, blood-red mouth, behind a door-curtain of greenery, for another imposing footman has that moment courteously called him by his mangled name.

In a quarter of an hour it will be my turn. I look at myself in the mirror and find myself ugly, deprived of the harsh electric-light which, in my dressing-room, floods the white walls, bathes the mirrors, penetrates one's make-up and gives it a velvety look. Will there be a carpet on the platform? If they could have risen, as Brague puts it, to a small row of footlights. This Salome wig grips my temples and makes my headache worse. I feel cold.

"Your turn, old girl! Go and do your stuff for them!"

Back again, Brague has already sponged his white face streaked with lines of sweat, and put on his coat while he is speaking.

"They're obviously people of standing. They don't make too much row. They talk, of course, but they don't laugh too loud. By the way, here's the two francs fifteen for my share of the taxi. I'm off."

"Aren't you going to wait for me?"

"What's the point? You go to Les Ternes and I to Montmartre, it's not the same way. Besides, I've got to give a lesson at nine tomorrow. So long, till tomorrow."

Now is the moment for my turn. My misshapen little pianist is already seated. With a hand trembling with stage-fright, I wrap round myself the veil which constitutes almost my whole costume, a circular veil of blue and violet measuring fifteen yards round.

At first I cannot distinguish anything through the fine mesh of my gauze cage. My bare feet are aware that they are treading on the short, firm pile of a fine Persian carpet. There are, alas, no footlights.

The bluish chrysalis which I represent awakens at the sound of a short prelude, and begins to writhe as my limbs slowly loosen. Little by little, the veil unwinds, fills, billows out and falls, revealing me to the eyes of the beholders, who have stopped their frantic chatter to gaze at me.

I see them. In spite of myself I see them. As I dance and crawl and turn, I see them, and I recognise them!

In the first row is a woman, still young, who was for quite a long time the mistress of my ex-husband. She was

not expecting to see me this evening, and I was not
thinking of her. Her sorrowful blue eyes, her one beauty,
express as much fear as amazement. It is not me she fears;
but my sudden presence has confronted her, brutally,
with her own memories, she who suffered for Adolphe,
she who was ready to leave everything for him, and
wanted, with loud cries and noisy, imprudent tears, to
kill her husband, and me too, and flee with Adolphe. By
then he had already ceased to love her, and found her
heavy on his hands. He used to confide her to my care
for whole days together, charging me—what am I saying,
ordering me—not to bring her back till seven o'clock;
and never were there more harrowing tête-à-têtes than
those of those two betrayed women who hated each
other. Sometimes the poor creature, at the end of her
tether, would burst into humiliated tears, and I would
watch her weep, without pity for her tears, proud of
controlling my own.

There she is, in the front row. They have used every
inch of space and her chair is so close to the platform
that I could bestow an ironical caress on her hair, which
she dyes blonde because it is growing grey. She has aged
in the past four years, and she looks at me with terror.
She is looking through me at her sin, her despair, and her
love which has perhaps ended by dying.

Behind her I recognise another woman too . . . and
then one more. They used to come and have tea every
week at my house in the days when I was married. Perhaps they slept with my husband; it does not matter if
they did. None of them gives any sign of knowing me,
but something reveals that they have recognised me,
since one of them pretends to let her attention wander
and talks very animatedly in a low voice to her neighbour,
another exaggerates her short-sightedness, and a third,

busy fanning herself and shaking her head, keeps whispering: "How hot it is, how terribly hot!"

They have changed their hair styles since the year when I abandoned all these false friends. Every one of them now conforms to the mode of swathing the hair round over the ears like a cap, binding it with a wide bandeau of ribbon or metal, which makes them look as though they were convalescent and not very clean. One no longer sees tempting napes of necks, or temples haloed in curls; one sees nothing but little muzzles—jaws, chins, mouths and noses—to which this year's fashion undeniably gives a markedly bestial appearance.

Round the sides and at the back there is a dark row of men, standing. Packed closely together they crane forward with that curiosity, that cynical courtesy which men of the world display towards a woman who is considered "déclassée", the woman whose finger-tips one used to kiss in her drawing-room and who now dances, half-naked, on a platform.

Come now, this won't do, I'm too clear-sighted this evening, and if I don't pull myself together my dancing will suffer for it. I dance and dance. A beautiful serpent coils itself along the Persian carpet, an Egyptian amphora tilts forward, pouring forth a cascade of perfumed hair, a blue and stormy cloud rises and floats away, a feline beast springs forwards, then recoils, a sphinx, the colour of pale sand, reclines at full length, propped on its elbows with hollowed back and straining breasts. I have recovered myself and forget nothing. Do these people really exist, I ask myself? No, they don't. The only real things are dancing, light, freedom and music. Nothing is real except making rhythm of one's thought and translating it into beautiful gestures. Is not the mere swaying of my back, free from any constraint, an insult to those bodies cramped by their long corsets, and enfeebled by a fashion which insists that they should be thin?

But there is something more worth while than humiliating them; I want, for one moment only, to charm them! It needs only a little more effort: already their heads, under the weight of their jewels and their hair, sway vaguely as they obediently follow my movements. At any moment now the vindictive light in all those eyes will go out, and the charmed creatures will all give in and smile at the same time.

The end of the dance, and the noise of the very controlled applause, break the spell. I disappear, to return and bow with a smile all round the room. At the back of the room a man's silhouette gesticulates and calls out "Bravo!" I know that voice and that tall black figure.

Why, it's my imbecile of the other evening! It's the Big-Noodle! Any doubts I may have about it are soon dispelled when I see him enter, with bent head, the little room where my pianist rejoins me. He is not alone, he is accompanied by another tall black noodle, who has the air of being the master of the house.

"Madame . . ." says he, bowing.

"Monsieur . . ."

"Will you permit me to thank you for having been so kind as to take part, on the spur of the moment, in . . . and to express to you all the admiration . . ."

"Really, Monsieur . . ."

"I am Henri Dufferein-Chautel."

"Ah, of course."

"And this is my brother, Maxime Dufferein-Chautel, who is extremely anxious to be presented to you."

My Big-Noodle of yesterday bows once more and manages to seize and kiss a hand which was busy gathering up the blue veil. Then he remains standing and saying nothing, much less at his ease than in my dressing-room.

Meanwhile Dufferein-Chautel No. 1 is awkwardly crumpling a closed envelope:

"I . . . I'm not sure whether it is to Monsieur Salomon, your impresario, or to you yourself that I should hand . . ."

Dufferein-Chautel No. 2, suddenly crimson under his brown skin, casts a furious, hurt glance at him, and there they both stand, each as foolish-looking as the other!

What is there embarrassing about all that? I cheerfully put them out of their misery: "Why, to me myself, Monsieur, it's quite simple! Give me that envelope, or rather slip it in with my music—for I will confess to you in confidence that my dancer's costume has no pockets!"

They both burst into relieved and slightly naughty laughter whereupon, declining the sly offer of Dufferein-Chautel No. 2, who fears on my behalf the toughs of Les Ternes, I am at last free to go home alone, joyfully clasping the five hundred francs that are my share, and to go to bed and sleep.

SIX

THIS Friday evening, in order to slip my hand into the box where they put the letters—a little case nailed to the side of the box-office—I have to disturb a fine "pimp" in a cap, one of those classic types that abound in this district.

Even though his costume has been popularised in pictures and caricatures, in the theatre and the *café-concert*, the "bully" remains faithful to his sweater or his coloured, collarless shirt, to his cap and the jacket which he strains flatteringly tight round his hips by plunging his hands in the pockets, to his fag-end and his noiseless slippers.

On Saturdays and Sundays these gentlemen fill half our *Empyrée-Clichy*, outlining the gallery and stumping up two francs twenty-five to reserve in advance the cane-bottomed seats that practically touch the stage. They are the faithful, the devotees, who exchange remarks with the artistes, hiss or applaud them, and have a gift for interjecting the ribald criticism, the lewd exclamation that set the whole house in a roar.

Sometimes their success goes to their heads and then the whole thing becomes a riot. From one gallery to another they exchange pre-arranged remarks in spicy slang, followed by cat-calls and missiles which in turn lead to the prompt arrival of the police. It is as well for the artist on the stage to await the end of the storm with an expressionless face and a modest bearing, if he does not want to see the oranges, the programmes rolled into a ball, and the small coins change their direction. Simple prudence also cautions him not to go on with his interrupted song.

But these, I repeat, are brief storms, skirmishes reserved for Saturdays and Sundays. Order is very well maintained at the *Empyrée-Clichy*, where one feels the hand of Mme la Directrice—the Boss!

Dark and lively, covered with jewels, the Boss presides this evening, as every evening, in the box-office. Her brilliant, darting eyes miss nothing, and the theatre cleaners, in the mornings, do not dare to forget the dust in the dark corners. At the moment of my arrival those terrible eyes are withering a genuine apache, a hefty fellow not to be spurned, who has come to reserve one of the best cane-bottomed seats, close to the stage, those in the front row whose occupants squat like toads, with their arms on the railing in front and their chins on their crossed hands.

The Boss is turning him away, without any fuss, but with the demeanour of a lion-tamer!

"Pick up your money and hop it!"

The stalwart swings his arms and rocks like a bear: "What for, Madame Barnet? What've I done?"

"You and your, 'What've I done?' D'you think I didn't see you last Saturday? It was you in seat No. 1 in the gallery, wasn't it?"

"As if I could remember!"

"It was you who stood up during the pantomime, wasn't it, shouting out: 'She's only showing one bub, I want to see the two of 'em! I've paid two bob, one for each bub!' "

The stalwart turns crimson and protests, with his hand on his heart: "Me? Me? Now look here, Madame Barnet, I know how to behave, I know what's not done! Cross my heart, Madame Barnet, it wasn't me who . . ."

The queen of the *Empyrée* raises an inexorable right hand: "No fibs! I saw you, didn't I? So that's enough. There'll be no place for you for a week from today. Pick

up your money and don't let me see you before Saturday
or Sunday next. And now get out!"

The exit of the stalwart, barred for eight days, is well
worth my losing a few minutes more. He goes off on
his noiseless felt shoes, his back humped, and does not
resume his insolent expression until he is on the pavement
again. But his heart is not in it, his bearing is forced
and, for a short while, there is no difference between
this dangerous brute and a small boy deprived of his
favourite pudding.

On the iron staircase, mingling with the air rising from
the hot pipes, which smells of plaster, coal and ammonia,
the voice of Jadin reaches me in snatches. The little
wretch has found her familiar public again and got
back her hold on them! You only have to hear, in the
distance, the stormy laughter and the contented muttering with which they accompany and support her.

That warm harsh contralto, husky already from dissipation and perhaps the beginnings of consumption,
finds its way to one's heart by the lowest and surest
paths. If a "discriminating and artistic" producer were
to stray in here and listen to Jadin singing, he would
cry: "I'll take her and launch her, and in three months
you'll see what I'll make of her!"

An arrogant and embittered failure, that is what he
would make of her. Experiences of that kind are never
encouraging; where could the ill-kempt Jadin shine
better than here?

There she is on the staircase, just as she went away,
would you believe it, with her over-long frock frayed
out by her heels, and her Marie-Antoinette fichu, yellowed by the smoke of the auditorium, gaping open to
show her gaunt, youthful thinness, her hunched shoulder,

and her sulky mouth with its curled upper lip on whose down a moustache of powder lingers.

It gives me a keen and genuine pleasure to see that foul-mouthed child again, and she on her side rushes down the last steps to fall on me and squeeze my hands in her warm paws: for some unknown reason her "spree" has brought us closer together.

She follows me into my dressing-room where I risk a discreet reproach. "You know, Jadin, it was a rotten thing to do! You don't let people down like that!"

"I went to see my mother," says Jadin with great gravity.

But on catching sight of herself in the mirror in the act of lying, her whole childish face breaks into laughter and becomes one wide slit, like the faces of very young Persian cats.

"That's a good 'un, ain't it? . . . How bored you must all have been here without me!"

She radiates confident pride, surprised at heart that the *Empyrée-Clichy* had not put up its shutters during her absence.

"Haven't changed, have I? . . . Oh what lovely flowers! 'Scuse me."

With the swift gesture of a pickpocket, skilled from childhood at stealing oranges from the stalls, she seizes a huge purple rose before I have even opened the little envelope fastened to the side of a great sheaf of flowers which is standing waiting for me on the little make-up shelf.

MAXIME DUFFEREIN-CHAUTEL

With his respectful compliments

Dufferein-Chautel! At last I have found again the name of the Big-Noodle! Ever since the other evening, too

lazy to open a *Tout-Paris*, I have called him success-
ively Thureau-Dangin, Dujardin-Beaumetz, or Duguay-
Trouin!

"Those are flowers all right, I'll say!" says Jadin while
I undress. "They from your friend?"

I protest, with useless sincerity: "Dear me, no! Just
someone thanking me . . . for an evening performance. . . ."

"That's a pity!" declares Jadin, as one who knows all
about these things. "Only a gentleman gives flowers like
that. The chap I did a bunk with the other day gave me
just that kind."

I burst out laughing: Jadin airing her views on the
quality of flowers and "chaps" is irresistible. She turns
quite red under her flour-powder and takes offence:

"What is it? P'raps you don't believe he was a gentleman? All right then, ask Canut, the stage-setter, to let
you see what I brought back in the way of brass, last
night when you'd just gone!"

"How much?"

"Sixteen hundred francs, dearie! Canut saw them, it
isn't a yarn!"

Do I look sufficiently impressed? I fear not.

"And what are you going to do with it, Jadin?"

She plucks unconcernedly at the threads hanging from
her old blue and white dress: "Don't suppose there'll be
any for savings. I stood the stage hands a round of drinks.
And then I lent—as she calls it—fifty francs to Myriame
to pay for her coat. And the girls keep asking one after
the other and saying they haven't got a bean. I really
don't know! I say, there's Bouty! Hullo, Bouty!"

"Hullo, reveller!"

Bouty, having politely assured himself that my desha-
bille is covered by a kimono, pushes open the door of my

dressing-room and shakes the hand that Jadin holds out, repeating "Hullo!" in a tender voice but with a rough gesture. But Jadin immediately forgets him and continues her conversation, standing behind me, and addressing herself to my image in the glass: "You know it makes me feel quite sick to have *as much money as that*!"

"But . . . won't you buy yourself some frocks . . . at least one . . . to replace this one?"

With the back of her hand she thrusts aside the straggling locks of her thin, straight hair: "What an idea! This dress'll do very well till the *Revue* comes on. Whatever would *they* say, if they saw I'd gone off up town to pick up enough brass to bring back a swell new outfit!"

She is right. *They* means her famous local public, exigent and jealous, whom she has slightly betrayed but who forgive her on condition that she reappears before them badly turned out, badly shod, got up like an old rag-bag, but just the same as before her escapade, before her lapse.

After a pause Jadin goes on, quite at ease before the embarrassed silence of Bouty: "You see I bought myself what I needed most: a hat and a muff, as well as a scarf. And what a hat! You'll see it soon. . . . So long. You staying, Bouty? You know, Bouty, I'm rich, I'll stand you anything you like!"

"Not my line, thanks."

I've never seen Bouty so cold and disapproving. If I were to say aloud that he loves Jadin I should cover myself with ridicule; so I must be content to think it.

The little comedian departs soon after and I am left alone with my sheaf of roses, a large commonplace sheaf tied with pale green ribbon, just the sheaf one would expect from a "big noodle" such as my new admirer.

"With his respectful compliments. . . ." During the

past three years I have received a good many compliments, if I may say so, but there was nothing respectful
about them. And my old middle-class respectability,
always vigilant, is secretly gratified, just as if those compliments—however veiled with respect they hope they
are—were not asking for the same thing, always the same
thing.

My short-sightedness does not prevent me from seeing,
in the front row of the stalls, M. Dufferein-Chautel, junior,
stiff and grave, with his black hair shining like the silk of
a top-hat. Happy because he has seen from my look that
I have recognised him, he follows my movements, my
comings and goings on the stage, with his head, just as
my dog Fossette does when I am dressing to go out.

SEVEN

THE days pass. There is nothing new in my life, except a patient man lying in wait for me.

We have just got over Christmas and the first of January. The Christmas evening performance was a hectic affair which shook the whole "dump" to its foundations. The public, more than half drunk, yelled like one man; the bespangled stage-boxes hurled mandarines and twopenny cigars at the upper galleries; Jadin, tipsy from lunch time on, lost the thread of her song and danced a frightful "cancan" on the stage, pulling up her skirts over her laddered stockings, a great lock of hair flapping down her back. A gala evening with our Boss presiding in her box, totting up the princely takings, with one eye on the sticky glasses cluttering the little shelves nailed to the backs of the stalls.

Brague also had been tipsy since dinner and was bubbling over with lewd fantasies like a little black goat. Alone in his dressing-room he improvised an extraordinary monologue of a moonstruck person defending himself against spectres, with cries of "Oh no, stop, let me alone!" or "Not that! Not that! Well, just once then . . ." and sighs and protests as of a man tortured by diabolical voluptuousness.

As for Bouty, writhing with the cramp his enteritis gave him, he sat sipping his bluish milk.

By way of a New Year's Eve celebration, I ate the beautiful hot-house grapes which my old friend Hamond had brought me, all alone with Fossette, who was crunching sweets sent by the Big-Noodle. But it needed a great deal of self-mockery not to fall a prey to the hurt jealousy of a child whom they have forgotten to ask to the party.

What in fact would I have liked? To have supper with Brague, or with Hamond, or with Dufferein-Chautel? Heavens, no! Well then, what? I am neither better nor worse than the rest of the world, and there are times when I should like to forbid others to enjoy themselves when I am bored.

It is a fact worth remarking that all my friends, the real, true ones like Hamond, are people who never have any luck and are incurably sad. Is it the "solidarity of ill-fortune" which binds us together? I don't think so. It seems to me rather that I attract and keep the friendship of those melancholy, solitary persons who are pledged to loneliness or the wandering life, as I am. Birds of a feather . . .

I brood on these cheerful ideas on my way back from visiting Margot. Margot is the younger sister of my ex-husband. Ever since childhood she has lugubriously borne this playful pet name which suits her about as well as a ring in the nose. She lives alone and, with her bobbed hair turning grey, her shirt blouse adorned with Russian embroidery, and her long black jacket, she looks rather like a Rosa Bonheur, turned Nihilist.

Fleeced by her husband, sponged on by her brother, robbed by her lawyer and cheated by her servants, Margot has taken refuge in a grim serenity made up of incurable kindness of heart and silent contempt. Everyone around her is so used to exploiting her that they continue to eat into her income and she lets it happen, merely giving way sometimes to sudden rages and dismissing her cook for a too-flagrant overcharge of a penny.

"I don't mind being robbed," she says, "but I do think they should take care how they do it." After which she relapses for days on end into her all-embracing contempt.

During my married life I knew Margot very little. Kind though she was, she was always cold and far from talkative, and this reserve of hers did not encourage me to confide in her. But on the day when my break with Adolphe seemed final, she politely and briefly closed the door to my astonished husband and never saw him again. It was then I learnt that I had in Margot an ally, a friend and a support, since it is from her that I get the fifteen pounds a month which keep me from destitution. "Go on, take it!" said Margot. "You won't be doing me any harm. It's only the ten bob a day that Adolphe has always touched me for!"

It is true that I should never turn to Margot for consolation or for that tonic cheerfulness that they tell me will be good for me. But at least Margot loves me in her own way, her discouraged and discouraging way, though prophesying that I shall come to a wretched end.

"As for you, my girl," she said to me once again today, "you'll be lucky if you don't get caught up all over again with a man just like Adolphe. Like me, you're made to be imposed on. But it's a waste of my time talking to you. Burnt child though you are, you'll go back to the fire, you mark my words! You're so obviously one of those who need more than one Adolphe to teach them."

"Really, Margot, you're extraordinary! Every time I see you, you take me to task like this," I reproached her, laughingly. " 'You're this, you're that, you're one of those who, one of those that . . .' Do at least wait until I've sinned, it'll be time enough to blame me for it afterwards."

Margot put on one of those expressions that make her look very tall, so lofty do they seem.

"I'm not blaming you, my girl. And I shan't blame you any more when you have sinned, as you put it. Only, it will be very difficult for you to refrain from committing *the* folly, for there is only one: the folly of beginning all over again. I know what I'm talking about. Even though," she added with a strange smile, "*I* never had any senses!"

"Well then, Margot, what ought I to do? What do you feel is wrong with my present life? Do you think I ought to shut myself up, as you do, for fear of a worse ill, and like you love nothing but little short-haired Brabançon terriers?"

"Take jolly good care you don't!" burst out Margot, with a sudden childlike gaiety. "Little Brabançon terriers indeed! They're the nastiest brutes possible. Look at that creature," she went on, pointing to a little tawny bitch who looked like a shorn squirrel. "I sat up with her for fifteen nights when she had bronchitis. Yet if I happen to leave her alone for an hour in the house, the little horror pretends not to recognise me and growls at my heels as if I were a tramp. . . . But apart from all those things, are you well, my child?"

"Very well, thank you, Margot."

"Tongue? Whites of the eyes? Pulse?"

She turns back my eyelids and presses my wrist with an assured, professional hand, exactly as if I were a little Brabançon. For Margot and I both know the value of health, and the misery of losing it. One manages to live alone and one gets used to it; but to languish alone in fever, to cough through an interminable night, to stagger on tottering legs to a window whose panes are lashed with rain, and then to return to a rumpled, sagging bed —alone, alone, alone!

For a few days last year I knew the horror of lying, vaguely delirious, and dreading, in my half-lucidity, that I might die slowly, far from everyone and forgotten. Ever

since then, following Margot's example, I take good care
of myself and look after my insides, my throat, my
stomach and my skin, with the slightly fanatical strictness
of a proprietor who is devoted to his possessions.

I have been thinking today of that odd remark of
Margot's, that she for her part "never had any senses".
And what about me and my senses? Now I come to think
of it, it's a very long time since I thought of them.

Margot appears to think that the whole "question of
the senses" is important. If I am to believe literature—the
best and the worst too—no voice can compete with the
voice of the senses. What is one to believe?

Brague once said to me, in the tone of one giving
medical advice: "You know, it's not healthy to live as you
do." And, like Margot, he added: "Anyway, you'll come
to it, like all the others. Remember what I'm telling you."

I don't like thinking of that. Brague is always ready to
lay down the law and play at being infallible. It doesn't
mean a thing. All the same I don't like thinking of it.

At the music-hall I join, without the slightest affectation of prudery, in conversations where they discuss "the
question of the senses" with statistical and surgical preci-
sion, and I take the same detached and respectful interest
in them as I do in reading in a newspaper of the ravages
of the plague in Asia. I am quite ready to be moved but
I prefer to remain half incredulous. All the same I don't
much like thinking of it.

And besides, there is that man—the Big-Noodle—who
contrives to live in my shadow and tread in my footsteps
with the obstinacy of a dog. I find flowers in my dressing-
room and Fossette gets a little nickel trough for her
meals; three minute animal mascots sit chatting nose to
nose on my writing-table: an amethyst cat, a chalcedony
elephant and a turquoise toad. A circlet of jade, green as

a tree-frog, bound the stalks of a bunch of greenish lilies which was handed to me on New Year's Day. And in the street I too often run into that same Dufferein-Chautel, who bows with a look of surprise that would deceive no one.

He forces me to remember, too often, the existence of desire, that imperious demi-god, that unleashed faun who gambols round love and does not obey love; and to remember that I am alone, healthy, still young, and rejuvenated by my long, moral convalescence.

Senses? Yes, I have them . . . or I had them in the days when Adolphe Taillandy condescended to concern himself with them. Shy senses they were, normal senses, glad of the conventional caress which was enough for them, afraid of any refinements or erotic complications, slow to rouse but slow to quench, in short, healthy senses.

Betrayal and long-drawn-out grief have anaesthetised them . . . for how much longer, I wonder? On days when I am gay and light-hearted, the pleasure of feeling myself pure, and cut off from what made me a woman like any other, is enough to make me say to myself "For ever!" But there are also lucid days when I reason harshly with myself. "Take care! Be always on guard! Everyone who approaches you is suspect, but you are your own worst enemy. Don't proclaim that you are dead, empty, light: the beast whom you forget is hibernating, and fortifying himself with a long sleep."

And then I forget once again the memory of what I was, in the fear of becoming once more *alive*; I want nothing, I regret nothing . . . until the next time my confidence lands me in disaster, until that inevitable moment of crisis when, with terror in my eyes, I see advancing towards me, with gentle, powerful hands, the sadness that guides and accompanies one in all the pleasures of the flesh.

EIGHT

For several days past Brague and I have been rehearsing a new act. There will be a forest, a grotto, an old troglodyte, a young hamadryad, and a faun in the prime of life.

The faun is Brague, I am to be the woodland nymph, and as for the old troglodyte, we haven't yet thought about him. He only appears at intervals, and to play this part, Brague says: "There's a young ruffian of eighteen among my pupils who'll make a perfect prehistoric!"

They have kindly lent us the stage at the *Folies* from ten to eleven in the mornings for our rehearsals. Stripped of its backcloths, the whole of the deep, bare stage is visible. How sad and grey it all looks when I arrive, with no corset on, a sweater instead of a blouse, and black satin knickers under my short skirt.

I envy Brague for being, at no matter what hour, always himself, alert, swarthy and authoritative. I struggle feebly against the cold, and the sluggish, sickening atmosphere not yet rid of the stale smells of the night before and still smelling of humanity and sour punch. The tinny old rehearsal piano grinds out the new music, my hands grip each other and part with difficulty, my gestures are constricted, close to my body, I hunch my shoulders with the cold and feel myself mediocre, awkward, lost.

Brague, used to my morning inertia, has also learnt the secret of how to cure it. He badgers me without respite, running round me like a terrier, showering brief encouragements and sharp exclamations which make me tingle as though I had been lashed.

A cloud of dust rises from the auditorium: it is the hour when the cleaners are brushing away the mud that has dried on the carpets, together with all the rubbish dropped the evening before: papers, cherry-stones, cigarette-ends, and dried dung from the soles of shoes.

Towards the back of the stage—for we are only lent a section of it, a strip about two yards wide—a troupe of acrobats are at work on their thick carpet: they are handsome, fair-haired, rosy Germans, silent and intent on the job. Their working tights are dirty, and by way of relaxation and pastime during the intervals of their act, they keep on exercising; two of them, laughing sleepily, attempt a miracle of unattainable equilibrium . . . which they will perhaps achieve next month. When the rehearsal is over, they concentrate very seriously on the perilous education of the youngest of the troupe, an urchin with the face of a little girl, beneath long fair curls, whom they throw in the air and catch on a foot or a hand, an airy little creature who seems to fly, with his locks streaming out horizontally behind him or standing on end like a flame above his head while he falls back to earth, feet together and pointing downwards and arms glued to his body.

"As you were!" cries Brague. "You've bungled that movement again! Of all the lackadaisical rehearsals! Can't you possibly attend to what you're doing?"

It's difficult, I must admit. Overhead now there are some gymnasts swinging on three trapezes, and exchanging shrill cries like the cries of swallows. The glittering nickel of the metal trapezes, the squeak of rosined hands on the polished bars, all that expenditure of elegant and supple strength going on around me, that methodical contempt of danger, finally exalt and fire me with the desire to emulate them. And that is the moment when they turn us out, just when I was beginning to be conscious of the beauty of a perfected gesture, the rightness of an expression of horror or desire, suddenly adorning my body like a rich ornament.

Roused thus too late, I use up the rest of my energy in returning on foot with Fossette, whom rehearsals fill with a silent rage which she works off outside on dogs bigger than herself. Like a brilliant mime, she terrorises them with a single twitch of her Japanese dragon-mask, a hideous grimace which makes her black eyes start out of her head, and curls back her lips to reveal, beneath their pink undersides, a few white teeth set askew like palings of a fence blown in all directions by the wind.

As a result of having grown up in the profession, Fossette knows the music-hall better than I do; she trots about in dark basements, bowls along corridors, and finds her way by the familiar smell of soapy water, rice powder and ammonia. Her brindled body is used to being clasped in arms coated with pearl white; she condescends to eat the sugar that the supers scrounge from the saucers in the café downstairs. A creature of whims, sometimes she insists that I should take her with me in the evenings, and on other days, coiled round like a turban in her basket, she watches me go with the contempt of a dowager who, for her part, likes to digest her meal slowly.

"It's Saturday, Fossette, we must hurry! Hamond will have arrived before us!"

Instead of taking a cab, we have run like two mad creatures, because the air, this morning, is full of that soft and surprising sweetness that comes before the spring. We catch up with Hamond just as he reaches my white box of a house, the colour of sculptured butter.

But Hamond is not alone: he is talking on the pavement

with . . . with Dufferein-Chautel, junior, christened
Maxime, and *known* as the Big-Noodle.

"What! You again!"

Without giving him time to protest, I questioned
Hamond severely. "You know M. Dufferein-Chautel?"

"Certainly I do," says Hamond calmly. "So do you, I
see. But I knew him when he was quite small. I still have
in a drawer a photograph of a boy with a white arm-
band: 'In memory of the First Communion of Maxime
Dufferein-Chautel, May 15th 18 . . .' "

"So you have!" cries the Big-Noodle. "Mother sent it
you because she thought I looked so beautiful."

I don't join in their laughter. I am not pleased that they
know each other. And I feel uncomfortable under the
strong, noonday light, with my hair out of curl under my
fur cap, my nose shiny for lack of powder, and my mouth
dry with hunger and thirst.

I hide my shapeless, laced rehearsal boots under my skirt.
The kid is so rubbed now that it shows the blue, but they
grip my ankles well and their worn soles are as supple as
those of dancing slippers. Especially as the Big-Noodle
is looking me over as if he had never seen me before.

I stifle a sudden childish longing to cry and instead I
ask him, as if I were about to bite him: "What is it?
Have I got a smut on my nose?"

He takes his time to reply: "No . . . but . . . it's odd . . .
when one has only seen you in the evening one would
never believe you have grey eyes. They look brown on
the stage."

"Yes, I know. I've been told so before. You know,
Hamond, the omelette will be cold. Goodbye, Monsieur."

Come to that, I too had never seen him so well, in full
daylight. His deep-set eyes are not black, as I thought,
but a rather tawny brown, like the eyes of sheep-dogs.

I thought they would never stop shaking hands! And
that little tart, Fossette, saying "goodbye to the gentleman", and grinning like an ogress from ear to ear! And
the Big-Noodle putting on the look of a beggar at the
pastry-cook's window, just because I spoke of an
omelette! If he thinks I'm going to invite him!

Quite unfairly, I lay the blame for all of it on Hamond.
So I remain silent as I hurriedly give my face and hands a
brief wash before rejoining my old friend in the little
study where Blandine is laying the table. For I have suppressed once and for all that sad and useless room known
as a dining-room and used for only one hour in the
twenty-four. But I must admit that Blandine sleeps in,
and that an extra room would have cost me too much.

"Well, well, so you know Maxime!" cries Hamond as
he unfolds his napkin.

I was expecting that!

"I? I don't know him at all! I had an evening engagement at his brother's house, where I met him. That's all."

I forbear—why, I wonder?—to mention the first
interview, when the Big-Noodle, in a state of excitement,
burst into my dressing-room.

"Well, he knows you. And he admires you a great deal.
In fact I rather think he is in love with you."

Subtle Hamond! I look at him with that sly, feline
mirth that masculine naïvety inspires in us.

"He knows you like roses, and sweets flavoured with
pistachio. He's ordered a collar for Fossette . . ."

I spring to my feet: "He's ordered a collar for Fossette! . . . Oh well, after all that's nothing to do with me!"
I say, laughing. "Fossette's a creature with no morals:
she'll accept, she's quite capable of it!"

"We spoke of you, naturally. I thought you were very
good friends."

"Oh Hamond, I would have told you!"

His friendly jealousy flattered, my old friend lowers his eyes.

"He's a very nice chap, I assure you."

"Who is?"

"Maxime. I met his mother, who is a widow, in . . . let's see now, it must be thirty . . . no, thirty-five. . . ."

Off he goes, and I have to endure the history of the Dufferein-Chautels, mother and son. A managing woman, she runs the whole estate, saw mills in the Ardennes, acres of forest land. Maxime, rather lazy, is the youngest and most spoilt of her sons, much more intelligent than he seems, thirty-three and a half years old. . . .

"Fancy! Just like me!"

Hamond leans towards me, over the little table, with the attention of a miniaturist: "Are you thirty-three, Renée?"

"Alas!"

"Don't say it. No one would know."

"Oh, I know very well that on the stage . . ."

"Nor in everyday life either."

That is as far as his compliment gets and Hamond goes on with the history of the Dufferein-Chautels. Displeased, I suck some grapes. The Big-Noodle is insinuating himself into my life more than I have allowed him. At this hour Hamond and I ought, as our custom is, to be stirring up those bad old memories that blossom weekly in the bitter aroma of our steaming cups.

Poor Hamond! It is for my sake that he is departing from his beloved, gloomy habit. I well know that my solitude makes him anxious; if he dared he would say to me, like a paternal go-between:

"There is the lover you need, my dear! Good health, doesn't gamble, doesn't drink, well-enough off. . . . You'll thank me!"

NINE

FOUR days more and I leave the *Empyrée-Clichy*! Every
time I come to the end of a rather long engagement
at a *café-concert*, I have the odd impression, during the
last days, of being given a freedom I have not desired.
Happy though I am to be free and able to spend my evenings at home, I am not in a hurry to enjoy it, and when
I stretch and say "At last!" there is a lack of spontaneity
about it.

All the same this time I really believe I am glad, and
as I sit in Brague's dressing-room I give him a list, at
which he mocks, of the urgent tasks which are going to
fill my holidays.

"I'm having all the divan cushions re-covered, you
know. And then I'm pushing the divan itself right into
the corner, and I'm going to have an electric lamp fixed
above it."

"Splendid! It'll look just like a brothel," says Brague
gravely.

"Silly ass! And besides that, oh well, I've heaps of
things to do. It's such ages since I paid any attention to
my home."

"It certainly is!" agrees Brague, drily. "And who are
you doing all this for?"

"What d'you mean, who for? For myself, of course!"

Brague turns from the mirror a moment, showing a
face in which the right eye, the only one he has rubbed
with blue, looks as if it were ringed with terrific bruises.

"For yourself? Just for yourself? You'll forgive me
but I find that a bit . . . fatuous. Besides, d'you suppose

I'm going to let *The Pursuit* lie dormant? You'd better be ready to be off at a moment's notice for one of those first-rate establishments in the provinces and abroad. And by the way, Salomon, the agent, asked me to tell you to drop round and see him."

"Oh! already?"

Brague shrugs his shoulders and says, sharply: "There you go as usual, with your 'Oh! already?' Yet if I were to tell you there was nothing doing, you'd keep on like a mosquito: 'When do we start? When do we start?' You're all exactly alike, you womenfolk."

"My view too," agrees the melancholy voice of Bouty, behind us.

He has grown thinner than ever this past month, has Bouty, and he "tires" more and more. I steal a glance at him when he is not looking, so as not to hurt him; but what can one make out under that red mask with the white-rimmed eyes? Silently we listen to the voice of Jadin above us:

> "My sweet little Mignonet-te
> I pray you may never regret
>   The wonderful day
>   When I gave you a spray,
> A spray—of mignonette!"

The composer of the *Waltz of the Mignonette*, an experienced man who knows his job, has cunningly contrived a suggestive pause in the middle of the last line of the chorus.

"So in four days more you'll be making tracks?" asks the little funny-man abruptly, raising his head.

"Yes, in four days. I've enjoyed being here. It's so peaceful."

"So peaceful!" protests Bouty, sceptically. "I can think of places more peaceful than this. You'll easily find better. I'm not running down our public, but all the same they're a pretty low lot. Oh, I know one can keep up one's standard anywhere," he goes on, seeing me shrug as if I thought that unimportant. "But all the same . . . just listen to them bawling now! How d'you suppose a woman, a young woman I mean, with no proper notions, always up to larks and ready to go on the spree, can learn good behaviour in the middle of all that? When she's a scatterbrained, rackety girl, I mean . . . like Jadin, for instance?"

Poor little Bouty, it is your unhappy love that has suddenly given you these aristocratic ideas, this contempt for a public which applauds you; and in seeking and finding an excuse for Jadin, you spontaneously invent the theory of the influence of environment, in which I don't believe!

The Russian dancers have gone, and Antonieff—the "grand-duke"—and his dogs have gone too. Where? No one knows. None of us has had the curiosity to find out. Other turns have come to take their place, some engaged for seven days and others for four, since the *Revue* is now so imminent; on the stage and in the corridors I run into new faces with which, by way of a friendly and discreet greeting, I exchange a half-smile or a questioning look.

The only ones who remain from the former programme are ourselves, Jadin, who is to create—Heavens above!— various roles in the *Revue*, and Bouty. We chat in a melancholy way in the evenings, like veterans of the *Empyrée-Clichy* forgotten when the young regiment marched away.

Where shall I find again those whom I have known here? In Paris, Lyons, Vienna or Berlin? Perhaps never, perhaps nowhere. We shall meet for five minutes in the office of Salomon, the agent, with noisy greetings and stagey handclasps, just long enough to know that we still exist and to utter the indispensable "What are you doing?" and to learn in reply that "things are going nicely" or that "things aren't shaping too well".

Things aren't shaping too well. . . . This is the vague circumlocution my wandering companions use to cover hard times, "restings", money troubles, and destitution. Puffed up and sustained by that heroic vanity which endears them to me, they never admit. A few of them, at the end of their tether, find a little part to fill in a *real* theatre, and oddly enough they never boast of this. Patient and obscure, they wait there for the renewal of luck which will bring them an engagement at a music-hall, the blessed hour which will see them in a spangled skirt again, or evening clothes smelling of benzine, once more facing the spotlight *in their repertoire*!

"No, things aren't shaping well," some will tell me, adding: "I'm trying the films again."

The cinematograph, which threatened the humble *café-concert* artistes with ruin, is now their salvation. In it they adapt themselves to an anonymous labour which brings them no fame, which they do not like, which upsets their habits and changes the times of their meals, their leisure and their work. Hundreds live by it in times of unemployment, and many settle down in it. But if the films become glutted with supers and stars, what will they do?

"Things aren't shaping well . . . no, things aren't shaping well."

They utter the phrase in a casual but at the same time serious way, without overdoing it and without whining, swinging their hat or a pair of old gloves in their hands.

They swagger, tightly buttoned in a full-skirted overcoat of the fashion of two seasons ago; for the essential, the indispensable thing, is not the possession of a clean suit but of a "really classy" overcoat which covers everything: threadbare waistcoat, shapeless jacket, trousers yellowed at the knees; a dashing, flashy overcoat, which makes an impression on the director or the agent, and which in the last resort enables one to throw off a "things aren't shaping well" in the jaunty tone of a man of means.

Where shall we be next month? In the evenings Bouty prowls aimlessly up and down the corridor of the dressing-rooms, and keeps up a gentle coughing until I half open my door to invite him to sit down for a moment in my room. He squeezes his flanks, like a lean dog's, into a rickety chair with its white paint flaking off, and tucks his feet under him so as not to interfere with my movements. Brague comes to join us and crouches like a gipsy, with his behind against the hot pipes. Standing between them, I finish dressing, and my red skirt, embroidered with yellow, fans them as I pass. Though we have no wish to talk, we chatter to overcome a brooding longing to be silent, to huddle against each other and grow sentimental.

Brague manages better than the rest of us to remain clear-sighted, interested and active; he is still commercially eager for the future. For me the future, whether it is here or there, is . . . My lately acquired and rather artificial liking for uprootings and travel fits in happily with the peaceful fatalism natural to the bourgeoise that I am. A gipsy henceforth I certainly am, and one whom tours have led from town to town, but an orderly gipsy, careful to mend her well-brushed garments herself; a gipsy who nearly always carries her slender fortune on her person;

but in the little suède bag, the coppers are in one compartment, the silver in another, while the gold is preciously hidden in a secret pocket.

A vagabond, maybe, but one who is resigned to revolving on the same spot like my companions and brethren. It is true that departures sadden and exhilarate me, and whatever I pass through—new countries, skies pure or cloudy, seas under rain the colour of a grey pearl —something of myself catches on it and clings so passionately that I feel as though I were leaving behind me a thousand little phantoms in my image, rocked on the waves, cradled in the leaves, scattered among the clouds. But does not a last little phantom, more like me than any of the others, remain sitting in my chimney corner, lost in a dream and as good as gold as it bends over a book which it forgets to open?

PART TWO

ONE

"WHAT a charming, cosy nest! I must say it's hard to imagine your existence in the music-hall when one sees you here between this rosy lamp and that vase of carnations."

Such was the parting remark of my admirer the first time he came to dinner at my flat, with Hamond the go-between. For I have an admirer. Only this old-fashioned name seems to suit him: he is neither my lover, nor my flame, nor my gigolo; he is my admirer.

"What a charming, cosy nest!" That evening I laughed bitterly behind his back. To think that a shaded lamp, a crystal vase filled with sparkling water, an easy chair drawn up close to the table, and a divan whose shabbiness is masked by a cunning disorder of cushions—to think that all that can so dazzle the casual visitor as to make him imagine, between these faded green walls, the secluded, contemplative and studious life of a gifted woman. Ah, but he hasn't noticed the dusty inkpot, the dry pen and the uncut book on the empty box of stationery!

An old spray of holly, contorted as though it had been through fire, curls over the edge of an earthenware pot. The cracked glass of a little pastel (one of Adolphe Taillandy's sketches) waits in vain to be replaced. Round the electric bulb which lights the fireplace I have carelessly pinned, and then forgotten, a torn sheet of paper. A pile of five hundred postcards—scenes from *The Pursuit*—, banded with grey paper, lies on a fifteenth-century carved ivory and threatens to crush it.

The whole place gives an impression of indifference, neglect, hopelessness, almost of imminent departure. Cosy? Could one so describe anything that happens in the evening here, under the lamp with its faded shade?

After my two guests had left I laughed, and sighed with weariness, and the night that followed was so troubled by an obscure sense of shame, born of the very admiration of the Big-Noodle, that it seemed endless. His belief in me, the innocent belief of a man very much in love, enlightened me about myself that evening just as an unexpected mirror, at a street corner or on a staircase, suddenly reveals blemishes and saggings in one's face and figure.

But since then there have been other evenings when Hamond came with my admirer, or my admirer without Hamond. My old friend conscientiously performs what he calls his sordid task. Sometimes he presides with the brilliant ease of a former wit over the visits of his pupil who, without him, I admit in all sincerity, would be too much for me. Sometimes he effaces himself, though not for long, or keeps us waiting, just long enough, exercising on my behalf that social diplomacy of his which was getting rusty.

I do not dress up for them, and change neither my pleated shirt-blouse nor my plain dark skirt. I "let my face go" when they are there, mouth tired and shut and eyes deliberately dull, and to my admirer's persistence I oppose the passive bearing of a girl whom her parents want to marry against her will. The only thing I take trouble over, for my own sake more than theirs, is the sketchy, deceptive interior where I live so little; Blandine has condescended to explore the dusty corners of the study, and the cushions of the armchair in front of the table are still flattened from the last time I rested there.

I have an admirer. Why should it be this one and not another? I have no idea. I look in astonishment at this man who has managed to worm his way into my flat. My word, how desperately he wanted to! Luck was on his side every time, and Hamond helped him. One day, when I was all alone, I opened the door to a timid ring; and how could I possibly have thrust out this creature standing there awkwardly waiting, his arms full of roses, with Hamond beside him gazing imploringly at me? He has managed to worm his way in here, and no doubt it was bound to happen.

Every time he comes now, I have to get to know his face as though I had never seen it before. On each side of his nose there is a crease, already quite deep, which disappears under his moustache, and he has the rather swarthy red lips which you find in people who are almost too dark. His hair and his eyebrows and lashes are as black as the devil, and it needed a very bright ray of sunshine one day to show me that, beneath all that black, my admirer's eyes are a tawny grey, and very deep set.

Standing up, he really is a Big-Noodle, stiff, awkward and nothing but bones. Sitting, or half-reclining on the divan, he seems to grow supple all of a sudden, and to enjoy the pleasure of being quite a different man, lazy and relaxed, moving his hands gracefully as he settles his head indolently back against the cushions.

When I know that he cannot see me, I observe him, feeling vaguely shocked at the thought that I do not know him at all and that the presence of this young man in my flat is as unexpected as a piano in a kitchen.

How is it that he, who is in love with me, is not in the
least disturbed that he knows me so little? He clearly
never gives that a thought, and his one idea is first to
reassure me and afterwards to conquer me. For if he has
very quickly learnt—on Hamond's advice, I'll bet—to
hide his desire and subdue his look and his voice when
he speaks to me, if he pretends, cunning as an animal,
to have forgotten that he wants to possess me, neither
does he show any eagerness to find out what I am like,
to question me or read my character, and I notice that he
pays more attention to the play of light on my hair than
to what I am saying.

How strange all that is! There he sits close to me, the
same ray of sun gliding over his cheek and mine, and if
it makes his nostrils glow ruby-red, it must be tinting
mine bright coral. He is not there, he is a thousand
leagues away! I keep wanting to get up and say to him:
"Why are you here? Go away!" And I do nothing of the
kind.

Does he think? Does he read? Does he work? I believe
he belongs to that large rather commonplace class of
persons who are interested in everything and do absolutely nothing. Not a trace of wit, a certain quickness of
comprehension, a very adequate vocabulary enhanced by
a beautiful rich voice, that readiness to laugh with a
childish gaiety that one sees in many men—such is my
admirer.

To be entirely honest, let me mention what I like best
in him: a look that is sometimes absent and seeking, and
that kind of private smile in the eyes which one sees in
sensitive people who are both violent and shy.

He has travelled, but just like everyone else: not very
far and not often. He has read what everyone reads, he
knows "quite a few people" and cannot name three

intimate friends, in addition to his elder brother. I forgive him all this ordinariness for the sake of a simplicity which has nothing humble about it, and because he finds nothing to say about himself.

His glance rarely meets mine, which I turn aside. I cannot forget the reason for his presence and for his patience. And yet what a difference between the man sitting there on this divan and the cruel animal, full of fierce desire, who forced the door of my dressing-room! Nothing about me shows that I remember our first meeting, except the fact that I hardly talk to the Big-Noodle. Whatever subject he tries, I answer him briefly, or else I address to Hamond the reply destined for my admirer. This type of indirect conversation gives our meetings a slowness and a false gaiety that are quite indescribable.

TWO

I AM still rehearsing the new act with Brague. Sometimes in the mornings the *Folies-Bergère* takes us in,
or else the *Empyrée-Clichy* lends us its stage for an hour;
or else we wander from the *Brasserie Gambrinus*, which is
used to the noise of Baret's tours, to the Cernuschi
dancing-hall.

"It's beginning to look like something," says Brague,
as eager for compliments for others as for himself.

The Old Troglodyte rehearses with us: he is a famished-
looking youth of eighteen, whom Brague assists, dumb-
founds and shatters with insults till I am moved to pity:
"You're really going too far, Brague, he's going to cry!"

"Just let him cry and I'll boot him in the backside!
He's got to work, not weep!"

Perhaps he is right. The Old Troglodyte gulps back his
tears, humps his back in what he hopes is a "prehistoric"
way, and sets himself to guarding a Hamadryad attitu-
dinising in a white knitted sweater.

One morning last week Brague took the trouble to
come in person to warn me that there would be no
rehearsal the following day. He found Hamond,
Dufferein-Chautel and myself finishing lunch. I had to
keep Brague a few minutes, offer him coffee and introduce
him to my guests. And I saw his bright little black eyes
linger furtively on my admirer with a curious satisfaction,
a sort of security, which made me feel stupidly uncomfortable.

When I accompanied him to the door again my comrade did not question me or permit himself any familiar

allusions, and my embarrassment was redoubled. It would
have been too absurd to explain: "That's a friend of
Hamond's who came to lunch. He's just a pal, you
know."

Fossette is now wearing a collar of red morocco with
gilded studs, in deplorable sporting taste. I have not
dared to say that I found it ugly. Wretched little servile
female that she is, she fawns on the well-dressed gentleman who smells of man and tobacco, and knows just the
right way to pat her back.

Blandine outdoes herself, cleaning the windows and,
without being asked, bringing in the tea-tray when my
admirer is there.

All of them, following the example of my old friend
Hamond, look as if they are plotting against me in favour
of Maxime Dufferein-Chautel. Alas, it costs me so little
effort to remain invulnerable! Invulnerable, and worse
than insensitive: shrinking. For when I give my hand to
my admirer, the touch of his long hand, warm and dry,
surprises and displeases me. I cannot brush against the
stuff of his jacket without a little nervous shudder, and
when he speaks I involuntarily avoid his breath, healthy
though it is. I could never bring myself to tie his tie, and
I would rather drink from Hamond's glass than from his.
Why?

It is because . . . this fellow is *a man*. In spite of myself
I cannot forget that he is *a man*. Hamond is not a man,
he is a friend. And Brague is a comrade; so is Bouty.
The slender, muscular acrobats who reveal, beneath their
shimmering tights, the most flattering details of their
anatomy, well, they are just acrobats!

Has it ever occurred to me that Brague, who in *The
Pursuit* clasps me hard enough to bruise my ribs, and

looks as if he were crushing my mouth under a passionate kiss, had a sex? No. And yet the most fleeting glance from my admirer, the most correct handshake, remind me why he is there and what he hopes. What a delightful pastime he would be for a coquette! What an agreeable flame, provocative and determined!

The trouble is that I do not know how to flirt. I have neither the disposition, nor the experience, nor the light touch necessary, and above all—oh above all—I have the memory of my husband.

If for a single instant I call to mind Adolphe Taillandy when he was on the job, by which I mean working, with that ruthless unswerving pursuit characteristic of him, to seduce a woman or a young girl, I immediately grow frigid, shrinking, and utterly hostile to "the business of love". I see again, too well, his look of conquest, with lowered lids, sly, childish mouth, and that trick of dilating his nostrils when a particular perfume drifted by. Ugh! All that manœuvring, those elaborate preparations for love, for a goal that one cannot even call love, am I to encourage and even to imitate that sort of thing? Poor Dufferein-Chautel! Sometimes it seems to me that it is you who are being deceived here, and that I ought to tell you . . . to tell you what? That I have become an old maid again with no temptations, and that the four walls of my dressing-room at the music-hall are for me a cloister?

No, I shall not tell you that because, like those who have got to the tenth lesson at the Berlitz School, we only know how to exchange elementary phrases where the words *bread, salt, window, temperature, theatre* and *family* play a great part.

You are a *man*, so much the worse for you! Everyone in my house seems to remember it, not in the way I do, but in order to congratulate you because of it, from Blandine who gazes at you with a never-wearying satisfaction, to Fossette whose wide doggy smile says just as clearly: "At last *a man* in the house—behold THE MAN!"

I don't know how to talk to you, poor Dufferein-Chautel. I hesitate between my own *personal* language, which is rather brusque, does not always condescend to finish its sentences, but sets great store on getting its technical terms exact—the language of a one-time bluestocking—and the slovenly, lively idiom, coarse and picturesque, which one learns in the music-hall, sprinkled with expressions like: "You bet!" "Shut your trap!" "I'm going to hop it!" "Not my line!"

Unable to decide, I choose silence.

THREE

"DEAR Hamond, how happy I am to be lunching with you! No rehearsal today, but sunshine, and you, it's all perfect!"

My old friend, who is suffering from stabs of rheumatism, smiles at me, flattered. He is at present very thin and looks older and somehow light. Being very tall, too, all that, and his bony, aquiline nose gives him a great resemblance to the Knight of the Dolorous Countenance.

"Yet I rather think we have already had the pleasure of lunching together this week? What overflowing affection for my old carcass, Renée!"

"That's just it, I *am* overflowing! It's a fine day, I feel gay, and . . . we're all alone!"

"Which means?"

"That the Big-Noodle isn't here, you've guessed it!"

Hamond shakes his long, melancholy head: "It's an aversion, there's no doubt of it!"

"Not at all, Hamond, not at all! It's . . . it's nothing. All right then, I'll tell you, I've been thinking of being frank with you for some days past: the trouble is I can't discover that I have the slightest feeling for Dufferein-Chautel, unless perhaps it is distrust."

"That's something."

"I haven't even any opinion about him."

"Well then it'll be a pleasure for me to offer you mine. The honest creature has no history."

"Not enough!"

"Not enough? You're really too difficult! You don't encourage him to tell you what he has."

"That would be the last straw! Can't you see him, with his large hand on his large heart: 'I am not a man like other men. . . .' That's what he'd say, isn't it? Men always say the same thing as women do, at such times."

Hamond's eyes dwell on me with an ironic look.

"I always like you, Renée, when you assume an experience which—happily—you lack. 'Men do this . . . men say that. . . .' Where did you glean such assurance? Men! Men! Have you known so many?"

"Only one. But what a one!"

"That's just it. But you aren't accusing Maxime of reminding you of Taillandy, are you?"

"Heavens, no! He reminds me of nothing at all. Nothing, I tell you! He isn't witty . . ."

"People in love are always a bit idiotic. Take me, for instance, when I was in love with Jeanne . . ."

"Not to mention me, when I was in love with Adolphe! But that was a conscious idiocy, almost voluptuous. Do you remember the evenings when we dined out, Adolphe and I, and I would put on my poor look, my 'look of a dowerless daughter', as Margot used to say? My husband held forth, smiled, laid down the law and shone. No one had eyes for anyone but him. If anyone cast a glance at me I am sure it was to pity him. I was made to understand so well that, without him, I didn't exist."

"Oh, come now, that's a bit exaggerated."

"Not very much, Hamond! Don't protest! I wholeheartedly tried to efface myself as much as possible. I was so fatuously in love with him!"

"I was just the same, just the same!" says Hamond, warming up. "D'you remember when my small chit of a Jeanne used to give her opinion on my pictures? 'Henri was born conscientious and old-fashioned', she would declare. And I never said a word."

We laugh and feel happy, rejuvenated by this stirring up of humiliating and bitter memories. Why must my old friend spoil this Saturday, so much in harmony with all our traditions, by bringing in the name of Dufferein-Chautel?

I make a cross face. "There you go again! Do give me a bit of a rest from that gentleman, Hamond! What do I know about him? That he's clean, well brought up, is fond of bulldogs and smokes cigarettes. That he happens, into the bargain, to be in love with me is not—to be modest—a very special characteristic."

"But you do everything in your power never to get to know him!"

"Well, I have every right."

That irritates Hamond, who clucks his tongue disapprovingly: "Your right, your right! My dear friend, you argue like a child, I do assure you!"

I take away my hand, which he had covered with his own, and speak fast, in spite of myself: "You do assure me of what? That he's a gilt-edged security? What is it you really want? That I should go to bed with this gentleman?"

"Renée!"

"Well, one might as well say it! You want me to act like everyone else? To make up my mind? Him or someone else, what's it matter! You want to upset my newly-recovered peace, to make me exchange the keen, invigorating, natural care of earning my own living for a care of a different kind? Or perhaps you're advising me to take a lover for health reasons, as a blood-purifier? But what for? I'm in good health and, thank God, I love no one, no one, and never again will I love anyone, anyone, anyone!"

I shouted that so loud that all of a sudden I fall silent,

quite abashed. Hamond, who is not so carried away as I, gives me time to get a grip on myself while my blood, which had risen to my cheeks, runs slowly back to my heart.

"You'll never again love anyone? Alas, that may be true! And that would be saddest of all. To think of you, young and strong, and affectionate. . . . Yes, that would be saddest of all."

Indignant, and on the verge of tears, I gaze at the friend who dares to speak thus to me: "Oh Hamond, can it be you who say that to me! After what has happened to you . . . to us, could you still hope for love?"

Hamond turns away his gaze, stares at the window with those eyes that are so young in his old face, and replies vaguely: "Yes. It's true I'm very happy as I am. But just because of that, to answer for myself and definitely say: 'I shall never love again,' good lord no, I wouldn't dare!"

That strange answer from Hamond put an end to our discussion, for I don't like talking of love. The broadest of broad jokes doesn't scare me, but I don't like talking of love. If I had lost a beloved child, it seems to me that I should never again be able to pronounce its name.

FOUR

"COME and have a bite at Olympe's this evening," said Brague to me at the rehearsal. "And afterwards we'll go and say hullo to the boys in the *Revue* at the *Emp'-Clich'*."

There's no danger of my misunderstanding: this is not an *invitation* to dinner; we are two *comrades*, and the protocol—for there is one—governing comradeship between artistes banishes all ambiguity.

So I rejoin Brague this evening at Olympe's bar, whose doubtful reputation does not in the least disturb me. Now that I need give no thought to my own reputation, I feel neither apprehension nor pleasure when I enter this little Montmartre restaurant, which is silent from seven to ten and resounds all the rest of the night with what seems rather a deliberate din made up of shouts, the clatter of crockery and the twanging of guitars. I sometimes used to go and dine there in haste, alone or with Brague, last month, before we went on to the *Empyrée-Clichy*.

This evening a waitress from the country, tranquil and slow in the midst of the calls for her, serves us with pickled pork and cabbage, a filling, nourishing dish, rather heavy for the stomachs of the poor little local prostitutes who sit eating near us, by themselves, with that aggressive look which animals and under-nourished women adopt when a heaped plate is put before them. No, indeed, the place is not always gay!

Brague, mocking but compassionate at heart, speaks slightingly of two thin young women who have just entered, with idiotic hats balanced precariously on their curly heads. One of them is striking, and carries her head with a kind of angry insolence; every line of her exaggerated slenderness shows, in all its grace, beneath a tight sheath of pink Liberty silk, bought from the second-hand clothes woman. On this freezing February evening all she has to cover her is a cloak, a sort of light cape, also of Liberty silk, blue and embroidered with tarnished silver. She is frozen, almost beside herself with cold, and her furious grey eyes repulse all compassion; she is ready to insult, or even to claw, the first person who says to her, sympathetically, "Poor child!"

Young women of this kind, slowly dying of misery and pride, beautiful in their stark poverty, are by no means uncommon in this district of Montmartre. I meet them here and there, trailing their flimsy garments from table to table at supper-time on the Butte, gay, drunk, and fierce, always ready to bite, never gentle, never affectionate, resenting their profession and "working" all the same. The men call them "wretched little sluts", with a contemptuous but admiring laugh, because they belong to a breed which never gives in, never admits to cold or hunger or love; little sluts who die saying: "I'm not ill," who may bleed under blows, but hit back all the same.

Yes, I know something of those girls, and it is of them that I am reminded as I watch the proud, frozen young girl who has just come into Olympe's.

A hungry half-silence reigns in the bar. Two painted young men exchange barbed repartee from opposite ends of the room, without any conviction. A street-girl with short legs, who is dining on a crème-de-menthe with water while awaiting a problematical supper, throws out a few half-hearted retorts. A bulldog bitch, in pup to bursting point, pants painfully on the threadbare carpet, her balloon of a stomach studded with knob-like teats.

Brague and I chat, relaxed by the warmth of the gas. I think of all the mediocre restaurants in all the towns which have seen us thus seated at table, tired, indifferent and curious, before strange meats. The hog-wash of station buffets and hotel restaurants is never too much for Brague's iron stomach; but as for me, if the plain veal or the leg of mutton *bonne femme* are so leathery that they defeat me, I make up on the cheese and the omelette.

"I say, Brague, that man over there with his back to us, isn't it Stephen-the-Dancer?"

"Where? Yes, that's him all right . . . with a tart."

Such a "tart", in fact, that I remain flabbergasted at the sight of that fifty-year-old brunette with her dark moustache. And as if he felt our eyes on him, Stephen-the-Dancer half turns to throw us one of those knowing looks which are used in the theatre to convey: "Not a word! It's a mystery!" discreetly enough to be noticed by the whole house.

"Poor wretch, he certainly earns any money *he* gets," whispers Brague. "Coffee, Mademoiselle," he calls, "we've got to skedaddle."

The coffee is an olive-black ink which leaves a clinging stain on the sides of the cups. But as a result of never drinking good coffee any more, I have come to like these hot, bitter brews which smell of liquorice and quinine. In our profession we can do without meat but not without coffee.

Quickly as they serve us ours, Stephen-the-Dancer "skedaddles" before us—he is *rinking* in the *Revue* at the *Emp'-Clich'*—in the wake of his companion. Behind her back he shamelessly imitates for us the gesture of the athlete who "heaves" the four hundred pound weight, and we are cowardly enough to laugh. Then we leave this sad, so-called "pleasure" haunt, where by this time everyone is getting drowsy under the pink lights: the pregnant bitch, the exhausted street-girls, the waitress from the country and the manager with his waxed moustache.

Once outside, the outer boulevard and the Place Blanche, round which an icy wind circles, revive us, and I feel myself joyfully seized once more with an active passion, a real need to *work*, a mysterious and undefined need which I could satisfy equally well by dancing, writing, running, acting, or pulling a hand-cart.

As if the same desire had seized him, Brague suddenly says to me: "By the way, I've had a word from the agent, Salomon. The tour I spoke about's taking shape. He's fixing up one day here and two there, a week in Marseilles and another in Bordeaux. You can still go?"

"Me? Right away! Why not?"

He darts a sharp sideways glance at me.

"Oh, I don't know. Sometimes a mere trifle . . . I know what life is . . ."

So that's it! My comrade remembers Dufferein-Chautel and thinks that . . . My sudden laugh, instead of undeceiving him, bewilders him still further, but this evening I feel in a gay and teasing mood, and as light-hearted as if we had set off already. Oh, how lovely to go away, to move from one place to another, to forget who I am and the name of the town which sheltered me the day before, scarcely to think, to receive and retain no impressions but that of the beautiful landscape which unfolds and changes as the train runs past, of the lead-coloured pool in which the blue sky is reflected green, and the open-work spire of a belfry encircled with swallows.

I remember a day, a May morning, when I was leaving Rennes. The train very slowly followed a track under repair between coppices of white hawthorn, pink apple-trees which cast a blue shadow, and very young willows with leaves of jade. A child, standing at the edge of the wood, watched us pass, a little girl of twelve whose resemblance to myself struck me. A serious child with frowning brows, and tanned round cheeks—as mine were—, and hair a little bleached by the sun, she was holding a leafy shoot in her sunburnt hands covered with scratches—as mine were. Her unsociable look, too, and those ageless, almost sexless, eyes which seemed to take everything seriously, were mine also, really mine. It was indeed my own shy childhood which stood there, dazzled by the sun, at the edge of that coppice and watched me pass.

"Whenever you like, then!"

My comrade's curt invitation brings me back to earth in front of the *Emp'-Clich'*, glittering with mauve lights, whose glare, as Brague says, hurts "the back of your eyes". We descend to the basement, where the familiar smell of plaster, ammonia, *Crème Simon* and rice-powder, rouses in me a disgust that is almost pleasant. We've come to see our pals in the *Revue*, we have, and not the *Revue* itself!

I find my old dressing-room, at present inhabited by Bouty, and Brague's, which is now filled with the dazzling presence of Jadin who is playing three parts in the *Emp'-Clich'-Revue*.

"Stir your stumps!" she calls to us. "You're just in time for my song, *Night-time in Paris*."

Alas, they have dressed Jadin as a street-walker! A black skirt, a low-cut black bodice, cobweb-fine stockings, a red ribbon round her neck and, on her head, the traditional helmet-shaped wig with a blood-red camellia in it. There is not a trace left of the endearing, guttersnipe charm of that young girl with the hunched shoulder.

It was, I suppose, inevitable that they should quickly turn my sulky young apache into the ordinary little *café-concert* singer. While we exchange the "How goes it?" "What's the news?" "Things shaping?" I watch her moving about her dressing-room, and realise with a shock that Jadin walks like a tart, as all of them do, with her stomach drawn in and her chest out, that she is careful to *pitch* her voice when she speaks, and that she has not once said "B—— it!" since we arrived.

Bouty, who is to dance the inevitable cancan with her, beams at us under his silk cap and says nothing. One feels he might at any moment say "Now what about it?", and point at the little creature with a proprietary gesture. Has he at last vanquished his comrade? At any rate I guess that it is he who is making Jadin commonplace and now there they both are, talking of doing a "sensational turn", very well paid, at the Crystal Palace in London!

How quickly everything changes, especially women! In a few months this one will lose nearly all her piquancy, her natural and unconscious pathos. Will that hare-brained, eighteen-year-old Jadin, so prodigal of herself and her scanty cash, suddenly reveal an upsurge of craftiness, the craftiness of concierges and grasping small tradesmen? Why in her presence am I reminded of the Bells, German acrobats with an English name, whom Brague and I knew in Brussels? Of unequalled strength and grace in their cerise tights which made their fair skin look paler still, the five of them lived in two rooms without furniture, where they cooked for themselves on a

little iron stove. And all day long, the impresario told
us, it was nothing but mysterious discussions, consult-
ings of financial newspapers, and fierce disputes concern-
ing gold-mines, railway shares and the Egyptian Land
Loan. Money, money, money.

Jadin's empty chatter enlivens our visit, which needs
enlivening. After Bouty, who is slightly less thin, has
given us news of his health and announced that, "things
are shaping" for the following winter, we fall silent and
embarrassed, chance friends whom chance has separated.
I fiddle with the grease-paint and pencils on the little
shelf, with that greedy exasperation, that itch for make-
up, familiar to anyone who has ever trodden the boards.
Fortunately, the little bell tinkles and Jadin jumps to her
feet: "Look sharp, up we go! The fireman'll give you
his stage-box and you'll see what a hit I make in my
Night-time in Paris song."

The sleepy fireman does in fact lend me his straw-
bottomed stool and his little box. Sitting there, with my
nose to the grating which frames a square of warm, reddish light, I can see, without myself being seen, half of
two rows of the stalls and three uncurtained boxes, as
well as a stage-box. In this stage-box I can make out a
lady in an enormous hat, with pearls, rings and sequins,
and two men who are. Dufferein-Chautel senior and
Dufferein-Chautel junior, both of them looking very
black and white, and very sleek and smart. They are
relentlessly illuminated and, framed by my grating, they
take on an extraordinary importance.

The woman is not a woman, she is a *lady*: Madame
Dufferein-Chautel senior, no doubt. My admirer, for his
part, seems to be greatly amused by the march past of
the girl rag-pickers, and of the girl cabbies who follow
them and, after singing a couplet, dance casually off.

Finally comes Jadin, who announces herself: "And I —I am the Queen of Night-time Paris: I am the Street Walker!"

I see my admirer bend rather eagerly over the programme and then raise his head and study my little comrade closely, from her helmet of hair to her open-work stockings.

By a curious transposition, he it is who becomes the spectacle for me, for I can only see little Jadin in profile; the blinding footlights make her face look like a skull, with black nostrils and a lip foreshortened above a gleaming row of teeth, as if her face had been eaten by the light. With her neck stretched out gargoyle-fashion, a red rag knotted round it, this young girl suddenly resembles some lewd spectre by Félicien Rops.

When, at the end of her number, she twice returns to take her call, her heels together and her fingers to her lips, my admirer claps her with his big brown hands so loudly that, before she disappears, she throws him a little kiss all for himself, with a forward thrust of her chin.

"What's the matter, are you asleep? This is the second time I've told you that you can't stay there; they're setting the scene for Heliopolis!"

"All right, all right, I'm coming."

I think in fact that I must have fallen asleep, or else I am just emerging from one of those moments when one's mind goes blank before some painful idea is set in motion, moments which are the prelude to a slight loss of morale.

FIVE

"COME on now, either make up your mind or don't.
Does it seem to you all right, or doesn't it?"

There they both are, Brague and Salomon, harrying
me with their looks and their voices. Salomon laughs to
reassure me, while Brague keeps muttering. Then
Salomon lays his heavy hand on my shoulder and says:
"As contracts go, it's pretty good, I think!"

I have the typed contract in my hand, and I re-read it
for the tenth time for fear there may be some hidden
snare, some suspicious clause, lurking among its fifteen
short lines. Above all I re-read it to gain time. And then
I look at the window, the curtains of starched net, and
behind them the sad, clean courtyard.

I look as if I am reflecting, but I am not reflecting.
Hesitating is not reflecting. Absentmindedly, I examine
the contents of the English-type desk I have seen so
many times before, covered with foreign photographs:
half-length portraits of ladies in low-necked frocks, with
Viennese smiles; men in evening dress who might
equally well be singers or acrobats, mimes or ring-masters
—impossible to say which.

A six weeks tour at a hundred and fifty francs a day,
that makes six thousand francs. Pretty good. But . . .

"But," I finally say to Salomon, "I don't want to put
six hundred francs in your fat purse. Ten per cent, all
said and done, is sheer murder."

I have found my voice again and the art of using it,
and the right vocabulary for the occasion. Salomon turns
the colour of his hair, brick-red; even his shifty eyes go

bloodshot, but from his full, pleasant mouth pours a flood of almost amorous supplications.

"My darling, my pet, don't start saying silly things. I've been working at your itinerary for a month now, a whole month. Ask Brague! For a month I've been wearing myself out to find first-class houses for you, absolutely first-class. And posters like . . . like Madame Otéro, think of it! And that's the way you thank me! Haven't you got a heart? Ten per cent? Why it's twelve, not ten, you ought to give me, d'you hear?"

"Yes, I hear. But I don't want to put six hundred francs in your fat purse. You aren't worth such a sum."

Salomon's little red eyes grow smaller still. The heavy hand caressing my shoulder would like to crush me.

"Oh, you ungrateful wretch! Look at her, Brague! A child who owed her first engagement to me!"

"A child who's now jolly well of age, my friend, and in need of some new clothes. D'you realise my costume for *The Pursuit* is worn out? Thirty pounds for a character costume, plus the slippers, plus the veil for my dance—all the accessories, in short. You're not going to pay me for all those separately, are you, old skinflint?"

"Look at her, Brague!" repeats Salomon. "I feel ashamed for her in front of you. Whatever will you think of her?"

"I think," says Brague tranquilly, "that she would be right to accept the tour and wrong to give you six hundred francs."

"All right then. Give me back the papers."

The fat hand lets go of me. Frowning and pale, Salomon goes back to his English-style desk without a glance at us.

"Come now, Salomon, let's stop pretending. I'm an absolute bitch when I want to be, and if anyone irritates me I don't care a fig if the whole thing goes down the drain!"

"Madame," answers Salomon, very dignified and stiff, "you've spoken to me as though you despised me, and I've taken it to heart."

"Silly ass!" interrupts Brague, without raising his voice. "Stop playing the fool! Six hundred for her share, four hundred and forty for mine . . . d'you take us for German acrobats? Give me the forms; we aren't going to sign to-day. I want twenty-four hours to consult my family."

"In that case, it's up the spout," splutters Salomon excitably. "All those people are directors of very smart houses, people who don't like being trifled with, people . . ."

"Yes, yes, I know, who go up in smoke if you cross them," interrupts my comrade. "All right, then, tell them I'll be back tomorrow. Coming, Renée? Salomon, it's seven and a half per cent for the two of us. And I call that big and generous."

Salomon wipes his dry eyes and his damp forehead.

"There you go again, I still think you're a pretty pair of sharpers."

"Well, Salomon, I can't say you're so very handsome yourself."

"Leave him alone, Renée, he's a dear creature really. He'll do as we want. In the first place, he loves you. Don't you, Salomon?"

But Salomon is sulking. He turns his back like a big child and says in a tearful voice: "No. Take yourselves off. I don't want to see you any more. I'm really hurt. It's the very first time, since I started to book engagements, that anyone has inflicted such a humiliation on me. Off with you! I want to be alone. I don't want to see you any more."

"Right you are. Till tomorrow!"

"No, no! It's all over between us three."

"Five o'clock?"

Seated at his desk, Salomon lifts his tearful pink face towards us. "Five o'clock? Well I'm blowed, I suppose I must now miss my rendezvous at the Alhambra for you? Not before six, d'you hear?"

Disarmed, I squeeze his stubby fist, and we leave.

The street is so crowded that conversation is impossible, so we are silent. I dread the comparative solitude of the Boulevard Malesherbes, where Brague will begin to argue and convince me. I am convinced in advance and have made up my mind to go. Hamond will not be pleased. Margot will say to me: "You're quite right, my girl!" though she will be quite sure I am not, but she will give me excellent advice, and three or four boxes of "specialities" against headaches, fever and constipation.

And to come down to Dufferein-Chautel, what will he say? It amuses me to think of his face. He will console himself with Jadin, that's all. And I shall depart . . . already I begin to ask how soon.

"What was the date, Brague? I paid no attention to that, just fancy!"

Brague shrugs his shoulders and stands close to me among the cluster of pedestrians waiting submissively until the white baton cleaves the line of carriages, and opens a passage for us from the pavement of the Boulevard Haussmann to the island on the Place Saint-Augustin.

"If we had to depend on you to button up the engagements, my poor friend! Madame rants, and mounts her high horse, Madame wants this, won't have that, and then, at the end of it all, 'Fancy, I paid no attention to the date!'"

Deferentially, I let him enjoy his superiority. It is one of Brague's keenest pleasures to treat me as a novice, a blundering pupil. Protected by the policeman's baton, we hurry as far as the Boulevard Malesherbes.

"From April 5th to May 15th," finishes Brague. "You've nothing against that? Nothing to keep you?"

"Nothing."

We walk up the boulevard, panting a little because of the steam which rises from the damp pavement as from a warm bath. The thaw has set in with a slight, almost stormy, shower; the lights are reflected, elongated and iridescent, in the blackish pavement. The top of the avenue is lost to view in a blurred mist, faintly rosy in the lingering dusk. Involuntarily I look back and all about me, searching for . . . what? Nothing. No, nothing keeps me here, or elsewhere. No dear face will rise from the mist, like a flower emerging from dark water, to beg tenderly: "Don't go away!"

So I shall leave, once again. The fifth of April is a long way off—it is now February 15th—but it is as if I had already left, and I pay no heed as Brague lists in my ear the names of towns and hotels and figures, figures, figures. . . .

"Are you at least listening to me?"

"Yes."

"So you're not doing anything between now and April 5th?"

"Not that I know of!"

"You wouldn't consider a little act, just any kind of little silly thing, something rather elegant, to occupy you between now and then?"

"My goodness, no."

"If you like, I'll look for a little weekly engagement for you?"

I thank my comrade, on parting from him, because I feel touched that he should want to save me from hard times and the idleness which demoralises out-of-work

actors, diminishing their powers and making them go
to pieces.

Three heads are raised when I enter my study:
Hamond's, Fossette's, and Dufferein-Chautel's. All three
huddled round a little table under the pink lampshade,
they were playing *écarté* while they waited for me.
Fossette knows how to play cards in the bulldog manner:
perched on a chair, she follows the come and go of hands,
ready to seize as it flies past any card thrown too far.

Hamond cries "At last!", Fossette "Wuff!", and
Dufferein-Chautel says nothing, but he very nearly barked
too.

To leave the fetid fog outside, for this joyful welcome
under the softly-shaded light, so raises my spirits that in
a burst of affectionate joy I cry: "Greetings! What d'you
think, I'm going away!"

"You're going away? How d'you mean? When?"

In spite of himself a slightly curt and inquisitorial note
has crept into my admirer's voice; but I pay no attention
to that as I roll up my gloves and take off my hat.

"I'll tell you all about it over dinner. You'll both stay:
it's almost a farewell dinner already. Stay where you are
and go on with your little game; I'll send Blandine to get
some cutlets and go and slip into a dressing-gown; I'm
worn out!"

When I return, enveloped in the folds of a rose-
coloured flannel kimono, I notice that both Hamond and
Dufferein-Chautel have the too-casual look of people who
have been plotting something. What does it matter? My
adorer this evening is reaping the benefit of an optimism
which embraces every living thing: I invite him to offer
us some of the Saint-Marceaux from the grocer next door,

to "drink to the tour", and he runs off at once without his hat, returning with two bottles under his arm.

Feeling feverish and a little tipsy, I bend on my admirer a trustful look which he has never seen on my face before. I laugh aloud with a laugh he has never heard, I roll the wide sleeves of my kimono back to my shoulder, revealing arms which he says are "the colour of a peeled banana". I feel kind and gentle, and for two pins I would offer him my cheek: what does it matter? I'm going away, I shall never see this young man again! It's only for forty days? Oh, but we shall certainly all be dead by the time they're over!

Poor admirer, how badly I've treated him, all the same! Now he seems to me pleasant, clean, well-groomed, and considerate . . . like someone one will never see again! For when I come back I shall have forgotten him, and he too will have forgotten me . . . with little Jadin, or with someone else. But more likely with little Jadin.

"I say, what about that little Jadin!"

I have uttered this remark, which seems to me extremely funny, at the top of my voice. My admirer, who finds it difficult to laugh this evening, wrinkles his coal-miner's eyebrows as he looks at me: "What d'you mean, that little Jadin?"

"She rather took your fancy the other day, didn't she? At the *Emp'-Clich'*?"

Dufferein-Chautel bends towards me, intrigued. As his face emerges from the zone of shadow cast by the lamp-shade, I can see the exact shade of his brown eyes, tawny and gold-flecked like certain agates from the Dauphiné.

"Were you in the audience? I didn't see you."

I empty my glass before replying, mysteriously: "Ah, you see!"

"Well, well, so you were there! Yes, she's charming, is little Jadin. You know her? I find her very charming."

"More than me?"

This imprudent, idiotic remark, so unworthy of me, might well have deserved a different reply from the astonished silence with which he greeted it. I could have kicked myself. Oh well, what does it matter? I'm going away! I describe my itinerary: a complete tour of France, but only the big towns! Posters like . . . like Madame Otéro! And the lovely places I shall see, and the sun I shall find in the South, and . . . and . . .

The champagne—three glasses, but that is quite enough—finally lulls my happy chatter. What an expenditure of energy talking is for someone who remains silent for days together! My two friends are smoking now, and slowly, slowly, they recede behind their veil of smoke. How far away I feel, as if I had already left, cut adrift, and taken refuge in my journey! Their voices grow muffled and fade into the distance, mingling with the rumbling of trains, with whistlings and the lulling swell of an imaginary orchestra. Ah, what a delicious departure, what a sweet sleep, which wafts me towards an invisible shore!

"Hullo? is it six o'clock? Good, thank you. . . . Ah, it's you?"

I was asleep and dreaming of the journey: a hotel servant was knocking with his fist against the door of my dream, and calling out that it was six o'clock. And I come to, sitting up with a start in the hollow of my old divan where weariness and my slight tipsiness have made me doze off. Standing beside me, the Big-Noodle looms as high as the room. My eyes, opened too soon, blink at the lamp; the edges of the lampshade and the corners of the lighted table are like gleaming blades which wound my sight.

"It's you? Where's Hamond?"

"Hamond's just gone."

"What time is it then?"

"It's midnight."

"Midnight!"

I've slept for more than an hour! Mechanically I push up my flattened hair, combing it with my fingers, and then pull down my dressing-gown to the very tips of my bedroom slippers.

"Midnight? Why didn't you leave with Hamond?"

"We were afraid you might feel alarmed at finding yourself alone here. So I stayed."

Is he making fun of me? His face is so far above me in the shadow that I can't make it out.

"I was tired, you understand."

"I understand very well."

What is the meaning of this curt and scolding tone? I am quite staggered. Really, if I were easily frightened, this might seem just the moment to call for help, finding myself alone with this black-avised creature addressing me from such a height! Perhaps he has been drinking, too.

"I say, Dufferein-Chautel, are you ill?"

"I'm not ill."

Thank goodness, he begins to move about; I had had enough of seeing him towering so close to me!

"I'm not ill, I'm angry."

"Oh, that's it!"

I consider for a moment, and then add, stupidly enough: "Is it because I'm going away?"

Dufferein-Chautel stops short.

"Because you're going away? I never gave it a thought. Since you're still here, there's no need for me to think

that you're going away. No. I'm cross with you. I'm
cross with you because you were sleeping."

"Really?"

"It's crazy to fall asleep like that! Before Hamond, and
even before me! It's obvious you've no idea how you
look when you're asleep. Unless you do it on purpose,
and that's unworthy of you."

He sits down abruptly, as though he were breaking
himself in three, and this brings him close to me, with his
face on a level with mine.

"When you sleep you don't look as though you were
asleep. You look . . . well, to be frank, you look as though
you had closed your eyes to hide a joy that is too much
for you. You really do. You haven't the face of a woman
asleep, you . . . well, damn it, you know very well what
I'm trying to say! It's revolting. When I think that you
must have slept in that way before a heap of people, I
don't know what I couldn't do to you!"

He is seated sideways on a flimsy chair, and he half
turns away his distracted face, divided by two great
wrinkles, one on his forehead and the other running
down his cheek, as though the explosion of his wrath
had just cracked him. I am not afraid; on the contrary,
it is a relief to me to find him sincere, like the man who
entered my dressing-room two months earlier.

Once again, then, there reappears before me, with his
childish rage, his bestial persistence, his calculated sincerity, my enemy and my tormentor: love. There is no
mistaking it. I have already seen that forehead, those eyes,
and those hands convulsively gripping each other, yes, I
have seen all that . . . in the days when Adolphe Taillandy
desired me.

But what am I going to do with this one? I am not
offended, I am not even moved—or only a very little!

But what am I going to do? How shall I answer him? This continuing silence becomes more embarrassing than his avowal. If only he would go away . . . but he does not budge. I dare not risk the slightest movement, for fear a sigh, or a ripple of my gown, might be enough to rouse my adversary; I no longer dare say my admirer, no, he loves me too much.

"That's all you have to say to me?"

The sound of his voice, softened, causes me such keen pleasure that I smile with relief at being released from the suffocating silence.

"Well, I really don't see . . ."

He turned towards me with the clumsy gentleness of a big dog.

"That's quite true, you don't see. You have an absolute talent for not seeing. Whenever I'm concerned, you don't see, you see nothing. You look through me, you smile above my head, you speak to one side of me. And I act as though I didn't see that you don't see. How clever that is! And how worthy of you and of me!"

"Listen, Dufferein-Chautel . . ."

"And you call me Dufferein-Chautel! I know very well I've got a ridiculous name, the sort of name for a member of Parliament or an industrialist, or a director of a discount bank. It isn't my fault. All right, go on, laugh! It's a bit of luck, anyway," he adds in a lower tone, "that I can make you laugh."

"Well, then, what d'you want me to call you? Dufferein or Chautel? Or Duduffe? Or . . . just Maxime, or Max? I say, do pass me the hand-mirror, there, on the little table, and the powder puff: I must look a sight, what with the champagne, and sleeping, and no powder on my nose."

"That doesn't matter," he says impatiently. "Whoever d'you want to put powder on for, at this hour?"

"For myself, in the first place. And then for you."

"There's no need to bother on my account. You treat me like a man who is paying court to you. What if I were, quite simply, a man who loves you?"

I look at him, more distrustful than ever before, disconcerted to find in this man, as soon as it is a question of love between us, a remarkable intelligence and ease which his Big-Noodle-like appearance entirely belies. What I divine in him is, in fact, an aptitude for love, by virtue of which he both surpasses and embarrasses me.

"Tell me frankly, Renée, is it hateful, or a matter of indifference, or vaguely agreeable to you to know that I love you?"

He is neither insulting, nor humble, nor plaintive, nor is there anything timid or cunning about him. Copying his simplicity, I pluck up courage to reply: "I simply don't know."

"That's just what I thought," he said gravely. "Well then . . ."

"Well then?"

"There's nothing for me to do but to go away."

"It's half an hour after midnight."

"No, you haven't understood me. What I mean is: not to see you any more, to leave Paris."

"Leave Paris? Why?" I say, simply. "There's no need for that. And I haven't forbidden you to see me again."

He shrugs his shoulders.

"Oh, I know myself! When things aren't going well, when I have . . . well, worries, I go off home."

There was something provincial and tender in the way he said "home".

"Is it pretty, where you live?"

"Yes. It's forest land. Lots of firs and quite a few oaks. I love the new fellings, you know, when they've thinned out the woods, and all that remains is the saplings and the great circles left by the charcoal fires, where wood strawberries will grow the next summer."

"And lilies of the valley . . ."

"And lilies of the valley. And foxgloves too. You know? They're as tall as that, and when you're a kid you poke your fingers in the bells."

"I know."

He describes it badly, my wood-cutter from the Ardennes, but I see so well what he describes!

"I motor down there during the summer. I shoot a little too, in the autumn. It's mother's house, of course. Mother Ever-Cut!" says he, laughing. "She cuts and cuts and saws and sells."

"Oh!"

"But she doesn't damage anything, you know. She knows what wood is, she's as knowledgeable about it as a man, better than a man."

I listen to him with a new attraction, glad that he should forget me for a moment, and that he should talk, like a worthy wood-cutter, of his mother's forest. I had not remembered that he was from the Ardennes, and he had not bothered to inform me that he loved his country-side. Now I know why he has the look of a noodle! It is because he wears his clothes rather as if they were "party clothes", with an ineradicable and endearing awkwardness, like a handsome peasant in his Sunday best.

". . . Only, if you send me away, Renée, my mother will understand at once that I have come for her to 'look after' me, and she'll want once again to get me married. Look what you're exposing me to!"

"Let yourself get married."

"You don't say that seriously?"

"Why not? Because I've had an unfortunate experience myself? What does that prove? You ought to get married, it would suit you very well. You look married already. Though you're a bachelor, you have all the appearance of a young father of a family, you adore a fireside, you're affectionate and jealous and obstinate, as lazy as a spoilt husband, a despot at heart, and mono- gamous from birth!"

Stupefied, my admirer stares at me without saying a word, then leaps to his feet.

"I'm all that!" he cries. "I'm all that! She's said it! I'm all that!"

I coldly check his cries and gestures.

"Do be quiet! What's possessed you? Why should being . . . well, egoistical, and lazy, and a fireside-lover make you want to dance?"

He sits down again opposite me, very meekly, but his sheep-dog's eyes rest on me with a look of victorious sagacity.

"No. It doesn't matter a bit to me that I am all you say: what makes me want to dance is the fact that you know it!"

Ah, fool that I am! There he is, triumphant, encour- aged by my confession, the confession of my curiosity, if not of a sharper interest. There he is, arrogant, trembling with the longing to reveal himself further. If he dared, he would cry: "Yes, I am all that! So you have deigned to see me, while I was losing hope that I should ever exist in your eyes? Look at me again! Reveal me completely, invent weaknesses and absurdities in me, overwhelm me with imaginary vices! My worry is not that you should know me as I am: create your admirer according to your liking, and afterwards, artfully and little by little, I will make myself resemble him, as a master touches up and re-does the mediocre work of a beloved pupil."

Shall I speak my thought aloud to him to embarrass him? Careful! I nearly did another clumsy thing. He will not be embarrassed, he will listen, ravished, to his sooth-sayer, and praise to the skies the second sight that love confers. And what is he waiting for now? For me to fall into his arms? Nothing astonishes a man in love. I could wish him far off. I'm struggling with the need to rest, to relax, to raise my hand and beg: "Pax! Stop! I don't know the game. If I find I want to, we'll begin again another time; but I haven't the strength to follow you, and I shall get caught every time, as you well see."

His watchful eyes dart rapidly from my eyelids to my mouth, from my mouth to my eyelids, and seem to read my face. Suddenly he rises and turns aside, with brusque discretion.

"Goodbye, Renée," he says in a lower voice. "I ask your pardon for staying so late, but Hamond suggested to me . . ."

With a sense of social embarrassment, I protest: "Oh, it doesn't matter at all . . . on the contrary . . ."

"Does your concierge sleep very soundly?"

"I hope not."

This is so pitifully silly that I recover some of my gaiety.

"Listen!" I say suddenly. "I would rather you didn't waken the concierge: you shall leave by the window."

"By the window? Oh, Renée!"

"It's the ground floor."

"I know. But aren't you afraid that . . . that I shall be seen? One of the other tenants might return just at that moment."

"Whatever d'you suppose that would matter to me?"

In spite of myself, there is so much contemptuous

indifference in the way I answered him and shrugged my shoulders, that my admirer no longer dares to rejoice. In his heart, this exit at one in the morning by the window—from my bedroom, if you please—must make him feel as gleeful as a student. Ah, what youthfulness!

"Jump! That's right. Goodbye!"

"Till tomorrow, Renée?"

"If you like, my friend."

What youthfulness! Yet he is thirty-three, this man. I too. Thirty-four in six months.

I heard him running along the pavement, under a fine, clinging rain which makes the paving stones sticky and moistens the window-sill where I remain propped on my elbows, like a lover. But, behind me, no one has rumpled the big, commonplace bed, with its fresh, uncreased sheets on which my uncomplaining insomnia will leave no trace.

He has gone. He will return tomorrow, and the following days, since I have given him permission. He will return almost happy, awkward but full of hope, with that look as though he were saying: "I'm not asking for anything", which, in the end, has the same exasperating effect on me as the mechanical prayer of a beggar. And to think it would have been so simple to wound him with a refusal before he had got to the dangerous stage, and to let him go while the cut was fresh and curable!

The thin rain, falling past the square of my lighted window, looks like damp, finely-sifted flour, white against the black background of the road.

I must confess that, in allowing this man to return tomorrow, I was giving way to my desire to keep, not an admirer, not a friend, but an eager spectator of my life and my person. "One has to get terribly old," said Margot to me one day, "before one can give up the vanity of living in the presence of someone else."

Could I sincerely declare that, for a few weeks past, I have not taken pleasure in the attention of this passionate spectator? I denied him my brightest look, my freest smile; I was careful of the tone of my voice when I spoke to him, and my whole face remained closed against him. But was it not so that, distressed and humbled, he should realise that all my reticences were addressed to him, and that for his sake I was taking the trouble to exist less? There is no disguise without coquetry, and it needs as much care and vigilance to make oneself ugly all the time as to adorn oneself.

If my admirer, in the shadow, is watching my open window, he has reason to be proud. I am neither regretting him nor wanting him, but I am thinking of him. I am thinking of him as though I were taking stock of my first defeat.

The first? No, the second. There was an evening—oh, what a bitter memory, and how I curse it for rising up at this moment—an evening when, propped on my elbows like this, I was leaning out over an invisible garden. My long, long hair hung down from the balcony like a silk rope. The certainty of love had just swooped down on me, and, far from weakening under it, my young strength bore it proudly. Neither doubt, nor even the sweetest melancholy sobered that triumphal and solitary night, crowned with wistaria and roses. What did the man who aroused it do with that blind, that innocent exaltation?

Shut the window, shut the window! I tremble too much lest I should see rising, through the veil of the rain, a country garden, green and black, silvered by the rising moon across which passes the shadow of a young girl dreamily winding her long plait round her wrist, like a caressing snake.

SIX

"M ARSEILLES, Nice, Cannes, Toulon . . ."
     "No, Mentone before Toulon . . ."
"And Grenoble! We've got Grenoble too!"

We reckon up the towns of our tour like children
counting their marbles. Brague has decided that we
should take two "numbers": *The Pursuit* and *The Dryad*.

"For the big burgs where we do four or six days," he
declares, "it's just as well to have a second string."

I readily agree to that. I readily agree to anything. No
one could be kindlier and more appreciative than I am
this morning. There is hardly a sound to be heard at
Cernuschi's studio, where we are working, except
Brague's outbursts and the laughter of the "Old Troglodyte" who is thrilled with the idea of going on tour and
earning fifteen francs a day: his famished young face,
with its sunken blue eyes, beams with uninterrupted
happiness, and goodness knows he is paying for it!

"You fat-headed louse!" yells Brague. "Take that
ballet-dancer's smirk off, can't you? Anyone'd think
you'd never seen a troglodyte. Twist your mug sideways,
I tell you! More still! And make your eyes start out!
And your jaw quiver! Sort of like Chaliapine, that's the
kind of thing."

He wipes his forehead and turns towards me, discouraged: "I can't think why I wear myself out over that
clod; when I talk to him of Chaliapine, he thinks I am
using rude words to him. And you too, what are you up
to, gaping at the ceiling?"

"Oh, so it's my turn now? I was just saying to myself,
it's a long time since Brague murmured some love-words
to me."

My comrade-professor eyes me with a look of theatrical contempt: "Love-words! I leave those to others: I don't suppose you're short of them, are you? And now, off with you! The meeting's adjourned. Tomorrow, dress rehearsal with scenery and accessories, which is to say that you'll have a veil for your dance, while this gentle-man here will carry a packing-case full of candles to represent the rock he brandishes over our heads. I'm tired of seeing you both, you with a handkerchief the size of one of my buttocks, and him with his *Paris-Journal* rolled into a ball instead of his lump of granite. Ten o'clock tomorrow, here. Them's my orders."

Just when Brague stops speaking, a ray of sunshine gilds the glass ceiling, and I raise my head as if I had suddenly heard someone calling me from above.

"D'you hear me, you chit of a Renée?"

"Yes."

"Yes? Well then off with you. It's time for grub. Go and wallow in the sun outside. You're dreaming of the country, isn't that it?"

"Nothing escapes you. Till tomorrow."

I'm dreaming of the country, yes, but not in the way that my infallible companion supposes. And the joyful hubbub of the Place Clichy at midday in no wise dispels a nagging memory that is still fresh and keen.

Yesterday Hamond and Dufferein-Chautel took me to the woods at Meudon, like two art-students taking out a little milliner. My admirer was showing off a new car that smelt of morocco leather and turpentine: a magni-ficent toy for grown-ups. His dark youthful face was alight with longing to offer me this beautiful, gleaming, vibrating object for which I had not the slightest wish. But I laughed because, for this outing to Meudon,

Hamond and Dufferein-Chautel were wearing identical wide-brimmed brown hats with a dint in the crown, and I looked so small between those two tall creatures.

Sitting opposite me on one of the tip-up seats, my admirer tucked his legs discreetly under him so that my knees should not touch his. The clear, grey day, very mild and spring-like, showed me all the details of his face, darker than ever under the bronze felt, with the smoky tone of his eyelids and the double row of stiff, thick eyelashes. His mouth, half-hidden under his rusty-black moustache, intrigued me, as did the faint network of little wrinkles below his eyes, and the thick, rather untidy eyebrows that extended beyond their orbit, bristling rather like those of hunting griffons. I suddenly began to grope, with an anxious hand, for the looking-glass in my little bag.

"Have you lost something, Renée?"

But I had already changed my mind: "No, nothing; thank you."

What would be the sense of examining, in front of him, the blemishes of a face which is losing the habit of being looked at in daylight? And what could my mirror have taught me, since yesterday, as on all other days, a skilful make-up of brown pencil, bluish kohl, and red lipstick managed to draw attention to my eyes and my mouth, the three lights, the three loadstars of my face. No rouge on my rather hollow cheeks, nor beneath the eyelids which weariness and frequent blinking have already delicately chequered.

The happiness of Fossette, who sat on my knees craning towards the door, provided us with occasional conversation, as did also the charm of that still wintry wood, with its grey twigs against a chinchilla sky. But whenever I leant forward to drink in a little of the gentle breeze, laden with the bitter musk of old, decayed leaves, I felt the gaze of my admirer dwelling confidently on my whole person.

Between Paris and the woods of Meudon we had not exchanged a hundred phrases. The country never makes me talkative, and my old Hamond feels bored as soon as he passes beyond the fortifications. Our silence might have cast a gloom over anyone but an admirer, sufficiently recompensed by the private satisfaction of having me there under his eyes, a passive prisoner in his car, vaguely enjoying the outing and smiling at the bumps in the damp and rutted road.

With a short bark, Fossette imperiously decided that we should go no further, and that some urgent business was calling her from the depths of those bare woods, on that forest road where the pools left by a recent downpour shone like round mirrors. We all three followed her without protest, with the long strides of people used to walking.

"It smells good," says the Big-Noodle suddenly, sniffing the air. "It smells like it does at home."

I shook my head: "No, not like *your* home, like mine! Hamond, what does it smell like?"

"It smells like autumn," says Hamond in a weary voice.

Whereupon we said no more and stood still, gazing up at a rivulet of sky imprisoned between very tall trees, and listening to the liquid call, clear and quavering, of a blackbird defying the winter, that came to us through the living, whispered murmur that rises from a forest.

A little red-brown creature started up from under our feet, a stoat or a weasel Fossette pretended she had put to flight, and we followed the stupid, excited bitch who kept showing off and barking: "I see it! I've got it!" as she followed an imaginary track.

In the end, catching the excitement, I set off after her

down the path, giving myself up to the animal pleasure
of the chase, my skunk cap pulled well down to my ears,
and grasping my skirt in both hands to leave my legs
free. When I stopped, out of breath, I found Maxime
behind me.

"Oh, you followed me? Why didn't I hear you
running?"

He was breathing fast, his eyes shining under his
uneven eyebrows, his hair ruffled by the chase, very much
the amorous wood-cutter and rather alarming.

"I followed you . . . I was careful to run at the same
pace as you so that you shouldn't hear my steps. It's
quite simple."

Yes, it's quite simple. But it had to be thought of. For
my part I shouldn't have thought of it. Provoked and
imprudent, a nymph-like brutality took possession of me
and I laughed full in his face, defying him. I was tempted,
and wanted to light again the wicked yellow light in the
depths of those beautiful eyes flecked with grey and red-
brown. The menace duly appeared in them, but I refused
to yield, obstinate as a cheeky child who expects and asks
for a slap. And the chastisement came, in the form of a
badly-planted, irascible kiss, a bungled kiss in short,
which left my mouth punished and disappointed.

As I follow the Boulevard des Batignolles, I carefully weigh all the moments of the day out yesterday, not
in order to re-live them complacently, nor to find an
excuse. There is no excuse, except for the man whom I
provoked. "How unlike me that was!" I mentally exclaimed to myself, yesterday, while we were returning
towards Hamond, dissatisfied with each other and in a
defiant mood. But was it? How do I know? "You have
no more redoubtable enemy than yourself!" A pretended

thoughtlessness, a pretended imprudence—these are to be found at the bottom of the most mischievously impulsive women, and I am not one of them. One should be severe with those of them who cry: "Oh, I no longer know what I am doing!" and realise that there is in their confusion a large admixture of premeditated cunning.

I do not at all say that I am not responsible, even partly. What shall I say to this man, this evening, if he wants to clasp me in his arms? That I do not want, that I never did want to tempt him, and that it is a game? That I offer him my friendship for the period of one month and ten days which separates us from the tour? No, the time has come to make up my mind, the time has come to make up my mind.

I walk on and on, quickening my steps every time I see my reflection in a shop window, because the expression of anxious determination which I see on my face looks to me rather too theatrical, with eyes not sufficiently in earnest under frowning brows. I know that face. It puts on a mask of austerity, of renunciation, the better to wait for the little miracle, the sign of my master, Chance, the phosphorescent word that he will write on the black wall when I turn out my light tonight.

How good the air smells round these little barrows full of wet violets and white jonquils! An old man all mossy with beard is selling up-rooted snowdrops with their bulbs clotted with earth and their pendant flowers shaped like a bee. Their scent resembles that of the orange-flower, but so faint as to be almost imperceptible.

Come now, come, the time has come to make up my mind! I walk and walk as if I did not know that, in spite of my bursts of energy, my scruples and all that inner penitence which I try to inflict on myself, as if I did not know, already, that I shall not take *that* course, but the *other*!

SEVEN

HEAVENS, how tired I am, absolutely worn out! I fell asleep after lunch, as I sometimes do on rehearsal days, and I've wakened up utterly weary, feeling as though I had come from the ends of the earth, astonished and sad and barely able to think, eyeing my familiar furniture with a hostile gaze. Just such an awakening, in fact, as the most horrible of those I used to experience in the days of my suffering. But since I am not suffering now, what can the reason be?

I feel unable to move. I look at my hand hanging down as though it did not belong to me. I don't recognise the stuff of my frock. Who was it, while I slept, who loosened the coronet of plaits coiled about my brows like the tresses of a grave young Ceres? I was ... I was ... there was a garden ... a peach-coloured sunset sky ... a shrill childish voice answering the cries of the swallows ... yes, and that sound like distant water, sometimes powerful and sometimes muffled: the breath of a forest. I had gone back to the beginning of my life. What a journey to catch up with myself again, where I am now! I cry for the sleep that has fled, the dark curtain which sheltered me and now has withdrawn itself, leaving me shivering and naked. Sick people who think they are cured experience these fresh attacks of their malady which find them childishly astonished and plaintive: "But I thought it was over!" For two pins I could groan aloud, as they do.

O dangerous and too-kindly sleep which in less than an hour obliterates the memory of myself! Whence come

I, and on what wings, that it should take me so long, humiliated and exiled, to accept that I am myself? Renée Néré, dancer and mime. . . . Was my proud childhood, my withdrawn and passionate adolescence, which welcomed love so fearlessly, to lead to no end but that?

O Margot, my discouraging friend, if only I had strength to get up, and run to you, and tell you. . . . But my courage is the only thing you admire and I should not dare to falter before you. I feel pretty sure that your virile gaze and the clasp of your dry little hand, chapped by cold water and household soap, would know better how to reward a victory over myself than to help me in my daily efforts.

And what of my approaching departure? And freedom? Ah, no! The only moment when freedom is truly dazzling is at the dawn of love, of first love, when you can say, as you offer it to the person you love: "Take! I wish I could give you more."

As for the new cities and new countrysides, so briefly glimpsed, so quickly passed that they grow blurred in the memory, are there such things as new countries for one who spins round and round in circles like a bird held on a string? Will not my pathetic flight, begun anew each morning, inevitably end up each evening at the fatal "first-class establishment" which Salomon and Brague praise so highly to me?

I have seen so many *first-class establishments* already! On the side of the public there is an auditorium cruelly flooded with light, where the heavy smoke hardly tones down the gilt of the mouldings. On the artistes' side there are sordid, airless cells, and a staircase leading to filthy lavatories.

Must I really, for forty days, endure this struggle against fatigue, the bantering ill-will of the stage-hands,

the raging pride of provincial conductors, the inadequate
fare of hotels and stations? Must I discover and perpetu-
ally renew in myself that rich fund of energy which is
essential to the life of wanderers and solitaries? Must I,
in short, struggle—ah, how could I forget it?—against
solitude itself? And to achieve what? What? What?

When I was small they said to me: "Effort brings its
own reward", and so, whenever I had tried specially
hard, I used to expect a mysterious, overwhelming recompense, a sort of grace to which I should have surrendered
myself. I am still expecting it.

The muffled trill of a bell, followed by the barking of
my dog, delivers me at last from this bitter reverie. And
suddenly I am on my feet, surprised to find I have jumped
lightly up and begun quite simply to live again.

"Madame," says Blandine in a low voice, "may
M. Dufferein-Chautel come in?"

"No . . . just a minute."

To powder my cheeks, redden my lips, and comb out
the tangled locks which hide my forehead is a rapid
mechanical task which does not even need the help of a
mirror. One does it as one brushes one's nails, more for
manners than vanity.

"Are you there, Dufferein-Chautel? You can come in.
Wait a moment, I'll turn on the light."

I feel no embarrassment at seeing him again. The fact
that our mouths met yesterday, abortively, does not
make me feel the least awkward at this moment. A
bungled kiss is much less important than an understanding exchange of looks. And I almost feel surprised
that he for his part should look unhappy and frustrated.
I called him Dufferein-Chautel as usual, as though he
had no Christian name. I always call him "You" or

"Dufferein-Chautel". Is it for me to put him at his ease? I suppose it is.

"So there you are! Are you well?"

"Thank you, I'm well."

"You don't look it."

"That's because I'm unhappy," he does not fail to reply.

Really, what a Big-Noodle! I smile at his unhappiness, the trifling unhappiness of a man who has embraced clumsily the woman he loves. I smile at him from rather far away, from the other side of the chaste black stream where I was bathing a while back. I hand him a little vase filled with his favourite cigarettes, made of a sweet, golden tobacco which smells like spice-bread.

"You're not smoking today?"

"Yes, of course. But I'm unhappy all the same."

Sitting on the divan, with his back against the low cushions, he exhales at regular intervals long jets of smoke from his nostrils. I smoke too, for something to do and to keep him company. He looks better bare-headed. A top-hat makes him uglier and a soft felt hand-somer to the point of flashiness. He smokes with his eyes on the ceiling, as though the seriousness of the words he is preparing prevented him from paying any attention to me. His long, shining eyelashes—the one sensuous, feminine ornament of that face whose fault is excess of virility—blink frequently, betraying agitation and hesitancy. I can hear him breathing. I can also hear the tick-tock of my little travelling-clock, and the screen in the fireplace which the wind suddenly rattles.

"Is it raining outside?"

"No," he says with a start. "Why do you ask me that?"

"So's to know. I haven't been out since lunch, I don't know what the weather's like."

"Just ordinary . . . Renée!"

All of a sudden he sits up and throws away his cigarette. He takes my hands and looks very closely at me, so closely that his face appears to me almost too big, with the details strongly emphasised, the texture of the skin, and the moist and quivering corner of his large eyes. What love there is, yes, love, in those eyes! How speaking they are, and gentle, and wholly enamoured! And those big hands which clasp mine with such steady, communicative strength, how much in earnest I feel them!

It is the first time that I leave my hands in his. At first I feel I have to overcome my repugnance, then their warmth reassures and persuades me, and in a moment I shall yield to the surprising, brotherly pleasure, for so long unfamiliar, of confiding without words in a friend, of leaning for a moment against him, of finding comfort in the nearness of a warm, motionless being, affectionate and silent. Oh, to throw my arms round the neck of a creature, dog or man, a creature who loves me!

"Renée! What is it, Renée, you're not crying?"

"Am I crying?"

He's quite right, I am! The light dances in my brimming tears in a thousand broken, criss-cross rays. I wipe them quickly with a corner of my handkerchief, but I don't dream of denying them. And I smile at the idea that I was about to cry. How long is it since last I cried? It must be years and years.

My friend is overcome. He draws me towards him and forces me—not that I protest much—to sit beside him on the divan. His eyes, too, are moist. After all he is only a man, capable of feigning an emotion, no doubt, but not of hiding it.

"My darling child, what is the matter?"

Will he forget the stifled cry, the shudder which

answers him? I hope so. "My darling child!" His first word of tenderness is "My darling child!" The same word and almost the same accent as *the other* . . .

A childish fear wrenches me from his arms, as if *the other* had just appeared at the door with his Kaiser William moustache, his false, veiled gaze, his terrible shoulders and his short, peasant's thighs.

"Renée, my darling, if only you would talk to me a little!"

My friend is quite pale and does not try to take me in his arms again. May he at least never know the pain he has just, so innocently, given me! I no longer want to cry. My delicious, cowardly tears slowly return to their source, leaving a burning sensation in my eyes and throat. While I wait for my voice to steady itself, I reassure my friend with a nod.

"I've made you angry, Renée?"

"No, my friend."

I sit down beside him again, of my own accord, but timidly, for fear my gesture and my words should provoke another tender exclamation as familiar and hateful as the last.

His instinct warns him not to rejoice at my sudden docility. I feel no desire to embrace me in the arm which supports me, and the dangerous, grateful communicative warmth is no longer there. No doubt he loves me enough to guess that, if I lay an obedient head on his strong shoulder, it is a question of a trial more than a gift.

Can this be my forehead on a man's shoulder? Am I dreaming? I am neither dreaming nor wandering. Both my head and my senses are calm, ominously calm. Yet there is something better and more than indifference in the ease which keeps me there, and the fact that I can let my hand play innocently and unthinkingly with the plaited gold chain on his waistcoat shows that I feel myself sheltered and protected, like the lost cat one rescues, who only knows how to play and sleep when it has a house.

Poor admirer . . . I wonder what he is thinking of as he sits there motionless, respecting my silence? I lean my head back to look at him, but immediately lower my lids, dazzled and abashed by the expression on this man's face. Ah, how I envy him for loving so deeply, for the passion that confers such beauty on him!

His eyes meet mine and he smiles bravely.

"Renée . . . do you think a time will ever come when you will love me?"

"Love you? How I wish I could, my friend! *You*, at least, don't look cruel. Don't you feel that I am beginning to get fond of you?"

"To get fond of me . . . that's just what I'm afraid of, Renée; that hardly ever leads to love."

He is so profoundly right that I do not protest.

"But . . . be patient . . . you never know. It may be that, when I come back from my tour . . . And then, after all, a great, great friendship . . ."

He shakes his head. Obviously he has no use for my friendship. For my part I should be very glad to have a friend who was less old, less *worn out*, than Hamond, a real friend. . . .

"When you come back. . . . In the first place, if you really hoped to love me one day, Renée, you wouldn't think of going away from me. In two months' time, just as now, it will be the same Renée who will stretch out her cold little hands, with eyes that shut me out, and that mouth which, even when it offers its lips, does not surrender itself."

"It's not my fault. Yet here it is, this mouth. See . . ."

With my head on his shoulder once more, I close my

eyes, more resigned than curious, only to open them
again at the end of a moment, surprised that he does not
swoop down with the greedy haste of yesterday. All he
has done is to turn a little towards me and encircle me
comfortably with his right arm. Then he gathers my two
hands into his free hand and bends forward, and I see
slowly approaching the serious unfamiliar face of this
man whom I know so little.

Now there is hardly any space or air between our two
faces, and I try and jerk myself free, breathing fast as if I
were drowning. But he holds my hands and tightens his
arm round my waist. In vain I bend my neck back, just
at the moment when Maxime's mouth reaches mine.

I have not closed my eyes. I frown in an attempt to
threaten those eyes above me, which try to subjugate and
extinguish mine. For the lips which kiss me are just the
same as yesterday, gentle, cool and impersonal, and their
ineffectiveness irritates me. But all of a sudden they
change, and now I no longer recognise the kiss, which
quickens, insists, falters, then begins again with a
rhythmical movement, and finally stops as if waiting for
a response which does not come.

I move my head imperceptibly, because of his moustache which brushes against my nostrils with a scent of
vanilla and honeyed tobacco. Oh! . . . suddenly my
mouth, in spite of itself, lets itself be opened, opens of
itself as irresistibly as a ripe plum splits in the sun. And
once again there is born that exacting pain that spreads
from my lips, all down my flanks as far as my knees, that
swelling as of a wound that wants to open once more and
overflow—the voluptuous pleasure that I had forgotten.

I let the man who has awakened me drink the fruit he
is pressing. My hands, stiff a moment ago, lie warm and
soft in his, and my body, as I lie back, strives to mould

itself to his. Drawn close by the arm which holds me, I burrow deeper into his shoulder and press myself against him, taking care not to separate our lips and to prolong our kiss comfortably.

He understands and assents, with a happy little grunt. Sure at last that I shall not flee, it is he who breaks away from me, to draw breath and contemplate me as he bites his moist lips. I let my lids fall, since I no longer need to see him. Is he going to undress me and take possession of me completely? It doesn't matter. I am lapped in a lazy, irresponsible joy. The only urgent thing is that that kiss should begin again. We have all our time. Full of pride, my friend gathers me up in his arms as though I were a bunch of flowers, and half lays me on the divan where he rejoins me. His mouth tastes of mine now, and has the faint scent of my powder. Experienced as it is, I can feel that it is trying to invent something new, to vary the caress still further. But already I am bold enough to indicate my preference for a long, drowsy kiss that is almost motionless—the slow crushing, one against the other, of two flowers in which nothing vibrates but the palpitation of two coupled pistils.

And now comes a great truce when we rest and get our breath back. This time it was I who left him, and got up because I felt the need to open my arms, to draw myself up and stretch. Anxious to arrange my hair and see what my new face looked like, I took up the hand-mirror, and it makes me laugh to see we both have the same sleepy features, the same trembling, shiny, slightly swollen lips. Maxime has remained on the divan and his mute appeal receives the most flattering of responses: my look of a submissive bitch, rather shame-faced, rather cowed, very much petted, and ready to accept the leash, the collar, the place at her master's feet, and everything.

EIGHT

H<small>E</small> has gone. We dined together, rather a scratch meal;
Blandine did us some cutlets in gravy, with gherkins.
I was consumed with hunger. *"Et l'amour comblant tout,
hormis . . ."*, said he, to show he had read Verlaine.

We did not fall into each other's arms when dinner was
over, and we have not become lovers, since he is shy and
I dislike doing things on the spur of the moment. But I
have pledged and promised myself, joyfully and without
coquetry.

"We've got plenty of time, haven't we, Max?"

"Not too much, darling. I've grown so old while I've
I've been waiting for you!"

So old! He does not know how old I am.

He has gone, and he will return tomorrow. He could
hardly tear himself away from me, and I was so afraid I
might weaken that I held him at arms' length. I felt warm
and he sniffed me ecstatically, as though he were about
to bite me. But at last he has gone. I say "at last", because
now I shall be able to think about him, and about us.

"Love" was what he said. Is it love? I should like to
be sure of it. Do I love him? My sensuality frightened me;
but perhaps it will prove to be only a moment of crisis,
an overflowing of forces pent up for such a long time,
and afterwards no doubt I shall find I love him. What if
he were to come back and knock on my shutter? Yes,
certainly I love him. I brood tenderly over the memory
of certain inflexions in his voice today—the echo of his
little amorous grunt is enough to make me catch my
breath—and then how good and strong he was, and what
a comfort in my solitude when I laid my head on his

shoulder! Oh yes, I do love him. What is it that has made me so timorous? I did not make so much fuss when . . .

Imprudently my train of thought has stumbled on a grave. Too late to flee, I find myself once again face to face with that pitiless mentor who speaks to me from the other side of the looking-glass:

"You didn't make so much fuss when love swept down on you and found you so mad and brave. You didn't ask yourself, that day, *if it was love*. You couldn't mistake it; it was love indeed, *first love*. That was what it was and never again will be. Your maiden simplicity recognised love without hesitation, and begrudged him neither your body nor your childish heart. It was then love made his appearance unannounced, unchosen, unquestioned. And never again will it be he. He took from you what you can only give once: trust, the religious wonder of the first caress, the novelty of your tears, the flower of your first suffering. Love, if you can; no doubt this will be granted you, so that at the summit of your poor happiness you may again remember that nothing counts, in love, except the first love, and endure at every moment the punishment of remembering, and the horror of comparing. Even when you say: 'Ah, this is better!' you will feel the pang of knowing that nothing which is not unique is good. There is a God who says to the sinner: 'You would not seek me if you had not already found me!' But Love is not so merciful. 'You, who have found me once,' he says, 'you shall lose me for ever!' Did you think, when you lost him, that you had reached the limit of suffering? It is not over yet. In striving now to be again what once you were, you will realise the height from which you fell; and the first, the only love will instil its poison into each feast of your new life, if you do not stem its flow."

NINE

I SHALL have to speak to Margot and tell her of this event, this touch of the sun which sets my life aflame. For it has come to that, we love each other. It has come to that and, besides, I have made up my mind to it. I have sent to the devil all my memories-and-regrets, and my obsession about what I call sentimental high-water marks, and my *ifs* and *fors* and *buts* and *howevers*.

We spend every moment together, he sweeps me off my feet, dazes me with his presence and prevents me from thinking. He decides, he almost commands, and I surrender to him not only my liberty but my pride too, since I let him fill my flat with a wasteful abundance of flowers and of next summer's fruits, and I wear a little glittering arrow, pinned against my neck as though it were driven into my throat, all bleeding with rubies.

And yet we are not lovers. Max has grown patient now, and imposes on himself and me a curiously exhausting period of betrothal which in less than a week has already made us languid and slightly thinner. It is not vice in him which makes him act thus, but the coquetry of a man who wants to make himself desired and, at the same time, leave me an illusory "free will" for as long as I want.

In any case there is not much left for me to desire. And the only thing which makes me tremble at present is that unsuspected ardour which leapt into life at the first contact and is always fiercely ready to obey him. I agree he is right to postpone the hour which will unite us completely. I know my value now, and the splendour of the

gift which he will receive. I shall surpass his wildest
hopes, I am sure of it. In the meantime let him cull a
little of the fruit in his orchard if he wants.

And he does often want. For my pleasure and to my
disturbance chance has willed that in this tall young man,
with his straightforward, symmetrical good looks, there
is a subtle lover, born for women, and so skilled at
divining that his caresses seem to know the thoughts
behind my desire. He makes me think—and I blush for it—
of the saying of a lascivious little music-hall comrade who
boasted of the cleverness of a new lover: "My dear, one
couldn't do better oneself!"

But . . . I shall have to let Margot know! Poor Margot,
whom I was forgetting. As for Hamond, he has disappeared. He knows everything, thanks to Max, and keeps
away from my house like a discreet relation.

And Brague! I can't forget how he looked at our last
rehearsal. He greeted me on my arrival in Max's car with
his best Pierrot's grimace, but he still says nothing. He
even displayed an unusual and undeserved courtesy, for
that morning I was blundering and absent-minded, and
kept blushing and excusing myself. Finally he burst out:
"Be off with you! Go back to it! Take your fill and don't
come back here till you've had all you can take!"

The more I laughed, the more he fulminated, looking
like a little oriental fiend: "Laugh away, go on, laugh!
If you could see the look on your face!"

"My look?"

"Yes, a look that's absolutely asking for it, craving for
it. Don't raise your eyes to me, Messalina! Look at her,"
he cried, calling invisible gods to witness, "she shows
those orbs there in broad daylight. And when I ask her
to put that much and a bit more too into the Dryad's
love scene, and to hot the whole thing up a bit, she trots

out the chilly charm of a young girl at her first communion."

"Does *that* really show?" I asked Max, who was taking me home. The same mirror which the other evening reflected a countenance glorying in its defeat, now frames a pointed face with the defiant smile of a friendly fox. Yet an indefinable flame keeps flickering over it, painting it, as it were, with a kind of tormented youthfulness.

I have decided to confess everything to Margot: my relapse, my happiness, and the name of the man I love. It won't be easy. Margot is not a woman to say: "I told you so!" but I feel pretty sure that I shall sadden and disappoint her, although she will not show it. "Burnt child though you are, you'll go back to the fire!" I am indeed going back to it, and with what joy!

I find Margot unchangeably true to herself in the big studio where she sleeps, eats and breeds her Brabançon dogs. Tall and upright, in her Russian blouse and long black jacket, she bends her pale face, with its lean cheeks framed in her rough grey bobbed hair, over a basket in which a minute dog in a flannel shirt, a little yellow monster, is groping about and gazing up at her with the beautiful, imploring eyes of a squirrel, under the bumpy forehead of a bonze. Round me yap and wriggle six cheeky little creatures whom a crack of a whip sends scampering to their straw kennels.

"What, Margot, another Branbançon? It's a passion!"

"Lord, no!" says Margot, sitting down opposite me and cradling the sick animal on her knees. "I don't love this poor little wretch."

"Someone gave her to you?"

"No, I bought her, of course. That will teach me not to

walk in future past that old blackguard of a Hartmann, the dog-dealer. If you'd seen this Brabançon in the window, with her little face like a sick rat's and this spine protruding like a rosary, and above all those eyes. . . . Hardly anything touches me now, you know, except the expression of a dog for sale. So I bought her. She's half dead with enteritis; that never shows at the dealer's; they dope them with cacodylate. . . . Well now, my child, it's a long time since I saw you; are you working?"

"Yes Margot, I'm rehearsing."

"I can see that, you're tired."

With that familiar gesture of hers, she takes hold of my chin to tilt my face up and draw it towards her. Embarrassed, I close my eyes.

"Yes, you're tired. You've got older," she says in a very grave tone.

"Older! Oh, Margot!"

In that cry of pain and the flood of tears that follows it, my whole secret leaks out. I bury myself against my stern friend, and she strokes my shoulder and comforts me with the same "Poor little one!" that she used a moment ago to the sick Brabançon.

"There, there now, poor little one, there, there. It'll soon be all right. Look, here's some boracic lotion to bathe your eyes, I'd just prepared it for Mirette's. Not with your handkerchief! Take some cotton-wool . . . there! Poor little one, so your beauty's very necessary to you at present, is it?"

"Oh yes! . . . Oh Margot!"

" 'Oh, Margot!' Anyone might think I'd beaten you. Look at me. Are you very sore with me, poor little one?"

"No, Margot."

"You know very well," she goes on in her gentle, level voice, "that you can always count on finding here every kind of help, even the kind that hurts most: the truth. What was it I said to you? I said: you've got older."

"Yes . . . Oh, Margot . . ."

"Now don't begin again! But you've got older *this week*. You've got older *today*. Tomorrow, or in an hour's time, you'll be five years younger, ten years younger. If you'd come yesterday, or tomorrow, no doubt I should have said: 'My word, you've got younger!' "

"Just think, Margot, I shall soon be thirty-four."

"Don't expect me to pity you, I'm fifty-two!"

"It isn't the same thing, Margot, it's so important for me to be pretty, and young, and happy. I've . . . I . . ."

"You've got a lover?"

Her voice is still gentle, but the expression of her face has changed slightly.

"I haven't got a lover, Margot. Only, it's certain that I . . . I shall have one. But . . . I love him, you see!"

This kind of silly excuse amuses Margot.

"Ah, you love him? And he, too, loves you?"

"Oh!"

With a proud gesture, I protect my friend from the least suspicion.

"That's good. And . . . how old is he?"

"Just my age, Margot: very nearly thirty-four."

"That's . . . that's good."

I can't find anything else to add. I am horribly ill at ease. I had hoped, once the first embarrassment was over, to chatter about my happiness, and to tell everything about my friend, the colour of his eyes, the shape of his hands, his goodness, his honesty.

"He's . . . he's very nice, you know, Margot," I risked, shyly.

"So much the better, my child. You've made some plans, the two of you?"

"Plans? No . . . we haven't yet thought of anything. There's time."

"Yes of course, there's plenty of time. And what's happening about your tour, with all this?"

"My tour? Oh, this makes no difference to that."

"You're taking your . . . your fellow with you?"

Bathed in tears though I am, I can't help laughing when Margot refers to my friend with such squeamish discretion, as if she were speaking of something dirty.

"Taking him along, taking him . . . well . . . as a matter of fact, Margot, I don't at all know. I'll see."

My sister-in-law raises her eyebrows.

"You don't at all know, you have no plans, you'll see! My word, what an astonishing pair you are! What can you be thinking about? After all, it's the only thing you've got to do, to plan and prepare your future."

"The future. . . . Oh, Margot, I don't like preparing the future. It prepares itself without any help, and it comes so soon!"

"Is it a question of marriage or living in sin?"

I do not answer all at once, embarrassed for the first time by the chaste Margot's rather crude vocabulary.

"It isn't a question of anything. We're getting to know each other, finding out what we're like. . . ."

"You're finding out what you're like!"

With her mouth pursed and a cruel gaiety in her bright little eyes, Margot observes me.

"You're finding out what you're like! I see, you're at the stage when you're showing off to each other, is that it?"

"I assure you, Margot, we hardly show off at all," I say, forcing myself to smile. "That game's well enough for very young lovers, but he and I are no longer very young lovers."

"All the more reason," answers Margot, pitilessly. "You have more things to hide from each other. My little one," she added gently, "you know well enough you must laugh at my mania. Marriage seems to me such a monstrous thing. Haven't I often enough made you laugh by telling you how, from the very first days of my married life, I refused to share a bedroom with my husband because I thought it immoral to live at such close quarters with a young man who was a stranger to my family? I was born that way, that's the trouble, and I shall never change. . . . You haven't brought Fossette to see me today?"

Like Margot, I make an effort to cheer up.

"No, Margot. Your pack gave her such a poor welcome last time!"

"That's true. My pack isn't in very good shape at present. Come along, cripples!"

They do not have to be asked twice. From a row of kennels there emerge half a dozen dogs, a shivering, miserable little bunch, the biggest of which could be held in the crown of a hat. Saved by Margot from the "dog-dealer", wrested from that stupid, noxious trade which pens together in a window creatures that are sick, fattened up, starving or doped, I know nearly all of these. A few of them have become again, in her house, healthy, gay, robust animals; but others never get rid of their upset stomachs, their scabby skins, and their ineradicable hysteria. Margot looks after them as well as she can, discouraged by the thought that her charity is all to no purpose and that there will everlastingly be "luxury dogs" for sale.

The sick bitch has gone to sleep. I can find nothing to say. I look at the big room which, with its uncurtained windows, always has somewhat the appearance of an infirmary. On a table there are rows of chemists' bottles, rolled bandages, a diminutive thermometer, a tiny little rubber pear for dogs' enemas. The room smells of iodine and Jeyes fluid. I suddenly feel I must go away, I must find again without an instant's delay my warm narrow room, with the hollowed divan, and the flowers, and the friend I love.

"Goodbye, Margot, I'm going."

"Off you go then, my child."

"You're not too cross with me?"

"What about?"

"For being so foolish, and ridiculous, for being in love, I mean. I had so sworn to myself . . ."

"Cross with you? My poor little one, that would be too unkind. A new love . . . you mustn't feel uncomfortable. Poor little one!"

I am in a hurry to get home. I feel frozen, shrunken, and so sad. Never mind, it's done, what a relief! I've told Margot everything. I have received the cold douche I expected and I run to shake it off, to dry myself and expand in the warmth again. I lower my veil to hide the traces of my upset, and I run—run to him!

TEN

"MONSIEUR MAXIME is here, waiting for Madame."
My charwoman Blandine now says "Monsieur
Maxime" in a tender tone, as if she were speaking of her
foster-child.

He is here!

I rush to my room and shut myself in: he mustn't see
my face! Quick! Rice-powder, kohl, lip-stick. . . . Oh
dear, look at that shiny groove under my eye, still moist
from my tears! "You've got older." Silly thing, to go
and cry like a little girl! Haven't you learnt to suffer
"dry-eyed"? Where are the days when my glistening
tears rolled down the velvet of my cheeks without wetting it? There was a time when, to conquer my husband
all over again, I knew how to adorn myself with my
tears, weeping with my face lifted towards him and my
eyes wide open, and shaking but not drying the slow
pearls which made me more beautiful. How poor I have
become!

"There you are at last, my darling, my scented one,
my appetising one, my . . ."

"Goodness, how silly you are!"

"Thank Heaven, yes!" sighs my friend in a tone of
blissful conviction.

He begins to indulge in his favourite game of lifting
me up in his arms till I touch the ceiling, and then kissing
my cheeks, chin, ears and mouth. I resist enough to force
him to show his strength, but he gets the upper hand in
the struggle and then he tips me right over on his arm,
head down and feet in air until I cry "Help!", when he

sets me upright again. The dog rushes to my defence and mingles her hoarse barks with our laughter and cries, in this rough game which I much enjoy.

What a good thing this healthy silliness is! And what a gay companion I have in him, as little concerned to appear clever as to avoid rumpling his tie. How warm it is here, and how quickly our laughter changes from the laughter of two opponents, confronting each other, to a voluptuous challenge. He devours his "appetising one", tasting her slowly, like a gourmet.

"How good you would be to eat, my darling. Your mouth is honeyed, but your arms, when I bite them, are salty, just a tiny bit, and so are your shoulders and knees. I feel sure you're salty from head to foot, like a cool shell, aren't you?"

"You'll know that only too soon, Big-Noodle!"

For I still call him "Big-Noodle", but . . . in a different tone.

"When? This evening? It's Thursday today, isn't it?"

"I think so . . . yes . . . why?"

"Thursday . . . that's a very good day."

Lying back among the cushions, and very happy, he says foolish things. A lock of his hair has fallen over his eyes, which have the vague look that a great wave of desire gives them, and he half opens his mouth to breathe. Whenever he adopts an abandoned attitude, he turns again into a handsome country lad, a wood-cutter "taking a nap" on the grass—not that I dislike that!

"Get up, Max; we must talk seriously."

"I don't want to be hurt!" he sighs plaintively.

"Really, Max!"

"No! I know what talking seriously means. Mother always calls it that when she wants to speak of business, or money-matters, or marriage."

He snuggles into the cushions and closes his eyes. It is
not the first time that he has shown that determination
to be frivolous.

"Max, you've not forgotten that I'm going away on
the fifth of April?"

He half opens his eyelids with their feminine lashes,
and favours me with a long look.

"You're going away, darling? Whoever decided that?"

"Salomon, the impresario, and I."

"Good. But I haven't yet given my consent. Well, so
be it then, you're going away. But if so, you're going
away with me."

"With you!" I say, alarmed. "Don't you know what a
tour is, then?"

"Of course I do. It's a journey . . . with me."

"With you?" I repeat. "For forty-five days! But
haven't you anything to do, then?"

"Certainly I have. Since I've known you, I haven't a
minute to myself, Renée."

That is prettily answered, but . . .

I gaze, disconcerted, at this man who has nothing to
do, who always finds money in his pocket. He has nothing
to do, that is a fact, I had never thought about it. He has
no profession and no sinecure behind which to conceal
his lazy freedom. How strange that is! Till I met him I
never knew an idle man. He can give himself up entirely,
day and night, to love, like . . . like a prostitute.

This quaint idea that, of the two of us, it is he who is
the courtesan, causes me a sudden gaiety, and he quickly
draws his touchy eyebrows together in a frown.

"What's the matter? Are you laughing? You shan't
go!"

"I like that! And what about my forfeit?"

"I'll pay it."

"And Brague's forfeit? And the Old Troglodyte's?"

"I'll pay them."

Even if it is a joke, I do not altogether like it. Can I any longer doubt that we love each other? Here we are on the verge of our first quarrel.

I was mistaken, for here is my friend close to me, almost at my feet.

"My Renée, you shall do whatever you want, you know that."

But he has laid his hand on my forehead, and his eyes are fixed on mine, to read obedience there. Whatever I want? Alas! for the moment all I want is him.

"Is it still *The Pursuit* that you're taking on tour?"

"We're taking *The Dryad* too. Oh, what a lovely violet tie you have! It makes you look quite yellow."

"Leave my tie alone! *The Pursuit*, and *The Dryad*, and everything else, is an excuse to show your beautiful legs, and the rest."

"It's not for you to complain. Wasn't it on the boards that the 'rest' had the honour of being introduced to you?"

He presses me to him until it hurts.

"Be quiet! I remember. Every evening for five days I said hurting things to myself, final things every time. I thought I was a fool to go to the *Emp'-Clich'* as you call it, and when your act was over I would leave, calling myself every kind of name. And then next day I would weakly compromise: 'This truly is the last evening I shall be seen at that dump! But I just want to make sure what colour Renée Néré's eyes are. And besides, yesterday I didn't manage to arrive for the beginning.' In short, I was idiotic already."

"Idiotic already! You have a gift for putting things attractively, Max. It seems so queer to me that anyone can fall in love with a woman merely by looking at her."

"That depends on the woman one looks at. You know nothing about these things, Renée Néré. Just imagine, after I'd seen you mime *The Pursuit* for the first time, I spent at least an hour trying to sketch a diagram of your face. I succeeded, and I repeated I don't know how many times, in the margins of a book, a little geometric design that conveyed something to me alone. There was also, in your mime, a moment that filled me with unbearable joy: the moment when you sat on the table and read the threatening letter from the man you were deceiving. D'you know? You slapped your thigh, throwing back your head to laugh, and one could hear that your thigh was bare under your thin dress. The gesture was so robust you might have been a young fishwife, but your face glowed with a wonderfully sharp, refined wickedness, worlds apart from your accessible body. D'you remember?"

"Yes, yes . . . like this. Brague was pleased with me in that scene. But that, Max, is . . . is admiration, desire! Has it changed into love since then?"

"Changed?" He looked at me, very surprised. "I've never thought about it. I expect I loved you from that very moment. There are lots of women more beautiful than you, but . . ."

With a gesture of his hand he expresses all that is incomprehensible and irremediable in love. . . .

"But Max, what if, instead of a nice little bourgeoise like me, you'd chanced on a cold and calculating shrew, as tormenting as the itch! What then? Didn't the fear of that hold you back?"

"It never occurred to me," he said, laughing. "What a comic idea! When you love you don't think of so many things, you know."

He sometimes makes remarks like that which I, who think of so many things, feel as a rebuke.

"Little one," he murmurs, "why do you go in for this *café-concert* business?"

"Big-Noodle, why don't you go in for cabinet-making? Don't answer that you have the means to live otherwise, I know you have. But as for me, what would you have me do? Sewing, or typing, or street-walking? The music-hall is the job of those who never learnt one."

"But . . ."

I can hear from his voice that he is going to say something serious and embarrassing. I raise my head, which was resting on his shoulder, and gaze attentively at that face with its straight, firm nose, its fierce eyebrows sheltering the tender eyes, and the thick moustache under which hides a mouth with experienced lips.

"But, darling, you no longer need the music-hall now that I am there, and that . . ."

"Shh!"

Agitated and almost terrified, I urge him to stop. Yes, he is there, and ready for every kind of generosity. But that doesn't concern me, I don't want it to concern me. I cannot see that the fact that my friend is rich has anything to do with me. I cannot manage to fit him in to my future in the way he would like. No doubt that will come. I shall get used to the idea. I ask nothing better than to mingle my mouth with his and feel in advance that I belong to him, yet I can't associate his life with mine. If he were to announce to me: "I'm getting married," I feel I should answer politely: "All my congratulations!", thinking in my heart: "That doesn't concern me." And yet I wasn't exactly pleased, a fortnight ago, that he should eye little Jadin with such attention.

All these sentimental complications, fusses, hair-splittings, and psychological soliloquies, goodness how absurd I am! Would it not at bottom be more honest, and more worthy of a woman in love, to answer him: "Yes indeed you're there, and since we love each other, I'll ask you for everything. It's so simple. If I truly love you, you owe me everything, and any bread which does not come to me from you is impure."

What I have just thought is the right way to look at it. I ought to say it out loud, instead of remaining wheedlingly silent, rubbing my cheek against his shaven cheek, which has the smoothness of a very smooth piece of pumice-stone.

ELEVEN

My old Hamond had persisted for so many days in remaining at home, pleading rheumatism, influenza, or urgent work, that I ordered him to come at once. He delayed no longer and, when he came, his discreet and casual air, like that of a relation visiting some newly-weds, doubled my joy at seeing him again.

So here we are again, in affectionate tête-à-tête, like the old days.

"Like the old days, Hamond. Yet what a change!"

"Thank goodness, my child. Are you at last going to be happy?"

"Happy?"

I look at him with genuine astonishment.

"No, I shan't be happy. I don't even think of it. Why should I be happy?"

Hamond clacks his tongue; that is his way of scolding me. He thinks I have an attack of neurasthenia.

"Oh, come now, Renée. Isn't it going as well as I thought, then?"

I burst out laughing, very gay.

"Yes, of course it's going well, Hamond, only too well. I'm afraid we're beginning to adore each other."

"Well then?"

"Well then! D'you think that's a reason why I should be happy?"

Hamond cannot help smiling, and now it is my turn to look on the gloomy side.

"What torments you've thrust me into all over again, Hamond! For you'll admit it was your doing. Torments," I added in a lower tone, "that I wouldn't exchange for the greatest joys."

"Well," bursts out Hamond, relieved, "at least you're saved from that past which was fermenting inside you. I'd really had enough of seeing you gloomy and defiant, entangled in your memory and fear of Taillandy. Forgive me, Renée, but I would have stooped to pretty low things to endow you with a new love."

"You would, would you! D'you think that a new love, as you call it, destroys the memory of the first or . . . resuscitates it?"

Disconcerted by the asperity of my question, Hamond does not know what to say. But he has touched my sore spot so clumsily! And besides, he is only a man: he does not understand. He must have loved so many times: he no longer understands. His consternation makes me relent.

"No, my friend, I'm not happy. I'm . . . better or worse than that. Only . . . I don't at all know where I'm going. I want to say that to you before I become Maxime's mistress completely."

"Or his wife!"

"His wife?"

"Why not?"

"Because I don't want to."

My quick answer flies ahead of my reasoning, like an animal jumping wide of the snare before it sees it.

"Anyway that's of no importance," says Hamond carelessly. "It's the same thing."

"You think it's the same thing? For you, perhaps, and for many men. But for me! D'you remember, Hamond, what marriage was for me? No, I'm not thinking of the betrayals, you mistake me. I'm thinking of conjugal domesticity, which turns so many wives into a sort of nurse for a grown-up. Being married means . . . how shall I put it? It means trembling lest Monsieur's cutlet should be overdone, his Vittel water not cold enough, his shirt badly starched, his stiff collar soft, or the bath too hot! It means playing the exhausting part of an intermediary buffer between Monsieur's ill humour, his avarice, his greed, his laziness . . ."

"You're forgetting lust, Renée," interrupts Hamond gently.

"No, I jolly well am not! The part of mediator, I tell you, between Monsieur and the rest of humanity. You can't know, Hamond, you've been so little married! Marriage means . . . means: 'Tie my tie for me! . . . Get rid of the maid! . . . Cut my toe-nails! . . . Get up and make me some camomile! . . . Prepare me an emetic. . . .' It means: 'Give me my new suit, and pack my suit-case so that I can hurry to join her!' Steward, sick-nurse, children's nurse—enough, enough, enough!"

I end by laughing at myself and at the long scandalised face of my old friend.

"Oh, for goodness' sake, Renée, if you knew how this mania of yours for generalising gets on my nerves! 'In this country all the servant-girls are red-haired.' One doesn't always marry Taillandy! And I give you my word that, for my humble part, I should have blushed to ask a woman one of those petty services which . . . very much the contrary!"

I clap my hands. "Oh fine, I'm going to learn everything! Very much the contrary: I'm sure there was no one to touch you at buttoning up boots or flattening the press-studs on a tailored skirt? Alas, everyone can't marry Hamond!"

After a silence, I go on in a tone of weariness: "Let me generalise, as you say, even though I've had only one experience, as a result of which I'm still feeling shattered. I'm no longer young enough, or enthusiastic enough, or generous enough to go in for marriage again, or married life, if you prefer. Let me stay alone in my closed bedroom, bedecked and idle, waiting for the man who has chosen me to be his harem. I want to know nothing of him but his tenderness and his ardour, I want nothing from love, in short, but love."

"I know a good many people," says Hamond after a silence, "who would call that kind of love libertinism."

I shrug my shoulders, vexed at having made myself so little understood.

"Yes," insists Hamond, "libertinism. But since I know you . . . a little, I'd rather suppose that there is in you a fanciful, childish longing for the unrealisable: the loving couple, imprisoned in a warm room, isolated by four walls from the rest of the world—the normal dream of any young girl very ignorant of life."

"Or of a woman already mature, Hamond."

He protests, with a polite, evasive gesture, and avoids a direct answer.

"In any case, my dear child, it is not love."

"Why?"

My old friend throws away his cigarette almost angrily.

"Because! You said to me just now: 'Marriage for a woman means accepting a painful and humiliating domesticity; it means *tie my tie, prepare me an emetic, keep an eye on my cutlet, put up with my bad temper and my betrayals.*' You ought to have said *love* and not *marriage*. For only love makes the bond-service you speak of easy and joyful and glorious. You hate it at present, you repudiate it and spew it from you, because you no longer love Taillandy. But remember the time when, in the name of love, the tie, the footbath and the camomile tea became sacred symbols, revered and terrible. Remember the

miserable part you played! I used to shake with indignation at seeing you being used almost like a go-between,
aiding and abetting Taillandy and his women friends,
but when one day I lost all discretion and all patience,
you answered me: 'To love is to obey.' Be frank, Renée,
be clear-sighted, and tell me whether all your sacrifices
haven't only lost their value in your eyes since you
recovered your free will? You assess them at their true
worth *now that you no longer love*. Before—I've seen you at
it, I know you, Renée—did you not unconsciously enjoy
the merciful numbness which love dispenses?"

What is the good of answering? Nevertheless I am
ready to argue, with all the unfairness in the world: the
only thing that could rouse my pity today is this poor
man who lists my conjugal misfortunes while thinking
of his own. How young and "hurtable" he is, and quite
saturated with the poison he longed to get rid of! We've
moved a long way from my adventure and from Maxime
Dufferein-Chautel.

I wanted to confide in Hamond and ask his advice.
What is it that always leads us, scratched all over with
dead thorns, invincibly back to the past? I have the feeling that, if Maxime came in, Hamond and I would not
have time enough to change those faces of ours that no
one ought to see: Hamond is all yellow with bile, with
a little nervous tic in his left cheek, and as for me, my
brows are knitted as if in the throes of a migraine, and
my neck is thrust tensely forward, that strong neck that
is beginning to lose the smooth suppleness of its youthful
flesh.

"Hamond," I say very gently, "to change the subject,
you aren't forgetting that I have to go off on tour?"

"To go off. . . . Yes, of course," he says, like a man
being wakened from sleep. "What of it?"

"What of it! What about Maxime?"

"You're taking him, naturally?"

" 'Naturally!' It's not as simple as you seem to think. Life on tour is terrible . . . for a couple. There are the awakenings and departures in the early hours or the middle of the night, and interminable evenings for the one who waits, and then the hotel! What a beginning for a honeymoon! Even a woman of twenty wouldn't dare to risk being surprised at dawn, or sleeping in the train, that sleep that comes at the end of exhausting days, when one looks like a slightly swollen corpse. No, no, that's too great a danger for me. And besides, he and I deserve better than that. I'd vaguely thought of postponing our . . ."

"Heart-to-heart . . ."

"Thank you . . . until the end of the tour, and then to begin a life, oh! such a life! Not to think any more, Hamond, to go to ground somewhere, with him, in a country where, within reach of my mouth and my hands, I should find everything that offers itself and then escapes from me on the other side of the train window: moist leaves, flowers nodding in the wind, fruits with the bloom on their skins, and above all, streams of free, wayward, living water. You know, Hamond, when you've been living in a train for thirty days, you can't think how the sight of running water, between banks of new grass, parches your whole skin with a kind of indefinable thirst. During my last tour, I remember, we used to travel all morning and often all afternoon too. At noon, the farm girls would be milking the cows in the fields: I could see, in the deep grass, pails of burnished copper where the foaming milk squirted in thin straight jets. What a thirst, what an agonised longing I used to feel for that warm milk, topped with foam. It was a real little daily torture, I assure you. That is why I want to enjoy, all at the same time, everything I lack: pure air, a generous country where everything is to be found, and my love."

Involuntarily, I stretch out my arms, with my hands clasped, in the effort to invoke all I desire. Hamond goes on listening as though I had not stopped speaking.

"And then, my child, afterwards?"

"What d'you mean, 'afterwards'?" I say vehemently. "Afterwards? But that's all. I don't ask for anything more."

"That's fortunate," he murmurs to himself. "I mean, how will you live after, with Maxime? You'll give up your tours? You won't . . . work any longer in the music-hall?"

This question of his, so natural, is enough to bring me up short, and I look at my old friend defiantly, anxiously, almost intimidated:

"Why shouldn't I?" I say, feebly.

He shrugs his shoulders.

"Come now, Renée, think for a moment. Thanks to Maxime you can live comfortably, even luxuriously, and take up again, as we all hope, that witty pen which is growing rusty. And then perhaps a child; what a fine little chap he would be!"

Rash Hamond! Is he yielding to his impulse as an ex-genre painter? This little picture of my future life, between a faithful lover and a beautiful child, produces in me the most inexplicable and disastrous effect. And he elaborates it, the poor wretch. He labours the point, without noticing the horrid gaiety dancing in my eyes which avoid his, and that the only replies he is getting from me are an occasional bored "yes", and the "I don't know, I suppose so", of a schoolgirl who is finding the lesson too long.

TWELVE

A BEAUTIFUL child; a faithful husband; after all there
was nothing to laugh at in that. I am still wondering
what was the reason for my cruel hilarity. A beautiful
child; I confess that I have never thought of it. When I
was married I had not the time, being occupied first
with love and then with jealousy, monopolised, in a
word, by Taillandy, who in any case was not at all
anxious to encumber himself with an expensive progeny.

So here am I, having spent thirty-three years without
ever considering the possibility of being a mother. Am I
a monster? A beautiful child: grey eyes, a sharp little
nose, and the look of a little fox, like his mother, big
hands and broad shoulders, like Maxime. It's no good;
no matter how much I try I can't *see* him and I don't love
him, the child I might have had, that I perhaps shall have.

"Tell me, what d'you feel about it, darling Big-
Noodle?"

He has just come in, very quietly, already so much a
part of my mind that I go on with my soul-searching in
his presence.

"What d'you feel about the child we might have? It's
Hamond who wants one, would you believe it!"

My friend opens enormous eyes and a round, astonished Pierrot mouth, and cries: "Long live Hamond! He
shall have his kid, right away if you like, Renée."

I defend myself, for he goes for me with a mixture of
roughness and passion, biting a little and kissing a lot,
with that famished air which makes me feel just pleasantly
frightened.

"A child!" he cries, "a little one of our own! I'd never

thought of it, Renée. How intelligent Hamond is! It's a brilliant idea."

"D'you think so, my darling? Selfish brute that you are! It doesn't matter a scrap to you that I should be deformed and ugly, and that I should suffer, does it?"

He laughs again and pins me down on the divan at arms' length.

"Deformed? Ugly? What a goose you are, Madame! You'll be magnificent, and so will the little one too, and it will all be the greatest fun."

Then all at once he stops laughing and draws his fierce eyebrows together above his gentle eyes.

"And then, at least, you'd never be able to leave me and go gadding about the world all alone, would you? You'd be caught."

Caught. I give in, and play lazily with the fingers which hold me. But giving in is also a ruse of the weak. Caught. He did indeed say that, in a transport of egoism. I summed him up correctly, the time when I laughingly called him a monogamous bourgeois, and a home-loving paterfamilias.

So I might end my days, peacefully, dwarfed by his large shadow? Would his faithful eyes still love me when my graces had faded one by one? Ah, what a difference, what a difference from *the other*! Except that *the other* also spoke as a master and knew how to say under his breath, as he gripped me with a rough grasp: "Keep your head up and walk on, I'm holding you!" How I suffer! Their differences hurt me and so do their resemblances. And I stroke the forehead of this one, so unaware and innocent, and call him "my little one".

"Don't call me your 'little one', darling, it makes me ridiculous."

"I'll make you ridiculous if I want to. You are my little

one because you're younger than . . . than your age,
because you've suffered very little, and loved very little,
because you aren't cruel. . . . Listen to me, my little one:
I'm going away."

"Not without me, Renée!"

How he cried out! It makes me shiver with pain and
pleasure.

"Without you, my darling, without you. I must. Listen
to me. No . . . Max . . . I shall speak all the same, after . . .
Listen Max. D'you mean you don't want to, you can't,
wait for me? Don't you love me enough then?"

He tears himself from my hands and draws violently
away from me.

"Not enough, not enough! Oh, these womanish reasonings! I don't love you enough if I follow you, and
not enough if I stay. Admit it: if I'd answered you: 'Very
well, darling, I'll wait for you', what would you have
thought of me? And you, who go away when you could
quite well not go away, how d'you expect me to believe
that you love me? After all . . ."

He plants himself in front of me, head thrust forward
and suddenly suspicious: "After all, you've never said it
to me."

"Said what?"

"That you love me."

I feel myself blushing as if he had caught me out in
something.

"You've never said it to me," he repeats obstinately.

"Oh Max!"

"You've said to me . . . you've said to me: 'Darling . . .
my beloved Big-Noodle . . . Max . . . my darling love',
and you groaned aloud, as though you were singing, the
day when . . ."

"Max!"

"Yes, that day when you couldn't prevent yourself from calling me 'My love', but you've never said to me: 'I love you.' "

It is true. I had desperately hoped that he would not notice it. One day, another lovely day, I sighed so loudly in his arms that the words "love you" breathed from me like a slightly louder sigh, and all at once I became silent and cold.

"Love you." I don't want to say it again, never again. I never want to hear again that voice, my voice of other days, broken and low, irresistibly murmuring that word of long ago. Only, I know no other that will do. There is no other.

"Tell me, tell me that you love me. Tell me, I implore you."

My lover has knelt down before me and his imperious prayer will give me no peace. I smile in his face, as if I were resisting him for fun, and all of a sudden I want to hurt him so that he may suffer a little too. But he is so gentle, so far away from my suffering. Why should I hold him responsible for it? He doesn't deserve that.

"Poor darling, don't be naughty, don't be sad. Yes, I love you, I love you, oh, I do love you. But I don't want to say it to you. I'm so proud at heart, if you only knew."

Leaning against my breast, he closes his eyes, accepts my lie with a fond assurance, and goes on hearing me say "I love you" when I have ceased to speak.

What a strange burden he seems to these arms that have been empty for so long! I don't know how to rock so big a child, and how heavy his head is! But let him rest there, sure of me. Sure of me because he is a prey to a time-honoured delusion which makes him jealous of my present and my roving future, but lets him rest trustfully against this heart that another inhabited for so long. Rash and honest lover that he is, it does not occur to him that he shares me with a memory, and that he will never taste that best of all glories, the glory of being able to say to me: "I bring you a joy and a sorrow that you have never known."

There he is, on my breast. Why he, and not another? I don't know. I gaze down at his brow, I feel I want to protect him against myself, to excuse myself for giving him only a heart that has been deconsecrated, if not cleansed. I would like to safeguard him against the harm I can do him. Well, there it is as Margot foretold: I'm going back to the fire. But a reliable fire this time, with nothing infernal about it; in fact much more like a family kettle.

"Wake up, darling."

"I'm not asleep," he murmurs, without lifting his beautiful lashes. "I'm breathing you in."

"You'll wait for me in Paris, while I'm on tour? Or will you go to your mother's in the Ardennes?"

He gets up without answering and smooths his hair with the flat of his hand.

"Well?"

He takes his hat from the table and turns to go with lowered eyes, still silent. With a bound I am on him, clinging to his shoulders: "Don't go away, don't go away! I'll do whatever you want, come back, don't leave me alone, oh, don't leave me alone!"

Whatever has happened to me? I've suddenly become nothing but a poor wisp of a thing, drenched with tears. It seemed to me that if he went away, with him would go warmth and light and that second love all mingled with the burning ashes of the first, but so dear, so unhoped for. I cling to my lover with the hands of a

drowning person, and stammer over and over again
without hearing it: "Everyone leaves me, I'm all alone."

Loving me as he does, he well knows that there is no
need of words or reasonings to calm me, but only cradling arms, a warm murmur of vague caressing words,
and kisses, endless kisses.

"Don't look at me, my darling, I'm ugly, my eye-black
has got rubbed off and my nose is red. I'm ashamed to
have been so foolish."

"My Renée, my little, little one, what a brute I've been.
Yes, yes, I'm just a big brute. You want me to wait for
you in Paris? I will. You want me to go to mother's?
I'll go to mother's."

Undecided, and embarrassed by my victory, I no
longer know what I want.

"Listen, Max darling, this is what we must do. I shall
go away, alone, about as eagerly as a whipped dog. We'll
write to each other every day. And we'll put up with it
heroically, won't we, so as to get to the date, the beautiful
fifteenth of May, which will reunite us?"

The hero agrees sadly, with a resigned nod.

"The fifteenth of May, Max! I feel," say I in a lower
voice, "that that day I shall throw myself into your arms
as I would throw myself into the sea, as freely and as
irremediably."

He replies to this with a look and an embrace which
make me lose my head a little.

"And then, listen. If we can't wait, well never mind,
you'll come and join me, I'll send for you. Now are you
happy? After all, it's silly to be heroic and life's so short.
That's fixed then. Whoever is the unhappier will join the
other, or write to the other to come. But we'll still try,
because a honeymoon in the train . . . Is it all right now?
What are you looking for?"

"I'm thirsty, can you believe it, absolutely dying of thirst. Would you mind ringing for Blandine?"

"No need for her. You stay there and I'll go and get the things."

Happy and passive, he lets himself be waited on, and I watch him drinking as though he were granting me a great favour. If he wants me to, I'll tie his tie and decide what we'll have for dinner. And I'll bring him his slippers. And he shall ask me: "Where are you going?" as though he were my master. A female I was and, for better or worse, a female I find myself to be.

Relying on the dusk to hide my face whose ravages I have hastily restored, I sit on his knee and let him drink from my lips the breath that is still uneven from my sobs of a moment ago. One of his hands slides down from my forehead to my breast and I kiss it as it passes. Held in his arms, I fall back again into the state of a cherished victim who protests feebly against something she would not prevent if she could.

But all of a sudden I spring to my feet, struggle with him for a few seconds without saying a word, and finally manage to free myself crying "No!"

I had very nearly let myself be taken by surprise, there on that corner of the divan, his attempt was so swift and so clever. Out of reach, I look at him without anger and merely reproach him with: "Why did you do that? That was very naughty, Max."

Obedient and repentant, he sidles towards me, knocking over a little table and some chairs on his way, and murmuring "Forgive me . . . won't do it again . . . darling, it's so hard to wait . . ." in a somewhat exaggerated tone of childish supplication.

It is nearly dark now and I can no longer make out his

features clearly. But I suspected that the suddenness of that attempt a moment ago was due as much to calculation as loss of control. "You would have been caught, and then you would no longer have gone off wandering about the world all on your own."

"Poor Max," I say to him, gently.

"Are you laughing at me? Have I been silly?" He humbles himself nicely, and cleverly. He wants to bring my thoughts back to the gesture itself, and so to prevent me from thinking of his true motives. And I lie a tiny bit, to reassure him.

"I'm not laughing at you, Max. There are precious few men, you know, who would risk losing all their prestige by throwing themselves on a woman as you did, you great idiot. It's your clumsy peasant air which saves you, and those eyes, like an amorous wolf's. You looked like a day labourer tumbling a girl by the roadside on his way home from work at nightfall."

I leave him, to go and encircle my eyes again with the blue outline which makes them velvety and shining, to put on a coat and to pin on my head one of those bell-shaped hats whose form and whose colours remind Max of Champfleury's "Animated Flowers", those little flower-fairies who wear on their heads a poppy inside-out, the cup of a lily-of-the-valley, or a big iris with drooping petals.

We go off together for a gentle drive in the motor in the darkness of the Bois. These evening promenades are dear to me, when I hold my love's hand in the dim light, to know that he is there and for him to know that I am there. Then I can close my eyes and dream that I am going away with him to an unknown country where I shall have no past and no name, and where I shall be born again with a new face and an untried heart.

THIRTEEN

O<small>NE</small> week more and I leave.

Shall I really leave? There are hours and days when I doubt it. Especially days of premature spring, when my love takes me to those parks outside Paris, flattened and rutted with motors and bicycles, yet made mysterious all the same by the sharp, fresh season. Towards the end of the afternoon, a mauve mist veils the avenues so that you do not know where they end, and the unexpected discovery of a wild hyacinth, with its three slender bells of artless blue swaying in the wind, has all the charm of a stolen joy.

On a sunny morning last week we went for a long walk in the Bois, where the grooms gallop their horses. Walking side by side, we felt energetic and happy but not very talkative, and I was humming a little song which makes you walk fast. At a bend in a deserted riding-track we stopped, nose to muzzle before a very young hind with a golden coat, who lost countenance at sight of us and stopped short instead of fleeing.

She was panting with emotion and her delicate knees trembled, but her long eyes, made longer still by a brown line—like mine—expressed more embarrassment than fear. I would have liked to touch her ears, which were pointed towards us and plushy like the leaves of mullein, and that soft velveteen muzzle. But when I stretched out my hand, she turned her forehead away timidly and disappeared.

"You wouldn't have killed her, out hunting, Max?"

"Kill a hind? Why not a woman?" he answered, simply.

That day we lunched at Ville-d'Avray, like everyone else, in that restaurant with the curious terraces, terraces for eating and sleeping, that overhang the edge of the water, and we were as sensible as lovers already surfeited with pleasure. I was glad to find that the open air and the pure wind and the trees inspired in Max the same exhilarating serenity with which they always fill me. I gazed at the smooth water of the pool, turbid water with patches of iridescence on its surface, and at the hazel bushes with their hanging catkins. Then my eyes returned to this good comrade who had come into my life, full of the firm hope that I might build for him a happiness that would endure as long as that life itself.

Shall I really leave? There are times when I busy myself, as if in a dream, with my departure. My sponge-bag, my rolled-up rug and my waterproof, unearthed from cupboards, have reappeared in the light of day, streaked and shapeless and looking as though they were worn out with travelling. Full of disgust, I turned out containers filled with rancid cold cream and yellowed vaseline stinking of paraffin.

For the time being I take no pleasure in handling these tools of my trade. And when Brague came round to see how I was getting on, I received him so absent-mindedly and offhandedly that he departed in a huff and, much more serious, with a very polite "au revoir, dear friend". Never mind, there will be plenty of time to see him and smooth him out during those forty days. I am expecting him very soon now, to give me my final instructions. Max will come a little later.

"Good-morning, dear friend."
I thought as much; my comrade is still ruffled.
"No really, Brague, that's enough. That high-falutin'

style doesn't suit you at all. We're here to talk business. You remind me of Dranem as the Sun-King when you call me 'dear friend'."

Quickly amused, Brague protests: "High-falutin' style indeed, and why not? I can outdo Castellane when I want to. Have you never seen me in a dress suit?"

"No."

"Neither have I. I say, it's dark in this little . . . boudoir of yours. Why don't we go into your bedroom? We could see better to talk."

"All right, let's go into my bedroom."

Brague immediately spots, on the mantelpiece, a photograph of Max: Max looking stiff in a new suit, the black of his hair too black, the white of his eyes too white, formal and slightly absurd but very handsome all the same.

Brague examines the portrait, as he rolls his cigarette. "Definitely your 'friend', this chap, isn't he?"

"It's . . . my friend, yes." And I simper, idiotically.

"He's smart, there's no denying it. You'd take him for someone in the government. What are you laughing at?"

"Nothing. Just the thought that he might be in the government. That's hardly his line."

Brague holds a match to his cigarette and watches me out of the corners of his eyes.

"Taking him with you?"

I shrug my shoulders: "No, of course not. I couldn't. How could you expect . . ."

"But I don't *expect*, that's just it," cried Brague, his equanimity restored. "I think that's very right of you, my girl. You wouldn't believe how many tours I've seen bitched up because Madame wouldn't leave Monsieur, or because Monsieur wanted to keep an eye on Madame. It's nothing but arguments, billings and cooings,

quarrels, reconciliations when they simply can't get out
of bed, or else they totter feebly about the stage with
black-ringed eyes: in short, it ruins the whole thing. Give
me a cheerful trip where we're all pals. You know how
I've always said that love and work don't go together,
and I've never changed my mind about that. Besides, after
all, forty days isn't eternity; you write to each other and
when it's over you meet and team up again. Has he got
an office, your friend?"

"An office? No, he hasn't got an office."

"Well, does he . . . make motor-cars? I mean, he's got
some sort of business?"

"No."

"He does nothing?"

"Nothing."

Brague lets out a whistle that might be interpreted in
at least two ways.

"Absolutely nothing at all?"

"Nothing. That's to say, he owns some forests."

"It's staggering."

"What staggers you?"

"That anyone can live like that. No office. No factory.
No rehearsals. No racing stables. Doesn't it seem comic
to you?"

I look up at him with an embarrassed and slightly
conspiratorial air. "Yes."

I cannot make any other answer. My friend's idleness,
that mooning about like a schoolboy on perpetual holiday, often fills me with dismay and almost scandalises me.

"It would kill me," declares Brague, after a silence.
"A matter of habit."

"No doubt."

"Now," says Brague, sitting down, "let's be brief and
to the point. You've got everything you need?"

"Of course I have! My Dryad's costume, the new one, is a dream. Green as a little grasshopper and weighs less than a pound. The other's been done up and re-embroidered and cleaned, and you'd swear it was new: it can do another sixty shows without showing any signs of wear."

Brague purses his mouth.

"H'm . . . you sure? You ought to have managed to stump up a new rig for *The Pursuit*."

"That's right, and you'd have paid me for it, wouldn't you? And talking about *The Pursuit*, what about your embroidered buckskin breeches that have taken on the colour of all the boards that have covered them with polish, am I reproaching you with them?"

My comrade lifts a dogmatic hand: "Don't let's confuse things, if you don't mind. My breeches are magnificent. They've taken on a patina, a richness; they have the colour of fine earthenware. It would be a crime to replace them."

"You're just a skinflint," I tell him, shrugging my shoulders.

"And you're a harpy."

It does us a world of good to go for each other a bit, it refreshes us. We're both just sufficiently roused for the dispute to seem like a lively rehearsal.

"Break it up!" cried Brague. "The costume question is settled. Now for the baggage question."

"As if I needed you for that! This isn't exactly the first time we've been away together, you know. Are you going to teach me how to fold my chemises?"

From between eyelids wrinkled by his grimaces on the stage, Brague casts on me a crushing look.

"You poor thing. Lop-sided and ill-shapen brain, go on. Talk, natter away, rouse your bee and let it buzz.

Am I going to teach you? As if I could teach you!
Listen, and try to take it in: we have to pay for our
excess baggage ourselves, don't we?"

"Shh!"

I sign to him to stop, agitated because I have heard
two discreet rings on the bell in the antechamber. It is
he, and Brague is still there. After all, they know each
other.

"Come in, Max, come in. It's Brague. We're talking of
the tour; it won't bore you?"

No, it does not bore him; but it embarrasses me a
little. These music-hall matters are poor, precise, commercial things, which I want to keep separate from my
love, my darling lazy love.

Brague, very nice when he wants to be, smiles at Max.

"You don't mind, sir? It's our professional mixture
we're stirring, and I pride myself on being an economical
cook who wastes nothing and doesn't make a bit on the
side."

"Oh, please go on," cries Max. "On the contrary, it
will amuse me, since it's all new to me. I shall learn."

Liar. For a man who is being amused, he looks very
bad-tempered and very sad.

"As I was saying," Brague begins, "on the last tour,
the September one, if you remember we got through ten
or eleven francs for excess baggage every day, as if we'd
been Carnegie."

"Not all the time, Brague."

"No, not all the time. There were days when we paid
three francs or four francs excess. Even that's too much.
As far as I'm concerned, I've had enough of it. What have
you got in the way of luggage, besides your suitcase?"

"My black trunk."

"The big one? It's madness. I won't have it."

Max coughs.

"This is what you'll do: you'll use mine. In the top-layer: stage costumes. Second compartment; our under-things, your chemises, your knickers and your stockings, my shirts, my pants, etcetera."

Max fidgets.

". . . and at the bottom, shoes, change of suit for you and me, oddments, etcetera. Understand?"

"Yes, not a bad idea."

"All the same . . ." says Max.

"Like that," goes on Brague, "we've got just one piece of big luggage (the Troglodyte'll manage somehow. His mother, who's a poultry plucker, will lend him a basket) *one*, in all and for all. That means no excess, and reduction of tips to station porters, stage hands, etcetera. If we don't each make five francs a day on that, I'm a Dutch-man. You change your underwear every how often, on tour?"

I blush, because of Max.

"Every two days."

"That's your affair. We can get our washing done in the big burgs, Lyons, etcetera. So I reckon twelve chemises and twelve little pantikins, and the rest in pro-portion; isn't that big and generous? In short, I rely on you to be reasonable."

"Don't worry."

Brague gets up and grasps Max's hand.

"You see it doesn't take long to button up, sir. As for you, rendezvous at the station, at quarter past seven on Tuesday morning."

I accompany him as far as the antechamber and, when I come back, a tempest of protestations, lamentations and reproaches greets me.

"Renée, it's monstrous, it isn't possible, you've lost

your head. Your chemises, your own chemises, and your far-too-short little pantaloons, my darling love, hugger-mugger with the underdrawers of that individual. And your stockings with his socks, I dare say. How contemptible and how sordid!"

"How d'you mean, how sordid? It mounts up to two hundred francs."

"That's just what I mean, it's all so paltry."

I restrain a reply which would wound him: where could he, the spoilt child, have learnt that money, the money one earns, is a respectable, serious thing which one handles with care and speaks about solemnly?

He wipes his forehead with a beautiful handkerchief of violet silk. For some time past my friend has shown a great concern for elegance: he has magnificent shirts, handkerchiefs to match his ties, and shoes with doe-skin spats. I have not failed to notice this for, on this dear Big-Noodle with his somewhat heavy build, the slightest detail of dress takes on an almost shocking importance.

"Why do you agree to it?" he asks me reproachfully. "It's odious, this promiscuity."

Promiscuity. I was expecting that word. It is widely used. The "promiscuity of the stage".

"Tell me, darling," I say, tapering the points of his silky, rusty-black moustache between two fingers, "if it were a question of *your* shirts and *your* underdrawers, that wouldn't be *promiscuity*? You must remember that I'm only a very sensible little '*caf'conc*'' who lives by her job."

He suddenly embraces me, crushing me a little on purpose.

"The devil take your job. Ah, when I have you all to myself, you'll see. I'll absolutely load you with first-class carriages, and racks full of flowers, and frocks and frocks, and every beautiful thing I can find and everything I can invent."

His beautiful sombre voice ennobles this commonplace promise. Beneath the words I can hear, vibrating in it, his desire to lay the whole universe at my feet.

Frocks? I realise he must find my tailored suits of grey, brown and dark blue very monotonous and severe, a kind of neutral crysalis which I exchange, once the foot-lights are lit, for painted gauzes, shining spangles, and iridescent swirling skirts. First-class carriages? What for? They don't go any further than the others.

Fossette has squeezed between us her bonze-like skull, which gleams like rosewood. My little companion scents a departure. She has recognised the suitcase, with its rubbed corners, and the waterproof, she has seen the black-enamelled English tin box and the make-up case. She knows that I shall not take her, and resigns herself in advance to a life, petted it must be added, of rambles on the fortifications, evenings with the concierge, dinners in town and teas in the Bois. "I know you'll come back," say her slit eyes, "but when?"

"Max, she's very fond of you; you'll look after her?"

There now, the mere fact of bending together over this anxious little creature makes our tears overflow. I hold mine back with an effort which makes my throat and nose sting. How beautiful my love's eyes look, enlarged by the two lustrous tears which wet his eyelashes. Ah, why leave him?

"In a little while," he murmurs in a stifled voice, "I'll go and fetch a . . . beautiful little handbag . . . that I've ordered for you . . . very strong . . . for the journey. . . ."

"Oh, Max, have you?"

"In . . . pigskin. . . ."

"Max, come now, be a bit braver than I am."

He blows his nose, rebelliously.

"Why should I? I don't want to be brave, I don't. On the contrary."

"We're absurd. Neither would have dared to give way to our feelings on our own account, but Fossette has set us off. It's the trick of the 'little table' in *Manon*, and of the one-armed man in *Poliche*, d'you remember?"

Max dries his eyes, very slowly and carefully, with the simplicity with which he does everything, and which saves him from ridicule.

"I daresay you're right, my Renée. Anyway, if ever you want to turn me into a fountain, you need only talk to me of everything which surrounds you here in this little flat, everything that I shan't see again until you return. This old divan, the armchair where you sit to read, and your portraits, and the ray of sunshine gliding over the carpet from midday until two o'clock." He smiles, very moved. "Don't talk to me of the coal-shovel, of the hearth or the tongs or I shall break down!"

He has gone to get the beautiful little pigskin handbag.

"When we live together," he said to me wheedlingly, before he went out, "will you give me the furniture of this little sitting-room? I'll have some more made for you."

I smiled, to avoid refusing. These bits and pieces at Max's? For lack of money I have never replaced these relics of my conjugal home, which Taillandy let me take by way of contemptible compensation for the author's rights of which he formerly cheated me. What a "little table" aria I could sing about that would-be Dutch fumed oak, about that old divan worn into hollows by wanton games to which I was not bidden! Haunted furniture it is, amidst which I have often awakened with the mad fear that my liberty was only a dream. A strange wedding-present for a new lover. A shelter, and not a home, that is all I leave behind me: first- and second-class travelling boxes, hotels of every type, and sordid music-hall dressing-rooms in Paris and the provinces and abroad, have been more familiar and more benevolent to me than this place which my love calls "a charming, cosy nest".

How many times, in fleeing from myself, have I not fled from this ground floor? Today when, beloved and in love, I am leaving, I would like to be still more loved, still more loving, and so changed as to be unrecognisable in my own eyes. No doubt it is too soon, and the time has not yet come. But at least I am leaving with a troubled mind, overflowing with regret and hope, urged to return and reaching out towards my new lot with the glorious impulse of a serpent sloughing off its dead skin.

PART THREE

ONE

"GOODBYE, my dear love. My trunk is shut. My lovely pigskin bag, my travelling costume, and the long veil to go over my hat are laid out on our big divan, looking sad and sensible and awaiting my awakening tomorrow. Out of reach of you and my own weakness, I feel I have left already, so I give myself the joy of writing you my first love-letter.

"You'll receive this express-letter tomorrow morning, just at the time when I'm leaving Paris. It's merely an au revoir, written before I sleep, to let you know that I love you so much, that you mean so much to me! I am desolate at leaving you.

"Don't forget that you've promised to write to me 'all the time', and to console Fossette. And on my side I promise to bring you back a Renée tired of touring, grown thinner with solitude, and freed from everything, except you.

Your
Renée."

The swift shadow of a bridge passes rapidly over my eyelids which I was keeping closed, and I open them again to see, receding rapidly on the left of the train, that little field of potatoes that I know so well, huddled against the high wall of the fortifications.

I am alone in the compartment. Brague, severely economical, is travelling second with the Old Troglodyte. A wet day, languid as a grey dawn, lies heavy over the countryside with its trails of smoke from factories. It is eight o'clock and the first morning of my trip. After a short period of dejection, following the agitation of departure, I had fallen into a glum immobility which made me hope for sleep.

I pull myself together and proceed to make my preparations, mechanically, like an old campaigner: I unfold the camel-hair travelling-rug, blow up the two silk-covered rubber cushions—one for my back and one for the nape of my neck—and hide my hair under a veil of the same bronze colour. I do all that methodically and carefully, though a sudden indescribable anger makes my hands tremble the while. A real fury, yes, and against myself. I am leaving, each turn of the wheel carries me further from Paris, I am leaving, while an icy spring adorns the tips of the oak branches with frozen pearls; all is cold and damp, with a mist which smells of winter still, and I am leaving when I might at this hour be lying, relaxed with pleasure, against the warm side of a lover. I feel as though my anger were whetting in me a devouring appetite for all that is pleasant, luxurious, easy and selfish, a need to let myself slide down the softest slope, and embrace with arms and lips a belated happiness that is tangible and ordinary and delicious.

How tedious to me is everything that I see in this familiar suburb, with its pallid villas where the yawning housewives in their camisoles rise late to shorten the empty days. I would have done better not to have left Brague, to have remained with him in the dirty, blue-cushioned seats of the second-class carriages, among the good-natured chatter, the human odour of the crowded compartment, and the smoke of cigarettes at sixpence the packet.

The ta-ta-tam of the train, which I hear in spite of myself, acts as an accompaniment to the dance motif of

The Dryad, which I hum with the persistence of one possessed. How long will this impression of having dwindled last? For I feel myself diminished, and weakened, as though I had been bled. During my saddest days the sight of a quite ordinary landscape, as long as it was receding rapidly to right and left, and as long as it was veiled from time to time with a ribbon of smoke that got torn on the thorn hedges, acted all the same on me like a health-giving tonic. I am cold. A wretched morning sleep numbs me, and I feel as though I were fainting rather than sleeping, agitated by childish arithmetical dreams in which this wearisome question keeps recurring: "if you have left half of yourself behind, does that mean you have lost fifty per cent of your original value?"

TWO

Dijon, April 3rd.

"YES, yes, I'm well. Yes, I found your letter; yes, I'm having a success. Ah, my darling, know the whole truth. When I left you I sank into the most absurd, the most impatient despair. Why did I go away? Why did I leave you? Forty days! I shall never be able to bear that, now. And I'm only at the third town.

> *At the third town*
> *Her lover puts on her*
> *A gown of gold and a silver gown.*

"*Alas, my lover, I need neither silver nor gold, but only you. It rained at my first two stopping-places, to make me realise better my hateful desertion, there between hotel walls papered with chocolate and beige, and in those imitation oak dining-rooms which the gas makes darker still.*

"*You don't know what discomfort is, you spoilt son of Madame Ever-Cut. When we're together again, just to rouse your indignation and make you cherish me still more, I'll tell you of the returns at midnight to the hotel, with the make-up box weighing heavily on my tired arm, the waiting at the door under the fine mist while the night-porter slowly wakes, the horrible room with its badly-dried sheets, the minute jug of hot water which has had time to get cold. And should I make you share these daily joys? No, my darling, let me exhaust my own powers of resistance before I cry to you 'Come, I can't bear it another minute!'*

"*Anyway, it's fine here at Dijon, and I welcome this sun timidly, like a present that's going to be quickly taken away from me.*

"*You promised me to console Fossette. She's yours as much as mine. Take care not to overwhelm her with attentions whilst I'm away, or she won't forgive you. Her bulldog sensibility is such as to impose on her an exquisite repression of her feelings, and when I desert her, she greatly resents it if some affectionate third person notices her grief, even by an attempt to distract her from it.*

"Goodbye, goodbye, I kiss you and I love you. Such a cold twilight today, you can't imagine. The sky's as green and pure as it is in January when it's freezing hard. Write to me, love me, warm your

Renée."

April 10th.

"My last letter must have made you unhappy. I'm not pleased with myself, nor with you either. You have a beautiful writing, bold and round, and at the same time slender, elegant and curly, like the plant that in my part of the world we call 'flowering osier'; it fills four or even eight pages with loving maledictions and the most burning regrets and a few 'I adore you's'. It can be read in twenty seconds and I'm sure you genuinely think you've written me a long letter. Moreover, you talk of nothing but me in it.

"My darling, I've just passed through, without stopping, a region which belongs to me because I spent my childhood there. I felt as though a long caress were stroking my heart. One day, promise me, we'll go there together? No, no—what am I writing —we won't go there. In your memory your Ardennes forests would put to shame my coppices of oaks and brambles and white-beam, and you would not see, as I do, trembling above them and the shadowy waters of the springs, and above the blue hill adorned with the tall flowers of the thistle, the slender rainbow which magically enshrines all things in the place where I was born.

"Nothing has changed there. A few new roofs, bright red, that's all. Nothing has changed in my part of the world—

except me. *Ah, my darling love, how old I am! Can you really love such an old young woman? I blush for myself, here. Why did you not know the tall child who used to trail her regal plaits here, silent by nature as a wood nymph? All that, which once I was, I gave to another, to another than you! Forgive me for this cry, Max, it is the cry of my torment, which I've kept in ever since I loved you. And now that it's too late, are not the things you love in me the things which change me and deceive you, my curls clustering thick as leaves, my eyes which the blue kohl lengthens and suffuses, the artificial smoothness of my powdered skin? What would you say if I were to reappear, if I appeared before you with my heavy, straight hair, with my fair lashes cleansed of their mascara, in short with the eyes which my mother gave me, crowned with brief eyebrows quick to frown, grey, narrow, level eyes in the depths of which there shines a stern, swift glance which I recognise as that of my father?*

"*Don't be afraid, my darling love, I shall return to you more or less as I left you, a little more weary, a little more tender. Every time I touch the fringes of it, my own country casts a spell on me, filling me with sad, transitory rapture; but I would not dare to stop there. Perhaps it is only beautiful because I have lost it.*

"*Goodbye, dear, dear Max. We have to leave very early tomorrow, for Lyons, otherwise we shouldn't have our rehearsal with the orchestra, which I look after while Brague, never tired, sees to the programmes, the putting of our posters in the frames, and the sale of our postcards.*

"*Oh, how cold I was, last night again, in the flimsy dress I wear for* The Pursuit. *Cold is my enemy, it paralyses my life and my thoughts. You know that, you in whose hands my own seek refuge, curled up like two leaves under the frost. I miss you, my dear warmth, as much as I miss the sun.*

Your
Renée."

THREE

ON we go. I eat, sleep, walk, mime and dance. No zest,
but no effort. There is just one moment of excitement in the whole day, the moment when I ask the porter
at the music-hall if there is "any post" for me. I read my
letters like one starved, leaning against the greasy door-
post of the artistes' entry, in the foetid draught that smells
of cellars and ammonia. But they make time hang more
heavily afterwards, when there is no more left to read,
when I have deciphered the date of the postmark and
turned the envelope inside out as if I hoped to see a
flower or a photo fall out of it.

I pay no attention to the towns where we play. I know
them and have no wish to explore them again. So I just
tack on to Brague, who goes about like a good-humoured
conqueror taking possession once more of those familiar
"little old burgs"—Rheims, Nancy, Belfort and
Besançon.

"That little cookshop's still at the corner of the quay,
did you notice? I bet they recognise me when we go and
tuck in to their sausage with white wine this evening."

He takes deep breaths, darts down the streets with the
joy of a vagabond, loiters round the shops, and climbs up
to the cathedrals. Last year it was I who led him, but
now I accompany him. He trails me along in his shadow,
and sometimes we take the Old Troglodyte in tow too,
though normally he goes off alone, gaunt and seedy-
looking in his thin jacket and over-short trousers. Where
does he sleep? Where does he eat? I don't know. When
I asked Brague he answered briefly: "Where he likes.
I'm not his nurse."

The other evening, at Nancy, I caught sight of the Troglodyte in his dressing-room. He was standing there biting into a pound loaf and holding a slice of brawn delicately between two fingers. The sight of that poor man's meal, and the voracious movement of his jaws, made my heart contract and I went to find Brague.

"Brague, has the Troglodyte enough to live on on tour? He really does earn fifteen francs, doesn't he? Why doesn't he feed better?"

"He's saving," answers Brague. "*Everyone* saves on tour. *Everyone* isn't Vanderbilt or Renée Néré, to treat themselves to rooms at five francs and *café-au-laits* served in their rooms. The Troglodyte owes me for his costume, which I advanced him; he pays me for it at the rate of five francs a day. In twenty days he'll be able to guzzle oysters and wash his feet in cocktails if he likes. That's his affair."

Thus rebuked, I say no more. And I too "save", first out of habit and then to imitate my companions, so as to excite neither their jealousy nor their contempt. Can she be Max's love, that woman with the calm, indifferent, unsociable look of those who belong neither here nor elsewhere, reflected in the smoke-blackened mirror of a "Brasserie Lorraine" where she is dining, that traveller with the dark-ringed eyes, a travelling veil knotted under her chin, and everything about her, from her hat to her boots, the colour of the road? Can she be Max's lover, the pale lover whom he used to embrace half-naked in a rose-coloured kimono, that tired comedienne who comes along, in corset and petticoat, to hunt in Brague's trunk for her chemise, her linen for the next day, and to put away her spangled draperies?

Every day I wait for my love's letter. Every day it consoles me and disappoints me at the same time. He writes

simply but obviously not with ease. His beautiful
flowery writing slows up the natural impetus of his
hand. And then his tenderness and his sadness both con-
strain him, as he ingenuously laments: "When I've told
you a hundred times that I love you and that I'm horribly
cross with you for having left me, what more can I say?
My darling wife, my little blue-stocking of a wife, you'll
laugh at me but I don't care. My brother is leaving for
the Ardennes and I'm going with him. Write to me at
Salles-Neuves, care of my mother. I'm going to collect
some money, some money for us, for our home, little
sweetheart."

This is the way he tells me of his doings and what is
happening to him, with no commentary and without
frills. He associates me with his life and calls me his wife.
He has no idea that by the time his warm solicitude
reaches me it has become no more than a beautifully even
writing, all cold on the paper; so far apart, what help to
us are words? One needs—oh, I don't know—perhaps
some passionate drawing, all glowing with colour.

FOUR

"SO now you're getting Blandine to tell your fortune from the cards! This really is the limit. My darling, you're lost. Whenever I leave the house, that girl always prophesies the most picturesque catastrophes. If I go on tour she dreams of cats and serpents, turbid waters and folded sheets, and reads in the cards the tragic adventures of Renée Néré (the Queen of Clubs) with the False Young Man, the Soldier and the Rustic. Don't listen to her, Max. Count the days as I do, and smile—oh, that smile that makes hardly perceptible wrinkles in your nostrils—to think that the first week is almost over.

"I myself prophesy to you that, in one month and four days, I shall 'steer my course' to rejoin the 'Big-hearted Man' and that 'you will have great joy of it' and that the False Young Man will be 'thwarted', as will also the mysterious 'Woman of Ill-Fame', by whom I mean the Queen of Diamonds.

"Here we are for five days at Lyons. That'll be a rest, did you say? Yes, if by that you mean that for four mornings running I shall be able to wake up with a start at daybreak, scared to death of missing my train, and then fall back on my bed in a state of exhausted laziness that drives sleep away, and listen for a long time to the servants getting up round me, to the bells, and the traffic in the street. It is much worse, my darling, than the daily departure at dawn. I have the impression that I'm looking on, from the depths of my bed, at a fresh start from which I'm excluded, that the world is beginning to 'turn' without me. And then it is in the depths of my bed, too, when I'm a prey to my memories and overcome with boredom, that I most long for you.

"O dear enemy, we might have spent five days together here.

*Don't mistake this for a challenge; I don't want you to come.
Don't worry, I shan't die of it, lord no! You always seem to
think that being away from you has killed me already. My
handsome peasant, all it does is to benumb me, I'm hibernating.*

"*It's stopped raining and it's mild and damp and grey, the
best kind of Lyons weather. It's rather absurd, the way these
meteorological reports crop up in all my letters, but if you only
knew how, on tour, both our fate and our moods hang on the
colour of the sky. 'Wet weather, dry pocket,' says Brague.*

"*In the last four years I've spent seven or eight weeks in
Lyons. My first visit was to see the deer in the park of Saint-
Jean, those little blonde fawns with their unseeing, tender gaze.
There are so many of them, and all so alike, that I can't single
one out; they follow me down the length of the wire-netting with
a trot which pits the soil like hail, and beg black bread with
clear, persistent, timid bleats. The smell of the turf, of the
churned-up earth, is so strong in this garden, under the still air
at the end of the day, that it would be able to carry me back to
you if I attempted to escape.*

"*Goodbye, darling. Here in Lyons I've run again into some
wanderers of my own sort whom I met here or elsewhere. If I
were to tell you that one is called Cavaillon, a comic singer, and
the other Amalia Barally, who plays the duennas in comedies,
you wouldn't be much the wiser. Yet Barally is almost a friend,
for we played together in a three-act play all round France, two
years ago. She is a one-time beauty, a dark woman with a Roman
face, an accomplished trouper, who knows by name every inn in
the world. She has sung in operetta in Saigon, acted in comedies
in Cairo, and enlivened the evenings of I don't know what
khedive.*

"*What I appreciate in her, in addition to her gaiety which is
proof against poverty, is her protective nature, that skill in
looking after people, a delicate motherliness in her gestures
which you find in women who have sincerely and passionately*

loved women; it confers on them an indefinable attraction which you men will never perceive.

"Heavens, how I write to you! I could spend my whole time writing to you, I believe I find it easier to write than to talk to you. Take me in your arms; it's nearly dark now, the worst moment of the day; hold me very close, very close.

Your
Renée."

April 15th.

"My darling, how kind of you! What a good idea! Thank you, thank you with all my heart for that badly-developed snapshot, yellow with hyposulphite; you're both there, my dear ones, ravishing, the pair of you. And now of course I can't any longer scold you for having taken Fossette to Salles-Neuves without my permission. She looks so happy in your arms. She's put on her photograph face, that makes her look like a beefy wrestler, holder of the Gold Belt.

"It's clear—as I observe with a slightly jealous gratitude— that at that moment she had no thoughts at all for me. But what about your eyes, that I can't see because they're gazing paternally down at Fossette, what were they dreaming about? The tender awkwardness of your arms holding that little dog both moves and amuses me. I slip this portrait of you, with the two others, into the old leather pocket-book—you remember?—which you thought had a mysterious and sinister air.

"Send me still more photos, will you? I've brought four with me and I compare them, examining you in them with a magnifying glass, to find again in each one, notwithstanding the smears of the retouching and the exaggerated lighting, a little of your secret self. Secret? Heavens no, there's nothing deceptive in you. It seems to me that any little goose would know you at a glance, as I do.

"I say that, you know, but I don't believe a word of it.

Behind my teasing there's a nasty little desire to simplify you, to humiliate in you the old adversary: that's what I've always called the man who is destined to possess me.

"Is it true there are so many anemones in your woods, and violets? I saw some violets near Nancy when I was crossing that undulating eastern countryside, blue with firs and slashed with bright, sparkling rivers where the water is green-black. Was that you, that tall boy standing bare-legged in the icy water, fishing for trout?

"Goodbye. Tomorrow we leave for Saint-Etienne. I must grumble to you about Hamond, who hardly ever writes to me, so you must try and write to me a lot, my dear, in case I should complain to Hamond. I kiss you.

Renée."

FIVE

WE have just dined at Berthoux's—an artistes' restaurant—Barally, Cavaillon, Brague, I and the Troglodyte, whom I had invited. He does not talk, his one idea is to eat. It was a typical "barnstormers' " dinner, noisy but with rather a false gaiety. Cavaillon stood us a bottle of Moulin-à-Vent.

"You must be horribly bored here," chaffed Brague, "to stump up the price of such a classy wine."

"I'll say," replied Cavaillon briefly.

Cavaillon, young but already famous in the music-hall world, is envied by everyone there. They say of him that "Dranem is afraid of him", and that "he earns whatever he chooses". We have run into this tall young man of twenty-two once or twice already; he walks like a human serpent, as though he had no bones, his heavy fists swinging at the end of his frail wrists. His face, under his fair hair cut in a fringe, is almost pretty, but his mauve glance, anxious and restless, reveals acute neurasthenia, near to madness. His favourite expression is: "I'm killing myself." He spends his whole day waiting till it is time for his act, and while it lasts he forgets, enjoys himself, and carries the public away. He neither drinks nor goes on the loose. He invests his money and is bored.

Barally, who is "spinning out" a season at the *Celestins*, has laughed so much, showing her beautiful teeth, and talked so much, relating terrific binges when she was young, that it has gone to her head. She tells us of the colonial theatres of twenty years ago, when she used to sing in operetta in Saigon, in a hall lit by eight hundred oil lamps. Penniless and already old, she is the old-fashioned Bohemian incarnate, likeable and incorrigible.

A pleasant dinner all the same: we work each other up and come close together for an instant round the over-small table, and then goodbye. A goodbye without regrets, for the next day, or the next moment, we forget each other. . . . At last we are off again. Five days in Lyons can be interminable.

Cavaillon accompanies us to the Kursaal; it is too early for him since he only takes ten minutes to make up; but, a prey to solitude and grown silent and gloomy again, he clings to us. The Troglodyte, transported and slightly tipsy, sings to the stars, and I dream, and listen to the black wind rising and sweeping up the banks of the Rhone with a roar like the sea. Why do I feel as though I were rocked on an invisible swell like a ship set afloat by the sea? It is the kind of evening that makes one want to sail to the other side of the world. My cheeks are cold, my ears frozen and my nose moist: my whole animal self feels fit and vigorous and adventurous . . . until we get to the threshold of the Kursaal, where the musty warmth of the basement chokes my cleansed lungs.

As glum as government clerks, we arrive at those peculiar artists' dressing-rooms which resemble at the same time lofts in provincial houses, and servants' attics, papered in cheap grey and white. Cavaillon, who shed us on the staircase, is already in his dressing-room where I see him, sitting before his make-up shelf, his elbows propped on it and his head in his hands. Brague tells me that that is how this comic actor passes his lugubrious evenings, utterly worn out and silent. I shiver. I should like to shake off the memory of that man sitting there and hiding his face. I am afraid of becoming like him, that wretched, stranded creature, lost in our midst and conscious of his solitude.

SIX

"YOU'RE *afraid I'm forgetting you? That's a new idea!
Max darling, don't start 'playing the tart', as I call
it. I think of you and gaze at you from far off with such keen
attention that you ought, every now and again, to feel some
mysterious intimation of it. Don't you? Across the distance that
separates us I watch you intently, unwearyingly. I see you so
clearly. The hours of our rapid intimacy have now yielded up all
their secrets to me, and I slowly unfold all our words, all our
silences, our looks and our gestures, faithfully recorded with all
their pictorial and musical values. And this is the time you choose
to complain coquettishly, a finger in the corner of your mouth:
'You're forgetting me, I feel you've gone further away from me!'
Really, the second sight of lovers!*

"*It is true I'm going further away, my dear. We have just left
Avignon behind, and when I woke in the train yesterday after
a nap of two hours, I might have thought I had slept for two
months; spring had come to meet me, a spring such as one
imagines in fairy-tales, the exuberant, ephemeral, irresistible
spring of the South, rich and fresh, springing up in sudden bursts
of greenery, in plants already tall which sway and ripple in the
wind, in mauve Judas trees and paulownias the colour of grey
periwinkles, in laburnums, wistarias and roses.*

"*The first roses, my dear one! I bought them in the station at
Avignon, little more than buds, of sulphur yellow touched with
carmine, transparent in the sun as an ear aglow with bright
blood, adorned with tender leaves and curved thorns of polished
coral. They are on my table now. They smell like apricot and
vanilla, like a very fine cigar, and like some dark, curled and
scented beauty—the exact scent, Max, of your dry, dark-
skinned hands.*

"Dear one, I'm letting myself be dazzled and revived by this new season, this hard, strong sky, and that rare, gold colour of rocks that have been caressed by the sun all the year round. No, no, don't pity me for leaving at dawn, since dawn in this country breaks, naked and rosy, from a milky sky, filled with the sound of bells and flights of white pigeons. . . . Oh I beseech you, do understand that you mustn't write me 'thought out' letters, that you mustn't think of what you are writing to me. Write no matter what, the kind of weather you're having, what time you woke up, how cross you feel with your 'salaried gipsy'; fill your pages with the same tender word, repeated like the cry of a mating bird. My dear lover, I want you to feel the same disturbance as this spring which has thrust its way out of the earth and is burning itself up with its own haste."

I rarely re-read my letters, but I've re-read this one and let it go with the strange impression that I was doing a clumsy thing, making a mistake, and that it was on its way to a man who ought not to have read it. I have felt a bit light-headed since we left Avignon. The regions of mist have melted away behind the curtains of cypress that bend under the mistral. That day the silky rustle of the long reeds came in through the lowered window of the compartment, together with a scent of honey and pine, of varnished buds and unopened lilac, that bitter scent of the lilac before it flowers, like turpentine and almond mingled. The cherry trees cast a violet shadow on the reddish earth already cracking with thirst. The train cuts across or runs along beside white roads where a chalky dust rolls in low clouds and powders the bushes. A pleasantly exciting murmur, like that of a distant swarm of bees, buzzes incessantly in my ears.

Alive to that excess of scent and colour and warmth, and unable to resist although I had foreseen it, I let myself be taken by surprise, carried away and conquered. Can it be that there is no danger in such sweetness?

Below the balcony, the deafening Canebière teems at my feet, that Canebière which rests neither day nor night, and where idling takes on the importance and assurance of a job. If I bend forward I can see the water of the port glittering at the end of the street behind the geometrical lace of the riggings, a fragment of dark blue sea dancing in little short waves.

My hand, on the edge of the balcony, crumples the last note from my love, in answer to my letter from Lyons. Unluckily he recalls from it that my comrade Amalia Barally was not a lover of men and, like the "normal" and "well-balanced" being that he is, he has not failed to cast a bit of a slur on my old friend, by poking fun at her, and to vilify something that he does not understand. What would be the good of explaining to him? Two women enlaced will never be for him anything but a depraved couple, he will never see in them the melancholy and touching image of two weak creatures who have perhaps sought shelter in each other's arms, there to sleep and weep, safe from man who is so often cruel, and there to taste, better than any pleasure, the bitter happiness of feeling themselves akin, frail and forgotten. What would be the good of writing, and pleading, and discussing? My voluptuous friend can only understand love.

SEVEN

April 24th.

"DON'T *do that, I implore you, don't do that! Landing here without a word of warning, you haven't seriously thought of it, have you?*

"*What should I do if I saw you suddenly entering my dressing-room, as you did five months ago at the* Empyrée-Clichy? *Goodness me, I should keep you here, you can be sure of that. But that is why you mustn't come. I should keep you, my darling, against my heart, against my breast that you have so often caressed, against my mouth which is wilting from not being kissed any more. Ah, how I should keep you! That is why you must not come.*

"*Stop invoking our common need of taking fresh courage, of drawing from each other the strength for a new separation. Let me devote myself wholly to my job, which you do not like. After all, it's only twenty days more before I return. Let me finish my tour, putting into it an almost soldierly sense of duty and that sort of honest worker's application with which one mustn't mix our happiness. Your letter frightened me, my darling. I thought I was going to see you walk in. Take care not to over-whelm your love and do not lavish on her unexpected sorrows, or joys either.*

Renée."

The canvas awning flaps above our heads, chequering with light and shade the terrace of the restaurant on the port where we have just been lunching. Brague reads the newspapers, uttering exclamations from time to time and talking to himself. I don't hear him, I scarcely see him.

A habit already of long standing has suppressed all politeness, coquetry and modesty between us—all the insincere things. We have just been eating sea-urchins, tomatoes, and a *brandade* of cod. In front of us, between the oily sea lapping the sides of the boats and the perforated wooden balustrade which encloses this terrace, there is a stretch of pavement where busy people with the happy faces of idlers pass up and down; there are fresh flowers, carnations tied up in stiff bunches, like leeks, soaking in green pails; there is a street-stall loaded with black bananas smelling of ether, and shell-fish dripping with sea-water: sea-urchins, "*violets*", clams, blue mussels and cockles, dotted about with lemons and little flasks of pink vinegar.

I cool my hand on the belly of the white water-cooler, ribbed like a melon, which stands exuding moisture on the table. Everything there belongs to me and possesses me. I shall not think tomorrow that I am taking this picture away with me, but it seems to me that a shadow of myself, detached from me like a leaf, will remain here, a little bowed with fatigue, its transparent hand stretched out and laid on the side of an invisible water-cooler.

I contemplate my changing kingdom as though I had almost lost it. Yet nothing threatens this easy, wandering life, nothing, except a letter. It is there, in my little bag. My word, how my love writes when he wants to! How clearly he makes himself understood! Here, in eight pages, is something that I can at last call a real love-letter. It has the incoherence of a love-letter, the spelling groggy in places, the tenderness and . . . the authority. A superb authority which disposes of me, my future, and the whole of my little life. Absence has done its work; he has suffered without me and so he has thought things out and carefully planned a lasting happiness: he offers me marriage as if he were offering me a sunny enclosure, bounded by solid walls.

"My mother certainly cried a little, but I let her cry. She has always done what I wanted. You will win her heart, and besides, we shan't be spending much time with her. You love travelling, don't you, my darling wife? You shall have so much that you'll get tired of it; the whole world shall be yours, until you come to love nothing but a little corner of our own where you will no longer be Renée Néré but My Lady Wife. You'll have to be content to be billed as that in future! I'm already arranging to . . ."

What is he already arranging? I unfold the thin sheets of foreign writing-paper which rustle like bank notes: he is arranging to move, since the second floor of his brother's house was never suitable for anything but a bachelor flat. He has his eye on something in the neighbourhood of the *Rue Pergolèse*.

Impelled by a cruel hilarity, I crumple the letter, exclaiming to myself: "That's all very well, but what about me, am I not to be consulted? What do I become in all that?"

Brague raises his head, then takes up his paper again, without a word. It takes more than that to startle him out of his discretion, which is part reserve and part indifference.

I was not lying when I wrote to Max two days ago: "I see you so clearly, now that I'm far away." I only hope I do not see him too clearly. Young, too young for me, idle, free, affectionate, but spoilt: "My mother has always done what I wanted." I hear his voice pronouncing those words, his beautiful sombre voice with its seductive modulations, as though he had learnt in the theatre how to use it, that voice which gives beauty to the words, and I hear, like a diabolical echo, another voice which rises, muffled, from the depths of my memories: "The woman who will order me about is not yet born." Coincidence, if you will, but all the same it seems to me as though I had just swallowed a small piece of sharp glass.

Yes, what do I become in all that? A happy woman? This sunlight, imperiously penetrating the "dark room" of my inmost being, makes it difficult to think.

"I'm going in, Brague, I'm tired."

Brague looks at me over the top of his paper, his head on one side to avoid the thread of smoke rising from the half-extinguished cigarette in the corner of his mouth.

"Tired? Not ill? It's Saturday you know. The public at the *Eldo* will be pretty lively, so keep up to the mark."

I don't deign to answer. Does he take me for a beginner? We know all about this Marseilles public, decent but excitable, despising timidity and punishing conceit, not to be won over unless one throws one's whole self into it.

The migraine which was beginning vanishes as I get undressed and feel on my skin the coolness of a bluish shantung kimono, that has been washed twenty times. I do not lie down on my bed, for fear of going to sleep; I have not come here to rest. Kneeling on an armchair against the open window, I prop my elbows on the back of it and rub my bare feet against each other behind me. A few days ago I fell again into the habit of planking myself down on the edge of a table, perching on the arm of an easy chair, and remaining for a long time in awkward attitudes on uncomfortable seats, as though for these brief pauses on my way it was not worth while installing myself, or taking trouble to rest properly. Anyone might think that, with my coat thrown here and my hat there, I was only spending a quarter of an hour in the bedrooms where I sleep. It is in railway carriages that I show myself to be methodical to the point of mania, surrounded by my handbag, my rolled rug, my books and papers, the rubber cushions which support me when, with the promptitude of a hardened traveller, I fall into a rigid sleep which disturbs neither my veil, tied like a nun's head-band, nor my skirt drawn down to my ankles.

I am not resting. I want to force myself to think, and my mind jibs, escapes, darts down a path of light that a sunbeam, falling on the balcony, opens before it, and goes on its way across a mosaic roof of green tiles down below, where it childishly stops to play with a reflection, the shadow of a cloud. I struggle, lashing myself on. Then I give up for a minute, only to begin again. It is duels such as this which give to exiles like me those wide-open eyes, so slow to detach their gaze from some invisible lure. These are the gloomy gymnastics of the solitary.

Solitary! How can I think such a thing when my lover is calling to me, ready to take care of me all my life long? But I don't know what "all my life long" means. Three months ago I pronounced those terrible words "ten years", "twenty years", without understanding. Now the time has come when I must understand. My lover offers me his life, the improvident and generous life of a young man of about thirty-four, like me. He thinks I am young too, and he does not see the *end*—my end. In his blindness he will not admit that I must change and grow old, although every second, added to the second that is fleeting, is already snatching me away from him.

I still have what it takes to please him, and more still,

to dazzle him. I can put off this face of mine as one takes off a mask; I have another, more beautiful face, which he has glimpsed. And where others adorn themselves, I disrobe, trained as I have been, first as Taillandy's model and then as a dancer, to avoid the dangers that lie in nudity and to move naked under the light as though it were a complicated drapery. But for how many years more am I still thus armed?

My friend offers me his name and his fortune, with his love. Decidedly my master Chance is doing things handsomely, and is anxious to reward by one large gesture my desultory worship of him. It is both unexpected and crazy; it is also a bit too much!

Dear good man, he will be awaiting my reply impatiently and watching for the postman on the road, in company with Fossette, my Fossette who is thrilled at acting the Lady of the Manor, riding in a motor and playing inner circle round the saddled horses. I am sure his joy must be intensified by the naïve legitimate pride of a gentleman who has been decent enough to raise from below stage at the *Emp'-Clich'* to his own level on the white terrace of Salles-Neuves, a nice little "*caf'-conc'*" actress.

Dear, dear, heroic *bourgeois*! Ah, why doesn't he love one of his own kind? How happy she would make him! It seems to me that I shall never be able to.

If it were only a question of giving myself! But voluptuous pleasure is not the only thing. In the limitless desert of love it holds a very small place, so flaming that at first one sees nothing else; but I am not a green young girl, to be blinded by the brilliance of it. All about this flickering hearth there lies the unknown, there lies danger. What do I know of the man whom I love and who wants me? After we have risen from a short embrace, or even from a long night, we shall have to begin to live at close quarters to each other, and in dependence on each other. He will bravely hide the first disappointments that I shall cause him, and I shall keep silent about mine, out of pride and shame and pity, and above all because I shall have expected them, *because I shall recognise them*. I who shrink right up when I hear myself called "my darling child", I who tremble before certain gestures of his, certain intonations that rise up from the past, what an army of ghosts is lying in wait for me behind the curtains of a bed that is still unopened?

No reflection dances now on the green-tiled roof down below. The sun has started to sink; a lake of sky, azure a moment ago between two spindles of motionless cloud, now pales serenely, passing from turquoise to lemon-green. My arms, propped on their elbows, and my bent knees, have gone to sleep. The unprofitable day is drawing to its end and I have decided nothing and written nothing, nor have I torn from my heart one of those irresistible impulses whose wild guidance I once upon a time accepted, without further thought, ready to call it "divine".

What shall I do? For today I'll write—briefly, for time is short—and lie to him.

"My darling, it is nearly six o'clock and I've spent the whole day struggling against a terrible migraine. The heat is so great and so sudden that it makes me groan but, like Fossette before too bright a fire, without resentment. And then your letter on top of all that! You and the sky overwhelm me with your gifts, it's just too much sun, too much light at the same time; that's all I have strength for today, to sigh 'It's too much!' A friend like you, Max, and lots of love and lots of happiness and lots of money . . . how strong you must think me! I am, usually, it is true, but not today. Give me time.

"Here is a photograph for you. I've just received it from Lyons where Barally took this snapshot. Don't you think I look terribly dark and small, and sort of lost dog, with those folded hands and that beaten look? Frankly, my dear love, that humble stray feels ill-equipped to bear the excess of honour and wealth that you promise her. She is looking in your direction and her defiant fox's muzzle seems to say to you 'Is it really for me, all that? Are you sure?'

"Goodbye, my darling love. You are the best of men, and you deserved the best of wives. Will you not regret having chosen only
                                        Renée Néré?"

I have forty-eight hours before me.

And now I must hurry and get ready to dine on the terrace at Basso's, in the cool breeze and the scent of lemons and wet mussels, and then rush to the *Eldorado* along avenues bathed in pink electric light, snapping, at last, for a few hours, the thread which unceasingly draws me away back there.

EIGHT

Nice, Cannes, Mentone. . . . On I spin, followed by my ever-growing torment: a torment so lively, so ever-present, that I sometimes fear I may see the shape of its shadow beside mine on the pale freestone of the jetties that enclose the sea, or on the hot pavement where banana skins lie fermenting. My torment tyrannises over me; it comes between me and the joy of living, contemplating, and breathing deeply. One night I dreamt that I did not love, and that night, released from all bonds, I lay as though in a kind of soothing death.

To my ambiguous letter from Marseilles Max replied with a calm and happy one, full of thanks from beginning to end without a word crossed out, and friendly, confident love proud of giving everything and receiving more; in short a letter which might have made me suppose I had written: "On such a day, at such an hour, I will be yours and we will go away together."

Is it really settled then? Am I as much committed as that? And this bad mood which makes me find the time drag so between one day and another, one town and another, one night and another, is it due to impatience or to haste? At Mentone yesterday I was listening, in a boarding-house drowsing among gardens, to the birds and the flies waking up, and the parakeet on the balcony. The dawn wind made the palm trees rustle like dead reeds and I recognised all the sounds, the whole music, of a similar morning the year before. But this year the whistling of the parakeet, the buzzing of the wasps as the

sun rose, and the stiff breeze in the palms all receded far
away from me and seemed like a murmured accompaniment to my anxiety, acting as a pedal to my obsession,
love.

In the garden, under my window, an oblong bed of
violets which the sun had not yet touched made a blue
patch in the dew, beneath mimosas yellow as a chick.
And against the wall there were climbing roses, too,
which I guessed were scentless from their colour, greenish
and sulphury yellow, the same indeterminate shade as the
sky, which was not yet blue. The same roses and the same
violets as the year before; but why was I not able to
greet them yesterday with that involuntary smile, reflecting a harmless, half-physical felicity, in which the silent
happiness of solitary people expresses itself?

I suffer. I cannot attach myself to what I see. For just
a minute longer, just one more, I cling to what would be
the greatest folly, the irremediable unhappiness of the
rest of my existence. Clinging and leaning, like a tree
which has grown over an abyss, and the weight of whose
blossoming bends it towards its destruction, I still resist,
and who can say if I shall succeed?

As soon as I grow calmer and accept the thought of my
brief future, in which I shall belong utterly to the man
who awaits me back there, a little picture, a little photographic picture casts me back into my torment, and into
prudence. It is a snapshot of Max playing tennis with a
young girl. It has no significance: the young girl is a
casual acquaintance, a neighbour come for tea at Salles-
Neuves, and he was not thinking of her when he sent me
his photograph. But I think of her and I was already
thinking of her before I saw her. I do not know her name,
I can hardly see her face, turned up to the sun, and dark,
with a cheerful grin revealing a shining line of white

teeth. Ah, if I had my lover there at my feet, between my hands, I should say to him. . . .

No, I should say nothing to him. But to write is so easy. To write, to write, to cover white pages with the rapid, uneven writing which he says is like my mobile face, exhausted from expressing too much. To write sincerely, almost sincerely! I hope it may bring me relief, that sort of interior silence which follows a sudden utterance, a confession.

"*Max, my dear love, I asked you yesterday the name of that young girl playing tennis with you. I need not have bothered. As far as I am concerned she is called* a girl, all the girls, all the young women *who will be my rivals a little later on, soon, tomorrow. She is called the unknown, my junior, the one with whom I shall be cruelly and lucidly compared, yet with less cruelty and clearsightedness than I shall use myself.*

"*Triumph over her? How often? And what is triumph when the struggle is exhausting and never-ending? Understand me, please understand me! It is not suspicion, not your future betrayal, my love, which is devastating me, it is my own inadequacy. We are the same age; I am no longer a young woman. Oh my love, imagine yourself in a few years' time, as a handsome man in the fullness of your age, beside me in mine! Imagine me, still beautiful but desperate, frantic in my armour of corset and frock, under my make-up and powder, in my young, tender colours. Imagine me, beautiful as a full-blown rose which one must not touch. A glance of yours, resting on a young woman, will be enough to lengthen the sad crease that smiling has engraved on my cheek, but a happy night in your arms will cost my fading beauty dearer still. I am reaching—you know it—the age of ardour. It is the age of fatal imprudences. Understand me! Will not your fervour, if I let it convince and reassure me, lead me into the fatuous security of women who are loved? I have seen satisfied, amorous women in whom, for a few brief and dangerous minutes, the affected ingénue reappears and allows herself girlish tricks which make her rich and heavy flesh quiver. I have shuddered at the lack of awareness of a friend in her forties who, unclothed and all breathless with love, clapped on her head the cap of her lover, a lieutenant of Hussars.*

"*Yes, I know, I'm rambling, and frightening you. You don't understand. What this letter lacks is a long preamble containing all the thoughts I am hiding from you, the thoughts that have been poisoning me for so long. Love is so simple, isn't it? You never supposed it had this ambiguous, tormented face? We love and give ourselves to each other, and there we are, happy for life, isn't that it? Ah, how young you are, and worse than young, you whose only suffering is waiting for me! Your hell is limited to not possessing what you desire, a thing which some people have to put up with all their lives. But to possess what one loves and every minute to feel one's sole treasure disintegrating, melting, and slipping away like gold dust between one's fingers! And not to have the dreadful courage to open one's hand and let the whole treasure go, but to clench one's fingers ever tighter, and to cry and beg to keep . . . what? a precious little trace of gold in the hollow of one's palm.*

"*Don't you understand? My little one, I would give anything in the world to resemble you, I wish I might never have suffered except because of you, and that I could fling away my old, well-tried distress. Help your Renée, as you can if you will, but, my love, if I no longer hope except in you, am I not already half-way to despair?*"

My hand still grips the wretched, over-thin penholder. On the table, four large sheets of paper bear witness to the haste with which I have written, no less than does the untidiness of the manuscript where the writing slopes upwards and downwards, sometimes bigger and sometimes smaller, responsive to my mood. Will he be able to make me out in all this untidiness? No. I am still concealed in it. To speak the truth is one thing, but the whole truth, that cannot, must not, be said.

Before me, on the square, swept by a wind which was keen a short while back but now weakens and drops like a tired wing, the arched wall of the arena at Nîmes rears its red-brown, rugose substance against a stretch of opaque, slate-coloured sky which foretells a storm. The burning air drifts about my room. I want to see again, under this heavy sky, my Elysian refuge, the Gardens of the Fountain.

A ramshackle cab and a worn-out horse take me as far as the black railings which protect this park where nothing changes. Can last year's spring have lasted magically until this hour, to wait for me? It is so fairy-like in this place, where the spring hangs motionless over all things, that I tremble lest I should see it swallowed up and melt into a cloud.

Amorously, my hand caresses the warm stone of the ruined temple and the varnished leaves of the spindle-trees, which seem damp. The baths of Diana, over which I lean, still, as always, reflect the Judas trees, the tere-binths, the pines, the paulownias with their mauve flowers, and the double purple thorns. A whole garden of reflections is spread out there below me, turning, as it decomposes in the aquamarine water, dark blue, the violet of a bruised peach, and the maroon of dried blood. Oh beautiful garden and beautiful silence, where the only sound is the muted plashing of the green, imperious water, transparent and dark, blue and brilliant as a bright dragon.

A harmonious double alley, between walls of clipped yew, leads up to the Tour Magne, and I stop to rest for a moment on the edge of a stone trough full of stagnant water, green with fine watercress and chattering tree-frogs with tiny delicate hands. At the top, the very top, a dry bed of scented pine-needles receives us, me and my torment.

The beautiful garden lies spread out below, with open spaces in a geometrical design. The approach of the storm has driven away all intruders, and the hurricane, with its hail, rises slowly from the horizon, borne along in the billowing flanks of a thick cloud rimmed with white fire.

All this is still my kingdom, a small portion of the splendid riches which God distributes to passers-by, to wanderers and to solitaries. The earth belongs to anyone who stops for a moment, gazes and goes on his way; the whole sun belongs to the naked lizard who basks in it.

Underlying all my anxiety there is a great bargaining going on, a kind of bartering which weighs up undisclosed values and half-hidden treasures; and this dispute is slowly rising up and forcing its way into the daylight. Time presses. The whole truth, which I could not tell to Max, I owe to myself. It is not a beautiful truth, and it is still a bit feeble and scared, and slightly perfidious. So far all it can do is to whisper to me in short sighs: "I don't want . . . I mustn't . . . I'm afraid."

Afraid of getting old, of being betrayed, of suffering. A subtle choice guided my partial sincerity while I was writing that to Max. That particular fear is the hair-shirt which clings to the skin of nascent Love and contracts there as he grows. I have worn that hair-shirt; one does not die of it. I would wear it again if . . . *if I could not do otherwise*.

"If I could not do otherwise. . . ." This time the formula is clear. I saw it written in my mind and I see it there still, printed like a judgment in small, bold capitals. Now at last I have taken the true measure of my paltry love and brought my real hope into the open: the hope of escape.

But how to achieve it? Everything is against me. The first obstacle I run into is the female body lying there, which bars my way, a voluptuous body with closed eyes, deliberately blind, stretched out and ready to perish rather than leave the place where its joy lies. That woman there, that brute bent on pleasure, is I myself. "You are your own worst enemy." Don't I know it, my word, don't I know it! Shall I also be able to overcome the lost child, a hundred times more dangerous than that greedy beast, who trembles inside me, weak and nervous and ready to stretch out her arms and implore: "Don't leave me alone!" She is afraid, that child, of night, solitude, illness and death, in the evenings she draws the curtains over the dark window pane which frightens her, and pines merely because she is not cherished enough. And you, Max, my well-beloved adversary, how will lacerating myself help me to get the better of you? You would only have to appear and . . . But I am not calling to you to come!

No, I am not calling to you to come. It is my first victory.

Now the stormy cloud is passing over my head, letting fall, one by one, sluggish, scented drops of water. A star of rain plops on the corner of my mouth and I drink it, warm and sweetened with a dust that tastes of jonquils.

NINE

Nîmes, Montpellier, Carcassonne, Toulouse . . . four days without respite, and four nights. We arrive, wash, eat, dance to the accompaniment of an orchestra reading at sight and not sure of itself, go to bed—is it worth while?—and leave again. We grow thin with weariness and no one complains, pride before everything. We change music-halls, dressing-rooms, hotels and rooms with the indifference of soldiers on manœuvres. The make-up box is peeling and showing its tin. The costumes are beginning to wear and, hastily cleaned with petrol before the show, give out a sour smell of rice-powder and cleaning-spirit. I re-paint with carmine my cracked sandals for *The Pursuit*; my tunic for *The Dryad* is losing its acid, grass-green, grasshopper shade. Brague is superb in dirt of all colours: his Bulgarian breeches of emboidered leather, stiff with the artificial blood which spatters them each night, look like the hide of a newly-skinned ox. The Old Troglodyte spreads terror on the stage in a tow-wig which is moulting and some discoloured and evil-smelling hare-skins.

Hard days indeed, where we gasp between a blue sky swept with occasional long clouds, wispy as though they had been frayed by the mistral, and an earth cracking and splitting with thirst. And besides, I have a double burden to bear. My two companions, when they land in a new town, free their shoulders from the strap that bows them, and then, light of heart, think of nothing but a foaming half-pint and an aimless stroll. But for me there is the hour when the post arrives. The post: that means Max's letters.

In the glass-fronted rack and on the greasy tables where the porter scatters the papers with the back of his hand, I see, immediately and electrically, the round, flowery script and the bluish envelope: farewell to rest!

"Give it me, that one! Yes, yes, I tell you it's for me." Oh my goodness, what will there be in it? Reproaches, prayers, or perhaps merely: "I'm coming . . ."

I have waited four days for Max's reply to my letter from Nîmes; and for four days I have written tenderly to him, hiding my profound agitation under a wordy gentleness, as though I had forgotten that letter from Nîmes. At such a distance any epistolary dialogue is bound to be disjointed, and a sad note creeps in by fits and starts when things happen not to go well. Four days have I waited for Max's answer, and felt impatient and ungrateful when all I found was the tall, old-fashioned, graceful Italian hand of my friend Margot, the microscopic scribble of my old Hamond, and Blandine's postcards.

Ah, that letter from Max, I've got it at last, and I read it with a too-familiar palpitation, made more painful by a certain memory: was there not a period in my life when Taillandy "the man whom no woman ever dropped", as he always said, got suddenly furious at my absence and my silence and wrote me lover's letters? The mere sight of his spiky writing used to make me turn pale, and I would feel my heart bounding about like something very small and hard and round—just like today, just like today.

What if I were to crumple up this letter from Max without reading it, fill my lungs with air like a hanged man taken down in time, and flee? But I can't. It was only a passing temptation. I must read.

Thank my stars, my friend has not understood. He thought the whole trouble was a fit of jealousy, the coquettish alarm of a woman who wants to receive, from the man she loves, an explicit assurance in the most flattering terms. And so he gives me this assurance and I cannot help smiling because he praises his "beloved soul", sometimes as though she were a very respected sister, and sometimes as though she were a beautiful mare. "You will always be the most beautiful!" he writes, and no doubt he thinks it too. But could he answer anything else? Perhaps, at the moment of writing those words, he raised his head and looked at the deep forest before him, with a hardly perceptible hesitation, a suspension of thought. And then he will have shaken his shoulders, as one does when one is cold, and written bravely and slowly: "You will always be the most beautiful!"

Poor Max! The best of myself seems to conspire against him now. The day before yesterday we left before dawn and, as soon as we were in the train, I was just resuming my shattered sleep, broken and begun again twenty times, when a breath of salt air smelling of fresh seaweed made me open my eyes again: the sea! Sète and the sea! There it was again, running along beside the train, when I had quite forgotten it. The seven o'clock sun, still low on the horizon, had not yet penetrated it; the sea was refusing to let itself be possessed and, hardly awake, still kept its nocturnal colour of ink-blue crested with white.

Salt-pans filed past, edged with grass glittering with salt, and sleeping villas, white as the salt, between their dark laurels, their lilacs and their Judas trees. Half asleep, like the sea, and yielding to the swaying of the train, I thought I was skimming the waves, so close at hand, with a swallow's cutting flight. And then I experienced one of those perfect moments, the kind of happiness that comes to a sick person, unable to think, when a sudden *memory*, an image, a name, turned me once again into an ordinary creature, the creature of yesterday and the days before. How long had it lasted, that moment when for the first time I had forgotten Max? Yes, forgotten him, as though I had never known his gaze, nor the caress of his mouth, forgotten him as if the one dominating anxiety in my life were to seek for words, words to express how yellow the sun is, how blue the sea, and how brilliant the salt like a fringe of white jet. Yes, forgotten him, as if the only urgent thing in the world were my desire to possess through my eyes the marvels of the earth.

In that same hour an insidious spirit whispered to me: "And if indeed that were the only urgent thing? If everything, save that, were merely ashes?"

TEN

I LIVE in a turmoil of thoughts which go round and round unceasingly, and only with difficulty and patience do I find again my vocation of silence and dissimulation. Once more it is easy for me to follow Brague across a town, from top to bottom, through squares, cathedrals and museums, and into the smoke of little taverns where "one eats amazingly well". Our form of cordiality speaks little and rarely smiles, but sometimes shouts with laughter as if gaiety came more naturally to us than gentleness. I laugh easily at Brague's stories and make my laughter as shrill as I can, just as he, when he speaks to me, exaggerates a coarseness that is quite unnatural.

We are both sincere but not always very simple. We have time-honoured jests which provoke time-honoured amusement: Brague's favourite—which exasperates me— is the Game of the Satyr, which is played in trams, where my comrade chooses as a victim sometimes a timid young woman and sometimes an aggressive old maid. Sitting opposite her and lolling back, he fixes a lustful gaze on her to make her blush and cough, fidget with her veil and turn her head aside. The "satyr's" look persists, lasciviously, and then all the features of his face—mouth, nostrils, eyebrows—combine to express the particular joy of an erotomaniac.

"It's a wonderful facial exercise," Brague declares. "When the Conservatoire founds a miming class for me, I shall make all my feminine pupils rehearse it together and separately."

I laughed because the poor scared lady never fails to leave the tram very quickly, but the grimacing perfection of the wicked game gets on my nerves. My body, rather exhausted, has fits of unreasonable chastity, out of which I fall into a brazier lit in a second by the remembrance of a scent, a gesture or a tender cry, a brazier which kindles delights which I have not had and in whose flames I let myself be consumed, motionless and with my knees together, as though at the slightest movement I were in danger of enlarging my burns.

Max. . . . He writes to me and waits for me. How hard to bear his trustfulness is! Harder to bear than to deceive, for I too write, with a fullness and a freedom difficult to explain. I write on wobbly pedestal tables, sitting sideways on chairs that are too high, I write with one foot shod and one bare, the paper lodged between the breakfast tray and my open handbag, all among the brushes, the bottle of scent and the button-hook; I write sitting at a window that frames part of a courtyard, or the most delicious gardens, or misty mountains. I feel myself at home amid this disorder of a camp, this no matter where and no matter how, and freer than among my haunted furniture.

ELEVEN

"SOUTH AMERICA, what d'you say to that?"

This odd question from Brague fell like a stone yesterday into my after-dinner reverie, during that brief hour when I struggle against sleep and my reluctance to undress and put on my make-up just when I'm in the middle of digesting.

"South America? That's a long way away."

"Slacker!"

"You don't understand, Brague. I say 'it's a long way away' as I would say 'it's beautiful'."

"Oh well, all right if that's it. Salomon's been sounding me about going there. Well?"

"Well?"

"Can we consider it?"

"We can consider it."

Neither of us is taken in by our feigned indifference. I have learnt, to my cost, not to "put ideas" into the impresario's head about a tour, by showing my eagerness to go. Brague, on the other hand, unfailingly takes care not to present the matter to me in an advantageous light, for fear I will ask for a greater share of "the gross fee".

South America! At the sound of those two words I felt the dazzlement of an illiterate person who sees the New World through an enchanted web of falling stars, giant flowers, precious stones and humming birds. Brazil, the Argentine . . . what glittering names! Margot told me that she was taken there when she was quite small, and the longing and amazement she evoked remain fixed to

the picture she gave me of a spider with a silver stomach
and a tree covered with fireflies.

Brazil, the Argentine, but . . . what about Max?

What about Max? Ever since yesterday I've been
prowling round this question mark. What about Max?
What about Max? It is no longer a thought, it is a refrain,
a noise, a little rhythmic croaking which inevitably
brings on one of my "fits of coarseness". Who is the
foul-mouthed ancestor who goes on barking inside me
with a violence not only verbal but sentimental? I have
just crumpled up the letter I had begun to my love,
swearing under my breath.

"What about Max! What about Max! What, again?
However long am I going to go on finding this creature
getting under my feet? What about Max! What about
Max! What about me, then, do I merely exist to bother
my head about this cumbersome capitalist? A truce, Lord,
I beseech you, I've had enough fusses and idylls and
lost time, and enough of men! Look at yourself, my poor
girl, look at yourself, you're not an old woman, by a
long chalk, but you're already a kind of confirmed
bachelor. You've got the fads of such, and the difficult
character, and the finicking sensibility—enough of them
to cause you suffering and make you unbearable. What
will you do in that galley, or rather in that tub of a
houseboat, firmly moored, in solemn attendance on the
master's needs? If you could just manage to indulge in a
nice little infatuation for the chap, say fifteen days, three
weeks or two months and then goodbye! No strings on
either side, just a mutual enjoyment. You ought to have
learnt, when you were with Taillandy, how to drop
people!"

On and on I rant. I display a crude and wicked ingen-
uity in finding ways to insult my friend and myself; it is

a kind of game in which I provoke myself to say true
things that I do not think, that I have not so far thought.
And it goes on until the moment when I notice that it is
raining in torrents: the roofs on the other side of the
road are streaming, and the gutter overflowing. A long,
cold water-drop rolls down the window and falls on my
hand. Behind me the room has grown dark. How good
it would be to lean now against the shoulder of the man
I was humiliating a moment ago by calling him a cumbersome capitalist.

I switch on the ceiling-light and, for something to do,
try a temporary arrangement of the writing-table, opening the blotter between the cheval-glass and the bunch
of narcissus; I'm trying to make the place look like home
and what I long for is hot tea, golden bread, my familiar
lamp with its pink shade, the barking of my dog and the
voice of my old Hamond. A large sheet of white paper
lying there tempts me, and I sit down:

*"Max, my darling, yes, I'm coming back; I return a little
every day. Is it possible that only twelve nights separate me from
you? Nothing is less sure; it seems to me that I shall never see
you again. How terrible that would be! And how wise!"*

I stop short: is it not too clear? No. Besides, I wrote
"it would be", and no lover would ever take a condi-
tional tragically. I can continue in the same reassuring
vein, risking a few melancholy generalities and a few
timorous taboos. And since, all the same, I dread a
brusque decision which would bring Max here in less
than twelve hours, I do not forget to drown the whole
letter in a flood of tendernesses which, alas, draw me on.

Rather disgusting, all that.

TWELVE

How time flies! Where are the Pyrenees with their blossoming cherries, the great austere mountain which seemed to follow us, glittering with a snow which makes you thirsty, slashed with vertiginous shadows, rent with blue chasms and blotched with bronze forests? Where are the narrow valleys, turf-carpeted, and the wild orchids white as gardenias, and where the little Basque village square where we drank steaming dark chocolate? How far away already is the icy Gave, that graceful dangerous river with its waters clouded by the melting of the snows to the milky transparency of moonstones!

We are leaving Bordeaux now, after giving five shows in three days. "A nice town," sighed Brague at the station. "I treated myself to a little Bordelaise . . . a dainty dish! One of those small helpings you can get for the asking in all the main streets, can't you just see? High as your heart, plenty of breast, short in the leg, a plump little foot, and so plastered with eye-black and powder and frizzed hair that I defy you to tell whether they're pretty or not. They sparkle and chatter and wriggle—they're just my dish!"

He exuded tranquil happiness and I looked at him with a rather disgusted hostility, as I look at people eating when I am no longer hungry.

The timid spring flees before us, growing younger hour by hour and closing again leaf by leaf and flower by flower as we get further north. In the sparser shade of the hedges, the April daisies have reappeared, and the last faded violets. The paler blue of the sky, the shorter grass and an acid humidity in the air give one the illusion of growing younger and going back in time.

If only I could wind back again the months that have expired up to that winter day when Max walked into my dressing-room. . . . When I was small and learning to knit, they made me undo rows and rows of stitches until I had found the little unnoticed fault, the dropped stitch, which at school was called "a lapse". A "lapse"! That's all that he would have been in my life, then, this poor second love of mine whom I used to call my dear warmth, my light. He is there, quite close at hand, I can take hold of him—and I flee.

For I shall flee. A premeditated escape is being organised far away, down in the depths of my being, without my taking so far any direct part in it. At the decisive moment, when all that remains will be to cry, as though in panic: "Quick, Blandine, my suitcase and a taxicab!" I shall perhaps be taken in by my own confusion, but O dear Max, whom I wanted to love, I confess here, with the most genuine sorrow, that from this moment all is resolved.

Except for this sorrow, have I not become again *what I was*, that is to say free, horribly alone and free? The momentary grace which touched me now withdraws itself from me, since I refused to lose myself in it. Instead of saying to it: "Take me!" I ask it: "What are you giving me? Another myself? There is no other myself. You're giving me a friend who is young, ardent, jealous and sincerely in love? I know: that is what is called a master, and I no longer want one. He is good and simple, he admires me and he is straightforward? In that case he is my inferior and I should be making a misalliance. A look of his can rouse me and I cease to belong to myself if he puts his mouth on mine? In that case he is my enemy, he is the thief who steals me from myself. I shall have everything, everything that money can buy, and I shall lean over the edge of a white terrace smothered with the roses of my gardens? But it is from there that I shall see the lords of the earth, the wanderers, pass by! Come back to me, beseeches my love, leave your job and the shabby sadness of the surroundings where you live, come back among your equals. I have no equals, I have only my fellow wayfarers."

Windmills revolve on the horizon. In the little stations through which the train passes, Breton head-dresses, the first white head-dresses, blossom like daisies. Dazzled, I enter into the yellow kingdom of the brooms and the gorses. Gold, copper, and vermilion too—for the pale rape is there as well—set these poor heathlands ablaze with an unendurable light. I press my cheek and my outspread hands against the carriage windows, surprised not to feel it warm. We are crossing the conflagration, leagues and leagues of gorse in flower, wasted riches which rebuff even the goats, and where butterflies, made languorous by the warm scent like half-ripe peaches and pepper, flutter about with torn wings.

THIRTEEN

At Caen, two days before our return, I find a letter from Max consisting of only one line, with no signature: "My Renée, do you no longer love me?"

That is all. I had not foreseen that gentleness and the simplicity of that question, which confound all my literature. What was it I wrote then, the last time?

That doesn't matter. If he loves me, it is not in my letters that he read the warning. If he loves me, he knows those mysterious shocks, that light, hurtful finger which strikes the heart, those small thunderbolts which suddenly arrest a gesture or cut short a burst of laughter. He knows that treason, desertion and lies can strike from a great way off, and he knows the brutality and infallibility of a *presentiment*.

Poor, poor friend that I wanted to love! You might have died, or deceived me, and I should have known nothing of it, I whom the best-hidden treachery wounded by telepathy once upon a time.

"My Renée, do you no longer love me?" I did not melt into passionate tears, but I jotted down on a sheet of paper the abbreviated message of a vaguely reassuring telegram: "*Shall be home five o'clock day after tomorrow. All love.*"

I am subtly jealous of this man who is suffering. I re-read his complaint and talk to this letter as if I were speaking to him, with his firm mouth and angry eyebrows.

"*You love and suffer and complain. That makes you just as I was when I was twenty. I am leaving you and, thanks to me,*

*you may perhaps acquire what now you lack. Already you can
see through protecting walls; does that not astonish you, you
great, dense male? Nerves grown sensitive, an innocent, burning,
suffering, hope for ever renewing itself, green and strong, like a
mown field, all that was my portion and now it will be yours. I
cannot take it away from you, but I begrudge it you."*

There was a packet of letters with that of Max. Even
Blandine writes: *"Madame, Monsieur Maxime has brought
Fossette back, she has another new collar. Monsieur Maxime
asks for news of Madame, he doesn't look very happy and one
can see he's been missing Madame."*

There's a letter from Hamond, who talks simply but
writes with an almost ceremonious courtesy; and a letter
from Margot who has nothing to tell me and fills two
sheets with a nun-like tittle-tattle. They are all in a hurry
to write to me now I am about to return, as if their conscience were pricking them slightly for having neglected
me for such a long time.

Whom shall I confide in when I get back? In Hamond?
In Margot? In neither. I tear up all this trifling stuff
before leaving the stifling tomb known as the "star's
dressing-room" at the *Folies-Caennaises*, to go up on to
the stage. We are in an old-style *café-chantant*: to reach
the stage door one has to cross a part of the auditorium,
and this is the worst moment of the evening. The public
elbows us and bars our way on purpose so as to stare at
us longer; my bare arm leaves its powder on a jacket, a
hand slyly pulls at my embroidered shawl, and furtive
fingers feel my hips. With heads high, we bear like proud
prisoners the contempt and desire of this suffocating
crowd.

FOURTEEN

A HALF-HOUR strikes, very far away. The train from Calais, which is to take me back to Paris, is not due for fifty minutes.

I am returning alone, by night, without warning anyone. Brague and the Old Troglodyte, their thirst slaked thanks to me, are now asleep somewhere in Boulogne-sur-Mer. We killed three-quarters of an hour in doing our accounts, and chattering, and discussing plans for our South American tour, and then I found myself in this station at Tintelleries, so deserted at this hour that one might think it was no longer in use. They have not switched on the electric globes of the platform, just for me. A cracked bell tinkles timidly in the shadows, as though it were hanging from the neck of a paralysed dog.

The night is cold and moonless. Near by, in an invisible garden, there are scented lilacs which rustle in the wind. Far away I can hear the call of foghorns at sea.

Who would guess that I am here, right at the end of the platform, huddled in my coat? How well hidden I am! Neither darker nor lighter than the shadows.

With the first light I shall let myself noiselessly into my flat, like a thief, for I am not expected so soon. I shall wake Fossette and Blandine and then will come the hardest moment.

I deliberately imagine the details of my arrival; I conjure up, with necessary cruelty, the memory of the two-fold scent which clings to the hangings: English tobacco and rather too-sweet jasmine; in imagination I press the satin cushion with its two pale stains, the traces of two tears which fell from my eyes in a moment of very great

THE VAGABOND 223

happiness. I can hardly hold back the little stifled "ah!" of one who has been wounded and jolts her wound. I am doing it on purpose. It will hurt me less by and by.

From far away I am saying my goodbyes to all which would keep me there, and to him who will have nothing left of me, except a letter. A cowardly, rational wisdom persuades me not to see him again: no "frank explanations" between us! A heroine who is only human, like myself, is not strong enough to triumph over all the demons. Let him despise me and even curse me a little, it will be all the better if he does; poor dear, he'll recover more quickly. No, no, there mustn't be too much honesty. And not too many phrases either, since by keeping silent I shall spare him.

A man crosses the rails with sleepy steps, pushing a trunk on a hand-cart, and suddenly the electric globes of the station come on. I get up, feeling numb, I had not noticed I was very cold. At the end of the platform a lantern jerks in the darkness, swinging from an invisible arm. A distant whistle answers the harsh foghorns: it is the train. Already!

FIFTEEN

"GOODBYE, *my darling. I am going away, to a village not very far from here; after that I shall no doubt leave for America, with Brague. I shall not see you again, my darling. When you read this you will not think it is a cruel game, since the day before yesterday you wrote to me; 'My Renée, do you no longer love me?'*

"*I am going away, it is the least hurt I can do you. I am not cruel, Max, but I feel myself quite worn out, as though unable to resume the habit of loving and afraid lest I should have to suffer again because of it.*

"*You did not think I was so cowardly, my darling? What a small heart mine is! Yet once upon a time it could have been worthy of yours, which offers itself so simply. But now . . . what could I give you, oh my darling? In a few years' time the best of myself would be that frustrated maternity that a childless woman transfers to her husband. You do not accept that and neither do I. It is a pity. There are days when I, who watch myself growing older with a resigned terror, think of old age as a recompense.*

"*My darling, one day you will understand all this. You will understand that I must not belong to you or to anyone, and that in spite of a first marriage and a second love, I have remained a kind of old maid, like some among them who are so in love with Love that no love appears to them beautiful enough, and so they refuse themselves without condescending to explain; who repel every sentimental misalliance and return to sit for life before a window, bent over their needle, in solitary communion with their incomparable vision. Like them, I wanted everything; a lamentable mistake punished me.*

"*I no longer dare, my darling, that is the whole trouble, I no*

*longer dare. Don't be cross if I have hidden so long from you my
efforts to resuscitate in myself the enthusiasm, the adventurous
fatalism, the blind hope, the whole cheerful escort of love. The
only delirium I feel is that of my senses. And alas, there is none
whose intervals are more lucid. You would have consumed me to
no purpose, you whose gaze, whose lips, whose long caresses,
whose moving silence cured, for a little while, a distress which is
not your fault.*

*"Goodbye, my darling. Seek far from me that youth, that
fresh, unspoilt beauty, that faith in the future and in yourself,
in a word, the love that you deserve, the love that once upon a
time I could have given you. Don't seek me out. I have just
enough strength to flee from you. If you were to walk in here,
before me, while I am writing to you . . . but you will not
walk in.*

*"Goodbye, my darling. You are the one being in the world
whom I call my darling, and after you I have no one to whom to
give that name. For the last time, embrace me as if I were cold,
hold me very close, very close, very close. . . .*

Renée."

I have written very slowly; before signing my letter
I re-read it, rounded the loops, added the dots and the
accents, and dated it: *May 15th, 7 a.m.*

But though signed and dated and finally stuck down,
it still remains an unfinished letter. Shall I open it again?
I suddenly shiver as if, in closing the envelope, I had
blocked out a luminous opening through which a warm
breath of air was still blowing.

It is a sunless morning and the winter cold seems to
have taken refuge in this little sitting-room behind the
shutters that have been padlocked for forty days. Crouching at my feet, my dog is silent, her eyes on the door: she
is waiting. She is waiting for someone who will not come

again. I can hear Blandine shifting the casseroles, I smell
the smell of ground coffee; hunger gnaws sullenly at my
stomach. A worn sheet covers the divan, a damp, blue
mist tarnishes the mirror. I was not expected so soon.
Everything is shrouded in old linen and dampness and
dust, everything here still wears the slightly funereal air
of departure and absence, and I pass furtively through
this refuge of mine without taking off the white dust-
sheets, without writing a name on the bloom of dust,
without leaving any other trace of my passage than that
letter, unfinished.

Unfinished. Dear intruder, whom I wanted to love, I
spare you. By going away, I leave you your one chance
of growing bigger in my eyes. Reading my letter will
only give you pain. You will not know the humiliating
comparison you are escaping, nor the dispute of which
you were the prize, the prize which I disdain.

For I reject you and I choose . . . all that is not you. I
have met you before, and I recognise you. Are you not
he who, thinking he is giving, takes for himself? You
came to share my life. To share, yes: *to take your share!*
To be a partner in everything I do, to insinuate yourself
at every moment in the secret temple of my thoughts,
isn't that it? Why you, more than another? I have barred
it to everyone.

You are good and, with the best faith in the world,
you meant to bring me happiness, since you saw me
deprived and solitary. But you counted without my
beggar-woman's pride: I refuse to see the most beautiful
countries of the world microscopically reflected in the
amorous mirror of your eyes.

Happiness? Are you sure that happiness is enough for
me henceforward? It is not only happiness that gives

value to life. You wanted to brighten me with that commonplace dawn, for you pitied me in my obscurity. Call it obscurity, if you will: the obscurity of a room seen from without. I would rather call it dark, not obscure. Dark, but made beautiful by an unwearying sadness: silvery and twilit like the white owl, the silky mouse, the wings of the clothes-moth. Dark, with the red gleams of an agonising memory. But you are he in whose presence I should no longer have the right to be sad.

I escape from myself, but I am still not free of you, I know it. A vagabond, and free, I shall sometimes long for the shade of your walls. How many times shall I return to you, dear prop on which I rest and wound myself? How many times shall I cry for what you were able to give me: a long-drawn-out voluptuousness, suspended, fanned, renewed, the winged fall, the swooning in which one's strength is renewed by its own death . . . the musical drumming of the maddened blood . . . the scent of burning sandal-wood and trodden grass. . . . Ah, how long shall I not thirst for you upon my road!

I shall desire you as I desire in turn the fruit that hangs out of reach, the far-off water, and the blissful little house that I pass by. In each place where my desires have strayed, I leave thousands and thousands of shadows in my own shape, shed from me: one lies on the warm blue rocks of the combes in my own country, another in the damp hollow of a sunless valley, and a third follows a bird, a sail, the wind and the wave. You keep the most enduring of them: a naked, undulating shadow, trembling with pleasure like a plant in the stream. But time will dissolve it like the others, and you will no longer know anything of me until the day when my steps finally halt and there will fly away from me a last little shadow.

CHÉRI

Translated by
Roger Senhouse

"Give it me, Léa, give me your pearl necklace! Do you hear me, Léa? Give me your pearls!"

No answer came from the huge brass-bedecked wrought-iron bedstead that glimmered in the shadows like a coat of mail.

"Why won't you let me have your necklace? It looks every bit as well on me as on you—even better!"

At the snap of the clasp, ripples spread over the lace frilled sheets, and from their midst rose two magnificent thin-wristed arms, lifting on high two lovely lazy hands.

"Leave it alone, Chéri! You've been playing long enough with that necklace."

"It amuses me. . . . Are you frightened I'll steal it?"

He was capering about in front of the sun-drenched rosy pink curtains—a graceful demon, black against a glowing furnace; but when he pranced back towards the bed, he turned white again from top to toe, in his white silk pyjamas and white Moorish slippers.

"I'm not frightened," the soft, deep voice answered from the bed. "But you'll wear out the thread. Those pearls are heavy."

"They certainly are," Chéri said with due respect. "Whoever gave you this lot never meant to make light of you!"

He was standing in front of a pier-glass framed in the

space between two windows, gazing at the reflection of
a very youthful, very good-looking young man, neither
too short nor too tall, hair with the blue sheen of a blackbird's plumage. He unbuttoned his pyjamas, displaying a
hard, darkish chest, curved like a shield; and the whites
of his dark eyes, his teeth, and the pearls of the necklace
gleamed in the over-all rosy glow of the room.

"Take off that necklace!" The female voice was
insistent. "Do you hear what I say?"

The young man, motionless in front of his image,
laughed softly to himself: "Yes, yes, I heard you. I know
so well you're terrified I'll make off with it!"

"No, I'm not. But if I did offer it to you, you're quite
capable of taking it."

He ran to the bed and bounded into it. "You bet I
am! I rise above the conventions. Personally, I think it's
idiotic for a man to allow a woman to give him a single
pearl for a tie-pin, or two for a pair of studs, and then to
consider himself beyond the pale if she gives him
fifty. . . ."

"Forty-nine."

"Forty-nine—as if I hadn't counted! I dare you to say
they don't look well on me! Or that I'm ugly!"

Léa sat up in bed. "No, I won't say that. For one thing,
because you'd never believe me. But can't you learn to
laugh without crinkling up your nose like that? I suppose
you won't be happy till you've wrinkles all up the side
of your nose!"

He stopped laughing at once, let the skin on his forehead relax, and drew in the fold under his chin like a
coquettish old woman. They looked at each other in open
hostility—she, leaning on her elbow in a flurry of frills
and lace; he, sitting side-saddle on the edge of the bed.
He was thinking 'Who's she to talk of any wrinkles

I may have one day?' and she 'Why is he so ugly wnen he laughs?—he who's the very picture of beauty!' She thought for a moment, then finished aloud: "It's because you look so ill-natured when you're joking. You never laugh except unkindly—*at* people, and that makes you ugly. You're often ugly."

"That's not true!" Chéri exclaimed, crossly.

Anger knitted his eyebrows close above his nose, magnified his eyes, glittering with insolence behind a palisade of lashes, and parted the chaste bow of his disdainful mouth. Léa smiled to see him as she loved him best: rebellious only to become submissive, enchained lightly but powerless to free himself. She put a hand on his young head, which impatiently shook off the yoke. Like someone quieting an animal, she murmured, "There, there! What is it? What is it, then?"

He fell upon her big beautiful shoulder, nuzzling and butting his way into his favourite resting-place with eyes already shut, seeking his customary long morning sleep in the protection of her arms. But Léa pushed him away. "None of that now, Chéri! You're having luncheon with our national Harpy, and it's already twenty to twelve!"

"Not really? I'm lunching at the old girl's? You too?"

Lazily Léa settled deeper into the bed.

"Not me, I'm off duty. I'll go for coffee at half-past two, or tea at six, or for a cigarette at a quarter to eight. Don't worry; she'll always see enough of me. And besides, I've not been asked."

Chéri's sulky face lit up with malice.

"I know, I know why! We're going to have high society. We're going to have the fair Marie-Laure, and that poisonous child of hers."

Léa brought her big blue wandering eyes to rest.

"Oh, really! The little girl's charming. Less so than her mother, but charming. Now take off that necklace, once and for all."

"Pity," Chéri sighed, as he undid the clasp. "It would look so well in the trousseau."

Léa raised herself on her elbow: "What trousseau?"

"Mine," Chéri said with ludicrous self-importance. "*My* trousseau, full of *my* jewels, for *my* marriage!"

He bounded in the air, executed a perfect *entrechat-six*, returned to earth, butted his way through the door-curtains, and disappeared, shouting: "My bath, Rose! And quick about it! I'm lunching at the old girl's!"

'That's that,' Léa thought. 'We'll have a lake in the bathroom and eight towels floating in it, and razor scrapings in the basin. If only I had two bathrooms!'

But, as on former occasions, she soon saw that this would mean getting rid of a wardrobe and lopping off a corner of her dressing-room, and so concluded, as on former occasions: 'I shall simply have to put up with it till Chéri gets married.'

She lay down again on her back and noticed that Chéri, undressing the night before, had thrown his socks on the mantelpiece, his pants on the writing-table, his tie round the neck of her portrait bust. She could not help smiling at this hasty masculine disorder, and half closed her large tranquil eyes. Their blue was as beautiful as ever, and so were the thick chestnut lashes.

At the age of forty-nine, Léonie Vallon, called Léa de Lonval, was nearing the end of a successful career as a richly kept courtesan. She was a good creature, and life had spared her the more flattering catastrophes and exalted sufferings. She made a secret of the date of her birth; but willingly admitted—with a look of voluptuous condescension for Chéri's special benefit—that she was

approaching the age when she could indulge in a few
creature comforts. She liked order, fine linen, wines in
their prime, and carefully planned meals at home. From
an idolised young blonde she had become a rich middle-
aged *demi-mondaine* without ever attracting any outrageous
publicity. Not that she went in for any pretences. Her
friends remembered a Four-in-Hand Meet at Auteuil,
about 1895, when the sub-editor of *Gil Blas* had addressed
her as "dear artist" and she had answered: "Artist! Oh
come, my good friend, my lovers must have been telling
tales. . . ."

Her contemporaries were jealous of her imperturbable
good health, and the younger women, whose figures
were padded out in front and behind after the fashion of
1912, scoffed at her opulent bust. Young and old
alike envied her the possession of Chéri.

"Though, good heavens!" Léa used to say, "there's no
reason why they should. They're welcome to him!
I don't keep him on a lead. He goes out by himself."

But in this she was not altogether speaking the truth,
for she was proud of a liaison—sometimes, in her weakness for the truth, referring to it as "an adoption"—that
had lasted six years.

'Trousseau,' Léa said over again. 'Marriage for Chéri!
It's not possible, it's not . . . human . . . you can't give an
innocent girl to Chéri! Why, it would be throwing a doe
to the hounds! People don't know what Chéri is!'

As if telling the beads of a rosary, she ran her fingers
over the necklace which Chéri had tossed on the bed.
She put it away at night now because, with his passion
for fine pearls and his fondness for playing with them
in the morning, he would have noticed too often that
her throat had thickened and was not nearly so white,
with the muscles under its skin growing slack. She

fastened the pearls round her neck without getting up, and took a hand-mirror from the bedside-table.

'I look like a gardener's wife,' was her unflattering comment, 'a market-gardener's wife. A market-gardener's wife in Normandy, off to the potato-fields wearing a pearl necklace. I might as well stick an ostrich feather in my nose—and that's being polite!'

She shrugged her shoulders, severely critical of everything she no longer loved in herself: the vivid complexion, healthy, a little too ruddy—an open-air complexion, well suited to emphasise the pure intensity of her eyes, with their varying shades of blue. Her proud nose still won her approval. "Marie-Antoinette's nose!" Chéri's mother was in the habit of saying, without ever forgetting to add: "and in another two years, our Léa will have a chin like Louis Seize'." Her mouth, with its even row of teeth, seldom opened in a peal of laughter; but she smiled often, a smile that set off to perfection the lazy flutter of her large eyes—a smile a hundred times lauded, sung, and photographed—a deep, confiding smile one never tired of watching.

As for her body—"Everyone knows," Léa would say, "that a well-made body lasts a long time." She could still afford to show her body, pink and white, endowed with the long legs and straight back of a naiad on an Italian fountain; the dimpled hips, the high-slung breasts, "would last," Léa used to say, "till well after Chéri's wedding."

She got out of bed, and, slipping into a wrap, went to draw back the long curtains. The noonday sun poured into the gay, rosy, over-decorated room. Its luxury dated: double lace curtains, rose-bud watered silk on the walls, gilded woodwork, and antique furniture upholstered in modern silks. Léa refused to give up either this cosy room or its bed, a massive and indestructible masterpiece of wrought iron and brass, grim to the eye and cruel to the shins.

"Come, come!" Chéri's mother protested, "it's not as bad as all that. Personally, I like this room. It belongs to a period. It has a style of its own. It suggests La Païva."

The remembrance of this dig made Léa smile as she pinned up her hair. She hurriedly powdered her face on hearing two doors slam, and the thud of a male foot colliding with some delicate piece of furniture. Chéri came back into the room in shirt and trousers, his ears white with talcum powder. He was in an aggressive mood.

"Where's my tie-pin? What a wretched hole this is! Have they taken to pinching the jewellery?"

"Marcel must have stuck it in his tie to go to the market," Léa gravely replied.

Chéri, who had little or no sense of humour, was brought up short by the little quip like an ant by a lump of coal. He stopped his angry pacing up and down, and found nothing better to say than: "Charming! and what about my boots?"

"Your what?"

"The calf, of course!"

Léa smiled up at him from her dressing-table, too affectionately. "You said it, not I," she murmured in caressing tones.

"The day when a woman loves me for my brains," he retorted, "I shall be done for. Meanwhile I must have my pin and my boots."

"What for? You don't wear a tie-pin with a lounge suit, and you've got one pair on already."

Chéri stamped his foot. "I've had enough of this!

There's nobody here to look after me, and I'm sick of it all."

Léa put down her comb. "Very well, say goodbye to it all for good!"

He shrugged his shoulders, like a young tough. "You wouldn't like it if I did!"

"Be off with you! I hate guests who complain of the cooking and leave bits and pieces all over the place and cream-cheese sticking to the mirrors. Go back to your sainted mother, my child, and stay there."

Unable to meet Léa's gaze, he lowered his eyes, and broke out into schoolboy protests. "Soon I shan't be allowed to open my mouth! Anyhow, you'll let me have your motor to go to Neuilly?"

"No."

"Why not?"

"Because I'm going out in it myself at two, and because the chauffeur is having his dinner."

"Where are you going at two?"

"To say my prayers. But if you need three francs for a taxi . . . Idiot," she added tenderly. "At two I'll probably come to your lady mother's for coffee. Does that satisfy you?"

He tossed his head like a young buck. "You bite my head off, you won't give me anything I ask for; they hide my things away, they . . ."

"Will you never learn to dress yourself?"

She took the tie from Chéri's hands and tied it for him.

"There! And that frightful purple tie. . . . However, it's just the thing for the fair Marie-Laure and family. . . . And you wanted to wear a pearl on top of all that! You little dago. . . . Why not earrings into the bargain?"

His defences were down. Blissful, languid, irresolute,

supine, he surrendered again to a lazy happiness and closed his eyes. . . .

"Nounoune darling . . ." he murmured.

She brushed the hair off his ears, combed a straighter parting in the bluish locks of his black hair, dabbed a little scent on his temples, and gave him a quick kiss, unable to resist the tempting mouth so close to her own.

Chéri opened his eyes, and his lips, then stretched out his hands.

She moved away. "No. It's a quarter to one! Be off now, and don't let me see you again!"

"Never?"

"Never," she laughed back at him with uncontrollable tenderness.

Left to herself, she smiled proudly, and a sharp little sigh of defeated desire escaped her as she listened to Chéri's footsteps crossing the courtyard. She saw him open and close the gates, drift away on his winged feet, only to encounter the adoring glances of three shop-girls walking along arm in arm.

"Lawks! He's too good to be true! Let's touch him to see if he's real!"

But Chéri took it all for granted and did not even turn round.

"MY bath, Rose! Tell the manicurist she can go, it's far too late now. My blue coat and skirt—the new one—the blue hat with the white under brim, and the little shoes with the straps . . . No, wait . . ."

Léa, with one leg across the other, rubbed her ankle and shook her head.

"No, the blue kid laced boots. My legs are a little swollen to-day. It's the heat."

Her elderly maid, butterfly-capped, raised understanding eyes to Léa. "It's . . . it's the heat," she repeated obediently, shrugging her shoulders as much as to say: "We know . . . Nothing lasts for ever. . . ."

With Chéri out of the house, Léa became herself again, very much alive, cheerful, and on the spot. Within an hour, she had been given her bath, followed by a spirit-rub scented with sandal-wood, and was ready dressed, hatted, and shod. While the curling-tongs were heating, she found time to run through the butler's book and send for Emile, the footman, and call his attention to the blue haze on one of the looking-glasses. She ran an experienced eye—rarely taken in—over everything in the room, and lunched in solitary bliss, with a smile for the dry Vouvray and for the June strawberries, served, with their stalks, on a plate of Rubelles enamel as green as a tree-frog after rain. Someone in the past who appreciated good food must have chosen the huge

Louis Seize looking-glasses and the English furniture
of the same period, for this rectangular dining-room:
light, airy side-boards, high pedestalled dumb-waiters,
spindly yet strong Sheraton chairs, in a dark wood with
delicate swags. The looking-glasses and the massive
silver caught the full light of day, with a touch of green
reflected from the trees in the Avenue Bugeaud. Léa, as
she ate, examined a fork for any suspicion of pink
cleaning-powder left in the chasing, and half-closed one
eye the better to judge the quality of the polish on the
dark wood. Standing behind her, the butler watched this
performance nervously.

"Marcel!" Léa said, "for the last week or so, the wax
on your floors has been smeary."

"Does Madame think so?"

"Madame does think so. Add a little turpentine while
you're melting it in a double saucepan; it's quite easy to
do again. You brought up the Vouvray a little too soon.
Close the shutters as soon as you've cleared the table;
we're in for a heat-wave."

"Very good, Madame. Will Monsieur Ch—Monsieur
Peloux be dining?"

"Probably. . . . No *crème-surprise* to-night. We'll just
have a strawberry water ice. Coffee in the boudoir."

As she rose from the table, straight and tall, the shape
of her legs visible under a dress that moulded her hips,
she had ample time to note the ""Madame is beautiful" in
the butler's discreet glance, and this did not displease her.

"Beautiful," Léa whispered on her way up to the
boudoir. "No. . . . No longer. I have now to wear something white near my face, and very pale pink underclothes
and tea-gowns. Beautiful! Pish. . . . I hardly need to be
that any longer."

All the same, she allowed herself no siesta in the painted

silk boudoir, when she had finished with coffee and the newspapers. And it was with battle written on her face that she gave her chauffeur the order: "To Madame Peloux's."

The tree-lined road through the Bois, dry beneath the young, already wind-faded June foliage—the toll-gate—Neuilly—Boulevard d'Inkermann—'How many times have I come this way?' Léa wondered. She began to count, then tired of counting and softened her step on the gravel outside Madame Peloux's house to overhear any sounds coming from it.

'They're in the garden-room,' she concluded.

She had put on more powder before approaching the house and tightened the fine-meshed, misty blue veil under her chin. Her answer to the manservant's formal request to pass through the house was: "No; I'd rather go round by the garden."

A real garden—almost a park—completely surrounded the vast white villa, typical of the outer suburbs of Paris. Madame Peloux's villa had been called "a country residence" in the days when Neuilly was still on the outskirts of Paris. This was apparent from the stables, converted into garages, the other offices with their kennels and wash-houses, not to mention the size of the billiard-room, entrance hall and dining-room.

"This is a handsome investment of Madame Peloux's," her female devotees never tired of repeating—the old toadies who, in exchange for a dinner or a glass of brandy, came there to take a hand against her at bezique or poker. And they added: "But then, where has Madame Peloux not got money invested?"

Walking along in the shade of the acacia trees, between trellised roses and huge clumps of rhododendrons in full blaze, Léa could hear the murmur of voices, and, rising above it, Madame Peloux's shrill nasal trumpet notes and Chéri's dry cackle.

'That child's got an ugly laugh,' she thought. She paused a moment to listen more attentively to a new feminine note; weak, pleasing, quickly drowned by the redoubtable trumpeting. 'That must be the girl,' she said to herself, and a few quick steps brought her to the garden-room with its glass front, from which Madame Peloux burst out with a "Here comes our beautiful friend!"

A little round barrel of a woman, Madame Peloux—in reality Mademoiselle Peloux—had been a ballet-dancer from her tenth to her sixteenth year. Occasionally Léa would search for some trace in Madame Peloux that might recall the once chubby little fair-haired Eros, or the later dimpled nymph, and found nothing except the big implacable eyes, the delicate aggressive nose, and a still coquettish way of standing with her feet in 'the fifth position', like the members of the *corps de ballet*.

Chéri, coming to life in the depths of a rocking-chair, kissed Léa's hand with involuntary grace and ruined his gesture by exclaiming: "Hang it all! you've put on a veil again, and I loathe veils."

"Will you leave her alone!" Madame Peloux interposed. "You must never ask a woman why she is wearing a veil. We'll never be able to do anything with him," she said to Léa affectionately.

Two women had risen to their feet in the golden shade of a straw blind. One, in mauve, rather coldly offered her hand to Léa, who looked her over from head to foot.

"Goodness, how lovely you are, Marie-Laure! you're perfection itself!"

Marie-Laure deigned to smile. She was a red-haired young woman with brown eyes, whose physical presence alone was enough to take your breath away. She drew attention, almost coquettishly, to the other young woman, by saying: "But would you have recognised my daughter Edmée?"

Léa held out a hand which the girl was reluctant to shake.

"I should have known you, my child, but a schoolgirl alters so quickly, and Marie-Laure alters only to become always more disconcertingly lovely. Are you quite finished with school now?"

"I should hope so, I should hope so," exclaimed Madame Peloux. "You can't go on for ever, hiding her under a bushel, such a miracle of grace and charm, and she's nineteen already!"

"Eighteen," said Marie-Laure, sweetly.

"Eighteen, eighteen! . . . Yes of course, eighteen! Léa, you remember? This child was just making her first Communion the year that Chéri ran away from school, surely you remember? Yes, yes, you did, you little good-for-nothing, you ran away and Léa and I were driven nearly out of our wits!"

"I remember perfectly," Léa said, and she exchanged an imperceptible little nod with Marie-Laure—something corresponding to the '*touché*' of a punctilious fencer.

"You must get her married soon, you must get her married soon!" pursued Madame Peloux, who never failed to repeat a basic truth at least twice. "We'll all come to the wedding."

She brandished her little arms in the air, and the young girl glanced at her with ingenuous alarm.

'She's just the daughter for Marie-Laure,' thought Léa, gazing at her more closely. 'She has all her mother's dazzling qualities, but in a quieter key: fluffy, ash-brown hair, that looks as if it were powdered; frightened, secretive eyes, and a mouth she avoids opening even to speak or smile. . . . Exactly what Marie-Laure needs as a foil—but how she must hate her!'

Madame Peloux insinuated a maternal smile between Léa and the young girl: "You ought to have seen how well these two young people were getting on together in the garden!"

She pointed to where Chéri stood smoking a cigarette on the other side of the glass partition, his cigarette-holder clenched between his teeth, and his head tilted back to avoid the smoke. The three women looked at the young man who—forehead held at an angle, eyes half-shut, feet together, motionless—looked for all the world like a winged figure hovering dreamily in the air. Léa did not fail to observe the expression of fright and sub-jugation in the girl's eyes, and she took pleasure in making her tremble by touching her on the arm. Edmée quivered from head to foot, withdrew her arm, and whispered almost savagely, "What?"

"Nothing," Léa replied, "I dropped my glove."

"Come along, Edmée!" Marie-Laure called, negli-gently.

Silent and docile, the girl walked towards Madame Peloux, who flapped her wings: "Leaving already? Surely not? We must meet again soon, we must meet again soon!"

"It's late," Marie-Laure said, "and you'll be expecting any number of people as it's Sunday afternoon. The child is not accustomed to company."

"Of course not, of course not," Madame Peloux said

tenderly. "She's had such a sheltered existence . . . such a lonely life!"

Marie-Laure smiled, and Léa gave her a look as much as to say, "That's one for you!"

"But we'll call again soon."

"Thursday, Thursday! Léa, you'll come to luncheon on Thursday?"

"I'll be here," Léa answered.

Chéri had rejoined Edmée at the entrance to the room and stood beside her, disdaining all conversation. He heard Léa's promise, and turned round: "Splendid, then we can go for a run in the motor."

"Yes, yes, just the thing for you young people," Madame Peloux insisted, touched by his proposal. "Edmée can sit in front next to Chéri, at the wheel, and the rest of us will go at the back. Youth at the helm, youth at the helm! Chéri, my love, will you ask for Marie-Laure's motor?"

Her small stumpy feet kept slipping on the gravel, but she managed to take her two visitors to the corner of the path, where she handed them over to Chéri. On her return, she found that Léa had taken off her hat and was smoking a cigarette.

"Aren't they sweet, those two!" Madame Peloux gasped. "Don't you think so, Léa?"

"Delicious," Léa breathed out in the same puff as her cigarette smoke. "But really, that Marie-Laure!"

"What's Marie-Laure been up to?" asked Chéri, as he rejoined them.

"How lovely she is!"

"Ah! Ah!" Madame Peloux began in formal assent. "That's true, that's true. She has been really lovely."

Chéri and Léa caught each other's eye and laughed.

"Has been?", Léa emphasized the past tense. "But she's

the picture of youth. Not a single wrinkle! And she can
wear the palest mauve, such a foul colour! I loathe it
and it loathes me."

Madame Peloux raised her big pitiless eyes and thin
nose from her brandy-glass.

"The picture of youth, the picture of youth!" yapped
Madame Peloux. "Pardon me, pardon me! Marie-Laure
had Edmée in 1895, no . . . '94. She'd just run away with
a singing-teacher, leaving Khalil Bey flat, though he'd
given her the famous pink diamond which . . . No, no!
Wait! . . . That must have been the year before!"

The trumpet notes were shrill and off key. Léa put a
hand over her ear, and Chéri declared, with some feeling:
"Everything would be heavenly on an afternoon like
this, if only we could be spared my mother's voice!"

She looked at her son with no sign of anger, accustomed to his insolence. Dignified, feet dangling, she
settled herself back in a basket chair too high for her
short legs. In one hand she warmed her glass of brandy.
Léa, rocking herself gently to and fro, glanced occasionally at Chéri, who lay sprawled on a cool cane settee,
coat unbuttoned, a cigarette dying between his lips, a
lock of hair over one eyebrow. 'He's a handsome young
blackguard,' she thought admiringly.

There they remained, peacefully side by side, making
no effort to talk or be sociable, happy after their own
fashion. Years of close familiarity rendered silence
congenial, and Chéri slipped back into his lethargy,
Léa into her calm. As the afternoon became hotter,
Madame Peloux pulled her narrow skirt up to her
knees, displaying her tight little sailor's calves, and
Chéri ripped off his tie—reproved by Léa in an audible
"Tch, tch."

"Oh! leave the child alone," Madame Peloux protested,

as from the depths of a dream. "It's much too hot! Would you care for a kimono, Léa?"

"No, thank you. I'm perfectly comfortable."

Their unbuttoned siestas disgusted her. Never once had her young lover caught her untidily dressed, or with her blouse undone, or in her bedroom slippers during the day. "Naked, if need be," she would say, "but squalid, never!"

She picked up her picture paper again, but did not read it. 'These Pelouxs—mother and son alike!' she thought dreamily. 'They've only to sit themselves down at a good meal or in the heart of the countryside and— snap!—the mother whisks off her stays and the son his waistcoat. They behave like publicans out on a holiday, the pair of them.' She cast a vindictive eye on one of the publicans in question, and saw that he had fallen asleep, his eyelashes spread against his pallid cheeks, his mouth closed. His upper lip, lit from below, reflected two silver pinpoints of light at the twin curves of its delicious Cupid's bow, and Léa was forced to admit that he looked far more like a sleeping god than a licensed victualler.

Without moving from her chair, she gently plucked the lighted cigarette from between Chéri's fingers and put it in the ash-tray. The hand of the sleeper relaxed and the tapering fingers, tipped with cruel nails, drooped like wilting flowers: a hand not strictly feminine, yet a trifle prettier than one could have wished; a hand she had kissed a hundred times—not in slavish devotion—but kissed for the pleasure of it, for its scent.

From behind her paper, she glanced at Madame Peloux. Was she asleep too? Léa always liked to remain awake while mother and son dozed, allowing her a quiet hour's self-communing in the dappled sunlight of a broiling afternoon. But Madame Peloux was not asleep. She was

sitting bolt upright in her wickerwork chair, like a
Buddha staring into space, and sipping her *fine-champagne*
with the absorption of an alcoholic baby.

'Why doesn't she go to sleep?' Léa wondered. 'It's
Sunday. She's lunched well. She's expecting her sponging
old cronies to drop in for her five o'clock tea. By rights
she ought to be having a snooze. If she's not snoozing,
it's because she's up to some devilment or other.'

They had known each other for twenty-five years.
Theirs was the hostile intimacy of light women, enriched
and then cast aside by one man, ruined by another: the
tetchy affection of rivals stalking one another's first
wrinkle or white hair. Theirs was the friendship of two
practical women of the world, both adepts at the money
game; but one of them a miser, and the other a sybarite.
These bonds count. Rather late in their day, a stronger
bond had come to link them more closely: Chéri.

Léa could remember Chéri as a little boy—a marvel
of beauty with long curls. When quite small he was
known as Fred, and had not yet been nicknamed Chéri.

Sometimes forgotten and sometimes adored, Chéri
grew up among wan housemaids and tall sardonic men-
servants. Although his birth had mysteriously brought
wealth to the house, no "Fräulein", no "Miss" was ever
to be seen at Chéri's side; and his mother had preserved him, to the accompaniment of piercing shrieks,
from "these ghouls".

"Charlotte Peloux, you belong to another age." The
speaker was the moribund, mummified, but indestructible
Baron de Berthellemy. "Charlotte Peloux, in you I salute
the only light woman who ever had the courage to bring

up her son as the son of a tart! You belong to another
age! You never read, you never travel, you make a
point of knowing your neighbour's business, and you
abandon your child to the tender mercies of the servants.
How perfect! How absolutely About![1] . . . Or, better
still, how like a novel by Gustav Droz. . . . And to
think that you've never heard of either! . . ."

Chéri had enjoyed the full freedom of a profligate
upbringing. When barely able to lisp, he was quick to
pick up all the backstairs gossip. He shared in the
clandestine suppers of the kitchen. His ablutions varied
between milky immersions in his mother's orris-root
baths and scanty cat-licks with the corner of a towel. He
suffered from indigestion after a surfeit of sweets, or
from pangs of hunger when no one remembered to give
him his supper. He was wretchedly bored at every Battle
of Flowers, where Charlotte Peloux would exhibit him—
half-naked and catching cold—sitting on drenched roses;
but it so happened, when he was twelve, that he had a
glorious adventure in an illicit gambling-den, when an
American woman allowed him to play with a fistful of
louis d'or, and called him 'a little masterpiece'. At about
the same time, Madame Peloux imposed a tutor on her
son—an Abbé, whom she packed off at the end of ten
months "because," she confessed, "whenever I caught
sight of that black robe trailing along the passages, it
made me think I was housing a female relation: and God
knows there are few things more depressing than having
a poor relation to stay!"

At the age of fourteen, Chéri had a taste of school. He

Edmond About (*Roman d'un brave homme*, etc.) and Gustav Droz
(*Monsieur, Madame et Bébé*, etc.) light popular novelists of the last half of
the nineteenth century, some of whose books appeared in English
translation. (*Papa, Mamma and Baby*, illustrated by Morin 1887.)

didn't believe in it. He broke prison and ran away. Madame Peloux not only found the energy to incarcerate him a second time, but also, when faced with her son's tears and insults, took to her heels with hands over her ears screaming, "I can't bear the sight of it! I can't bear the sight of it!" So sincere were her cries that she actually fled from Paris, in the company of a man who was young but far from scrupulous. Two years later she came back, alone. It was the last time she succumbed to an amorous impulse.

She found, on her return, that Chéri had shot up too fast; that his cheeks were hollow and his eyes black-ringed; that he dressed like a stable-lad and spoke with a worse accent than ever. She beat her breast, and snatched him back from the boarding school. He utterly refused to work; demanded horses, carriages, jewels; insisted on a substantial monthly allowance; and, when his mother began to beat her breast and shriek like a pea-hen, he put a stop to her cries by saying: "Madame Peloux, ma'am, don't carry on so. My venerable mother, if no one except me drags you down into the gutter, you're likely to die a comfortable death in your downy bed; I don't altogether fancy a trustee for my estate. Your cash is mine. Let me go my own way! Men friends cost next to nothing—a dinner and a bottle of champagne. As for the fair sex, surely Ma'me Peloux, seeing that I take after you, you can trust me not to treat 'em to more than a trinket—if that!"

He pirouetted about while she shed tears and proclaimed herself the happiest of mothers. When Chéri began buying motor-cars, she trembled once more; but he simply advised her: "Keep an eye on the petrol, Ma'me Peloux, if you please!" and sold his horses. He was not above checking the two chauffeurs' books. His calculations were quick and accurate, and the figures he jotted down on slips of paper—dashed off rapidly, round and regular—were in marked contrast to his rather slow and childish handwriting.

At seventeen he was like a little old man, always fussing over his expenses: still good-looking—but skinny and short-winded. More than once Madame Peloux ran into him on the cellar steps, coming up from checking the bottles in the racks and bins.

"Would you believe it?" she said to Léa. "It's too wonderful."

"Much too wonderful," Léa answered, "he'll come to a bad end. Chéri! Show me your tongue!"

He put out his tongue, made a face, and showed other signs of disrespect. Léa took no notice. She was too intimate a friend, a sort of doting godmother, whom he called by her Christian name.

"Is it true," Léa enquired, "that you were seen last night at a bar, sitting on old Lili's knees?"

"Her knees!" scoffed Chéri. "She hasn't had any for ages. They foundered years ago."

"Isn't it true," Léa persisted with greater severity, "that she made you drink gin laced with pepper? You know gin is bad for the breath!"

On one occasion, Chéri, hurt, snapped back at Léa: "I can't think why you bother me with all these questions. You must have seen what I was up to; you were tucked away in that cubby-hole at the back, with Patron your prize-fighter friend."

"That's perfectly correct," Léa answered, unmoved. "There's nothing of the dissipated schoolboy about Patron. He has other attractions, and a good deal more to recommend him than a perky little face and two black rings round his eyes."

That week Chéri had been out on the razzle in Montmartre and les Halles, consorting with ladies of the town
who called him "poppet" and "my pet vice", but he had
got no kick out of it: he suffered from migraines and a dry
cough. Madame Peloux poured out her heart-breaking
woes—"Life is nothing but a series of crosses for us
mothers"—to her masseuse, to her stay-maker, Madame
Ribot, to old Lili, to the Baron de Berthellemy, and
thus passed painlessly from the state of being the
happiest-of-parents to that of the martyr-mother.

A night in June, when Madame Peloux and Léa and
Chéri were together in the garden-room at Neuilly,
was to change the destinies of the young man and the
middle-aged woman. Chéri's friends had gone off for the
evening—little Baxter, a wholesale wine-merchant, and
the Vicomte Desmond, a hanger-on of his, barely of age,
difficult and arrogant—and so Chéri had returned to the
maternal fold, and habit had drawn Léa there also.

For one more evening, in a whole sequence of such
occasions, these two women, each suspicious of the
other, found themselves together. They had known
each other for twenty years; they shared a past made up
of similarly dull evenings; they lacked other friends;
and, in their later days, they had become mistrustful,
self-indulgent, and cut off from the world, as women
are who have lived only for love.

Both were staring in silence at Chéri, who never spoke.
Madame Peloux lacked the strength to take her son's
health in hand, but hated Léa a little more each time she
bent her white neck and glowing cheeks over Chéri's
pallid cheek and transparent ear. She would willingly

have bled that healthy female neck, already wrinkled by the so-called lines of Venus, in order to give a touch of colour to her slim lily-green son: yet it never occurred to her to take her darling away to the country.

"Chéri, why are you drinking brandy?" Léa scolded.

"Out of politeness to Ma'me Peloux—who would otherwise be drinking alone," Chéri answered.

"What are you going to do to-morrow?"

"Dunno, and you?"

"I'm off to Normandy."

"With?"

"That's none of your business."

"With our friend Spéleïeff?"

"Don't be so stupid. That was over two months ago. You're behind the times. Spéleïeff's in Russia."

"Chéri, darling, what can you be thinking of?" sighed Madame Peloux. "Don't you remember going last month to the charming dinner given by Léa to celebrate the end of the affair? Léa, you've never let me have the recipe for those langoustines I enjoyed so much."

Chéri sat up, his eyes sparkling. "Yes, yes, langoustines, swimming in a creamy sauce! How I'd like some now!"

"You see," Madame Peloux said reproachfully, "he's got no appetite to speak of and yet he's asking for langoustines."

"Shut up!" Chéri snapped. "Léa, are you off to the shady woods with Patron?"

"Certainly not, my boy. Patron and I are merely friends. I'm going on my own."

"Nice to be so rich!" Chéri threw out.

"I'll take you with me, if you like: there'll be nothing to do but eat and drink and sleep. . . ."

"Where is this place of yours?" He had risen to his feet and was standing over her.

"You know Honfleur—the Côte de Grâce—don't you? Sit down; you're green in the face. Now as you go down the Côte de Grâce, you know those farm gates where we always say, in passing, your mother and I . . ."

She turned round to where Madame Peloux was sitting. Madame Peloux had disappeared. The discretion with which she had faded away was something so unlike the normal Charlotte Peloux, that they looked at each other and laughed in surprise.

Chéri sat down close to Léa. "I'm tired," he said.

"You're ruining your health."

He drew himself up in his chair, with offended vanity. "Oh! I'm still in good enough fettle, you know."

"Good enough! For others perhaps . . . but not . . . not for me, I'd have you know."

"Too green?"

"The very word I was looking for. So why don't you come down to the country? No nonsense, of course. Ripe strawberries, fresh cream, cakes, grilled spring chicken . . . that's just what you need—and no women."

He let himself snuggle up to Léa's elbow and shut his eyes.

"No women . . . grand . . . Léa, tell me, you're my pal? You are? Then let's be off. Women indeed! I'm fed up with 'em. Women! I've seen all they've got to show."

These vulgarities were muttered in a drowsy voice. Léa listened to his soft tone, and felt his warm breath against her ear. He had taken hold of her long string of pearls and was rolling the larger ones between his fingers. She slipped her arm under his head and so accustomed

was she to treating the boy in this way that, almost
without thinking, she pulled him towards her and rocked
him in her arms.

"How comfy I am!" he sighed. "You're a good pal.
I'm so comfy."

Léa smiled, as though hearing praise she valued
intensely. Chéri seemed to be ready to drop off to sleep.
She looked very closely at his glistening, almost dewy,
eyelashes sunk flat against the cheeks, and then at the
cheeks themselves, hollowed by his joyless dissipation.
His upper lip, shaved that morning, was already bluish,
and the pink lampshades lent his mouth an artificial
colour.

"No women!" Chéri exclaimed, as though dreaming.
"Then . . . kiss me!"

Taken by surprise, Léa made no movement.

"Kiss me, I tell you!"

He rapped out his order, frowning, and Léa felt
embarrassed by the rekindled gleam in his eyes. It was
as if someone had switched on the light. She shrugged
her shoulders and kissed the forehead so close to her lips.
He drew his arms tighter around her neck, and pulled
her down towards him.

She shook her head only at the very instant that their
lips touched, then she remained absolutely motionless,
and held her breath like someone listening. When he
released his hold, she broke away from him, rose to her
feet, took a deep breath, and put a hand up to tidy her
unruffled hair. She turned to him, rather pale and with
rueful eyes, and said, teasingly: "That was a bright
idea!"

He lay far back in the rocking-chair, speechless, and
scrutinized her with a suspicious, questioning gaze, so
that she asked: "What is it?"

"Nothing," Chéri said. "I know what I wanted to know."

She blushed with humiliation, then skilfully defended herself.

"What do you know? That I like your mouth? My poor child, I've kissed uglier. What does that prove? D'you think I'm going to fling myself at your feet and cry, 'Take me!' You talk as if you've known only nice young girls! D'you imagine I'm going to lose my head because of a kiss?"

She grew calmer while speaking and wished to prove her self-control.

"Listen, child," she persisted, as she leaned over him, "d'you think a handsome mouth means anything to me?"

She smiled down at him, completely sure of herself, but unaware that there remained on her face a sort of very faint quiver, an appealing sadness, and that her smile was like a rainbow after a sudden storm.

"I'm perfectly calm. Even if I were to kiss you again, or even if we . . ." She stopped and pouted with scorn. "No, no, I really can't see you and me doing that."

"Nor could you see us doing what we did just now," Chéri said, taking time over his words. "And yet you don't mind doing it, and not in a hurry, either. So now you're thinking of going further, are you? *I* never suggested such a thing."

They faced each other like enemies. Léa was afraid to reveal a desire she had not yet had time to develop or to disguise; she resented this child, so suddenly cold and perhaps derisive.

"You're right," she conceded lightly. "Let's say no more about it. Shall we say instead that I'm offering to put you out to grass! And the food will be good . . . *my* food, in other words."

"We'll see," Chéri answered. "Shall I bring the Renouhard tourer?"

"Of course; you're not going to leave it behind with Charlotte."

"I'll pay for the petrol, but you'll feed the chauffeur."

Léa burst out laughing. "I'll feed the chauffeur! Ha! Ha! There speaks the son of Madame Peloux! Get along with you! You forget nothing. . . . I'm not usually inquisitive, but I should love to eavesdrop when you're making up to a woman."

She sank into a chair and fanned herself. A sphinx-moth and a number of long-legged mosquitoes hovered round the lamps; scents of the countryside drifted in from the garden, now that night had fallen. A sudden waft from an acacia burst in upon them, so distinct, so active, that they both turned round, half expecting to see it advancing towards them.

"It's the rose-acacia," Léa said.

"Yes," Chéri said. "But to-night it has sipped a draught of orange-flower water."

She stared at him, in vague admiration, astonished that he had hit upon such an idea. He was breathing in the scent in helpless rapture, and she turned away, suddenly fearful lest he might call her; but he did call, and she went to him.

She went to kiss him, on an impulse of resentment and selfishness, and half thinking to chastise him. 'Just you wait, my boy. . . . It's all too true that you've a pretty mouth, and, this time, I'm going to take my fill because I want to—and then I'll leave you, I don't care what you may say. Now . . .'

Her kiss was such that they reeled apart, drunk, deaf, breathless, trembling as if they had just been fighting. She stood up again in front of him, but he did not move from the depths of his chair, and she taunted him under her breath, "Well? . . . Well?" and waited for an insult. Instead, he held out his arms, opened his vague beautiful hands, tilted his head back as if he had been struck, and let her see beneath each eyelash the glint of a shining tear. He babbled indeterminate words—a whole animal chant of desire, in which she could distinguish her name—"darling"—"I want you"—"I'll never leave you"—a song to which she listened, solicitous, leaning over him, as if unwittingly she had hurt him to the quick.

WHEN Léa recalled their first summer in Normandy, she would sum it up impartially: "I've had other naughty little boys through my hands, more amusing than Chéri, more likeable, too, and more intelligent. But all the same, never one to touch him."

"It's funny," she confided to the old Baron de Berthellemy, towards the end of the summer of 1906, "but sometimes I think I'm in bed with a Chinee or an African."

"Have you ever had a Chinaman or a Negro?"

"Never."

"Well then?"

"I don't know. I can't explain. It's just an impression."

The impression had grown upon her slowly, also an astonishment she had not always been able to conceal. Her earliest memories of their idyll were abundantly rich, but only in pictures of delicious food, superb fruit, and the pleasure of taking pains over her country larder. She could still see Chéri—paler in the blazing sunlight—dragging along his exhausted body beneath the lime-tree tunnels in Normandy, or asleep on the sun-warmed paving beside a pond.

Léa used to rouse Chéri from sleep to cram him with strawberries and cream, frothy milk, and corn-fed chicken. With wide, vacant eyes, as though dazed, he would sit at dinner watching the mazy motions of the moths round the bowl of roses, and then look at his wrist-watch to see whether the time had come to go to bed: while Léa, disappointed but unresentful, pondered over the unfulfilled promises of the kiss at Neuilly and good-naturedly bided her time.

"I'll keep him cooped up in this fattening-pen till the end of August, if need be. Then, back in Paris again—ouf!—I'll pack him off to his precious studies."

She went to bed mercifully early, so that Chéri—after nuzzling against her till he had hollowed out a selfishly comfortable position—might get some sleep. Sometimes, when the lamp was out, she would watch a pool of moonlight shimmering over the polished floor, or listen, through the chorus of rustling aspens and shrilling crickets, unceasing by night or day, to the deep, retriever-like sighs that rose from Chéri's breast.

'Why can't I go to sleep? Is there something wrong with me?' she vaguely wondered. 'It's not this boy's head on my shoulder—I've held heavier. The weather's wonderful. I've ordered him a good plate of porridge for to-morrow. Already his ribs stick out less. Then why can't I go to sleep? Yes, of course, I remember. . . . I'm going to send for Patron, the boxer, to give the boy some training. We've plenty of time between us, Patron and I, to spring a surprise on Madame Peloux.'

She fell asleep, lying stretched out on her back between the cool sheets, the dark head of her naughty little boy resting on her left breast. She fell asleep, to be aroused sometimes—but all too rarely—by a waking desire of Chéri's towards the break of day.

Patron actually arrived after they had been two months in their country retreat, with his suitcase, his small pound-and-a-half dumb-bells, his black tights, his six-ounce gloves, and his leather boxing-boots, laced down to the toe. Patron, with his girlish voice, his long eye-lashes, and his splendid tanned skin, as brown as the leather of his luggage—he hardly looked naked when he took off his shirt. And Chéri, by turns peevish, listless, or jealous of Patron's smooth strength, started the slow, oft-repeated movements. They were tiresome, but they did him good.

"One . . . sss . . . two . . . sss . . . I can't hear you breathing . . . three . . . sss. . . . Don't think I can't see you cheating there with your knee . . . sss. . . . ."

An awning of lime foliage filtered the August sunlight. The bare bodies of instructor and pupil were dappled with purple reflections from the thick red carpet spread out upon the gravel. Léa watched the lessons with keen attention. Sometimes during the quarter of an hour's boxing, Chéri, drunk with new-found strength, lost all control and, red-faced with anger, attempted a foul blow. Rock-like, Patron stood up to his swings, and from the height of his Olympian glory let fall oracular words—words of wisdom that packed more weight than his proverbial punch.

"Steady on now! That left eye's wandering a bit! If I hadn't stopped myself in time, it would have had a nasty taste of the stitches on my right glove."

"I slipped," Chéri said, enraged.

"It's not a question of balance," Patron went on, "it's a question of morale. You'll never make a boxer."

"My mother won't let me, isn't that a pity?"

"Whether your mother lets you or not, you'll never make a boxer, because you've got a rotten temper. Rotten tempers and boxing don't go together. Aren't I right, Madame Léa?"

Léa smiled, and revelled in the warm sun, sitting still and watching the bouts between these two men, both young and both stripped. In her mind she kept comparing them. 'How handsome Patron is—as solid as a house! And the boy's shaping well. You don't find knees like his running about the streets every day of the week, or I'm no judge. His back, too, is . . . will be . . . marvellous. Where the devil did Mother Peloux drop her line to fish up a child like that? And the set of his head! quite a statue! But what a little beast he is! When he laughs, you'd swear it's a greyhound snarling!' She felt happy and maternal—bathed in quiet virtue. 'I'd willingly change him for anyone else,' she said to herself, with Chéri naked in the afternoon beside her under the lime-tree-bower, or with Chéri naked in the morning on her ermine rug, or Chéri naked in the evening on the edge of the warm fountain. 'Yes, handsome as he is, I'd willingly make a change, if it weren't a question of conscience!'

She confessed her indifference to Patron.

"And yet," Patron objected, "the lad's very nicely made. There's muscles on him now such as you don't see on our French lads; his are more like a coloured boy's —though he couldn't look any whiter, I must say. Nice little muscles they are, and not too showy. He'll never have biceps like melons."

"I should hope not, Patron! But then, you know, I didn't take him on for his boxing!"

"Of course not," Patron acquiesced, letting his long lashes droop, "there's—your feelings to be considered."

He was always embarrassed by Léa's unveiled allusions to sex, and by her smile—the insistence of the smiling eyes she brought to bear on him whenever she spoke of love.

"Of course," Patron tried another tack, "if he's not altogether satisfactory . . ."

Léa laughed: "Altogether! no . . . but I find being disinterested is its own reward. Just as you do, Patron."

"Oh! me . . ." He waited in fear and hope for the question that did not fail to follow.

"Always the same, Patron? You still won't give way an inch?"

"I won't give way, Madame Léa, and I've just had a letter from Liane by the midday post. She says she's all alone, that I've no good reasons for refusing, and that her two admirers have left her."

"Well?"

"Well, I don't believe it! I won't give way, because she won't give way. She's ashamed, she says, of a man who works for his living—specially when it pulls him out of bed so early every day for his training—a man who gives boxing lessons and teaches Swedish gymnastics. We've only got to meet, and the row starts all over again. 'Anyone'd think,' she shouts at me, 'that I'm not in a position to support the man I love!' That shows very nice feelings, I don't say it doesn't, but it doesn't fit in with my ideas. Everyone's funny about something. It's just like you said, Madame Léa, it's all a question of conscience."

They were talking in low tones under the trees: he prudish and half naked; she dressed in white, the colour flaming in her cheeks. They were enjoying the pleasure of a friendly understanding: they shared the same taste for the simple things of life, good health and a sort of plebeian decency. And yet Léa would not have been shocked had Patron received handsome presents from a beautiful and expensive woman like Liane. "Fair exchange is no robbery." And she did her best to break down Patron's "funny feelings" by arguments based on homespun justice. These leisurely conversations always revealed their worship of the same twin deities—love

and money, and would drift away from money and love
to come back to Chéri and his deplorable upbringing, to
his exceptional good looks ("harmless, after all," as Léa
would say) and to his character ("virtually non-existent,"
as Léa would say). They had a taste for sharing confidences, and a dislike of new words or ideas, which
they satisfied in these long talks. They were often disturbed by the preposterous apparition of Chéri, whom
they thought either asleep or motoring down some
baking hot road—Chéri, looming into sight, half naked,
but equipped with an account book, a stylo behind his
ear.

"Look at our Mister Adding-machine," Patron said
admiringly. "All got up as a clerk in a bank."

"What can this mean?" Chéri shouted from afar.
"Three hundred and twenty francs for petrol? Somebody
must be swilling the stuff! We've been out four times in
the last fortnight—and seventy-seven francs for oil!"

"The motor goes to the market every day," Léa
replied. "And while we're on the subject, it appears your
chauffeur had three helpings of the joint for his dinner.
Don't you think that's stretching our agreement a bit
far? . . . Whenever a bill sticks in your throat, you look
just like your mother."

At a loss for an answer, he stood uncertain for a
moment, shifting from one slender foot to the other,
poised with winged grace like a young Mercury. This
always made Madame Peloux swoon with delight and
yelp, "Me when I was eighteen! Winged feet! winged
feet!" He cast about for some insolent retort, his whole
face a-quiver, his mouth half-open, his forehead jutting
forward, in a tense attitude that showed off to advantage
the peculiar and diabolic upward twist of his eyebrows.

"Don't bother to think of an answer," Léa said kindly.

"I know you hate me. Come and kiss me. Handsome devil. Fallen angel. Silly goose. . . ."

He came, calmed by the softness of her voice, yet ruffled by her words. Seeing them together, Patron once again let the truth flower on his guileless lips.

"As far as first-rate bodies go, Monsieur Chéri, you have one all right. But whenever I look at it, Monsieur Chéri, I feel that if I was a woman I'd say to myself: 'I'll come back again in ten years' time'."

"You hear, Léa? He says in ten years' time," Chéri said insinuatingly, pushing away the head of his mistress as she leaned towards him. "What do you think of that?"

But she did not deign to listen. The young body owed to her its renewed vigour, and she began patting it all over, touching it anywhere and everywhere, on the cheek, on the leg, on the behind, with the irreverent pleasure of a nanny.

"What d'you get out of being spiteful?" Patron then asked.

Chéri allowed a savage, inscrutable gaze to sweep over every inch of the waiting Hercules before he answered. "I find it comforting. You wouldn't understand."

In fact, Léa herself understood precious little about Chéri after three months' intimacy. If she still talked to Patron, who now came only on Sundays, or to Berthellemy, who arrived without being invited but left again two hours later, about "sending Chéri back to his blessed studies", it was because the phrase had become a kind of habit, and as though to excuse herself for having kept him there so long. She kept on setting a limit to his stay, and then exceeding it. She was waiting.

"The weather is so lovely. And then his trip to Paris last week tired him. And, besides, it's better for me to get thoroughly sick of him."

For the first time in her life, she waited in vain for what

had never before failed her: complete trust on the part of her young lover, a self-surrender to confessions, candours, endless secrets — those hours in the depths of the night when, in almost filial gratitude, a young man unrestrainedly pours out his tears, his private likes and dislikes, on the kindly bosom of a mature and trusted friend.

'They've always told me everything in the past,' she thought obstinately. 'I've always known just what they were worth—what they were thinking and what they wanted. But this boy, this brat . . . No, that would really be the limit.'

He was now strong, proud of his nineteen years, gay at meals and impatient in bed; even so he gave away nothing but his body, and remained as mysterious as an odalisque. Tender? Yes, if an involuntary cry or an impulsive hug is an indication of tenderness. But the moment he spoke, he was "spiteful" again, careful to divulge nothing of his true self.

How often at dawn had Léa held him in her arms, a lover soothed, relaxed, with half-closed lids! Each morning his eyes and his mouth returned to life more beautiful, as though every waking, every embrace, had fashioned them anew! How often, at such moments, had she indulged her desire to master him, her sensual longing to hear his confession, and pressed her forehead against his, whispering, "Speak. Say something. Tell me . . ."

But no confession came from those curved lips, scarcely anything indeed but sulky or frenzied phrases woven round "Nounoune"—the name he had given her when a child and the one he now used in the throes of his pleasure, almost like a cry for help.

"Yes, I assure you, he might be a Chinee or an African," she declared to Anthime de Berthellemy, and added, "I can't tell you why." The impression was strong but confused, and she felt lazily incompetent to find words for the feeling that she and Chéri did not speak the same language.

It was the end of September when they returned to Paris. Chéri went straight to Neuilly, the very first evening, to "spring a surprise" on Madame Peloux. He brandished chairs, cracked nuts with his fist, leaped on to the billiard-table and played cowboy in the garden at the heels of the terrified watch-dogs.

"Ouf!" Léa sighed, as she entered her house in the Avenue Bugeaud, alone. "How wonderful!—a bed to myself!"

But at ten o'clock the following night, she was sipping coffee and trying not to find the evening too long or the dining-room too large, when a nervous cry was forced from her lips. Chéri had suddenly appeared, framed in the doorway—Chéri, wafted on silent, winged feet.

He was not speaking or showing any sign of affection, but just running towards her.

"Are you mad?"

Shrugging his shoulders, disdaining all explanations, just running towards her. Never asking "Do you love me?", "Have you already forgotten me?". Running towards her.

A moment later they were lying in the middle of Léa's great brass-encumbered bed. Chéri pretended to be worn out and sleepy. This made it easier to grit his teeth and keep his eyes tight shut, suffering as he was from a furious attack of taciturnity. Yet, through his silence, she was listening as she lay beside him, listening with delight to the distant delicate vibration, to the imprisoned tumult thrumming within a body that sought to conceal its agony, its gratitude and love.

"WHY didn't your mother tell me this herself at dinner last night?"

"She thought it better it should come from me."

"No!"

"That's what she said."

"And you?"

"What about me?"

"Do you think it better?"

Chéri raised uncertain eyes to Léa's. "Yes." He appeared to think it over a moment and repeated: "Yes, far better, in fact."

In order not to embarrass him, Léa looked away towards the window.

The August morning was dark with warm rain, which fell vertically on the already rusted foliage of the three plane-trees in the garden court.

"It might be autumn," she said, and sighed.

"What's the matter?" Chéri asked.

She looked at him in astonishment. "Nothing, I don't like the rain, that's all."

"Oh! All right, I thought . . ."

"What?"

"I thought something was wrong."

She could not help giving a frank laugh. "Wrong with me, because you're getting married? No, listen . . . you're . . . you're so funny."

She seldom laughed outright, and her merriment vexed Chéri. He shrugged his shoulders and made the usual grimace while lighting a cigarette, jutting out his chin too far and protruding his lower lip.

"You oughtn't to smoke before luncheon," Léa said.

He made some impertinent retort she did not hear. She was listening to the sound of her own voice and its daily lectures, echoing away down the past five years. 'It's like the endless repetition in opposite looking-glasses,' she thought. Then, with a slight effort, she returned to reality and cheerfulness.

"It's lucky for me that there'll soon be someone else to stop you smoking on an empty stomach."

"Oh! *she* won't be allowed to have a say in anything," Chéri declared. "She's going to be my wife, isn't she? Let her kiss the sacred ground I tread on, and thank her lucky stars for the privilege. And that will be that."

He exaggerated the thrust of his chin, clenched his teeth on his cigarette-holder, parted his lips, and, as he stood there in his white silk pyjamas, succeeded only in looking like an Asiatic prince grown pale in the impenetrable obscurity of palaces.

Léa drew the folds of her pink dressing-gown closer about her—the pink she called "indispensable". She was lazily turning over ideas which she found tiresome, ideas that she decided to hurl, one by one, as missiles against Chéri's assumed composure.

"Well, why are you marrying the child?"

He put both elbows on the table and, unconsciously, assumed the composed features of his mother. "Well, you see, my dear girl . . ."

"Call me Madame or Léa. I'm neither your housemaid nor a pal of your own age."

She sat straight up in her armchair and clipped her

words without raising her voice. He wanted to answer back. He looked defiantly at the beautiful face, a little pale under its powder, and at the frank blue light of her searching eyes. But he softened, and conceded, in a tone most unusual for him, "Nounoune, you asked me to explain. . . . It had to come to this in the end. And besides, there are big interests at stake."

"Whose?"

"Mine," he said without a smile. "The girl has a considerable fortune of her own."

"From her father?"

He rocked himself to and fro, his feet in the air. "Oh, how do I know? What a question! I suppose so. You'd hardly expect the fair Marie-Laure to draw fifteen hundred thousand out of her own bank account, would you? Fifteen hundred thousand, and some decent family jewels into the bargain."

"And how much have you?"

"Oh, I've more than that of my own," he said with pride.

"Then you don't need any more money?"

He shook his smooth head and it caught the light like blue watered silk. "Need . . . need . . . ? You know perfectly well we don't look at money in the same way. It's something on which we never see eye to eye."

"I'll do you the justice to say that you've spared me any reference to it during the last five years." She leaned towards him and put her hand on his knee. "Tell me, child, how much have you put by from your income in these five years?"

He cavorted like a clown, laughed, and rolled at Léa's feet, but she pushed him aside with her toe.

"No, tell me the truth . . . fifty thousand a year, or sixty? Tell me, sixty? Seventy?"

He sat down on the carpet facing away from Léa, and laid his head back on her lap. "Aren't I worth it, then?"

He stretched out to his full length, turned his head to look up at her, and opened his eyes wide. They looked black, but their true shade, Léa knew, was a dark almost reddish brown. As though to indicate her choice of what was rarest among so much beauty, she put her forefinger on his eyebrows, his eyelids and the corners of his mouth. At moments this lover, whom she slightly despised, inspired her with a kind of respect by his outward form. 'To be as handsome as that amounts to nobility,' she said to herself.

"Tell me, child, how does this young person feel about you?"

"She loves me. She admires me. She never says a word."

"And you—how do you behave with her?"

"I don't," he answered simply.

"Delightful love duets," Léa said, dreamily.

He sat up, crossing his legs tailor-fashion.

"You seem to me to be thinking a lot about her," he said severely. "Don't you think of yourself at all, in this upheaval?"

She gazed at Chéri with an astonishment that made her look years younger—eyebrows raised and lips half open.

"Yes, you, Léa. You, the victimized heroine. You, the one sympathetic character in all this, since you're being dropped."

He had become rather pale, and his tough handling of Léa seemed to be hurting him.

Léa smiled. "But, my darling, I've not the slightest intention of changing my life. Now and then, during the next week, I'll come across a pair of socks, a tie, a handkerchief on my shelves . . . and when I say a week

. . . you know in what excellent order my shelves are
kept! Oh, yes, and I'll have the bathroom re-done. I've
got an idea of putting in encrusted glass. . . ."

She fell silent and assumed an almost greedy look as
she traced a vague outline with her finger. Chéri continued to look vindictive.

"You aren't pleased! What do you want, then? Do
you expect me to go to Normandy to hide my grief?
To pine away? To stop dyeing my hair? To have Madame
Peloux rushing to my bedside?" And she imitated
Madame Peloux, flapping her arms and trumpeting:
" 'The shadow of her former self, the shadow of her
former self! The poor unfortunate creature has aged a
hundred years, a hundred years!' Is that what you want?"

He had been listening with a smile that died on his
lips, and a trembling of the nostrils that might be due to
emotion. "Yes!" he cried.

Léa rested her smooth, bare, heavy arms on Chéri's
shoulders.

"My poor boy! But at that rate, I ought to have died
four or five times already! To lose a little lover. . . . To
exchange one naughty little boy. . . ." She added in
lower, lighter tones: "I've grown used to it!"

"We all know that," he said harshly. "I don't give a
damn—d'you hear me?—I don't give a single damn that
I wasn't your first lover. What I should have liked, or
rather what would have been . . . fitting . . . decent . . .
is to be your last." With a twist of his shoulders, he
shrugged off her superb arms. "After all, what I am
saying to you now is for your own good."

"I understand perfectly. You think only of me. I
think only of your fiancée. That's all very nice, all very
natural. It's clear that we both have hearts of gold."

She rose, waiting for some outrageous rejoinder. But

he said nothing, and it hurt her to see for the first time a look of discouragement on his face.

She bent over and put her hands under his armpits.

"Now then, come along, get your clothes on. I've only to put on my dress, I'm ready underneath, and what in the world is there to do on a day like this except to go to Schwabe and choose a pearl for you? You see, I must give you a wedding-present."

He jumped up, his face aglow: "Top-hole! A pearl for my shirt-front! A pale pink pearl. I know the very one!"

"Not on your life! A white one, something masculine for pity's sake! Don't tell me, I know which one just as well as you. It'll ruin me, as usual. However, think of the money I'm going to save when you're out of the way!"

Chéri adopted a more reticent attitude. "Oh, that . . . that depends on my successor."

Léa turned back at the door of her boudoir and gave him her gayest smile, showing her strong teeth and the fresh blue of her eyes skilfully darkened by bistre.

"Your successor? A couple of francs and a packet of cigarettes! And a glass of cassis on Sunday—that's all the job will be worth! And I'll settle money on your children."

THEY both became extremely gay for the next few weeks. Chéri's official duties as a fiancé separated them for a few hours each day, sometimes for a night or two. "We mustn't let them lose confidence," Chéri declared. Léa, kept by Madame Peloux at a safe distance from Neuilly, satisfied her curiosity by plying Chéri with a hundred questions. Whenever he came back to Léa's house, he was full of his own importance and heavy with secrets which he at once divulged. He was like a schoolboy playing truant.

"Oh my sainted aunt!" he shouted one day, cramming his hat down on Léa's portrait-bust. "The goings-on at the Peloux Palace Hôtel ever since yesterday!"

She began by scolding him, laughing already in anticipation.

"Take your hat off that, in the first place. And in the second, don't invoke your wretched aunt in my house. Well, what's been happening now?"

"A riot, Nounoune! A riot's broken out among the ladies. Marie-Laure and Ma'me Peloux are scratching each other's eyes out over the marriage settlement!"

"No!"

"Yes! It was a superb sight. (Look out for the olives. . . . I'm going to impersonate Ma'me Peloux as a windmill. . . .) 'Separate bank accounts! Separate bank accounts! Why not a trustee? It's a personal insult, a personal insult. You forget that my son has his own fortune! . . . May I inform you, Madame . . .' "

"She called her Madame?"

"She most certainly did. 'Let me tell you, Madame, that my son has never had a ha'porth of debts since he came of age and the list of his investments bought since 1910 is worth . . .' is worth this, that and the other, including the skin off my nose, plus the fat off my bottom. In short, Catherine de Medici in person! But even more artful, of course!"

Léa's blue eyes glistened with tears of merriment. "Oh Chéri! you've never been funnier in your life! What about the other? The fair Marie-Laure?"

"Her? Oh! terrible, Nounoune. That woman must have at least a dozen corpses in her wake. Dolled up in jade green, red hair, painted to look eighteen, and the inevitable smile. The trumpetings of my revered Mamma failed to make her bat an eyelid. She held her fire till the assault was over, then she came out with: 'It might perhaps be wiser, dear Madame, not to talk too loudly about all the money your son put by in 1910 and the years following. . . .' "

"Bang! Straight between the eyes! . . . Between yours. Where were you while all this was going on?"

"Me? In the large armchair."

"You were actually in the room?" She stopped laughing, and eating. "You were there? What did you do?"

"Cracked a joke, of course. Ma'me Peloux had just seized hold of a valuable piece of bric-à-brac, to avenge my honour, when I stopped her without even getting up. 'My adored mother, calm yourself. Follow my example, follow that of my charming mother-in-law, who's being as sweet as honey . . . as sweet as sugar.'

And that's how I managed to arrange that the settlement should apply only to property acquired after marriage."

"I simply don't understand."

"The famous sugar plantations that the poor little Prince Ceste left to Marie-Laure by his will. . . ."

"Yes?"

"Forged will! Fury of the Ceste family! Lawsuit pending! Now d'you get it?"

He crowed.

"I get it. But how did you get hold of the story?"

"Ah! I'll tell you! Old Lili has just pounced with her full weight upon the younger of the Ceste boys, who's only seventeen and religious. . . ."

"Old Lili? What a nightmare!"

"And he babbles family secrets in her ear between every kiss. . . ."

"Chéri! I feel sick!"

"And old Lili tipped me off at Mamma's At Home last Sunday. She simply adores me! Besides, she respects me because I've never wanted to go to bed with her. . . ."

"I should hope not!" Léa sighed. "Yet all the same . . ." She broke off to reflect, and it seemed to Chéri her enthusiasm was flagging.

"Well, you must say it was pretty smart of me, eh?"

He leaned across the table; and the sunshine, playing over the silver and the white table-cloth, lit him up like a row of footlights.

"Yes . . ." 'All the same,' she was thinking, 'that poisonous Marie-Laure simply treated him like a ponce . . .'

"Is there any cream cheese, Nounoune?"

"Yes . . ." ' . . . and he showed no more surprise than if she had thrown him a flower. . . .'

"Nounoune, will you let me have that address? the address of the place where you get your cream cheese—for the new cook I've engaged for October?"

"Are you mad? It's home-made. I *have* a cook, you know. Think of the *sauce aux moules* and *vol-au-vent*!"

'. . . it's true I've practically kept the boy for the last five years. . . . But all the same he has an income of three hundred thousand francs a year. That's the point. Can you be a ponce with three hundred thousand a year? But why ever not? It doesn't depend on the amount, but on the man. . . . There are some men I could have given half a million to, and that wouldn't make them a ponce. But how about Chéri? After all, I have never actually given him any money. All the same . . .'

"All the same," she broke into speech. "She treated you like a gigolo!"

"Who did?"

"Marie-Laure!"

He brightened at once, like a child.

"Didn't she? Didn't she just, Nounoune? That's what she meant, wasn't it?"

"So it seems to me."

Chéri raised his glass of Château-Chalon, almost the colour of brandy. "So here's to Marie-Laure! What a compliment, eh? And if anyone can still say it of me when I'm your age, I shan't ask anything better!"

"If that's enough to make you happy . . ."

She listened to him absent-mindedly till the end of luncheon. Accustomed to her half-silences and her worldly wisdom, he asked for nothing better than the usual maternal homilies—"Take the brownest crusts. Don't eat so much new bread. . . . You've never learnt how to choose a fruit. . . ." All the time, secretly disgruntled, she was reproaching herself, 'I must make up my mind

what I want! What would I really have liked him to do?
Get up on his hind legs and hiss "Madame, you have
insulted me! Madame, I am not what you take me for!"
I'm responsible, when all's said and done. I've spoon-fed
him, I've stuffed him with good things. . . . Who in the
world would have thought that one day he'd want to
play the paterfamilias? It never occurred to me! Even
supposing it had—as Patron would say, "Nature will out."
Even supposing Patron had accepted Liane's proposals,
his nature would have come out all right if anyone had
hinted at the fact in his hearing. But Chéri . . . has
Chéri's nature. He's just Chéri. He's . . .'

"What were you saying, child?" she interrupted her
thoughts to ask. "I wasn't listening."

"I was saying that never again—never, do you hear
me—will anything make me laugh so much as my
scene with Marie-Laure!"

—'There you are,' Léa concluded her thoughts,
'it . . . it merely made him laugh.'

Slowly she rose to her feet, as though tired. Chéri put
an arm round her waist, but she pushed it away.

"What day is your wedding to be, now I come to
think of it?"

"Monday week."

His candour and detachment terrified her. "That's
fantastic!"

"Why fantastic, Nounoune?"

"You don't look as if you were giving it a thought!"

"I'm not," he said, calmly. "Everything's been
arranged. Ceremony at two o'clock, saving us all the fuss
and rush of a wedding breakfast. Instead, a tea party
at Ma'me Peloux's. After that, sleepers, Italy, the
Lakes. . . ."

"Are the Lakes back in fashion?"

"They are. There'll be villas, hotels, motor-drives, restaurants, like Monte-Carlo, eh?"

"But the girl! There's always the girl. . . ."

"Of course there's the girl. She's not much, but she's there!"

"And I'm no longer there."

Chéri had not expected her to say this and showed it. His face became disfigured, and he suddenly turned white about the mouth. He controlled his breath to avoid an audible gasp, and became himself again.

"Nounoune, you'll always be there."

"Monsieur overwhelms me."

"There'll always be you, Nounoune . . ." and he laughed awkwardly, "whenever I need you to do something for me."

She did not answer. She bent to pick up a tortoiseshell comb that had fallen to the floor and pushed it back in her hair, humming to herself. She went on humming a little snatch of a song in front of a looking-glass, pleased with herself, proud of having kept her self-control so easily, covered up so successfully the only emotional moment of their separation, proud of having held back words that must never be said: "Speak . . . beg for what you want, demand it, put your arms round my neck. . . . You have suddenly made me happy. . . ."

MADAME PELOUX must have been talking a great deal and for a long time before Léa appeared. The high colour on her cheeks emphasised the sparkle of her large eyes, which expressed only an indiscreet and inscrutable watchfulness. This Sunday she was wearing a black afternoon dress with a very narrow skirt, and nobody could fail to have observed that her feet were tiny and her stays too tight. She stopped talking, took a little sip from the petal-thin brandy glass warming in her hand, and nodded at Léa in lazy contentment.

"Isn't it a lovely day? Such weather, such weather! Would any one believe we're in the middle of October?"

"Oh, no, never. . . . Most certainly not!" two obsequious voices answered in chorus.

Beside the curving garden path a stream of red salvias wound between the banks of grey-mauve Michaelmas daisies. Golden butterflies flitted as if it were summer and the scent of chrysanthemums, strengthened by the hot sun, was wafted into the garden-room. A yellowing birch tree trembled in the wind above beds of tea roses, where the last of the bees still were busy.

"But what's this weather," yelled Madame Peloux, suddenly waxing lyrical, "but what's this weather, when compared to what *they* must be having in Italy?"

"Yes, indeed! . . . Just what I was thinking!" the attendant voices echoed.

Léa turned with a frown in their direction. 'If only they would hold their tongues,' she thought.

The Baroness de la Berche and Madame Aldonza were sitting at a card-table, playing piquet. Madame Aldonza, an aged ballerina, with legs eternally swathed in bandages, was distorted with rheumatism, and wore her shiny black wig a little askew. Opposite her, a head or more taller, the Baroness squared her rigid shoulders like a country priest's. Her face was large and had grown alarmingly masculine with age. She was a bristling bush of hair—hair in her ears, tufts in her nostrils and on her lip, and rough hairs between her fingers.

"Baroness, don't forget I made ninety," Madame Aldonza bleated like a goat.

"Score it, score it, my good friend! All I want is to see everyone happy."

An endless flow of honied words masked her savage cruelty. Léa looked at her closely as if for the first time, felt disgusted, and turned back to Madame Peloux. 'Charlotte, at least, *looks* human,' she thought.

"What's the matter with you, my Léa? You don't seem your usual self?" Madame Peloux enquired tenderly.

Léa drew up her handsome figure and answered: "Of course I am, Lolotte dear . . . it's so comfortable here in your house, I was merely relaxing," thinking all the while, 'Careful now . . . she's just as cruel as the other,' and she at once assumed an expression of flattering contentment, of dreamy repletion, and accentuated it by sighing, "I lunched too well. . . . I really must get thinner. I shall start a strict diet from to-morrow."

Madame Peloux flapped her hands and simpered.

"Isn't a broken heart enough to do that?"

"Oh, oh, oh! Ha-ha! Ho-ho!" guffawed Madame Aldonza and the Baroness de la Berche. "Ha-ha-ha!"

Léa rose to her full height in her autumn dress of sombre green, handsome under her satin hat trimmed with seal-skin, youthful among these old ruins over whom she cast a gentle eye. "Oh, la-la, my dears! Give me a dozen such heart-breaks, if that would help me to lose a couple of pounds!"

"Léa, you're astounding," the old baroness shot at her in a puff of smoke. "Madame Léa, think of me, please, when you throw away that hat," old Madame Aldonza begged. "Madame Charlotte, you remember your blue one? It lasted me two years. Baroness, when you've quite finished ogling Madame Léa, perhaps you'll be kind enough to deal the cards to me."

"Very well, my sweet, and may they bring you luck!"

Léa stopped for a moment by the door, then stepped out into the garden. She picked a tea rose, which shed its petals. She listened to the breeze in the birch, to the trams in the Avenue, to the whistle of the local train. The bench she sat on was warm, and she closed her eyes, letting her shoulders enjoy the warmth of the sun. When she opened her eyes again, she hurriedly turned her head in the direction of the house, feeling positive that she was going to see Chéri standing in the garden entrance with his shoulder against the doorway.

'What can be the matter with me?' she wondered. Piercing screams of laughter and a little chorus of greeting from indoors brought her, trembling slightly, to her feet. 'Can I be suffering from nerves?'

"Ah, here they are, here they are!" Madame Peloux trumpeted, and the deep bass of the Baroness chimed in "Here come the happy pair!"

Léa shivered, ran as far as the door and stopped short: there, in front of her, were old Lili and her adolescent lover, Prince Ceste, just arriving.

Perhaps seventy years of age, with the corpulence of a eunuch held in by stays, old Lili was usually referred to as 'passing all bounds', without these 'bounds' being defined. Her round pink painted face was enlivened by a ceaseless girlish gaiety, and her large eyes and small mouth, thin-lipped and shrunken, flirted shamelessly. Old Lili followed the fashion to an outrageous degree. A strik-ing blue-and-white striped skirt held in the lower part of her body, and a little blue jersey gaped over her skinny bosom crinkled like the wattles of a turkey-cock; a silver fox failed to conceal the neck, which was the shape of a flower-pot and the size of a belly. It had engulfed the chin.

'It's terrifying,' Léa thought. She was unable to tear her eyes away from details that were particularly sinister —a white sailor hat, for instance, girlishly perched on the back of a short-cut, strawberry-roan wig; or, again, a pearl necklace visible one moment and the next interred in a deep ravine which once had been termed a "*collier de Vénus*".

"Léa, Léa, my little chickabiddy!" old Lili exclaimed as she did her best to hasten towards Léa. She walked with difficulty on round swollen feet, tightly swaddled in high-heeled laced boots with paste buckles on the ankle-straps, and was the first to congratulate herself on this performance: "I waddle like a duckling! it is a special little way I have. Guido, my passion, you remem-ber Madame de Lonval? Don't remember her too well or I'll tear your eyes out. . . ."

A slim youth with Italian features, enormous empty eyes and a weak receding chin, kissed Léa's hand hastily and retired into the shadows without a word. Lili caught him in flight, pulled his head down to her scaly chest, calling the onlookers to witness: "Do you know what this is, Madame, do you know what this is? This, ladies, is the love of my life!"

"Restrain yourself, Lili!" Madame de la Berche advised in her masculine voice.

"But why? But why?" from Charlotte Peloux.

"For the sake of decency," said the Baroness.

"Baroness, that's not nice of you! I think they're so sweet. Ah!" she sighed, "they remind me of my own children."

"I was thinking of them," Lili said, with a delighted smile. "It's our honeymoon too, Guido's and mine. Indeed, we've just come to ask about the other young couple! We want to hear all about them."

Madame Peloux became stern. "Lili, you don't expect me to go into details, do you?"

"Oh yes, yes, I do," Lili cried, clapping her hands. She tried to skip, but succeeded only in raising her shoulders and hips a little. "That's always been my besetting sin, and always will be! I adore spicy talk! I'll never be cured of it. That little wretch there knows how I adore it."

The silent youth, called to bear witness, did not open his mouth. The black pupils of his eyes moved up and down against the whites, like frantic insects. Léa watched him, rooted to the spot.

"Madame Charlotte told us all about the wedding ceremony," bleated Madame Aldonza. "The young Madame Peloux was a dream in her wreath of orange-blossom!"

"A madonna! A madonna!" Madame Peloux corrected at the top of her voice, with a burst of religious fervour. "Never, never, has anyone looked so divine. My son was in heaven! In heaven, I tell you! . . . What a pair they made, what a pair!"

"You hear that, my passion? Orange blossom!"
Lili murmured. "And tell me, Charlotte, what about
our mother-in-law, Marie-Laure?"

Madame Peloux's pitiless eyes sparkled: "Oh her!
Out of place, absolutely out of place. In tight-fitting
black, like an eel wriggling out of the water—you could
see everything, breasts, stomach—everything!"

"By Jove!" muttered the Baroness de la Berche with
military gusto.

"And that look of contempt she has for everybody,
that look of having a dose of cyanide up her sleeve and
half a pint of chloroform inside her handbag! As I said,
out of place—that exactly describes her. She behaved
as if she could only spare us five minutes of her precious
time—she'd hardly brushed the kiss off her lips, before
she said, 'Au revoir, Edmée, au revoir, Fred,' and off
she flew."

Old Lili was breathing hard, sitting on the edge of her
chair, her little grandmotherly mouth, with its puckered
corners, hanging half open. "And who gave the usual
advice?" she threw out.

"What advice?"

"The little talk—oh, my passion, hold my hand while
I say it!—instruction for the young bride. Who gave her
that?"

Charlotte Peloux took offence and stared at her.
"Things may well have been done in that way when you
were young, but the practice has fallen into disuse."

The sprightly old girl plumped her fists on her thighs:
"Disuse? Disuse or not, how would you know anything
about it, my poor Charlotte? There's so little marrying
in your family!"

"Ha-ha-ha!" the two toadies imprudently guffawed.
But a single glance from Madame Peloux made them

tremble. "Peace, peace, my little angels! You're each enjoying your paradise on earth, so what more do you want?" The Baroness stretched out a strong arm, like a policeman keeping order, between the purple faces of Lili and Madame Peloux. But Charlotte scented battle like a war-horse. "If you're looking for trouble, Lili, you don't have to look further than me! Because of your age, I must treat you with respect, and if it weren't for that . . ."

Lili shook with laughter from chin to thigh. "If it weren't for that, you'd get married yourself just to give me the lie? I know—it's not so hard to get married! Why, I'd marry Guido like a shot, if only he were of age!"

"Not possible!" gasped Charlotte, so taken aback that she forgot her anger.

"But, of course . . . Princess Ceste, my dear! *la piccola principessa! Piccola principessa,* that's what my little Prince always calls me!"

She nipped hold of her skirt, and, in turning, displayed a gold curb-chain where her ankle ought to have been. "Only," she continued mysteriously, "his father . . ."

By now out of breath, she made a sign to the silent young man, who took up the tale in a low rapid voice as if he were reciting his piece: "My father, the Duke of Parese, threatens to put me in a convent if I marry Lili."

"In a convent!" Charlotte Peloux squealed. "A man in a convent!"

"A man in a convent!" neighed Madame de la Berche in her deep bass, "Egad! if that isn't exciting!"

"They're barbarians," Aldonza lamented, joining her misshapen hands together.

Léa rose so abruptly that she upset a glass.

"It's uncoloured glass," Madame Peloux observed

with satisfaction. "You'll bring good luck to my young couple. Where are you running off to? Is your house on fire?"

Léa managed to squeeze out a sly little laugh: "On fire? In a sense, perhaps. Ssh! no questions! It's a secret."

"What? Already? It's not possible!" Charlotte Peloux cheeped enviously. "I was just saying to myself that you looked as if . . ."

"Yes, yes! You must tell us! Tell us everything," yapped the three old women.

Lili's quilted fists, old Aldonza's deformed stumps, Charlotte Peloux's hard fingers had seized upon her wrist, her sleeve, her gold-mesh bag. She snatched her arm away from all these claws and succeeded in laughing again, teasingly: "No, it's far too early in the day, it would spoil everything! It's my secret." And she rushed away to the hall.

But the door opened in front of her and a desiccated old fellow, a sort of playful mummy, took her into his arms: "Léa, lovely creature, a kiss for your little Berthellemy, or he won't let you pass!"

She gave a cry of fright and impatience, struck off the gloved bones retarding her progress, and fled.

Neither in the avenues of Neuilly, nor on the roads through the Bois, turning to blue in the fast-falling twilight, did she allow herself a moment's reflection. She shivered slightly and pulled up the windows of the motor-car. She felt restored by the sight of her clean house, the comfort of her pink bedroom and boudoir, overcrowded with furniture and flowers.

"Quick, Rose, light the fire in my room!"

"But, Madame, the pipes are already at their winter temperature. Madame should not have gone out with only a fur round her neck. The evenings are treacherous."

"A hot-water bottle in my bed at once, and for dinner a cup of thick chocolate beaten up with the yolk of an egg, some toast, and a bunch of grapes. . . . Hurry, dear, I'm freezing. I caught cold in that junk-shop at Neuilly. . . ."

Once under the sheets, she clenched her teeth to stop them chattering. The warmth of the bed eased her stiffened muscles, but still she did not altogether relax, and she went through the chauffeur's expense book till the chocolate arrived. This she drank at once, frothy and scalding. She chose her *chasselas* grapes one by one, the long greenish-amber bunch dangling by its stem against the light.

Then she turned out the bedside lamp, settled herself in her favourite position, flat on her back, and gave way.

'What can be the matter with me?'

She succumbed again to anxiety and started to shiver. She was obsessed by the vision of an empty doorway, with clumps of red salvia on either side. 'I can't be well,' she thought, 'one doesn't get into a state like this over a door!' Again she saw the three old women, Lili's neck, and the beige rug that Madame Aldonza had trailed about with her for the past twenty years. 'Which of them am I going to look like in ten years' time?'

Though she did not feel alarmed at this prospect, her anxiety increased still further. She let her mind wander from one incident of her past life to another, from this scene to that, trying to rid her thoughts of the empty doorway framed by red salvia. She was growing restless in her bed and trembled slightly. Suddenly she jumped as though shot, racked by a pain so deep that at first she thought it must be physical, a pain that twisted her lips and dragged from them, in a raucous sob, a single name: "Chéri!"

Tears followed, beyond all control at first. As soon as she had regained her self-control, she sat up, wiped her face, and turned on the lamp again. 'Ah! That's what it is! Now I understand!'

She took a thermometer from the drawer of her bedside table and put it under her arm. 'My temperature's normal, so it's nothing physical. I see. I'm just unhappy. Something must be done about it.'

She drank some water, got out of bed, bathed her inflamed eyes, put on a little powder, poked the fire, and went back to bed. She was on her guard, full of mistrust for an enemy she had never known: grief. She had just said goodbye to thirty years of easy living: years spent pleasantly, intent often on love, sometimes on money. This had left her, at almost fifty, still young and defenceless.

She made fun of herself, ceased to feel her grief, and smiled. 'I think I was out of my mind just now. There's nothing wrong with me any longer.'

But a movement of her left arm, which bent automatically to hold and shelter a sleeping head, brought back all her agony, and she sat up with a jump. "Well, this *is* going to be fun!" she said out loud and sternly.

She looked at the clock and saw that it was barely eleven. Overhead passed the slippered tread of the elderly Rose, on her way up the stairs to the attic floor. Then there was silence. Léa resisted the impulse to call out for help to this deferential old body. 'Don't give the servants anything to gossip about. We mustn't have that.'

She left her bed again, wrapped herself up warm in a

quilted silk dressing-gown and toasted her feet. Then she
half opened her window and listened for she knew not
what. A moist and milder wind had brought clouds in
its wake, and the lingering leaves in the neighbouring
Bois sighed with every gust. Léa shut the window again,
picked up a newspaper and looked at the date—'October
the twenty-sixth. Exactly a month since Chéri was
married?' She never said 'Since Edmée was married.'

Following Chéri's example, she did not yet count his
young wraith of a wife as really alive. Chestnut-brown
eyes, ashy hair which was very lovely with the vestige
of a crimp in it—all the rest melted away in her
memory like the contours of a face seen in a dream.

'At this very moment, of course, they'll be in each
other's arms in Italy. And . . . and I don't mind that in
the least.'

She was not boasting. The picture of the young couple
she had called up, the familiar attitudes it evoked—even
Chéri's face, as he lay exhausted for a minute, with the
white line of light between his tired eyelids—aroused in
her neither curiosity nor jealousy. On the other hand,
an animal convulsion again racked her body, bending her
double, as her eye fell on a nick in the pearl-grey wainscot
—the mark of some brutality of Chéri's. "The lovely
hand which here has left its trace, has turned away from
me for ever," she said. 'How grandly I'm talking! Soon
grief will be turning me into a poet!'

She walked about, she sat down, she went to bed again
and waited for daylight. At eight o'clock Rose found her
writing at her desk, and this upset the old lady's-maid.

"Is Madame not well?"

"So-so, Rose. Age, you know. . . . Doctor Vidal
thinks I ought to have a change of air. Will you come
with me? It promises to be a cold winter here in Paris.

We'll go south to the sun, and eat meals cooked in oil."

"Whereabouts will that be?"

"You want to know too much. Simply have my trunks brought down, and give my fur rugs a good beating."

"Madame will be taking the motor-car?"

"I think so. I'm sure of it, in fact. I'll need all my creature comforts now, Rose. Just think of it, this time I'm going all on my own. It's going to be a pleasure trip."

During the next five days Léa rushed all over Paris; wrote, telegraphed, and received telegrams and answers from the south. And she said goodbye to Paris, leaving behind a short letter addressed to Madame Peloux which she started no less than three times:

> *My dear Charlotte,*
>
> *You'll forgive me if I go away without saying goodbye to you, and keep my little secret to myself. I'm making a perfect fool of myself . . . and why not? It's a short life, let's make it a gay one.*
>
> *I send you an affectionate kiss. Remember me to the child when he comes back.*
>
> > *Your incorrigible*
> > *Léa.*
>
> *PS.—Don't trouble to come and interview my butler or concierge; no member of my household knows anything at all about it.*

"Do you know, my adored treasure, I don't think you're looking very well."

"It's the night in the train," Chéri answered shortly.

Madame Peloux did not dare to say just what she thought. She found her son changed. 'He's . . . yes, he's sinister!' she decided; and she ended by exclaiming enthusiastically, "It's Italy!"

"If you like," Chéri conceded.

Mother and son had just finished breakfasting together, and Chéri had condescended to praise with an oath his cup of "housemaid's coffee", made with creamy milk, well sugared, slowly re-heated, with buttered toast crumbled into it and browned till it formed a succulent crust.

He felt cold in his white woollen pyjamas and was clasping his knees to his chest. Charlotte Peloux, anxious to look pretty for her son, had put on a brand new marigold négligée, and a boudoir-cap fitting tight across the forehead. This made her face stand out, bare and macabre.

Finding her son's eye fixed upon her, she simpered: "You see, I've adopted the grandmother style. Very soon, I'll powder my hair. Do you like this cap? Rather eighteenth-century, don't you think? Dubarry or Pompadour? How do I look in it?"

"Like an old convict," Chéri said witheringly. "Next time you must run up a warning signal."

She groaned, then shrieked with laughter: "Ha-ha-ha. You've a sharp tongue in your head and no mistake!"

But he did not laugh. He was staring out at the lawn powdered with snow after last night's fall. His nervous state was visible only in the spasmodic twitching of his jaw muscles. Madame Peloux was intimidated. She, too, was silent. The faint tinkle of a bell sounded.

"That's Edmée, ringing for her breakfast," said Madame Peloux.

Chéri did not answer. "What's wrong with the heating? It's freezing in here!" he said a moment later.

"It's Italy!" Madame Peloux repeated lyrically. "You come back here, your eyes and your heart full of the warm sun of the south, and find you've landed at the Pole—at the North Pole. There hasn't been a flower on the dahlias for the last week. But don't worry, my precious! Your love-nest will soon be finished. If the architect hadn't gone down with paratyphoid, it would be ready for you now. I warned him. If I told him once, I told him twenty times: 'Monsieur Savaron . . . ' "

Chéri, who was standing by the window, turned round sharply. "What was the date on that letter?"

Madame Peloux opened her large child-like eyes: "What letter?"

"The letter from Léa you showed me."

"She put no date on it, my love; but I got it the night before my last Sunday At-home in October."

"I see. And you don't know who it is?"

"Who what is, my paragon?"

"Whoever it was she went away with, of course."

Malice clothed Madame Peloux's stark features. "No. Would you believe it, nobody has an idea! Old Lili is in

Sicily, and none of my set has a clue! A mystery, an
enthralling mystery! However, you know me, I've
managed to pick up a few scraps here and there . . . "

Chéri's dark eyes expanded: "What's the tattle?"

"It seems it's a young man . . ." Madame Peloux
whispered. "A young man not . . . not particularly
desirable, if you know what I mean . . . very well made,
of course!" She was lying, careful to insinuate the worst.

Chéri shrugged his shoulders.

"Well made, did you say. Don't make me laugh! My
poor Léa! I can see him from here—a hefty little fellow
from Patron's training-quarters—black hairs on his
wrists and clammy hands. . . . Well, I'm going back to
bed now; you make me tired."

Trailing his bedroom slippers, he went back to his
room, dawdling in the long corridors and on the spacious
landings of the house he seemed to be discovering for the
first time. He ran into a pot-bellied wardrobe, and was
amazed. 'Damned if I knew that thing was there. . . . Oh,
yes, I vaguely remember. . . . And who the devil's this
chap?' He was addressing an enlarged photograph, in a
deep black frame, hanging funereally near a piece of
coloured pottery, equally unfamiliar to Chéri.

Madame Peloux had been installed in this house for
the last twenty-five years, and had kept every unfortunate
result of her bad taste and acquisitiveness. "Your house
looks just like the nest of a magpie gone batty," was
old Lili's reproachful comment. She herself had a hearty
appetite for modern pictures, and still more for modern
painters. To this Madame Peloux had replied: "I believe
in letting well alone."

If the muddy green paint—"The green of hospital
corridors," Léa called it—flaked off in one of the passages,
Madame Peloux would have it repainted a similar muddy

green; or if the maroon velvet on a *chaise-longue* needed replacing, she was careful to choose the same maroon velvet.

Chéri paused by the open door of a dressing-room. Embedded in the dark red marble-topped wash-stand were jug and basin of plain white with a monogram, and over the two electric-light fittings were lily-shaped bead shades. Chéri shuddered as though caught in a violent draught—'Good God, how hideous, what an old junk-shop!'

He hurried away. At the end of the passage, he came upon a window edged with small pieces of red and yellow stained glass. 'That's the last straw!' he said grumpily.

He turned to the left and roughly opened a door—the door of his nursery—without knocking. A little cry came from the bed where Edmée was just finishing her breakfast. Chéri closed the door and stared at his wife without going any closer.

"Good morning," she said with a smile. "You do look surprised to see me here!"

She lay bathed in a steady blue light reflected from the snow outside. Her crimped ashy chestnut hair was down, but barely covered her prettily curved shoulders. With her pink-and-white cheeks matching her nightgown, and her rosy lips paler than usual from fatigue, she looked like a light toned picture, not quite finished and rather misty.

"Aren't you going to say good morning to me, Fred?" she insisted.

He sat down close beside his wife and took her in his arms. She fell back gently, dragging him with her. Chéri propped himself on his elbow to look down more closely at her. She was so young that even when tired she still looked fresh. He seemed astonished by the smoothness of her fully rounded lower eyelids, and by the silvery softness of her cheeks.

"How old are you?" he asked suddenly.

Edmée opened her eyes, which she had closed voluptuously. Chéri stared at the brown of their pupils and at her small square teeth.

"Oh, come! I shall be nineteen on the fifth of January, and do try and remember it."

He drew his arm away roughly and the young woman slipped into the hollow of the bed like a discarded scarf.

"Nineteen, it's prodigious! Do you know that I'm over twenty-five?"

"But of course I know that, Fred. . . ."

He picked up a pale tortoiseshell mirror from the bed-table and gazed at himself. "Twenty-five years old!"

Twenty-five years of age and a face of white marble that seemed indestructible. Twenty-five, but at the outer corners of the eye and beneath it—delicately plagiarising the classical design of the eyelid—were two lines, visible only in full light, two incisions traced by the lightest, the most relentless, of fingers.

He put back the mirror: "You're younger than I am. That shocks me."

"Not me!"

She had answered in a biting voice. full of hidden meaning. He took no notice.

"Do you know why my eyes are beautiful?" he asked in all seriousness.

"No," Edmée said. "Perhaps because I love them?"

"Stuff!" Chéri said, shrugging his shoulders. "It's because they're shaped like a sole."

"Like what?"

"Like a sole."

He sat down near her to give a demonstration.

"Look—here—the corner next the nose is the head of the sole. And then—the upper curve, that's the back of the sole; whereas the lower line runs perfectly straight and that's its belly. And the other corner that tapers up to my temples, that's the sole's tail."

"Oh?"

"Yes, but if I had an eye shaped like a flounder, that's to say, with the lower part as much curved as the top, then I should look silly. See? You've passed your matric., and you didn't know that?"

"No, I must admit . . ."

She broke off, feeling guilty, because he had spoken sententiously and with exaggerated passion, like someone with a mania. 'There are moments when he looks like a savage,' she thought, 'like a man from the jungle. Yet he knows nothing about plants or animals, and sometimes he doesn't seem even to know about human beings.'

Sitting close beside her, Chéri put one arm round her shoulders and with his free hand began to finger the small, evenly matched, very round and very beautiful, pearls of her necklace. Intoxicated by the scent which Chéri used too much of, she began to droop like a rose in an overheated room.

"Fred! Come back to sleep! We're both tired. . . ."

He seemed not to have heard. He was staring at the pearls with obsessed anxiety.

"Fred!"

He shivered, leaped to his feet, furiously tore off his pyjamas and jumped naked into bed, seeking the place to rest his head on a shoulder where the delicate collar-bone was still youthfully sharp. The whole of Edmée's body obeyed his will as she opened her arms to him. Chéri closed his eyes and never moved. She took care to remain

awake, a little smothered under his weight, and thinking
him asleep. But almost at once he turned over away from
her with a sudden pitch, imitating the groans of someone
fast asleep, and rolled himself up in the sheet at the other
side of the bed.

'He always does that,' Edmée noted.

All through the winter, she was to awaken in this
square room with its four windows. Bad weather delayed
the completion of the new house in the Avenue Henri-
Martin—bad weather, and Chéri's whims. He wanted a
black bathroom, a Chinese drawing-room, a basement
fitted up with a swimming pool and gymnasium. To the
architect's objections he would answer: "I don't care a
damn. I pay, I want the work done. To hell with the
cost." But every now and again he would cast a ruthless
eye over an estimate and proclaim "You can't bamboozle
young Peloux." Indeed, he held forth on standardisa-
tion, fibro-cement and coloured stucco with unexpected
glibness and a memory for exact figures that compelled
the contractor's respect.

Rarely did he consult his young wife, although he
paraded his authority for her benefit and took pains,
when occasion arose, to cover his deficiencies by giving
curt commands. She was to find that he possessed an
instinctive eye for colour, but had only contempt for
beauty of shape and period differences.

"You simply clutter up your head with all that stuff
and nonsense, what's your name, yes, you, Edmée.
An idea for the smoking-room? All right, here's one:
Blue for the walls—a ferocious blue. The carpet purple
—a purple that plays second fiddle to the blue of the

walls. Against that you needn't be afraid of using as much black as you like and a splash of gold in the furniture and ornaments."

"Yes, you're right, Fred. But it will be rather drastic with all those strong colours. It's going to look rather charmless without a lighter note somewhere . . . a white vase or a statue."

"Nonsense," he interrupted, rather sharply. "The white vase you want will be me—me, stark naked. And we mustn't forget a cushion or some thingumabob in pumpkin-red for when I'm running about stark naked in the smoking-room."

Secretly attracted and at the same time disgusted, she cherished these fanciful ideas for turning their future home into a sort of disreputable palace, a temple to the greater glory of her husband. She offered little resistance, just gently requested "some little corner" for a small and precious set of furniture upholstered with needle-work on a white ground—a present from Marie-Laure.

This gentleness masked a determination that was young yet far from inexperienced; it stood her in good stead during the four months of camping out in her mother-in-law's house. It enabled her to evade, throughout these four months, the enemy stalking her, the traps laid daily to destroy her equanimity, her still susceptible gaiety, and her tact. Charlotte Peloux, over-excited at the proximity of so tender a victim, was inclined to lose her head and squander her barbs, using her claws indiscriminately.

"Keep calm, Madame Peloux," Chéri would throw out from time to time. "What bones will there be left for you to pick next winter, if I don't stop you now?"

Edmée raised frightened, grateful eyes to her husband, and did her best not to think too much, not to look too much at Madame Peloux. Then one evening, Charlotte, almost heedlessly, three times tossed across the chrysanthemum table-piece Léa's name instead of Edmée's.

Chéri lowered his satanic eyebrows: "Madame Peloux, I believe your memory is giving way. Perhaps a rest-cure is indicated?"

Charlotte Peloux held her tongue for a whole week, but Edmée never dared to ask her husband: "Did you get angry on my behalf? Was it me you were defending? Or was it that other woman, the one before me?"

Life as a child and then as a girl had taught her patience, hope, silence; and given her a prisoner's proficiency in handling these virtues as weapons. The fair Marie-Laure had never scolded her daughter: she had merely punished her. Never a hard word, never a tender one. Utter loneliness, then a boarding-school, then again loneliness in the holidays and frequent relegations to a bedroom. Finally, the threat of marriage—any marriage—from the moment that the eye of a too beautiful mother had discerned in the daughter the dawn of a rival beauty, shy, timid, looking a victim of tyranny, and all the more touching for that. In comparison with this inhuman gold-and-ivory mother, Charlotte Peloux and her spontaneous malice seemed a bed of roses.

"Are you frightened of my respected parent?" Chéri asked her one evening.

Edmée smiled and pouted to show her indifference: "Frightened? No. You aren't frightened when a door slams, though it may make you jump. It's a snake creeping under it that's frightening."

"A terrific snake, Marie-Laure, isn't she?"

"Terrific."

He waited for confidences that did not come and put

a brotherly arm round his wife's slender shoulders: "We're sort of orphans, you and I, aren't we?"

"Yes, we're orphans, and we're so sweet!"

She clung to him. They were alone in the big sitting-room, for Madame Peloux was upstairs concocting, as Chéri put it, her poisons for the following day. The night was cold and the window panes reflected the lamp-light and furnishings like a pond. Edmée felt warm and protected, safe in the arms of this unknown man. She lifted her head and gave a cry of alarm. He was staring up at the chandelier above them with a look of despera-tion on his magnificent features, and two tears hung glistening between the lids of his half-closed eyes.

"Chéri, Chéri, what's the matter with you?" On the spur of the moment she had called him by the too en-dearing nickname she had never meant to pronounce. He answered its appeal in bewilderment and turned his eyes down to look at her.

"Chéri, oh God! I'm frightened. What's wrong with you?"

He pushed her away a little, and held her facing him. "Oh! Oh! You poor child, you poor little thing! What are you frightened of?"

He gazed at her with his eyes of velvet, wide-open, peaceful, inscrutable, all the more handsome for his tears. Edmée was about to beg him not to speak, when he said, "How silly we are! It's the idea that we're orphans. It's idiotic. It's so true."

He resumed his air of comic self-importance, and she drew a breath of relief, knowing that he would say no more. He began switching off all the lights with his usual care, and then turned to Edmée with a vanity that was either very simple or very deceitful: "Well, why shouldn't I have a heart like everybody else?"

"WHAT are you doing there?"

He had called out to her almost in a whisper, yet the sound of Chéri's voice struck Edmée so forcibly that she swayed forward as if he had pushed her. She was standing beside a big open writing-desk and she spread her hands over the papers scattered in front of her.

"I'm tidying up . . ." she said in a dazed voice. She lifted a hand and it remained poised in mid-air as though benumbed. Then she appeared to wake up, and stopped lying.

"It's like this, Fred. You told me that when we came to move house you'd hate to be bothered over what you'd want to take with you, all the things in this room . . . the furniture. I honestly wanted to tidy, to sort things. Then the poison, temptation came . . . evil thoughts . . . one evil thought. . . . I implore your forgiveness. I've touched things that don't belong to me. . . ."

She trembled bravely and waited.

He stood with his forehead jutting forward, his hands clenched in a threatening attitude; but he did not seem to see his wife. His eyes were strangely veiled, and ever after she was to retain the impression of having spoken with a man whose eyes were deathly pale.

"Ah, yes," he said at length. "You were looking . . . you were looking for love-letters." She did not deny it. "You were hunting for my love-letters."

He laughed his awkward, constrained laugh.

Edmée felt hurt, and blushed. "Of course you must

think me a fool. As if you were the kind of man not to
lock them away in a safe place or burn them! And then,
anyhow, they're none of my business. I've only got what I
deserved. You won't hold it too much against me, Fred?"

Her pleading had cost her a certain effort, and she
tried deliberately to make herself look appealing, pouting
her lips a little and keeping the upper half of her face
shadowed by her fluffy hair. But Chéri did not relax his
attitude, and she noticed for the first time that the
unblemished skin of his cheeks had taken on the trans-
parence of a white rose in winter, and that their oval
contour had shrunk.

"Love-letters," he repeated. "That's howlingly funny."

He took a step forward, seized a fistful of papers and
scattered them: post-cards, restaurant bills, tradespeople's
announcements, telegrams from chorus girls met one
night and never seen again, *pneumatiques* of four or five lines
from sponging friends; and several close-written pages
slashed with the sabre-like script of Madame Peloux.

Chéri turned round again to his wife: "I have no
love-letters."

"Oh!" she protested. "Why do you want . . ."

"I have none," he interrupted; "you can never understand. I've never noticed it myself until now. I can't have
any love-letters because——" He checked himself.
"But wait, wait. . . . Yes, there was one occasion, I
remember, when I didn't want to go to La Bourboule,
and it . . . Wait, wait."

He began pulling out drawers and feverishly tossing
papers to the floor.

"That's too bad! What can I have done with it? I could
have sworn it was in the upper left-hand . . . No. . . ."

He slammed back the empty drawers and glowered at
Edmée.

"You found nothing? You didn't take a letter which began 'But what do you expect, I'm not in the least bored. There's nothing better than to be separated one week in every month,' and then went on to something else. I don't remember what, something about honey-suckle climbing high enough to look in at the window."

He broke off, simply because his memory refused to come to his aid, and he was left gesticulating in his impatience.

Slim and recalcitrant, Edmée did not quail before him. She took refuge in caustic irritability. "No, no, I *took* nothing. Since when have I been capable of *taking* things? But if this letter is so very precious to you, how is it you've left it lying about? I've no need to enquire whether it was one of Léa's?"

He winced, but not quite in the manner Edmée had expected. The ghost of a smile hovered over his hand-some, unresponsive features; and, with his head on one side, an expectant look in his eyes, and the delicious bow of his mouth taut-stretched, he might well have been listening to the echo of a name.

The full force of Edmée's young and ill-disciplined emotions burst forth in a series of sobs and tears, and her fingers writhed and twisted as if ready to scratch. "Go away! I hate you! You've never loved me. I might not so much as exist, for all the notice you take of me! You hurt me, you despise me, you're insulting, you're, you're . . . You think only of that old woman! It's not natural, it's degenerate, it's . . . You don't love me! Why, oh why, did you ever marry me? . . . You're . . . you're . . ."

She was tossing her head like an animal caught by the neck, and as she leaned back to take a deep breath, because she was suffocating, the light fell on her string of small, milky, evenly matched pearls. Chéri stared in stupefaction at the uncontrolled movements of the lovely throat, at the hands clasped together in appeal, and above all at the tears, her tears. . . . He had never seen such a torrent of tears. For who had ever wept in front of him, or wept because of him? No one. Madame Peloux? 'But,' he thought, 'Madame Peloux's tears don't count.' Léa? No. Searching his memory, he appealed to a pair of honest blue eyes; but they had sparkled with pleasure only, or malice, or a rather mocking tenderness. Such floods of tears poured down the cheeks of this writhing young woman. What could be done about all these tears? He did not know. All the same, he stretched out an arm, and as Edmée drew back, fearing some brutality perhaps, he placed his beautiful, gentle, scented hand on her head and patted her ruffled hair. He did his best to copy the tone and speech of a voice whose power he knew so well: "There, there. . . . What's it all about? What's the matter, then? There . . . there. . . ."

Edmée collapsed suddenly, fell back huddled in a heap on a settee, and broke out into frenzied and passionate sobbing that sounded like yells of laughter or howls of joy. As she lay doubled up, her graceful body heaved and rocked with grief, jealousy, fury and an unsuspected servility. And yet, like a wrestler in the heat of a struggle, or a swimmer in the hollow of a wave, she felt bathed in some strange new atmosphere, both natural and harsh.

She had a good long cry, and recovered by slow degrees, with periods of calm shaken by great shudders and gasps for breath. Chéri sat down by her side and continued to stroke her hair. The crisis of his own emotion was over, and he felt bored. He ran his eyes over Edmée as she lay sideways upon the unyielding settee. This straggling body, with its rucked-up frock and trailing scarf, added to the disorder of the room; and this displeased him.

Soft as was his sigh of boredom, she heard it and sat up. "Yes," she said, "I'm more than you can stand. . . . Oh! it would be better to . . ."

He interrupted her, fearing a torrent of words: "It's not that. It's simply that I don't know what you want."

"What I want? How d'you mean, what I . . ."

She lifted her face, still wet with tears.

"Now listen to me." He took her hands.

She tried to free herself. "No, no, I know that tone of voice. You're going to treat me to another of those nonsensical outbursts. When you put on that tone of voice and face, I know you're going to prove that your eye is shaped like a striped super-mullet, or that your mouth looks like the figure three on its side. No, no, I can't stand that!"

Her recriminations were childish, and Chéri relaxed, feeling that after all they were both very young. He pressed her warm hands between his own.

"But you must listen to me! . . . Good God! I'd like to know what you've got to reproach me with! Do I ever go out in the evenings without you? No! Do I often leave you on your own during the day? Do I carry on a secret correspondence?"

"I don't know—I don't think so——"

He turned her this way and that like a doll.

"Do I have a separate room? Don't I make love to you well?"

She hesitated, smiling with exquisite suspicion. "Do you call that love, Fred?"

"There are other words for it, but you wouldn't appreciate them."

"What you call love . . . isn't it possible that it may be,

really, a . . . kind . . . of alibi?" She hastened to add, "I'm merely generalising, Fred, of course . . . I said '*may* be', in certain cases. . . ."

He dropped Edmée's hands. "That," he said coldly, "is putting your foot right in it."

"Why?" she asked in a feeble voice.

He whistled, chin in air, as he moved back a step or two. Then he advanced upon his wife, looking her up and down as if she were a stranger. To instil fear a fierce animal has no need to leap. Edmée noticed that his nostrils were dilating and that the tip of his nose was white.

"Ugh!" he breathed, looking at his wife. He shrugged his shoulders, turned, and walked away. At the end of the room he turned round and came back again. "Ugh!" he repeated, "Look what's talking!"

"What are you saying?"

"Look what's talking, and what it says. Upon my word, it actually has the cheek to . . ."

She jumped up in a rage. "Fred," she said, "don't dare to speak to me again in that tone? What do you take me for?"

"For a woman who knows exactly how to put her foot in it, as I've just had the honour of informing you."

He touched her on the shoulder with a rigid fore-finger, and this hurt her as much as if he had inflicted a serious bruise. "You've matriculated; isn't there some-where some kind of a proverb which says, 'Never play with knives or daggers' or whatever it may be?"

"Cold steel," she answered automatically.

"That's right. Well, my child, you must never play with cold steel. That's to say, you must never be wounding about a man's . . . a man's favours, if I may so express it. You were wounding about the gifts, about the favours, I bestow on you."

"You . . . you talk like a cocotte," she gasped.

She blushed, and her strength and self-control deserted her. She hated him for remaining cool and collected, for keeping his superiority: its whole secret lay in the carriage of his head, the sureness of his stance, the poise of his arms and shoulders.

The hard forefinger once more pressed into Edmée's shoulder.

"Excuse me, excuse me . . . It'll probably come as a great surprise when I state that, on the contrary, it's you who have the mentality of a tart. When it comes to judging such matters, there's no greater authority than young Peloux. I'm a connoisseur of 'cocottes', as you call them. I know them inside out. A 'cocotte' is a lady who generally manages to receive more than she gives. Do you hear what I say?"

What she heard above all was that he was now addressing her like a stray acquaintance.

"Nineteen years old, white skin, hair that smells of vanilla; and then, in bed, closed eyes and limp arms. That's all very pretty, but is there anything unusual about it? Do you really think it so very unusual?"

She had started at each word, and each sting had goaded her towards the duel of female *versus* male.

"It may be very unusual," she said in a steady voice, "how could *you* know?"

He did not answer, and she hastened to take advantage of a hit. "Personally, I saw much handsomer men than you when we were in Italy. The streets were full of them. My nineteen years are worth those of any other girl of my age, just as one good-looking man is as good as the next. Don't worry, everything can be arranged. Nowadays, marriage is not an important undertaking. Instead of allowing silly scenes to make us bitter . . ."

He put a stop to what she had to say by an almost pitying shake of the head.

"My poor kid, it's not so simple as that."

"Why not? There's such a thing as quick divorce, if one's ready to pay."

She spoke in the peremptory manner of a runaway schoolgirl, and it was pathetic. She had pushed back the hair off her forehead, and her anxious, intelligent eyes were made to look all the darker by the soft contours of her cheeks now fringed with hair: the eyes of an unhappy woman, eyes mature and definitive in a still undeveloped face.

"That wouldn't help at all," Chéri said.

"Because?"

"Because . . ." He leaned forward with his eyelashes tapered into pointed wings, shut his eyes and opened them again as if he had just swallowed a bitter pill. "Because you love me."

She noticed that he had resumed the more familiar form of addressing her, and above all the fuller, rather choked tones of their happiest hours. In her heart of hearts she acquiesced: 'It's true, I love him. At the moment, there's no remedy.'

The dinner bell sounded in the garden—a bell which was too small, dating from before Madame Peloux's time, a sad clear bell reminiscent of a country orphanage. Edmée shivered. "Oh, I don't like that bell. . . ."

"No?" said Chéri, absent-mindedly.

"In our house, dinner will be announced. There'll be no bell. There'll be no boarding-house habits in our home—you'll see."

She spoke these words without turning round, while walking down the hospital-green corridor, and so did not see, behind her, either the fierce attention Chéri paid to her last words, or his silent laughter.

HE was walking along with a light step, stimulated by the rathe spring, perceptible in the moist gusty wind and the exciting earthy smells of squares and private gardens. Every now and again a fleeting glimpse in a glass would remind him that he was wearing a becoming felt hat, pulled down over the right eye, a loose-fitting spring coat, large light-coloured gloves and a terra-cotta tie. The eyes of women followed his progress with silent homage, the more candid among them bestowing that passing stupefaction which can be neither feigned nor hidden. But Chéri never looked at women in the street. He had just come from his house in the Avenue Henri-Martin, having left various orders with the upholsterers: orders contradicting one another, but thrown out in a tone of authority.

On reaching the end of the Avenue, he took a deep breath of the good spring scents carried up from the Bois on the heavy moist wing of the west wind, and then hurried on his way to the Porte Dauphine. Within a few minutes he had reached the lower end of the Avenue Bugeaud, and there he stopped. For the first time in six months his feet were treading the familiar road. He unbuttoned his coat.

'I've been walking too fast,' he said to himself. He started off again, then paused and, this time, trained his eyes on one particular spot: fifty yards or so down the road: bareheaded, shammy-leather in hand, Ernest the concierge—Léa's concierge—was "doing" the brass-work of the railings in front of Léa's house. Chéri began to hum, realised from the sound of his voice that he never did hum, and stopped.

"How are things, Ernest? Hard at work as usual?"

The concierge brightened respectfully.

"Monsieur Peloux! It's a pleasure to see Monsieur again. Monsieur has not changed at all."

"Neither have you, Ernest. Madame is well, I hope?"

He turned his head away to gaze up at the closed shutters on the first floor.

"I expect so, Monsieur, all we've had has been a few post-cards."

"Where from? Was it Biarritz?"

"I don't think so, Monsieur."

"Where is Madame?"

"It wouldn't be easy for me to tell you, Monsieur. We forward all letters addressed to Madame—and there's none to speak of—to Madame's solicitor."

Chéri pulled out his note-case, and cocked an eye at Ernest.

"Oh, Monsieur Peloux, money between you and me? Don't think of it. A thousand francs won't make a man tell what he doesn't know. But if Monsieur would like the address of Madame's solicitor?"

"No thanks, there's no point. And when does she return?"

Ernest threw up his hands: "That's another question that's beyond me. Maybe to-morrow, maybe in a month's time. . . . I keep everything in readiness, just the same. You have to watch out where Madame is concerned. If you said to me now, 'There she comes round the corner of the Avenue,' I shouldn't be surprised."

Chéri turned round and looked towards the corner of the Avenue.

"That's all Monsieur Peloux wants? Monsieur just happened to be walking by? It's a lovely day. . . ."

"Nothing else, thank you, Ernest. Good-bye, Ernest."

"Always at Monsieur's service."

Chéri walked up as far as the Place Victor-Hugo, swinging his cane as he went. Twice he stumbled and almost fell, like people who imagine their progress is being followed by hostile eyes. On reaching the balustraded entrance to the Métro, he leaned over the ramp to peer down into the pink-and-black recesses of the Underground, and felt utterly exhausted. When he straightened his back, he saw that the lamps had been lighted in the square and that the blue of dusk coloured everything around him.

'No, it can't be true. I'm ill.'

He had plumbed the depths of cavernous memories and his return to the living world was painful. The right words came to him at last. 'Pull yourself together, Peloux, for God's sake! Are you losing your head, my boy? Don't you know it's time to go back home?'

This last word recalled a sight that one hour had sufficed to banish from his mind: a large square room— his own nursery; an anxious young woman standing by the window; and Charlotte Peloux, subdued by a Martini.

"Oh, no," he said aloud. "Not that! That's all over."

He signalled to a taxi with his raised stick.

"To the . . . er   . to the Restaurant du Dragon Bleu."

Chéri crossed the grill-room to the sound of violins
in the glare of the atrocious electric light, and this had a
tonic effect. He shook the hand of a maître d'hôtel who
recognised him. Before him rose the stooping figure
of a tall young man. Chéri gave an affectionate gasp.
"Desmond, the very man I wanted to see! Howdydo?"

They were shown to a table decorated with pink
carnations. A small hand and a towering aigrette beckoned
towards Chéri from a neighbouring table.

"It's La Loupiote," Vicomte Desmond warned him.

Chéri had no recollection of La Loupiote, but he
smiled towards the towering aigrette and, without
getting up, touched the small hand with a paper fan
lying on his table. Then he put on his most solemn
"conquering hero" look, and swept his eyes over an
unknown couple. The woman had forgotten to eat since
he had sat down in her vicinity.

"The man with her looks a regular cuckold, doesn't he?"

He had leaned over to whisper into his friend's ear,
and his eyes shone with pleasure as if with rising tears.

"What d'you drink, now you're married?" Desmond
asked, "Camomile tea?"

"Pommery," Chéri said.

"And before the Pommery?"

"Pommery, before and after." And, dilating his
nostrils, he sniffed as he remembered some sparkling,
rose-scented old champagne of 1889 that Léa kept for
him alone.

He ordered a meal that a shop-girl out on the spree
might choose—cold fish *au porto*, a roast bird, and a piping
hot soufflé which concealed in its innards a red ice,
sharp on the tongue.

"Hello!" La Loupiote shouted, waving a pink carnation at Chéri.

"Hello," Chéri answered, raising his glass.

The chimes of an English wall-clock struck eight. "Blast!" Chéri grumbled, "Desmond, go and make a telephone call for me."

Desmond's pale eyes were hungry for revelations to come.

"Go and ask for Wagram 17–08, tell them to put you through to my mother, and say we're dining together."

"And supposing young Madame Peloux comes to the telephone?"

"Say the same thing. I'm not tied to her apron-strings. I've got her well trained."

He ate and drank a lot, taking the greatest care to appear serious and blasé; but his pleasure was enhanced by the least sound of laughter, the clink of glasses, or the strains of a syrupy valse. The steely blue of the highly glazed woodwork reminded him of the Riviera, at the hour when the too blue sea grows dark around the blurred reflection of the noonday sun. He forgot that very handsome young men ought to pretend indifference; he began to scrutinise the dark girl opposite, so that she trembled all over under his expert gaze.

"What about Léa?" Desmond asked suddenly.

Chéri did not jump: he was thinking of Léa. "Léa? She's in the South."

"Is all over between you?"

Chéri put his thumb in the armhole of his waistcoat.

"Well, of course, what d'you expect? We parted in proper style, the best of friends. It couldn't last a lifetime. What a charming, intelligent woman, old man! But then, you know her yourself! Broadminded . . . most remarkable. My dear fellow, I confess that if it hadn't been for the question of age . . . But there *was* the question of age, and you agree . . ."

"Of course," Desmond interrupted.

This young man with lack-lustre eyes, though he knew just how to perform the wearing and difficult duties of a parasite, had just yielded to curiosity and blamed himself for such rashness. Chéri, circumspect and at the same time highly elated, never stopped talking about Léa. He made all the right remarks, showed all the sound sense of a married man. He spoke in praise of marriage, while giving Léa's virtues their due. He extolled the submissive sweetness of his young wife, and thus found occasion to criticise Léa's independence of character. "Oh, the old devil, she had her own ideas about everything, I can tell you!"

He went a step further in his confidences, speaking of Léa with severity, and even impertinence. He was sheltering behind idiotic words, prompted by the suspicions of a deceived lover, and at the same time enjoying the subtle pleasure of being able to speak of her without danger. A little more, and he would have sullied her name, while his heart was rejoicing in his own memories of her: sullied the soft sweet name which he had been unable to mention freely during the last six months, and the whole gracious vision he had of Léa, leaning over him with her two or three irreparable wrinkles, and her beauty, now lost to him, but—alas— ever present.

About eleven o'clock they rose to go, chilled by the emptiness of the almost deserted restaurant. However, at the next table, La Loupiote was busy writing letters and had called for telegraph-forms. She raised her white, inoffensive, sheep-like head as the two friends passed by. "Well, aren't you even going to say good evening?"

"Good evening," Chéri condescended to say.

La Loupiote drew her friend's attention to Chéri's good looks. "Would you believe it! And to think that he's got such pots of money. Some people have everything!"

But when Chéri merely offered her an open cigarette-case, she became vituperative. "They have everything, except the knowledge of how to make proper use of it. Go back home to your mother, dearie!"

"Look here," Chéri said to Desmond when they were outside in the narrow street, "Look here, I was about to ask you, Desmond . . . Wait till we get away from this beastly crowd. . . ."

The soft damp evening air had kept people lingering in the streets, but the theatre-goers from the Rue Caumartin onwards had not yet packed the Boulevard. Chéri took his friend by the arm: "Look here, Desmond . . . I wanted you to make another telephone call."

Desmond stopped, "Again?"

"You'll ask for Wagram . . ."

"17–08."

"You're marvellous . . . Say that I've been taken ill in your flat. Where are you living?"

"Hôtel Morris."

"Splendid—and that I won't be back till morning, and that you're making me some mint tea. Go on, old man. Here, you can give this to the telephone-girl, or else keep it yourself. But come back quickly. I'll be sitting waiting for you outside Weber's."

The tall young man, arrogant and serviceable, went off crumpling the franc-notes in his pocket, without permitting himself a comment. When Desmond rejoined him, Chéri was slouched over an untouched orangeade in which he appeared to be reading his fortune.

"Desmond . . . Who answered you?"

"A lady," the laconic messenger replied.

"Which?"

"Dunno."

"What did she say?"

"That it was all right."

"In what tone of voice?"

"Same as I'm speaking to you in."

"Oh, good. Thanks."

'It was Edmée,' thought Chéri.

They were walking towards the Place de la Concorde and Chéri linked arms with Desmond. He did not dare to admit that he was feeling dog-tired.

"Where do you want to go?" Desmond asked.

"Well, old man," Chéri sighed in gratitude, "to the Morris; and as soon as we can. I'm fagged out."

Desmond forgot to be impassive. "What? It can't be true. To the Morris? What d'you want to do? No nonsense! D'you want to . . ."

"To go to bed," Chéri answered. And he closed his eyes as though on the point of dropping off, then opened them again. "Sleep, I want to sleep, got it?"

He gripped his friend's arm too hard.

"Let's go there, then," Desmond said.

Within ten minutes they were at the Morris. The sky-blue and white bedroom and the imitation Empire furniture of the sitting-room smiled at Chéri like old friends. He took a bath, borrowed one of Desmond's silk night-shirts which was too tight for him, got into bed, and, wedged between two huge soft pillows, sank into dreamless bliss, into the dark depths of a sleep that protected him from all attacks.

HE began to count the shameful days as they went by. "Sixteen . . . seventeen . . . When three weeks are up, I'll go back to Neuilly." He did not go back. Though he saw the situation quite clearly, he no longer had the strength to cure it. At night, and in the morning sometimes, he flattered himself that he would get over his cowardice within an hour or two. "No strength left? . . . Please, please, I beg of you . . . Not yet strength enough. But it's coming back. What's the betting I'll be in the Boulevard d'Inkermann dining-room at the stroke of twelve? One, two . . ." The stroke of twelve found him in the bath, or else driving his motor, with Desmond at his side.

At every mealtime, he felt optimistic for a moment about his marriage. This feeling was as regular as a recurrent fever. As he sat down facing Desmond at their bachelor table, the ghost of Edmée would appear, and plunge him into silent thoughts of his young wife's inconceivable deference. "Really, that young thing's too sweet! Did you ever see such a dream of a wife? Never a word, never a complaint! I'll treat her to one of those bracelets when I get back. . . . Upbringing, that's what does it! Give me Marie-Laure every time for bringing up a daughter!" But one day in the grill-room at the Morris, abject terror was written on his face when he caught sight of a green dress with a chinchilla collar just like one of Edmée's dresses.

Desmond found life wonderful and was getting a little fat. He reserved his arrogance for moments when Chéri—encouraged by him to pay a visit to some "prodigious English girl, riddled with vice", or to some "Indian potentate in his opium palace"—refused point blank or else consented with unconcealed scorn. Desmond had long since despaired of understanding Chéri's ways; but Chéri was paying—and better than during the best of their bachelor days together. They ran across the blonde La Loupiote a second time, when they visited a friend of hers, a woman who boasted such an ordinary name that nobody ever remembered it; "What's-her-name . . . you know perfectly well . . . that pal of La Loupiote's."

The Pal smoked opium, and gave it to others. The instant you came into her modest, ground-floor flat, you smelt escaping gas and stale drugs. She won the hearts of her guests by a tearful cordiality and by a constant incitement to self-pity—both objectionable traits. She treated Desmond, when he paid her a visit, as "a great big desperately lonesome boy," . . . and Chéri as "a beauty who has got everything and it only makes him more miserable." Chéri never touched the pipe; he looked at the small box of cocaine with the repugnance of a cat about to be dosed, and spent most of the night with his back against the cushioned dado, sitting up on a straw mat between Desmond, who went to sleep, and the Pal, who never stopped smoking. For most of the night he breathed in the fumes that satisfy all hunger and thirst, but his self-control and distrust persisted. He appeared to be perfectly happy, except that he stared now and then, with pained and questioning intensity, at the Pal's withered throat—a skinny, far too red throat, round which shimmered a string of false pearls.

Once, he stretched out a hand and with the tip of his

fingers touched the henna-tinted hair on the nape of her neck. He judged the weight of the big light hollow pearls with his hand, then snatched it back with the nervous shiver of someone who catches his finger-nail on a piece of frayed silk. Not long after, he got up and went.

"Aren't you sick to death of all this," Desmond asked Chéri, "sick of these poky holes where we eat and drink and never have any girls? Sick of this hotel with the doors always slamming? Sick of the night-clubs where we go in the evenings, and of dashing in that fast car of yours from Paris to Rouen, Paris to Compiègne, Paris to Ville d'Avray? . . . Why not the Riviera for a change? The season down there isn't December and January, it's March, April, or . . ."

"No," said Chéri.

"Then what?"

"Then nothing."

Chéri affected to become amiable and put on what Léa used to call "his air of worldly superiority".

"Dear old boy . . . you don't seem to appreciate the beauty of Paris at this time of the year. . . . This . . . er . . . indecisive season, this spring that doesn't seem willing to smile, the softness of the light . . . as opposed to the commonplace Riviera. . . . No, don't you see, I like it here."

Desmond all but lost his lackey patience. "Yes, and besides, it may be that the young Peloux's divorce will . . ."

Chéri's sensitive nostrils blenched. "If you've arranged to touch a commission from some lawyer friend, you can drop the idea at once. There'll be no such thing as 'young Peloux's divorce'."

"My dear fellow! . . ." Desmond protested, doing his best to look hurt, "You have a very curious way of behaving to a man who has been a friend since your childhood, and who has always . . ."

Chéri was not listening. Instead, he pushed towards Desmond's face a pointed chin and a mouth pursed like a miser's. For the first time in his life he had heard a stranger disposing of his possessions.

He began to reflect. Young Peloux's divorce? Many nights and days had he spent in thinking over these words till they had come to spell liberty, a sort of second boyhood, perhaps something even better. But Desmond's voice, with its affected nasal twang, had just called up the image he had been looking for: Edmée, resolute in her little hat with its long motoring veil, moving out of the house at Neuilly on her way to an unknown house to join an unknown man. "Of course, that would settle everything," and his Bohemian side was delighted. At the same time a surprisingly timorous Chéri jibbed, "That's not the sort of way one behaves!" The image became focused in sharper colour and movement. Chéri could hear the heavy musical note of the iron gate swinging to, and could see beyond it fingers wearing a grey pearl and a white diamond. "Farewell," the small hand said.

Chéri jumped up, pushing back his seat. "Those are mine, all of them! The woman, the house, the rings . . . they all belong to me!"

He had not spoken out loud, but his features expressed such savage violence that Desmond thought his last hour of prosperity had struck. Chéri spoke to him pityingly but without kindness.

"Poor pussy-cat, did I scare you? What it is to be descended from the Crusaders! Come along, and I'll buy

you pants as fine as my shirts, and shirts as fine as your
pants. Desmond, is to-day the seventeenth?"

"Yes, why?"

"The seventeenth of March. In other words, spring.
Desmond, people who think themselves smart, I mean
those in the height of fashion, women or men—can they
afford to wait any longer before buying their spring
wardrobes?"

"Hardly——"

"The seventeenth, Desmond! Come along at once;
everything's all right. We're going to buy a huge bracelet
for my wife, an enormous cigarette-holder for Madame
Peloux, and a tiny tie-pin for you."

On more than one such occasion he had felt an
overwhelming presentiment that Léa was on the point
of returning; that she was already back in her house;
that the first-floor shutters had been opened, allowing a
glimpse of the flowered pink net curtains across the
windows, the lace of the full-length curtains at each side
and the glint of the looking-glasses. . . . The fifteenth of
April went by and still there was no sign of Léa.

The mournful monotony of Chéri's existence was
tempered by several provoking incidents. There was a
visit from Madame Peloux, who thought she was
breathing her last when she found Chéri looking as thin
as a greyhound, eyes wandering and mouth tight shut.
There was the letter from Edmée: a letter all in the same
surprising tone, explaining that she would stay on at
Neuilly "until further orders," and had undertaken to
pass on to Chéri "Madame de la Berche's best regards."
. . . He thought she was laughing at him, did not know
what to answer, and ended by throwing away the
enigmatic screed; but he did not go to Neuilly.

April advanced, leafy, cold, bright, and scenting all

Paris with tulips, bunches of hyacinths, paulownias and laburnums like dropping-wells of gold. Chéri buried himself all the deeper in austere seclusion. The harassed, ill-treated, angry but well-paid Vicomte Desmond was given his orders: now to protect Chéri from familiar young women and indiscreet young men; now to recruit both sections and form a troop, who ate, drank, and rushed screaming at the top of their voices between Montmartre, the restaurants in the Bois, and the cabarets on the left bank.

One night the Pal was alone in her room, smoking opium and bewailing some shocking disloyalty of La Loupiote's, when her door opened to reveal the young man, with satanic eyebrows tapering towards his temples. He begged for "a glass of really cold water" to allay some secret ardour that had parched his beautiful lips. He showed not the slightest interest in the Pal and the woes she poured out. She pushed towards him the lacquer tray with its pipe: he would accept nothing, and took up his usual position on the mat, to share with her the semi-obscurity in silence. There he stayed till dawn, moving as little as possible, like a man who fears that the least gesture may bring back his pain. At dawn, he questioned the Pal: "Why weren't you wearing your pearls to-day; you know, the big ones?" and politely took his leave.

Walking alone at night was becoming an unconscious habit with him. With rapid lengthy strides he would make off towards some positive but inaccessible goal. Soon after midnight he would escape from Desmond, who discovered him again only towards daybreak, asleep on his hotel bed, flat on his stomach, his head pillowed on his folded arms, in the posture of a fretful child.

"Oh, good, he's here all right," Desmond would say
with relief. "One can never be sure with such a crackpot."

One night, when out on a tramp, his eyes wide open
in the darkness, Chéri had felt compelled to walk up
the Avenue Bugeaud; for during the day he had dis-
regarded the superstition that made him return there once
every twenty-four hours. There are maniacs who cannot
go to sleep without having first touched the door-knob
three times; a similar obsession made him run his hand
along the railings, then put his first finger to the bell-
push, and call out Hullo! under his breath, as if in fun,
before making off in haste.

But one night, that very night, as he stood before the
railings, his heart jumped almost into his mouth: there,
in the court, the electric globe shone like a mauve moon
above the front door·steps, the back-door stood wide
open shedding a glow on the paved courtyard, while, on
the first floor, the bedroom lights filtered through the
shutters to make a golden comb. Chéri supported himself
against the nearest tree and lowered his head.

"It can't be true. As soon as I look up, it will all be
dark again."

He straightened up at the sound of a voice. Ernest,
the concierge, was shouting in the passage: "At nine
to-morrow, Marcel will help me carry up the big black
trunk, Madame."

Chéri turned round in a flash and ran as far as the
Avenue du Bois. There he sat down. In front of his eyes
danced the image of the electric globe he had been
staring at—a dark purple ball fringed with gold, against
a black group of trees in bud. He pressed his hand to his
heart, and took a deep breath. Early lilac blossom
scented the night air. He threw his hat away, undid the

buttons of his overcoat and, leaning back on a seat, let himself go, his legs outstretched and his hands hanging feebly by his sides. A crushing yet delicious weight had just fallen upon him. "Ah!" he whispered, "so this is what they call happiness. I never knew."

For a moment he gave way to self-pity and self-contempt. How many good things had he missed by leading such a pointless life—a young man with lots of money and little heart! Then he stopped thinking for a moment, or possibly for an hour. Next, he persuaded himself there was nothing in the world he wanted, not even to go and see Léa.

When he found himself shivering in the cold, and heard the blackbirds carolling the dawn, he got up and, stumbling a little but light-hearted, set off towards the Hôtel Morris without passing through the Avenue Bugeaud. He stretched himself, filled his lungs with the morning air, and overflowed with goodwill to all.

"Now," he sighed, the devil driven out of him, "now . . . Oh now you'll see just how nice to the girl I shall be."

Shaved, shod and impatient—he had been up since eight—Chéri shook Desmond. Sleep gave him a swollen look, livid and quite frightful, like a drowned man. "Desmond! Hey, Desmond! Up you get. . . . You look too hideous when you're asleep!"

The sleeper woke, sat up, and turned towards Chéri eyes the colour of clouded water. He pretended to be fuddled with sleep so that he could make a long and close examination of Chéri—Chéri dressed in blue, pathetic, superb, and pale under the lightest coat of powder.

There were still moments when Desmond felt pain-

fully aware of the contrast between his ugly mask and
Chéri's good looks. He pretended to give a long yawn.
'What's he up to now?' he wondered; 'The idiot is in far
better looks than yesterday—especially his eyelashes,
and what eyelashes he has . . .' He was staring at the
lustrous sweep of Chéri's thick lashes and the shadow
they shed on the dark pupils and bluish whites of his eyes.
Desmond noticed also that, this morning, the contemptuously arched lips were moist and fresh, and that he was
breathing through them as if he had just that moment
finished making love.

Quickly he relegated his jealousy to the back of his
mind—where he kept his personal feelings—and asked
Chéri in tones of weary condescension: "May one enquire
whether you are going out at this hour of the morning,
or just coming in?"

"I'm going out," Chéri said. "Don't worry about me.
I'm off shopping. I'm going to the florist's, the jeweller's,
to my mother's, to my wife's, to . . ."

"Don't forget the Papal Nuncio!"

"I know what's what," Chéri answered. "He shall
have some imitation gold studs and a sheaf of orchids."

It was rare for Chéri to respond to jokes: he usually
accepted them in stony silence. His facetious reply
proved that he was pleased with himself, and revealed
this unaccustomed mood to Desmond. He studied
Chéri's reflection in the looking-glass, noted the pallor
of his dilated nostrils, observed that his eyes were
continually on the rove, and ventured to put the most
discreet of questions.

"Will you be coming back for luncheon? . . . Hey,
Chéri, I'm speaking to you. Are we lunching together?"

Chéri answered by shaking his head. He whistled
softly, arranging himself in front of the pier-glass so that

it framed his figure exactly like the one between the two windows in Léa's room—the one which would soon frame in its heavy gold, against a sunny pink background, the reflection of his body—naked or loosely draped in silk—the magnificent picture of a young man, handsome, loved, happy, and pampered, playing with the rings and necklaces of his mistress. 'Perhaps her young man's reflection is already there, in Léa's lookingglass!' This sudden thought cut so fiercely into his exhilaration that it dazed him, and he fancied he had heard it actually spoken.

"What did you say?" he asked Desmond.

"I never said a word," his well-trained friend said stiffly. "It must have been someone talking outside in the courtyard."

Chéri went out, slamming the door behind him, and returned to his own rooms. They were filled with the dim continual hubbub of the fully awakened Rue de Rivoli, and Chéri, through the open window, could see the spring foliage, the leaves stiff and transparent like thin jade knives against the sun. He closed the window and sat down on a useless little chair which stood against the wall in a dingy corner between his bed and the bathroom door.

"How can it be? . . ." he began in a low voice, and then said no more. He did not understand why it was that during the last six and a half months he had hardly given a thought to Léa's lover. "*I'm making a perfect fool of myself,*" were the actual words of the letter so piously preserved by Charlotte Peloux.

'A perfect fool?' Chéri shook his head. 'It's funny, but that's not how I see her at all. What sort of a man can she be in love with? Somebody like Patron—rather than like Desmond, of course. An oily little Argentine? Maybe.

Yet all the same . . .' He smiled a simple smile. 'Apart from me, who is there she could possibly care for?"

A cloud passed over the sun and the room darkened. Chéri leaned his head against the wall. "My Nounoune . . . My Nounoune . . . Have you betrayed me? Are you beastly enough to deceive me? . . . Have you really done that?"

He tried to give a sharper edge to his suffering by a misuse of his imagination: the words and sights it presented left him more astonished than enraged. He did his best to evoke the elation of early morning delights when he was living with Léa, the solace of the prolonged and perfect silences of certain afternoons, with Léa—the delicious sleepy hours in winter spent in a warm bed in a freshly aired room, with Léa . . . ; but, all the time, in the suffused cherry-coloured afternoon light aflame behind the curtains of Léa's room, he saw in Léa's arms one lover and one lover only—Chéri. He jumped up, revived by a spontaneous act of faith. 'It's as simple as that! If I'm unable to see anyone but myself beside her, then it's because there is no one else to see.'

He seized the telephone, and was on the point of ringing her up, when he gently replaced the receiver. "No nonsense, . . ."

He walked out into the street, erect, with shoulders squared. He went in his open motor to the jeweller's, where he became sentimental over a slender little bandeau of burning blue sapphires invisibly mounted on blue steel, "so exactly right for Edmée's hair," and took it away with him. He bought some stupid, rather pompous flowers. As it had only just struck eleven, he frittered away a further half-hour, drawing money from the Bank, turning over English illustrated papers at a kiosk, visiting his scent-shop and a tobacconist's that specialised

in Oriental cigarettes. Finally, he got back into his
motor, and sat down between his sheaf of flowers and a
heap of little beribboned parcels.

"Home."

The chauffeur swivelled round on his basket-seat.

"Monsieur? . . . What did Monsieur say? . . ."

"I said Home—Boulevard d'Inkermann. D'you require a map of Paris?"

The motor went full speed towards the Champs-
Elysées. The chauffeur drove much faster than usual and
his thoughts could almost be read in his back. He seemed
to be brooding uneasily over the gulf which divided the
flabby young man of the past months—with his "As you
like," and his "Have a glass of something, Antonin?"—
from young Monsieur Peloux, strict with the staff and
mindful of the petrol.

"Young Monsieur Peloux" leaned back against the
morocco leather, hat on knees, drinking in the breeze
and exerting all his energy in an effort not to think.
Like a coward, he closed his eyes between the Avenue
Malakoff and the Porte Dauphine to avoid a passing
glimpse of the Avenue Bugeaud, and he congratulated
himself on his resolution.

The chauffeur sounded his horn in the Boulevard
d'Inkermann for the gate to be opened, and it sang on
its hinges with a heavy musical note. The capped concierge hurried about his business, the watch-dogs barked
in recognition of their returning master. Very much at
his ease, sniffing the green smell of the newly mown
lawns, Chéri entered the house and with a master's step
climbed the stairs to the young woman whom he had
left behind three months before, much as a sailor from
Europe leaves behind, on the other side of the world, a
little savage bride.

Léa sat at her bureau, throwing away photographs from the last trunk to be unpacked. "Heavens, how hideous people are! The women who had the nerve to give me these! And they think I'm going to put them up in a row on the mantelpiece—in plated frames or little folding-cases. Tear them all up quick, and straight into the waste-paper basket!"

She picked up the photographs again and, before throwing them away, subjected each to the closest scrutiny of which her blue eyes were capable. A post-card with a dark background of a powerful lady encased in full-length stays, doing her best to veil her hair and the lower part of her face with a wisp of tulle, in the teeth of a strong sea-breeze. "*To dearest Léa, in memory of exquisite hours spent at Guéthary. Anita.*" Another photograph, stuck on the middle of a piece of cardboard with a surface like dried mud, portrayed a large and lugubrious family. They might have been a penal colony, with a dumpy, heavily-painted grandmother in charge. Holding above her head a tambourine tricked out with favours, she was resting one foot on the bent knee of what looked like a robust and crafty young butcher-boy. "That should never have seen the light of day," Léa said decisively, crumpling the rough-cast cardboard.

She smoothed out an unmounted print, to disclose two old provincial spinsters. An eccentric, loud-voiced

and aggressive couple, they were to be found every
morning on a bench somewhere along a promenade, and
every evening between a glass of Cassis and their needle-
work-frames, on which they were embroidering black
pussy-cats, fat toads, or a spider. *"To our beautiful fairy!
From her little friends at Le Trayas, Miquette and Riquette."*

Léa destroyed these souvenirs of her travels—and
brushed a hand across her forehead. "It's horrible.
And there'll be dozens and dozens more after these, just
as there were dozens before them, all much the same.
There's nothing to be done about it. It's life. Maybe
wherever a Léa is to be found, there at once spring from
the earth a myriad creatures like Charlotte Peloux, de la
Berche, and Aldonza, or old horrors who were once
handsome young men, people who are . . . well, who are
impossible, impossible, impossible. . . ."

She heard, so fresh was her memory, voices that had
called out to her from the top of hotel steps or hailed her
with a "Hoo-hoo" from afar, across golden sands, and
she lowered her head in anger like a bull.

She had returned, after an absence of six months,
thinner, more flabby, less serene. Now and again a
nervous twitch of the jaw jerked her chin down against
her neck, and careless henna-shampooing had left too
orange a glint in her hair; but her skin had been tanned
to amber by sea and wind. This gave her the glowing
complexion of a handsome farmer's wife, and she might
have done without rouge. All the same, she would have
to arrange something carefully round her neck, not to
say cover it up completely; for it had shrunk and was
encircled with wrinkles that had been inaccessible to
sunburn.

Still seated, she dawdled over tidying away her various
odds and ends, and her eyes began to glance round the

room, as if some chair were missing. But what she was looking for was her old energy, the old anxiety to see at once that everything was as it should be in her comfortable home.

'Oh! That trip!' she sighed. 'How could I? How exhausting it all is!'

She frowned, once again with that irritable jerk of her chin, when she noticed the broken glass of a little picture by Chaplin which she thought perfectly lovely—the head of a young girl, all silver and rose.

"And I could put both hands through that tear in the lace curtains.... And that's only the beginning.... What a fool I was to stay away so long! And all in *his* honour! As if I couldn't just as well have nursed my grief here, in peace and comfort!"

She rose, disgruntled, and, gathering up the flounces of her tea-gown, went over to ring the bell, saying to herself, "Get along with you, you old baggage!"

Her maid entered, under a heap of underclothes and silk stockings.

"Eleven o'clock, Rose. And my face hasn't been done yet. I'm late."

"There's nothing to be late for. There aren't any old maids now to drag Madame off on excursions, or turn up at crack of dawn to pick every rose in the place. There's no Monsieur Roland to drive Madame mad by throwing pebbles through her window...."

"Rose, there's only too much to keep us busy in the house. The proverb may well be true that three moves are as bad as a fire, but I'm quite convinced that being away from home for six months is as bad as a flood. I suppose you've noticed the hole in the curtain?"

"That's nothing.... Madame has not yet seen the linen-room: mouse-droppings everywhere and holes nibbled in the floor. And it's a funny thing that I left Émérancie with twenty-eight glass-cloths and I come back to find twenty-two."

"No!"

"It's the truth—every word I say, Madame."

They looked at each other, sharing the same indignation, both of them deeply attached to this comfortable house, muffled in carpets and silks, with its well-stocked cupboards and its shiny white basement. Léa gave her knee a determined slap.

"We'll soon change all that, my friend. If Ernest and Émérancie don't want their week's notice, they'll manage to find those six glass-cloths. And did you write to Marcel, and tell that great donkey which day to come back?"

"He's here, Madame."

Léa dressed quickly, then opened the window and leaned out, gazing complacently at her avenue of trees in bud. No more of those fawning old maids, and no more of Monsieur Roland—the athletic young heavyweight at Cambo. . . . 'The idiot,' she sighed.

She forgave this passing acquaintance his silliness, and blamed him only for having failed to please her. In her memory—that of a healthy woman with a forgetful body —Monsieur Roland was now only a powerful animal, slightly ridiculous and, when it came to the point, so very clumsy. Léa would now have denied that, one rainy evening when the showers were falling in fragrance on the rose-geraniums, a flood of blinding tears had served to blot out Monsieur Roland behind the image of Chéri.

This brief encounter had left Léa unembarrassed and unregretful. In the villa she had taken at Cambo, the "idiot" and his frolicking old mother would have been made just as welcome as before. They could have gone

on enjoying the well-arranged meals, the rocking-chairs
on the wooden balcony, all the creature comforts that
Léa dispensed with such justifiable pride. But the idiot
had felt sore and gone away, leaving Léa to the attentions
of a stiff, handsome officer, greying at the temples, who
aspired to marriage with "Madame de Lonval".

"Our years, our fortunes, the taste we both have for
independence and society, doesn't everything show that
we were destined for each other?" murmured the
colonel, who still kept his slim waist.

She laughed, and enjoyed the company of this dry,
dapper man, who ate well and knew how to hold his
liquor. He mistook her feelings and he read into the
lovely blue eyes, and the trustful, lingering smiles of his
hostess, the acceptance he was expecting. The end of
their dawning friendship was marked by a decisive
gesture on her part: one she regretted in her heart of
hearts and for which she was honest enough to accept
the blame. 'It's my own fault. One should never treat a
Colonel Ypoustègue, descendant of an ancient Basque
family, as one would treat a Monsieur Roland. I've never
given anyone such a snub. All the same, it would have
been gentlemanly, and intelligent too, if he had come
back as usual the next day in his dog-cart, to smoke his
cigar, meet the two old girls and pull their legs.'

She failed to understand that a middle-aged man could
accept his dismissal, but not certain glances—glances
appraising his physique, comparing him in that respect
so unmistakably with another, unknown and invisible.
Léa, caught in his sudden kiss, had subjected him to the
searching, formidable gaze of a woman who knows
exactly where to find the tell-tale marks of age. From the
dry, well cared-for hands, ribbed with veins and tendons,
her glance rose to the pouched chin and furrowed brows,

returning cruelly to the mouth entrapped between double lines of inverted commas. Whereupon all the aristocratic refinement of the "Baroness de Lonval" collapsed in an "Oh, la la," so insulting, so explicit, so common, that the handsome figure of Colonel Ypoustègue passed through her door for the last time.

'The last of my idylls,' Léa was thinking, as she leaned out over her window-ledge. But the weather over Paris was fine, her echoing courtyard was dapper, with its trim bay trees rising ball-shaped in green tubs, and from the room behind her a breath of scented warmth came playing over the nape of her neck: all this gradually helped her to recover her good humour, and her sense of mischief. She watched the silhouettes of women passing on their way down to the Bois. 'So skirts are changing again,' Léa observed, 'and hats are higher.' She planned sessions with her dressmaker, others with her milliner; the sudden desire to look beautiful made her straighten her back. 'Beautiful? For whom? Why, for myself, of course. And then to aggravate old Ma Peloux!'

Léa had heard about Chéri's flight, but knew no more than that. While disapproving of Madame Peloux's private-detective methods, she did not scruple to listen to a young *vendeuse*, who would show her gratitude for all Léa's kindnesses by pouring gossip in her ear at a fitting, or else by sending it to her, with "a thousand thanks for the delicious chocolates" on a huge sheet of paper embossed with the letter-head of her establishment. A postcard from Lili, forwarded to Léa at Cambo—a postcard scribbled by the dotty old harridan in a trembling hand without commas or full stops—had recounted

an incomprehensible story of love and flight and a young
wife kept under lock and key at Neuilly.

'It was weather like this,' Léa recalled, 'the morning
I read Lili's postcard in my bath at Cambo.'

She could see the yellow bathroom, the sunlight
dancing on the water and ceiling. She could hear the thin-
walled villa re-echoing with a great peal of laughter—her
own laughter, rather ferocious and none too spontaneous
—then the cries that followed it: "Rose! Rose!"

Breasts and shoulders out of water, dripping, robust,
one magnificent arm outstretched, looking more than
ever like a naiad on a fountain, she had waved the card
with the tips of her wet fingers. "Rose, Rose! Chéri . . .
Monsieur Peloux has done a bunk! He's left his wife!"

"That doesn't surprise me, Madame," Rose had said.
"The divorce will be gayer than the wedding, when the
dead seemed to be burying the dead."

All through that day Léa had given way to unseemly
mirth. "Oh! that fiendish boy. Oh! the naughty child!
Just think of it!"

And she shook her head, laughing softly to herself,
like a mother whose son has stayed out all night for the
first time.

A bright varnished park-phaeton flashed past her
gates, sparkled behind its prancing high-steppers and
vanished almost without a sound on its rubber wheels.

'There goes Spéleïeff,' Léa observed; 'he's a good
sort. And there goes Merguillier on his piebald: eleven
o'clock. It won't be long before that dried-up old
Berthellemy passes on his way to thaw out his bones on
the Sentier de la Vertu. Curious how people can go on

doing the same thing day after day! I could almost believe I'd never left Paris, except that Chéri isn't here. My poor Chéri! He's finished with, for the present. Night-life, women, eating at any hour, drinking too much. It's a pity. He might have turned into a decent sort, perhaps, if he'd only had pink chaps like a pork-butcher and flat feet. . . .'

She left the window, rubbing her numbed elbows, and shrugged her shoulders. 'Chéri could be saved once, but not a second time.' She polished her nails, breathed on a tarnished ring, peered closely at the disastrous red of her hair and its greying roots, and jotted down a few notes on a pad. She did everything at high speed and with less composure than usual, trying to ward off an attack of her old insidious anxiety. Familiar as this was, she denied its connection with her grief and called it "her moral indigestion". She began wanting first one thing, then suddenly another—a well-sprung victoria with a quiet horse appropriate to a dowager; then a very fast motor-car; then a suite of Directoire furniture. She even thought of doing her hair differently; for twenty years she had worn it high, brushed straight off the neck. 'Rolled curls low on the neck, like Lavallière? Then I should be able to cope with this year's loose-waisted dresses. With a strict diet, in fact, and my hair properly hennaed, I can hope for ten—no, let's say five years more of . . .'

With an effort she recovered her good sense, her pride, her lucidity. 'A woman like me would never have the courage to call a halt? Nonsense, my beauty, we've had a good run for our money.' She surveyed the tall figure, erect, hands on hips, smiling at her from the looking-glass. She was still Léa.

'Surely a woman like that doesn't end up in the arms of an old man? A woman like that, who's had the luck

never to soil her hands or her mouth on a withered stick!
Yes, there she stands, the "vampire", who needs must
feed off youthful flesh.'

She conjured up the chance acquaintances and lovers
of her early days: always she had escaped elderly lechers;
so she felt pure, and proud of thirty years devoted to
radiant youths and fragile adolescents.

'And this youthful flesh of theirs certainly owes me a
great debt. How many of them have me to thank for
their good health, their good looks, the harmlessness of
their sorrows! And then their egg-nogs when they
suffered from colds, and the habit of making love un-
selfishly and always refreshingly! Shall I now, merely
to fill my bed, provide myself with an old gentleman of
... of ...' She hunted about and finished up with majestic
forgetfulness of her own age, 'An old gentleman of
forty?'

She rubbed her long shapely hands together and
turned away in disgust. 'Pooh! Farewell to all that! It's
much prettier. Let's go out and buy playing-cards, good
wine, bridge-scorers, knitting-needles—all the paraphernalia to fill a gaping void, all that's required to disguise
that monster. an old woman.'

In place of knitting-needles, she bought a number of
dresses, and négligées like the gossamer clouds of dawn.
A Chinese pedicure came once a week, the manicurist
twice, the masseuse every day. Léa was to be seen at
plays, and before the theatre at restaurants where she
never thought of going in Chéri's time.

She allowed young women and their friends—as well
as Kühn, her former tailor, now retired—to ask her to

their box or to their table. But the young women treated
her with a deference she did not appreciate; and when
Kühn, at their first supper together, called her "my dear
friend," she retorted: "Kühn, I assure you it doesn't
suit you at all to be a customer."

She sought refuge with Patron, now a referee and
boxing promoter. But Patron was married to a young
person who ran a bar, a little creature as fierce and
jealous as a terrier. To join the susceptible athlete, Léa
went as far out as the Place d'Italie, at considerable risk
to her dark sapphire-blue dress, heavy with gold embroidery, to her birds of paradise, her impressive jewels,
and her new rich red-tinted coiffure. She had had enough
after one sniff of the sweat, vinegar and turpentine exuded
by Patron's "white hopes", and she left, deciding never
to venture again inside that long low gas-hissing hall.

An unaccountable weariness followed her every· attempt to get back into the bustling life of people with
nothing to do.

'What can be the matter with me?'

She rubbed her ankles, a little swollen by evening,
looked at her strong teeth, and gums that had hardly
begun to recede; and thumped her strong ribs and
healthy stomach as if sounding a cask. Yet some undefin-
able weight, now that the chock had been knocked from
under her, was shifting within her, and dragging her
down. It was the Baroness de la Berche—met by chance
in a "public bar" where she was washing down two
dozen snails with cabbies' white wine—who in the end
informed her of the prodigal's return to the fold, and of
the dawn of a crescent honeymoon in the Boulevard
d'Inkermann. Léa listened calmly to this Moral Tale;
but she turned pale with emotion the following day
when she recognised the blue limousine outside her

gates and saw Charlotte Peloux on her way to the house.

"At last, at last! Here you are again, Léa, my beauty!
... Lovelier than ever! Thinner than last year! Take care,
Léa, we mustn't get too thin at our age! So far, and no
further! And yet ... But what a treat it is to see you!"

Never had that bitter tongue sounded so sweet to Léa.
She let Madame Peloux prattle on, thankful for the
breathing-space afforded by this acid stream. She had
settled Charlotte Peloux into a deep armchair, in the soft
light of the little pink-panelled salon, as in the old days.
Automatically she had herself taken the straight-backed
chair, which forced her to lift her shoulders and keep up
her chin, as in the old days. Between them stood the
table covered by a cloth of heavy embroidery, and on it,
as in the old days, the large cut-glass decanter half full
of old brandy, the shimmering petal-thin goblets, iced
water, and shortbread biscuits.

"My beauty, now we'll be able to see each other again
in peace, in peace. You know my motto: 'When in
trouble, shun your friends: let them only share your
luck!' All the time Chéri was playing truant, I purposely
didn't show you any sign of life, you understand. Now
that all's well and my children are happy again, I shout
it aloud, I throw myself into your arms, and we start our
pleasant existence all over again. . . ." She broke off and
lit a cigarette, as clever with her pauses as an actress,
". . . without Chéri, of course."

"Of course," Léa acquiesced with a smile.

She was watching and listening to her old enemy in
satisfied astonishment. The huge inhuman eyes, the
chattering lips, the restless, tight little body—all that was
facing her across the table had come simply to test her
powers of resistance, to humiliate her, as in the old days,
always as in the old days. But, as in the old days, Léa

knew when to answer, when to be scornful, when to
smile, and when to retaliate. Already that sorry burden,
which had weighed so heavily the day before and the
days before that, was beginning slowly to lift. The light
seemed normal once more, and familiar, as it played over
the curtains and suffused the little drawing-room.

'Here we are again,' Léa thought, in lighter vein.
'Two women, both a little older than a year ago, the same
habits of backbiting and the same stock phrases; good-
natured wariness at meals shared together; the financial
papers in the morning, scandalmongering in the afternoon: all this will have to be taken up again, since it's
Life, my life. The Aldonzas and the de la Berches, the
Lilis and a few homeless old gentlemen: the whole lot
squeezed round a card table, with the packs jostling the
brandy-glasses, and perhaps, thrown in, a pair of little
woollen shoes, begun for a baby who's soon to be born.
. . . We'll start all over again, since it is ordained. Let's
enter on it cheerfully. After all, it's only too easy to sink
back into the grooves of the old life.'

And she settled back, eyes bright and mouth relaxed,
to listen to Charlotte Peloux, who was greedily ex-
patiating upon her daughter-in-law.

"My Léa, you should know, if anyone, that what I've
always longed for is peace and quiet. Well now, I've got
them. Chéri's escapade, you see, was nothing more than
sowing a few wild oats. Far be it from me to reproach
you, Léa dear, but as you'll be the first to admit, from
eighteen to twenty-five he really never had the time to
lead the life of a bachelor! And now he's done it with a
vengeance!"

"It's a very good thing that he did," Léa said, without
the flicker of a smile; "it acts as a sort of guarantee to
his wife for the future."

"The very word, the very word I was hunting for!"
barked Madame Peloux, beaming. "A guarantee! And
ever since that day—one long dream! And, you know,
when a Peloux does come home again after being properly
out on the spree, he never goes off again!"

"Is that a family tradition?" Léa asked.

But Charlotte took no notice.

"And what's more, he was very well received when he
did return home. His little wife—ah, there's a little wife
for you, Léa!—and I've seen a fair number of little wives
in my time, you know, and I don't mind telling you I've
never seen one to hold a candle to Edmée!"

"Her mother is so remarkable," Léa said.

"Think, just think, my beauty—Chéri left her on my
hands for very nearly three months! and between you
and me she was very lucky to have me there."

"That's exactly what I was thinking," Léa said.

"And then, my dear, never a word of complaint, never
a scene, never a tactless word! Nothing, nothing! She
was patience itself, and sweetness . . . and the face of a
saint, a saint!"

"It's terrifying," Léa said.

"And then, what d'you suppose happened when our
young rascal walked in one morning, all smiles, as
though he'd just come in from a stroll in the Bois?
D'you suppose she allowed herself a single comment?
Not one. Far from it. Nothing. As for him, though at
heart he must have felt just a little ashamed . . ."

"Oh, why?" Léa asked.

"Well, really! After all . . . He was welcomed with open
arms, and the whole thing was put right in their bedroom
—in two ticks—just like that—no time lost! Oh, I can
assure you, for the next hour or so there wasn't a happier
woman in the world than me."

"Except, perhaps, Edmée," Léa suggested.

But Madame Peloux was all exaltation, and executed a superb soaring movement with her little arms: "I don't know what you can be thinking of. Personally, I was only thinking of the happy hearth and home."

She changed her tune, screwed up her eyes and pouted: "Besides, I can't see that little girl frantic with passion, or sobbing with ecstasy. Twenty, and skinny at that. . . . Pah! at that age they stammer and stutter. And then, between ourselves, I think her mother's cold."

"Aren't you being carried away by your sense of family?" Léa said.

Charlotte Peloux expanded her eyes to show their very depths, but absolutely nothing was to be read there.

"Certainly not, certainly not! Heredity, heredity! I'm a firm believer in it. Look at my son, who is fantasy incarnate . . . What? You don't know that he's fantasy incarnate?"

"It must have escaped my memory," Léa apologised.

"Well, I have high hopes for my son's future. He'll love his home as I love mine, he'll look after his fortune, he'll love his children, as I loved him. . . ."

"For goodness' sake, don't paint such a depressing picture," Léa begged. "What's it like, the young people's home?"

"Sinister!" shrieked Madame Peloux. "Positively sinister. Purple carpets. Purple! A black-and-gold bathroom. A salon with no furniture in it, full of Chinese vases larger than me! So, what happens is that they're always at Neuilly. Besides, without being conceited, I must say that girl adores me."

"Her nerves have not been upset at all?" Léa asked, anxiously.

Charlotte Peloux's eyes brightened. "No danger of

that! She plays her hand well, and we must face the fact."

"Who d'you mean by 'we'?"

"Forgive me, my beauty, pure habit. We're dealing here with what I call a brain, a real brain. You should see the way she gives orders without raising her voice, and takes Chéri's teasing, and swallows the bitterest pills as if they were lollipops. . . . I begin to wonder, I really begin to wonder, whether there is not positive danger lying ahead for my son. I'm afraid, Léa dear, I'm afraid she may prove a damper on his originality, on his . . ."

"What? Is he being an obedient little boy?" Léa interrupted. "Do have some more of my brandy, Charlotte, it comes from Spéleïeff and it's seventy-four years old—you could give it to a new-born babe."

" 'Obedient' is hardly the right word, but he's . . . inter- impertur . . ."

"Imperturbable?"

"That's the word! For instance, when he knew I was coming to see you . . ."

"Did he know, then?"

An impetuous blush leapt to Léa's cheeks, and she cursed her hot blood and the bright daylight of the little drawing-room. Madame Peloux, a benign expression in her eyes, fed on Léa's confusion.

"But of course he knew. That oughtn't to bring a blush to your cheeks, my beauty. What a child you are!"

"In the first place, how did you know I was back?"

"Oh, come, Léa, don't ask such foolish questions. You've been seen about everywhere."

"Yes, but Chéri—did you tell him I was back?"

"No, my beauty, it was he who told me."

"Oh, it was he who . . . That's funny."

She heard her heart beating in her voice and dared not risk more than the shortest answers.

"He even added: 'Madame Peloux, you'll oblige me by going to find out news of Nounoune.' He's still so fond of you, the dear boy."

"How nice!"

Madame Peloux, crimson in the face, seemed to abandon herself to the influence of the old brandy and talked as in a dream, wagging her head from side to side. But her russet eyes remained fixed and steely, and she kept a close watch on Léa, who was sitting bolt upright, armed against herself, waiting for the next thrust.

"It's nice, but it's quite natural. A man doesn't forget a woman like you, Léa dear. And . . . if you want to know what I really think, you've only to lift a finger and . . ."

Léa put a hand on Charlotte Peloux's arm. "I don't want to know what you really think," she said gently.

The corners of Madame Peloux's mouth fell: "Oh, I can understand, I approve," she sighed in a passionless voice. "When one has made other arrangements for one's life, as you have . . . I haven't even had a word with you about yourself!"

"But it seems to me that you have."

"Happy?"

"Happy."

"Divinely happy? A lovely trip? Is *he* nice? Where's his photo?"

Léa, relieved, sharpened her smile and shook her head. "No, no, you'll find out nothing, search where you will. Have your detectives let you down, Charlotte?"

"I rely on no detectives," Charlotte answered. "It's certainly not because anyone has told me . . . that you'd been through another heart-breaking desertion . . . that you'd been terribly worried, even over money. . . . No, no, you know what small attention I pay to gossip!"

"No one knows it better than me. My dear Lolotte, you

can go back home without any fears on my behalf. And
please reassure our friends, and tell them that I only
wish they had made half what I did out of Oil shares
between December and February."

The alcholic cloud-screen, which softened the features of
Madame Peloux, lifted in a trice; a clear, sharp, thoroughly
alert face emerged. "You were in on Oil? I might have
known it! And you never breathed a word to me."

"You never asked me about it. . . . You were thinking
only of your family, as was natural. . . ."

"Fortunately, I was thinking of Compressed Fuel at
the same time." The muted trumpet resembled a flute.

"Ah! and you never let on to me either!"

"Intrude upon love's young dream? Never! Léa, my
dear, I'm off now, but I'll be back."

"You'll come back on Thursday, because at present,
my dear Lolotte, your Sundays at Neuilly . . . they're
finished for me. Would you like it if I started having a
few people here on Thursdays? Nobody except old
friends, old Ma Aldonza, our Reverend-Father-the-
Baroness—poker for you, knitting for me. . . ."

"Do you knit?"

"Not yet, but it will soon come. Well?"

"I jump for joy at the idea! See if I'm not jumping!
And you may be sure I won't say a word about it at home.
That bad boy would be quite capable of coming and
asking for a glass of port on one of your Thursdays.
Just one more little kiss, my beauty. . . . Heavens, how
good you smell. Have you noticed that as the skin gets
less firm, the scent sinks in better and lasts much longer?
It's really very nice."

'Be off, be off . . .' Quivering, Léa stood watching
Madame Peloux as she crossed the courtyard. 'Go on
your mischievous way! Nothing can stop you. You
twist your ankle, yes—but it never brings you down.
Your chauffeur is careful not to skid, so you'll never
crash into a tree. You'll get back safely to Neuilly, and
you'll choose your moment—to-day, or to-morrow, or
one day next week—to come out with words that should
never pass your lips. You'll try and upset those who,
perhaps, are happy and at peace. The least harm you'll
do is to make them tremble a little, as you made me, for
a moment. . . .'

She was trembling at the knees, like a horse after a
steep pull, but she was not in pain. She felt overjoyed
at having kept so strict a control over herself and her
words. Her looks and her colour were enhanced by her
recent encounter, and she went on pulping her handkerchief to release her bottled-up energy.

She could not detach her thoughts from Madame
Peloux. 'We've come together again,' she said to herself,
'like two dogs over an old slipper which both have got
used to chewing. How queer it is! That woman is my
enemy, and yet it's from her I now draw my comfort.
How close are the ties that bind us!'

Thus, for a long time, she mused over her future,
veering between alarm and resignation. Her nerves were
relaxed, and she slept for a little. As she sat with one
cheek pressed against a cushion, her dreams projected
her into her fast-approaching old age. She saw day
follow day with clockwork monotony, and herself beside
Charlotte Peloux—their spirited rivalry helping the time
to pass. In this way she would be spared, for many
years, the degrading listlessness of women past their
prime, who abandon first their stays, then their hair-dye,

and who finally no longer bother about the quality of their underclothes. She had a foretaste of the sinful pleasures of the old—little else than a concealed aggressiveness, day-dreams of murder, and the keen recurrent hope for catastrophes that will spare only one living creature and one corner of the globe. Then she woke up, amazed to find herself in the glow of a pink twilight as roseate as the dawn.

"Ah, Chéri!" she sighed.

But it was no longer the raucous hungry cry of a year ago. She was not now in tears, nor was her body suffering and rebellious, because threatened by some sickness of the soul. Léa rose from her chair, and rubbed her cheek, embossed by the imprint of the embroidered cushion.

'My poor Chéri! It's a strange thought that the two of us—you by losing your worn old mistress, and I by losing my scandalous young lover—have each been deprived of the most honourable possession we had upon this earth!'

Two days went by after the visit of Charlotte Peloux: two grey days that passed slowly for Léa. She faced this new life with the patience of an apprentice. 'Since this is going to be my new life,' she said to herself, 'I'd better make a start.' But she set about it clumsily, altogether too conscientiously, so that it was a strain on her perseverance. On the second day, about eleven in the morning, she was seized with a desire to go for a walk through the Bois as far as the Lakes.

'I'll buy a dog,' she thought. 'He'll be a companion, and force me to walk.' And Rose had to hunt through the bottom of the summer cupboards for a pair of strong-

soled brown boots and a tweed coat and skirt, smelling
of alpine meadows and pine forests. Léa set off with the
resolute stride proper to the wearer of heavy footwear
and rough country clothes.

'Ten years ago, I should not have feared to carry a
stick,' she said to herself. When still quite near the
house, she heard behind her a brisk light tread, which
she thought she recognised. She became unnerved,
almost paralysed by a compelling fear; and before she
could recover she let herself unwittingly be overtaken,
and then passed, by an unknown young man. He was in a
hurry, and never even glanced at her.

'I really am a fool,' she breathed in her relief.

She bought a dark carnation to pin on her jacket and
started off again. But thirty yards ahead of her, looming
out of the diaphanous mist above the grass verges of the
Avenue, the silhouette of a man was waiting.

'This time I do recognise the cut of that coat and that
way of twirling a cane. . . . Oh, no thank you, the last
thing I want is for him to see me shod like a postman and
wearing a thick jacket that makes me look stocky. If I
must run into him, I'd far rather he saw me in something
else . . . and he never could stand me in brown, anyhow.
. . . No, no . . . I'm off home. . . . I . . .'

At that moment the waiting man hailed an empty
taxi, stepped in, and drove past Léa: he was a young man
with fair hair and a small close-clipped moustache.
But this time Léa did not smile or feel relief. She turned
on her heel and walked back home.

"One of my off-days, Rose. . . . Bring me the peach-
blossom tea-gown, the new one, and the big embroidered
cloak. I'm stifling in these woollen things."

'It's no good being obstinate,' Léa thought. 'Twice in
succession it's turned out not to be Chéri: the third time

it would have been. I know the little jokes Fate plays
on one. There's nothing to be done about it. I've no
fight left in me to-day, I'm feeling limp.'

She spent the rest of the day once more trying patiently
to learn to be alone. After luncheon she enjoyed a cigarette and a look at the papers, and welcomed with a
short-lived joy a telephone call from Baroness de la
Berche, then another from Spéleïeff, her former lover,
the handsome horse-coper, who had seen her in the street
the previous evening and offered to sell her a spanking
pair.

There followed an hour of complete and frightening
silence. 'Come, come . . .' She began to walk up and
down, with her hands on her hips, her arms free of the
heavy gold rose-embroidered cloak, its magnificent
train sweeping the floor behind her.

'Come, come. . . . Let's try to take stock. This isn't the
moment to become demoralised—now that I'm no
longer in love with the boy. I've been living on my own
now for six months. I managed perfectly well when I
was in the south. To start with, I moved about from
place to place. And the people I got to know on the
Riviera or in the Pyrenees did me good; I felt positively
refreshed each time any of them went away. Starch
poultices may not cure a burn, but they do bring relief
when constantly renewed. My six months of keeping on
the move reminds me of the story of that hideous Sarah
Cohen, who married a monster of ugliness. "Each
time I look at him, I think that I am pretty."

'But I knew what it was like to live alone before these
last six months. What sort of life did I lead after I'd left
Spéleïeff, for instance? Oh yes, I went chasing round
bistros and bars with Patron, and then all of a sudden
Chéri came into my life. But before Spéleïeff, there was

little Lequellec: when his family dragged him away from me to lead him to the altar, his beautiful eyes were brimming with tears, poor boy. . . . After him, I was all alone for four months, I remember. The first month, I cried a great deal. Oh, no, it was for Bacciocchi I cried so much. But when I was through with my tears, there was no holding me. It was so delightful to find myself alone. Yes, but at the Bacciocchi time I was twenty-eight, and thirty after Lequellec, and in between these two, I had known . . . Well, no matter. After Spéleïeff, I became disgusted—so much money so ill spent. Whereas now, after Chéri, I'm . . . I'm fifty, and I was unwise enough to keep him for six whole years!"

She wrinkled her forehead, and looked ugly with her mouth in a sulky droop.

'It serves me right. At my age, one can't afford to keep a lover six years. Six years! He has ruined all that was left of me. Those six years might have given me two or three quite pleasant little happinesses, instead of one profound regret. A liaison of six years is like following your husband out to the colonies: when you get back again nobody recognises you and you've forgotten how to dress.'

To relieve the strain, she rang for Rose, and together they went through the contents of the little cupboard where she kept her lace. Night fell, set the lamps blossoming into light, and called Rose back to the cares of the house.

'To-morrow, Léa said to herself, 'I'll order the motor and drive out to Spéleïeff's stud-farm in Normandy. I'll take old La Berche, if she wants to come: it will remind her of the past glories of her own carriages. And, upon my word, should the younger Spéleïeff cast an eye in my direction, I'm not saying I . . .'

She carefully smiled a mysterious and provocative smile, to delude what ghosts there might be hovering round the dressing-table or round the formidable bed, glimmering in the shadows. But she felt entirely frigid, and full of contempt for the pleasures other people found in love.

She dined off grilled sole and pastries, and found the meal a recreation. She chose a dry champagne in place of the Bordeaux, and hummed as she left the table. Eleven o'clock caught her by surprise, still taking the measurements of the space between the windows in her bedroom, where she planned to replace the large looking-glasses with old painted panels of flowers and balustrades. She yawned, scratched her head, and rang for her maid to undress her. While Rose knelt to take off her silk stockings, Léa reviewed her achievements of the day already slipping into the pages of the past, and was as pleased with her performance as if she had polished off an imposition. Protected for the night against the dangers of idleness, she could look forward to so many hours of sleep, so many when she would lie awake. Under cover of night, the restless regain the privilege of yawning aloud or sighing, of cursing the milkman's cart, the street-cleaners, and the early morning sparrows.

During her preparations for the night, she thought over a number of mild projects that would never come into being.

'Aline Mesmacker has a restaurant bar and is simply coining money. . . . Obviously, it gives her something to do, as well as being a good investment. . . . But I can't see myself sitting at a cash-desk; and if one employs a manageress, it's no longer worth while. Dora and that fat Fifi run a night-club together, Mother La Berche told me. Everybody's doing it now. And they wear stiff

collars and dinner jackets, to attract a special clientèle.
Fat Fifi has three children to bring up—they're her
excuse. . . . Then there's Kühn, who's simply kicking
his heels, and would gladly take some of my capital to
start a new dressmaker's.' Naked, and brick-pink from
the reflection of her Pompeian bathroom, she sprayed
herself with her favourite sandalwood, and, without
thinking about it, enjoyed unfolding a long silk night-
gown.

'All that's so much poppycock! I know perfectly well
that I dislike working. To bed with you, Madame! You'll
never have any other place of business, and all your
customers are gone!'

The coloured lining of the white gandoura she put on
was suffused with a vague pink. She went back to her
dressing-table, and combed and tugged at the hairs
stiffened by dye, lifting both her arms, and thus framing
her tired face. Her arms were still so beautiful, from the
full deep hollow of the armpit up to the rounded wrists,
that she sat gazing at them in the looking-glass.

"What lovely handles for so old a vase!"

With a careless gesture she thrust a pale tortoiseshell
comb into the back of her hair, and, without much hope,
picked a detective story from the shelf of a dark closet.
She had no taste for fine bindings and had never lost the
habit of relegating books to the bottom of a cupboard,
along with cardboard boxes and empty medicine bottles.

As she stood smoothing the cool linen sheets on her
huge uncovered bed, the big bell in the courtyard rang
out. The full, solemn, unwonted peal jarred on the
midnight hour.

"What in the world . . . ?" she said out loud.

She held her breath while listening, her lips parted.
A second peal sounded even louder than the first, and

Léa, with an instinctive movement of self-preservation and modesty, ran to powder her face. She was about to ring for Rose when she heard the front door slam, followed by footsteps in the hall and on the stairs, and the sound of two voices mingling—her maid's and someone else's. She had no time to make up her mind: the door of her room was flung open by a ruthless hand. Chéri stood before her—his top-coat unbuttoned over evening clothes, his hat on his head—pale and angry-looking.

He leaned back against the door now shut behind him, and did not move. He looked not so much at Léa as all round the room, with the quick shifting glance of a man about to be attacked.

Léa, who that morning had trembled at the half-surmised outline of a figure in the mist, felt at first only the resentment of a woman caught at her toilet. She drew her wrap more closely about her, settled her comb, and with one foot hunted for a missing slipper. She blushed, yet by the time the high colour died down she had already recovered the semblance of calm. She raised her head and appeared taller than the young man who was leaning, all in black, against the white of the door.

"That's a nice way to come into a room," she said in a rather loud voice. "You might at least take your hat off and say good evening."

"Good evening," Chéri said in surly tones.

The sound of his voice seemed to astonish him. He looked all round less like an angry animal, and a sort of smile drifted from his eyes down to his mouth, as he repeated a gentler "Good evening."

He took off his hat and came forward a few steps.

"May I sit down?"

"If you like," Léa said.

He sat down on a pouffe and saw that she remained standing.

"Are you in the middle of dressing? Aren't you going out?"

She shook her head, sat down far away from him, picked up her nail-buffer and never said a word. He lit a cigarette, and asked her permission only after it was alight.

"If you like," Léa repeated indifferently.

He said nothing more and dropped his gaze. Noticing that his hand with the cigarette in it was shaking, he rested it on the edge of a table. Léa continued polishing her nails deliberately and from time to time cast a brief glance at Chéri's face, especially at his lowered eyelids and the dark fringe of his lashes.

"It was Ernest who opened the front door to me as usual," Chéri said at last.

"And why shouldn't it have been Ernest? Ought I to have changed my staff because you got married?"

"No . . . I mean, I simply said that . . ."

Again silence fell, broken by Léa.

"May I know whether you intend to remain for some time, sitting on that pouffe? I don't even ask why you take the liberty of entering my house at midnight. . . ."

"You may ask me why," he said quickly.

She shook her head. "It doesn't interest me."

He jumped up precipitately, sending the pouffe rolling away behind him, and bore down upon Léa. She felt him bending over her as if he were going to strike her, but she did not flinch. The thought came to her: 'What in this world is there for me to be frightened of?'

"So you don't know what brings me here! You don't want to know what brings me here!"

He tore off his coat and sent it flying on to the chaise-longue, then he crossed his arms, and shouted quite close to Léa's face, in a strained but triumphant voice, "I've come back!"

She was using a delicate pair of tweezers, and these she carefully put away before wiping her fingers. Chéri dropped into a chair, as though his strength was completely exhausted.

"Good," Léa said. "You've come back. That's very nice! Whose advice did you take about that?"

"My own," Chéri said.

She got up in her turn, the better to dominate him. Her surging heartbeats had subsided, allowing her to breathe in comfort. She wanted to play her role without a mistake.

"Why didn't you ask me for my advice? I'm an old friend who knows all your clownish ways. Why did it never occur to you that your coming here might well embarrass . . . someone?"

Lowering his head, he searched every corner of the room from under his eyebrows—the closed doors, the bed, metal-girt and heaped with luxurious pillows. He found nothing exceptional, nothing new, and shrugged his shoulders.

Léa expected more than that and drove home her point. "You understand what I mean?"

"Perfectly," he answered. " 'Monsieur' has not come in yet? 'Monsieur' is sleeping out?"

"That's none of your business, child," she said calmly.

He bit his lip and nervously knocked off his cigarette ash into a jewel tray.

"Not in that, I keep on telling you!" Léa cried. "How many times must I . . . ?"

She broke off to reproach herself for having

unconsciously adopted the tone of their old familiar quarrels. But he did not appear to have heard and went on examining one of Léa's rings—an emerald she had purchased on her recent trip.

"What's . . . what's this?" he stammered.

"That? It's an emerald."

"I'm not blind. What I mean is, who gave it you?"

"No one you know."

"Charming!" Chéri said bitterly.

The note in his voice was enough to restore Léa's authority, and she pressed her advantage, taking pleasure in leading him still further astray.

"Isn't it charming? I get compliments on it wherever I go. And the setting, you've seen it . . . the filigree of diamonds . . ."

"Enough!" bawled Chéri furiously, smashing his fist down on the fragile table.

A few roses shed their petals at the impact, and a china cup slithered without breaking on to the thick carpet. Léa reached for the telephone, but Chéri caught her hand in a rough grasp. "What are you going to do with that telephone?"

"Call the police," Léa said.

He took hold of both her arms, pretending to be up to some playful nonsense as he pushed her away from the instrument.

"Oh go on with you, that's all right. Don't be silly! Can't I even open my mouth without your getting all melodramatic?"

She sat down and turned her back on him. He remained standing, with nothing in his hands: his parted lips were swollen, giving him the look of a sulky child; one black lock hung down over his eyebrow. Surreptitiously, Léa watched him in a looking-glass, till his reflection vanished when he sat down. In her turn, Léa was embarrassed when she felt him staring at her back, broadened by the loose folds of her gandoura. She returned to her dressing-table, smoothed her hair, re-arranged her comb, and, as if for want of something better to do, began unscrewing the top of a scent-bottle. Chéri turned his head as the first whiff reached his nostrils.

"Nounoune!" he called.

She did not answer.

"Nounoune!"

"Beg my pardon," she ordered, without turning round.

"Not likely!" he sneered.

"I can't force you. But you'll leave the house. And at once. . . ."

"I beg your pardon," he said at once, peevishly.

"Better than that."

"I beg your pardon," he repeated, quite low.

"That's better."

She went over to him and ran her hand lightly over his bowed head. "Come, tell me all about it."

He shivered, trembling under her touch. "What do you want me to tell you? It's not very complicated. I've come back, that's all."

"Tell me! Come along, tell me!"

He rocked backwards and forwards on his seat, pressing his hands between his knees, and raised his head towards Léa without meeting her eyes. She watched the quivering of his nostrils, and she heard him trying to control his rapid breathing. She had only to say once more, "Come, tell me all about it," and give him a prod with her finger, as if to push him over. At once he cried out, "Nounoune darling! Nounoune darling!" and threw all his weight upon her, clasping her long legs, so that they gave way under her.

Once seated, she let him slither to the floor and sprawl over her with tears, and inarticulate words, and groping fingers that caught at her lace and her pearls and hunted feverishly under her dress for the shape of her shoulder and under her hair to touch her ears.

"Nounoune darling! We're together again, my Noun-oune! Oh, my Nounoune! your shoulder, and your scent, and your pearls, my Nounoune, oh, it's so stunning . . . and that little burnt taste your hair has, oh, it's . . . it's stunning. . . ."

He leaned back to breathe out this silly word with what might have been the last breath of his body: then, still on his knees, he clasped Léa in his arms, offering her a forehead shadowed under tousled hair, a trembling mouth moist with tears, and eyes bright with weeping and happiness. She was so lost in contemplating him, so perfectly oblivious of everything that was not Chéri, that she never thought of kissing him. She twined her arms round his neck and gently hugged him to her, rocking him to the rhythm of murmured words.

"My pet . . . my naughty boy . . . You're here . . . You've come back again. . . . What have you been up to now? You're so naughty . . . my pretty. . . ."

He was moaning softly, keeping his lips together and hardly speaking, as he listened to Léa. He rested his cheek on her breast and begged her to go on, if for a moment she ceased her tender lullaby. And Léa, fearful that her own tears would flow, went on with her scolding.

"Wicked monster . . . heartless little devil . . . Get along with you, you great slut!"

He looked at her in gratitude: "That's right . . . Go on slanging me! Oh, Nounoune!"

She held him at arm's length to see him properly. "So you love me, then?"

He lowered his eyes in childish confusion: "Yes, Nounoune."

A little burst of uncontrollable laughter warned Léa that she was on the verge of giving way to the most terrible joy of her life. An embrace, followed by collapse, the uncovered bed, two bodies joined together like the two living halves of an animal that has been cut through. 'No, no,' she said to herself, 'not yet, oh, not yet. . . .'

"I'm thirsty," Chéri sighed. "Nounoune, I'm thirsty."

She rose quickly and put a hand on the now tepid jug of water; hardly had she hurried from the room before she was back again. Chéri, curled up in a ball, was lying with his head on the pouffe. "Rose will bring you some lemonade," Léa said. "Don't stay there. Come and sit on the chaise-longue. Does the lamp hurt your eyes?"

She was trembling with delight in her imperious solicitude. She sat down at the other end of the chaise-longue and Chéri half stretched out to nestle against her.

"Perhaps now you'll tell me a little . . ."

They were interrupted by the entry of Rose. Chéri, without getting up, languidly turned his head in her direction: "Evening, Rose."

"Good evening, Monsieur," Rose said, discreetly.

"Rose, to-morrow at nine, I'd like . . ."

"Brioches and chocolate," Rose finished for him.

Chéri shut his eyes again with a sigh of contentment. "And that's that. . . . Rose, where am I going to dress to-morrow morning?"

"In the boudoir," Rose answered accommodatingly. "Only I had better take the settee out, I suppose, and put back the shaving-mirror, as it used to be?"

She sought confirmation in the eye of Léa, who was proudly displaying her spoilt child, supported by her arm as he drank.

"If you like," Léa said. "We'll see. You can go, Rose."

Rose retired, and during the ensuing moment's silence nothing could be heard except the vague murmuring of the wind and the cry of a bird bewildered by the brightness of the moon.

"Chéri, are you asleep?"

He gave one of his long-drawn sighs like an exhausted retriever. "Oh, no, Nounoune, I'm too happy to sleep."

"Tell me, child . . . You haven't been unkind over there?"

"At home? No Nounoune, far from it. I swear to you."

He looked up at her, without raising his trusting head.

"Of course not, Nounoune. I left because I left. The girl's very nice. There was no fuss at all."

"Ah!"

"I wouldn't swear that she didn't have an inkling all the same. This evening she was wearing what I call her 'orphanage look', you know, pathetic dark eyes under her pretty head of hair. . . . You know how pretty her hair is?"

"Yes."

She threw out these monosyllables in a whisper as if intent on the words of someone talking in his sleep.

"I even think," Chéri continued, "that she must have seen me going through the garden."

"Oh?"

"Yes. She was on the balcony, in her white sequin dress, congealed whiteness. Oh! I don't like that dress. . . . Ever since dinner it had been making me long to cut and run."

"No."

"Yes it had, Nounoune. I can't say whether she saw me. The moon wasn't up. It came up while I was waiting."

"Where were you waiting?"

Chéri waved a vague hand in the direction of the avenue. "There. I was waiting, don't you understand. I wanted to see. I'd waited a long time."

"But what for?"

He hastily jumped away and sat further off. He resumed his expression of primitive distrust. "I wanted to be sure there was nobody here."

"Oh, yes. . . . You thought that . . ."

She could not resist a scornful laugh. A lover in her house! A lover while Chéri was still living! It was grotesque. 'How stupid he is!' she thought in her enthusiasm.

"You're laughing?"

He stood up in front of her and put his hand on her forehead, forcing back her head. "You're laughing! You're making fun of me. You're . . . Then you have a lover! There is someone!"

He leaned over her as he spoke, pushing her head back against the end of the chaise-longue. She felt the breath of an insulting mouth on her eyelids, and made no effort to be free of the hand that was crushing her hair against her forehead.

"I dare you to say you have a lover!"

She fluttered her eyelids, dazzled by the radiance of the face bearing down on her, and finally, in a toneless voice, she said: "No, I have no lover. I . . . love you. . . ."

He relaxed his hold and began pulling off his dinner jacket and waistcoat; his tie whistled through the air and ended up round the neck of Léa's bust—up on the mantel-piece. Meanwhile, he never moved away from her, and kept her, wedged between his knees, where she sat on the chaise-longue.

When she saw him half-naked, she asked, with a note of sadness: "Do you really want to? . . . Do you? . . ."

He did not answer, carried away by the thought of his approaching pleasure and the consuming desire to take her again. She gave way and served her young lover like a good mistress, with devout solicitude. Nevertheless, she anticipated with a sort of terror the moment of her own undoing; she endured Chéri as she might a torture, warding him off with strengthless hands, and holding him fast between strong knees. Finally, she seized him by the arm, uttered a feeble cry and foundered in the deep abyss, whence love emerges pale and in silence, regretful of death.

They remained enfolded in their close embrace and no words troubled the prolonged silence of their return to life. The upper part of his body had slipped down and he lay across Léa's thigh, his pendent head, with eyes closed, resting upon the sheets as if he had been stabbed to death over the body of his mistress. She, meanwhile, partly turned away from him, bore almost the full weight of this unsparing body. She breathed softly but unevenly. Her left arm ached, crushed beneath her. Chéri could feel the back of his neck growing numb. Both were waiting, concentrated and motionless, for the abating tempest of their pleasure to recede.

'He's asleep,' Léa thought. With her free hand, she was still clinging to Chéri's wrist and she squeezed it gently. One of her knees was being crushed by a knee —how well she knew its lovely shape! About the level of her own heart she could feel the steady muffled beating of another. Chéri's favourite scent—insistent, clinging, reminding her of fat waxy flowers and exotic glades—was all pervasive. 'He is here!' she whispered, immersed in a feeling of blind security. 'He is here for ever!' her senses re-echoed. The well-ordered prudence, the happy common sense that had been her guide through life, the humiliating vagaries of her riper years and the subsequent renunciations, all beat a retreat and vanished into thin air before the presumptuous brutality of love. 'He is here!' she thought. 'He has left his own home and his pretty silly little wife to come back, to come back to me! Who can take him from me now? Now at last I'll be able to organise our existence. He doesn't always know what he wants; but I do. No doubt we shall have to go away. We shan't go into hiding, but we'll look for somewhere peaceful. For I must find time to look at him. When I was unaware I loved him, I can't ever have looked at him properly. I must find a place where there'll be room enough for his whims and my wishes. I'll do the thinking for both of us—let him do the sleeping.'

While she was painstakingly withdrawing her left arm, cramped and pricking with pins and needles, and her numbed shoulder, she glanced at Chéri's averted face and found that he was not asleep. She could see the whites of his eyes and the flutter of the little black wings of his long eyelashes.

"Why, you're not asleep!"

She felt him tremble against her, before he turned over in a single movement.

"But you're not asleep, either, Nounoune!"

He stretched a hand out to the bedside table and switched on the lamp: a flood of rosy light covered the big bed, throwing the patterns of the lace into high relief, hollowing out shadowed valleys between swelling hills in the quilted folds of the eiderdown. Chéri, stretched out at full length, surveyed the field of his victory and of his peace. Léa, leaning on one elbow beside him, stroked his beloved, long eyebrows, and swept back the rebellious locks. Lying with his hair dishevelled over his forehead, he looked as if he had been blown over by a raging wind.

The enamel clock struck. Chéri straightened himself at a bound and sat up. "What time is it?"

"I don't know. What difference can it make to us?"

"Oh, I just asked. . . ."

He gave a short laugh, and did not immediately lie down again. Outside, the first milkcart clinked out its tinkling carillon, and he made a vague movement in the direction of the avenue. The strawberry-coloured curtains were slit through by the cold blade of dawning day. Chéri turned back to look at Léa, and stared at her with the formidable intensity of a suspicious dog or a puzzled child. An undecipherable thought appeared in the depths of his eyes; their shape, their dark wallflower hue, their harsh or languorous glint, were used only to win love, never to reveal his mind. From sheets crumpled as though by a storm, rose his naked body, broad-shouldered, slim-waisted; and his whole being breathed forth the melancholy of perfect works of art.

"Ah, you . . ." sighed the infatuated Léa.

He did not smile, accustomed as he was to accepting personal praise.

"Tell me, Nounoune. . . ."

"What, my pretty?"

He hesitated, fluttered his eyelids, and shivered. "I'm tired . . . and then to-morrow, how will you manage about——"

Léa gave him a gentle push and pulled the naked body and drowsy head down to the pillows again.

"Don't worry. Lie down and go to sleep. Isn't Nounoune here to look after you? Don't think of anything. Sleep. You're cold, I'm sure. . . . Here, take this, it's warm. . . ."

She rolled him up in the silk and wool of a little feminine garment, retrieved from somewhere in the bed, and put out the light. In the dark, she lent him her shoulder, settled him happily against her side, and listened till his breathing was in rhythm with her own. No desires clouded her mind, but she did not wish for sleep. 'Let him do the sleeping; it's for me to do the thinking,' she repeated to herself. 'I'll contrive our flight with perfect tact and discretion; I believe in causing as little suffering and scandal as possible. . . . For the spring we shall like the south best. If there were only myself to be considered, I'd rather stay here, in peace and quiet; but there's Ma Peloux and the young Madame Peloux. . . .' The vision of a young wife in her nightgown, anxiously standing beside a window, checked Léa only long enough for her to shrug her shoulders with cold impartiality. 'I can't help that. What makes one person's happiness . . .'

The black silky head stirred on her breast, and her sleeping lover moaned in his dream. With a zealous arm, Léa shielded him against nightmares, and rocked him gently so that—without sight, without memory, without plans for the future—he might still resemble that "naughty little boy" never born to her.

HE had lain awake for some little while, taking great care not to stir. Cheek on folded arms, he tried to guess the time. Under a clear sky, the avenue must be vibrating with heat too insistent for early morning, since no shadow of a cloud passed across the lambent rose-red curtains. 'Ten o'clock, perhaps?' He was tormented by hunger; he had eaten little the previous evening. A year ago he would have bounded out of bed, roughly aroused Léa from sleep by ferocious shouts for cream-frothed chocolate and butter off the ice.

He did not stir. He was afraid, did he move, of crumbling away what remained to him of his rapture, the visual pleasure he derived from the shining curtains and from the steel and brass spirals of the bed, twinkling in the coloured aura of the room. Last night's great happiness had dwindled, it seemed, had melted, and sought refuge in the dancing iridescence of a cut glass jug.

On the landing, Rose trod the carpet with circumspect step; a discreet besom was sweeping the courtyard; and Chéri heard the tinkle of china coming from the pantry. 'How the morning drags on,' he said to himself. 'I'll get up'. But he remained without moving a muscle, for, behind him, Léa yawned and stretched her legs. He felt the touch of a gentle hand on his back. He shut his eyes again, and, for no good reason, his whole body began to act a lie, feigning the limpness of sleep. He was aware of

Léa leaving the bed and of her dark silhouette between
him and the curtains, which she drew half apart. She
turned round to look at him, and with a toss of the head
smiled in his direction—in no sense a smile of triumph,
but a resolute smile, ready to accept all dangers. She was
in no hurry to leave the room, and Chéri kept watch on
her through hardly parted eyelashes. He saw her open a
railway time-table and run her finger down the columns;
then she seemed absorbed in some calculation, brow
puckered and face upturned. Not yet powdered, a meagre
twist of hair at the back of her head, double chin and
raddled neck, she was exposing herself rashly to the
unseen observer.

She moved away from the window, and, taking her
cheque-book from a drawer, wrote and tore out several
cheques. Then she put a pair of white pyjamas at the
foot of the bed, and silently left the room.

Alone, Chéri took several deep breaths, realising that
he had hardly dared to breathe since Léa had left the bed.
He got up, put on the pyjamas, and opened a window.
'It's stifling in here,' he gasped. He had the vague uncomfortable feeling of having done something repre-
hensible. 'Because I pretended to be asleep? But I've
watched Léa a hundred times just after she's got out
of bed. Only, this time, I made the pretence of being
asleep.'

The dazzling light restored the rose-pink glow of the
room, and the delicate nacreous tints of the picture by
Chaplin smiled down at him from the wall. Chéri bowed
his head and shut his eyes, in an effort to remember the
room as it had looked the night before—the mysterious
colour, like the inside of a water-melon, the enchanted
dome of lamp-light, and, above all, his exaltation when
reeling under the intensity of his pleasures.

"You're up! The chocolate's already on its way."

He was pleased to note that it had taken Léa only these few moments to do her hair, touch up her face, and spray herself with the familiar scent. The room seemed suddenly to be filled with the cheerful sound of her lovely voice, and with the smell of chocolate and hot toast. Chéri sat down beside the two steaming cups and was handed the thickly buttered toast by Léa. She did not suspect that he was trying to find something to say, for she knew that he was seldom talkative, especially when he was eating. She enjoyed a good breakfast, eating with the haste and preoccupied gaiety of a woman who, her trunks packed, is ready to catch her train.

"Your second piece of toast, Chéri?"

"No, thank you, Nounoune."

"Not hungry any more?"

"Not hungry."

With a smile, she shook her finger at him. "You know what you're in for! You're going to swallow down two rhubarb pills!"

He wrinkled his nose, shocked. "Listen, Nounoune. You've got a mania for fussing . . ."

"Ta ti ta ta! That's my look out. Put out your tongue. You won't show it me! Then wipe off your chocolate moustache, and let's have a quick sensible talk. Tiresome subjects can't be dealt with too quickly."

She stretched across the table to take Chéri's hand and hold it between her own.

"You've come back. That was our fate. Do you trust yourself to me? I'll be responsible for you."

She could not help breaking off, and closed her eyes as if hugging her victory. Chéri noticed the flush on his mistress's face.

"Oh!" she continued in a lower voice, "When I think

of all that I never gave you, all that I never said to you! When I think that I believed you merely a passing fancy, like all the others—only a little more precious than all the others! What a fool I was not to understand that you were my love, *the* love, the great love that comes only once!"

When she opened her blue eyes, they seemed to have become bluer, gaining depth in the shade of her eyelids, and her breathing was uneven.

'Oh,' Chéri prayed inwardly, 'Don't let her ask me a question, don't let her expect an answer from me now! I couldn't speak a single word.'

She gave his hand a little shake. "Come along, let's be serious. As I was saying—we're leaving, we've already left. What will you do about *over there?* Let Charlotte arrange all the settlement details—it's much the wisest— and make her be generous, I beg of you. How will you let them know *over there?* A letter, I imagine. None too easy, but the less ink spilled, the better. We'll see about that between us. Then there's the question of your luggage. I've none of your things here any more. Such little details are far more upsetting than a major decision, but don't worry too much. . . . Will you kindly stop tearing the skin off the side of your toe all the time! That's the way to get an ingrowing toe-nail!"

Automatically, he let his foot drop to the floor. Under the weight of his sullen taciturnity, he found it a strain to focus his jaded attention on what Léa was saying. He stared at his mistress's happy, animated, imperious features, and asked himself vaguely: 'Why does she look so happy?'

His bewilderment became so obvious that Léa stopped in the middle of her monologue on their chances of buying old Berthellemy's yacht from him. "Could anyone believe that you've not got one word of advice to give? Oh, you might still be twelve!"

Chéri, snatched from his stupor, put a hand to his forehead and looked at Léa, his eyes filled with melancholy.

"Being with you, Nounoune, is likely to keep me twelve for half a century."

She blinked her eyes several times as if he had breathed on their lids, and let silence settle again.

"What are you trying to say?" she asked at last.

"Nothing, except what I did say, Nounoune. Nothing but the truth. And can you deny it, you, the most honest person alive?"

She decided to laugh, but her gaiety masked a terrible fear.

"But half your charm lies in your childishness, stupid! Later on it will be the secret of your eternal youth. Why complain of it? And you have the cheek to complain of it to *me*!"

"Yes, Nounoune. Do you expect me to complain to anyone but you?" and he caught hold of the hand she had taken away. "My own Nounoune, dearest, darling Nounoune, I'm not only complaining of myself: I'm accusing you!"

She felt the grip of his firm hand. Instead of looking away, his large dark eyes with lashes gleaming clung pitifully to hers. She was determined not to tremble, yet. 'It's nothing, it's nothing,' she thought. 'It calls only for two or three sharp words and he'll become insulting, then sulky, and then I'll forgive him. . . . It's no more than that.' But she failed to find the quick rebuke which would change the expression on his face. "Come, come, child . . . You know quite well there are certain jokes I will not tolerate." But at the same moment she knew her voice to be sounding false and feeble. 'How badly I said that . . . bad theatre. . . .'

It was half-past ten, and the sun was now shining on the table between them. Léa's polished nails twinkled in its beams; but the light fell also on the soft flabby skin on the back of her well-shaped hands and on her wrists. This emphasised—like criss-crossings on a clay soil when heavy rain is followed by a dry spell—the complicated network of tiny concentric grooves and miniature parallelograms. Léa rubbed her hands absent-mindedly, turning her head to make Chéri look out of the window; but he persisted in his miserable, hang-dog moodiness. The two hands were pretending, as if in disgrace, to toy with a loop of her belt. Brusquely he pounced upon them, kissed and kissed them again, then pressed his cheek against them, murmuring "My Nounoune. . . . Oh, my poor Nounoune . . ."

"Let me alone," she cried with inexplicable anger, snatching her hands away from him.

She took a moment to regain her control, frightened of her weakness, for she had been on the verge of tears. As soon as she was able, she smiled and spoke.

"So now it's me you're sorry for! Why did you accuse me a moment ago?"

"I was wrong," he said, humbly. "For me you have been always . . ." He made a gesture to express his inability to find words worthy of her.

"*You have been*?" she underlined in a biting voice. "That sounds like an obituary notice, my good child!"

"You see . . ." he began reproachfully.

He shook his head, and she saw only too well that she could not rouse any anger in him. She tightened all her muscles, and reined in her thoughts with the help of those few words, ever the same, and inwardly repeated again and again: 'Here he is, in front of my eyes. I've only to look to see he's still there. He's not out of reach. But is he still here, with me, really and truly?'

Her thoughts escaped from the domination of these repeated phrases, only to sink into a great unvoiced lament. 'Oh! if only, if only I could somehow be returned to the moment when I was saying, "Your second piece of toast, Chéri!" for that moment's only just round the corner—it's not yet lost and gone for ever! Let's start again from there. The little that's taken place since won't count—I'll wipe it out, I'll wipe it out. I'm going to talk to him as though we're back where we were a moment ago. I'm going to talk to him about our departure, our luggage.'

She did, in fact, speak, and said, "I see . . . I see I cannot treat as a man a creature who, from sheer feebleness of character, can drive two women to distraction. Do you think that I don't understand? You like your journeys short, don't you? Yesterday at Neuilly, here to-day, but to-morrow! To-morrow, where? Here? No, no, my child, no need to lie, that guilty look would never take in even a woman stupider than I am, if there is one like that over there. . . ."

She threw out an arm to indicate Neuilly with so violent a gesture that she upset a cake-stand, which Chéri picked up again. Her words had sharpened her grief into anguish, an angry jealous anguish pouring forth like a young wife's outburst. The rouge on her cheek turned to the deep purple of wine-lees; a strand of her hair, crimped by the curling-tongs, wriggled down her neck like a small dry snake.

"And even the woman over there, even your wife won't be found waiting there every time you choose to come back home! A wife, my child, may not always be

easy to find, but she's much easier to lose! You'll have
yours kept under lock and key by Charlotte, eh? That's a
marvellous idea! Oh, how I'll laugh, the day when . . ."

Chéri got up, pale and serious. "Nounoune! . . ."

"Why Nounoune? What d'you mean, Nounoune?
Do you think you're going to frighten me? You want to
lead your own life, do you? Go ahead! You're bound to
see some pretty scenes, with a daughter of Marie-Laure's.
She may have thin arms and a flat behind, but that won't
prevent her from . . ."

"I forbid you, Nounoune!"

He seized her by the arm; but she rose, vigorously
shook herself free, and broke into hoarse laughter:
"Why, of course, 'I forbid you to say a word against my
wife!' Isn't that it?"

He walked round the table, trembling with indignation,
and went straight up to her. "No, I forbid you—d'you
hear me?—I forbid you to spoil my Nounoune!" She
retreated to the end of the room, babbling, "What's
that? what's that?" He followed her as though bent on
chastising her. "You heard what I said. Is that the way
for Nounoune to speak? What do you mean by such
behaviour? Cheap little jibes like Madame Peloux's,
is that what you go in for? To think they could come
from you, Nounoune, from you. . . ."

Arrogantly he threw back his head. "I know how
Nounoune should speak. I know how she ought to think.
I've had time to learn. I've not forgotten the day when
you said to me, just before I married, 'At least don't be
cruel. Try not to make her suffer. I have the feeling that
a doe is being thrown to a greyhound.' Those were your
words. That's really you. And the night before I married,
when I ran away to come and see you, I remember you
said to me . . ."

He could not go on, but all his features were bright with the memory.

"Darling, pull yourself together." He put his hands on Léa's shoulders. "And even last night," he went on, "it wasn't the first time you asked me whether I might not have hurt somebody *over there*! My Nounoune, I knew you as a fine woman, and I loved you as a fine woman, when we first started. If we have to make an end of it, must you start behaving like all the other women?"

She dimly felt the cunning behind the compliment and sat down, hiding her face in her hands.

"How hard you are, how hard," she stammered. "Why did you come back? . . . I was so calm on my own, getting so used to . . ."

She heard herself lying and stopped.

"Well, *I* wasn't!" Chéri said quickly. "I came back because . . . because . . ."

He raised his arms, let them drop and lifted them again. "Because I couldn't go on without you, there's no point in looking for any other explanation."

For a moment no word was spoken.

Quite overcome, she looked at this impatient young man, who with light feet and open arms, as white as a seagull, seemed poised for flight.

Chéri let his dark eyes rove all over her body.

"Oh, you can be proud of yourself," he said suddenly. "You can be proud of yourself for having made me— and what's more for three months—lead such a life, such a life!"

"I did?"

"Who else, if it wasn't you? If a door opened, it was Nounoune; the telephone rang, Nounoune; a letter in the garden postbox, perhaps Nounoune. . . . In the very

wine I drank, I looked for you, and I never found a
Pommery to equal yours. And then at nights . . . Oh,
heavens above!"

He was walking up and down the carpet with rapid,
noiseless steps. "I know now what it is to suffer for a
woman, and no mistake! After you, I know what all the
other women will be . . . dust and ashes! Oh, how well
you've poisoned me!"

She drew herself up slowly in her chair, and, letting
her body turn now this way, now that, followed Chéri's
movements. Her cheeks were dry, rather shiny, and their
fevered flush made the blue of her eyes almost intolerable.
He was walking up and down, head lowered, and he
never stopped talking.

"Imagine Neuilly with you not there, the first days
after my return! For that matter, everything—with you
not there! I almost went mad. One night, the child was
ill—I no longer remember what it was, headache, pains,
something. I felt sorry for her, but I had to leave the
room; otherwise nothing in the world could have stopped
me saying, 'Wait, don't cry, I'll go and fetch Nounoune
and she'll make you well'—and you would have come,
wouldn't you, Nounoune? Great heavens, what a life
it was. . . . I took on Desmond at the Hôtel Morris, paid
him well into the bargain, and sometimes at night I
would tell him stories. . . . I used to speak as if you were
unknown to him. 'Old boy, there's never been a skin
like hers. . . . Take one look at that cabochon sapphire of
yours, and then hide it away for ever, because no light
can turn the blue of *her* eyes to grey!' I used to tell him
how you could be tough when you wanted to be; and
that no one had ever got the better of you, least of all me!
I used to say, 'That woman, old boy, when she's wearing
just the right hat—the dark blue one with the white

wing, Nounoune, last summer's—and with the way she
has of putting on her clothes—you can match her against
any other woman you may choose—and she'll put
every one of them in the shade!' And then that wonderful
manner you have of walking—of talking—your smile—
the erect way you hold yourself, I used to say to him—to
Desmond: 'Ah! A woman like Léa *is* something!' "

He snapped his fingers with proprietary pride and
stopped, quite out of breath from his talking and walking.
'I never said all that to Desmond,' he thought, 'and yet
I'm not telling lies. Desmond understood all right.'

He wanted to go on and glanced at Léa. She was still
ready to listen. Sitting bolt upright now, she exposed to
him in the full light her noble face in its disarray, the skin
shining like wax where the hot tears had dried. Her
cheeks and chin were pulled down by an invisible weight,
and this added a look of sadness to the trembling corners
of her mouth. Chéri found intact amidst this wreckage
of beauty the lovely commanding nose and the eyes as
blue as a blue flower.

"And so you see, Nounoune, after months of that sort
of life, I come back here, and . . ." He pulled himself
up, frightened by what he had nearly said.

"You come back here, and find an old woman," Léa
said calmly, in a whisper.

"Nounoune! Listen, Nounoune!"

He threw himself on his knees beside her, looking like
a guilty, tongue-tied child no longer able to hide his
misdemeanour.

"And you find an old woman," Léa repeated. "So
what are you afraid of, child?"

She put her arms round his shoulders, and felt his body
rigid and resistant, in sympathy with the hurt she was
suffering. "Come, cheer up, my Chéri. Don't cry, my

pretty. . . . What is it you're afraid of? Of having hurt me? Far from it: I feel so grateful to you."

He gave a sob of protestation, finding no strength to gainsay her.

She put her cheek against his tousled black hair. "Did you say all that, did you really think all that of me? Was I really so lovely in your eyes, tell me? And so kind? At the age when a woman's life is so often over, was I really the loveliest for you, the most kind, and were you really in love with me? How grateful I am to you, my darling! The finest, did you say? . . . My poor child."

He let himself go, while she supported him in her arms.

"Had I really been the finest, I should have made a man of you, and not thought only of the pleasures of your body, and my own happiness. The finest! Oh no, my darling, I certainly wasn't that, since I kept you to myself. And now it's almost too late. . . ."

He seemed to be asleep in Léa's arms; but his obstinately tight-shut eyelids quivered incessantly, and with one lifeless hand he was clutching hold of her négligée and slowly tearing it.

"It's almost too late, it's almost too late. But all the same . . ." She leaned over him. "Listen to me, my darling. Wake up, my pretty, and listen to me with your eyes open. Don't be afraid of looking at me. I am, after all, the woman you were in love with, you know, the finest woman . . ."

He opened his eyes, and his first tearful glance was already filled with a selfish, mendicant hope.

Léa turned away her head. 'His eyes . . . Oh, we must get this over quickly. . . .' She put her cheek against his forehead.

"It was I, child, it was my real self who said to you, 'Don't cause unnecessary pain; spare the doe. . . .' I had quite forgotten, but luckily you remembered. You are breaking away from me very late in the day, my naughty little boy; I've been carrying you next to my heart for too long, and now you have a load of your own to carry: a young wife, perhaps a child. . . . I am to blame for everything you lack. . . . Yes, yes, my pretty, here you are, thanks to me, at twenty-five, so light-hearted, so spoilt, and at the same time so sad. . . . I'm very worried about you. You're going to suffer and make others suffer. You who have loved me. . . ."

His fingers tightened their grip on her négligée, and Léa felt the sharp nails of her "naughty child" bite into her breast.

"You who have loved me," she went on after a pause, "will you be able to? . . . I don't know how to explain what I mean. . . ."

He drew back in order to listen: and she could barely restrain herself from saying, "Put your hand back on my breast and your nails where they have left their mark; my strength abandons me as soon as your flesh is parted from mine." Instead, she leaned over him as he knelt in front of her, and continued: "You have loved me, and you will regret . . ."

She smiled at him, looking down into his eyes.

"What vanity, eh! . . . But you will regret me! I beg of you, when you're tempted to terrify the girl entrusted to your care and keeping, do restrain yourself! At such moments, you must find for yourself the wisdom and kindness you never learned from me. I never spoke to you of the future. Forgive me, Chéri—I've loved you as if we were both destined to die within the same hour. Because I was born twenty-four years before you, I was doomed, and I dragged you down with me. . . ."

He was listening very attentively, which made his face

look hard. She put her hand on his forehead to smooth the furrows of anxiety.

"Can you see us, Chéri, going out to lunch together at Armenonville! . . . Can you see us inviting Monsieur and Madame Lili! . . ."

She gave a sad little laugh, and shivered.

"Oh, I'm just about as done for as that old creature. . . . Quick, quick, child, run off after your youth! Only a small piece of it has been snipped off by ageing women: all the rest is there for you and the girl who is waiting for you. You've now had a taste of youth! It never satisfies, but one always goes back for more. Oh, you had started to make comparisons before last night. . . . And what am I up to now, doling out all this advice and displaying the greatness of my soul! What do I know of you two? She loves you: it's her turn to tremble; but her misery will come from passion and not from perverted mother love. And you will talk to her like a master, not capriciously, like a gigolo. Quick, quick, run off. . . ."

She spoke in tones of hasty supplication. He listened, standing planted before her, his chest bare, his hair tempestuous: and so alluring, that she had to clasp her hands to prevent their seizing hold of him. He guessed this, perhaps, and did not move away. For an instant they shared a lunatic hope—do people feel like this in mid-air when falling from a tower?—then the hope vanished.

"Go," she said in a low voice. "I love you. It's too late. Go away. But go away at once. Get dressed!"

She rose and fetched him his shoes, spread out his crumpled shirt and his socks. He stood helpless, moving his fingers awkwardly as if they were numb. She had to find his braces and his tie; but she was careful not to go too close to him and offered him no further help. While

he was dressing, she glanced into the courtyard several
times, as if she were expecting a carriage at the door.

He looked even paler when he was dressed, and a halo
of fatigue round his eyes made them seem larger.

"You don't feel ill?" she asked him. And she added
timidly, lowering her eyes, "You could always lie down
for a little." But at once she pulled herself together and
came over to him, as though he were in great danger.
"No, no, you'll be better at home. Hurry, it's not yet
midday; a good hot bath will soon put you to rights, and
then the fresh air . . . Here are your gloves. . . . Your
hat? On the floor, of course. Put your coat on, there's a
nip in the air. Au revoir, my Chéri, au revoir. That's
right. And tell Charlotte that . . ." She closed the door
behind him, and silence put an end to her vain and
desperate words. She heard Chéri stumble on the staircase and she ran to the window. He was going down the
front steps and then he stopped in the middle of the
courtyard.

"He's coming back! He's coming back!" she cried,
raising her arms.

An old woman, out of breath, repeated her movements in the long pier-glass, and Léa wondered what she
could have in common with that crazy creature.

Chéri continued on his way towards the street. On the
pavement he buttoned up his overcoat to hide his crumpled shirt. Léa let the curtain fall back into place; but
already she had seen Chéri throw back his head, look up
at the spring sky and the chestnut trees in flower, and
fill his lungs with the fresh air, like a man escaping from
prison.

THE LAST OF CHÉRI

Translated by
Roger Senhouse

CHÉRI closed the iron gate of the little garden behind him and sniffed the night air: "Ah! it's nice out here!" In the same breath, he changed his mind: "No, it isn't."

The thickly planted chestnut trees weighed heavily upon the heat pent up beneath. A dome of rusted leaves vibrated above the nearest gas-lamp. The Avenue Henri-Martin, close-set with greenery, was stifling; only with the dawn would a breath of fresh air come up from the Bois de Boulogne.

Bare-headed, Chéri turned back to look at the house, empty now but still lit up. He heard the clink of roughly handled glass, followed by the clear ring of Edmée's voice, sharp with reproof. He saw his wife come to the window of the gallery on the first floor and lean out. The frosted beads on her evening dress lost their snowy whiteness, caught for a moment a greenish glint from the lamp, then flamed into yellow as she touched the gold lamé curtains.

"Is that you on the pavement, Fred?"

"Who else could it be?"

"You didn't take Filipesco home, then?"

"No, I didn't; he'd hopped it already."

"All the same, I'd rather have liked . . . Oh well, it doesn't matter. Are you coming in now?"

"Not just yet. Far too hot. I'll just stretch my legs."

"But . . . Oh well, just as you like."

She broke off a moment, and must have been laughing, for he could see the quiver of her frost-spangled dress.

"All I can see of you from here is a white shirt-front and a white face cut out on black. Exactly like a poster for a night club. It looks devastating."

"How you adore my mother's expressions!" he said reflectively. "You can tell everyone to go to bed. I've got my key."

She waved a hand in his direction. He watched the lights go out one by one in all the windows. One particular light—a dull blue gleam—told Chéri that Edmée was going through her boudoir into their bedroom, which looked out on the garden at the back of the house. 'The boudoir will soon come to be known as the study, and no mistake,' he thought.

The clock of Janson-de-Sailly began to strike and Chéri cocked his ear to catch the chiming notes in flight, like drops of rain. 'Midnight! She's in a hurry to get to bed. . . . Yes, of course, she has to be at her Hospital by nine to-morrow morning.' He took a few nervous steps, shrugged his shoulders, and grew calmer.

'It's as if I'd married a ballet-dancer. Nine o'clock sharp, the class: it's sacrosanct. It has to come before everything else.'

He walked on as far as the entrance to the Bois. The day's dust, hanging in the pallid sky, dimmed the brightness of the stars. Step for step, a second tread echoed Chéri's: he stopped and waited for it to catch up with him. He disliked anyone walking behind him.

"Good evening, Monsieur Peloux," said the nightwatchman, touching his cap.

Chéri answered by raising a finger to his forehead

with the condescension of an officer—a trick he had
picked up during the war from his fellow quartermaster-
sergeants—and walked on past the night-watchman,
who was trying the locks on the iron gates to the little
private gardens.

From a couple of lovers on a bench just inside the
Bois, came the rustle of crushed clothes and the whisper
of smothered endearments. Chéri listened for an instant
to the clasped bodies and invisible lips, a sound like the
ripple of a ship's prow cleaving calm waters.

'The man's a soldier,' he noticed. 'I've just heard him
unbuckle his belt.'

He was not thinking, which left his every sense on
the alert. On many a calm night during the war Chéri had
derived complex pleasure and subtle terror from his
primitive keenness of hearing; his fingers, even when
caked with mud and pocket fug, had been quick to
distinguish the image on medal or coin, and to tell, by
leaf or stalk, plants whose name he did not know. "Hi,
there, Peloux lad, just tell us what I've got ahold of
here?" Chéri recalled the ginger-headed lad who, under
cover of darkness, would push into his hand a dead mole,
a small snake, a tree-frog, an over-ripe fruit, or some piece
of filth, and then exclaim, "Blimey, he gets it every
time!" The memory made him smile, but with no pity
for the ginger-headed lad, now dead. Yet he was haunted
sometimes by the picture of his pal Pierquin, lying there
on his back asleep for ever, with a look of distrust still on
his face. He often spoke of him.

This very evening, at home, when dinner was over,
Edmée had deftly steered the conversation round to the
pathetic little tale, put together with such studied
clumsiness. Chéri had it off by heart and it ended with the
words: "And then Pierquin said to me, 'I had a dream

about cats, old lad; and then I'd another dream about
our river at home and it looked fair mucky. . . . The
meaning of that's pretty clear. . . .' It was at this very
moment he was picked off, by the smallest scrap of
shrapnel. I wanted to carry him back. They found the
two of us, him on the top of me, not a hundred yards from
the spot. I tell you about him because he was a rare good
sort . . . and he had quite a lot to do with my being given
this."

And, as he ended on this modest note, Chéri had
lowered his eyes to his green-and-red riband and knocked
the ash off his cigarette, as though to keep himself in
countenance. He considered it nobody's business that a
chance explosion had thrown one of them across the
other's shoulders, leaving Chéri alive and Pierquin dead.
The truth—more ambiguous than falsehood—was that
the terrific weight of a Pierquin, suddenly struck dead,
had kept Chéri alive and half-suffocated, indignant and
resentful. Chéri still bore a grudge against Pierquin.
And, further, he had come to scorn the truth ever since
the day when, years ago, it had suddenly fallen from
his mouth like a belch, to spatter and wound one whom
he had loved.

But at home this evening, the Americans—Majors
Marsh-Meyer and Atkins, and Lieutenant Wood—had
not appeared to listen to him. With the vacant faces of
athletic first-communicants, with fixed and expressionless
eyes, they had simply been waiting to go to a night club,
waiting with almost painful anxiety. As for Filipesco!
'Needs watching,' Chéri decided laconically.

The lake in the Bois was encircled with a fragrant mist
that rose rather from the scythed slopes of its banks
than from the stagnant water. Chéri was about to lean
against a tree, when, from the shadows, a woman boldly

brushed against him. "Good evening, kid . . ." The last word made him start; it was uttered in a low parched voice, the very voice of thirst, of dusty roads, of this dry hot night. . . . He made no answer, and the dim figure came a step nearer on soft-soled shoes. But he caught a whiff of black woollens, soiled linen, dank hair, and turned back with long springy strides towards his own home.

The dull blue light was still on: Edmée had not yet left her boudoir-study. In all probability she would still be seated at her desk, signing chits for drugs and dressings, reading through the day's notes and the short reports made by her secretary. Her pretty school-marm head, crimped hair with a reddish tint, would be bent over her papers.

Chéri pulled out the small flat key on the end of its thin gold chain. 'Here we go. In for another carefully measured dose of love. . . .'

As was his habit, he entered his wife's boudoir without knocking. Edmée showed no sign of surprise, but went on with her telephone conversation. Chéri listened.

"No, not to-morrow. . . . You won't want me there for that. The General knows you perfectly well. And at the Ministry of Commerce, there's . . . What do you mean? 'Have I got Lémery?' No, certainly not! He's charming, but . . . Hullo? . . . Hullo? . . ." She laughed, showing her small teeth. "Oh come! that's going too far. . . . Lémery makes up to every woman, provided she's not blind or lame. . . . What? Yes, he's come in, he's here at my elbow. No, no, I'll be very discreet. . . . Goodbye. . . . See you to-morrow. . . ."

A plain white wrap, the white of her pearl necklace,

was slipping off one shoulder. She had taken the pins from her chestnut hair, which, slightly frizzed by the dry atmosphere, followed every movement of her head.

"Who was that?" Chéri asked, as she put back the receiver and turned to ask him:

"Fred, you'll let me have the Rolls to-morrow morning, won't you? It will look better for bringing the General back here to lunch."

"What General?"

"General Haar."

"Is he a Boche?"

Edmée frowned. "Really, Fred, you're too old for such jokes! General Haar is coming to inspect my Hospital to-morrow. Then he can go back to America and tell them all that my Hospital can compare with any effort of the sort over there. Colonel Beybert will be showing him round, and they'll both come back here for luncheon afterwards."

Chéri took off his dinner-jacket and sent it flying in the direction of a chair.

"I don't give a damn! I'm lunching out."

"What d'you mean. What's all this?"

A spasm of rage crossed Edmée's face; but she smiled, picked up the dinner-jacket with care, and changed her tone of voice. "Didn't you ask me a moment ago who that was on the telephone? Your mother."

Chéri collapsed into an armchair and said nothing. His features were set in their most beautiful and impassive mould. Over his forehead hovered an air of serene disapproval. This was apparent, too, on his lowered eyelids, faintly shadowed now at the approach of his thirtieth year, and on his mouth, which he was careful never to compress too tightly, keeping his lips gently apart as in sleep.

"You know," Edmée continued, "she wants Lémery, of the Ministry of Commerce, to do something about her three cargo-loads of leather. There are three ships filled with leather, at present held up in harbour at Valparaiso. There is something in the idea, you know! The only thing is that Lémery won't grant the necessary import licence . . . at least, that's what he says. Do you know how much money the Soumabis offered your mother as a minimum commission?"

With a wave of the hand, Chéri brushed aside ships, leather, and commission.

"Not interested," he said simply.

Edmée dropped the subject, and affectionately approached her husband.

"You will have luncheon here to-morrow, won't you? There'll probably be Gibbs—the reporter from *Excelsior*, who's going to photograph the Hospital—and your mother."

Chéri shook his head with no sign of impatience.

"No," he said. "General Hagenbeck . . ."

"Haar."

" . . . and a Colonel, and my mother in her uniform. Her tunic—what d'you call it? her jacket?—with its little leather buttons; her elastic uplift-belt; epaulettes; high colonel's collar and her chin cascading over . . . and her cane. No, really, I don't pretend to be braver than I am. I'd rather go out."

He was laughing quietly to himself, and his laugh seemed mirthless. Edmée put a hand, already trembling with irritation, upon his arm; but her touch was light.

"You can't mean that seriously?"

"Certainly I can. I shall go for lunch to *Brekekekex*, or somewhere else."

"With whom?"

"With whom I choose."

He sat down and kicked off his pumps. Edmée leant against a black lacquer cabinet and racked her brain for words to make him behave sensibly. The white satin front of her dress rose and fell in rhythm to the quickened pace of her breathing, and she crossed her hands behind her back like a martyr. Chéri looked at her with an air of pretended indifference. 'She really does look a lady,' he thought. 'Hair all anyhow, in her chemise, on her way to the bath—she always looks a lady.'

She lowered her eyes, caught Chéri's, and smiled.

"You're teasing me," she said plaintively.

"No," Chéri replied. "I shan't lunch here to-morrow, that's all."

"But why?"

He rose, walked as far as the open door into their room—which was in darkness and filled with night scents from the garden—and then came back to her.

"Because I shan't. If you compel me to explain myself, I shall speak out and perhaps be rude. You'll burst into tears, and 'in your distress', as the saying goes, you'll let your wrap slip to the floor and . . . and unfortunately it won't have the slightest effect on me."

Another spasm of rage passed over his wife's features, but her much-tried patience was not yet exhausted. She smiled and shrugged the one bare shoulder peeping from under her hair.

"It's quite easy to *say* that it won't have any effect on you."

He was walking to and fro, clad in nothing but his short white silk pants. All the time he was testing the elasticity of his instep and calf muscles, and kept rubbing his hand over the twin brown scars under his right breast, as if to preserve their fading hue. Lean, with less flesh on his body than he had had at twenty, at the same time in better shape and training, he liked to parade up and down in front of his wife as a rival rather than a lover. He knew himself to be the more perfect specimen and, as a connoisseur, could condescend to admire in her the slim hips, the small breasts, and the graceful, almost imperceptible lines which Edmée knew so well how to clothe in tubular frocks and slinky tunics. "Are you fading away, then?" he would sometimes ask her, just for the fun of annoying her. He would watch her whole body writhe in anger, and note its sudden and unsuspected vigour.

This reply of his wife's was distasteful to him. He wanted her to look well-bred, and to be silent, if not unresponsive, in his arms. He came to a halt, puckered his brow, and looked her up and down. "Pretty manners, I must say. Do you learn them from your Physician-in-charge? The war, Madame!"

She shrugged her bare shoulder.

"What a child you are, my poor Fred! It's lucky we're by ourselves. To go on at me like that just because of a little joke . . . which was really a compliment. And for you to try and teach me manners, you . . . you! And after seven years of marriage!"

"Where do you get the seven years from?"

He sat down, naked as he was, as though for a prolonged discussion, his legs wide apart with all the ostentation of an athlete.

"Well . . . really . . . nineteen-thirteen . . . nineteen-nineteen . . ."

"Excuse me! it's clear that we don't reckon by the same calendar. Now, I count from . . ."

Edmée arched a knee, taking the weight of her body on the other leg, a confession of her weariness; but Chéri interrupted her with: "Where's all this talk leading us? Come on, let's go to bed. You've got your ballet-class at nine to-morrow, haven't you?"

"Oh! Fred!"

Edmée crushed a rose from a black vase and threw away its petals. Chéri fanned the flames of anger still smouldering in her eyes, now moist with tears, by saying: "That's the name I give that job-lot of wounded, when I'm not thinking."

Without looking at him, she murmured through trembling lips: "You brute . . . you brute . . . you loathsome monster!"

He laughed, quite untouched.

"What d'you want me to say? As far as you're concerned, we all know you're carrying out a sacred mission. But what about me? You might just as well *have* to go to the Opera every day and practise in the Rotunda, for all the difference it would make. That would leave me just as much . . . just as much out of it. And those men I called your 'job-lot', well, they're wounded, aren't they? wounded who are a little luckier than others, perhaps. I've got absolutely nothing to do with them either. With them, too, I'm . . . out of it."

She turned round to face him so impulsively that it made her hair fly out from her temples: "My darling, don't be so unhappy! You're not out of it at all, you're above all that!"

He got up, drawn towards a jug of iced water, on the sides of which the moisture was slowly condensing into bluish tears. Edmée hurried forward: "With or without lemon, Fred?"

"Without, thanks."

He drank, she took the empty glass from his hands, and he went towards the bathroom.

"By the way," he said. "About that leak in the cement of the bathing-pool. It ought . . ."

"I'm having it seen to. The man who makes those glass mosaics happens to be a cousin of Chuche, one of my wounded, and he won't need to be asked twice, believe me."

"Good." Then, as he was moving away, he turned round. "Tell me, this business of the Ranch shares we were talking about yesterday morning, ought we to sell or not? Supposing I went to see old Deutsch about them to-morrow morning, and had a chin-wag with him?"

Edmée gave a shriek of schoolgirl laughter.

"Do you think I waited for you about that? Your mother had a stroke of genius this morning, while we were giving the Baroness a lift home."

"You mean that old La Berche woman?"

"Yes, the Baroness. Your mother, as you so elegantly put it, had a chin-wag with her. The Baroness is one of the original shareholders, and never leaves the Chairman of the Board alone for a moment. . . ."

"Except to cover her face in flour."

"Must you interrupt me the whole time? . . . and by two o'clock, my dear, the whole lot had been sold—every bit of it! The little flare up on the Bourse this afternoon—it lasted only a very short time—raked us in something like two hundred and sixteen thousand francs, Fred! That'll pay for piles of medicine and bandages. I wanted to keep the news till to-morrow, and then give you one of these topping note-cases. Kiss?"

He stood, naked and white-skinned, holding back the folds of the door-curtain, and looking closely at the expression on his wife's face.

"That's all very well . . ." he said at last, "but where do I come in?"

Edmée gave a mischievous shake of the head: "Your power of attorney still stands, my love. 'The right to sell, purchase, draw up or sign an agreement made out in my name . . . etcetera'—which reminds me, I must send the Baroness something as a souvenir."

"A briar pipe," said Chéri, after pretending to have given the matter his attention.

"No, don't laugh. The good soul is so valuable to us."

"And who are 'us'?"

"Your mother and me. The Baroness knows how to talk to the men in a way they understand. She speaks their language. She tells them rather risky stories, but in such a way . . . They dote on her."

The strangest of laughs trembled on Chéri's lips. He let go his hold on the dark curtain, and it fell back into place behind him, thus obliterating him completely, as sleep obliterates the figment of a dream. He walked along a passage dimly lit by a blue globe, without making a sound, like a figure floating on air; for he had insisted upon having thick carpets laid on every floor, from top to bottom of the house. He loved silence, and furtiveness, and never knocked at the door of the boudoir, which his wife, since the war, called her study. She showed no annoyance, and sensing Chéri's presence, never jumped when he came into the room.

He took a shower bath without lingering under the cool water, sprayed himself with scent absent-mindedly, and returned to the boudoir.

He could hear the sound of someone rumpling the sheets in the bedroom next door, and the tap of a paper-knife against a cup on the bedside table. He sat down and rested his chin in his hand. On the little table beside him, he caught sight of the morrow's menu, duly made out for the butler, according to daily routine. On it he read: "*Homard Thermidor, Côtelettes Fulbert-Dumonteil, Chaud-froid de canard, salade Charlotte, Soufflé au curaçao, Allumet-tes au Chester.*" . . . 'No alteration required,' he murmured to himself. "*Six places?*"—'Ah, yes, that I must alter.' He corrected the number, and once more cupped his chin in his hand.

"Fred, do you know what time it is?"

He did not answer the soft voice, but went into their room and sat down facing the bed. With one shoulder bare and the other half-hidden by a wisp of white night-gown, Edmée was smiling, despite her tired state, aware that she looked prettier in bed than out. But Chéri remained seated, and once again cupped his chin in his hand.

"Rodin's *Penseur*," said Edmée, to encourage him to smile or to move.

"There's many a true word spoken in jest," he answered sententiously.

He pulled the folds of his Chinese dressing-gown closer over his knees and savagely crossed his arms.

"What the hell am I doing here?"

She did not understand, or had no wish to do so.

"That's what I'd like to know, Fred. It's two o'clock, and I get up at eight. To-morrow's going to be another of those pleasant little days. . . . It's unkind of you to dawdle like this. Do come along; there's a nice breeze rising. We'll go to bed with it on our faces, and imagine we're sleeping out of doors."

He weakened, and hesitated only an instant before hurling his silk wrap to a far corner of the room, while Edmée switched out the remaining light. She nestled up against him in the dark, but he neatly turned her over with her back to him and held her round the waist with strong arms, murmuring, "Like that. That's like being on a bob-sleigh," and fell asleep.

The following day, from the little window of the linen-room where he was hidden, he watched them leave. The duck's-egg green motor and another long American automobile were purring very quietly in the avenue under the thick overhanging chestnut trees. The green shade and the recently watered pavement exuded a pretence of freshness, but Chéri knew very well that in the garden at the back of the house the heat of this June morning— the month that scorches Paris—was already shrivelling the lovely deep blue of a pool of forget-me-nots within their edging of pinks.

His heart began to beat with a sort of nervousness when he saw, approaching the iron gates to his house, two figures in khaki, with gold stars on their breast and crimson velvet bands round their caps.

"In uniform, of course, the crackpot!"

This was the nickname Chéri had bestowed on the Physician-in-Charge at Edmée's Hospital, and without really knowing it, he loathed the man and his red-gold hair and the caressing tones he put into technical terms when talking to Edmée. He muttered vague hearty curses, against the Medical Corps in particular, and against all who insisted on wearing uniform in peace-time. The American officer was growing fat, so Chéri sneered: "I thought the Americans went in for sport. What's he doing with a belly like that?"but he said not a word when Edmée, in a white dress and white shoes, vivaciously held out her white-gloved hand to the Doctor. She greeted him in loud, quick, cheerful tones. Chéri had not missed a single word that fell from her red mouth, which parted in a smile over such tiny teeth. She had walked out as far as the motors, come back to tell a footman to fetch a notebook she had forgotten and stood chatting while she waited for it. She had spoken in English to the American Colonel, and lowered her voice, in automatic deference, when replying to Doctor Arnaud.

Chéri was keeping a sharp look-out from behind the muslin curtains. His characteristic mistrust and slyness froze his features into immobility directly he concealed a strong emotion, and he kept a strict watch on himself, even when alone. His eyes travelled from Edmée to the Doctor, and then from the American Colonel back to Edmée, who had more than once looked up to the first floor, as though she knew of his hiding-place.

'What are they waiting for?' he grumbled under his breath. 'Ah, so this is it. . . . God in heaven!'

Charlotte Peloux had arrived, in a sports-car driven by an impersonal and impeccable young chauffeur. Bursting out of her gabardine uniform, she held her head stiffly upright under its little tight-fitting hat with a military peak, and the ends of her bobbed red hair could be seen popping out at the back. She did not set foot to ground, but suffered them to come and pay their respects to her. She received Edmée's kiss and apparently asked after her son, for she too raised her head in the direction of the first floor, thus unveiling her magnificent eyes, over which drifted, as over the huge eyes of an octopus, some dark inhuman dream.

"She's wearing her little military cap," Chéri murmured.

He gave a curious shudder, which made him angry with himself, and smiled when the three motors drove away. He waited patiently until his "bachelor's runabout" drew up against the kerb punctually at eleven o'clock, and he kept it waiting for some considerable time. Twice he stretched out his hand to lift the receiver of the telephone, and twice he let it fall again to his side. His sudden impulse to invite Filipesco soon vanished and he thought he would like to collect young Maudru and his girl. 'Or, better still, Jean de Touzac. . . . But at this hour he'll still be furiously snoring. Gosh! all that lot . . . not one of them, I must be fair, a patch on Desmond. . . . Poor old boy.'

He regarded Desmond as a war casualty; but with greater compassion than he ever vouchsafed the dead. Desmond, who was alive yet lost to him, had the power of inspiring him with an almost tender melancholy, as well as with the jealous respect due to a man with a "job". Desmond ran a night club, and sold antiques to Americans. A gutless wash-out during the whole of the war, when he had carried anything and everything but a rifle—official papers, billy-cans, any dirty hospital receptacle—Desmond had bitten deep into peacetime with a warlike fervour, and rich had been his immediate reward, very much to Chéri's astonishment. *Desmond's* had been started in quite a small way in a private house in the Avenue d'Alma, and now it sheltered frenzied and silent couples behind its heavy ashlar masonry, beneath ceilings decorated with swallows and hawthorn, and hemmed in by the bulrushes and flamingoes of its stained-glass windows. They danced at *Desmond's*, night and day, as people dance after war: the men, young and old, free from the burden of thinking and being frightened— empty-minded, innocent; the women, given over to a pleasure far greater than any more definite sensual delight, to the company of men: that is to say, to physical contact with them, their smell, their tonic sweat, the certain proof of which tingled in every inch of their bodies—the certainty of being the prey of a man wholly alive and vital, and of succumbing in his arms to rhythms as personal, as intimate, as those of sleep.

'Desmond will have got to bed at three, or three-thirty,' Chéri reckoned. 'He'll have had enough sleep.'

But once again he let drop the hand he had stretched out to the telephone. He went down the stairs in double quick time, aided by the springy thick pile that covered every floor board in his house. As he passed by the dining-room he looked without anger at the five white plates set in a diadem round a black crystal bowl, in which floated pink water-lilies, matching the pink of the tablecloth; and he did not pause till face to face with the looking-glass, fixed to the back of the heavy door of the reception-room on the ground floor. He feared, yet was attracted by, this looking-glass, which drew what little light it had from the french windows immediately facing it across the corridor, their opaque blue panes further obscured by the dark foliage of the garden. Every time he bumped into his own image, Chéri was brought up sharp by a slight shock when he recognised it as his own. He never could understand why this glass did not reflect the faithful image of a young man of twenty-four. He could not detect the precise points where time, with invisible finger, marks first the hour of perfection on a handsome face, and then the hour of that more blatant beauty, the herald of a majestic decline.

To Chéri's mind, there could be no question of a decline, and he could never have noticed it on his own features. He had just happened to bump into a thirty-year-old Chéri and failed to recognise him; and he sometimes asked himself "What's wrong with me?" as though he were feeling a little off-colour or had thrown his clothes on anyhow. Now he hurried past the reception-room door, and thought no more about it.

Desmond's, being a properly organised establishment, was up and doing by midday, despite the late hours it kept. The concierge was hosing the paved courtyard, a waiter was sweeping the steps clean, brushing away a heap of high-class rubbish—fine light dust, silver paper, corks with metal caps, stub-ends of gold-tipped cigarettes, and crumpled drinking-straws—rubbish which bore daily witness to the prosperity of *Desmond's*.

Chéri cleared at a bound the residue of last night's brisk business; but the smell inside the house barred further progress like a rope stretched across his path. Forty couples, packed like sardines, had left behind the smell—the memory of their sweat-soaked clothes—stale, and tainted with tobacco fumes. Chéri plucked up courage and leapt up the staircase, narrowed by heavy oak banisters supported on caryatids. Desmond had wasted no money on changing the stuffy sumptuosities of 1880. After removing two dividing walls, installing a refriger-ator in the basement, engaging a jazz-band regardless of cost, no further outlay would be necessary for at least another year. "I'll bring it up to date to attract customers," so Desmond said, "when dancing isn't such a rage."

He slept on the second floor, in a room where con-volvulus ran riot on the walls and storks on the stained-glass windows; his bath was of enamelled zinc, bordered by a tiled frieze of river-plants, and the ancient heating-apparatus wheezed like a bulldog past its prime. But the telephone shone as brightly as a weapon kept polished by daily use, and Chéri, after bounding up four steps at a time, discovered his friend, lips to the chalice, apparently imbibing the murky breath of its mouthpiece. His wandering glance came down to earth, and hardly settled on Chéri before it was off and up again to the convolvulus-wreathed cornice. His yellow-gold pyjamas cast a blight over a morning-after-the-night-before face, but Desmond was inflated by prosperity and no longer worried about being ugly.

"Good morning," said Chéri. "I came through all right. What a stench there is on your stairs. Worse than a dug-out."

". . . You'll never get *Desmond's* custom at twelve," Desmond was saying to an invisible listener. "I have no difficulty in buying Pommery at that price. And for my private cellar, Pommery ought to be eleven when minus labels . . . hullo . . . yes, the labels that came off in the general rumpus. That's what I want . . . hullo?"

"You're coming out to lunch. I've got the runabout at the door," Chéri said.

"No, and twice times no," said Desmond.

"What?"

"No, and a thousand times no. Hullo? . . . Sherry! What d'you take me for? This isn't a bar. Champagne, or nothing. Don't go on wasting your time and mine. Hullo. . . . That's quite possible. Only I'm all the rage at the moment. Hullo. . . . At two o'clock precisely. A very good day to you, Monsieur."

He stretched himself, before offering a limp hand. He still looked like Alfonso XIII, but thirty summers and the war had rooted this uncertain creature in the soil he needed. To have come through the war without firing a shot, to have eaten regularly, taken every advantage of it, and malingered in general, were so many personal victories from which he had emerged strengthened

and self-confident. Assurance and a full pocket had
made him less ugly, and you could be sure that, at sixty,
he would give the illusion of having once passed for a
handsome man with a large nose and long legs. He
looked at Chéri condescendingly, but with a friendlier
eye. Chéri turned away his head and said: "What! Are
you reduced to this? Come on, old boy. It's midday and
you're not up yet."

"In the first place, I *am* ready," Desmond replied,
unbuttoning his pyjamas to show a white silk shirt and a
bronze-coloured bow tie. "And in the second, I'm not
going to lunch out."

"So that's it," said Chéri. "Well, of all . . . I'm speechless. . . ."

"But if you like I can give you two fried eggs, and half
my ham, my salad, my stout and my strawberries. No
extra charge for coffee."

Chéri looked at him in impotent fury. "Why?"

"Business," said Desmond, with a deliberately nasal
twang. "Champagne! You heard what I was saying a
moment ago. Oh! these wine-merchants! If one didn't
put on the screw . . . But I'm a match for them."

He knotted his fingers and the knuckle-joints cracked
with commercial pride.

"Yes or no?"

"Yes, you swine."

Chéri chucked his soft felt hat at his head; but Desmond
picked it up and brushed it with his forearm, to show that
this was not the moment for childish jokes. They had
eggs in aspic, ham and tongue, and good black stout with
coffee-coloured foam on it. They spoke little, and Chéri,
gazing out on to the paved courtyard, was politely bored.

'What am I doing here? Nothing, except that I'm not
at home, sitting down to cutlets Fulbert-Dumonteil.'

He visualised Edmée in white, the baby-faced American Colonel, and Arnaud, the Physician-in-Charge, in whose presence she acted the docile little girl. He thought of Charlotte Peloux's epaulettes, and a sort of fruitless affection for his host was coming over him, when the latter asked him an abrupt question:

"Do you know how much champagne was drunk here last night, between four o'clock yesterday and four o'clock this morning?"

"No," said Chéri.

"And do you know how many bottles were returned empty from those delivered here between May the first and June the fifteenth?"

"No," said Chéri.

"Say a number."

"No idea," Chéri grunted.

"But say something! Say a number! Have a guess, man! Name some figure!"

Chéri scratched the table cloth as he might during an examination. He was suffering from the heat, and from his own inertia.

"Five hundred," he got out at last.

Desmond threw himself back in his chair and, as it swerved through the air, his monocle shot a piercing flash of sunlight into Chéri's eye.

"Five hundred! You make me laugh!"

He was boasting. He did not know how to laugh: his nearest approach was a sort of sob of the shoulders. He drank some coffee, to excite Chéri's curiosity, and then put down his cup again.

"Three thousand, three hundred, and eighty-two, my boy. And do you know how much that puts in my pocket?"

"No," Chéri interrupted, "and I don't give a damn.

That's enough. My mother does all that for me if I want
it. Besides . . ." He rose, and added in a hesitant voice:
"Besides, money doesn't interest me."

"Strange," said Desmond, hurt. "Strange. Amusing."

"If you like. No, can't you understand, money doesn't
interest me . . . doesn't interest me any more."

These simple words fell from his lips slowly. Chéri
spoke them without looking up, and kicked a biscuit
crumb along the carpet; his embarrassment at making
this confession, his secretive look, restored for a fleeting
instant the full marvel of his youth.

For the first time Desmond stared at him with the
critical attention of a doctor examining a patient, 'Am I
dealing with a malingerer?' Like a doctor, he had recourse
to confused and soothing words.

"We all go through that. Everyone's feeling a little
out of sorts. No one knows exactly where he stands.
Work is a wonderful way of putting you on your feet
again, old boy. Take me, for instance. . . ."

"I know," Chéri interrupted. "You're going to tell
me I haven't enough to do."

"Yes, it's your own fault." Desmond's mockery was
condescending in the extreme. "For in these wonderful
times . . ." He was going on to confess his deep satisfaction with business, but he pulled himself up in time.
"It's also a question of upbringing. Obviously, you never
learned the first thing about life under Léa's wing.
You've no idea how to manage people and things."

"So they say." Chéri was put out. "Léa herself wasn't
fooled. You mayn't believe me, but though she didn't
trust me, she always consulted me before buying or
selling."

He thrust out his chest, proud of the days gone by,
when distrust was synonymous with respect.

"You've only got to apply yourself to it again—to money matters," Desmond continued, in his advisory capacity. "It's a game that never goes out of fashion."

"Yes," Chéri acquiesced rather vaguely. "Yes, of course. I'm only waiting."

"Waiting for what?"

"I'm waiting. . . . What I mean is . . . I'm waiting for an opportunity . . . a better opportunity. . . ."

"Better than what?"

"What a bore you are. An excuse—if you like—to take up again everything the war deprived me of years ago. My fortune, which is, in fact . . ."

"Quite considerable?" Desmond suggested. Before the war, he would have said "enormous," and in a different tone of voice. A moment's humiliation brought a blush to Chéri's cheek.

"Yes . . . my fortune. Well, the little woman, my wife, now makes that her business."

"Oh, no!" exclaimed Desmond, in shocked disapproval.

"Oh, yes, I promise you. Two hundred and sixteen thousand in a little flare-up on the Bourse the day before yesterday. So, don't you see, the question now arises, 'How am I to interfere?' . . . Where do I stand, in all this? When I suggest taking a hand, they say . . ."

"They? Who are 'they'?"

"What? Oh, my mother and my wife. They start saying: 'Take it easy. You're a warrior. Would you like a glass of orangeade? Run along to your shirt-maker, he's making you look a fool. And while you are going the rounds, you might call in and collect my necklace, if the clasp's been mended . . .' and so on, and so forth."

He was growing excited, hiding his resentment as best he could, though his nostrils were quivering, and his lips as well.

"So must I now tout motor-cars, or breed Angora
rabbits, or direct some high-class establishment? Have I
got to engage myself as a male nurse or accountant in
that bargain-basement, my wife's Hospital?" He walked
as far as the window, and came back to Desmond
precipitately. "Under the orders of Doctor Arnaud,
Physician-in-Charge, and pass the basins round for him?
Must I take up this night club business? Can't you *see*
the competition!"

He laughed in order to make Desmond laugh; but
Desmond, no doubt a little bored, kept a perfectly straight
face.

"How long ago did you start thinking of all this? You
certainly had no such ideas in the spring, or last winter,
or before you were married."

"I had no time for it," Chéri answered quite simply.
"We went off on our travels, we began furnishing the
house, we bought motors just in time to have them
requisitioned. All that led up to the war. Before the war
. . . before the war I was . . . a kid from a rich home.
I was rich, damn it!"

"You still are."

"I still am," Chéri echoed.

He hesitated once more, searching for words. "But
now, it's not at all the same thing. People have got the
jitters. And work, and activity, and duty, and women who
serve their country—not half they don't—and are crazy
about oof . . . they're such thorough-going business-
women that they make you disgusted with the word
business. They're such hard workers it's enough to make
you loathe the sight of work." He looked uncertainly at
Desmond, "Is it really wrong to be rich, and take life
easy?"

Desmond enjoyed playing his part and making up

for past subservience. He put a protective hand on Chéri's shoulder.

"My son, be rich and live your own life! Tell yourself that you're the incarnation of an ancient aristocracy. Model yourself on the feudal barons. You're a warrior."

"*Merde*," said Chéri.

"Now you're talking like a warrior. Only, you must live and let live, and let those work who like it."

"You, for instance."

"Me, for instance."

"Obviously, you're not the sort to let yourself be messed about by women."

"No," said Desmond curtly. He was hiding from the world a perverse taste for his chief cashier—a gentle creature with brown hair scraped well back, rather masculine and hairy. She wore a religious medallion round her neck, and smilingly confessed, "For two pins I'd commit murder: I'm like that."

"No. Emphatically, no! Can't you mention anything without sooner or later dragging in 'my wife, women,' or else 'in Léa's time'? Is there nothing else to talk about in 1919?"

Beyond the sound of Desmond's voice, Chéri seemed to be listening to some other, still unintelligible sound. 'Nothing else to talk about,' he repeated to himself. 'Why should there be?' He was daydreaming, lulled by the light and the warmth, which increased as the sun came round into the room. Desmond went on talking, impervious to the stifling heat, and as white as winter endive. Chéri caught the words "little birds" and began to pay attention.

"Yes, I've a whole heap of amusing connections, with whom, of course, I'll put you in touch. And when I say 'birds', I'm speaking far too frivolously of what amounts to a unique collection, you understand, utterly unique. My regulars are tasty pieces, and all the tastier for the last four years. Just you wait and see, old boy! When my capital is big enough, what a restaurant I'll show the world! Ten tables, at most, which they'll fall over each other to book. I'll cover in the court-yard. . . . You may be sure my lease provides for all additions I make! Cork-lino in the middle of the dance-floor, spot-lights. . . . That's the future! It's out there. . . ."

The tango merchant was holding forth like a founder of cities, pointing towards the window with outstretched arm. Chéri was struck by the word "future," and turned to face the spot indicated by Desmond, somewhere high up above the courtyard. He saw nothing, and felt limp. The reverberations of the two o'clock sun smote glumly down upon the little slate roof of the old stables, where the concierge of *Desmond's* had his lodging. "What a ballroom, eh?" said Desmond with fervour, pointing to the small courtyard. "And it won't be long now before I get it!"

Chéri stared intently at this man who, each day, expected and received his daily bread. 'And what about me?' he thought, inwardly frustrated.

"Look, here comes my swipes-merchant," Desmond shouted. "Make yourself scarce. I must warm him up like a bottle of Corton."

He shook Chéri's hand with a hand that had changed its character: from being narrow and boneless, it had become broad, purposeful, disguised as the rather firm hand of an honest man. 'The war . . .' thought Chéri, tongue in cheek.

"You're off? Where?" Desmond asked.

He kept Chéri standing on the top of the steps long

enough to be able to show off such a decorative client to his wine merchant.

"Over there," said Chéri, with a vague gesture.

"Mystery," murmured Desmond. "Be off to your seraglio!"

"Oh no," said Chéri, "you're quite wrong."

He conjured up the vision of some female—moist flesh, nakedness, a mouth. He shuddered with impersonal disgust, and, repeating 'You're quite wrong' under his breath, got into his runabout.

He carried away with him an all too familiar uneasiness, the embarrassment and irritation of never being able to put into words all that he really wanted to say; of never meeting the person to whom he would have to confide a half-formed admission, a secret that could have changed everything, and which, for instance, this afternoon would have dispersed the ominous atmosphere from the bleached pavements and the asphalt, now beginning to melt under a vertical sun.

'Only two o'clock,' he sighed, 'and, this month, it stays light till well after nine.'

The breath of wind raised by the speed of his motor was like a hot dry towel being flapped in his face, and he yearned for the make-believe night behind his blue curtains, to the accompaniment of the simple drip-drop-drip of the Italian fountain's sing-song in the garden.

'If I slip quickly through the hall, I'll be able to get in again without being seen. *They'll* be having coffee by now.'

He could almost catch a whiff of the excellent luncheon, of the lingering smell of the melon, of the dessert wine which Edmée always had served with the fruit; and, ahead of time, he saw the verdigrised reflection of Chéri closing the door lined with plate glass.

'In we go!'

Two motors were dozing in the shade of the low-hanging branches just inside the gates, one his wife's and the other American, both in the charge of an American chauffeur who was himself taking a nap. Chéri drove on as far as the deserted Rue de Franqueville, and then walked back to his own front door. He let himself in without making a sound, took a good look at his shadowy form in the green-surfaced mirror, and softly went upstairs to the bedroom. It was just as he had longed for it to be—blue, fragrant, made for rest. In it he found everything that his thirsty drive had made so desirable: and more besides, for there was a young woman dressed in white, powdering her face and tidying her hair in front of a long looking-glass. Her back was turned to Chéri, and she did not hear him enter. Thus he had more than a moment to observe in the glass how flushed luncheon and the hot weather had made her, and to note her strange expression of untidiness and triumph and her general air of having won an emotionally outrageous victory. All at once Edmée caught sight of her husband and turned to face him without saying a word. She examined him critically from top to toe, waiting for him to speak first.

Through the half-open window facing the garden, floated up the baritone notes of Doctor Arnaud's voice, singing, "*Oy Marie, Oy Marie.*"

Edmée's whole body seemed to incline towards this voice, but she restrained herself from turning her head in the direction of the garden.

The slightly drunken courage visible in her eyes might well forebode a serious situation. Out of contempt or cowardice, Chéri, by putting a finger to his lips, enjoined silence upon her. He then pointed to the staircase with the same imperative finger. Edmée obeyed. She went resolutely past him, without being able to repress, at the moment when she came closest to him, a slight twist of the hips and quickening of the step, which kindled in Chéri a sudden impulse to strike her. He leant over the banisters, feeling reassured, like a cat that has reached safety at the top of a tree; and, still thinking of punishing, smashing, and taking flight, he waited there, ready to be wafted away on a flood of jealousy. All that came to him was a mediocre little feeling of shame, all too bearable, as he put his thoughts into words, 'Punish her, smash up the whole place! There's better to do than that. Yes, there's better to do.' But what, he did not know.

Each morning for him, whether he woke early or late, was the start of a long day's vigil. At first he paid but scant attention, believing it to be merely the persistence of an unhealthy habit picked up in the army.

In December, 1918, after putting his knee-cap out of joint, he had eked out in his bed at home a short period of convalescence. He used to stretch himself in the early morning and smile. 'I'm comfortable. I'm waiting for the time when I feel much better. Christmas this year is really going to be worth while.'

Christmas came. When the truffles had been eaten, and the holly twig dipped in brandy set alight on a silver platter, in the presence of an ethereal Edmée, very much the wife, and to the acclamations of Charlotte, of Madame de La Berche, and members of the nursing staff of the Hospital, together with a sprinkling of Rumanian officers and athletic adolescent American colonels, Chéri waited. 'Oh, if only those fellows would go away! I'm waiting to go to sleep, head in the cool air and feet warm, in my own good bed!' Two hours later, he was still waiting for sleep, laid out as flat as a corpse, listening to the mocking call of the little winter owls in the branches—a challenge to the blue light of his unshuttered room. At last he fell asleep; but a prey to his insatiable vigilance from the peep of dawn, he began to wait for his breakfast, and gave utterance to his hearty impatience: "What the hell do they think they're doing with the grub downstairs?" He did not realise that whenever he swore or used "soldiers' slang", it always went with an affected state of mind. His jolliness was a method of escape. Breakfast was brought to him by Edmée; but in his wife's bustling movements he never failed to discern haste and the call of duty, and he would ask for more toast, or for another hot roll which he no longer really wanted, simply from a malicious wish to delay Edmée's departure, to delay the moment when he would once more, inevitably, resume his period of waiting.

A certain Rumanian lieutenant used to be sent off by Edmée to look for concentrated disinfectant and absorbent cotton wool, or again to press a demand upon Ministers —"What the government refuses point-blank to a Frenchman, a foreigner gets every time," she affirmed. He used to bore Chéri stiff by cracking up the duties of a soldier, fit or nearly fit, and the paradisal purity of the Coictier Hospital. Chéri went along there with Edmée, sniffed the smells of antiseptics which relentlessly suggest underlying putrefaction, recognised a comrade among the "Trench Feet" and sat down on the edge of his bed, forcing himself to assume the cordiality prescribed by war novels and patriotic plays. He knew well enough, all the same, that a man in sound health, who had come through unscathed, could find no peer or equal among the crippled. Wherever he looked, he saw the fluttering white wings of the nurses, the red-brick colour of the faces and hands upon the sheets. An odious sense of impotence weighed upon him. He caught himself guiltily stiffening one of his arms as if held in a sling, or dragging one of his legs. But the next moment he could not help taking a deep breath and picking his way between the recumbent mummies with the light step of a dancer. He was forced reluctantly to reverence Edmée, because of her authority as a non-commissioned angel, and her aura of whiteness. She came across the ward, and, in passing, put a hand on Chéri's shoulder; but he knew that the desire behind this gesture of tenderness and delicate possession was to bring a blush of envy and irritation to the cheek of a young dark-haired nurse who was gazing at Chéri with the candour of a cannibal.

He felt bored, and consumed by the feeling of weariness that makes a man jib at the serried ranks of masterpieces before him as he is being dragged round a museum. The plethora of whiteness, thrown off from the ceiling and reflected back from the tiled floor, blotted out all corners, and he felt sorry for the men lying there, to whom shade would have been a charity, though no one offered it. The noonday hour imposes rest and privacy upon the beasts of the field, and the silence of deep woodland undergrowth upon the birds of the air, but civilised men no longer obey the dictates of the sun. Chéri took a few steps towards his wife, with the intention of saying: "Draw the curtains, install a punkah, take away that macaroni from the poor wretch who's blinking his eyes and breathing so heavily, and let him eat his food when the sun goes down. Give them shade, let them have any colour you like, but not always and everywhere this eternal white." With the arrival of Doctor Arnaud, he lost his inclination to give advice and make himself useful.

The Doctor, with his white linen belly and his red gold hair, had taken no more than three steps across the ward, before the hovering non-commissioned angel glided to earth again, to minister as a humble seraph, rosy with faith and zeal. Chéri thereupon turned to Filipesco, who was distributing American cigarettes, shouted "Are you coming?" in contemptuous tones, and bore him away; but not before he had bidden farewell to his wife, to Doctor Arnaud, to nurses male and female, with the haughty affability of an official visitor. He crossed the rough gravel of the little courtyard, got into his car, and allowed himself no more than a dozen words' soliloquy: 'It's the regular thing. The correct move for the Physician-in-Charge.'

Never again did he cross the threshold of the Hospital, and thereafter Edmée invited him on State occasions only, out of official courtesy, much as one might, at a dinner party, politely offer the snipe to a vegetarian guest.

He was now given over to reflection, and a prey to idleness. Before the war his idleness had been so light and varied, with the resonant ring of a flawless empty glass. During the war, too, he had endured periods of inertia under military discipline, inertia modified by cold, mud, risk, patrols, and even, on occasion, a little fighting. Conditioned to indolence by his upbringing and the life of a sensual young man, he had watched, himself untouched, the fresh young vulnerable companions all round him pine away in silence, solitude, and frustration. He had witnessed the ravages inflicted on intelligent people by the lack of newspapers as if they were being deprived of a daily drug. Whereas he had relapsed into contemplative silence—like a cat in a garden at night—content with a short letter, a postcard, or a cunningly packed parcel, other men, so-called superior men, had appeared to him to be showing every symptom of ruinous mental starvation. Thus he had learned to take pride in bolstering up his patience, and had brooded over two or three ideas, over two or three persistent memories, as highly coloured as a child's, and over his inability to imagine his own death.

Time and again, throughout the war, on coming out of a long dreamless sleep or a fitful bout of spasmodically interrupted rest, he would awake to find himself somewhere outside the present time and, his more recent past sloughed off, restored to the days of his boyhood —restored to Léa. Later, Edmée would suddenly rise up from the past, distinct and clear in every detail, and this evocation of her form, no less than its almost immediate disappearance, had always put Chéri in good spirits. "That gives me two of them," he reckoned. Nothing came to him from Léa; he did not write to her. But he received postcards signed by the crabbed fingers of old mother Aldonza, and cigars chosen by the Baroness de La Berche. Sometimes he dreamed of a long soft-wool scarf, as blue as a pair of blue eyes and with a very faint suggestion of the scent associated with it throughout long hours of warmth and slumber. He had loved this scarf and hugged it to him in the dark, until it had lost its fragrance and the freshness of the blue eyes, and he had thought of it no more.

For four years he had not bothered his head about Léa. Her trusty old cronies, had occasion arisen, would have forwarded news of any events in her life. He

never imagined anything happening to her. What had
Léa in common with sickness, or Léa with change?

In 1918 he could not believe his ears when the Baroness
de La Berche casually mentioned "Léa's new flat".

"Has she moved, then?"

"Where have you sprung from?" the Baroness answered. "The whole world knows it. The sale of her
house to the Americans was a brilliant deal, you bet! I've
seen her new flat. It's small, but it's very cosy. Once you
sit down in it, you never want to get up again."

Chéri clung to the words "small, but cosy". Unable
to imagine anything different, he supplied an over-all rose-
pink background, threw in that huge galleon of gold and
steel—the bed with its lace rigging—and hung Chaplin's
pearly-breasted nymph from some floating cloud.

When Desmond began looking about for a sleeping
partner for his night club, Chéri had spasms of alarm
and anxiety. "The blackguard's certain to try and tap
Léa, or get her mixed up in some fishy business . . . I'd
better tip her off on the telephone." He did nothing of
the sort, however. Telephoning to a discarded mistress
is riskier far than holding out your hand in the street to
a nervous enemy who tries to catch your eye.

He went on biding his time, even after surprising
Edmée in front of the looking-glass, after that flagrant
exhibition of over-excitement, flushed cheeks, and
untidiness. He let the hours slip by, and did not put into
words—and so accentuate—his certainty that a still
almost chaste understanding existed between his wife
and the man who had been singing "Oy Marie!" For he
felt much lighter in spirit, and for several days stopped
uselessly consulting his wrist-watch as soon as daylight

began to fade. He developed the habit of sitting out under the trees in a basket-chair, like a newly arrived guest in an hotel garden. There he marvelled to see how the oncoming night blotted out the blue of the monkshood, producing in its stead a hazier blue into which the shapes of the flowers were fused, while the green of their leaves persisted in distinct clumps. The edging of rose-coloured pinks turned to rank mauve, then the colour ebbed rapidly and the July stars shone yellow between the branches of the weeping ash.

He tasted at home the pleasures enjoyed by a casual passer-by who sits down to rest in a square, and he never noticed how long he remained there, lying back with his hands dangling. Sometimes he gave a fleeting thought to what he called "the looking-glass scene" and the atmosphere in the blue room when it had been secretly troubled by a man's sudden appearance, theatrical behaviour, and flight. He whispered over and over, with foolish mechanical regularity, "That's one point established. That's what's called a point-t-established", running the two words together into one.

At the beginning of July he bought a new open motor, and called it his Riviera Runabout. He drove Filipesco and Desmond out along drought-whitened roads, but returned to Paris every evening, cleaving alternate waves of warm and cool air, which began to lose their good smells the nearer the motor drew to Paris.

One day he took out the Baroness de La Berche, a virile companion, who, when they came to the barriers of the Octroi, raised her forefinger to the little felt hat pulled well down on her head. He found her agreeable, sparing of words, interested in wayside inns overgrown with wistaria, and in village wine-shops with their cellar-smell and wine-soaked sand. Rigid and in silence, they

covered two hundred miles or more, without ever opening their mouths except to smoke or feed. The following
day Chéri again invited Camille de La Berche with a curt
"Well, how about it, Baroness?" and whisked her off
without further ado.

The trusty motor sped far afield through the green
countryside, and came back at nightfall to Paris like
a toy at the end of a string. That evening, Chéri, while
never taking his eye off the road, could distinguish on
his right side the outline of an elderly woman, with a
man's profile as noble as that of an old family coachman.
It astonished him to find her worthy of respect because
she was plain and simple, and when he was alone in her
company for the first time and far away from town-life,
it began to dawn on him that a woman burdened with
some monstrous sexual deformity needs must possess a
certain bravura and something of the dignified courage
of the condemned.

Since the war this woman had found no further use for
her unkindness. The Hospital had put her back in her
proper place, that is to say, among males, among men
just young enough, just tamed enough by suffering, for
her to live serenely in their midst, and forget her frustrated
femininity.

On the sly, Chéri studied his companion's large nose,
the greying hairy upper lip, and the little peasant eyes
which glanced incuriously at ripe cornfields and scythed
meadows.

For the first time he felt something very like friendship
for old Camille, and was led to make a poignant comparison: "She is alone. When she's no longer with her
soldiers or with my mother, she's alone. She too. Despite
her pipe and her glass of wine, she's alone."

On their way back to Paris, they stopped at a

"hostelry" where there was no ice, and where, trained against the plinths of columns and clinging to ancient baptismal fonts dotted about the lawn, the rambler-roses were dying, frizzled by the sun. A neighbouring copse screened this dried-up spot from any breeze, and a small cloud, scorched to a cherry hue, hung motionless, high in the heavens.

The Baroness knocked out her short briar pipe on the ear of a marble fawn.

"It's going to be grilling over Paris to-night."

Chéri nodded in agreement, and looked up at the cloud. The light reflected from it mottled his white cheeks and dimpled chin, like touches of pink powder on an actor's face.

"Yes," he said.

"Well, you know, if the idea tempts you, let's not go back till to-morrow morning. Just give me time to buy a piece of soap and a tooth-brush. . . . And we'll telephone your wife. Then, to-morrow morning we can be up and on our way by four o'clock, while it's fresh."

Chéri sprang to his feet in unthinking haste. "No, no, I can't."

"You can't? Come, come!"

Down near his feet he saw two small mannish eyes, and a pair of broad shoulders shaking with laughter.

"I didn't believe that you were still held on such a tight rein," she said. "But, of course, if you are . . ."

"Are what?"

She had risen to her feet again, robust and hearty, and clapped him vigorously on the shoulder.

"Yes, yes. You run around all day long, but you go back to your kennel every night. Oh, you're kept well in hand."

He looked at her coldly: already he liked her less.

"There's no hiding anything from you, Baroness. I'll fetch the car, and in under two hours we'll be back at your front door."

Chéri never forgot their nocturnal journey home, the sadness of the lingering crimson in the west, the smell of the grasses, the feathery moths held prisoner in the beam of the headlamps. The Baroness kept watch beside him, a dark form made denser by the night. He drove cautiously; the air, cool at faster speeds, grew hot again when he slowed down to take a corner. He trusted to his keen sight and his alert senses, but he could not help his thoughts running on the queer massive old woman motionless at his right side, and she caused him a sort of terror, a twitching of the nerves, which suddenly landed him within a few inches of a waggon carrying no rear lamp. At that moment a large hand came lightly to rest on his forearm.

"Take care, child!"

He certainly had not expected either the gesture or the gentle tone of the voice. But nothing justified the subsequent emotion, the lump like a hard fruit stone in his throat, 'I'm a fool, I'm a fool,' he kept repeating. He continued at a slower speed, and amused himself by watching the refraction of the beams, the golden zigzags and peacock's feathers, that danced for a moment round the headlamps when seen through the tears that brimmed his eyes.

'She told me that it had a hold on me, that I was held well in hand. If she could see us, Edmée and me. . . . How long is it since we took to sleeping like two brothers?' He tried to count: three weeks, perhaps more? 'And the joke about the whole business is that Edmée makes no demands, and wakes up smiling.' To himself, he always used the word "joke" when he wished to avoid

the word "sad". 'Like an old married couple, what!
like an old married couple ... Madame and her Physician-
in-Charge, Monsieur ... and ... his car. All the same, old
Camille said that I was held. Held. Held. Catch me ever
taking that old girl out again. . . .'

He did take her out again, for July began to scorch
Paris. But neither Edmée nor Chéri complained about the
dog-days. Chéri used to come home, polite and absent-
minded, the backs of his hands and the lower part of his
face nut-brown. He walked about naked between the
bathroom and Edmée's boudoir.

"You must have been roasted to-day, you poor
townees!" Chéri jeered.

Looking rather pale and almost melting away, Edmée
straightened her pretty odalisque back and denied that
she was tired.

"Oh well, not quite as bad as that, you know. There
was rather more air than yesterday. My office down there
is cool, you know. And then, we've had no time to think
about it. My young man in bed twenty-two, who was
getting on so well . . ."

"Oh yes!"

"Yes, Doctor Arnaud isn't too pleased about him."

She didn't hesitate to make play with the name of the
Physician-in-Charge, much as a player moves up a decisive piece on the chess-board. But Chéri did not bat an
eyelid, and Edmée followed his movements, those of
a naked male body dappled a delicate green from the
reflected light of the blue curtains. He walked to and
fro in front of her, ostentatiously pure, trailing his aura
of scent, and living in another world. The very self-
confidence of this naked body, superior and contemptuous, reduced Edmée to a mildly vindictive immobility.
She could not now have claimed this naked body

for her own except in a voice altogether lacking the tones and urgency of desire—that is, in the calm voice of a submissive mate. Now she was held back by an arm covered with fine gold hairs, by an ardent mouth behind a golden moustache, and she gazed at Chéri with the jealous and serene security of a lover who covets a virgin inaccessible to all.

They went on to talk about holidays and travelling arrangements, in light-hearted and conventional phrases.

"The war hasn't changed Deauville enough, and what a crowd . . ." Chéri sighed.

"There's simply no place where one can eat a good meal, and it's a huge undertaking to reorganise the hotel business!" Edmée affirmed.

One day, not long before the Quartorze Juillet, Charlotte Peloux was lunching with them. She happened to speak of the success of some business deal in American blankets, and complained loudly that Léa had netted a half share of the profits. Chéri raised his head, in astonishment. "So you still see her?"

Charlotte Peloux enveloped her son in the loving glances induced by old port, and appealed to her daughter-in-law as witness: "He's got an odd way of putting things—as if he'd been gassed—hasn't he? . . . It's disturbing at times. I've never stopped seeing Léa, darling. Why should I have stopped seeing her?"

"Why?" Edmée repeated.

He looked at the two women, finding a strange flavour in their kindly attention.

"Because you never talk to me about her . . ." he began, ingenuously.

"Me!" barked Charlotte. "For goodness sake . . .

Edmée, you hear what he says? Well at least it does credit to his feelings for you. He has so completely forgotten about everything that isn't you."

Edmée smiled without answering, bent her head, and adjusted the lace that edged the low-cut neck of her dress by tweaking it between her fingers. The movement drew Chéri's attention to her bodice, and through the yellow lawn he noticed that the points of her breasts and their mauve aureolas looked like twin bruises. He shuddered, and his shudder made him realise that the conventional beauty and all the most secret details of her charming body, that the whole of this young woman, in fact, so close and so disloyal, no longer aroused in him anything but positive repugnance. Nonsense, nonsense; but he was whipping a dead horse. And he listened to Charlotte's ever flowing stream of nasal burblings.

". . . and then again, the day before yesterday, I was saying in your presence, that motor for motor, well—I'd far rather have a taxi, a taxi, any day, than that prehistoric old Renault of Léa's—and if it wasn't the day before yesterday, it was yesterday, that I said—speaking of Léa—that if you're a woman living on your own and you've got to have a manservant, you might just as well have a good-looking one. And then Camille was saying, only the other day when you were there, how angry she was with herself for having sent a second barrel of Quarts-de-Chaumes round to Léa instead of keeping it for herself. I've complimented you often enough on your fidelity, my darling; I must now scold you for your ingratitude. Léa deserved better of you. Edmée will be the first to admit that!"

"The second," Edmée corrected.

"Never heard a word of it," Chéri said.

He was gorging himself with hard pink July cherries,

and flipping them from beneath the lowered blind at the sparrows in the garden, where, after too heavy a watering, the flower beds were steaming like a hot spring. Edmée, motionless, was cogitating on Chéri's comment, "Never heard a word of it." He certainly was not lying, and yet his off-hand assumed schoolboyishness, as he squeezed the cherry stones and took aim at a sparrow by closing his left eye, spoke clearly enough to Edmée. 'What can he have been thinking about, if he never heard a word?'

Before the war, she would have looked for the woman in the case. A month earlier, on the day following the looking-glass scene, she would have feared reprisals, some Red Indian act of cruelty, or a bite on the nose. But no . . . nothing . . . he lived and roamed about innocently, as quiet in his freedom as a prisoner in the depths of a gaol, and as chaste as an animal brought from the Antipodes, which does not bother to look for a kindred female in our hemisphere.

Was he ill? He slept well, ate according to his fancy— that is, delicately, sniffing all the meat suspiciously, and preferring fruit and new-laid eggs. No nervous twitch disfigured the lovely balance of his features, and he drank more water than champagne. 'No, he's not ill. And yet he's . . . something. Something that I should guess, perhaps, if I were still in love with him. But . . .' Once again she fingered the lace round the neck of her bodice, inhaled the warmth and fragrance that rose up from between her breasts, and as she bent down her head she saw the precious twin pink and mauve discs through the material of her dress. She blushed with carnal pleasure, and dedicated the scent and the mauve shadows to the skilful, condescending, red-haired man whom she would be meeting again in an hour's time.

'They've spoken of Léa in front of me every day, and I didn't hear. Have I forgotten her, then? Yes, I have forgotten her. But then what does it mean, "to forget"? If I think of Léa, I see her clearly, I remember the sound of her voice, the scent which she sprayed herself with and rubbed so lavishly into her long hands.' He took such a deep breath that his nostrils were indented and his lips curled up to his nose in an expression of exquisite pleasure.

"Fred, you've just made the most horrible face; you were the spit and image of that fox Angot brought back from the trenches."

It was the least trying hour of the day for the pair of them, awake and in bed with breakfast over. After a refreshing shower-bath, they were gratified to hear the drenching rain—three months ahead of the proper season—falling in sheets that stripped the false Parisian autumn of its leaves and flattened the petunias. They did not bother to find an excuse, that morning, for having wilfully remained behind in town. Had not Charlotte Peloux hit upon the proper excuse the previous evening? She had declared, "We're all good Parigots, born and bred, aren't we! True blue one and all! We and the concierges can claim that we've had a real taste of the first post-war summer in Paris!"

"Fred, are you in love with that suit? You never stop wearing it. It doesn't look fresh, you know."

Chéri raised a finger in the direction of Edmée's voice, a gesture which enjoined silence and begged that nothing should divert his attention while he was in the throes of exceptional mental labours.

'I should like to know if I have forgotten her. But what is the real meaning of "forgotten"! A whole year's gone by without my seeing her.' He felt a sudden little shock of awakening, a tremor, when he found that his memory had failed to account for the war years. Then he totted up the years and, for an instant, everything inside him stopped functioning.

"Fred, shall I never get you to leave your razor in the bathroom, instead of bringing it in here!"

Almost naked and still damp, he took his time in turning round, and his back was silver-flecked with dabs of talcum powder.

"What?"

The voice, which seemed to come from afar, broke into a laugh.

"Fred, you look like a cake that's been badly sugared. An unhealthy looking cake. Next year, we won't be as stupid as we have been this. We'll take a place in the country."

"Do you want a place in the country?"

"Yes. Not this morning, of course."

She was pinning up her hair. She pointed with her chin to the curtain of rain, streaming down in a grey torrent, without any sign of thunder or wind.

"But next year, perhaps . . . Don't you think?"

"It's an idea. Yes, it's an idea."

He was putting her politely at arm's length, in order to return to his surprising discovery. 'I really did think that it was only one year since I'd seen her. I never took the war into reckoning. I haven't seen her for one, two, three, four, five years. One, two, three, four. . . . But, in that case, have I really forgotten her? No! Because these women have spoken of her in front of me, and I've never jumped up and shouted, "Hold on! If that's true—then what about Léa?" Five years . . . How old was she in 1914?'

He counted once more, and ran up against an

unbelievable total. 'That would make her just about sixty to-day, wouldn't it? . . . How absurd!'

"And the important thing," Edmée went on, "is to choose it carefully. Let's see, a nice part of the world would be . . ."

"Normandy," Chéri finished for her, absent-mindedly.

"Yes, Normandy. Do you know Normandy?"

"No . . . Not at all well. . . . It's green. There are lime trees, ponds . . ."

He shut his eyes, as though dazed.

"Where do you mean? In what part of Normandy?"

"Ponds, cream, strawberries and peacocks. . . ."

"You seem to know a lot about Normandy! What grand country it must be! What else d'you find there?"

He appeared to be reading out a description as he leaned over the round mirror in which he made sure of the smoothness of chin and cheeks after shaving. He went on, unmoved, but hesitatingly. "There are peacocks. . . . Moonlight on parquet floors, and a great big red carpet spread on the gravel in front of . . ."

He did not finish. He swayed gently, and slithered on to the carpet. His fall was checked halfway by the side of the bed. As his head lay against the rumpled sheets, the overlying tan of his pallid cheeks had the greenish tinge of an old ivory.

Hardly had he reached the floor when Edmée, without uttering a sound, threw herself down beside him. With one hand she supported his drooping head, and with the other held a bottle of smelling-salts to his nostrils, from which the colour was visibly ebbing. But two enfeebled arms pushed her away.

"Leave me alone. . . . Can't you see I'm dying?"

He was not dying, however, and under Edmée's fingers his pulse retained its rhythm. He had spoken in a subdued whisper, with the glib, emphatic sincerity of very young would-be suicides who, at one and the same moment, both court death and fight shy of it.

His lips were parted over gleaming teeth and his breathing was regular; but he was in no haste to come right back to life. Safely ensconced behind his tightly shut eyes, he sought refuge in the heart of that green domain, so vivid in his imagination at the instant of his fainting fit—a flat domain, rich in strawberry-beds and bees, in pools of moonbeams fringed with warm stones. . . . After he regained his strength, he still kept his eyes shut, thinking 'If I open my eyes, Edmée will then see the picture in my mind.'

She remained on one knee, bending over him. She was looking after him efficiently, professionally. She reached out with her free hand, picked up a newspaper and used it to fan his forehead. She whispered insignificant but appropriate words, "It's the storm. . . . Relax. . . . No, don't try to move. . . . Wait till I slip this pillow under you. . . ."

He sat up again, smiling, and pressed her hand in thanks. His parched mouth longed for lemons or vinegar. The ringing of the telephone snatched Edmée away from him.

"Yes, yes. . . . What? Yes, of course I know it's ten. Yes. What?"

From the imperious brevity of her replies, Chéri knew that it was someone telephoning from the Hospital.

"Yes, of course I'm coming. What? In . . ." With a rapid glance she estimated Chéri's term of recovery. "In twenty-five minutes. Thanks. See you presently."

She opened the two glass doors of the french windows to their fullest extent, and a few peaceful drops of rain dripped into the room, bringing with them an insipid river smell.

"Are you better, Fred? What exactly did you feel? Nothing wrong with your heart, is there? You must be short of phosphates. It's the result of this ridiculous summer we're having. But what can you expect?"

She glanced at the telephone furtively, as she might at an onlooker.

Chéri stood up on his feet again without apparent effort. "Run along, child. You'll be late at your shop. I'm quite all right."

"A mild grog? A little hot tea?"

"Don't bother about me. . . . You've been very sweet. Yes, a little cup of tea—ask for it on your way out. And some lemon."

Five minutes later she was gone, after giving him a look, which she believed expressed solicitude only. She had searched in vain for a true sign, for some explanation of so inexplicable a state of affairs. As though the sound of the door shutting had severed his bonds, Chéri stretched himself and found that he felt light, cold, and empty. He hurried to the window and saw his wife crossing the small strip of garden, her head bowed under the rain. 'She's got a guilty back,' he pronounced, 'she's always had a guilty back. From the front, she looks a charming little lady. But her back gives the show away. She's lost a good half-hour by my having fainted. But "back to our muttons", as my mother would say. When I got married, Léa was fifty-one—at the very least—so Madame Peloux assures me. That would make her fifty-eight now, sixty perhaps. . . . The same age as General Courbat? No! That's too rich a joke!'

He tried his hardest to associate the picture of Léa at sixty with the white bristling moustache and crannied cheeks of General Courbat and his ancient cab-horse stance. 'It's the best joke out!'

The arrival of Madame Peloux found Chéri still given over to his latest pastime, pale, staring out at the drenched garden, and chewing a cigarette that had gone out. He showed no surprise at his mother's entrance, "You're certainly up with the lark, my dear mother."

"And you've got out of bed the wrong side, it would seem," was her rejoinder.

"Pure imagination. There are, at least, extenuating circumstances to account for your activity, I presume?"

She raised both eyes and shoulders in the direction of the ceiling. A cheeky little leather sports hat was pulled down like a vizor over her forehead.

"My poor child," she sighed, "if you only knew what I'm engaged on at this moment! If you knew what a gigantic task . . ."

He took careful stock of the wrinkles on his mother's face, the inverted commas round her mouth. He contemplated the small flabby wavelet of a double chin, the ebb and flow of which now covered, now uncovered, the collar of her mackintosh. He started to weigh up the fluctuating pouches under her eyes, repeating to himself: 'Fifty-eight . . . Sixty . . .'

"Do you know the task I've set myself? Do you know?" She waited a moment, opening wider her large eyes outlined by black pencil. "I'm going to revive the hot springs at Passy! *Les Thermes de Passy!* Yes, that means nothing to you, of course. The springs are there under the Rue Raynouard, only a few yards away. They're dormant; all they need is to be revived. Very active waters. If we go the right way about it, it will mean the ruination of Uriage, the collapse of Mont Dore, perhaps—but that would be too wonderful! Already I've made certain of the co-operation of twenty-seven Swiss doctors. Edmée and I have been getting to work on the Paris Municipal Council. . . . And that's exactly why I've come—I missed your wife by five minutes. . . . What's wrong with you? You're not listening to me. . . ."

He persisted in trying to relight his damp cigarette. He gave it up, threw the stub out upon the balcony, where large drops of rain were rebounding like grass-hoppers; then he gravely looked his mother up and down.

"I am listening to you," he said. "Even before you speak I know what you're going to say. I know all about this business of yours. It goes by the varying names of company promotion, wheezes, commissions, founders' shares, American blankets, bully-beef, etcetera. . . . You don't suppose I've been deaf or blind for the last year, do you? You are nasty, wicked women, that's all there is to it. I bear you no ill will."

He stopped talking and sat down, by force of habit rubbing his fingers almost viciously over the little twin scars beneath his right breast. He looked out at the green, rain-battered garden, and on his relaxed features weariness battled with youth—weariness, hollowing his cheeks and darkening his eye-sockets, youth perfectly preserved in the ravishing curve and full ripeness of his lips, the downiness of his nostrils, and the raven-black abundance of his hair.

"Very well, then," said Charlotte Peloux at length. "That's a nice thing to hear, I must say. The devil turned preacher! I seem to have given birth to a Censor of Public Morals."

He showed no intention of breaking the silence, or of making any movement whatever.

"And by what high standards do you presume to judge

this poor corrupt world? By your own honesty, I don't
doubt!"

Buckled into a leather jerkin, like a yeoman of old, she
was at the top of her form and ready for the fray. But
Chéri appeared to be through with all fighting, now
and for ever.

"By my honesty? . . . Perhaps. Had I been hunting for
the right word, I should never have hit upon that. You
yourself said it. Honesty will pass."

She did not deign to reply, postponing her offensive
until a later moment. She held her tongue that she might
give her full attention to her son's peculiar new aspect.
He was sitting with his legs very wide apart, elbows on
knees, his hands firmly locked together. He continued to
stare out at the garden laid flat by the lashing rain, and
after a moment he sighed without turning his head:
"Do you really call this a life?"

As might be expected, she asked: "What life?"

He raised one arm, only to let it fall again. "Mine.
Yours. Everything. All that's going on under our eyes."

Madame Peloux hesitated a moment. Then she
threw off her leather coat, lit a cigarette, and she too sat
down.

"Are you bored?"

Coaxed by the unusual sweetness of a voice that
sounded ethereally solicitous, he became natural and
almost confidential.

"Bored? No, I'm not bored. What makes you think
I'm bored? I'm a trifle . . . what shall I say? . . . a trifle
worried, that's all."

"About what?"

"About everything. Myself. . . . Even about you."

"I'm surprised at that."

"So am I. These fellows . . . this year . . . this peace."

He stretched his fingers apart as though they were sticky or tangled in overlong hair.

"You say that as we used to say 'This war' . . ." She put a hand on his shoulder and tactfully lowered her voice. "What is the matter with you?"

He could not bear the questioning weight of this hand; he stood up, and began moving about in a haphazard way. "The matter is that everyone's rotten. No!" he begged, seeing an artificial look of indignation on the maternal countenance, "No, don't start all over again. No, present company *not* excluded. No, I do *not* accept the fact that we are living in splendid times, with a dawn of this, a resurrection of that. No, I am *not* angry, don't love you any less than before, and there is nothing wrong with my liver. But I do seriously think that I'm nearly at the end of my tether."

He cracked his fingers as he walked about the room, sniffing the sweet-smelling spray of the heavy rain as it splashed off the balcony. Charlotte Peloux threw down her hat and her red gloves, a gesture intended as a peace-offering.

"Do tell me exactly what you mean, child. We're alone." She smoothed back her sparse hennaed hair, cut boyishly short. Her mushroom-coloured garb held in her body as an iron hoop clamps a cask. 'A woman. . . . She has been a woman. . . . Fifty-eight. . . . Sixty. . . .' Chéri was thinking. She turned on him her lovely velvety eyes, brimming with maternal coquetry, the feminine power of which he had long forgotten. This sudden charm of his mother's warned him of the danger lying ahead, and the difficulty of the confession towards which she was leading him. But he felt empty and listless, tormented by what he lacked. The hope of shocking her drove him on still further.

"Yes," he said, in answer to his own question. "You have your blankets, your macaroni and spaghetti, your légions d'honneur. You joke about the meetings of the Chambre des Députés and the accident to young Lenoir. You are thrilled by Madame Caillaux, and by the hot springs at Passy. Edmée's got her shopful of wounded and her Physician-in-Charge. Desmond dabbles in dance-halls, wines and spirits, and white slavery. Filipesco bags cigars from Americans and hospitals, to hawk them round night clubs. Jean de Touzac . . . is in the surplus store racket. What a set! What . . . ."

"You're forgetting Landru," Charlotte put in edge-ways.

His eyes twinkled as he gave the slyest of winks, in silent tribute to the malicious humour that rejuvenated his old pugilist of a mother.

"Landru? That doesn't count, there's a pre-war flavour about that. There's nothing odd about Landru. But as for the rest—well . . . well, to cut it short, there's not one who's not a rotter and . . . and I don't like it. That's all."

"That's certainly short, but not very clear," Charlotte said, after a moment. "You've a nice opinion of us. Mind you, I don't say you're wrong. Myself, I've got the qualities of my defects, and nothing frightens me. Only, it doesn't give me an inkling of what you're really after."

Chéri swayed awkwardly on his chair. He frowned so furiously that the skin on his forehead contracted in deep wrinkles between his eyes, as though trying to keep a hat on his head in a gusty wind.

"What I'm really after . . . I simply don't know. I only wish people weren't such rotters. I mean to say, weren't *only* rotten. . . . Or, quite simply, I should like to be able not to notice it."

He showed such hesitancy, such a need of coming to

terms with himself, that Charlotte made fun of it. "Why notice it, then?"

"Ah, well. . . . That's just the point, you see."

He gave her a helpless smile, and she noticed how much her son's face aged as he smiled. 'Someone ought constantly to be telling him hard-luck stories,' she said to herself, 'or else making him really angry. Gaiety doesn't improve his looks . . .' She blew out a cloud of smoke and in her turn allowed an ambiguous commonplace to escape her. "You didn't notice anything of that before."

He raised his head sharply. "Before? Before what?"

"Before the war, of course."

"Ah, yes . . ." he murmured, disappointed. "No, before the war, obviously. . . . But before the war I didn't look at things in the same way."

"Why?"

The simple word struck him dumb.

"I'll tell you what it is," Charlotte chid him, "you've turned honest."

"You wouldn't think of admitting, by any chance, that I've simply remained so?"

"No, no, don't let's get that wrong." She was arguing, a flush on her cheeks, with the fervour of a prophetess. "Your way of life before the war, after all—I'm putting myself in the position of people who are not exactly broad-minded and who take a superficial view of things, understand!—such a way of life, after all, has a name!"

"If you like," Chéri agreed. "What of it?"

"Well then, that implies a . . . a way of looking at things. Your point of view was a gigolo's."

"Quite possibly," said Chéri, unmoved. "Do you see any harm in that?"

"Certainly not," Charlotte protested, with the

simplicity of a child. "But, you know, there's a right time for everything."

"Yes . . ." He sighed deeply, looking out towards a sky masked by cloud and rain. "There's a time to be young, and there's a time to be less young. There's a time to be happy . . . d'you think it needed you to make me aware of that?"

She seemed suddenly to be upset, and walked up and down the room, her round behind tightly moulded by her dress, as plump and brisk as a little fat bitch. She came back and planted herself in front of her son.

"Well, darling, I'm afraid you're heading for some act of madness."

"What?"

"Oh! there aren't so many. A monastery. Or a desert island. Or love."

Chéri smiled in astonishment. "Love? You want me . . . in love with . . ." He jerked his chin in the direction of Edmée's boudoir, and Charlotte's eyes sparkled.

"Who mentioned her?"

He laughed, and from an instinct of self-preservation became offensive again.

"*You* did, and in a moment you'll be offering me one of your American pieces."

She gave a theatrical start. "An American piece? Really? And why not a rubber substitute as provided for sailors into the bargain?"

He was pleased with her jingoistic and expert disdain. Since childhood he had had it dinned into him that a French woman demeans herself by living with a foreigner, unless, of course, she exploit; him, or he ruins her. And he could reel off a list of outrageous epithets with which a native Parisian courtesan would brand a dissolute foreign woman. But he refused the offer, without irony.

Charlotte threw out her short arms and protruded her
lower lip, like a doctor confessing his helplessness.

"I don't suggest that you should work . . ." she risked
shamefacedly.

Chéri dismissed this importunate suggestion with a
shrug of the shoulders.

"Work," he repeated . . . "work, what you mean by
that is hobnobbing with fellows. You can't work alone,
short of painting picture post-cards or taking in sewing.
My poor mother, you fail to realise that, if fellows get
my goat, women can hardly be said to inspire me either.
The truth is, that I have no further use for women at all,"
he finished courageously.

"Good heavens!" Charlotte caterwauled. She wrung
her hands as though a horse had slipped and fallen at her
feet; but harshly her son enjoined silence with a single
gesture, and she was forced to admire the virile authority
of this handsome young man, who had just owned up
to his own particular brand of impotence.

"Chéri! . . . my little boy! . . ."

He turned to her with a gentle, empty, and vaguely
pleading look in his eyes.

She gazed into the large eyes that shone with an
exaggerated brilliance, due, perhaps, to their unblemished
white, their long lashes and the secret emotion behind
them. She longed to enter through these magnificent
portals and reach down to the shadowed heart which had
first started to beat so close to her own. Chéri appeared
to be putting up no defence and to enjoy being balked,
as if under hypnosis. Charlotte had, in the past, known
her son to be ill, irritable, sly; she had never known him
unhappy. She felt, therefore, a strange kind of excitement,
the ecstasy that casts a woman at a man's feet at the
moment when she dreams of changing a despairing

stranger into an inferior stranger—that is to say, of making him rid himself of his despair.

"Listen, Chéri," she murmured very softly. "Listen. ... You must ... No, no, wait! At least let me speak...."

He interrupted her with a furious shake of the head, and she saw it was useless to insist. It was she who broke their long exchange of looks, by putting on her coat again and her little leather hat, making towards the door. But as she passed the table, she stopped, and casually put her hand out towards the telephone.

"Do you mind, Chéri?"

He nodded his consent, and she began in a high-pitched nasal shrill like a clarinet. "Hullo ... Hullo ... Hullo ... Passy, two nine, two nine. Hullo ... Is that you, Léa? But of course it's me. What weather, eh! ... Don't speak of it. Yes, very well. Everyone's very well. What are you doing to-day? Not budging an inch! Ah, that's so like you, you self-indulgent creature! Oh, you know, I'm no longer my own mistress. ... Oh no, not on that account. Something altogether different. A vast undertaking. ... Oh, no, not on the telephone.... You'll be in all day then? Good. That's very convenient. Thank you. Goodbye, Léa darling!"

She put back the receiver, showing nothing but the curve of her back. As she moved away, she inhaled and exhaled puffs of blue smoke, and vanished in the midst of her cloud like a magician whose task is accomplished.

Without hurrying, he climbed the single flight of stairs up to Léa's flat. At six in the evening, after the rain, the Rue Raynouard re-echoed, like the garden of a boarding-school, with the chirrup of birds and the cries of small children. He glanced quickly, coldly, at everything, refusing to be surprised at the heavy looking-glasses in the entrance-hall, the polished steps, the blue carpet, or the lift-cage lavishly splashed with as much lacquer and gold as a sedan-chair. On the landing he experienced, for a moment, the deceptive sense of detachment and freedom from pain felt by a sufferer on the dentist's doorstep. He nearly turned away, but, guessing that he might feel compelled to return later, he pressed the bell with a determined finger. The maid, who had taken her time in coming to the door, was young and dark, with a butterfly cap of fine lawn on her bobbed hair: her unfamiliar face took from Chéri his last chance of feeling moved.

"Is Madame at home?"

The young servant, apparently lost in admiration of him, could not make up her mind.

"I do not know, Monsieur. Is Monsieur expected?"

"Of course," he said, with a return of his old harshness.

She left him standing there, and disappeared. In the half-light, he was quick to take in his surroundings, with eyes blurred by the gloom, and alert sensitive nostrils.

There was nowhere a vestige of that light golden scent, and some ordinary pine essence sputtered in an electric scent-burner. Chéri felt put out, like someone who discovers that he is on the wrong floor. But a great peal of girlish laughter rang out, its notes running down a deep descending scale. It was muffled by some curtain or other, but at once the intruder was cast into a whirl-pool of memories.

"Will Monsieur please come to the drawing-room."

He followed the white butterfly, saying over to himself as he went: "Léa's not alone. She's laughing. She can't be alone. So long as it's not my mother." Beyond an open door, he was being welcomed by rosy pink daylight and he waited, standing there, for the rebirth of the world heralded by this dawn.

A woman was writing at a small table, facing away from him. Chéri was able to distinguish a broad back and the padded cushion of a fat neck beneath a head of thick grey vigorous hair, cut short like his mother's. 'So I was right, she's not alone. But who on earth can this good woman be?'

"And, at the same time, write down your masseur's address for me, Léa, and his name. You know what I'm like about names. . . ."

These words came from a woman dressed in black, also seated, and Chéri felt a preliminary tremor of expectation running through him: 'Then . . . where is Léa?'

The grey-haired lady turned round, and Chéri received the full impact of her blue eyes.

"Oh, good heavens, child—it's you!"

He went forward as in a dream, and kissed an out-stretched hand.

"Monsieur Frédéric Peloux—Princess Cheniaguine."

Chéri bent over and kissed another hand, then took a seat.

"Is he your . . .?" queried the lady in black, referring to him with as much freedom as if he had been a deaf-mute.

Once again the great peal of girlish laughter rang out, and Chéri sought for the source of this laugh here, there, and everywhere—anywhere but in the throat of the grey-haired woman.

"No, no, he isn't! Or rather, he isn't any longer, I should say. Valérie, come now, what are you thinking of?"

She was not monstrous, but huge, and loaded with exuberant buttresses of fat in every part of her body. Her arms, like rounded thighs, stood out from her hips on plump cushions of flesh just below her armpits. The plain skirt and the nondescript long jacket, opening on a linen blouse with a jabot, proclaimed that the wearer had abdicated, was no longer concerned to be a woman, and had acquired a kind of sexless dignity.

Léa was now standing between Chéri and the window, and he was not horrified at first by her firm, massive, almost cubic, bulk. When she moved to reach a chair, her features were revealed, and he began to implore her with silent entreaties, as though faced with an armed lunatic. Her cheeks were red and looked over-ripe, for she now disdained the use of powder, and when she laughed her mouth was packed with gold. A healthy old woman, in short, with sagging cheeks and a double chin, well able to carry her burden of flesh and freed from restraining stays.

"Tell me, child, where have you sprung from? I can't say I think you're looking particularly well."

She held out a box of cigarettes to Chéri, smiling at

him from blue eyes which had grown smaller, and he was
frightened to find her so direct in her approach, and as
jovial as an old gentleman. She called him "child", and
he turned away his eyes, as though she had let slip an
indecent word. But he exhorted himself to be patient,
in the vague hope that this first picture would give place
to a shining transfiguration.

The two women looked him over calmly, sparing him
neither goodwill nor curiosity.

"He's got rather a look of Hernandez . . ." said Valérie
Cheniaguine.

"Oh, I don't see that at all," Léa protested. "Ten years
ago perhaps . . . and, anyhow, Hernandez had a much
more pronounced jaw!"

"Who's that?" Chéri asked, with something of an effort.

"A Peruvian who was killed in a motor accident about
six months ago," said Léa. "He was living with Maximilienne. It made her very unhappy."

"Didn't prevent her finding consolation," said Valérie.

"Like anyone else," Léa said. "You wouldn't have
wished her to die of it, surely?"

She laughed afresh, and her merry blue eyes disappeared, lost behind wide cheeks bulging with laughter.
Chéri turned away his head and looked at the woman in
black. She had brown hair and an ample figure, vulgar
and feline like thousands and thousands of women from
the south. She seemed in disguise, so very carefully was
she dressed as a woman in good society. Valérie was
wearing what had long been the uniform of foreign
princesses and their ladies—a black tailor-made of
undistinguished cut, tight in the sleeve, with a blouse
of extremely fine white batiste, showing signs of strain
at the breast. The pearl buttons, the famous necklace,
the high stiff whalebone collar, everything about Valérie

was as royal as the name she legitimately bore. Like royalty, too, she wore stockings of medium quality, flat-heeled walking shoes and expensive gloves, embroidered in black and white.

From the cold and calculating way she looked him over, Chéri might have been a piece of furniture. She went on with her criticisms and comparisons at the top of her voice.

"Yes, yes, there is something of Hernandez, I promise you. But, to hear Maximilienne to-day, Hernandez might never have existed . . . now that she has made quite certain of her famous Amerigo. And yet! And yet! I know what I'm talking about. I've seen him, her precious Amerigo. I'm just back from Deauville. I saw the pair of them!"

"No! Do tell us!"

Léa sat down, overflowing the whole armchair. She had acquired a new trick of tossing back her thick grey hair; and at each shake of the head, Chéri saw a quivering of the lower part of her face, which looked like Louis XVI's. Ostensibly, she was giving Valérie her full attention, but several times Chéri noticed a mischievous faltering in one of the little shrunk blue eyes, as they sought to catch those of the unexpected visitor.

"Well, then," Valérie started on her story, "she had hidden him in a villa miles outside Deauville, at the back of beyond. But that did not suit Amerigo at all —as you will readily understand, Monsieur!—and he grumbled at Maximilienne. She was cross, and said: 'Ah! that's what the matter is—you want to be on view to the world and his wife, and so you shall be!' So she telephoned to reserve a table at the Normandy for the following evening. Everyone knew this an hour later, and so I booked a table as well, with Becq d'Ambez and

Zahita. And we said to ourselves: 'We're going to be allowed to see this marvel at last!' On the stroke of nine there was Maximilienne, all in white and pearls, and Amerigo. . . . Oh, my dear, what a disappointment! Tall, yes, that goes without saying . . . in point of fact, rather too tall. You know what I always say about men who are too tall. I'm still waiting to be shown one, just one, who is well put together. Eyes, yes, eyes, I've got nothing to say against his eyes. But—from here to there, don't you see (she was pointing to her own face), from here to there, something about the cheeks which is too rounded, too soft, and the ears set too low. . . . Oh, a very great disappointment. And holding himself as stiff as a poker."

"You're exaggerating," said Léa. "The cheeks—well what about cheeks?—they aren't so very important. And, from here to there, well really it's beautiful, it's noble; the eyelashes, the bridge of the nose, the eyes, the whole thing is really too beautiful! I'll grant you the chin: that will quickly run to flesh. And the feet are too small, which is ridiculous in a boy of that height."

"No, there I don't agree with you. But I certainly noticed that the thigh was far too long in proportion to the leg, from here to there."

They went on to thrash out the question, weighing up, with a wealth of detail and point by point, every portion of the fore and hind quarters of this expensive animal.

'Judges of pedigree fat cattle,' Chéri thought. 'The right place for them is the Commisariats.'

"Speaking of proportions," Léa continued, "you'll never come across anything to touch Chéri. . . . You see, Chéri, you've come at just the right moment. You ought to blush. Valérie, if you can remember what Chéri was like only six, or say seven years ago . . ."

"But certainly, of course, I remember clearly. And Monsieur has not changed so very much, after all. . . . And you were so proud of him!"

"No," said Léa.

"You weren't proud of him?"

"No," said Léa with perfect calm, "I was in love with him."

She manœuvred the whole of her considerable body in his direction, and let her gay glance rest upon Chéri, quite innocently. "It's true I was in love with you, very much in love, too."

He lowered his eyes, stupidly abashed before these two women, the stouter of whom had just proclaimed so serenely that she and he had been lovers. Yet at the same time the voluptuous and almost masculine tone of Léa's voice besieged his memory, torturing him unbearably.

"You see, Valérie, how foolish a man can look when reminded of a love which no longer exists? Silly boy, it doesn't upset me in the least to think about it. I love my past. I love my present. I'm not ashamed of what I've had, and I'm not sad because I have it no longer. Am I wrong, child?"

He uttered a cry, almost as if someone had trodden on his big toe. "No, no, of course not! The very reverse!"

"It's charming to think you have remained such good friends," said Valérie.

Chéri waited for Léa to explain that this was his first visit to her for five years, but she just gave a good-humoured laugh and winked with a knowing air. He felt more and more upset. He did not know how to protest, how to shout out loud that he laid no claim to the friendship of this colossal woman, with the cropped hair of an elderly 'cellist—that, had he but known, he would never have come upstairs, never crossed her threshold, set foot on her carpet, never collapsed in the cushioned armchair, in the depths of which he now lay defenceless and dumb.

"Well, I must be going," Valérie said. "I don't mean to wait for crush-hour in the Métro, I can tell you."

She rose to face the strong light, and it was kind to her Roman features. They were so solidly constructed that the approach of her sixtieth year had left them unharmed: the cheeks were touched up in the old-fashioned way, with an even layer of white powder, and the lips with a red that was almost black and looked oily.

"Are you going home?" Léa asked.

"Of course I am. What d'you suppose my little skivvy would get up to if left to herself!"

"Are you still pleased with your new flat?"

"It's a dream! Especially since the iron bars were put across the windows. And I've had a steel grid fixed over the pantry fanlight, which I had forgotten about. With my electric bells and my burglar-alarms . . . Ouf! It's been long enough before I could feel at all safe!"

"And your old house?"

"Bolted and barred. Up for sale. And the pictures in store. My little entresol flat is a gem for the eighteen hundred francs it costs me. And no more servants looking like hired assassins. You remember those two footmen? The thought of them still gives me the creeps!"

"You took much too black a view, my dear."

"You can't realise, my poor friend, without having been through it all. Monsieur, delighted to have met you. . . . No, don't you move, Léa."

She enfolded them both in her velvety barbaric gaze, and was gone. Chéri followed her with his eyes until she reached the door, yet he lacked the courage to follow her example. He remained where he was, all but snuffed out by the conversation of these two women who had been speaking of him in the past tense, as though he were dead. But now Léa was coming back into the room, bursting with laughter. "Princess Cheniaguine! Sixty millions! and a widow!—and she's not in the least bit happy. If that can be called enjoying life, it's not my idea of it, you know!"

She clapped her hand on her thigh as if it were a horse's crupper.

"What's the matter with her?"

"Funk. Blue funk, that's all. She's not the sort of woman who knows how to carry such wealth. Cheniaguine left her everything. But one might say that it would have done her less harm if he'd taken her money instead of leaving her his. You heard what she said?"

She subsided into the depths of a well upholstered armchair, and Chéri hated to hear the gentle sigh of its cushions as they took the weight of her vast bulk. She ran the tip of her finger along the grooved moulding of the chair, blew away the few specks of dust, and her face fell.

"Ah! things are not at all what they were, not even servants. Eh?"

He felt that he had lost colour, and that the skin round his mouth was growing tighter, as during a severe frost. He fought back an overwhelming impulse to burst out in rancour mingled with entreaties. He longed to cry out loud: 'Stop! Show me your real self! Throw off your disguise! You must be somewhere behind it, since it's your voice I hear. Appear in your true colours! Arise as a creature reborn, with your hair newly hennaed this morning, your face freshly powdered: put on your long stays again, the blue dress with its delicate jabot, the scent like a meadow that was so much a part of you. In

these new surroundings I search for it in vain! Leave all
this behind, and come away to Passy—never mind the
showers—Passy with its dogs and its birds, and in the
Avenue Bugeaud we'll be sure to find Ernest polishing
the brass bars on your front door.' He shut his eyes,
utterly worn out.

"And now, my child, I'm going to tell you something
for your own good. What you need is to have your urine
tested. Your colour's shocking and you've got that
pinched look round your lips—sure signs, both of them:
you're not taking proper care of your kidneys."

Chéri opened his eyes again, and they took their fill
of this placid epitome of disaster seated in front of him.
Heroically he said: "D'you really think so? It's quite
possible."

"You mean, it's certain. And then, you've not got
enough flesh on you. . . . It's no use telling me that the
best fighting cocks are scraggy. You could do with a
good ten pounds more on you."

"Give them to me," he said with a smile. But he found
his cheeks singularly recalcitrant and opposed to smiling,
almost as though his skin had stiffened with age.

Léa burst into a peal of happy laughter, and Chéri
tasted a pleasure which he could not have borne for long;
he listened again to its full and rounded tones, the very
laugh which in the old days used to greet some outrageous
impertinence on the part of the "naughty little boy".

"That I could well afford! I've certainly been putting
on weight, haven't I? Eh? Look . . . here . . . would you
believe it? . . . and again here!"

She lit a cigarette, exhaled a double jet of smoke
through her nostrils, and shrugged her shoulders.
"It's age!"

The word flew out of her mouth so lightly that it gave

Chéri a sort of extravagant hope. 'Yes: she's only joking. In a flash she'll reappear as her real self.' For an instant she seemed to take in the meaning of the look he gave her.

"I've changed a lot, haven't I, child? Fortunately, it doesn't much matter. As for you, I don't like the look of you at all. . . . You've been fluttering your wings too much, as we used to say in the old days. Eh?"

He detested this new "Eh?" with which she peppered her sentences so freely. But he stiffened at each interrogation, and each time mastered his rising excitement, preferring to remain in ignorance of both its reason and its aim.

"I don't ask whether you have any troubles at home. In the first place, it's none of my business; and besides, I know your wife as if I were her mother."

He listened to the sound of her voice without paying much attention. He noticed, above all, that when she stopped smiling or laughing, she ceased to belong to any assignable sex. Despite her enormous breasts and crushing backside, she seemed by virtue of age altogether virile and happy in that state.

"And I know your wife to be thoroughly capable of making a man happy."

He was powerless to hide his inward laughter, and Léa quickly went on to say.

"What I said was 'a man', and not 'any man'. Here you are in my house, without a word of warning. You've not come, I take it, just to gaze into my beautiful eyes, eh?"

She turned on Chéri those once "beautiful blue eyes", now so diminished, marbled with tiny red veins, quizzical, neither kind nor unkind, alert and bright certainly, but . . . but where was now the limpid freshness that had laved their whites with palest blue? Where the contour of their orbs, with the roundness of fruit, breast, or hemisphere, and blue as a land watered by many a river?

Jestingly, he said, "Pooh! aren't you sharp! A real detective!" And it amazed him to find that he had fallen into such a carefree posture, with his legs crossed, like a handsome young man with bad manners. For inwardly he was watching his other self, hopelessly distracted and on his knees, waving his arms, baring his breast, and shrieking incoherently.

"I'm not a particularly stupid woman. But you must admit that you don't present me to-day with a very difficult problem!"

She drew in her chin and its lower folds spread over her neck: the kneeling ghost of his other self bowed its head like a man who has received a death-blow.

"You show every known sign of suffering from the disease of your generation. No, no, let me go on. Like all your soldier friends, you're looking everywhere for your paradise, eh! the paradise they owe you as a war hero: your own special Victory Parade, *your* youth, *your* lovely women. . . . They owe you all that and more, for they promised you everything, and, dear God, you deserved it. And what do you find? A decent ordinary life. So you go in for nostalgia, listlessness, disillusion and neurasthenia. Am I wrong?"

"No," said Chéri, for he was thinking that he would give his little finger to stop her talking.

Léa clapped him on the shoulder, letting her hand with its large rings rest there. As he bent his head down towards it, he could feel on his cheek the heat of this heavy hand.

"Oh!" Léa continued, raising her voice. "You're not the only one! I've come across dozens of boys, since the war ended, exactly in your state of . . ."

"Where?" Chéri interrupted.

The suddenness of the interruption and its aggressive character put an end to Léa's parsonic eloquence. She withdrew her hand.

"They're to be met with everywhere, my child. Is it possible to be so vain? You seem to think you're unique because you find the post-war world insipid. Don't flatter yourself to that extent!"

She gave a low chuckle, and a toss to her sportive grey hair, and then a self-important smile like a judge who has a nice taste in wine. "And you do flatter yourself, you know, always imagining that you're the only one of your kind."

She took a step back and narrowed her gaze, adding, perhaps a little vindictively: "You were unique only for . . . for a time."

Behind this veiled but carefully chosen insult, Chéri discovered something of her femininity at last. He sat bolt upright, delighted to find himself suffering less acutely. But by this time Léa had reverted to her milk and honey.

"But you didn't come here to have that said about you. Did you make up your mind on the spur of the moment?"

"Yes," said Chéri.

He could have wished that this monosyllable might have been the last word between the two of them. Shyly, he let his gaze wander to all the things that surrounded Léa. From the nearest plate he took a dry cake shaped like a curved tile, and then put it back, convinced that it would turn to brick-red grit in his mouth were he to take a bite out of it. Léa noticed this action, and the painful way he swallowed his saliva.

"Tut, tut, so we're suffering from nerves, are we? Peaky chin, and dark lines under the eyes. That's a pretty state of affairs!"

He closed his eyes, and like a coward decided to listen and not look.

"Listen to me, child, I know a little restaurant in the Avenue des Gobelins. . . ."

He looked up at her, in the full hope that she was going mad, that in this way he would be able to forgive her for both looking and behaving like an old woman.

"Yes, I know a little restaurant . . . Let me speak! Only, you must be quick, before the smart set and the newspapers take it into their heads to make it fashionable, and the good woman herself is replaced by a chef. She does all the cooking at present, and, my dear . . ." She brought thumb and forefinger together on the tip of her lips, and blew an imitation kiss. Chéri turned away to look out of the window, where the shadow thrown by a branch flicked at the steady shaft of sunlight, impatiently but at regular intervals, much as a bent reed or river-plant appears to strike at the ripples of a regularly flowing current.

"What an odd sort of conversation . . ." he ventured in strained tones.

"No more odd than your presence in my house," Léa snapped back at him.

With a wave of the hand he made it clear that he wanted peace, only peace, with as few words spoken as possible, and preferably none at all. He felt defeated in face of this elderly woman's boundless reserves of energy and appetite. Léa's quick blood was now rising and turning her bulging neck and her ears to purple. 'She's got a crop like an old hen,' he thought, with something of his old enjoyment of cruelty.

"And that's the truth!" she hurled at him excitedly. "You drag yourself round here, for all the world like an apparition, and when I do my best to find some way of putting things to rights, I who, when all's said and done, do happen to know you rather well . . ."

He smiled at her despondently, 'And how in the world should she know me? When far shrewder people than she, and even than I myself . . .'

"A certain kind of sickness of the soul, my child, of disillusion, is just a question of stomach. Yes, yes, you may laugh!" He was not laughing, but she might well think he was. "Romanticism, nerves, distaste for life: stomach. The whole lot, simply stomach. Love itself! If one wished to be perfectly sincere, one would have to admit there are two kinds of love—well-fed and ill-fed. The rest is pure fiction. If only I knew how to write, or to make speeches, my child, what things I could say about that! Oh, of course, it wouldn't be anything new, but I should know what I was talking about, and that would be a change from our present-day writers."

Something worse than this obsession with the kitchen was upsetting Chéri: the affectation, the false tone of voice, the almost studied joviality. He suspected Léa of putting on an act of hearty and sybaritic geniality, just as a fat actor, on the stage, plays "jovial" characters because he has developed a paunch.

As though defiantly, she rubbed her shiny, almost blotchy red nose with the back of her first finger, and fanned the upper part of her body with the aid of the two revers of her long jacket. In so doing, she was altogether too cheerfully inviting Chéri to sit in judgment on her appearance, and she even ran her hand through her thick grey locks as she shook them free of her head.

"Do you like my hair short?"

He deigned to reply only by a silent shake of the head, just like someone brushing aside an idle argument.

"Weren't you saying something just now about a little restaurant in the Avenue des Gobelins. . . ?"

It was now her turn to brush aside an irrelevance. She was beginning to understand, and he could see from the quivering of her nostrils that at last she was piqued. His animal instincts, which had been shocked into dullness, were now on the alert and it was as though a weight had been lifted from his mind. He intended somehow to find a way past this shameless flesh, the greying curls and "merry friar" joviality, and reach the being concealed behind them, to whom he was coming back, as to the scene of a crime. He remained close to this buried treasure, burrowing towards it spontaneously. 'How in the world did old age come upon her? All of a sudden, on waking up one morning? or little by little? And this surplus fat, this extra avoirdupois, under the weight of which armchairs groan? Was it some sudden shock that brought about this change and unsexed her? Could it, perhaps, have been grief on my account?' But he asked these questions of no one but himself, and without voicing them. 'She is piqued. She's on the way to understanding me. She's just going to tell me. . . .'

He watched her rise to her feet, walk over to the bureau, and start to tidy the papers lying on the open hinged flap. He noticed that she was holding herself more upright than when he had first entered the room, and that, under his following eye, she straightened her back still more. He accepted the fact that she was really colossal, her body seeming to run absolutely straight from armpit to hip. Before turning round again to face Chéri, she arranged a white silk scarf tightly round her neck, despite the heat of the room. He heard her take a deep breath, before she came towards him with the slow rolling gait of a ponderous animal.

She smiled at him. "I am not doing my duty as a hostess, it would seem. It's not very polite to welcome someone by giving them advice, especially useless advice."

From under a fold of her white scarf peeped insinuatingly a twisting, coiling, resplendent string of pearls, which Chéri at once recognised.

Held captive beneath the translucent skin, the seven colours of the rainbow flickered with some secret fire of their own all over the surface of each precious sphere. Chéri recognised the pearl with a dimple, the slightly egg-shaped pearl, and the biggest pearl of the string, distinguishable by its unique pink. 'These pearls, these at least, are unchanged! They and I remain unchanged.'

"So you've still got your pearls," he said.

She was astonished by the foolish phrase, and looked as though she wanted to interpret it.

"Yes, in spite of the war. Are you thinking that I could, or should, have sold them? Why should I have sold them?"

"Or 'for whom'?" he answered jokingly, in a tired voice.

She could not restrain a rapid glance towards the bureau and its scattered papers; and Chéri, in his turn, felt he knew the thought behind it, guessing that it was aimed at some yellowish postcard-photograph, probably the frightened features of a beardless boy in uniform. Disdainfully, he considered this imaginary face and said to himself, 'That's none of my concern,' adding a moment later, 'But what is there here that does concern me?'

The agitation which he had brought in his heart was now excited by everything around him; everything added to it—the setting sun, the cries of insect-chasing swallows, and the ember-glowing shafts of

light stabbing through the curtains. He remembered that
Léa carried with her wherever she went this incandescent
rose-pink, as the sea, on its ebb-tide, carries with it far
out from shore the earthy smells of pastures and new-
mown hay.

No word passed between them for a while, and they
were kept in countenance by pretending to listen to the
clear fresh notes of a child singing. Léa had not sat down
again. Standing massively in front of him, she carried
her irretrievable chin higher than before, and betrayed
some vague distress by the frequent fluttering of her
eyelids.

"Am I making you late? Have you to go out this
evening? Do you want to dress?" The questions were
abrupt, and forced Léa to look at Chéri.

"Dress? Good Lord, and in what do you wish me
to dress? I *am* dressed—irrevocably—once and for all."

She laughed her incomparable laugh, starting on a
high note and descending the scale by leaps of equal
interval till she got to the deep musical reaches reserved
for sobs and amorous moans. Chéri unconsciously
raised a hand in supplication.

"Dressed for life, I tell you! And how convenient that
is! Blouses, fine linen, and this uniform on top, and here
I am in full fig. Equally ready for dinner either at
Montagné's or somewhere modest, ready for the cinema,
for bridge, or for a stroll in the Bois."

"And what about love—which you're forgetting to
mention?"

"Oh, child!"

She blushed: and, though her face was dark with the
chronic red of sufferers from arthritis, the blush could
not be concealed. Chéri, after the first caddish satisfaction
of having said something outrageous, was seized with

shame and remorse at the sight of this maidenly reaction.

"I was only joking," he said, in some confusion. "Have I gone too far?"

"Of course not. But you know very well I have never cared for certain kinds of impropriety or for jokes that are not really funny."

She strove to control her voice, but her face revealed that she was hurt, and every coarsened feature gave signs of a distress that could perhaps be outraged modesty.

'Dear God, if she takes it into her head to cry!' and he imagined the catastrophic effect of tears coursing down each cheek into the single deep ravine near the mouth, and of her eyelids reddened by the salt of tears.

He hastened to intercept: "No, no, you mustn't think that! How could you! I never meant . . . Please, Léa. . . ."

From her quick reaction he realised suddenly that this was the first time he had spoken her name. Proud, as in the old days, of her self-control, she gently stopped him.

"Don't worry, child. I'm not offended. But I've only got you here for a few minutes, so don't spoil them by saying anything I shouldn't care to remember."

Her gentle tone left him cold, and her actual words seemed offensively tactful to him. 'Either she's lying, or she really has become the sort of person she pretends. Peace, purity, and the Lord knows what! She might as well wear a ring in her nose! Peace of heart, guzzling, and the cinema. . . . Lies, lies, all lies! She wants to make me think that women find growing old comfortable, positively enjoyable. How can she expect *me* to swallow that? Let her bore anyone else she likes with her fine talk about how cosy life is, and the little restaurants with the most delicious country dishes. I'm not having any! Before I could toddle, I knew all there is to know about reducing. I was *born* among ageing beauties! All my life I've watched them, my painted pixies, squabbling about their wrinkles, and, well into their fifties, scratching each other's eyes out over some wretched gigolo!'

"You sit there saying nothing, and I'm not used to it any more. I keep on thinking that there's something you want to say to me."

On her feet, separated from Chéri by an occasional table with a decanter and port glasses, she made no effort to defend herself against the severe inspection to which she was being subjected; but from the almost invisible tremors that passed over her body, Chéri noted the muscular effort required to keep in her spreading stomach. 'How many times must she have put on her full-length corset again, left it off, then valiantly put it on again, before abandoning it for ever? . . . How often of a morning must she have varied the shades of her face powder, rubbed a new rouge on her cheeks, massaged her neck with cold-cream and a small lump of ice tied up in a handkerchief, before becoming resigned to the varnished hide that now shines on her cheeks!' Impatience alone, perhaps, had made her tremble, yet this faint tremor led him to expect—so stubbornly blind was he to reality— some miraculous new blossoming, some complete metamorphosis.

"Why don't you say something?" Léa persisted.

Little by little she was losing her poise, though she was careful not to move. She was playing with her rope of large pearls, knotting and unknotting, round her big well-manicured and wrinkled fingers, their luminous, indescribably bedewed and everlasting lustre.

'Perhaps it's simply because she's frightened of me,' Chéri mused. 'A man who says nothing must always seem a bit cranky. She's thinking of Valérie Cheniaguine's terrors. If I put my hand out, would she scream for help? My poor Nounoune!' He lacked the courage to pronounce this name out loud, and, to protect himself from even a moment's sincerity, he spoke:

"What are you going to think of me?"

"It all depends," Léa answered guardedly. "At the moment you remind me of people who bring along a little box of cakes and leave it in the hall, saying to themselves: 'There'll be plenty of time to produce these later,' and then pick them up again when they go."

Reassured by the sound of their voices, she had begun to reason like the Léa of old, quick on the uptake, and as wily as a sharp-witted peasant. Chéri rose to his feet, walked round the table which separated him from Léa, and the daylight streaming through the pink curtains struck him full in the face. This made it easy for her to compute the passage of days and years from his features, which were all of them in danger, though still intact. There was something about so secret a falling away to tempt her pity and trouble her memory, and perhaps extract from her the word or gesture that would precipitate Chéri into a frenzy of humiliation. As he stood there, a sacrifice to the light, with eyes lowered as if he were asleep, it seemed to him this was his last chance of extorting from her one last affront, one last prayer, one final act of homage.

Nothing happened, so he opened his eyes. Once more he had to accept the true picture—in the shape of his stalwart old friend, who, prudently keeping her distance, was bestowing on him a certain degree of benevolence from small and slightly suspicious blue eyes.

Disillusioned and bewildered, he looked all over the room for her, except in the very spot where she stood.

'Where is she? Where is she? This old woman is hiding
her from me. She's bored by me, and she's waiting for
me to go, thinking it all an infernal nuisance, these
crowding memories and this returning ghost. . . . But if
by any chance I did ask for her help, if I beg her to give
me back Léa . . .' Deep inside him, his kneeling double
was still palpitating, like a body from which the life-
blood is being drained. With an effort of which he would
never have deemed himself capable, Chéri tore himself
away from this tortured image.

"I must be going," he said out loud, and he added on a
note of rather cheap wit, "and I'm taking my box of
cakes with me."

Léa's exuberant bosom heaved with a sigh of relief.
"As you like, my child. But I'm always here, you know,
if you're in any little trouble."

Though she seemed so obliging, Chéri could sense an
underlying resentment. Within that vast edifice of flesh
crowned with silvery thatch, femininity had for a moment
reasserted itself in tones resounding with an intelligent
harmony. But Chéri could not respond: like a ghost he
had come, and with the shyness of a ghost he must
vanish, in his own despite.

"Of course," Chéri replied, "and I thank you."

From that moment on, he knew, unerringly and
spontaneously, exactly how to manage his exit. All the
right words sprang to his lips, fluently, mechanically.

"You do understand, don't you, I came here to-day
. . . why not sooner, you may ask? I know I ought to have
come a long while ago. . . . But you will forgive me. . . ."

"Of course," Léa said.

"I'm even more hare-brained than before the war, you
know, so that . . ."

"I understand, I understand."

And because of this interruption, he thought that she must be impatient to see the last of him. A few words were exchanged during Chéri's retreat, in the intervals of bumping into some piece of furniture, crossing a strip of sunshine from the courtyard window—after the pink light in the drawing-room it seemed by comparison almost blue—kissing a puffy hand bulging with rings when it was raised to his lips. Another of Léa's laughs, which broke off abruptly half way down its usual scale, just like a fountain when the jet is turned off and the crest of the plume, suddenly bereft of its stem, falls back to earth in a myriad separate pearls. . . . The staircase seemed to glide away under Chéri's feet like a bridge connecting two dreams, and once more he was in the Rue Raynouard. Even the street was unfamiliar.

He noticed that the rosy tints of the sky were wonderfully reflected in the rain-filled gutters and on the blue backs of the low-skimming swallows. And now, because the evening was fresh, and because all the impressions he was bringing away with him were slipping back perfidiously into the recesses of his mind—there to assume their final shape and intensity—he came to believe that he had forgotten all about them, and he felt happy.

ONLY the sound of an old woman's bronchial cough, as she sat over her glass of crème-de-menthe, disturbed the peace of the bar room where the murmur of the Place de l'Opéra died away, as though muffled in an atmosphere too thick to carry any eddies of sound. Chéri ordered a long drink and mopped his brow: this precaution was a carry-over from the days when he had been a little boy and sat listening to the babble of female voices, as, with Biblical gravity, they bandied such golden rules as: "If you want your milk of cucumber with real cucumber in it, you must make it yourself . . .", or "Never rub the perspiration into your face when you're overheated, or the perspiration will get under your skin and ruin it."

The silence, and the emptiness of the bar, created an illusion of coolness, and at first Chéri was not conscious of the couple who, with heads bent close together across a narrow table, were lost in inaudible whisperings. After a few moments his attention was drawn to this unknown man and woman by an occasional hissing sibilant which rose above the main stream of their chatter, and by the exaggerated expressions on their faces. They looked like servants, underpaid, overworked, and patient.

He took a mouthful or two of the fizzy iced drink, leaned his head back against the yellow plush of the banquette, and was delighted to feel a slackening of the mental strain which, for the last fortnight, had been sapping his strength. The dead weight of the present had not accompanied him across the threshold of the bar, which was old-fashioned, with red walls, gilt festoons, plaster roses, and a large open hearth. The cloakroom attendant could be half-seen in her tiled kingdom, counting every stitch as she mended the linen, her white hair bowed beneath a green lamp.

A passer-by dropped in. He did not trespass upon the yellow room, but took his drink standing at the bar as though to be discreet, and left without a word. The Odol odour of the crème-de-menthe was the only thing distasteful to Chéri, and he frowned in the direction of the dim old woman. Under a black and battered soft hat, he could distinguish an old face, accentuated here and there by rouge, wrinkles, kohl, and puffiness—all jumbled together—rather like a pocket into which have been popped, higgledy-piggledy, handkerchief, keys, and loose change. A vulgar old face, in short—and common-place in its vulgarity, characterised, if at all, only by the indifference natural to a savage or a prisoner. She coughed, opened her bag, blew her nose vaguely, and replaced the seedy black reticule on the marble-topped table. It had an affinity with the hat, for it was made of the same black cracked taffeta, and equally out of fashion.

Chéri followed her every movement with an exagger-ated repugnance; during the last two weeks he had been suffering, more than he could reasonably be expected to bear, from everything that was at once feminine and old. That reticule sprawling over the table almost drove him from the spot. He wanted to avert his eyes, but did nothing of the sort: they were riveted by a small sparkling arabesque, an unexpected brilliance fastened to the folds of the bag. His curiosity surprised him, but half a minute later he was still staring at the point of sparkling light, and his mind became an absolute blank. He was roused from his trance by a subconscious flash of triumphant certainty, and this gave him back the freedom to think and breathe. 'I know! It's the two capital L's interlaced!'

He enjoyed a moment of calm satisfaction, not unlike the sense of security on reaching a journey's end. He actually forgot the cropped hair on the nape of that neck, the vigorous grey locks, the big nondescript coat buttoned over a bulging stomach; he forgot the contralto notes of the peal of youthful laughter—everything that had dogged him so persistently for the past fortnight, that had deprived him of any appetite for food, any ability to feel that he was alone.

'It's too good to last!' he thought. So, with a brave effort, he returned to reality. He looked more carefully at the offending object, and was able to reel off: 'The two initials, set in little brilliants, which Léa had designed first for her suède bag, then for her dressing-table set of light tortoise-shell, and later for her writing-paper!' Not for a moment would he admit that the monogram on the bag might represent some other name.

He smiled ironically. 'Coincidence be blowed! I wasn't born yesterday! I came upon this bag by chance this evening, and to-morrow my wife will go and engage one of Léa's old footmen—again by chance. After that I shan't be able to go into a single restaurant, cinema, or tobacconist's without running up against Léa at every turn. It's my own fault. I can't complain. I ought to have left her alone.'

He put some small change beside his glass, and got up before summoning the barman. He faced away from the old woman as he slipped between the two tables, holding himself in under his waistcoat, like a tomcat squeezing under a gate. This he managed so adroitly that the edge of his coat only just brushed against the glass of green crème-de-menthe. Murmuring an apology, he made a dash for the glass door, to escape into the fresh air beyond. Horrified, but not really in the least surprised, he heard a voice call out after him, "Chéri!"

He had feared—known indeed—that this was coming. He turned to find that there was nothing about the raddled old ruin to help him recall her name; but he made no second attempt to escape, realising that everything would be explained.

"Don't you recognise me? You don't? But how could you? More women were aged by the war than men were killed by it and that's a fact. All the same, it's not for me to complain; I didn't risk losing anyone in the war. . . . Eh! Chéri . . ."

She laughed; and recognition was complete, for he saw that what he had taken for decrepitude was only poverty and natural indifference. Now that she was holding herself upright and laughing, she did not look more than her age—sixty or thereabouts—and the hand with which she sought Chéri's was certainly not that of a doddering old grandmother.

"The Pal!" Chéri murmured, almost in tones of admiration.

"Are you really pleased to see me?"

"Oh, yes. . . ."

He was not telling a lie. He was gaining assurance step by step and thinking, 'It's only her . . . Poor Old Pal . . . I'd begun to fear . . .'

"Will you have a glass of something, Pal?"

"Just a whisky and soda, my pretty. My! haven't you kept your looks!"

He swallowed the bitter compliment which she tossed to him from the peaceful fringes of old age.

"And decorated, too," she added out of pure politeness.

"Oh! I knew all about it, you may be sure! We all knew about it."

The ambiguous plural failed to wrest a smile from Chéri, and the Pal thought she had shocked him.

"When I say 'we', I'm speaking of those of us who were your real friends—Camille de La Berche, Léa, Rita, and me. You may be sure Charlotte would never have told me a word about it. As far as she's concerned, I don't exist. But—and I may as well say so—she doesn't exist for me, either." She stretched out across the table a pale hand that had long forgotten the light of day. "You must understand that Charlotte will never again be anything to me but the woman who contrived to get poor little Rita arrested and detained for twenty-four hours. . . . Poor Rita, who had never known a word of German. Was it Rita's fault, I ask you, if she happened to be Swiss?"

"I know, I know. I know the whole story," Chéri broke in precipitately.

The Pal raised her huge dark watery eyes towards him, full of inveterate complicity and a compassion that was always misplaced. "Poor kid," she sighed. "I understand you. Forgive me. Ah! you've certainly had your cross to bear!"

He questioned her with a look, no longer accustomed to the overstatements that added a rich funereal tone to the Pal's vocabulary, and he feared she might be going to talk to him about the war. But she was not thinking of the war. Perhaps she never had, for it is the concern of two generations only.

She went on to explain. "Yes, I was saying that to have such a mother must have been a heavy cross to bear for a son like you—for a boy, that's to say, with a blameless life, both before marriage and after! A nice, quiet boy and all that; not one to sow his wild oats all over the place, or to squander his inheritance."

She wagged her head, and bit by bit he began to piece together the past. He rediscovered her, though she had the mask of a ravaged tragedy queen. Her old age was without nobility, yet bore no signs of illness, no tell-tale trace that betrayed her addiction to opium. The drug is merciful to those unworthy of it.

"Have you quite given up the pipe?" asked Chéri sharply.

She raised a white untended hand. "What do you suppose? That kind of foolishness is all very well when you're not all on your own. In the days when I used to shock you young men, yes. . . . You remember when you used to come back at nights? Ah! you were very fond of that. . . . 'Dear old Pal,' you used to say to me, 'just let me have another little pipeful, and pack it well!' "

Without turning a hair, he accepted this humble flattery, as he might from an old retainer, who fibs in order to fawn. He smiled knowingly, and scrutinised the folds of black tulle round her neck, looking in the shadows under the faded hat for a necklace of large fake pearls.

Almost mechanically and sip by sip, he drank the whisky which had been put in front of him by mistake. He did not care for spirits as a rule, but this evening he enjoyed the whisky, for it helped him to smile easily and softened to his touch unpolished surfaces and rough materials; it enabled him to listen kindly to an old woman for whom the present did not exist. They met again on the further side of the superfluous war-years and the young, importunate dead: the Pal spanned the gap by throwing across to Chéri a bridge of names— names of old men who bore charmed lives, of old women revitalised for the struggle or turned to stone in their ultimate shape, never to alter again. She recounted in detail a hard-luck story of 1913, some unhappiness that had taken place before August, 1914, and something trembled in her voice when she spoke of La Loupiote—a woman now dead—"The very week of your wedding, dear boy! you see what a coincidence it was? the hand of Fate was upon us, indeed"—dead after four years of a pure and peaceful friendship.

"We slanged each other day in, day out, dear boy, but only in front of other people. Because, don't you see, it gave them the impression that we were 'a couple'. Who would have believed it, if we hadn't gone for each other hammer and tongs? So we called each other the most diabolical names, and the onlookers chuckled: 'Have you ever seen such a devoted pair?' Dear boy, I'll tell you something else that will knock you flat—surely you must have heard about the will Massau was supposed to have made. . . ."

"What Massau?" Chéri asked, languidly.

"Oh, come. You knew him as well as you know yourself! The story of the will—so called—that he handed to Louise MacMillar. It was in 1909, and at the time I am speaking of, I was one of the Gérault pack, his pack of 'faithful hounds'—and there were five of us he fed every evening at *La Belle Meunière* down at Nice; but on the Promenade des Anglais, you must remember, we only had eyes for you—dolled up in white like an English baby, and Léa all in white as well. . . . Ah! what a pair you made! You were the sensation—a miracle, straight from the hands of the Creator! Gérault used to tease Léa: 'You're far too *young*, girlie, and what's worse you're too proud. I shan't take you on for fifteen or twenty years at least. . . .' And to think that such a man had to be taken from us! Not a tear at his funeral that wasn't genuine, the whole nation was in mourning. And now let me get on with the story of the will. . . ."

Chéri was deluged with a perfect flood of incidents, a

tide of bygone regrets and harmless resurrections, all declaimed with the ease and rapidity of a professional mourner. The two of them formed a symmetrical pattern as they leaned towards each other. The Pal lowered her voice when she came to the dramatic passages, giving out a sudden laugh or exclamation; and he saw in one of the looking-glasses how closely they seemed to resemble the whispering couple whose place they had taken. He got up, finding it imperative to put an end to this resemblance. The barman imitated his movement, but from afar, like a discreet dog when its master comes to the end of a visit. "Ah! well . . . yes . . ." said the Pal, "well, I'll finish the rest another time."

"After the next war," said Chéri, jokingly. "Tell me, those two capital letters. . . . Yes, the monogram in little brilliants. . . . It's not yours, Pal?"

He pointed at the black bag with the tip of his fore-finger, extending it slowly while withdrawing his body, as though the bag were alive.

"Nothing escapes you," the Pal said in admiration. "You're quite right. She gave it to me, of course. She said to me: 'Such bits of finery are far too frivolous for me nowadays!' She said: 'What the devil do you suppose I'd be doing with those mirrors and powder and things, when I've a great face like a country policeman's?' She made me laugh. . . ."

To stem the flood, Chéri pushed the change from his hundred-franc note towards the Pal. "For your taxi, Pal."

They went out on to the pavement by the tradesman's entrance, and Chéri saw from the fainter lamp-light that night was coming on.

"Have you not got your motor?"

"My motor? No. I walked; it does me good."

"Is your wife in the country?"

"No. Her Hospital keeps her in Paris."

The Pal nodded her invertebrate hat. "I know. She's a big-hearted woman. Her name's been put forward for a decoration, I understand from the Baroness."

"What?"

"Here, stop that taxi for me, dear boy, the closed one. . . . And Charlotte's going big guns in her support; she knows people round Clemenceau. It will make up a little for the story about Rita . . . a little, not very much. She's as black as Sin itself, is Charlotte, my boy."

He pushed her into the oven of the taxi, where she sank back and became enveloped in the shadow. She ceased to exist. It was as though he had never met her, now that he heard her voice no longer. He took stock of the night, filling his lungs with the dust-laden air that foretold another scorching day. He pictured, as in a dream, that he would wake up at home, among gardens watered every evening, among the scent of Spanish honeysuckle and the call of birds, resting alongside his wife's straight hips. . . . But the Pal's voice rose up from the depths of the taxi: "Two hundred and fourteen, Avenue de Villiers! Remember my address, Chéri! And you know that I often dine at the *Giraffe*, Avenue de Wagram, don't you, if ever you should want me. . . . You know, if ever you should be looking for me."

'That's really the limit,' thought Chéri, lengthening his step. ' "If I should ever be looking for her." I ask you! Next time I come across her, I'll turn round and walk the other way.'

Cooled off and calmer, he strode without effort along the *quais* as far as the Place de l'Alma, and from there took a taxi back to the Avenue Henri-Martin. The eastern sky was already burnished with dull copper-coloured tints, which seemed rather to betoken the

setting of some planet than the dawn of a summer day.
No clouds streaked the vault of the heavens, but a haze
of particles hung heavy and motionless over Paris, and
would presently flare up and smoulder with the sombre
glow of red-hot metal. As dawn breaks, the dog-days
drain great cities and their suburbs of the moist pinks,
floral mauves and dewy blues that suffuse the sky above
open country where plant life flourishes in profusion.

Nothing was stirring in the house when Chéri came to
turn the tiny key in the lock. The flagged hall still smelt
of the previous evening's dinner, and the cut branches of
syringa, arranged by the armful in white vases tall enough
to hide a man, filled the air with unbreathable poison.
A stray grey cat slipped past him, stopped dead in the
middle of the passage, and coldly inspected the intruder.

"Come here, little clerk of the Courts," Chéri called
in a low voice. The cat glared at him almost insultingly
and did not budge. Chéri remembered that no animal—
no dog, horse or cat—had ever shown him any signs of
affection. He could hear, across a span of fifteen years,
Aldonza's raucous voice prophesying: 'A curse lies on
those from whom animals turn away.' But when the cat,
now wide awake, began to play with a small green chestnut, bowling it along with its front paw, Chéri smiled
and went on up to his room.

He found it as dark and blue as a stage night. The dawn
penetrated no further than the balcony, bedecked with
well trained roses and pelargoniums fastened with
raffia. Edmée was asleep, her bare arms and toes peeping
out from under a light blanket. She was lying on her side,
her head inclined, one finger hooked through her pearls.
In the half-light she seemed to be immersed in thought
rather than sleep. Her wavy hair strayed over her cheek,
and Chéri could hear no sound of her breathing.

'She's enjoying a peaceful sleep,' thought Chéri. 'She's dreaming of Doctor Arnaud, or the Legion of Honour, or Royal Dutch shares. She's pretty. How pretty she is! . . . "Don't you worry, only another two or three hours, and you'll go to find your Doctor Arnaud. That's not so bad, is it? You'll meet again in the Avenue de l'Italie, in your beloved joint with its stink of carbolic. You'll answer 'Yes, Doctor; No, Doctor,' like a good little girl. You'll both of you put on really serious expressions; you'll jiggle with thermometers—ninety-nine point six, a hundred and two point four—and he'll take your small carbolicky paw in his great coal-tarry mitt. You're lucky, my girl, to have a romance in your life! Don't worry. I shan't deprive you of it. . . ." I wouldn't mind, myself. . . .'

All of a sudden Edmée woke up with such a start that Chéri caught his breath, as though rudely interrupted in the middle of a sentence.

"It's you! It's you! Why, it *is* you after all."

"If you were expecting someone else, I offer my apologies," said Chéri, smiling at her.

"That's very clever. . . ." She sat up in bed and tossed back her hair. "What time is it? Are you getting up? Oh no, I see you've not been to bed yet. . . . You've just come in. . . . Oh, Fred! What have you been up to this time?"

" 'This time' is a compliment. . . . If you only knew what I've been doing. . . ."

She was no longer at the stage where, hands over her ears, she besought him, "No, no! say nothing! Don't tell me!" But, faster than his wife, Chéri was leaving behind that childishly malicious period when, amidst floods of tears and stormy scenes which ended by her throwing herself into his arms in the early hours of the morning, he would draw her down with him into the deep sleep of reconciled antagonists. No more little games of that sort. . . . No more betrayals. . . . Nothing, now, but this enforced and unavowable chastity.

He chucked his dusty shoes to the other end of the room, and sat down on the soft lace-frilled sheets, offering his wife a pallid face accustomed to dissemble everything except his will to dissemble. "Smell me!" he said. "Come on! I've been drinking whisky."

She brought her charming mouth to his, putting a hand on her husband's shoulder. "Whisky . . ." she repeated wonderingly. "Whisky . . . why?"

A less sophisticated woman would have asked "With whom?" and her cunning did not pass unnoticed. Chéri showed that two could play at that game by answering, "With an old pal. Do you want to hear the whole truth?"

She smiled, now caught in the dawning light which, with growing boldness, touched the edge of the bed, the looking-glass, a picture-frame, and then the golden scales of a fish swimming round and round in a crystal bowl.

"No, Fred, not the whole truth. Only a half-veiled truth, suitable for the small hours." At the same time, her thoughts were busy. She was certain—or nearly so—that Chéri had not been drawn away from her either by love or by lust. She let her acquiescent body fall helplessly into his arms, yet he felt on his shoulder a thin, hard hand, unrelaxed in its guarded prudence.

"The truth is," he went on, "that I don't know her name. But I gave her . . . wait a moment . . . I gave her eighty-three francs."

"Just like that, all at once! The first time you met her? It's princely!"

She pretended to yawn, and slipped softly back into the depths of the bed, as though not expecting an answer. He gave her a moment's pity; then a brilliant horizontal ray brought into sharper relief the almost naked body lying beside him, and his pity vanished.

'She's . . . she has kept her good looks. It's not fair.'

She lay back, her lips parted, looking at him through half-closed eyes. He saw a gleam of the candid, calculating, uncharacteristically feminine expression that a woman bestows on the man who is going to pleasure her, and it shocked his unavowable chastity. From his superior position he returned this look with another —the uncommunicative, enigmatic look of the man who prefers to abstain. Not wishing to move away, he simply looked towards the golden daylight, the freshness of the watered garden, and the blackbirds, weaving liquid sequences of sound round the dry incessant chirps of the sparrows. Edmée could see signs of emaciation and prolonged fatigue on his features. His cheeks were blue with a day's growth of beard. She noticed that his fine hands were not clean, that his finger-nails had not been near soap and water since the previous evening, and that the dark lines which accentuated the hollows under his eyes were now spreading, in the shape of crow's feet, towards his nose. This handsome young man—she decided—without collar or shoes, looked ravaged, as if he had had to spend a night in prison. Without losing his looks, he had shrunk in accordance with some mysterious scaling down, and this enabled her to regain the upper hand. She no longer invited him to join her, sat up in bed, and put a hand on his forehead.

"Ill?"

Slowly he let his attention wander back from the garden to his wife.

"What? . . . No, no, nothing's wrong with me, except I'm sleepy. So sleepy that I can hardly bring myself to go to bed—if you know what I mean. . . ."

He smiled, showing dry gums and lips colourless on the insides. But, above all, this smile betrayed a sadness that sought no remedy, modest as a poor man's suffering. Edmée was on the point of questioning him categorically, but then thought better of it.

"Get into bed," she ordered, making room for him.

"Bed? It's water I need. I feel so filthy, I can't tell you."

He just had the strength to lift up a water bottle, take a gulp from the neck, then throw off his coat, before he fell back like a log on the bed, and lay there without moving again, drained by sleep.

For some little time Edmée gazed at the half-stripped stranger lying like a drugged man beside her. Her watchful eye wandered from bluish lips to hollowed eyes, from outflung hand to forehead sealed upon a single secret. She summoned her self-control and composed her features, as though afraid the sleeper might take her by surprise. She got out of bed softly, and, before shutting out the dazzling sunlight, drew a silk counterpane to hide the outstretched untidy body looking like a burglar who had been knocked out. She arranged this so as to give the beautiful rigid features their full splendour, carefully pulling it down over the drooping hand with a slight qualm of pious disgust, as though hiding a weapon that perhaps had killed.

He never twitched a muscle—having retired for a few moments within an impregnable fastness. In any case, Edmée's hospital training had given her fingers a professional touch, which, if not exactly gentle, was competent to go straight to the required spot without touching or in any way affecting the surrounding area. She did not get back into bed; but, sitting half-naked, enjoyed the unexpected freshness of the hour when the sun rouses the winds. The long curtains stirred, as if breathing and, dependent on the breeze, stippled Chéri's sleep with fitful flecks of dark blue.

As she gazed at him, Edmée was not thinking of the wounded, or of the dead, whose peasant hands she had joined together upon coarse cotton sheets. No invalid in the grip of a nightmare, not one among the dead, had ever resembled Chéri: sleep, silence, and repose made him magnificently inhuman.

Extreme beauty arouses no sympathy. It is not the prerogative of any one country. Time's finger had touched Chéri only to make him more austere. The mind —whose task it is to curb the splendour of mankind while degrading it piecemeal—respected Chéri as an admirable temple dedicated to instinct. What could avail the Machiavellian deceit, the ardour and the cunning self-sacrifice imposed by love, against this inviolable standard-bearer of light and his untutored majesty?

Patient and, on occasion, subtle as she was, it never occurred to Edmée that the feminine appetite for possession tends to emasculate every living conquest, and can reduce a magnificent but inferior male to the status of a courtesan. Her lower-middle-class wisdom made her determined not to relinquish the gains—money, ease, domestic tyranny, marriage—acquired in so few years and rendered doubly attractive by the war.

She gazed at the limp, worn-out, almost empty-looking body. 'That's Chéri,' she said to herself; 'yes, that's Chéri all right . . . That's how small a thing he is!' She shrugged a shoulder and added: 'That's what he's reduced to, this wonderful Chéri of theirs . . .' doing her best to induce contempt for the man lying thus supine. She called up memories of rapturous nights, of languid early mornings bathed in sunlight and pleasure, and, as a result—since he had progressively grown to disdain her

—she saw fit to pay but coldly vindictive homage to this body so sumptuously laid out under the pall of flowered silk and the refreshing wing of the curtains. She put one hand on the small, pointed breast set low on her slender body, and squeezed it like a pulpy fruit, as if calling this most tempting allurement of her young body to witness the injustice of his desertion. 'What Chéri himself needs is doubtless something else. What he needs is . . .'

But vain were her attempts to put her scorn into words. Even a woman loses the desire and the ability to despise a man who suffers in silence and alone.

All of a sudden, Edmée felt satiated with the spectacle: the shadows thrown by the curtains, the pallor of the sleeper, and the white bed helped to invest it with the romantic colouring of death and the nether world. She jumped to her feet, strong and ready to face this world, but determined to avoid any emotional attack upon the traitor lying on the disordered bed, the absentee seeking refuge in sleep, silent, ailing and repulsive. She was neither irritated nor unhappy. Her heart would beat more feverishly in her breast, the blood mount more quickly to her pearl-pale cheeks, only at the thought of the healthy red-haired man whom she called "dear master" or "chief" in tones of serious playfulness. Arnaud's thick gentle hands; his laugh; the points of light that sunshine or the lamp in the operating-theatre caused to twinkle on his red moustache; his very coat— the white surgery-coat he wore and even took off in the hospital, just like an intimate garment that never passes beyond the bedroom door. . . . Edmée sprang up as though for a dance.

'That, oh yes, *that*'s my life!' She gave a toss of the head that sent her hair flying out like a horse's mane, and went into the bathroom without turning round.

UNIMAGINATIVE in style, and in its very ordinary proportions, the dining-room made no pretence to luxury except in the panels of yellow stuff starred with purple and green. The grey and white stucco of the surrounding walls deflected too much light on the guests, deprived already of all shade by the merciless glare of the top lighting.

A galaxy of crystal sequins shimmered with every movement of Edmée's dress. For the family dinner, Madame Peloux was still wearing her tailor-made with leather buttons, and Camille de La Berche her nurse's veil, under the cowl of which she bore a striking resemblance to Dante, only far hairier. Because it was so hot, the women spoke little: so did Chéri, because it was his habit. A warm bath followed by a cold shower had triumphed over his fatigue; but the powerful light, ricocheting upon his cheeks, accentuated their cavities, and he kept his eyes lowered, to allow the shadow from his eyebrows to fall directly over the lids.

"To-night, Chéri doesn't look a day over sixteen," boomed the deep bass of the Baroness out of the blue.

No one took up her remark, and Chéri acknowledged it with a slight bow.

"Not for a long time," the Baroness continued, "have I seen the oval of his face so slender."

Edmée frowned imperceptibly. "I have. During the war, of course."

"That's true, that's true," piped Charlotte Peloux in

shrill agreement. "Heavens! how worn out he looked in 1916, at Vésoul! Edmée, my dear child," she went on in the same breath, "I've seen you-know-who to-day, and *everything* is going along very nicely. . . ."

Edmée blushed in a docile, unbecoming manner, and Chéri raised his eyes. "You've seen who? And what's going along nicely?"

"Trousellier's pension—my little soldier who's had his right arm off. He left the Hospital on June the twentieth. Your mother's taking up his case at the War Office."

She had not hesitated for words, and she let her calm golden gaze rest on Chéri: yet he knew she was lying.

"It's a question of whether he'll get his red riband. After all, poor boy, it's certainly his turn. . . ."

She was lying to him in front of two friends who knew that she was lying. 'Why don't I pick up the water-bottle and crash it down in the middle of them?' But he made no movement. What strength of feeling would have given him the impetus to brace his body and direct his hand?

"Abzac is leaving us in a week's time," began Madame de La Berche.

"That's not certain," Edmée took her up with an air of knowing better. "Doctor Arnaud isn't at all satisfied that he should be allowed to go off like that on his new leg. You can just see the man, liable to do any sort of silly thing, and always with the possibility of gangrene. Doctor Arnaud knows only too well that it was exactly that sort of thing, all through the war. . . ."

Chéri looked at her, and she stopped abruptly in the middle of her pointless sentence. She was fanning herself with a rose on a leafy stalk. She waved away a dish which she was offered, and put her elbows on the table. In her white dress and bare shoulders, even when sitting still, she was not exempt from a secret contentment, a self-satisfaction, which revealed her true nature. Something outrageous radiated from her soft outlines. Some tell-tale glow betrayed the woman bent on "arriving", who up till the present had met only with success.

'Edmée,' Chéri concluded, 'is a woman who should never grow older than twenty. How like her mother she's getting!'

The next moment the resemblance had vanished. Nothing obvious about Edmée recalled Marie-Laure: only in one respect did her daughter exhibit something of the poisonous, pink and white, impudent beauty exploited by the red-haired Marie-Laure to ensnare her victims during her palmy days—and that was in her shamelessness. Careful as she was not to shock anyone, those who still retained their native shrewdness, by instinct or from lack of education, were shocked by her all the same, as if by a second-rate race-horse, or a jewel that looked too new. The servants, as well as Chéri, were frightened of something in Edmée, whom they guessed to be more vulgar than themselves.

Authorised by Edmée, who was lighting a cigarette, the Baroness de La Berche slowly grilled the tip of her cigar before inhaling the first rapturous puff. Her white Red Cross veil fell over her manly shoulders and she looked like one of those grave-faced men who, at Christmas parties, adorn their heads with tissue paper Phrygian caps, programme-sellers' kerchiefs, or shakos. Charlotte undid the plaited leather buttons of her jacket and drew towards her a box of Abdullas; while the butler, mindful of the customs of the house, pushed within easy reach of Chéri a small conjuror's table on wheels—full of secret drawers, sliding double-bottomed compartments, and liqueurs in silver phials. Then he left the room; and there was no longer against the yellow panels the tall silhouette of an elderly Italian with a face carved out of box-wood, and crowned with white hair.

'Old Giacomo really does look an aristocrat," said the Baroness de La Berche, "and I know what I'm talking about."

Madame Peloux shrugged her shoulders, a movement that had long since ceased to lift her breasts. Her white silk blouse with a jabot sagged under the weight of her bosom, and her short, dyed, but still abundant hair glowed a livid red above large disastrous eyes and high forehead, suggesting a leader of the French Revolution.

"He's got the distinguished looks of all elderly Italians with white hair. They're all Papal Chamberlains, by the look of them, and they can write out the menu for you in Latin; but you've only to open a door and you'll find them raping a little girl of seven."

Chéri welcomed this outburst of virulence as a timely shower. His mother's malice had parted the clouds again, bringing back an atmosphere in which he could breathe. Not so long ago he had begun to enjoy discovering traces of the old Charlotte, who, from the safety of her balcony, would refer to a pretty woman passing below as "a tuppeny-ha'penny tart," and who, to Chéri's "Do you know her, then?" would reply, "No! Whatever next! Do you expect me to know that slut?" Only recently had he begun to take a confused pleasure in Charlotte's superior vitality, and, confusedly, he now preferred her to the other two creatures present; but he was unaware that this preference, this partiality, could perhaps be termed filial affection. He laughed, and applauded Madame Peloux for still being—and quite startlingly so—the woman he had known, detested, feared, and insulted. For an instant, Madame Peloux took on her authentic character in her son's eyes; that is to say, he estimated her at her proper value, a woman high-spirited, all-consuming, calculating and at the same time rash, like a high financier; a woman capable of taking a humorist's delight in spiteful cruelty. "She's a scourge, certainly," he said to himself, "and no more. A scourge, but not a stranger." Looking at the way the points of her hair impinged upon her Jacobin forehead, he recognised a similarity to the blue-black jutting points on his own forehead, which emphasised the whiteness of his skin and the blackbird sheen of his hair.

'She's my mother all right,' he thought. 'No one's ever told me I'm like her, but I am.' The "stranger" was sitting opposite, glimmering with the milky, veiled brilliance of a pearl. Chéri heard the name of the Duchess of Camastra thrown out by the deep voice of the Baroness, and on the stranger's face he saw a fleeting rapacity flicker and die, like the serpent of flame that suddenly flares up along a burnt vine-twig before it is consumed among the embers. But she did not open her mouth, and took no part in the volley of military curses which the Baroness was firing at a hospital-rival.

"They're properly in the soup, it appears, over some new-fangled injection or other. Two men died within two days of being given the needle. That needs some explaining!" said Madame de La Berche with a hearty laugh.

"You've got it wrong," corrected Edmée dryly. "That's an old story of Janson-de-Sailly resuscitated."

"No smoke without fire," sighed Charlotte charitably. "Chéri, are you sleepy?"

He was dropping with fatigue, but he admired the powers of resistance of these three women: neither hard work, the Parisian summer, nor perpetual movement and jabber could put them out of action.

"The heat," he murmured laconically. He caught

Edmée's eye, but she made no comment and refrained from contradicting him.

"Pooh, pooh, pooh," chanted Charlotte. "The heat! But, of course. . . . Pooh, pooh, pooh."

Her eyes, which remained fixed on Chéri's, overflowed with blackmailing tenderness and complicity. As usual, she knew everything there was to be known: back-stairs gossip, concierges' chatter. Perhaps Léa herself, for the pleasure of a feminine fib, of winning one last trick, had told Charlotte. The Baroness de La Berche emitted a little neigh, and the shadow of her large clerical nose covered the lower part of her face.

"God in Heaven!" swore Chéri.

His chair fell to the floor behind him, and Edmée, alert and on the watch, promptly jumped to her feet. She showed not the slightest astonishment. Charlotte Peloux and the Baroness de La Berche at once put themselves on the defensive, but in the old-fashioned way—hands clutching skirts, ready to gather them up and fly. Chéri, leaning forward with his fists on the table, was panting and turning his head to right and left, like a wild animal caught in a net.

"You, to start with, you . . ." he stammered. He pointed at Charlotte; used as she was to such scenes, she was galvanised by this filial threat in the presence of witnesses.

"What? What? What?" she barked in sharp little yelps. "You dare to insult me? a little whippersnapper like you, a wretched little whippersnapper who, were I to open my mouth . . ."

The wine-glasses quivered at the sound of her piercing voice, but her words were cut short by a shriller voice: "Leave him alone!"

After three such abrupt explosions the silence seemed

deafening, and Chéri, his physical dignity restored, shook himself, and a smile spread over his green face.

"I beg your pardon, Madame Peloux," he said mischievously.

She was already conferring blessings on him with eye and hand, like a champion in the ring, pacified at the end of a round.

"You're hot-blooded and no mistake!"

"He's a soldier all right," said the Baroness, as she shook hands with Edmée. "I must say goodbye, Chéri; they'll be missing me in my dug-out."

She refused a lift in Charlotte's motor, and insisted on going home on foot. The tall figure, the white nurse's veil, and the glow of her cigar would strike terror at night into the heart of the fiercest footpad. Edmée accompanied the two old women as far as the front door, an exceptional act of courtesy, which allowed Chéri time to draw what conclusions he could from his wife's wary action and her diplomatic peacemaking.

He drank a glass of cold water very slowly, as he stood beneath the cataract of light, thinking the matter over and savouring his terrible loneliness.

'She defended me,' he kept repeating to himself. 'She defended me with no love in her heart. She protected me as she protects the garden against blackbirds, her store of sugar against thieving nurses, or her cellar against the footmen. Little doubt she knows that I went to the Rue Reynouard, and came back here, never to go there again. She's not said a word about it to me, in any case—perhaps because she doesn't care. She protected me, because it wouldn't have done for my mother to talk. She defended me with no love in her heart.'

He heard Edmée's voice in the garden. She was testing his mood from afar. "You don't feel ill,

Fred, do you? Would you like to go straight to bed?"

She put her head through the half-open door, and he laughed bitterly to himself: 'How cautious she's being.'

She saw his smile and grew bolder. "Come along, Fred. I believe I'm just as tired as you, or I wouldn't have let myself go just now. I've been apologising to your mother."

She switched off some of the cruel light, and gathered the roses from the table-cloth to put them into water. Her body, her hands, her head bending over the roses and set off by a haze of fair hair from which the heat had taken most of the crimp—everything about her might have charmed a man.

"I said *a man*—I didn't say *any man*," Léa's insidious voice kept ringing in Chéri's ears.

'I can behave as I like to her,' he thought, as he followed Edmée with his eyes. 'She'll never complain, she'll never divorce me; I've nothing to fear from her, not even love. I should be happy enough, if I chose.'

But, at the same time, he recoiled with unspeakable repugnance from the idea of the two of them living together in a home where love no longer held sway. His childhood as a bastard, his long adolescence as a ward, had taught him that his world, though people thought of it as reckless, was governed by a code almost as narrow-minded as middle-class prejudice. In it, Chéri had learned that love is a question of money, infidelity, betrayals, and cowardly resignation. But now he was well on the way to forgetting the rules he had been taught, and to be repelled by acts of silent condescension.

He therefore ignored the gentle hand on his sleeve. And, as he walked with Edmée towards the room whence would issue no sound of endearment or reproach, he was overcome with shame, and blushed at the horror of their unspoken agreement.

HE found himself out of doors, dressed for the street and hardly conscious of having put on his soft hat and light raincoat. Behind him lay the drawing-room, misty with tobacco smoke; the overpowering scent of women and flowers; the cyanide smell of cherry brandy. There he had left Edmée, Doctor Arnaud, Filipesco, Atkins, and the two Kelekian girls, well-connected young women who, having done a little mild lorry-driving during the war, had no use now for anything but cigars, motors, and their garage-hand friends. He had left Desmond sitting between a real estate merchant and an Under-Secretary in the Ministry of Commerce, together with an invalided poet and Charlotte Peloux. Also a fashionable young married couple, who had obviously been put wise. Throughout dinner they had looked greedy but prudish, with a knowing expression and a simple-minded eagerness to be shocked—as though expecting Chéri to dance stark naked, or Charlotte and the Under-Secretary to make violent love to one another in the middle of the carpet.

Chéri had made off, aware that his behaviour had been stoical, with no other lapse than a sudden loss of interest in the present: an awkward thing to lose in the middle of a meal. Even so, his trance could have lasted little more than a moment, had been instantaneous, like a dream. But now he was putting a distance between himself and the strangers who thronged his house, and the

sound of his footfall on the sand was as light as the soft
padding of an animal. His light silver-grey coat shaded
into the mist that had fallen over the Bois; and a few
nocturnal loiterers must have envied a young man who
was in such a hurry to go nowhere in particular.

He was haunted by the vision of his crowded house.
He could still hear the sound of voices, and carried with
him the memory of faces, of smiles, and especially of the
shape of mouths. An elderly man had talked about the
war; a woman about politics. He remembered, too, the
new understanding between Desmond and Edmée, and
the interest his wife had taken in some building scheme.
'Desmond! . . . Just the husband for my wife!' And then,
dancing . . . the strange effect of the tango on Charlotte
Peloux. Chéri quickened his step.

The night was filled with the damp mist of a too early
autumn and the full moon was shrouded. A great milky
halo, ringed with a pallid iridescence, had replaced the
planet, and was sometimes itself hidden by fitful puffs
of scudding cloud. The smell of September was already
in the leaves that had fallen during the dog days.

'How mild it is,' Chéri thought.

He rested his weary limbs on a bench, but not for long.
He was rejoined by an invisible companion, to whom he
refused his seat on the bench—a woman with grey hair,
wearing a long coat, who poured forth a relentless gaiety.
Chéri turned his head towards the gardens of La Muette,
as though he could hear, even at that distance, the cymbals
of the jazz-band.

The time had not yet come for him to go back to the
blue room, where perhaps the two society girls were still
smoking good cigars, as they sat side-saddle on the blue
velvet of the bed, keeping the real estate merchant
amused with mess-room tales.

'Oh! for a nice hotel bedroom, a jolly pink room, very ordinary and very pink . . .' But would it not lose its very ordinariness the moment the light was turned out and total darkness gave the right of entry—a ponderous, mocking entry—to a figure with vigorous grey hair, dressed in a long, nondescript coat? He smiled at the intruder, for he was past the stage of fear. 'There, or in any other place, *she* will be just as faithful. But I simply can't go on living with those people.'

Day by day, hour by hour, he was becoming more scornful, more exacting. Already he was severely critical of the Agony Column heroes, and young war widows who clamoured for new husbands, like the parched for cold water. His uncompromising intolerance extended to the world of finance, without his realising how grave was the change. 'That Company for transporting raw hides they talked about at dinner. . . . How disgusting it was! And they don't mind discussing it at the top of their voices. . . .' But nothing in the world would have induced him to protest, to reveal that he was fast becoming a man utterly out of sympathy with his surroundings. Prudently, he kept quiet about that, as about everything else. When he had taken Charlotte Peloux to task for having disposed of several tons of sugar in rather a dubious fashion, had she not reminded him—and in no uncertain terms—of the time when he had shouted, without a trace of embarrassment, "Hand over five louis, Léa, so that I can go and buy some cigarettes"?

'Ah!' he sighed, 'they'll never understand anything, these women. It wasn't at all the same thing.'

Thus he let his thoughts run on, as he stood, bareheaded, his hair glistening, barely distinguishable in the mist. The shadowy form of a female passed close beside him, running. The rhythm of her steps and the crunch as each foot bit into the gravel betrayed anxiety and haste. Then the shadowy woman fell into the arms of a shadowy man who came to meet her, and down they fell together, breast to breast, as though struck by the same bullet.

'Those two are trying to hide,' Chéri thought. 'They're deceiving someone somewhere. The whole world's busy deceiving and being deceived. But I . . .' He did not finish the sentence, but a repugnance made him jump to his feet, an action that meant, 'But I am chaste.' A faint ray of light, flickering uncertainly over stagnant, hitherto unfeeling regions of his inmost being, was enough to suggest that chastity and loneliness are one and the same misfortune.

As night advanced, he began to feel the cold. From his prolonged, aimless vigils, he had learned that, at night, tastes, smells, and temperatures vary according to the hour, and that midnight is warm in comparison with the hour which immediately precedes the dawn.

'The winter will soon be on us,' he thought, as he lengthened his stride, 'and none too soon, putting an end to this interminable summer. Next winter, I should like . . . let me see . . . next winter . . .' His attempts at anticipation collapsed almost at once; and he came to a halt, head lowered, like a horse at the prospect of a long steep climb ahead.

'Next winter, there'll still be my wife, my mother, old gammer La Berche, Thingummy, What's-his-name, and the rest of them. There'll be the same old gang. . . . And for me there'll never again be . . .'

He paused once more, to watch a procession of low clouds advancing over the Bois, clouds of an indescribable pink, set upon by a gusty wind which buried its fingers in their misty tresses, twisting and dragging them across the lawns of heaven, to carry them off to the moon.

Chéri gazed with eyes well used to the translucent magic of the night, which those who sleep regard as pitch-dark.

The apparition of the large, flat, half-veiled moon among the scurrying vaporous clouds, which she seemed to be pursuing and tearing asunder, did not divert him from working out an arithmetical fantasy: he was computing—in years, months, hours and days—the amount of precious time that had been lost to him for ever.

'Had I never let her go when I went to see her again that day before the war—then it would have meant three or four years to the good; hundreds and hundreds of days and nights gained and garnered for love.' He did not fight shy of so big a word.

'Hundreds of days—a lifetime—life itself. Life as it was in the old days, life with my "worst enemy", as she used to call herself. My worst enemy! who forgave me all, and never let me off a single thing.' He seized hold of his past, to squeeze out every remaining drop upon his empty, arid present; bringing back to life, and inventing where necessary, the princely days of his youth, his adolescence shaped and guided by a woman's strong capable hands—loving hands, ever ready to chastise. A prolonged, sheltered, oriental adolescence, in which the pleasures of the flesh had their passing place, like silent pauses in a song. A life of luxury, passing whims, childish cruelty, with fidelity a yet unspoken word.

He threw back his head to look up at the nacreous halo which irradiated the whole sky, and he gave a low cry, 'It's all gone to hell! I'm thirty years old!'

He hurried on his way back home, heaping curses on himself to the rhythm of his quickened steps. 'Fool! The tragedy is not her age, but mine. Everything may be over for her, but, for me . . .'

He let himself in without making a sound, to find the house in silence at last; to be nauseated by the lingering stale smell of those who had dined, wined, and danced there. In the looking-glass fitted to the door in the hall he met face to face the young man who had grown so thin, whose cheeks had hardened, whose sad beautifully moulded upper lip was unshaven and blue, whose large eyes were reticent and tragic. The young man, in effect, who had ceased, inexplicably, to be twenty-four years old.

'For me,' Chéri completed his thought, 'I really do believe that the last word has been said.'

"WHAT I need is somewhere quiet, you understand. . . . Any little place would do. . . . A bachelor flat, a room, a corner. . . ."

"I wasn't born yesterday," said the Pal, reproachfully. She raised disconsolate eyes towards the festoons on the ceiling: "A little love, of course, of course, a little kiss—something to warm a poor lonely heart. . . . You bet I understand! Any special fancy?"

Chéri frowned. "Fancy? For whom?"

"You don't understand, my pretty. . . . Fancy for any particular district?"

"Ah! . . . No, nothing special. Just a quiet corner."

The Pal nodded her large head in collusion. "I see, I see. Something after my style—like my flat. You know where I rest my bones?"

"Yes."

"No, you don't know at all. I was certain you wouldn't write it down. Two hundred and fourteen Rue de Villiers. It's not big, and it's not beautiful. But you don't want the sort of place where the whole street knows your business."

"No."

"I got mine, of course, through a little deal with my landlady. A jewel of a woman, by the way, married, or as good as. Periwinkle blue eyes, and a head like a bird; but she bears the mark of Fate on her forehead, and I already know from her cards that she can't say no to anything, and that——"

"Yes, yes. You were saying just now that you knew of a flat. . . ."

"Yes, but not good enough for you."

"You don't think so?"

"Not for you . . . not for the two of you!"

The Pal hid a suggestive smile in her whisky, and Chéri turned from its smell—like wet harness. He put up with her quips about his imaginary conquests, for he saw, round her scraggy neck, a string of large faked pearls which he thought he recognised. Every visual reminder of his past halted him on his downward path, and, during such respites, he felt at peace.

"Ah!" sighed the Pal, "How I'd love to catch a glimpse of her! What a pair! . . . I don't know her, of course, but I can just see you two together! . . . Of course you'll provide everything yourself?"

"For whom?"

"Why, the furniture in your love-nest, of course!"

He looked at the Pal in bewilderment. Furniture . . . What furniture? He had been thinking only of one thing: a refuge of his own, with a door that opened and closed for him and no one else, safe from Edmée, Charlotte, all of them. . . .

"Will you furnish it in period or in modern style? La belle Serrano arranged her entire ground floor with nothing but Spanish shawls, but that was a bit eccentric. You're old enough, of course, to know your own mind. . . ."

He hardly heard her, far away in his dreams of a future home that would be secret, small, warm and dark. At the same time, he was drinking red currant syrup, like any young "miss", in the red-and-gold, out-of-date,

unchanging bar, just as it used to be when, a small boy,
Chéri had come there to sip his first fizzy drink through
a straw. . . . Even the barman himself had not changed,
and if the woman sitting opposite Chéri was now a
withered specimen, at least he had never known her
beautiful, or young.

'They all change, the whole of that set—my mother,
my wife, all the people they see—and they live for
change. My mother may change into a banker, Edmée
into a town councillor. But I . . .'

In imagination, he quickly returned to that refuge,
existing at some unknown point in space, but secret,
small, warm, and . . .

"Mine's done up in Algerian style," the Pal persisted.
"It's no longer in the fashion, but I don't mind—
especially as the furniture is hired. You'll be sure to
recognise many of the photos I've put up: and then
there's the portrait of La Loupiote. . . . Come and have a
look at it. Please do."

"I'd like to. Let's go!"

On the threshold he hailed a taxi.

"But d'you never have your motor? Why haven't you
got your motor? It's really quite extraordinary how
people with motors never have their motor!"

She gathered up her faded black skirts, caught the
string of her lorgnette in the clasp of her bag, dropped a
glove, and submitted to the stares of the passers-by with
the lack of embarrassment of a Negro. Chéri, standing
at her side, received several insulting smiles and the
admiring condolences of a young woman, who called out:
"Lord, what a waste of good material!"

In the taxi, patiently and half asleep, he endured the
old thing's tattle. And then some of her stories were soothing: the one about the ridiculous little dog which had held

up the return from the races in 1897, and then Mère La Berche eloping with a young bride on the day of her wedding in 1893.

"That's it over there. This door's stuck, Chéri, I can't get out. I warn you, there's not much light in the passage, nor, for that matter, is there much out here. . . . It's only a ground-floor flat, when all's said and done! . . . Wait where you are a second."

He waited, standing in the semi-darkness. He heard the jingle of keys, the wheezy old creature's gasps for breath and then her fussy servant's voice, "I'm lighting up. . . . Then you'll find yourself in a familiar landscape. I've got electricity, of course. . . . There, let me introduce you to my little morning-room, which is also my large drawing-room!"

He went in, and, from kindness—hardly bothering to glance at it—praised the room; it had a low ceiling and reddish walls, kippered by the smoke of innumerable cigars and cigarettes. Instinctively, he looked all round for the window, barricaded by shutters and curtains.

"You can't see in here? You're not an old night-bird like your Pal. Wait, I'll switch on the top light."

"Don't bother. . . . I'll just come in and——" He broke off, staring at the most brightly lit wall, covered with small frames and photographs pinned through the four corners. The Pal began to laugh.

"What did I say about a familiar landscape! I was quite sure you'd enjoy looking at them. You haven't got that one, have you?"

'That one' was a very large photographic portrait-study, touched up with water colours now quite faded. Blue eyes, a laughing mouth, a chignon of fair hair, and a look of calm yet exultant triumph. . . . High-breasted— in a First Empire corselet, legs showing through gauze skirts, legs that never finished, rounded out at the thigh, slender at the knee, legs that. . . . And a fetching hat, a hat that turned up on one side only, trimmed like a single sail to the wind.

"She never gave you that one, not that one, I bet! It makes her a goddess, a fairy walking on clouds! And yet it's absolutely her, of course. This big photo is the loveliest, to my way of thinking, but I'm still every bit as fond of the others. Here, for instance, look at this little one here—much more recent, of course—isn't it a sight for sore eyes?"

A snapshot, clinging to the wall with the help of a rusty pin, showed a woman standing in the shade against a sunlit garden.

'It's the navy-blue dress and the hat with the seagulls,' Chéri said to himself.

"I'm all for flattering portraits, myself," the Pal went on. "A portrait like this one. Come now—you must confess—isn't it enough to make you join your hands and believe in God?"

A degraded and smarmy art, to lend glamour to the "portrait photograph," had lengthened the neck line and modified those around the sitter's mouth. But the nose, just sufficiently aquiline, the delicious nose with its ravishing nostrils, and the chaste little dimple, the velvety cleft that indented the upper lip under the nose— these were untouched, authentic, respected by even the photographer.

"Would you believe it? She wanted to burn the lot, pretending that nobody to-day is the least interested in what she used to be like. My blood boiled, I shrieked like a soul in torment, and she gave me the whole collection the very same day that she made me a present of the bag with her monogram. . . ."

"Who's this fellow with her . . . here . . . in this one underneath?"

"What were you saying? What's that? Wait till I take off my hat."

"I'm asking you who this is—this fellow—here. Get a move on, can't you?"

"Heavens, don't bustle me about so. . . . That? It's Bacciocchi, come! Naturally, you can hardly be expected to recognise him, he dates from two turns before you."

"Two what?"

"After Bacciocchi, she had Septfons—and yet no—wait . . . Septfons was earlier than that. . . . Septfons, Bacciocchi, Spéleïeff, and you. Oh! do look at those check trousers! . . . How ridiculous men's fashions used to be!"

"And that photo over there; when was that taken?"

He drew back a step, for at his elbow the Pal's head was craning forward, and its magpie's nest of felted hair smelt like a wig.

"That? That's her costume for Auteuil in . . . in 1888, or '89. Yes, the year of the Exhibition. In front of that one, dear boy, you should raise your hat. They don't turn out beauties like that any more!"

"Pooh! . . . I don't think it so stunning."

The Pal folded her hands. Hatless, she looked older, and her high forehead was a buttery yellow under hair dyed greenish black.

"Not so stunning! That waist you could encircle with your ten fingers! That lily neck! And be good enough to let your eyes rest on that dress! All in frilled sky-blue chiffon, dear boy, and looped up with little pink moss-roses sewn on to the frills, and the hat to match! And the little bag to match as well—we called them alms-bags at that time. Oh! the beauty she was then! There's been

nothing since to compare with her first appearances: she
was the dawn, the very sun of love."

"First appearances where?"

She gave Chéri a gentle dig in the ribs. "Get along with
you. . . . How you make me laugh! Ah! the trials of life
must melt into thin air when you're about the house!"

His rigid features passed unobserved. He was still
facing the wall, seemingly riveted by several Léas—one
smelling an artificial rose, another bending over a book
with medieval hasps, her swan neck rising from a pleat-
less collar, a white and rounded neck like the bole of a
birch-tree.

"Well, I must be going," he said, like Valérie
Cheniaguine.

"What d'you mean—you must be going? What about
my dining-room? And my bedroom? just glance at
them, my pretty! Take a note of them for your little
love-nest."

"Ah! yes. . . . Listen; not to-day, because . . ." He
glanced distrustfully towards the rampart of portraits,
and lowered his voice. "I've an appointment. But I'll
come back . . . to-morrow. Probably to-morrow, before
dinner."

"Good. Then I can go ahead?"

"Go ahead?"

"With the flat."

"Yes, that's right. See about it. And thanks."

'I really begin to wonder what the world's coming to.
. . . Young or old—it's hard to tell which are the most
disgusting. . . . Two "turns" before me! . . . and "the first
appearances", said the old spider, "the dazzling first

appearances". . . . And all quite openly. No, really, what a world!'

He found that he had been keeping up the pace of a professional walker in training, and that he was out of breath. And all the more because the distant storm— which would not burst over Paris—had walled off what breeze there was behind a violet bastion, now towering straight up against the sky. Alongside the fortifications of the Boulevard Berthier, under trees stripped bare by the summer drought, a sparse crowd of Parisians in rope-soled sandals and a few half-naked children in red jerseys seemed to be waiting for a tidal wave to come rolling up from Levallois-Perret. Chéri sat down on a bench, forgetting that his strength was apt to play him tricks. He was unaware that his strength was being sapped in some mysterious manner ever since he had started to fritter it away on night vigils, and had neglected to exercise or nourish his body.

' "Two turns!" Really! Two turns before me! And after me, how many? Add the whole lot together, myself included, and how many turns d'you get?'

Beside a blue-clad, seagull-hatted Léa, he could see a tall, broad Spéleïeff, smiling expansively. He remembered a sad Léa, red-eyed with weeping, stroking his head when he was a small boy and calling him a "horrid little man in the making".

"Léa's lover" . . . "Léa's new pet" . . . Traditional and meaningless words—as common on everyone's lips as talk about the weather, the latest odds at Auteuil, or the dishonesty of servants. "Are you coming, kid?" Spéleïeff would say to Chéri. "We'll go out and have a porto at Armenonville, while we wait for Léa to join us. Nothing would drag her out of bed this morning."

"She's got a ravishing new little Bacciocchi," Madame

Peloux had informed her son, aged fourteen or fifteen at the time.

But, a bundle of sophistication and innocence, brought up in the midst of love, yet blinded by its proximity, Chéri, at that tender age, had talked love, as children learn a language by ear, picking up words, pleasant or filthy, merely as sounds without meaning. No vivid or voluptuous vision arose behind the shadow of this huge Spéleïeff so recently risen from Léa's bed. And was there really very much difference between this "ravishing little Bacciocchi" and a "prize Pekingese"?

No photograph or letter, no story from the only lips that might have told him the truth, had blighted the enclosed Paradise in which Léa and Chéri had dwelt for so many years. Next to nothing in Chéri existed which dated back beyond Léa: why, then, should he bother about a man who, before his day, had brought warmth or sadness or riches to his mistress?

A fair-haired little boy with fat knees came and planted his crossed arms on the bench beside Chéri. They glared at each other with identical expressions of offended reserve, for Chéri treated all children as strangers. For some time this boy let his pale blue eyes rest on Chéri, who watched some sort of indescribable smile, full of scorn, mount up from the small anæmic mouth to the flax-blue pupils of the eyes. Then the child turned away, and, picking up his dirty toys from the dust, began to play at the foot of the bench, blotting Chéri out of existence. Then Chéri got up and walked away.

Half an hour later, he was lying in a warm, scented bath, clouded by some milky bath essence. He lay revelling in its luxury and comfort, in the soft lather of the soap, and in the remote faint sounds about the house, as though they were the rewards of an act of great courage, or else blessings he was tasting for the last time.

His wife came into the room humming, broke off at the sight of him, and narrowly failed to disguise her speechless astonishment at finding Chéri at home and in his bath.

"Am I in your way?" he asked, with no irony.

"Not in the least, Fred."

She began to take off her day clothes with youthful abandon, with total disregard for modesty or immodesty, and Chéri was amused by her haste to be undressed and in a bath.

'How completely I'd forgotten her,' he thought, as he looked at the odalisque back, supple but well-covered, of the woman bending down to untie her shoelaces.

She did not speak to him, but went about her business like a woman who believes she is safely by herself, and in front of his eyes rose the figure of the child who, not long since, had been playing in the dust at his feet, resolutely ignoring his presence.

"Tell me . . ."

Edmée raised a surprised forehead, a soft half-naked body.

"What would you say to our having a child?"

"Fred! . . . What are you thinking of?"

It was almost a cry of terror, and already Edmée was clutching a wisp of lawn close to her bosom with one hand, while with the other she groped, fumbling, for the first kimono within reach. Chéri could not hold back his laughter.

"Would you like my revolver? I'm not going to assault you."

"Why are you laughing?" she asked, almost in a whisper. "You should never laugh."

"I seldom laugh. But do tell me . . . now that all is

SIX NOVELS

quiet and peaceful between us . . . do tell me why. Are
you really so terrified at the thought that we could have
had, could still have, a child?"

"Yes," she said cruelly, and her unexpected frankness
shocked even herself.

She never took her eyes off her husband, lying full
length in a low armchair, and she murmured distinctly
enough for him to hear, "A child . . . who'd be sure to
take after you. You twice over, you twice over in the
single lifetime of one woman? No. . . . Oh, no."

He began a gesture which she misinterpreted.

"No, I beg of you. . . . There's nothing more to be
said. I won't even discuss it. Let's leave things as they
are. We've only to be a little cautious, and go on . . . I
ask nothing of you . . ."

"That suits you?"

Her only answer was to put on a look, insulting in
its misery and plaintive helplessness, a seraglio look
that well suited her nakedness. Her freshly powdered
cheeks, the touch of colour on her youthful lips, the
light brown halo round her hazel eyes, the care bestowed
on every feature of her face, were in striking contrast
to the confusion of her body, bare except for the
crumpled silk shift she was clasping to her breasts.

'I can no longer make her happy,' thought Chéri,
'but I can still make her suffer. She is not altogether
unfaithful to me. Whereas I am not untrue to her . . . I
have deserted her.'

Turning away from him, she began to dress. She had
regained her freedom of movement and her disingenuous
tolerance. The palest of pink frocks now hid from
view the woman who, a moment since, had pressed her
last stitch of clothing to her bosom, as though to a wound.

She had recovered, too, her buoyant determination,

her desire to live and hold sway, her prodigious and feminine aptitude for happiness. Chéri despised her afresh; but a moment came when the rays of the evening sun, shining through her transparent pink dress, outlined the shape of a young woman who no longer bore any semblance to the wounded Circassian: a heaven-aspiring form, as supple and vigorous as a serpent about to strike.

'I can still hurt her, but how quickly she recovers! In this house, too, I am no longer needed, no longer expected. She has gone far beyond me, and is going further: I am, the old creature would say, her "first turn". It's now for me to follow her example, if only I could. But I can't. And then would I, if I could? Unlike some of us, Edmée has never come up against what one meets only once in a lifetime and is floored by completely. Spéleïeff was fond of saying that, after a really bad crash —which, however, involved no broken bones—some horses would let themselves be killed rather than take the fence again. I am just the same.'

He cast about for further sporting, and rather brutal, metaphors that would make his own fall and misfortunes seem an accident. But he had started his night too early, and, dog-tired, his dreams were haunted by sweet ghosts in sky-blue flounces, and half-remembered figures from the pages of the imperishable literature which finds its way into tawdry love-nests, from tales and poems dedicated to constancy and to lovers undivided in death: writings irresistible to adolescents and time-worn courtesans, who are akin in their credulity and passion for romance.

"THEN she said to me: 'I know who's at the back of all this: it's Charlotte again, making mischief about me. . . .' 'It's no more than you deserve,' I told her, 'you've only to stop going to see Charlotte as much as you do, and trusting her with all your secrets.' She retorted: 'I'm a much closer friend of Charlotte's than of Spéleïeff's and I've known her far longer. I assure you Charlotte, Neuilly, bezique and the child would be a far greater loss to me than Spéleïeff—you can't change the habits of a lifetime.' 'That doesn't prevent your faith in Charlotte costing you a pretty penny,' I said. 'Oh! well,' was her answer, 'what's good is worth paying for.' That's her all over, you'll agree: big-hearted and generous but no fool. And with that she went off to dress for the Races—she told me she was going to the Races with a gigolo. . . ."

"With me!" Chéri exclaimed bitterly. "Am I right? It was me?"

"I don't deny it. I simply tell you things as they took place. A white dress—of white crêpe-de-chine—Oriental-looking, edged with blue Chinese embroidery, the very dress you see her in here, in this snapshot, taken at the Races. And nothing will get it out of my head that this man's shoulder you can see behind her is you."

"Fetch it me!" Chéri ordered.

The old woman got up, pulled out the rusty drawing-pins tacking the photograph to the wall, and brought it back to Chéri. Lolling on the Algerian divan, he raised a tousled head, and, barely running his eyes over it, flung the snapshop across the room.

"When have you seen me wearing a collar that gapes at the back, and a short coat to go to the Races? Come, think again! I don't find that sort of thing at all funny."

She ventured a tut-tut of timid censure, bent her stiff knees to pick up the photograph, and went on to open the door into the passage.

"Where are you going?"

"I can hear the water for my coffee boiling. I'm going to pour it out."

"Good. But come back here again."

She disappeared in a shuffle of rustling taffeta and heelless slippers. Left to himself, Chéri settled his neck against the moquette cushion stamped with Tunisian designs. A new and startlingly bright Japanese kimono, embellished with pink wistaria on a ground of amethyst, had replaced his coat and waistcoat. The fag-end of a too-far-smoked cigarette was almost burning his lips, and his hair, falling fanwise down to the level of his eyebrows, half covered his forehead.

Wearing so feminine and flowered a garment did not make his appearance in any way ambiguous: he merely acquired an ignominious majesty that stamped every feature with its proper value. He seemed bent on death and destruction, and the photograph had flashed like a blade from his hand as he hurled it from him. Hard, delicate bones in his cheeks moved to the rhythm of his working jaws. The whites of his eyes flickered in the darkness round him like the crest of a wave, with the moonbeams interruptedly following its course.

Left alone, however, he let his head sink back against the cushion, and closed his eyes.

"Lord!" exclaimed the Pal coming back into the room, "you'll not look more handsome when laid out on your deathbed! I've brought in the coffee. Would you care for some? Such an aroma! It will waft you to the Isles of the Blest."

"Yes. Two lumps."

His words were curt, and she obeyed with a humility that suggested, perhaps, a deep subservient pleasure.

"You didn't eat anything for dinner?"

"I had enough."

He drank his coffee, without moving, supporting himself on one elbow. An Oriental curtain, draped like a canopy, hung from the ceiling directly above the divan, and in its shade lay an ivory and enamel Chéri, robed in exquisite silks, reclining upon an old worn dust-bedraggled rug.

The Pal set out, piece by piece upon a brass-topped table, the coffee-set, an opium lamp capped with a glass cowl, two pipes, the pot of paste, the silver snuff-box used for cocaine, and a flask, which, tight-stoppered as it was, failed to control the cold and treacherously volatile expansion of the ether. To these she added a pack of tarot cards, a case of poker chips, and a pair of spectacles, before settling herself down with the apologetic air of a trained hospital nurse.

"I've already told you," grunted Chéri, "all that paraphernalia means nothing to me."

Once again she stretched out her sickly white hands in protestation. In her own home she adopted what she called her "Charlotte Corday style": hair flowing loose, and wide white linen fichus crossed over her dusty

mourning, looking a mixture of decorum and fallen
virtue—like a heroine of the Salpêtrière Prison.

"No matter, Chéri. They're just in case. And it does
make me so happy to see the whole of my little armoury
set out in its proper order under my eyes. The arsenal
of dreams! the munitions of ecstasy! the gateway to
illusion!"

She nodded her long head and looked up to the
ceiling, with the compassionate eyes of a grandmother
who ruins herself on toys. Her guest partook of none of
her potions. Some sort of physical sense of honour still
survived in him, and his disdain for drugs was akin to
his distaste for brothels.

For a number of days—he had kept no count of them
—he had found his way to this black hole, presided over
by an attendant Norn. Ungraciously, and in terms that
brooked no argument, he had paid her for food, coffee
and her own liqueurs, and for his personal requirements
in the way of cigarettes, fruit, ice and soft drinks. He
had commanded his slave to buy the sumptuous Japanese
robe, scents and expensive soaps. She was moved less
by desire for money than by the pleasure of acting as
an accomplice. She devoted herself to Chéri with enthusiasm, a revival of her old zeal as a missionary of vice
who, with garrulous and culpable alacrity, would divest
and bathe a virgin, cook an opium pellet, and pour
out intoxicating spirits or ether. This apostolate was
fruitless, for her singular guest brought back no para-
mour, drank soft drinks only, stretched himself on the
dusty divan and delivered only one word of command:
"Talk."

She did talk, following, she believed, her own fancies;
but, now brutally, now subtly, he would direct the
muddied meanderings of her reminiscences. She talked

like a sewing-woman who comes in by the day, with the continuous, stupefying monotony of creatures whose days are given over to long and sedentary tasks. But she never did any sewing, for she had the aristocratic un-practicalness of a former prostitute. While talking, she would pin a pleat over a hole or stain, and take up again the business of tarot cards and patience. She would put on gloves to grind coffee bought by the charwoman, and then handle greasy cards without turning a hair.

She talked, and Chéri listened to her soporific voice and the shuffle of her felted slippers. He reclined at ease, magnificently robed, in the ill-kempt lodging. His guardian dared ask no questions. She knew enough: he was a monomaniac, as his abstemiousness proved. The illness for which she was ministering was mysterious; but it was an illness. She took the risk of inviting, as from a sense of duty, a very pretty young woman, childish and professionally gay. Chéri paid her neither more nor less attention than he would a puppy, and said to the Pal, "Are we going to have any more of your fashionable parties?"

She did not require snubbing a second time, and he never had cause to bind her to secrecy. One day she almost hit upon the simple truth, when she proposed asking in two or three of her friends of the good old days; Léa, for instance. He never batted an eyelid.

"Not a soul. Or I'll have to hunt out some better hole."

A fortnight went by, as funereal in its routine as life in a monastery; but it did not pall on either recluse. During the daytime, the Pal set forth on her old woman's junketings; poker parties, nips of whisky, and poisonous gossip, hole-and-corner gambling-dens, lunches of "regional dishes" in the stuffy darkness of a Norman or

Limousin restaurant. Chéri would arrive with the first
shadow of evening, sometimes drenched to the skin.
She would recognise the slam of his taxi-door and no
longer asked: "But why do you never come in your
motor?"

He would leave after midnight, and usually before
daybreak. During his prolonged sessions on the Algerian
divan, the Pal sometimes saw him drop off to sleep and
remain for an instant or two with his neck twisted against
his shoulder, as though caught in a snare. She never
slept herself till after his departure, having forgotten the
need for repose. Only once, in the small hours of the
morning, while he was putting back, meticulously and
one by one, the contents of his pockets—key on its
chain, note-case, little flat revolver, handkerchief,
cigarette-case of green gold—did she dare to ask:
"Doesn't your wife begin to wonder, when you come
in so late?"

Chéri raised long eyebrows above eyes grown larger
from lack of sleep: "No. Why? She knows perfectly well
I've been up to no harm."

"No child, of course, is easier to manage than you are.
. . . Shall you be coming again this evening?"

"I don't know. I'll see. Carry on as if I were coming
for certain."

Once more he gazed long at all the lily necks, all
the blue eyes, that flowered on one wall of his sanctuary,
before he went his way, only to return again, faithfully,
some twelve hours later.

By roundabout ways he considered cunning, he would
lead the Pal to talk of Léa, then he would clear the
narrative of all bawdy asides that might retard it. "Skip

it. Skip it!" Barely bothering to enunciate the words, he relied on the initial sibilants to speed up or curtail the monologue. He would listen only to stories without malice in them, and glorifications of a purely descriptive nature. He insisted upon strict respect for documentary truth and checked his chronicler peevishly. He stocked his mind with dates, colours, materials, and places, and the names of dressmakers.

"What's poplin?" he fired at her pointblank.

"Poplin's a mixture of silk and wool, a dry material . . . if you know what I mean; one that doesn't stick to the skin."

"Yes. And mohair? You said 'of white mohair.' "

"Mohair is a kind of alpaca, but it hangs better, of course. Léa was afraid to wear lawn in the summer: she maintained that it was best for underwear and handkerchiefs. Her own lingerie was fit for a queen, you'll remember, and in the days when that photograph was taken—yes, that beauty over there with the long legs— they didn't wear the plain underclothes of to-day. It was frill upon frill, a foam, a flurry of snow; and the drawers, dear boy! they'd have sent your head whirling. . . . White Chantilly lace at the sides and black Chantilly in between. Can't you just see the effect? But *can* you imagine it?"

'Revolting,' thought Chéri, 'revolting. Black Chantilly in between. A woman doesn't wear black Chantilly in between simply to please herself. In front of whose eyes did she wear them? For whom?'

He could see Léa's gesture as he entered her bathroom or boudoir—the furtive gesture as she drew her wrap across her body. He could see the chaste self-confidence of her rosy body as she lay naked in the bath, with the water turned to milk by some essence or other. . . . 'But, for others, she wore drawers of Chantilly lace. . . .'

He kicked one of the hay-stuffed moquette cushions to the floor.

"Are you too warm, Chéri?"

"No. Let me have another look at that photo . . . the large framed one. Tilt the what's-its-name of your lamp up a bit . . . a bit more . . . that's it!"

Abandoning his usual circumspection, he applied a searching eye to the study of every detail that was new to him, and almost refreshing. 'A high-waisted belt with cameos! . . . Never saw that about the place. And boots like buskins! Was she wearing tights? No, of course not, her toes are bare. Revolting. . . .'

"At whose house did she wear that costume?"

"I don't rightly remember. . . . A reception at the club, I believe . . . or at Molier's."

He handed back the frame at arm's length, to all appearances disdainful and bored. He left shortly afterwards, under an overcast sky, towards the close of a night that smelt of wood smoke and dankness.

He was deteriorating physically and took no account of it. He was losing weight through eating and sleeping too little, walking and smoking too much, thus bartering his obvious vigour for a lightness, an apparent return to youth, which the light of day repudiated. At home, he lived as he pleased, welcoming or running away from guests and callers. All that they knew of him was his name, his almost petrified good looks fined down little by little under an accusing chisel, and the inconceivable ease with which he would ignore them.

So he eked out his peaceful and carefully regimented despair until the last days of October. Then, one afternoon, he was seized by a fit of hilarity, because he caught a glimpse of his wife's unsuspected terror. His whole face lit up with the merriment of a man impervious to all feeling. 'She thinks I'm mad. What luck!'

His merriment was short-lived: for, on thinking it over, he came to the conclusion that, where the brute and the madman are concerned, the brute wins every time. She was frightened of the madman; otherwise would she not have stood her ground, biting her lips and forcing back her tears, in order to worst the brute?

'I am no longer even considered wicked,' he thought bitterly. 'And that's because I am no longer wicked. Oh! the harm the woman I left has done to me! Yet others left her, and she left others. . . . How, I wonder, does Bacciocchi exist at the present time? or Septfons, Spéleïeff, and all the rest of them? But what have we got in common, I and the rest of them? She called me "little bourgeois" because I counted the bottles in the cellar. "Little bourgeois", "faithful heart", "great lover"— those were her names for me—those were my real names: and, though she watched my departure with tears glistening in her eyes, she is still herself, Léa, who prefers old age to me, who sits in the corner by the fire counting over on her fingers: "I've had What's-his-name, and Thingummy-bob, and Chéri, and So-and-so . . ." I thought she belonged to me alone, and never perceived that I was only one among her lovers. Is there anyone left, now, that I am not ashamed of?'

Hardened by now to the exercise of impassivity, he sought to endure the capricious hauntings of such thoughts with resignation, and to be worthy of the devil by which he was possessed. Proud and dry-eyed, with a lighted match held between steady fingers, he looked sideways at his mother, well aware of her watchful eye. Once his cigarette was alight, with a little encouragement he would have strutted like a peacock in front of an invisible public, and taunted his tormentors with a "Good, isn't it?" In a confused way, the strength born of his dissimulation and resistance was gathering in his inmost self. He was beginning now to enjoy his extreme state of detachment, and dimly perceived that an emotional storm could be just as valuable and refreshing as a lull, and that in it he might discover the wisdom which never came to him in calmer moods. As a child, Chéri frequently had taken advantage of a genuine fit of temper, by changing it into a peevishness that would bring him what he wanted. To-day he was fast approaching the point at which, having attained to a definite state of unhappiness, he could rely on it to settle everything.

One gusty, wind-swept, September afternoon, with leaves sailing straight across the sky—an afternoon of blue rifts in the clouds and scattered raindrops—Chéri felt an urge to visit his dark retreat and its attendant, garbed in black, with a touch of white on the chest like a scavenging cat. He was feeling buoyant, and avid for confidences, though these would be sickly, like the fruit of the arbutus and as prickly leaved. Words and phrases of special though ill-defined significance kept running in his head: "Her monogram embroidered in hair on all her lingerie, dear boy, in golden hairs from her own head . . . faery handicraft! And, did I tell you, her masseuse used to pluck the hairs from the calves of her leg, one by one. . . ."

He turned round and left the window. He found Charlotte on a chair looking thoughtfully up at him; and in the restless waters of her great eyes he saw the formation of a prodigious, rounded, crystalline, glistening sphere which detached itself from the bronzed pupil, and then vanished, evaporating in the heat of her flushed

cheek. Chéri felt flattered and cheered. 'How kind of her!
She's weeping for me.'

An hour later, he found his ancient accomplice at her
post. But she was wearing some sort of parson's hat,
bunched up with shiny black ribbon, and she held out
to him a sheet of blue paper, which he waved aside.

"What's that? . . . I haven't the time. Tell me what's
written on it."

The Pal lifted puzzled eyes to his: "It's my mother."

"Your mother? You're joking."

She did her best to appear offended. "I'm not joking at
all. Please respect the departed! She is dead." And she
added, by way of an excuse, "She was eighty-three!"

"Congratulations. Are you going out?"

"No; I'm going away."

"Where to?"

"To Tarascon, and from there I take a little branch line
train that puts me down at . . ."

"For how long?"

"Four or five days . . . at least. There's the solicitor to
be seen about the will, because my younger sister . . ."

He burst out, hands to heaven: "A sister now! Why
not four children into the bargain?" He was conscious
of the unexpectedly high-pitched tone of his voice and
controlled it. "Good, very well. What d'you expect me
to do about it? Be off, be off. . . ."

"I was going to leave word for you. I'm catching the
7.30."

"Catch the 7.30."

"The time of the funeral service is not mentioned in
the telegram: my sister speaks only of the laying out,
the climate down there is very hot, they'll have to get
through it very quickly, only the business side can keep
me there, and over that one has no control."

"Of course, of course."

He was walking to and fro, from the door to the wall with the photographs and back to the door again, and in doing so he knocked against a squashed old travelling-bag. The coffee-pot and cups were steaming on the table.

"I made you your coffee, come what might. . . ."

"Thanks."

They drank standing up, as at a station, and the chill of departure gripped Chéri by the throat and made his teeth chatter secretly.

"Goodbye, then, dear boy," said the Pal. "You may be sure that I'll hurry things as much as I can."

"Goodbye—pleasant journey."

They shook hands, and she did not dare to kiss him. "Won't you stay here for a little while?"

He looked all round in great agitation. "No. No."

"Take the key, then?"

"Why should I?"

"You're at home here. You've fallen into the habit of it. I've told Maria to come every day at five and light a good fire and get the coffee ready. . . . So take my key, won't you? . . ."

With a limp hand he took the key, and it struck him as enormous. Once outside, he longed to throw it away or take it back to the concierge.

The old woman took courage on her way between her own door and the street, loading him with instructions as she might a child of twelve.

"The electric-light switch is on your left as you go in. The kettle is always on the gas-stove in the kitchen, and all you have to do is to put a match to it. And your Japanese robe—Maria has her instructions to leave it folded at the head of the divan and the cigarettes in their usual place."

Chéri nodded affirmation once or twice, with the look of courageous unconcern of a schoolboy on the last morning of the holidays. And, when he was alone, it did not occur to him to make fun of his old retainer with the dyed hair, who had placed the proper value both on the last prerogatives of the dead and on the little pleasures of one whom all had now deserted.

The following morning, he awoke from an indecipherable dream, in which a crush of people were all running in the same direction. Though he saw only their backs, each was known to him. As they hurried by, he identified his mother, Léa—unaccountably naked, and out of breath—Desmond, the Pal, and young Maudru . . . Edmée was the only one to turn and smile at him, with the grating little smile of a marten. "But it's the marten Ragut caught in the Vosges!" Chéri cried out in his dream, and this discovery pleased him immeasurably. Then he checked and recounted all the one-way runners, saying over to himself: 'There's one missing. . . . There's one missing. . . .' Once out of his dream, on this side of awakening, it came to him that the one missing was none other than himself: 'I must get back into it. . . .' But the efforts of exerting every limb, like an insect caught on flypaper, served only to widen the bar of blue between his eyelids, and he emerged into that real world in which he was frittering away his time and his strength. He stretched out his legs, and bathed them in a fresh, cool part of the sheets. 'Edmée must have got up some time ago.'

He was surprised to see beneath the window a new garden of marguerites and heliotrope, for in his memory there was only a summer garden of blue and pink. He

rang, and the sound of the bell brought to life a maid
whose face was unfamiliar.

"Where is Henriette?"

"I've taken her place, sir."

"Since when?"

"Why—for the last month, sir."

He ejaculated an "Ah!", as much as to say, "That
explains everything."

"Where's your mistress?"

"Madame is just coming, sir. Madame is ready to go
out."

Edmée, indeed, did appear, as large as life, but stopped
just inside the door in so marked a manner that Chéri
was secretly amused. He allowed himself the pleasure of
upsetting his wife a little by exclaiming, "But it's Ragut's
marten!" and watching her pretty eyes waver under his
gaze.

"Fred, I . . ."

"Yes, you're going out. I never heard you get up."

She coloured slightly. "There's nothing extraordinary
in that. I've been sleeping so badly these last few nights,
that I've had a bed made up on the divan in the boudoir.
You're not doing anything special to-day, are you?"

"But I am," he replied darkly.

"Is it important?"

"Very important." He took his time, and finished on
a lighter note: "I'm going to have my hair cut."

"But will you be back for luncheon?"

"No; I'll have a cutlet in Paris. I've made an appointment at Gustave's for a quarter past two. The man who
usually comes to cut my hair is ill."

He was childishly courteous, the lie flowering effortlessly on his lips. Because he was lying, his mouth took
on its boyhood mould—poutingly provocative and

rounded for a kiss. Edmée looked at him with an almost masculine satisfaction.

"You're looking well this morning, Fred. . . . I must fly."

"Are you catching the 7.30?"

She stared at him, struck dumb, and fled so pre-cipitately that he was still laughing when the front door slammed behind her.

'Ah! that does me good,' he sighed. 'How easy it is to laugh when you no longer expect anything from any-one. . . .' Thus, while he was dressing, did he discover for himself the nature of asceticism, and the tuneless little song he hummed through pursed lips kept him company like a silly young nun.

He went down to a Paris he had forgotten. The crowd upset his dubious emotional balance, now so dependent on a crystalline vacuity and the daily routine of suffering.

In the Rue Royale he came face to face with his own full-length reflection at the moment when the brightness of noon broke through the rain-clouds. Chéri wasted no thoughts on this crude new self-portrait, which stood out sharply against a background of newsvendors and shopgirls, flanked by jade necklaces and silver fox furs. The fluid feeling in his stomach, which he compared to a speck of lead bobbing about inside a celluloid ball, must come, he thought, from lack of sustenance, and he took refuge in a restaurant.

With his back to a glass partition, screened from the light of day, he lunched off selected oysters, fish and fruit. Some young women sitting not far away had no eyes for him, and this gave him a pleasant feeling, like that of a chilly bunch of violets laid on closed eyelids. But the smell of his coffee suddenly brought home the need to rise and keep the appointment of which this smell was an urgent reminder. Before obeying the summons, he went to his hairdresser's, held out his hands to be manicured, and slipped off into a few moments' inestimable repose, while expert fingers substituted their will for his.

The enormous key obstructed his pocket. 'I won't go, I won't go! . . .' To the cadence of some such insistent, meaningless refrain, he found his way without mishap to the Avenue de Villiers. His clumsy fumbling round the lock and the rasp of the key made his heart beat momentarily faster, but the cheerful warmth in the passage calmed his nerves.

He went forward cautiously, lord of this empire of a few square feet, which he now owned but did not know. The useless daily arrangement of the armoury had been laid out on the table by the well-trained charwoman, and an earthenware coffee-pot stood in the midst of charcoal embers already dying under the velvet of warm ashes. Methodically, Chéri emptied his pockets and set out one by one his cigarette case, the huge key, his own small key, the flat revolver, his note-case, handkerchief, and watch; but when he had put on his Japanese robe, he did not lie down on the divan. With the silent curiosity of a cat he opened doors and peered into cupboards. His peculiar prudishness shrank back before a primitive but distinctively feminine lavatory. The bedroom, all bed and little else, also was decorated in the mournful shade of red that seems to settle in on those of declining years; it smelt of old bachelors and eau-de-Cologne. Chéri returned to the drawing-room. He switched on the two wall lamps and the beribboned chandelier. He listened to faint far away sounds and, now that he was alone for the first time in this poor lodging, began trying out on himself the influence of its previous

inmates—birds of passage or else dead. He thought he
heard and recognised a familiar footstep, a slipshod,
shambling old animal pad-pad, then shook his head: 'It
can't be hers. She won't be back for a week, and when
she does come back, what will there be left for me in this
world? I'll have . . .'

Inwardly he listened to the Pal's voice, the worn-out
voice of a tramp. "But wait till I finish the story of the
famous slanging-match between Léa and old Mortier
at the Races. Old Mortier thought that with the aid of
a little publicity in *Gil Blas* he would get all he wanted
out of Léa. Oh! la la, my pretties, what a donkey he made
of himself! She drove out to Longchamp—a dream of
blue—as statuesque as a goddess, in her victoria drawn
by a pair of piebalds. . . ."

He raised his hand towards the wall in front of him,
where so many blue eyes were smiling, where so many
swan-necks were preening themselves above imperturbable bosoms. '. . . I'll have all this. All this, and nothing
more. It's true, perhaps, that this is a good deal. I've
found her again, by a happy chance, found her here on
this wall. But I've found her, only to lose her again for
ever. I am still held up, like her, by these few rusty nails,
by these pins stuck in slantwise. How much longer can
this go on? Not very long. And then, knowing myself
as I do, I'm afraid I shall demand more than this. I may
suddenly cry out: "I want her! I must have her! Now!
at this very moment!" Then what will become of me?'

He pushed the divan closer to the illustrated wall and
there lay down. And as he lay there, all the Léas, with
their downward gazing eyes, seemed to be showing
concern for him: 'But they only *seem* to be looking down
at me, I know perfectly well. When you sent me away,
my Nounoune, what did you think there was left for me

after you? Your noble action cost you little—you knew the worth of a Chéri—your risk was negligible. But we've been well punished, you and I: you, because you were born so long before me, and I, because I loved you above all other women. You're finished now, you have found your consolation—and what a disgrace that is!—whereas I . . . As long as people say, "There was the War," I can say "There was Léa." 'Léa, the War . . . I never imagined I'd dream of either of them again, yet the two together have driven me outside the times I live in. Henceforth, there is nowhere in the world where I can occupy more than half a place. . . .'

He pulled the table nearer to consult his watch. 'Half-past five. The old creature won't be back here for another week. And this is the first day. Supposing she were to die on the way?'

He fidgeted on his divan, smoked, poured himself out a cup of luke-warm coffee. 'A week. All the same, I mustn't ask too much of myself. In a week's time . . . which story will she be telling me? I know them off by heart—the one about the Four-in-Hand Meet, the one about the slanging-match at Longchamp, the one about the final rupture—and when I've heard every one, every twist and turn of them, what will there be left? Nothing, absolutely nothing. In a week's time, this old woman—and I'm already so impatient for her, she might be going to give me an injection—this old woman will be here, and . . . and she'll bring me nothing at all.'

He lifted beseeching eyes to his favourite photograph. Already this speaking likeness filled him with less resentment, less ecstasy, less heartbreak. He turned from side to side on the hard mattress, unable to prevent his muscles from contracting, like a man who aches to jump from a height, but lacks the courage.

He worked himself up till he groaned aloud, repeating over and over again "Nounoune", to make himself believe he was frantic. But he fell silent, ashamed, for he knew very well that he did not need to be frantic to pick up the little flat revolver from the table. Without rising, he experimented in finding a convenient position. Finally he lay down with his right arm doubled up under him. Holding the weapon in his right hand, he pressed his ear against the muzzle, which was buried in the cushions. At once his arm began to grow numb, and he realised that if he did not make haste his tingling fingers would refuse to obey him. So he made haste, whimpering muffled complaints as he completed his task, because his forearm was hurting, crushed under the weight of his body. He knew nothing more, beyond the pressure of his forefinger on a little lever of tempered steel.

THE RIPENING SEED

Translated by
Roger Senhouse

ONE

"ARE you going fishing, Vinca?"

With a haughty toss of her head, Vinca, the Periwinkle, with eyes the colour of April showers, replied that indeed she was going fishing. Her much-mended pullover and her sand-shoes hardened by brine showed that she was. Surely it was obvious that her blue-and-green-checked skirt, three years old and now well above her knees, belonged to shrimps and crabs. And did the two shrimping-nets across her shoulder, and her woollen beret, blue and thistly as the sea-holly on the dunes, denote any other rig than that for fishing?

She passed her questioner, and went on down towards the rocks with long strides of her well-shaped, slender legs, the colour of terra-cotta. Philippe watched her walking, comparing this year's Vinca with the Vinca of last year's holidays. Had she stopped growing yet? It was high time that she did! She had hardly filled out at all since a year ago. She had been letting her hair grow for the last four months yet, short and stiff, like a shock of burnished straw, it could neither be put up nor plaited. Her hands and cheeks were tanned almost black, but her neck under the hair was milk-white; her smile was reserved, her laugh spontaneous, and, though she was careful to fasten her blouses and jumpers over a non-existent bosom, she tucked up her skirt and knickers as high as she could when paddling with the unconcern of a small boy.

The companion who was watching her so intently lay stretched on a dune tufted with long wiry grass, his cleft chin resting on his crossed arms. Since Vinca had just turned fifteen and a half, he was sixteen and a half. All through their childhood they had been united: now adolescence was driving them apart. Already, the previous year, they were exchanging cutting remarks and sly punches: now, at any moment, silence would fall between them so heavily that they preferred a fit of the sulks to the effort of conversation. But Philippe, born hunter and gay deceiver, and cunning, cloaked his uncommunicativeness in mystery, and made a weapon of everything that embarrassed him. He would experiment with a few deprecatory gestures, throw out a "What's the use? You wouldn't understand . . ." while Vinca could only remain silent, tongue-tied, the victim of her desire to question and be answered, and fight against a precocious, overpowering instinct to give all; fight, too, against the fear that Philippe who was changing daily, and hourly gaining in strength, might sever the tenuous moorings that drew him back each year, from July to October, to the bushy copse that overhung the shore and the seaweed-bearded rocks. Already he had a disconcerting way of staring at Vinca without seeing her, as if she were transparent—fluid—negligible. . . .

Next year, perhaps, she will fall at his feet and use the speech of a grown-up woman: "Phil, don't be unkind to me. . . . I love you, Phil. Do what you like with me. . . . Say something to me, Phil!" But for the present she still preserves the wayward dignity of a child and offers resistance—a resistance that Phil resents.

His eyes followed the boyish, graceful figure on its way down the slope to the sea. He had no more wish to kiss than to beat her, but he wanted her to trust in him and promise to be his alone, to do what he liked with as he could with the treasures he was ashamed of: pressed flowers, agate marbles, seeds and shells, picture-books, and a small silver watch.

"Wait for me, Vinca! I'm going fishing with you!"

She slowed down without turning round. He caught up with her in a few bounds and seized hold of one of the shrimping-nets. "Why did you bring two?"

"I brought the small dip-net for the narrow holes, and my own because I always do."

His gentler dark eyes gazed penetratingly into the blue of hers. "So it wasn't for me then?"

At the same time he held out a hand to help her across an awkward fissure in the rocks, and Vinca blushed beneath her tan. An unexpected look or gesture was sufficient to confuse her. Yesterday they had explored the cliff-face and climbed down the clefts side by side—each taking risks unassisted by the other. . . . Lithe and active as Phil, she could not remember having asked for his help.

"Steady on now, Vinca!" he protested with a smile as she snatched back her hand too sharply. "What have I done to upset you now?"

She bit a lip cracked by the daily plunge and continued to pick her way over rocks that bristled with barnacles. The more she thought, the less certain of herself did she feel. What was he up to, in any case? Here he was, being charming and gallant, offering her his hand as he might to a lady. . . . Slowly she lowered the dip-net into a cavity where under the placid sea water she could clearly make out the various seaweeds, sea-cucumbers, blennies, wrasse, the father-lashers all head and fin, black-shell crabs etched with red, and shrimps. . . . Phil's shadow fell across the sunlit pool.

"Do get out of my light! You've gone and cast your shadow right over the shrimps and, what's more, this is my own special hole."

He moved away, and she fished by herself, impatiently, with less than her accustomed skill. Ten, twenty shrimps eluded the too precipitate dab with her net and darted away to ensconce themselves in crannies, where they tested the water with their delicate whiskers and defied capture.

"Phil! Do come here, Phil! This place is alive with shrimps, and they simply won't let themselves be caught."

He came back without much enthusiasm and leaned over the teeming little abyss.

"Of course they won't. You see, you don't know how. . . ."

"I know perfectly well how," Vinca interrupted shrilly. "I just haven't the patience, that's all."

Phil sank the shrimping-net down to the bottom and kept it there motionless.

"In the crevice of that rock," Vinca whispered over his shoulder, "beauties, such beauties. Don't you see their little horns?"

"No. That doesn't matter. They'll soon come along out."

"Do you really think so?"

She leaned further over and her hair, like the clipped wing of a captive bird, fluttered against her companion's cheek. She drew back, then involuntarily she came forward again, only to draw back once more. He seemed not to notice, but with his free hand he caught hold of her bare arm, tanned by sun and brine. "Look, Vinca! Here comes the belle of the ball!"

Vinca stealthily withdrew her arm and it slipped as far as the wrist through Phil's hand as through a bracelet, for he did not tighten his grip. "You'll never catch her, Phil. She's darted off again."

So as to watch the shrimp's antics better, Vinca let her arm slide back right up to the elbow through his half-closed hand again. In the green water the long agate-grey shrimp was frisking on the ring of the net, testing it now with its legs, now with its feelers. One turn of the wrist and . . . But the fisherman delayed, perhaps enjoying the stillness of the unresisting arm under his hand and the weight of a head veiled in hair against his shoulder, a head that leaned submissive for a moment and then was jerked shyly away. . . .

"Quick, Phil, quick, pull up the net! . . . Oh, she's got away! Why did you let her go?"

Phil drew in his breath, and gave his young friend a look in which pride, tinged with astonishment, seemed to make light of his triumph. He let go the arm that seemed in no hurry to be freed, saying, as he stirred up the whole limpid pool with great sweeps of the shrimping-net, "Oh, she'll come back. . . . It's just a question of waiting. . . ."

TWO

THEY were swimming side by side, his head round and black under his wet hair and his skin the whiter, hers the light gold that fair skins turn, a blue foulard round her head. The daily bathe, joy silent and complete, restored them to the peace and childhood they were in danger of losing at their difficult age. Vinca floated on her back, blowing water in the air like a young seal. Beneath the twisted foulard peeped two delicate pink ears, hidden by her hair during the day, and, on either temple, two clearings of white skin that saw the light only at bathing time. She smiled at Philippe, and under the eleven o'clock sun the delicious blue of her eyes took on a greenish reflection from the sea. All of a sudden he dived down, seized hold of one of her feet, and dragged her under the water. They "drank a draught" together, and came to the surface again spitting, spluttering and laughing, as though forgetful of their age, she of her fifteen years of tortuous love for her childhood companion, he of his sixteen years of domination, his debonair disdain, and the unreasonableness of his precocious sense of proprietorship.

"Race you to the rocks!" he shouted, cleaving the water.

But Vinca did not follow his lead, landing instead on the nearby sand.

"Are you getting out already?"

She tore off her cap as if she were scalping herself and shook out her stiff fair hair. "There's a gentleman coming to lunch. Papa said I must dress for it." Still wet, she started to run, tall and tomboyish but gracefully made, the muscles in her long legs hardly apparent. She drew up sharp at a word from Phil.

"Are you going to doll yourself up then? What about me? Can't I eat in a loose shirt in that case?"

"Of course you can, Phil. Anything you like. Besides, you look so much nicer in an open collar."

The periwinkle eyes, set in a small dripping sunburnt mask, suddenly expressed anxiety, a whim-of-the-moment desire for approval. Phil relapsed into haughty silence, and Vinca went on her way up the links starred with mauve scabious.

Left alone Phil muttered to himself as he churned up the water. Vinca's preferences meant little to him. 'I always look good to her . . . but this year she's never satisfied with anything.'

The apparent contradiction in these two sallies brought a smile to his lips. He turned turtle, and following her example floated on his back, letting the salt water fill his ears with rumbling silence. . . . Was it a wisp of cloud between him and the sun at its zenith? Phil opened his eyes to catch a glimpse overhead of the dun breast feathers—the dark legs forced back in flight—and the long tapering beaks of a pair of curlew.

'Of all the crazy ideas!' Philippe said to himself, 'No, it can't be true! What's come over her? She looks like an organ-grinder's monkey. She looks like a mulatto girl decked out in her Sunday best.'

Next to Vinca, and closely resembling her, a younger sister sat staring in front of her; she had china-blue eyes in a round sunburnt face under a thatch of wiry fair hair, and was resting her small fists on either side of her plate, like a well brought up child. Big and little sister alike were dressed in starched and ironed frocks of white flounced organdie.

'Sunday in Tahiti!' scoffed Philippe inwardly, 'I've never seen her look such a fright.'

Vinca's mother, Vinca's father, Vinca's aunt, Phil and his relations, and the visitor from Paris, made a fringe round the table of green jumpers, striped blazers, tussore jackets. The villa, rented each year by the two families of friends, smelt this morning of hot brioches and bees-wax. The grey-haired Parisian stood out from among the sun-tanned children and multi-coloured bathers as a stranger, delicate, pale, and over-dressed.

"How quickly you change, little Vinca!" he said to the little miss.

'Don't I know it!' Philippe muttered peevishly.

The stranger leaned towards Vinca's mother, to whisper confidentially, "She's going to be enchanting, really ravishing. Mark my words, in another two years . . ."

Vinca overheard this remark, favoured him with a swift, utterly feminine glance, and smiled. Her wine-red lips parted on a flash of white teeth, her fair lashes fluttered over eyes as blue as her name-flower, and even Philippe himself was dazzled. 'What's this? What's she up to now?'

Vinca served the coffee in the linen-panelled hall. She executed this intricate manœuvre deftly, with the accomplished poise of an acrobat. When a sudden gust threatened to overturn the flimsy table, she prevented a chair from toppling with her foot and with her chin a lace napkin from flying away, while at the same time she never stopped pouring an impeccable flow of coffee into one or other of the cups.

"Just look at her!" The stranger was in ecstasies, as he expatiated on her "tanagra" figure, insisted that she sip a chartreuse, and asked her the names of all the young men whose hearts she had broken at the Cancale Casino.

"That's a good one, the Cancale Casino! There is no casino at Cancale."

She laughed, showing the full range of her sound teeth, and spun round on the toes of her white shoes like a ballet-dancer. With coquettishness came guile: never once did she look toward Philippe, who, a

sullen figure lurking behind the piano and the large
copper jug filled with sea-holly, was watching her
every move. 'I must be wrong about her,' he confessed
to himself. 'She's really very pretty. Well, that's something new!'

When, at the sound of the gramophone, the stranger
asked her to teach him the latest dance-steps, Philippe
slipped out of doors, ran towards the beach and rolled
himself into a ball in one of the sandy hollows, before letting his head rest on his arms and his arms on his
knees. Behind his closed eyelids persisted the vision of
this new Vinca, full of insolent allurement: a coquettish
Vinca, quite suddenly endowed with rounded flesh
and conscious of her charms; or a naughty, rebellious
Vinca, according to choice.

"Phil, dear Phil, I've been looking for you everywhere. What's the matter?"

The enchantress was close beside him, panting, and
tugging ingenuously at his forelock to make him look
up.

"Nothing's wrong," he answered in a husky voice.

He opened his eyes fearfully, to find her on her knees
in the sand, ruining the ten flounces of her organdie
dress and crawling before him like a squaw.

"Please, please, Phil, don't be cross! Have I done
something to annoy you? Phil, you know I love you
best in the world. Do say something to me, Phil!"

He searched everywhere for a trace of the momentary splendour that had provoked him. All he could see
was a dismayed Vinca, a girl not yet fully mature,

beset beyond her years by the awkwardness, the self-abasement, the forlorn persistence of someone really in love. He snatched away the hand she was kissing. "Leave me alone can't you! You don't understand . . . you never understand anything! And do get up off the ground!"

And he sought, as he smoothed the crumpled folds, tied the sash, patted into place the stiff hairs all on end in the wind, he sought to change her back into the little goddess who, for a moment, had flashed before his eyes.

THREE

"WE'VE just another month and a half of the holidays left, haven't we?"

"Only a month," Vinca said. "You know well enough I have to be in Paris by the twentieth of September."

"Why? Your father's always had leave till the first of October in other years."

"I know, but Mummy and I, and Lisette, haven't so very much time, between the twentieth of September and the fourth of October, for all our autumn business. My new party dress—and a coat. A hat for me—same for Lisette. . . . I mean to say, you know, we women . . ."

Phil was lying on his back, chucking fistfuls of sand in the air.

"Oh rot! You women, indeed! You make far too much fuss over all that."

"We have to. . . . You, of course, find all your clothes laid out for you on the bed. All you worry about are your shoes, because you will buy them at a shop where your father forbids you to go. Apart from that, it's all plain sailing. Things are made so easy for you men. . . ."

Philippe sat bolt upright, ready to respond to her irony. But Vinca was not in joking mood. She was sewing, whipping a pink scallop on to a light linen frock that matched the colour of her eyes. Her fair hair, cut Joan-of-Arc style, was gradually growing longer. Sometimes she parted it at the back, tying it in two short whisks against her cheeks. She had lost one of her ribbons since lunch, and over that half of her face the hair flapped like a drawn curtain.

Philip frowned. "Lord, what a mess your hair's in, Vinca!"

She blushed under her holiday tan and a humble appeal crept into her eyes as she pushed back the hair behind her ear.

"I know it is. . . . It's bound to look untidy while it's kept so short. It's only trimmed this way, while waiting . . ."

"And you don't mind looking ugly in the meantime?" he asked harshly.

"I mind very much, Phil, I promise you I do."

He was shamed into silence by her quiet acquiescence, and she looked up at him in astonishment, for she expected no mercy. He believed in a short-lived truce once he had hurt her feelings, and made ready for the next insult, the next childish sarcasm, for what he called the "whippet-snaps" of his young friend. But she was smiling, a wistful, melancholy smile, addressed to the smooth sea and to the sky, where the high wind was drawing fern-patterns among the clouds.

"Whatever you may think, I really do want to look pretty, I promise you. Mummy says there's still a chance I may, but that I must have patience."

At fifteen, she had the pride and gawkiness of her age, but those years had given her a body trained for running and walking, conditioned to all weathers, lean, firm, and hardened, at times not unlike a riding-switch that cuts and slashes; but the startling blue of her eyes and the clear simple line of her mouth were already the perfected traits of feminine beauty.

"Patience, indeed!" Phil leapt to his feet and with the toe of his shoe began scraping at the dry sand of the dune, pearly with little empty snail-shells. A hated word had just poisoned his siesta, the siesta of a school-boy enjoying his holidays. In the full vigour of his seventeenth year, he could adapt himself to idleness and relaxation, but the idea of passive evolution, of having to wait patiently for developments, exasperated him. He clenched his fists, expanded his bare chest, and hurled defiance at the heavens.

"Patience! Good God! that's the one word you all of you have on the tip of your tongue! You, and my father, and my 'beaks'."

Vinca dropped her sewing to stare in admiration at the harmonious figure of her companion, whose proportions lost nothing by his gangling age. Dark, white-skinned, and of medium height, he had been slow in growing and since fourteen had resembled a small well-knit man, each year on a slightly larger scale.

"What else can we do, Phil? We have no choice. You always think that by stretching out your arms and swearing to heaven you can bring about some change or other. You'll prove no smarter than the others. You'll sit for your matric, and if you're lucky you'll get through."

"Shut up! You talk like my mother."

"And you like a child! What d'you hope to gain, my poor boy, by being so impatient?"

Philippe's dark eyes glared hatred at her because she had called him "my poor boy".

"I hope for nothing," he said tragically. "I don't even hope that you'll understand me. There you sit, with your pink scallop, babbling about going home, about your party dresses, and all that petty routine. Why, when I think that soon I'll be sixteen and a half . . ."

The periwinkle eyes, sparkling with humiliated tears, contrived to smile. "Oh, yes! Just because you're sixteen you consider yourself master of the whole world! Is that what the films have done for you?"

To prove his mastery, Phil seized her by the shoulder and shook her.

"Didn't I tell you to shut up! Every time you open your mouth you let out something fatuous. . . . I'm ready to explode, I tell you, when I think I'm only sixteen! All the years ahead—years of exams, matric, professional training, years of messing about and

groping in the dark—having to begin all over again if
you fail, or be crammed with the stuff you couldn't
digest properly the first time and so were ploughed.
When you have to pretend to your people that you're
dead keen on a career, so as not to distress them, while
all the time you can see what desperate efforts they're
making to appear infallible, though they know even
less about you than you know yourself. Oh, how I
detest this moment in my life, Vinca! Why can't I,
all at once, be twenty-five!"

He radiated intolerance and a sort of traditional
despair. In his haste to grow up and his contempt for
the period when body and soul are like buds ready to
burst into flower, this scion of a small Parisian industrial house was transformed into a hero of romance.
He flung himself down at Vinca's feet and continued his lamentations. "So many more years, Vinca,
of being almost a man, almost free, almost in love."

She put her hand on the raven locks tousled by the
wind and now on a level with her knees, but she voiced
none of the thoughts roused in her by an instinctive
feminine wisdom. 'Only almost in love? Isn't it
possible, then, to be no more than almost in love?'

Phil rounded on her violently. "And what about
you? You who put up with all that sort of thing, what
do you propose doing?"

Under his dark glance her features again took on a
look of uncertainty.

"The same as you, Phil. Only I'm not going to try
to matriculate."

"Then what are you going to do? Are you going in for industrial designing, or what? Or is it to be chemistry?"

"Mummy says . . ."

He kicked out in anger like a colt, though without standing up on his feet.

"Mummy says, mummy says! What a slavish little beast you are! And what does Mummy say?"

"She says," Vinca repeated the words submissively, "that she suffers from rheumatism, that Lisette is only eight, that there's plenty of work for me to do at home without my looking further afield, that soon I shall have to begin looking after the household accounts, help with Lisette's education, keep an eye on the maids, and all that sort of thing."

"All that sort of thing! Less than nothing, in fact!"

"She says that I shall get married . . ." She blushed and removed her hand from Philippe's head, seeming to hope for a word from him which never came. "And finally, that until I do get married, there's plenty I can be getting on with."

He turned round again and scanned her contemptuously.

"And that's enough for you, is it? That's enough for you for . . . let's see . . . for five or six years, perhaps more?"

Her blue eyes wavered but held his. "Yes, Phil, while waiting. . . . Since we're only sixteen and fifteen, you and I. . . . Since we're forced to wait. . . ."

The shock of this detestable word shook his

defences. Once again he was reduced to silence by the simplicity of his young friend, by the submissiveness she dared to put into words, by her way of paying homage, as a female, to trusty household gods, and, though disappointed by this, he felt vaguely appeased. Would he have welcomed a high-spirited Vinca, scenting adventure and pawing the ground, like a bridled filly, at the prospect of the long hard road through adolescence!

He pillowed his head against the dress of his childhood playmate. He felt her slender knees quiver, then press closer together, and with the sudden enthusiasm of youth, Philippe conjured up the vision of their delicate contours. But he closed his eyes, confiding the weight of his head to her safe keeping, and stayed like that, while waiting. . . .

FOUR

PHILIPPE was the first to reach the road—two ruts in the dry shifting-sand, mobile as a wave, with a median ridge of sparse salt-bitten grass—down which the carts went to gather sea-wrack after the neap tides. He was resting against the two poles of the shrimping-nets and carried a couple of creels slung over his shoulder, having left Vinca to carry the two slender gaffs baited with raw fish, and his fishing blazer—a precious relic, with amputated sleeves. He treated himself to a well-earned rest and condescended to wait for his fanatical little friend, whom he had abandoned in the desert of rocks and pools and sea-weed left uncovered by the August high tide. He tried to pick her out far below before he let himself slide down the bed of the road. Beyond the sandy declivity, among the scintillating sparks set off by the sun's rays striking a hundred little mirrors of water, a blue woollen beret, faded to the tint of sea-holly, marked the spot where Vinca was still hunting determinedly for shrimps and edible crabs.

'Ah, well, if it amuses her!' he said under his breath. Then he let himself go, his bare back extracting a delicious thrill from contact with the fresh sand as he slid along the track. Close to his ear he could hear, issuing from the creels, the moist susurrus of a fistful of shrimps and the sharp scraping of a large crab's claw against the lid.

Phil sighed, overcome by a sense of vague unclouded happiness, in which his agreeable fatigue, the twitch of muscles still tensed after rock-climbing, and the warmth and colour of a Breton afternoon suffused with vaporised saline, each severally played its part. He sat down, dazzled from staring at the milky sky, and was surprised to see the new bronze texture of his arms and legs—the arms and legs of a sixteen-year-old—slender, yet fully moulded over taut, unobtrusive muscles, which could equally have been the pride of a girl in her teens as of a growing boy. He had grazed his ankle and it was bleeding. After wiping the abrasion with his hand, he licked his fingers and tasted the mingled saltiness of blood and brine.

An off-shore breeze wafted the scent of the new-mown after-crop, farmyard smells, and the fragrance of bruised mint: little by little, along the level of the sea, a dusty pink was usurping the domain of blue unchallenged since the early morning. Philippe did not know how to express such a thought as: "All too few are the occasions in life when, with mind content, eyes surfeited with beauty, heart light, retentive, and almost empty, there comes a moment for the senses to be filled to overflowing: I shall remember this as just such a moment." Yet the bleat of a goat and the tinkle of the cracked bell round its neck were enough to make the corners of his mouth quiver with anguish and his eyes fill with tears of pleasure. He did not let his eyes linger on the dripping rocks where Vinca was roaming, did not even breathe her name when experiencing his pure emotion: at the crisis of such unheralded delights, a child of sixteen would not know how to call for succour to another child, herself perhaps in a similar predicament. . . .

"Hi, there, young fellow-me-lad!"

The voice that woke him from his day-dream was young, authoritative. Phil turned toward it without getting up, to find a lady dressed all in white who, not ten yards from him, was digging the point of her walking-stick and the high heels of her white shoes into the sandy cart-track.

"Tell me, young fellow, there's surely no sense in trying to drive my car any further down this way, is there?"

Politeness made Philippe rise to his feet and go closer; but only when he was upright and could feel on his bare body the touch of the cool breeze, and the eyes of the lady in white, did he blush. She smiled and changed her mode of approach. "Forgive me, monsieur . . . I was certain my chauffeur had made a mistake. He wouldn't listen to my word of warning. Surely this road ends up in a path that leads only to the sea?"

"Yes, madame. It's the sea-wrack road."

"Cirac? And how far away is Cirac?"

Phil could not retain a burst of laughter, which the white lady obligingly echoed.

"Did I say something funny? Take good care, or I shall be calling you 'young fellow' again. Now that you're laughing, you look no more than twelve."

But she was looking him in the eyes, like a man.

"Madame, it's the sea-wrack track, not Cirac. . . . It's . . . it's used for the sea-wrack."

"Most illuminating," said the white lady, "and I am much obliged to you for the explanation."

She was pulling his leg as a man might, and her bantering tone corresponded to the frank way she was gazing at him, so that Philippe felt suddenly tired, feeble and limp, overcome by an access of femininity that can paralyse an adolescent in front of a woman.

"Have you had a good catch, monsieur?"

"No, madame, nothing to speak of. . . . That's to say . . . Vinca caught more shrimps than I did."

"And who is Vinca? Your sister?"

"No, madame, she's a friend of mine."

"Vinca. . . . A foreign name?"

"No. . . . That's to say . . . It's short for Periwinkle."

"Is she a girl of your own age?"

"She's fifteen. I am sixteen."

"Sixteen . . ." the white lady repeated after him.

She made no comment, but added a moment later, "You've got sand on your cheek."

He rubbed his cheek so violently that he almost drew blood, and then his arm fell back to his side. 'I've got no feeling in my arms,' he thought, 'I believe I'm going to faint.'

The white lady relieved Phil of her tranquil gaze, and smiled.

"Here comes Vinca," she said, indicating the corner of the road round which the figure of a girl had just appeared. She was lugging a wooden tackle-box, and Philippe's blazer. "Good-bye, monsieur... ?"

"Phil," he answered automatically.

She did not hold out her hand, but nodded her head two or three times like a woman replying "Yes, yes," to her own hidden thoughts. She was not yet out of sight when Vinca ran up.

"Phil, who in the world was that lady?"

A shrug of the shoulders, and a blank look on every feature, expressed his complete ignorance.

"You don't know her, and yet you were speaking to her?"

In answer Phil gave her a scathing glance, inspired by a return of his old malice, and shook himself free of his momentary yoke. He was joyfully aware of their respective ages, of the rift in their friendship already perceptible, of his own despotic behaviour and Vinca's sometimes petulant devotion. Still dripping wet, her scarred knees were worthy of a Saint Sebastian and perfect under their ravaged surface: her hands would have done credit to a garden-help or cabin-boy; a greenish handkerchief was knotted round her throat and her jersey carried the whiff of live mussels. The blue of her shaggy beret no longer vied with the blue of her eyes and, except for her anxious, jealous, eloquent eye, she might well have been a student dressed for a college rag. Phil began to laugh, and Vinca stamped her foot as she threw his blazer at him.

"Will you answer me, or won't you?"

As if not deigning to reply, he thrust his bare arms through the open arm-holes of his jacket.

"Don't be so stupid! It was just a lady with a car who had lost her way. A little further, and the wheels would have sunk in the sand. I redirected her."

"Oh!"

Vinca had sat down and a shower of wet pebbles was pouring from her sand-shoes.

"And why did she go off in such a hurry just as I came into view?"

Philippe took his time before answering. Once more he savoured in secret the gestureless assurance, the frank gaze, and the thoughtful smile of the un-known lady. He recollected how serious she had been in calling him "Monsieur". But he also remembered how she had said "Vinca" in a familiar, if not derogat-ory way. He knitted his brows, permitting a protective look to cover the innocent disorder of his little friend. He thought a moment longer before he hit upon an ambiguous answer that satisfied both his secret taste for romance and his middle-class prudery.

"As things turned out, she did the right thing," was his reply.

FIVE

H E tried entreaty, "Vinca, look at me! Give me your hand. . . . Let's think about something else."

She turned away to the window and gently took her hand from his.

"Leave me alone. I'm miserable."

All that could be seen through the window was the westerly weather of August, bringing rain in its wake. The earth came to an abrupt end out there, on the brink of the links. One more squall, one more upheaval of the great grey field furrowed with parallel ridges of foam, and the house must surely float away like the ark. . . . But Phil and Vinca knew the August seas of old and their monotonous thunder, as well as the September seas and their crested white horses. They knew that this corner of a sandy field would remain impassable, and all through their childhood they had scoffed at the frothy foam-scuds that danced powerlessly up to the fretted edge of man's dominion.

For the second time Phil opened the french window, closing it behind him with an effort; he put his head down against the wind, and felt on his forehead the fine rain winnowed by the storm, the gentle drizzle, a little salty from the sea, that travelled through the air like drifting smoke. He started collecting the steel-weighted bowls and the boxwood jack they had left out on the terrace that morning, and picked up the light parchment racquets and the small rubber balls. These playthings that no longer amused him he stowed away in the shed, as one packs away the various bits and pieces of a disguise that may come in handy again one day. The periwinkle eyes followed his movements from behind the closed window, and the raindrops trickling down the panes seemed to be streaming from her eyes, troubled now, but of a blue unaffected by the variegated dull pewter of the heavens or the leaden green of the waves.

Phil folded up the wooden chairs and tipped the bamboo table on its side. He did not smile at his friend as he passed. Gone were the days when they had need to smile to make each other happy, and there was nothing about the present day to bring them joy.

'Only a few more days, less than three weeks,' Phil said to himself, as he wiped the sand off his fingers on a moist tuft of wild thyme covered with flowers and tiny wood-wasps, caught in the rain and waiting for the first ray of sunshine. He breathed in the pure fresh fragrance on the palms of his hands, and resolutely resisted a wave of enfeebling nostalgia that threatened to bring back the melancholy of his eleventh year. Instead, he looked up at the window, where, between the streaming tears of the rain and the twisted corollas of the moribund morning-glories, he could see on Vinca's face the grown-up expression she reserved for his eyes only and hid from all others behind the mask of a gay and sensible girl of fifteen.

A lull in the storm held the rain imprisoned in the clouds, and opened up a livid wound above the horizon, from which radiated an inverted fan of wan and dismal rays. Phil's heart leapt up when he beheld this omen in the sky, so eager was he to reap the just rewards and benefits to which his sixteen tormented years entitled him. Yet, though facing the sea, he was still aware of the closed window behind him with Vinca pressed against the panes. 'Only a few days more,' he repeated to himself, 'and then we'll be parted. What's to be done about it?'

It never crossed his mind that he had felt miserable and unhappy at the end of last year's holidays, until he returned to Paris and his day-school curriculum and became resigned to the consolations of Sunday. Last year Philippe had been fifteen: as each succeeding year came round, all that was not wrapped up with Vinca and himself he relegated to a dim and miserable past. Did he really love her as much as all that? he asked himself; and finding no other word but "love" in answer, he furiously tossed back the hair from his forehead. 'Perhaps I don't really love her as much as all that, but the truth is she belongs to me. And that's all there is to it.'

He turned round toward the house and shouted into

the wind, "Come on out, Vinca! It's stopped raining."

She opened the french window and stood there on the threshold like a convalescent, one shoulder hunched up to her ear, as if afraid.

"Do come on! The tide's on the turn and that means more rain."

She tied a white foulard round her head, knotting it at the back, so that it looked like a bandage.

"Come on down as far as the Point, at least. It'll be dry there under the rock."

She followed him without a word along the coast guard's path, cut in the cliff-face above the edge of the sea. They trod on pepper-scented marjoram and the last flowers of sweet clover. Below them the sea smacked like the flapping of torn flags and unctuously licked the foot of the rocks. Above them, near the top of the cliffs, its force drove back the warm gusts that wafted the odours of shell-fish and the earthly smell of the little ledges where seeds, sewn by the wind and birds in flight, throve on a scrappy sustenance.

They reached their retreat, an eyrie unprotected on three sides, dry, and well sheltered under its prow of overhanging rock, where one had the illusion of heading straight for the open sea. Philippe sat down close beside Vinca, and she let her head sink against his shoulder. She had all the appearance of being utterly exhausted, and closed her eyes at once. Her fresh round rosy cheeks, sunburnt as they were and powdered with freckles, with something vegetal about the softness of their velvety down, had lost much of their colour since the morning; so had her ripe lips, which always looked crinkled, like fruit scorched by the heat of the day.

After lunch, Vinca, who usually cut short the jeremiads of her "childhood sweetheart" by interposing with the stubborn, gentle, sound common sense of an intelligent little bourgeoise, had burst into tears, into protestations of despair and bitter recriminations. She had inveighed against everything that at their tender age they found so hateful—the future that looked so unattainable, the impossibility of running away, and a resignation they could not bring themselves to accept. She had shouted "I love you!" as some shout "Good-bye!", and "I can't ever bear to leave you!" with a look of horror in her eyes. Their love, which had grown up with them, had cast a spell over their childhood and protected their adolescence from vicarious friendships. Less ignorant than Daphnis, Phil had always treated Vinca as a brother, sometimes with respect, sometimes with roughness, but always with fondest affection, as though, after the manner of orientals, he and she had been married from the cradle. . . .

Vinca sighed, and opened her eyes again without raising her head.

"I'm not tiring you, am I, Phil?"

He shook his head, and gazed with admiration into her eyes, whose blue, each time more dear to his heart, flickered elusive between their fair-tipped lashes.

"Look out there," he said. "The storm is already dying down. There'll be another huge tide at four in the morning. . . . But we can trust in that rift and expect a lovely full moonrise to-night."

Instinctively he spoke of smooth seas and halcyon skies, to guide her thoughts toward serener images. But she gave no sign of response.

"You're coming to play tennis at the Jallons' to-morrow?"

She shut her eyes again and shook her head in sudden fury, as though refusing to eat or drink, or even to go on living.

"Vinca, you must!" Philippe was stern in his insistence. "We'll have to go."

Her lips parted and her eyes gazed searchingly out to sea, like those of a prisoner under sentence of death.

"We'll have to go, then," she repeated. "But what's the use of going? What's the use of not going? Nothing makes any difference."

The thoughts of both turned to the Jallons' garden, to tea and tennis. They thought, in the purity of their frenzied love, of the game they must play, for yet another to-morrow, in the guise of laughing children, and both felt worn out with fatigue.

'Only a few more days, and we'll be parted'— Philippe again took up the burden of his thoughts. 'We'll no longer wake up under the same roof, and I shan't see Vinca except on Sundays, either at home, or at her father's, or at the movies. And I'm sixteen! Sixteen and five make twenty-one. Hundreds and hundreds of days. . . . A few months in the hols, it's true; but then their last few days are always nightmarish. And to think that she belongs to me! That she's mine!'

It was then he noticed Vinca slowly slipping away from his shoulder. With eyes tight shut, she was slipping quietly, imperceptibly, deliberately, down the slope of the rocky ledge, so narrow, that her feet were already dangling over space. . . . He grasped the situation and felt no fear. He deliberated on the timeliness of her action, then tightened his arm round her waist so as never to be parted from her. As he pressed Vinca close, he was conscious of the full living reality, resilience, and vigorous perfection of her young body, ready to obey him in life, ready to drag him down with her to death. . . .

'Death! But what's the use of dying? . . . Not yet. Must I go down to the nether world without having really possessed all this, this girl who was born to be mine?'

On that sloping rock he dreamed of possession as a timid youth might dream, but also as an exacting man, as an inheritor grimly resolved to enjoy the fruits appointed him by time and the laws of man. For the first time it was for him to decide the fate of their future as lovers, and, as master of that fate, to choose whether to abandon her to the waves or plant her firmly on that jut of rock, like the stubborn seeds that flourished there with so little encouragement.

Tightening his arms round her like a belt, he

hoisted up the graceful young body so heavy to hold, and woke her by calling out a brief "Come along now, Vinca!"

She gazed up at him as he stood over her, and seeing him firmly resolute and impatient, it dawned on her that the hour for dying was over. With rapturous indignation she found the setting sun reflected in Phil's dark eyes, on his ruffled hair, on his mouth and on the shadow in the shape of two small wings of virile down above it, and she cried out, "You don't love me enough, Phil, you don't love me enough!"

He longed to say something, but all words failed him, for he had no stock heroics to offer her. He blushed and hung his head, guilty—at the moment when Vinca was slipping towards the bourne where love is powerless to torment its victims prematurely —of having treated his little friend as flotsam, as a precious bottle sealed upon a secret that alone was of importance, and of having refused to relinquish her to death.

SIX

For some days past, in the mornings, the scents of autumn had been drifting down as far as the sea.

These late August mornings smelt of autumn from daybreak till the hour when the sun-baked earth allowed the cool sea breezes to drive back the then less heavy aroma of threshed wheat, open furrows, and reeking manure. A persistent dew clung sparkling to the skirts of the hedgerows, and if, about noon, Vinca came upon a fallen aspen leaf, the white underside of its still green surface would be damp and glistening. Moist mushrooms poked up through the earth and, now that the nights were chillier, garden spiders retired in the evening to the shed where the playthings were kept, and there wisely took up their abode on the ceiling.

But the midday hours were free of the wisps of autumn mists and of the gossamer threads stretched over bramble bushes laden with blackberries, and the season showed every sign of going back to July. High in the sky the sun sucked up the dew, rotting the morning's mushrooms and smothering with wasps the antiquated vines and their puny clusters. Vinca and Lisette, out walking together, threw off with identical gestures the light woollies that since breakfast had protected their upper arms and bare necks, brown against the white of their frocks. A succession of fine days followed, calm, windless, and cloudless except for the milky "mare's tails" that trailed slowly across the noonday sky only to vanish into thin air: days so divinely akin to each other that Vinca and Philippe, at peace, almost believed the year to be ending at its sweetest moment, softly held in check by an August that would last for ever.

Under the spell of physical well-being, they thought less often of their September separation and were quit of the moody dramatics, induced at too tender an age, fifteen and sixteen, by their premature love, by the secrecy and silence it imposed, and by the bitterness of their periodic partings.

Some of the young friends, who had joined them for tennis or fishing, had left the coast for Touraine; the neighbouring villas were emptying; Philippe and Vinca remained at the seaside, in the big house where the varnished wood in the hall made it smell like a ship. They enjoyed perfect seclusion in the midst of relations whom they bumped into at all hours yet hardly noticed. Vinca, concerned as she was with Phil, still carried out all her duties as daughter of the house. In the wild garden she picked bunches of viburnum and fluffy clematis for the table, and in the kitchen garden the first pears and the last black-currants. She poured out the coffee, held a lighted match for Phil's father or her own, cut out and sewed little frocks for Lisette, and lived a strangely remote life among the ghostly throng of relatives whose faces she barely distinguished and whose voices she hardly heard; it was as if she were passing through the agreeable first stages of semi-blindness and semi-deafness that precede a trance. Her younger sister Lisette alone escaped the common fate and shone out in her own true colours. As far as that went, Lisette was as like the Periwinkle as a button-mushroom is to a bigger one.

"If I die," Vinca once said to Philippe, "you've always got Lisette. . . ."

But Philippe had shrugged his shoulders and had not laughed, for sixteen-year-old lovers admit neither change, nor illness, nor unfaithfulness, and refuse to countenance death, except to regard it as a reward, or as the decree of fate in the last resort, when no other means of escape can be found.

On the loveliest of these late August mornings, Phil and Vinca decided to desert the family table and take their lunch and bathing things packed in a picnic-basket, as well as Lisette, on a day's outing. In previous years they had often gone off alone, like explorers, to eat out of doors in one of the deep clefts in the cliffs: a time-honoured pleasure, at present in danger of becoming a doubtful one, owing to their state of uncertainty and misgiving. But this most radiant of mornings bid fair to rejuvenate the two young waifs, who sometimes turned back querulously towards the gate through which they had left the garden of their childhood.

Phil led the way down the coast guard's path, carrying the shrimping-nets for the afternoon's fishing and the string-bag, in which the litre of sparkling cider clinked against the smaller bottle of mineral water. Next came Lisette, wearing a pullover on top of her bathing-dress and swinging in a napkin a loaf still hot from the oven. Vinca brought up the rear, dressed in short white ducks and a blue sweater, and laden with panniers like an African donkey. At all the awkward corners Phil, without turning round, shouted "Hold on, I'll take one of the baskets!", to be answered by Vinca "Don't bother!" And, loaded as she was, she contrived to direct Lisette when the high bracken threatened to submerge the small head and its crown of stiff yellow hair.

They chose their chine, little more than a fault in the rocks, where the outgoing tide had spread a carpet of fine sand, a flat cornucopia widening out to the sea. Lisette took off her sandals and began to play with the stranded shells. Vinca rolled up the white ducks over her sunburnt thighs and dug a hole in the wet sand to keep the bottles cool.

"D'you need any help?" Phil asked a little feebly.

She did not deign to reply, but looked at him in silent laughter. For a moment the rare blue of her eyes, the warm bloom on her cheeks that resembled espalier nectarines, and the curved double strip of her teeth, irradiated such a flash of unidentifiable colours that

Phil felt as if transfixed. Then she turned away, and he watched her moving about effortlessly, bending down with the free, unhampered agility of a boy.

"It's easy to see that all you've come here for is to feed your face," she shouted. "Oh, you men!"

The "man" of sixteen accepted the implied flattery of this sudden sally. He called out sternly to Lisette when the feast was spread, ate the sandwiches buttered by Vinca, drank his cider neat, dipped his lettuce and his cube of gruyère in the salt, and licked the juice of the runny pears from his fingers. Vinca watched over the proceedings like a young cup-bearer, her forehead bound by a blue fillet. She boned the sardines for Lisette, portioned out the drinks, peeled the fruit, all before quickly settling herself down to eat with huge bites of her strong young teeth. The receding tide whispered low in the distance, a threshing-machine droned drowsily above their heads, and close at hand a thread of fresh water, smelling faintly of the earth, trickled from the rock fringed with grass and tiny yellow flowers. . . .

Philippe stretched out to full length and tucked one arm under his head.

"How lovely it is," he murmured.

Vinca, on her feet, busied over drying the knives and glasses, let the flash of her blue eyes fall on him. He did not stir, and hid the pleasure he always felt when under her admiring glance. He was aware of the handsome picture he must present, with a flush on his cheeks, a sparkle on his lips, and his forehead pillowed on a fine disorder of raven locks.

Vinca resumed her squaw-like chores without a word, and Philippe closed his eyes, lulled by the ebbing tide, the faraway chimes of a church-clock striking twelve, and the subdued hum of Lisette's little snatches of song. He fell at once into a light sleep, a siesta sleep, pierced by every sound yet weaving each into the pattern of a persistent dream: lying on the yellow sands after a nursery lunch, he was at one and the same time an ancient savage Phil, stripped of everything, but richly endowed in that he possessed a wife.

A shriller cry caused him to raise an eyelid: down by the edge of the sea, drained of all colour by the vertical rays and dazzle of the noonday sun, Vinca was bending over Lisette, attending to some scratch or removing a splinter from a small confiding upstretched hand. The vision in no sense disturbed the trend of his dream, and he once more closed his eyes. 'A child. . . . That's right, we've got a child."

Philippe's primeval dream, in which love, by out-stripping the requisite age for love, surpassed the generous limits of its own boundaries, had plunged him far back among solitudes where he was lord and master. He wandered past a grotto—a slung hammock hollowed by a naked form and the embers of a wood fire flickering at ground level—before the power of divination deserted him and the wings of his imagination were clipped, and he plummeted headlong down till he touched the cushioned depths of deepest sleep.

SEVEN

"I SIMPLY can't bring myself to believe that the days are drawing in!"

"Why can't you? You say the same thing every year precisely at this season. But if it's changing the solstice you want, Marthe, I'm afraid you have no say in the matter."

"And where does the solstice come in, I'd like to know? I ask nothing of the solstice, and I expect it to return the compliment."

"The ineptitude of some women at grasping certain facts is really most curious. Here's one, for example, to whom I must have explained the tidal system at least twenty times, yet her mind is a blank wall when faced with the syzygy!"

"You may be my brother-in-law, Auguste, but I see no reason why I should pay more attention to you than to anyone else. . . ."

"Heavens above, it's small wonder to me you've never found a husband, Marthe! . . . My dear spouse, would you mind passing me the ash-tray?"

"And if I do pass it to you, where d'you suppose Audebert's going to knock out his pipe?"

"Don't cudgel your brains over my little problems, Madame Ferret. There are plenty of those shells that the children leave about on every table."

"You're the one to blame for that, Audebert. Ever since you told them that ear-shells are pretty things and would make artistic ash-trays, their scrambles over the rocks have been transformed into a special mission. Isn't that so, Phil?"

"Yes, Monsieur Ferret."

"It was for that very mission your daughter abandoned her first attempt at money-making, Ferret. Would you believe it? Vinca had the bright idea of coming to some arrangement with Carbonieux —he's the big seed-merchant and bird-fancier, you know—by which she would supply him with cuttle-fish for his canaries to sharpen their beaks on. Say at once if I'm telling a fib, Vinca!"

"No, Monsieur Audebert."

"She's got a better eye for business than she's been given credit for, the little sly-boots. I feel like reproaching myself. . . .

"Please, Auguste, don't start on that over again!"

"I shall start on it over again if I think fit to do so. Here's a child you require should be kept at home, good. What scope does that allow her for moral and physical activity?"

"Why, the same scope as myself. You don't often find me twiddling my thumbs, I believe! And then, of course, I shall marry her off. That's my one aim in life."

"My sister's a stickler for the old traditions."

"Husbands are never the first to complain of that."

"No truer word . . . Madame Ferret! A girl's future . . . I know time is not of the essence. Fifteen! Vinca has plenty of time to discover her own vocation. . . . Isn't that so, Vinca? Are you listening? Prisoner-in-the-dock, what have you to say in your defence?"

"Nothing, Monsieur Audebert."

" 'Nothing, Monsieur Audebert!' That attitude isn't going to get you very far. I must say, Ferret, our children pay precious little attention to us! An ominous calm seems to be brooding over them this evening."

"They've been leading such a madcap existence. Vinca, one might almost say, has lost the seat off her pants."

"Marthe!"

"What d'you mean 'Marthe!' Just because I mentioned the word 'pants'? We're not English, I'd have you know!"

"Not in front of a young man."

"There's no young man here, there's only Phil. What are you drawing, Phil?"

"A turbine, Monsieur Ferret."

"Here's luck to the future engineer, say I! Audebert, have you noticed the moon over the Grouin? For the past fifteen years I've watched the August moon rising over the sea and my eyes have never grown tired of the sight. When one thinks that fifteen years ago the Grouin was bare rock, and that the wind alone is responsible for sowing all those little trees . . ."

"You're telling me the story, Ferret, as though I were a tourist. Fifteen years ago I was hunting along this coast for some little spot where I could blue the first wad of notes I'd ever managed to save."

"Was it really as long ago as that? Philippe must have been a mere toddler. . . . My dear spouse, do come and take a look at the moon. I don't suppose, in all these fifteen years, you've ever seen her quite the colour she is to-night. She's . . . she's green, I swear it, positively green."

Philippe turned an inquisitorial eye on Vinca. The talk had been of a time when she, though seen by none, might yet be said to have been in the land of the living. . . . He himself, naturally, had no very clear recollection of the days when they had toddled together on the yellow holiday sands: the midget form of that period—white muslin, brown skin—had faded from his memory. But when he said in his heart of hearts "Vinca!", the name, inseparably linked with his friend, evoked the memory of sand, warm to kneel on, or trickling out between fingers that held it in a tight squeeze. . . .

The periwinkle eyes caught Phil's, and, inscrutable as his, looked away again at once.

"Vinca, aren't you going up to bed?"

"Not just yet, Mummy, if you don't mind. I'm putting the finishing touches to Lisette's rompers."

She spoke softly, and then re-entered the world

shared by herself and Philippe, leaving outside it the
pale, almost non-existent Shades of the family circle.
Phil, after drawing his turbine, an aeroplane propeller,
and the mechanism of a milk-separator, sketched in on
each of his propeller blades a large shadowy eye like
that on the wing of a peacock butterfly, before adding
several delicate legs and antennae. Then he traced a
capital V, and with the aid of a blue pencil transformed
this into a blue eye fringed with long lashes—Vinca's
eye.

"Look, Vinca!"

She bent forward, put a hand that might have been
carved from mahogany—a Red Indian hand—on the
outstretched paper, and smiled.

"How silly you are!"

"What's he done now?" asked Monsieur Audebert.

The two young people turned toward the voice with
a look of rather haughty surprise.

"Nothing, Papa," Philippe replied. "Just doodles.
I've added legs to my turbine to make it go faster."

"When you show the first streak of intelligence, I'll
chalk it up on the mantel. The boy's still six, not
sixteen!"

Vinca and Philippe smiled out of politeness and
once more banished into outer darkness the vague
beings who were playing cards or stitching so close
beside them. They still overheard, as though catching
the sounds above a babbling brook, the gist of some
jesting remarks about Philippe's "vocation"—clearly
destined for mechanics and electrical appliances—

and on Vinca's matrimonial prospects. An explosion
of laughter all round the table greeted the suggestion
of marrying her to Phil. . . . "Ha, ha, ha! It would be
just like a sister marrying her brother. They know
each other far too well."

"Love, Madame Ferret, has to come unawares, like
a clap of thunder."

"*L'amour est enfant de Bohème*. . . ."

"Marthe, don't sing, please! Not when we're all so
keenly enjoying our fill of fine weather, and the
nor'-wester. . . ."

. . . An engagement between Vinca and himself! A
smile of pitying condescension played over Philippe's
features. An engagement! What would be the use?
Vinca belonged to him and he belonged to Vinca. In
their wisdom, they had already discounted any
troublesome effect a long-dated official announcement
might have on their age-old passion for each other.
They had anticipated the daily jokes at their expense,
the intolerable smirks, as well as their own attitude of
resistance. . . .

. . . Together they had reclosed the peep-hole
through which they sometimes communicated with
the world of reality from the fastness of their love.
In like manner they each envied their respective
parents their childishness, their easy laughter, and
their faith in a rosy future.

'How cheery they seem!' Philippe said to himself, as
he scanned his father's greying temples for some sign
of enlightenment, or at least some trace of a scar.

'Oh,' he decreed pontifically, 'he's never really been in love, the poor man!'

Vinca tried her best to imagine a time when her mother, still in her teens perhaps, had suffered, and in silence, the pangs of secret love. She could see her only as she was now, hair prematurely white, gold-rimmed pince-nez, and the slight, elegant figure, which made Madame Ferret look so distinguished ... And she blushed on reaching the conclusion that she, and she alone, had suffered the shame of having to endure the physical and mental torments of being in love. Then she quitted the realm of unreal Shades to rejoin Philippe on the road where perforce they had to cover their tracks, and where they felt they might all too easily perish under the weight of a booty too rich, too burdensome, and one acquired too early in life.

EIGHT

AFTER turning the corner into the side road, Phil leapt from his bicycle, flinging it down on the near side and himself on the grass of the chalky verge opposite. 'I've had enough! I'm beat to the wide! What in the world made me offer to take that telegram?'

The eight mile stretch from the villa to Saint-Malo had not seemed to him too unbearable. A following breeze had sped him along, and while coasting down the two long declines a cool shaft of disturbed air had struck sharp against his bared chest. But the return journey had made him fed up with the summer, the bicycle, and his readiness to run errands. August was going out in flames. Philippe scrabbled his legs on the yellowing grass and licked the flinty road dust off his lips. Then he lay flat on his back, spread-eagling his arms above his head. The temporary constriction in his lungs had given him black patches under the eyes, so that he looked as if he had just come out of a boxing ring, while the number of holiday weeks and of days spent in rock-fishing were scored in white scars and black or red bruises on legs that were bronze right up to the line of his scanty running shorts.

'I should have brought Vinca along,' he thought half in jest, 'what a hullaballoo there'd have been!'

But a second Philippe, the one who worshipped Vinca, the Philippe ensnared in the toils of premature love like an orphan prince within the walls of a too vast palace, answered the wicked Philippe, 'You'd have carried her all the way home on your back, if she'd so much as uttered a word of complaint.' To which the wicked Philippe replied, 'That's not at all certain!' and, this time, the loving Philippe dared not pursue the argument.

He was lying beneath a garden wall overhung by blue pines and white aspens. Philippe knew the map of the coast like the back of his hand, had known it ever since he had learned to walk on his two legs or balance between the two wheels of a bicycle. 'This must be *Ker-Anna*. I can hear the dynamo that makes the electric light. But I've no notion who's rented it this season.' On the further side of the wall an engine was lap-lapping like the tongue of a panting dog, and the silver aspen leaves, twisted the wrong way by the wind, resembled ruffled wavelets. At peace with the world, Phil closed his eyes.

"You certainly look as if you deserve a glass of orangeade," said a tranquil voice.

Opening his eyes, Phil saw above his head, like an inverse reflection mirrored in a pool, the face of a woman leaning over him. From upside-down, her features presented a too fat chin, lips artificially reddened, the tip of a nose with close-set, irritable nostrils, and a pair of sombre eyes which had the shape

of twin crescents thus viewed from below. The whole
face, light amber in colour, was smiling with a
familiarity far from friendly. Philippe recognised it
as belonging to the Lady-in-white, whose car had
foundered in the sand on the sea-wrack road, the lady
who had addressed him first as "young fellow" and
then as "Monsieur". He sprang to his feet and greeted
her with all the politeness he could muster. She was
leaning over the wall on crossed arms left bare by her
short-sleeved white dress, looking him over from head
to foot, as on the first occasion.

"Tell me, Monsieur," she interrogated him in all
seriousness, "is it due to some vow or your own inclination that you wear no clothes, or practically none?"

Philip felt his cooled-off blood mount in a burning
up-rush to his ears and cheeks.

"Certainly not, madame," he cried shrilly, "it's
because I had to bike to the post office with a telegram
to one of papa's clients; there was nobody else in the
house ready and it would never have done for Vinca or
Lisette to be sent out on a day like this!"

"Don't take it so tragically," said the Lady-in-
white. "I'm fearfully susceptible. The very least thing
and I dissolve into tears."

Philippe was hurt by her words and by her inscrutable stare, for behind it seemed to hover the ghost
of a smile. He snatched up his bike by the handle-bars,
much as one pulls back a stumbling child by the arm,
and was about to jump on to the saddle.

"Do let me offer you a glass of orangeade, Monsieur

Phil. It's no trouble, I assure you." The screech of an
iron gate grinding on its hinges reached his ears just as
he rounded a bend in the wall, and his attempt at escape
landed him up exactly opposite an open door, a double
line of hectic pink hydrangeas, and the Lady-in-white.

"My name is Madame Dalleray."

"And mine's Philippe Audebert," said Phil with a
gulp.

This she waved airily aside with an "Oh!" of indifference, as much as to say it held no interest for her.

She walked by his side, and endured without
flinching the flaming sun on the lustrous coils of her
black hair. He began to feel dizzy, and thought it due
to a sun-stroke when he once again began to feel, in
the presence of Madame Dalleray, a similar fear, and a
similar hope, that he might faint and thus be spared the
agony of thinking, choosing, and having to obey.

"Totote, the orangeade!" Madame Dalleray called out.

Phil shivered and came to himself. 'The wall's over
there—it's not so very high. I'll leap over it and . . .',
but he refrained from adding . . . 'I shall be saved.'
As he went up the dazzling front steps in the wake of
the white dress, he summoned to his aid all the insolence of his sixteen years. 'After all, she's not going
to eat me! It's just that she's so set on getting rid of
her precious orangeade! . . .'

He followed her indoors, and thought he was going
to trip over his own feet when he entered a dark room,
closed against sun and flies. The low temperature
created by latched shutters and drawn curtains made

him catch his breath. He knocked his foot against
something soft, collapsed in a heap on a cushion,
heard a demoniacal little titter coming from he knew
not where, and nearly broke into tears of anguish.
An icy tumbler touched his hand.

"Don't drink it all at once," said the voice of
Madame Dalleray. "Totote, you were crazy to put ice
in it. It was cold enough from the cellar."

Three fingers of a white hand were dipped into the
glass and as speedily withdrawn. The sparkle of a
diamond glittered in the ice-cube held between the
three fingers. Philippe shut his eyes and, with a
tightening of the throat, took two sips but tasted
nothing, not even the acidity of the oranges; but on
reopening them, his more accustomed eyes discerned
the red and white of the wall-hangings, the black and
dull gold of the curtains. A female he had not before
noticed was leaving the room, carrying a tinkling
tray. A red and blue macaw, on a perch, spread one of
its wings with the snap of a fan, to display pink under-
feathers, the hue of livid flesh.

"How handsome he is!" Phil said in a hoarse voice.

"All the more handsome for being a non-talker,"
said Mme. Dalleray.

She had seated herself at some distance from
Philippe, and there rose between them a thread of
vertical smoke from an incense-burner that permeated
the room with fumes of resin and geranium. Philippe
crossed one bare leg over the other, and the Lady-in-
white smiled, to add to the atmosphere of nightmarish

luxury, of arbitrary arrest, of equivocal rape, so that Philippe was left without a stitch of composure.

"Your people come every year to this part of the coast, do they not?" said the soft, masculine voice of Mme. Dalleray, breaking the silence.

"Yes," he sighed, overwhelmed.

"It is, I must say, a delightful countryside, and one I was not acquainted with at all. Temperate for Brittany, too, hardly characteristic; but restful, and the colour of the sea is beyond compare."

Philippe did not answer. He was gathering what wits he had left to combat his progressive exhaustion, and expected to hear at any moment a regular, muffled drip-drip on the carpet as the last drops of his life-blood ebbed from his heart.

"You're in love with it all, are you not?"

"With whom?" he asked, almost somersaulting off his chair.

"This coast round Cancale?"

"Yes . . ."

"Are you not feeling well, Monsieur Phil? No? That's good. I'm a very efficient nurse, I must inform you. . . . But, on such a hot day, I couldn't agree with you more —far better to stay still and not talk. So let's not talk."

"I never said that . . ."

Ever since they had entered the darkened room, she had not made a move nor risked a remark that was not perfectly conventional. Yet each time he heard the sound of her voice, Philippe was afflicted with a sort of inexpressable trauma, and the threat of complete silence filled him with terror. His exit was pitiful and desperately contrived. He knocked his glass against a phantom small table, gave voice to a word or two he never heard himself speak, stumbled to his feet, clove his way to the door through heavy seas and past invisible objects, and was at his last gasp by the time he re-emerged into the light of day.

"Ah . . ." he managed in a whisper, as he pressed a pathetic hand to that part of the breast where we believe our heart to beat.

Then he quickly pulled himself together, laughed like a half-wit, gave Mme. Dalleray's hand a cavalier shake, picked up his bike and was gone. At the top of the last incline he found an anxious Vinca waiting for him.

"But what in the world have you been doing that's kept you so long, Phil?"

He kissed her on the eyelids, and behind them kissed the lovely blue of his sweetheart's eyes whose deeper shade they only served to enhance, before he answered exuberantly.

"What have I been doing! Why every sort of thing, what do you expect? I was set upon at the turning off the main road, shut up in a cellar, given powerful potions to quench my thirst, tied naked to a stake, tortured, put to the test . . ."

Vinca laughed as she leaned against his shoulder, while Philippe gave a shake of the head to detach from his eyelashes two tears caused by his nervous strain, and thought to himself, 'If only she knew the truth of every word I've been telling her. . . .'

NINE

Ever since the day when Mme. Dalleray had given him a glass of orangeade, Phil had felt the shock, the burning sensation of the iced drink on his lips and at the back of his throat. Also he began to imagine that never in his life had he drunk, and never again would drink, any orangeade so bitter. 'And yet it had no taste at all while I was drinking it. It was after . . . a long time after . . .' and the visit, kept a secret from Vinca, started to fester in his memory like a sensitive, throbbing spot, while its fever was amenable to being soothed or inflamed according to his mood.

Philippe's whole life belonged to Vinca, to the darling of his heart, born so close to him in time, a twelve-month after, attached to him as a twin sister is to her twin brother, and as anxiously concerned about his well-being as a mistress over a lover who must leave her the following day. But dreams, and nightmares most certainly, are not controlled by what happens in real life. A bad dream, a dream rich in lurid reds, velvety blacks and golds, and glacial shadows, was beginning to impinge on Phil's life.

The normal hours of his day were being diminished by his dream segmentally, as by an eclipse, ever since, one torrid afternoon in the *salon* at *Ker-Anna*, he had drunk the orangeade poured out by the grave and gracious Lady-in-white. The flash of her diamond at the edge of the glass . . . the die of glittering ice between her three pale fingers . . . the blue and red macaw, silent on its perch, the plumage of its crooked wing lined with white and peach-pink. . . . The poor fellow began to doubt his memory when it so constantly heightened these images by painting them in false and glowing colours—the décor a creation of sleep, perhaps, for sleep deepens to blue the tonal value of leafy greens, and adds sensational highlights to certain other shades.

He had derived no sense of pleasure from his visit. The very memory of the perfumes distilled by the incense-burner, on one occasion, had paralysed his appetite and induced a nervous aberration. "Vinca, don't you think the shrimps have a whiff of balsam to-day?"

Pleasure indeed! What pleasure had there been in his entry into the darkened room, bumping up against those soft and velvety objects! Or in his clumsy exit, with the hot sun like a cape thrown suddenly round his shoulders! No, no, the very reverse; so far from resembling pleasure, it was more like torture, like the continual embarrassment of an unredeemed debt . . .

'I really must repay her by some act of courtesy,' he said to himself one morning. 'There's no reason why she should take me for a blundering dragon. I must take her some flowers, and then never give her a further thought. But what kind of flowers?'

The long-stemmed marguerites in the kitchen garden, and the velvety snap-dragons, seemed to him contemptible. The last days of August had seen the end of the wild honey-suckle flowers and of the Dorothy Perkins' trained round the aspen boles. But somewhere among the dunes, between the villa and the sea, lay a hollow brimful of sea-holly—blue in flower, mauve the length of its breakable stalks—a flower worthy of being called "the mirror of Vinca's eyes".

'Sea-holly, of course. . . . I saw some in a big copper vase at Madame Dalleray's. . . . *Can* one present a bouquet of sea-holly, though? I'll hang them up on the wrought-iron gate. . . . I won't go in. . . .'

In the wisdom of his sixteen years, he waited for a day when Vinca, seemingly none too well, but looking tired and listless and a little on edge, with mauve rings round her eyes, went to lie down in the shade in preference to going for a walk or a bathe. He picked and tied up in secret a bunch of the finest flowers, tearing his fingers to pieces on their iron foliage. He set off on his bicycle in soft Breton weather, that veiled the earth in a ground-mist and mixed an immaterial milkiness in the blue of the sea. He pedalled along, hampered by his white linen trousers and his best woollen stockinnet jacket, till he reached the wall of *Ker-Anna*; then, crouching low, he crept along as far as the gate, where he longed to chuck his prickly bouquet over into the garden, as though ridding himself of a convicting piece of evidence. He worked out his best plan, crept back to where the surrounding wall almost touched the villa, and, curving his arm like a sling, he slung the bunch up into the air.

He heard a cry, footsteps running on the gravel, and a voice muffled with anger, which he none the less recognised, shouting, "If I can lay my hands on the idiot who did that . . ."

Feeling insulted, he gave up all idea of running away, and an infuriated Lady-in-white found him just outside the gate. She changed her expression when she saw who it was, stopped frowning, and gave a slight shrug.

"I might have known as much. . . . You would choose the easiest way of approach."

She waited for an apology which was not forthcoming, since Phil, lost in contemplation of her, was inwardly offering up thanks that she was once again dressed in white, and had added a discreet touch of rouge to her lips and pencilled a dark halo round her eyes. She raised a hand to her cheek.

"Look, I'm bleeding!"

"So am I," said Philippe roughly, and he held out his lacerated hands. She bent over and pressed out a tiny pearl of blood on one of their palms.

"Did you pick them for me?" she enquired casually.

He responded with no more than a nod, deriving a rustic kind of pleasure from behaving uncouthly in front of a lady so well-mannered and kind. But she showed neither annoyance nor surprise.

"Would you care to come in for a moment?"

He answered as before, and his mute refusal sent a flurry of hair flying out all round a face, at the moment devoid of all expression other than a strange severity.

"They're such a marvellous blue . . . a blue that's indescribable. . . . I'll arrange them in my big copper."

Phil's features relaxed a little.

"That's just what I was thinking," he said, "or perhaps in a grey-stone pot".

"Yes, if you like. . . . In a grey-stone pot."

Philippe was amazed by the note of docility in Mme. Dalleray's voice. Noticing this, she looked him straight in the eyes, before she resumed her easy almost masculine smile and changed her mode of approach.

"Tell me, Monsieur Phil. . . . Answer me just one simple question. Did you pick these lovely blue flowers especially for me, to give me pleasure?"

"Yes. . . ."

"How very kind. To give me pleasure. . . . But were you thinking more particularly of the pleasure it would give me to receive them—now listen carefully—than of the pleasure it gave you to pick them for me and present them to me?"

He did not listen properly, but stared at her like a deaf-mute, paying more attention to the words as they formed on her lips and to the flutter of her eyelids. He failed to grasp the meaning of her words and answered at random.

"I thought they would be nice for you to have . . . besides, you offered me your orangeade. . . ."

She removed the hand she had put on his arm, and pushed the half-closed gate wide open.

"Quite so. My boy, you must go away, and never return here again."

"What?"

"Nobody asked you to be nice to me. So forget the kindly solicitude that brought you here to-day, to bombard me with sea-holly. Good-bye, Monsieur Phil. Unless . . ."

She leaned forward challengingly against the scrolled iron-work of the gate she had so promptly shut between them, and looked at him quizzically as he stood rooted to the roadway.

"Unless, one fine day, I find you on this spot again, having come back, not to repay me for my orangeade with a bouquet of prickly flowers, but for another reason. . . ."

"Another reason?"

"How your voice echoes mine, Monsieur Phil! Next time we shall see whose pleasure is involved, yours or mine. I care only for starvelings and beggars, Monsieur Phil. So, if you do come back, come back empty-handed. . . . Now be off, Monsieur Phil! Shoo!"

She left the gate, and Philippe went off. Turned away, banished even, he still retained his manly pride and, in his memory, the vision of the black arabesques of the gate, like a branch of viburnum, mottling the face of a woman tattooed with the stigma of her own fresh blood.

TEN

"You'll trip up, Vinca, your espadrille's come untied. Hold on. . . ."

Phil bent down briskly, snatched hold of the two white tapes to cross them over a trembling ankle, brown and dry-skinned, the leg of a well-bred filly, conditioned to racing and jumping. Hardened skin and multiple scars did not detract from its shapeliness. With little flesh to cover the bone structure and just sufficient muscle to ensure the proper curve, Vinca's leg could not be said to excite desire, but rather the specialised appreciation of a connoisseur.

"Hold on, I tell you! How can I tie it if you will keep on going?"

"No, let go!"

Her bare linen-shod foot, as if winged, slipped from the fingers that held it and cleared Phil's head as he knelt before her. He caught a whiff of lavender, of well ironed linen and seaweed, the components of Vinca's particular brand of scent, and then saw her standing three paces away. She looked him up and down, shedding on him the dark troubled light of her eyes, whose blue never changed like the inconstant colours of the sea.

"What's got hold of you now? There's no end to your moods. I don't know how to tie a shoe, is that it? I promise you, Vinca, you're becoming impossible!"

Phil's chivalrous attitude was hardly in keeping with the offended look on a face that appeared cast in the mould of a young Roman god's, gilded by the sun, set off by a crown of black hair, its grace impaired only by the faintest shadow—the fluffy down of to-day, to-morrow's stiff hairs—of a nascent moustache.

"What's the matter? Did I hurt you? Have you got a thorn in your foot?"

She shook her head in prompt denial, let her body relax, and dropped to the ground among the meadow salvia and pink knot-grass, pulling the hem of her frock down as far as her ankles. Her every movement was governed by a quick and pleasing angularity, by a natural poise so exceptional that it would have rejoiced a choreographer's eye. Her happy and exclusive companionship with Phil had trained her to tomboyish games, and to a rivalry in sport as long-lived as her love and not yet undermined by it. There were still times when they could forget their love, despite the force that daily increased its tentacle hold and slowly but surely sapped their mutual trust and gentleness; and despite their very love itself, though it was changing the essence of their tender affection as coloured water changes the complexion of the rose that drinks it.

Philippe did not long submit to Vinca's gaze, though the deep clouded blue of her eyes harboured no resentment. Surprise alone was apparent there, and she was breathing fast, just as a hind, startled by a stroller in the forest, stays hesitantly poised instead of bounding away. She was questioning her own instincts and not the kneeling youth whose clutches she had fled, and it dawned on her that she had just obeyed an impulse of revulsion inspired by distrust and not by false modesty. There was no question of false modesty in a love as great as hers.

She had been quick to apprehend a feminine presence in Philippe's life, warned from the outset by the vigilance of her pure love. She could be said almost to have sniffed the air around him, as if he had been smoking in secret or eating forbidden sweets. She put an end to their talks with a silence as conclusive as a leap, or a look as sudden and weighty as a punch. Whilst they were strolling hand in hand along the road before dinner, she had untwined her shorter, more delicate, fingers from his, and withdrawn her hand from his friendly grasp.

Philippe had found some difficulty in concealing from Vinca his third and fourth visits to Mme. Dalleray. But what can walls and distances avail against invisible antennae which, when the heart is enamoured, are extended, sensitive to touch and feel, and, on detecting a blemish, are retracted. His small parasitic secret, attached to their own greater secret, was a blot perhaps on Philippe's scutcheon, yet left him untarnished by any smirch of moral delinquency. Vinca now found him gentle, whereas, by virtue of the despotism of his brotherly love, he should have treated her as his slave. Something of the amenity of erring husbands had crept into his behaviour and made him suspect in her eyes.

After roundly scolding her for acting so strangely, this time Philippe kept up his air of bravado and made his way back to the villa, though it was all he could do not to break into a run. Should he, he wondered, set off in an hour's time to enjoy the hospitality of *Ker-Anna*, as Mme. Dalleray had begged him to do? "Begged" was hardly the appropriate word for one who knew only how to issue orders and, with dissimulating firmness, dress down the recruit she had a mind to raise to the rank of starveling and beggar. A rebellious beggar, none the less, since he refused to be humbled and, once outside the sphere of her influence, might prove disloyal to the dispenser of cooling drinks, the peeler of luscious fruits, whose white hands were ready to tend and succour the well-set-up young novice who had stopped by her gate. But could he be termed a novice, this youth who since childhood had been dedicated to a love that would keep him pure till he attained to man's estate? Where she thought to find an easy victim, willing to submit to her enchantment, Mme. Dalleray discovered an enthralled but doughty opponent. For all the show of outstretched hands and parched lips, this beggar did not display the mien of a subjugated foe.

'He'll always be on his guard,' she surmised. 'He's keeping himself from me.' Mme. Dalleray had not yet reached the stage where she could say, '*She's* keeping him from me'.

On reaching the house, Philippe found it in him to shout back to the sandy meadow where Vinca was still sitting. "I'm off to the second post. Anything I can do for you?"

She replied with a negative shake of the head that turned her evenly cut hair into a gilded nimbus, and Philippe leapt on to his bicycle.

Mme. Dalleray was not expecting him, or so it seemed, for he found her reading. He felt assured of his welcome, however, when he saw the studied half-light in the *salon* and noticed the almost invisible table from which rose a pervasive aroma of slow-ripening peaches, of red cantaloup melon cut in slices the shape of crescent moons, and of black coffee poured over crushed ice.

Mme. Dalleray put down her book, and held out a hand without rising. Through the gloom he discerned the white dress and the white hand: her dark eyes, remote in their bistre halo, were more languid in their movement than usual.

"I hope you were not asleep?" Phil said, forcing himself to a conversational opening.

"No. . . . Certainly not. . . . Is it very hot? Are you hungry?"

"I don't know. . . ."

He sighed, sincere in his indecision, overcome from the moment of setting foot in *Ker-Anna* by some kind of thirst, by a susceptivity to the esculent smells that might have amounted to hunger had not his throat at the same time been constricted by a nameless anxiety. His hostess had risen to serve him, and soon he was sipping, from a small silver shovel, the sugar-sprinkled, anis-flavoured red flesh of the melon.

"Are your relatives enjoying good health, Monsieur Phil?"

He stared up at her in surprise. She looked slightly distraught and did not appear to have heard her own voice. He scooped up a spoon in his cuff and it fell on the carpet with the plaintive tinkle of a small bell.

"Clumsy! Just you wait . . ."

She caught hold of his wrist with one hand, and with the other she rolled up his sleeve as far as the elbow, keeping a firm grip on his bare arm with her hot hand.

"Let me go!" Phil cried in a piercing tone.

He jerked his arm away so violently that a saucer broke in pieces at his feet. The echo of Vinca's "Let go!" shrilled through the buzzing in his ears, and he turned to Mme. Dalleray with a glare of questioning fury. She had not moved, and the hand he had cast aside so roughly lay open on her lap like a hollow shell. It took Philippe some little time to weigh up the significance of her motionless attitude. He let his head drop forward, and in front of his eyes passed an incoherent vision of two or three self-images, in which he was either swimming ineluctably through the air, as one flies in dream, or plunging headlong down, as in a dive, at the very moment when the ripples rise up to strike the down-turned face; and then, without enthusiasm, but with deliberate slowness and calculated courage, he put his bare arm back into her open hand.

ELEVEN

Some time about one-thirty in the morning Philippe parted from the Lady-in-white.

Before leaving the family villa, he had been careful to wait till all noise and light had been extinguished. The french window that fastened on a latch, the barred gate that yielded to his push—beyond those lay the road to freedom. Freedom! He had walked on foot to *Ker-Anna* with a heavy heart, stopping every now and again to drink in a deep breath, when he would raise and lower his head like a dog baying the moon. At the top of the final crest he had turned round to glance back, halfway down the cliff, at the house where his parents lay sleeping—his and Vinca's, and Vinca herself. The third window along . . . the little wooden balcony . . . she would be asleep by now behind the two closed shutters. . . . In sleep she would be turned a little to one side, her face on her arm, like a child hiding its tears, her even hair like an open fan stretching from neck to cheek. How many times since their nursery days had he watched her asleep! How well he knew that gentle, rather sad, look on her sleeping face!

The fear of waking her telepathically had soon made

him turn back to the road, lying white under the milky radiance of the moon in her first quarter, thus making his way plain. He had felt reasonably certain of the suspension of his true love and its attendant anxieties, for even in the depths of his youthful sleep these still persisted, and never remained very far below the surface. Their weight, far more than the glacial fear that grips a young sixteen-year-old on the road to his first amorous adventure, their weight alone had threatened to turn his journey into a forced march, and—who could tell?—his pride in the delights ahead into a spunkless curiosity! But he had remained poised for no more than a moment before plunging forward again, with much the same antics of shortage of breath and appeals to the moon, as he had pursued his way down the further slope of the hill, which on his return journey, he was to climb more slowly.

"Two o'clock." Philippe counted the strokes with one ear cocked toward the village clock. The four crystalline quarters, followed by the two graver notes, travelled softly through the warm, salty mist. He added, as a ritual, "The wind must have veered, you can hear the church chimes and that means a change in the weather," and the sound of the familiar phrase came to him from far away, from a world that had turned a full circle. . . . He sat down on the grassy edge of a flower-bed in front of the villa, and burst into a flood of tears; he felt ashamed of his tears only at the moment of realising that he was enjoying a good cry.

Somebody close beside him fetched a heavy sigh: the caretaker's dog, hidden in the shadows at his feet, was dozing on the sandy path. Phil bent over and stroked the shaggy coat and hot nose of the friendly creature who had not barked at him.

"Fanfare . . . good old Fanfare. . . ." But the dog, who was old and of a Breton disposition, shuffled off out of reach to settle down again with the sound of an old sack.

Every few seconds the slack-water, slumbering under the mist at the foot of the links, sent a little extenuated wave rippling up the beach with the sound of a wet sheet being folded. Not a bird was astir, except for a little owl, which teasingly imitated the mew of a cat, now from the spindlewood hedge, now from the top of an aspen whiter than the mist.

Slowly, Philippe began piecing together the familiar but still unrecognisable features of the landscape. The stilly night, which frees man's spirit, offered him refuge and the necessary transition between his old life—the happy land of all his summers—and the world now newly opened to his eyes, with its whirl of indistinct, ever-shifting colours and scents and lights, whose concealed source could be as sharp as a dart or spread a pale restricted sheen. . . . Here all was topsy-turvy, the furniture disporting deer-like extremities, the flowers displaying the fluffy undersides of their leaves, their stiff stalks rigid in clear water. Treacherous place, treacherous atmosphere, where a woman's hand or mouth, at will, had the power of loosing

destruction on a quiet world, a catastrophe glorified
—as are the heavens when spanned by a bridge of light
after thunder—by the arched bow of a bare arm.

At least, he was leaving behind all the torments so
recently endured. He had come away with no more
than a swimmer's lassitude, and a survivor's vague and
all-embracing sense of comfort on feeling the ground
firm beneath his feet. More fortunate than many a
young man of his age who, to his lasting hurt, barters a
prolonged agony, fraught with limitless visions,
against a momentary pleasure that must thereafter
curb his dreams, he had returned in a stupor induced
by mere lack of sleep; conscious, as a man who has
drunk his fill is conscious, that he had only to move to
feel rumbling inside him the chilled residue of wine
from which the light intoxicating headiness had
evaporated.

Day was still far distant, but already one half of the
night sky was much lighter than the other. Some very
small creature, a hedgehog or rat, ran pattering past as
if scratching the ground. Forerunner of the dawn, the
first breath of wind bowled a few petals along the path,
only to relinquish them and vanish, when all became
still again. From the distant steeple the chimes of
three o'clock drifted dreamily, the first close and
limpid, the other two muffled in a gust of wind. A
pair of curlew passed above Philippe's head, low
enough for him to hear the straining of their taut
wings, and their plaintive cry from over the sea struck
deep down in his open and defenceless memory to the

very heart of his fifteen blameless years, spent moored to a golden strand and to a growing child who carried her golden head as upright as an ear of corn.

He rose to his feet in an effort to identify himself physically, to force the self who had sat down there to rest—beside the white barred gate, beside the sleeping dog—to be the same self who, the previous night, had turned his face fearfully toward *Ker-Anna* while leaning on the white gate, while giving the sleeping dog a parting pat. But he could not.

He put his hot hands to his face and felt them to be softer than was usual. They still carried vestiges of a scent so volatile that it vanished under his nostrils when he most wished to establish its essence, yet hung in the air like that of certain sweet-scented plants when their leaves are bruised. At that instant a light shone bright aslant the slats of the shutters in Vinca's room, and a little later went out. 'She's not asleep. She's just looked at the time. Why isn't she asleep?'

He knew, as certainly as if he could see through the walls, how by stretching out her arm Vinca had turned on her bedside lamp to look at the small watch hanging from her brass bedstead, and how, after turning it out again, she had thrown back her head on the pillow, her hair smelling of lavender soap like a well-cared-for child's. He knew, because the night was sultry, that her sunburnt shoulder would be bare, gartered with a thin white strip where protected by the shoulder-strap of her bathing-dress, and, with his mind's eye on her long vigorous body—a body he had watched every year as it grew in beauty—he was struck with sudden stupefaction.

What was there in common between her body, between what love would be able to make of it before it attained its inevitable perfection, and the ultimate destiny of another female body, dedicated to the gentle art of kidnapping, instrument of a relentlessly passionate enchantress, who, in the hypocritical guise of an instructress, was adept in despoiling green untutored youth?

"Never again!" he said out loud.

Only the day before he had been working out, with patient heart, how long it would be before Vinca belonged to him. Now, so much paler after an assignation that left his body as weak and trembling as though he had been beaten in a fight, Philippe recoiled in his whole being before a vision so rapacious.

"Never again!"

Dawn was breaking rapidly. But there was no wind to chase away the salty mist over which the roseate light was gaining by leaps and bounds. Phil went into the villa and up to his room, without making a sound. He found it filled with the heavy night air, and as he hurried to open the shutters he was confronted in the glass by his own reflection as a man. . . .

He saw a face drawn with fatigue, two tired eyes, their pupils enlarged, lips still smeared from contact with a rouged mouth, black dishevelled hair straggling over forehead—all signs of distress, resembling less the traits of a man than those of a violated girl.

TWELVE

At the moment when Philippe finally fell asleep, the sagacious goldfinches were already twittering for the handfuls of seed thrown them by Vinca early each morning. Their sharp cries penetrated his fitful sleep and, in his half-dreams, were transmuted into strips of thin metal ripped from an agonising helmet clamped to his skull. By the time he was fully awake, the too bright day resounded with the clucking of hens, the buzz of bees, and the drone of the threshing-machine. The sea was turning to green, ruffled by a fresh nor'wester, and beneath his window a white-frocked Vinca stood laughing.

"What's the matter with him? What can be the matter with him? Hi there, Phil! Are you down with sleeping sickness?"

And all round her the Shades, almost as inconspicuous as an old mark on the wall, as ivy or lichen, the Shades, regarded with indifference by the two young people, could be heard re-echoing her words: "What's the matter with him? What can be the matter with him? He must have been chewing poppy-seeds."

He looked down on them from the height of his window. His mouth was half-open, giving an affectedly simple look of horror to a face so pale that Vinca's laugh died on her lips, extinguishing that of the others.

"Oh, are you really ill?"

He recoiled from the window as though she had chucked a pebble at him.

"Ill! I'll soon show you whether I'm ill or not! But first tell me the time!"

Below him the laughs tuned up again.

"It's a quarter to eleven, sleepyhead! Come on down and bathe!"

He nodded his agreement, but once he had shut the window again and the tulle-curtained panes obscured the daylight, he felt an urge dragging him back towards the night abyss, from which the eddying ghost of a memory, dark and insidious, paraded among the luminous blobs that floated upwards to the full light, there to assume the colour of gold and flesh-tints, or the sudden flash of a moist eye, a ring, a finger-nail.

He tore off his pyjamas and impetuously pulled on his bathing-slip; but instead of going downstairs, as he usually did, half-stripped, he took care to knot the cord of his bath-robe.

Vinca was waiting for him on the links, peacefully letting the upper part of her legs and her sleeveless arms bake in the full sun to the brown of farmhouse bread. The incomparable blue of her eyes under the

faded blue foulard filled Philippe with a thirst for cold
water, and a yearning for the briny and the off-water
breeze. At the same time, he could not help noticing
the strength of a body growing each day more
feminine, the delicate oval of her knees under their
hard exterior, the lengthy muscles running down her
thighs, and the proud curve of her back. 'How she's
filling out!' he thought.

They dived in together, but whereas Vinca exuberantly splashed her arms and legs about in the listless
waves and spouted water as she sang, Philippe, white
to the gills and struggling against the shivers, swam
with clenched teeth. He stopped swimming the
moment Vinca's bare feet touched one of his, sank
like a stone, and reappeared only some few seconds
later; but he indulged in no reprisals and had recourse
to none of their usual pranks, the shouts and jousts and
seal-like frolics that made their morning bathe the
happiest hour of the day.

They came ashore on a strip of warm sand and
enjoyed a thorough good rub down. Vinca picked up a
pebble and aimed it at a little jutting reef with such
accuracy that Phil was grudgingly astonished and
forgot that his young playmate's proficiency in all
tomboyish games was due to his own instruction. He
felt soft-hearted, outside himself somehow, a feeling
akin to weakness, and not a spark of masculine
arrogance betrayed the fact that he had fled the house
of his childhood, the previous evening, to hasten to his
first amorous adventue.

"It's twelve o'clock, Phil. Can't you hear the church clock striking?"

Vinca was on her feet, shaking the last drops from the even tips of her wet hair. In her first few steps towards the villa, she trod on a small crab that cracked like a cob-nut, and Philippe was shocked when his heart cockled.

"What's wrong?" Vinca asked.

"You've just crushed a baby crab."

She turned back, and the sun shone full on her peach-brown cheeks, her lovely eyes, on her teeth and their surrounding pink.

"What if I did? It's not the first, by any means. And you don't seem to mind baiting the nets with bits of dissected crab!"

She ran on ahead, and cleared at a bound a hollow in the dunes. For the fraction of a second he saw her suspended in mid-air, her body strained forward, feet together, and her hands outstretched, as if she wished to gather an armful of air.

'I used to think she was tender-hearted,' Philippe mused.

The memory of his nocturnal adventures, that lay doggo during the noonday hour and barely stirred in the depths of its dark lair, was kept at bay throughout the family lunch, where he had to put up with compliments on his poetic pallor and criticism of his loss of speech and appetite. Vinca gobbled up everything put before her, and radiated a maddening cheerfulness. Phil looked at her with hostility, and took full note of the way she cracked the lobster claw with her strong hands, and flung back her hair with a haughty toss of the head.

'I suppose I ought to be thankful,' he thought. 'She suspects nothing.' But he was suffering, all the same, from her imperturbable serenity, and in his heart of hearts he was determined that she ought to be trembling like a blade of grass, horror-stricken by a betrayal which, in all conscience, she should have sensed floating in the air, as she would one of the latent storms that are apt to break, in summer, over any part of the Breton bay.

'She says she loves me. She does love me. Yet she was far more concerned *before* . . .'

After lunch Vinca danced, with Lisette, to the sound of the gramophone. She also insisted that Philippe dance too. She pored over the tidal charts, made ready the nets for the low tide at four o'clock, set Philippe and the whole villa in commotion with her schoolgirl shrieks for the tarred string and the old pocket-knife, and spread, wherever she went, the smell of iodine and seaweed that permeated her ragged old fishing-sweater. Philippe, feeling lax, and about to succumb to the sleep which follows close upon major disasters and all great happiness, kept a vindictive eye on her activities, and nervously clenched his fists.

'It wouldn't take more than two or three words to put a stop to all this!' But he knew that he would never bring himself to speak the two or three words, and in his lassitude he longed to go to sleep in a hollow of the warm dunes, his head on Vinca's lap.

Fishing the length of the foreshore, they came upon shrimps, and gurnards that extend their fan-like fins and puff out their rainbow gullets to intimidate their aggressors. But Phil went in passive pursuit of the smaller fry offshore and in the rock-pools. The glare from the mirrored sun hurt his eyes, and he slithered like a novice on the gluey patches of bladder-wrack. They captured a lobster, and Vinca raked about furiously in front of a conger eel's "hide-out".

"He's at home all right, you can see!" she shouted, showing him the tip of her iron hook stained with pinkish blood.

Phil turned white and shut his eyes.

"Let the poor creature alone!" he said in a stifled voice.

"The idea! I bet you I get him. What's wrong with you, anyway?"

He was doing his best to hide some inner pain he did not fully understand. What were, then, the fruits of his last night's victory in the scent-laden darkness, in the arms of one so eager to make him a man and proud of his conquest? Surely not the privilege of suffering such tortures, of fainting from weakness in front of an innocent, hardhearted girl! The privilege

of trembling so inexplicably in front of feeble, delicate
creatures and the sight of their spilt blood!

His next breath almost choked him and, covering
his face with his hands, he burst into tears. He was so
shaken by his sobbing that he had to sit down, while
Vinca remained on her feet, gripping the blood-stained
hook as though it were an instrument of torture. She
stooped over him, asking no questions, but listening
with a musician's trained ear to the new cadence that
gave his sobs an intelligible meaning. She put out her
hand to touch his forehead, but withdrew it before she
touched him. The expression of bewilderment on her
face gave way to one of severity, to an ageless grimace,
bitter and sorrowful, an altogether virile contempt
for the enigmatic weakness of the boy in tears. She
carefully picked up the raffia basket in which her catch
was flapping about, then her fishing-net, slipped the
iron hook under her belt like a sword, and, without
turning back, made off with a firm step.

THIRTEEN

H E did not see her again till close on dinner time. She had changed out of her fishing clothes into the pink-scolloped frock of blue crepon that so exactly matched her eyes. He saw that she was wearing white stockings and black suede shoes, and this Sunday attire disturbed him.

"Are there guests for dinner?" he asked one of the family Shades.

"You've only to count the places," the Shade replied with a shrug.

August was nearing its end, and already they were dining by lamp-light, with the door open on to the green sunset, where a spindle of coppery pink still floated. The sea was asleep, deserted, blue-black as the wing of a swallow, and during the breaks in conversation they could hear the tired, regular lap-lap of slack water. As they sat surrounded by the Shades, Philippe tried to catch Vinca's eye so as to test the strength of the invisible thread that had bound them together over so many years and had preserved them, pure and happy, from the melancholy that falls like a

dead weight at the close of meals, at the close of the
season, at the close of day. But she never raised her
eyes from her plate, and the light from the hanging
lamps lent a polished glow to her rounded eyelids,
the curve of her brown cheeks, and her small chin.
Then it was that he felt himself abandoned and
turned to look—beyond the peninsula, shaped like a
couchant lion surmounted by three twinkling stars—
for the road, white under the moon, that led to
Ker-Anna.

A few more hours, a little longer of the ashy blue in
the sky that lends the sunset a smattering of dawn, still
a few more ritual phrases: "Now, now, it's ten o'clock.
Don't you children realise that we go to bed at ten in
these parts?" and "I've done nothing out of the
ordinary, Madame Audebert, yet somehow I feel as if
I'd been on the go all day. . . ." Still another clink or
two from the pantry, the sharp rattle of dominoes on
the bare table, yet another squeal of protest from
Lisette who, though three parts asleep, would not go
up to bed. . . . Still one last attempt to regain contact
by a glance, by a secret smile of confidence and
understanding from the mysteriously aloof Vinca,
and then the hour would strike, the self-same hour
that had witnessed, the previous evening, Philippe's
furtive escape. His thoughts went back to it with no
definite desire, no set plan, as though he were being
driven by Vinca's ill-humour to beat a hasty retreat to
another refuge, to seek a more welcoming shoulder,
to find the warmth and comfort so urgently required

by a young convalescent from pleasure, utterly crushed by the passionate hostility of a girl too young.

One by one the rites were accomplished; a maid came to bear away the whimpering Lisette and, on the polished surface of the table, Mme. Ferret deposited the double-six.

"Are you coming outside, Vinca? It's awful the way these moths will batter themselves against the lamps!"

She followed him without answering and they found down by the sea, the still bright afterglow that twilight leaves to linger there.

"Wouldn't you like me to go and fetch you your scarf?"

"No thanks."

They walked side by side, bathed in the thin bluish vapour scented with wild thyme that rose from the links. Philippe refrained from taking her arm, and was horrified at his discretion. 'Oh God, what has come between us? Are we lost to each other? Since she doesn't know what took place *over there*, perhaps I have only to forget it myself for us to be as happy, and as unhappy, as before, and to be as one again.'

But this additional belief in hypnosis brought him small comfort, for there was Vinca walking beside him, cold and gentle, as if her great love had deserted her and left her unreceptive of her companion's anguish. And all the more because he himself felt his *hour* imminent, and was beginning to tremble in much the same way as when, the day after he had been stung on the arm by a stinging-ray, he had become feverish and experienced the same excruciating pain in the dressed wound when the rising tide covered it.

He stopped and wiped his forehead.

"I feel as if I'm suffocating. I'm not well, Vinca."

"No . . . not well," the voice of Vinca echoed.

Thinking her mood had changed, he was too eager in voice and gesture.

"Oh, how sweet you are! Oh, darling . . ."

"No, I'm not sweet," the voice interrupted.

The childish phrase left him still some hope, and he caught hold of her bare arm.

"I know what's the matter. You're angry with me because I cried to-day, like a woman."

"No, not like a woman. . . ."

He blushed in the dark and tried to explain.

"Can't you understand? When you were tormenting that conger in its hole . . . when the brute's blood got on your lobster hook . . . all of a sudden it made my heart turn. . . ."

"Oh I see, your heart . . . turn. . . ."

The tone of her voice was so full of meaning that Philippe caught his breath in dread. 'She knows all.' He waited for the shattering proof, the flood of tears and the moans. But Vinca remained silent, and after a long time, like the period of calm that follows a thunder clap, he risked asking a timid question. "And was my display of feebleness enough to make you pretend not to love me any more?"

Vinca turned her face toward him, bright under the moon yet a clouded blur between the two stiff hedges of her hair.

"Oh Phil, I love you all the time. Unfortunately, what you did makes no difference."

"You mean it? Then you can forgive me for being such a cry-baby, for making such a fool of myself?"

She hesitated for no more than a second.

"Of course I can forgive you, Phil. But there again, it makes no difference."

"To what?"

"To us, Phil."

She spoke with the persuasive calm of a prophetess, so that he dared not question her further, or take heart from what he had heard. Doubtless Vinca must have followed the trend of his thoughts to their inmost recesses, for there was subtlety in her answer.

"Do you remember, not three weeks ago, how you worked yourself up into a frenzy—and so did I— because we were both so impatient at having four, perhaps five more years of cooling our heels before we could get married. My poor Phil, I really believe I'd like to go back and be a child again, to-day . . ."

He waited, in case she should underline or comment further upon the so cunning, the insidious "To-day" that hung suspended before him in the blue August night. But Vinca was already practised in the art of silence.

"Then you're no longer angry with me?" he pursued

insistently. "To-morrow we'll be . . . we'll be Vinca-and-Phil again, just as we always were? And for ever?"

"For ever, if you wish it, Phil. . . . Come, let's go in. It's chilly."

She had not repeated his "as we always were", so he had to be content with an incomplete promise and a cold little hand for a moment clasped in his. For, at that precise minute, with the creak of the well-head chain and the clank of the empty pail, with the jingle of curtains along the length of their rod—the last human sounds of the day—Philippe's hour struck, the self-same hour for which he had waited, the previous night, before unfastening the door of the villa and hastening forth unseen. . . . Oh, the dim red glow in that unknown room! Oh, the dark ecstasy, the pro-tracted death, the return to life under slow-beating wings!

As if, ever since the day before, he had been expect-ing some sort of absolution from Vinca—the am-biguous absolution that she had just pronounced with such sincerity in her voice, such reticence in her words —he realised, quite suddenly, that he was a man and was able to appreciate the gift that a beautiful, authori-tative she-devil had bestowed upon him.

FOURTEEN

"Is the day of your return to Paris settled yet?"
Mme. Dalleray asked.

"We know we always have to be back there by the
twenty-fifth," Philippe answered. "Sometimes, de-
pending on what date Sunday falls, we leave on the
twenty-third or twenty-fourth, or maybe the twenty-
sixth. But it never varies by more than two days."

"Really! So, in short, you leave in a fortnight's
time. So to-day fortnight, at this time . . ."

Philippe stopped staring at the sea—flat and white
near the sands, and far out the colour of a tunny's back
under the low clouds—and turned towards Mme.
Dalleray. She was wrapped in the ample folds of some
white stuff such as Tahitian women wear, smoking
reflectively, her hair set, her powder matching her
skin; and there was nothing about her to show that the
young man sitting not far away, handsome and
sunburnt as herself, was anything else to her than a
younger brother.

"So, in a fortnight's time, at this hour, you'll be . .
where?"

"I'll be . . . oh, in the Bois, on the lake. Or more likely on the tennis-courts there, with . . . with some friends."

He blushed, for Vinca's name had been on the very tip of his tongue, and Mme. Dalleray smiled, the smile he had observed before, that gave her the appearance of a handsome lad. Philippe turned back to the sea, if only to hide his face, which showed the resentful petulance of an angry young god. A deliciously soft but firm hand was placed on his. Whereupon, without his gaze ever leaving the desultory grey sea, an expression of agonised happiness stole slowly up from his relaxed mouth to his eyes, in which the intermittent flash of white and black was finally extinguished behind closed lids.

"You mustn't be sad," Mme. Dalleray said, in a gentle voice.

"I'm not sad," he quickly protested. "You can't understand. . . ."

She bent her head, so beautifully lustrous.

"You are right. I can't understand. Not everything."

"Oh . . ."

Philippe gazed in awe, in reverent mistrust, at the woman who had revealed to him a terrifying secret. Did a low cry still re-echo in her small pink ears, like the smothered cry of someone whose throat is being cut? When he had felt light and on the point of fainting, her two arms, deceptively so much stronger than they looked, had borne him from this to another world; and her two lips, so sparing of words, had pressed upon his lips to impart a single all-powerful word, intoning an indistinct chant that was but a feeble echo rising from the depths of chaos and old night. . . . She knew everything. . . .

"Not everything," she repeated, as if Philippe's silence required an answer. "But you don't like my asking you questions. And sometimes I am a little tactless. . . ."

'Like a flash of lightning, yes,' Philippe thought. 'When it forks zigzagging across the sky, it does throw light on things that otherwise remain in shadow, even in broad daylight. . . .'

"And all I wanted to ask you was whether you'll be very pleased to leave me?"

The young man looked down at his bare feet. A loose-fitting garment of embroidered silk gave him the appearance of an Indian potentate and accentuated his good looks.

"What about you?" was his schoolboy retort.

The ash of the cigarette Mme. Dalleray was holding between her fingers dropped to the carpet.

"I don't come into it. This is a question that concerns Philippe Audebert and not Camille Dalleray."

He looked up at her in surprise on hearing once again this name which could belong to either sex. 'Camille. . . . Yes, of course that's her name. Well, she can keep it as far as I'm concerned. To myself I always call her *Madame Dalleray*, the *Lady-in-white*, or plain *She*.'

She was still smoking at her leisure and staring out

to sea. Could she be called young? Yes, she could
certainly be called young. Thirty to thirty-two.
Inscrutable, as are all calm persons, the extent of whose
facial expression never goes further than a tempered
irony, a smile, a certain gravity. Without turning
away from the stretch of sea over which a storm was
brooding, she once again put her hand on Philippe's
and squeezed it, entirely for her own pleasure and
with little thought for him. Under the pressure of
her small powerful hand, he spoke, constrainedly,
yielding up his confession, as a squeezed fruit oozes its
sweet juice.

"Yes, I shall be sad. But I hope I shan't be
unhappy."

"Really? And why do you hope so?"

He gave her a feeble little smile, looking shy and
touching, just as, secretly, she would have wished him
to be.

"Because," he answered, "I think you'll arrange
something. Yes, I'm sure you'll arrange something."

She lifted one shoulder, raised her Persian eyebrows.
It required an effort on her part to force her smile into
its habitual mould of serene disdain.

"Some . . . thing . . ." she repeated, "that means, if I
understand you correctly, that I am to invite you round
to my place, as I do here, if I still wish to, whereas all
you have to do is to join me there whenever your
school . . . and family ties permit?"

He showed surprise at the tone, but still held the eye
of Mme. Dalleray.

"Yes," he answered. "What else should I do? Do you blame me? I'm not a young gipsy, free to roam where I please. And I'm only sixteen and a half!"

The colour mounted slowly to her cheeks.

"I don't blame you for anything. But don't you imagine that any woman . . . any woman but me, that is, might well be shocked when she knew that all you wanted was one hour alone with her—that, and only that?"

Phil was listening to her with the loyal attention of a schoolboy, his eyes wide open, staring at her reticent mouth and at her jealous eyes, which, however, made no demands of him.

"No," he said, without hesitation, "I can't imagine why you should feel hurt. 'Only that?' Oh please, only that. . . ."

Then words failed him and the colour left his cheeks, confronted once again by concern for his future happiness, and Camille Dalleray's placid effrontery wavered as she computed the measure of respect she owed to her handiwork. Philippe, as though dazzled, let his head fall forward, and in her moment of triumph, she felt intoxicated by his gesture of submission.

"Do you love me?" she asked in a low voice.

He quaked and looked at her fearfully.

"Why . . . why do you ask me that?"

She recovered her self-control and, with it, her ambiguous smile.

"I was only joking, Philippe."

He did not at once stop questioning her with his

eyes, while inwardly censuring her for the temerity of her words.

'A fully developed man would have said yes in answer to my question,' she reflected. 'But if I insist, this boy will start to cry, and between his sobs and his kisses blurt out that he does not love me. Shall I insist? If I do, then I shall have to dismiss him, or perhaps sit trembling while I learn from his lips the precise limits of my influence over him.'

She felt a painful little contraction in the region of her heart and, as if oblivious of his existence, she rose and wandered aimlessly towards the open bay-window. Through it entered the smell of the small blue mussels, left stranded high and dry at the base of the rocks during the past four hours, and with it the thick heavy scent, reminiscent of an infusion of elder-bloom, that rose from the privet hedge in the last stage of its flowering.

As she leaned out with a faraway look, Mme. Dalleray was conscious of the presence of the young man lying down in the room behind her, and of the weight of a persistent little desire.

'He's waiting for me. He's calculating the amount of pleasure he can count on me giving him. What I got from him was to be had for the asking by the first passer-by. But this consciously timid, middle-class youth bridles when I ask him about his family, stands on his dignity when he speaks of his school, and immures himself behind a bastion of silence and offended modesty at the mere mention of the name

Vinca. . . . He's learnt nothing from me except the easiest. . . . Whenever he comes here, he brings with him, each time doffing and donning it with his clothes, his . . . his . . . !

She realised that she had just hesitated before the word "love", and she turned away from the window. Avidly Philippe watched her approach. She put her arms on his shoulders, and with a slightly brutal shove she forced his dark head down on to her bare arm. She hastened with her charge towards the narrow confines of the shadowy realm where she, in her pride, could interpret a moan as an avowal of weakness, and where beggars for favours of her sort drink in the illusion that they are the generous donors.

FIFTEEN

A LIGHT but persistent rain during the night had vaporised the salvias, glazed the privet and the motionless leaves of the magnolias and, without splitting the protective gauze of its covering, bedewed with tiny pearls the nest of the processionary caterpillars in one of the pines. The wind left the sea untroubled but sang under doors in a feeble, rather tentative voice, that brought back memories of the past year and mysteriously suggested ripe apples and roasting chestnuts. At its instigation, as soon as he was out of bed, Philippe put on a dark blue sweater under his linen jacket and came down last to breakfast— a frequent occurrence ever since his sleep was less pure and peaceful, and started later in the night. He hurried off in search of Vinca, as if he longed to find some sunny terrace after skirting a wall deep in shadow; but she was not in the hall, where the moist atmosphere accentuated the strong smell of varnish in the woodwork and of hemp in the hangings, and she was not to be seen on the terrace.

A fine impalpable sea-mist drifted through the air

and clung to his skin without wetting it. A yellow aspen-leaf, detached from its branch, hovered for an instant with intentional grace in front of Philippe's eyes, then tipped over and darted earthwards as if impelled by an invisible weight. He cocked one ear and listened to the winter sound of coal being shovelled on to the kitchen furnace. From another room rose a shrill protest from little Lisette that ended in a whimper.

"Lisette," he called. "Lisette, where's your sister?"

"I don't know," wailed a small voice blurred with tears.

A gust of blustery wind whipped a slate off the roof and hurled it crashing at his feet, where Philippe stared at it in stupefaction, as if before his very eyes fate had smashed to smithereens the mirror that brings seven years of bad luck. He became a small boy again, very far removed from good luck. He felt no desire to call out to the woman who, not so far away, in the pine-shadowed villa beyond the promontory shaped like a lion, would have rejoiced, none the less, at any sign of faint-heartedness on his part, or of looking for support from some source of indomitable female energy. He hunted all over the house without a glimpse of his young friend's fair head or of her frock, the blue of sea-holly, or again of her spongy cotton frock, the white of fresh mushrooms. No long brown legs with delicate dry-skinned knee-caps hastened to meet him, nor could he find a refreshing pair of blue eyes, en-enhanced by two or three shades of blue with a hint of mauve, to bring comfort to his own.

"Vinca! Where are you, Vinca?"

"Why, in here," answered a quiet voice close beside him.

"In the shed?"

"In the shed."

In the cold light peculiar to windowless outhouses where daylight enters only through the door, a crouched figure was sorting through a variety of garments spread out on a dust-sheet.

"What are you up to?"

"You can see for yourself. I'm sorting. I'm checking. We'll soon be leaving, so it's got to be done . . . mother said so."

She looked at Philippe and then squatted down, crossing her arms over her knees. He found it irritating to see her looking so poor and humble.

"There's not all that hurry! And why do you have to do it yourself?"

"Who else is there? If mother got down to it, she'd soon have a heart attack."

"But the maid could surely . . ."

Vinca shrugged her shoulders and went on with her job, talking to herself the while in a low voice, just as real work-girls keep up a humble little buzz like busy bees.

"There, that lot's Lisette's paddlers . . . the blue . . . the green . . . the striped . . . might as well throw them away and have done with it, for all the wear that's left in them. That's my frock with the pink scollops. . . . It might stand one more washing, I suppose. . . . One, two, three pair of espadrilles, all mine. . . . And this pair's Phil's. . . . Another of Phil's. . . . Two old cellular shirts of Phil's. They've gone a bit in the arm, but the fronts are still quite good. . . ."

She held up the openwork garments, discovered a couple of rents in them, and pursed her lips. Philippe was looking at her with no sign of gratitude in his pained and hostile expression. He was suffering from the grey light under the tiled roof, from seeing her so busied, and because he had left his bed too soon. He started to draw a comparison there and then, a comparison which did not originate in the love he concealed and the hours he had spent over at *Ker-Anna*, nor yet one that included Vinca; Vinca, the whole religion of his childhood, Vinca, deserted, but with all due respect, for the exciting and necessary intoxication of a first love affair.

He started making comparisons then and there, among the old garments spread over a mended sheet, between the four walls of unfaced brick, in the presence of a girl wearing a lavender overall faded on the shoulders. She was on her knees, and only interrupted her task to toss back her trimly-cut hair, kept damp and soft by the daily bathe and the salty air. Over the past fortnight she had lost something of her high spirits; she was much quieter, and her mood of stubborn equanimity was beginning to make Philippe uneasy. Had she, this young housewife with the Joan-of-Arc hair, had she really made up her mind to end her life with him rather than wait for the time when they

would be able to love freely and openly? With a
frown on his face, he stood measuring the effects of the
change that had taken place, and though his eyes were
on Vinca, his thoughts were far away. When she was
close beside him, the danger of losing her ceased to be
real, and he was no longer tormented by the urgent
desire to retrieve her. Yet it was on her account that
he had begun to make comparisons. His newly acquired
capacity for feeling, for suffering at unexpected
moments, together with a sense of intolerance be-
queathed him by a chartered libertine, flared up at the
least provocation. At the same time he felt justifiably
disloyal as, with heightened perception, he found
himself reproaching the second rate for their second-
rateness and their general attitude to life. He was
slowly discovering not only the world of emotions
which, for want of a better term, we call physical,
but also the need for some more material beauty to
clothe the obvious imperfections of the neophyte who
tended the altar at which he worshipped. He was
beginning to hanker after things gratifying to the
touch, the sight, the ear—velvets, the studied intimation of a voice, and pleasant scents. He made no bones
about it, since he knew all too well how much better he
felt when surrounded by intoxicating luxury, and how
a certain garb of oriental silk, slipped over his
shoulders in the secrecy and subdued light of *Ker-
Anna*, added to his stature and ennobled his soul.

He was tentatively groping after some vague and
generous new plan. Failing to grasp the fact that what

he really wanted was a Vinca beyond compare, well
dressed and smelling delicious, he was reduced to
trying to find out why it grieved him so to find her on
her knees, unlovely in her natural simplicity. He gave
vent to a few harsh words, to which Vinca paid no
heed. He became embittered, and she responded just
enough for him to become insulting, then ashamed
of his violence. He devoted a little time and trouble
to pulling himself together before he expressed some
sort of contrition in phrasing a lame excuse that
afforded him a fleeting pleasure. Vinca, meanwhile,
with patient hands, went on tying sandals together in
pairs and turning inside out the pockets of cast-off
jumpers full of pink shells and skeletal sea horses.

"And what's more," Philippe said in conclusion,
"it's all your fault. You never answer back. . . . So I
go on and on, working myself up and up. . . . You
let me bully you unmercifully. Why?"

She enveloped him in a look full of feminine
wisdom, that overflowed with the wiles and concessions of overweening love.

"All the time you're tormenting me," she said, "at
least I have you near me."

SIXTEEN

'THIS is where we come to an end this year,'
Philippe thought gloomily, as he gazed out to
sea. 'Vinca and I together are just sufficiently one
person to be twice as happy as either of us singly, and
this year the person who is Phil-and-Vinca is going to
die here. What a frightening thought! Is there nothing
I can do to prevent it? And here I am. ... And this evening, after ten o'clock, perhaps I shall be off once again
to *Ker-Anna*, for the last time these holidays.'

He dropped his head, and his black hair drooped,
disconsolate.

'If I had to go off there now, at this very moment,
to Mme. Dalleray's, I'd refuse to go. Why?'

Under a dismal sun, beset by two serried storm-
clouds, the road to *Ker-Anna* wound like a white
ribbon along the flank of the hill, and then disappeared among a thicket of stiff junipers, grey with
dust. Philippe turned away, struck by a repugnance
which did not deceive him. 'It's all very well. . . . But
what about to-night?'

After his third repast at *Ker-Anna*, he had given up
going there every night, from fear of rousing his

parents' suspicions and Vinca's qualms. Besides, his extreme youth made him tire of inventing alibis. He began to have his doubts, too, about the potent, clinging scent that pervaded everything in *Ker-Anna*, and most of all the body, naked or scantily clad, of her whom he had come to refer to in secret—dependent upon his alternating moods, either with the pride of a licentious schoolboy, or the stricken remorse of a husband who has deceived a beloved wife—as his mistress, and sometimes as his "master".

'Whether they find out or not, it means the end for us two. Why?'

Among all the many books he had read, propped on his elbows among the dunes or, for reasons of shyness rather than of fear, in the retirement of his own room, there was not one that had taught him that a chap must needs founder in so ordinary a shipwreck. A hundred pages or more of a novel would be taken up by the preliminaries to sexual desire, while the act itself was dismissed in a dozen lines, and Philippe searched his memory without recollecting a single story in which a young man cast off the shackles of childhood and chastity at one fell blow and did not continue to be shaken by strong, almost seismic tremors for many a long day after. . . .

He got to his feet and walked along the edge of the links, where the foreshore had been fretted and frayed by the equinoxial gales, till he came to a low gorse bush in its second flowering that grew leaning toward the beach, held and kept in position by a straggling network of roots. "When I was young," he said to himself, "this gorse bush didn't lean toward the beach. The sea has eaten away the ground between, more than three or four feet of it, while I've been growing up. Yet Vinca swears it's the gorse bush that's moved forward."

Not far from the furze bush lay the rounded hollow, carpeted with sea-holly, the hollow known as "Vinca's Eyes" because of the blue of its flowers. It was there Phil had cut a bunch of the finest plants, the prickly tribute tossed over the wall at *Ker-Anna*. . . . To-day the shrivelling flowers round the rim of the hollow looked desiccated. He stopped there for a moment, too young to smile at the mystic meaning that love lends to a dead flower, a wounded bird, a broken ring. Then, shrugging off his uneasiness and broadening his shoulders, he tossed back his hair with the traditional gesture of pride and cursed himself under his breath with a string of maledictions that would not have marred the pages of a Sunday-school adventure story.

'Come, enough of this shilly-shallying! At all events I can truthfully say, this year, that I've grown to be a man. As for what's to become of me . . .'

He caught himself thinking aloud and blushed. But then, what about his future! A month earlier he had been thinking along similar lines, but a month earlier he had envisaged a future painted in precise and childish detail against a broad vague background— his future and exams, starting his matric all over again, accepting thankless tasks not too ungrudgingly because "they have to be done, don't they"; his future and Vinca, all the former things made bearable because of her, his future cursed or blessed in the name of Vinca.

'I was hard put to it at the beginning of the hols,' he thought. 'But now!' and he gave a wry smile not unlike that of an unhappy man. Each day his upper lip was becoming more darkly shadowed, since the first fine down—which is to the moustache what a crop of spring hay is to coarse cutch-grass—had lent his mouth a slightly inflamed and swollen look, like a grief-stricken child's. It was to this mouth that Camille Dalleray's inscrutable, almost vindictive, glance would return again and again.

'But let's get back to my future! It's perfectly simple. If I don't watch out, it means my father's business—refrigerators for town and country houses, head-lamps, spare parts, motor accessories. Once I'm through my matric, then straight to the office stool—invoices, clients, correspondence. Papa just manages to scrape enough out of it to run a car. . . . Oh, I was forgetting my military service. What can I be thinking of! So let's go back and say that once I've passed . . .'

The flow of his thoughts came to a sudden stop, stemmed by an infinite boredom, by a profound indifference to no matter what a future without secrets might hold in store for him. "If your military service keeps you within easy distance of Paris, then during that time I shall . . ." At the back of his mind he could still hear the loving little voice of Vinca whispering more than a dozen plans, plans evolved during that very summer, and now lying flat and punctured, without life, substance, or colour. His rosy

hopes extended no further than the day's end, dinner-
time, and a game of chess with Vinca or Lisette—
preferably with Lisette, who, aggressively precocious
for her eight years, keen-eyed and calculating, solaced
his soulful preoccupations—till at last the moment
came for him to sally forth, a willing sacrifice to
pleasure. 'And besides,' he thought, 'it's none too
certain that I shall go. Not by a long chalk! Since I
don't behave like a love-sick loony, counting the
minutes and for ever turning my head toward *Ker-
Anna* like a sunflower to the light, I can well afford to
remain myself, and continue to take pleasure in all
that I enjoyed *before*. . . .'

He did not notice that in pronouncing the word
"before" he had firmly established it as a wedge
between the two periods of his existence. He could not
yet be sure for how long all the past events of his life
would come slap up against this stumbling-block, this
trite yet miraculous landmark. 'Ah yes, that was *before* . . .
Of course, I remember now, that was some time *after*.'

With a contempt tinged with jealousy, he thought of
his day-school pals, quaking at the knees as they
waited outside the portals of ill-fame from which they
would emerge whistling, liars and braggarts, sickened
with disgust. Then they would forget all about it,
then go back again, with no break in their work, their
games, clandestine cigars, debates on politics or sport.
'Whereas I . . . Then it can only be her fault. *She's* to
blame for the fact that I no longer desire anything any
more, not even *She* herself.'

A "blanket" of fog, coming from nowhere, enveloped the whole coastline. When over the sea it had been little more than a drifting frayed curtain, hardly thick enough to obscure a rocky islet. All of a sudden a strong stiff breeze had grappled and given it a good bracing, then deposited it pell mell, packed and opaque, over the bay. In a trice Philippe was drenched in fog, with just time enough to observe sea, beach and villa disappear, before he found himself choking in a vapour bath. Used as he was to the vagaries of the seaboard climate, he waited for the next bracing air stream to dissipate the temporary fog, and resigned himself to his limbo, to his symbolic blindness, in the depths of which gleamed a face, like a full moon, peering from windswept hair, and two idle, gestureless hands. 'She never moves. . . . But oh, let her give me back all that I've lost! The passage of time, eagerness, impatient haste, curiosity. . . . It isn't fair. . . . It isn't fair. . . . How much I grudge it her!'

He worked himself up into a state of rebellious ingratitude. No boy of sixteen and a half can realise that it is in the order of things that fair missionaries are thrown across the path of young men destinied by love to be lovers in too great haste to live and therefore impatient to die, and that the blandishments of these sirens cause time to stop, lull the spirit to sleep and rest, and bid the body ripen under their instruction.

The fog blanket suddenly lifted, drawn up into the air like a sheet being lifted from the drying-ground, and leaving behind it a momentary fringe of water on every blade of grass, a pearly dew on all the downy leaves, a wet varnish on the smooth.

The September sun cast a fresh clean yellow light over a sea blue in the distance and turning to green offshore, where sand lay beneath.

Once the sea fog had cleared, Philippe filled his lungs again as joyfully as if he had just come out from a stuffy corridor into the bright sun and air. He turned to face inland, where the gold of the gorse in its second flowering streamed down the rocky chines, and shuddered when he saw a small boy standing close behind him, like a wraith wafted by the fog and left forgotten.

"What do you want, young 'un? Aren't you the kid whose mother sells us fish at Cancale?"

"Yes," the small boy said.

"Was there no one in the kitchen? Are you looking for somebody?"

The urchin shook the dust out of his red hair.

"The lady told me . . ."

"What lady?"

"She said to me, 'Go and tell Monsieur Phil that I've gone away.'"

"What lady?"

"I don't know. She said to me 'You'll tell M. Phil that I have to go away to-day.'"

"Where did she tell you this? On the road?"

"Yes. . . . In her car."

"In her car. . . ."

Philippe shut his eyes for a moment and passed his hand over his forehead, letting out a deliberate whistle "Phe . . . ew. In her car. . . . Yes, I see. Phe . . . ew." He opened his eyes again to find his messenger no longer where he had been standing, and at once he was reminded of one of the short-lived dreams, crudely sketched, brutally effaced, that came to him during his after-lunch siestas. But he caught sight of the child of ill-tidings just as he was disappearing along the cliff path, picking him out by his carrotty thatch and the bluish patch on the seat of his pants.

Philippe threw himself into a becomingly foolish posture, as if the Cancale urchin could still see him.

'Right, and it doesn't make much odds if she has gone. One day, sooner or later—what's the difference, since she had to leave!'

But he was aware of some strange discomfort, almost entirely physical, in the pit of his stomach. He let himself give way to the pain, inclining his head thoughtfully, as if listening to mystical words of advice.

'Perhaps on a bike, I . . . But supposing she isn't alone? I never thought to ask the kid if there was anyone with her!'

Somewhere along the coast road a car hooted in the· distance. For one brief moment the prolonged blare made him forget his pain, but the next moment he felt his vitals contract, with the cramping effect of a low placed punch.

'At least I don't need to worry whether to go and see her to-night!'

Suddenly he thought of *Ker-Anna* standing barred and bolted in the moonlight—grey shutters, black

gate, imprisoned geraniums—and he shivered. He lay
down in a dry fold of the links, writhing like a
retriever puppy in the throes of distemper, and began
scratching up the sandy turf with regular movements
of his two feet. He closed his eyes, for the procession
of huge cumulus clouds with their fleecy billowing
whiteness brought on a feeling of nausea. He went on
and on digging at the sandy turf with rhythmical
kicks, in much the same way that a woman in the
pangs of childbirth rocks herself to and fro, her
groans becoming progressively louder and louder till
she gives vent to the final cry.

On opening his eyes, it took him more than a few
moments' astonishment to recover his senses. 'What's
up? What's wrong with me? I've always known she
had to leave before we did. I've got her Paris address
and her telephone number . . . so how can it affect me
if she's gone! She's my mistress, not my beloved. I
can get along without her.'

He sat upright and shelled the tall grass stalks of
their string of climbing snails so delectable to cows;
he indulged in a coarse laugh and a little ribaldry.
'So, she's quit, good! And I'll bet she's not gone off
alone, either, that piece! She was never too keen on
telling me about her little love affairs, not she! So
there we are. Alone or not alone, she's done a bunk.
And what do I lose by it? One night—to-night. One
night only before we ourselves go away. One night,
and I wasn't so sure myself that I wanted to go, a
moment since. I was thinking only of Vinca. . . . It

simply means we'll have to give up one pleasant evening, that's all!'

But some kind of cold wind blew over his spirit and swept away all his guttersnipe slang, his false confidence, his sarcasm, leaving his mind only a blank, cold surface, a clear understanding of what Camille Dalleray's departure really meant to him.

'Oh, she's gone away . . . she's gone beyond recall. The woman who gave me . . . who gave me . . . How can I express what it was she gave me? There is no name for it. She just gave. She's the only person who's given me anything since my early days when Christmas used to be so wonderful. Yes, she gave me something. She alone could take it back. She's taken it back.'

The colour mounted to his bronzed cheeks and his eyes pricked with tears. He tore open his shirt, ran the fingers of both hands through his hair, made himself look as if he had just left the ring after a gruelling round, panted, and cried aloud in a raucous, childish voice "And it's just this one more night I wanted most of all!"

Pressing his body up by the wrists, he craned his neck and gazed toward the invisible *Ker-Anna*: already the bare summit of the hill was overwhelmed by an advance mass of rain-clouds teeming in from the south; and Philippe accepted the fact that some threatening all-powerful Ifrit had expunged from the map the actual spot where he had known Camille Dalleray.

Someone coughed not so very far below him on the crumbling sandy path, where twenty times a year logs and flat stones were fitted to form rustic steps, and twenty times a year tumbled downhill to the beach. Philippe watched, on a level with his eye, a head with greying hair mount into full view; with the genius for dissimulation inherent in every child, he tidied himself up by smoothing away all the wild disorder of a man betrayed, before settling himself to wait, calm and collected, for his father to pass by.

"Ah, so here you are, young fellow!"

"Yes, Papa."

"All by yourself? Where's Vinca?"

"I don't know, Papa."

Almost without an effort, Phil was able to keep his face set in the becoming mask of an eager, sunburnt youth. His father, standing before him, looked like his father on any other day: a genial kind-hearted apparition, rather indistinct and woolly round the edges, like all other earthly creatures whose names were not Vinca, Philippe, or Camille Dalleray. Phil waited patiently for his father to recover his breath.

"Haven't you been fishing, Papa?"

"The idea! I've been for a walk. As it happens, Lequerec contrived to land an octopus. It had legs as long as my walking-stick here. Most remarkable. Lisette would have screamed had she seen it. You'd better have a care, all the same, when you're bathing."

"Oh, there's no real danger, you know!"

Too late Philippe realised that he had answered back on a note too childishly high-pitched and false. The grey, piercing eyes of his father were questioning his; and he could not tolerate for long a look that he found frank and straightforward, from eyes clear of the insolent and protective cloud behind which secret-ridden sons live in the midst of their relations.

"Are you worried by the thought of this departure, young man?"

"This departure! But Papa . . ."

"Yes, yes. If you're like me, you'll find it becomes more of a strain every year. The countryside, the villa. And then the Ferrets. . . . It's not always so easy—friends with whom one spends the summer each year—not to feel the wrench. Make the most of the time you have left, young man. Another two days of fine weather. There are thousands worse off than you."

Even while the words were still on his lips, he was drifting back among the shadows whence he had been brought into the open by an ambiguous word and a steady stare. To help him climb the disintegrating cliff, Philippe lent him an arm, with the cold, impartial attention a child condescends to bestow on a father, whenever the father is a quiet, middle-aged man, and the son a turbulent youngster, in the first flush of discovering love and its physical torments, and proud to be suffering alone in all the world, and not asking for help.

On reaching the flat, narrow terrace where the villa lay, Philippe let go his father's arm and made as if to go back down towards the beach, wishing to return to the spot chosen within the last hour as his own special corner of human solitude.

"Where are you off to, young man?"

"There, Papa . . . down there below. . . ."

"Are you in a great hurry? Come along here for a moment. I'd like to explain one or two things to you, about the villa. You know we've decided to buy it, Ferret and I, jointly? But of course you know all about it! We've been discussing it long enough in front of you children."

Phil made no answer, not daring to lie or to confess to the buzzing deafness that cut him off so completely from all family conversation.

"Come along and I'll explain. First, my idea— conjointly with Ferret—is to enlarge the villa by adding on two ground-floor wings, so that the roof will form two flat terraces for the best rooms on the first floor. Do you get the idea?"

Philippe nodded knowingly, and tried his level best to concentrate. But try as he would, he lost his bearings at the word "corbelling", and his mind slipped back down the slope to where the ill-omened little boy had said . . . 'corbelling . . . corbelling . . . I got stuck at corbelling.' Yet he kept on nodding his head and glancing, his look instinct with filial attention, from his father's face up to the Swiss chalet roof, and down from the roof to M. Audebert's hand, as it traced the new design in the air. 'Corbelling.'

"You've got the idea? That's what we shall do, Ferret and I. Or perhaps it will be you, in conjunction with the young Ferret girl. . . . For there's no telling who will be spared among us or who will die."

'Ah, I can hear once again!' Philippe gave an inward shout, turning a mental somersault at his deliverance.

"Do you find that funny? There's nothing to laugh at. You youngsters have no respect for death."

"But we do, Papa!"

'Death! A familiar word at last—one I can understand. An everyday word.'

"There seems every reason to suppose that you'll marry Vinca, later on. At least that's what your mother assures me. But then again, it's just as probable that you won't marry her. What makes you smile?"

"What you've just said, Papa."

'What you've just said, and the simplicity of all parents and grown-ups, and of those who, as they say, have lived: their ingenuousness and the disturbing purity of their minds.'

"Please note that I'm not asking for your opinion on that subject at the moment. If you were to tell me you wanted to marry Vinca, it would have much the same effect as if you declared that you did not want to marry Vinca.'

"Would it?"

"Yes. The time's not yet ripe. You're a pleasant enough lad, but . . ."

Once again the piercing grey eyes peered out from the general confusion and scanned Philippe.

". . . but you must wait. The Ferret girl won't have much more than a bean to her name. But what does that matter? For the first few years it's easy to do without silks and velvets and gold."

'Silks and velvets and gold! Oh, the velvet, the silk, and the gold, red and black and white: red, black, white.

And the cube of ice, cut like a diamond, in the glass of water. My velvet, my silk, my splendour, my mistress and my master. Oh, how can I do without such luxuries!'

"...Work....Hard times to start with....Serious.... Plenty of time to consider ... the age we live in...."

'Something's hurting me. Here, in the pit of my stomach. And I can't stand the sight of that purplish rock against the dull red of the background, black and white, now that I come to look into it more closely....'

"Family life ... pampered. ... *By Jove!* ... Having a good time. ... *Steady, young fellow, steady!*"

Voice and intermittent words were swamped in the gentle surge of incoming waters. Philippe knew nothing more, except for a slight shock to his shoulder and the tickle of dry grass against his cheek. Then the sound of several voices, like so many jagged island rocks, again broke through the pleasant, regular, booming of the water, and Philippe opened his eyes. His head was lying in his mother's lap, and all the Shades, in a circle, were bending over him with harmless expressions. A handkerchief sprinkled with lavender water touched his nostrils, and he smiled up at Vinca, as she broke through the barrier of the Shades, gold and rosy amber and crystalline blue. ...

"The poor pet!"

"Didn't I tell him he wasn't looking at all well!"

"We were both of us standing here chatting: he stood there, right in front of me—when all of a sudden—crash!"

"He's like every other boy of his age, quite incapable of looking after himself, pockets stuffed full of fruit ...."

"And now that he's begun to smoke. . . . Do you suppose those first cigarettes count for nothing."

"My poor darling. His eyes are filled with tears."

"Of course. It's the natural reaction."

"What's more, it can't have lasted more than thirty seconds—just the time it took to call you all here. As I was saying, here we were chatting together, and then . . ."

Phil got on to his feet, light-headed, his cheeks cold.

"Now do stay where you are. Don't try to walk!"

"Lean on my arm, young man."

But, with an expressionless smile, he took Vinca's hand.

"It's all over. Thanks, Mother. It's all over now."

"Wouldn't it be best if you went to lie down?"

"Oh, no. I'd much rather stay out of doors."

"Do look at Vinca's face, I ask you! Your Phil's not dead yet! Go along, take him with you. But stay on the terrace as long as you can."

The Shades drifted away, friendly hands and words of encouragement rising from the slow-moving throng; one last flashing smile from his mother and he was left alone with Vinca, who was not smiling. He attempted, with a tilt of the lips and a reassuring nod, to induce a gayer mood, but she shook her head to this without ever taking her eyes off him, staring at the greenish tint that had spread over his tan, at his black eyes with a touch of red in them from the sun, and at his lips parted over small closely set teeth. "How handsome you are, and how miserable am I!" Vinca's blue eyes seemed to say. . . . But he could read no pity there, and she let him hold her hand, hardened by tennis and fishing, as if she were offering him the handle of a walking-stick.

"Come along," Philippe urged her in a low voice. "I'll explain everything. It's nothing, really. But let's go to some quiet spot."

She went along, and together they chose as their secret chamber a flat slab of rock only occasionally washed over by the highest tide, which left behind it a coarse-grained sand, quickly dried. Neither of them ever dreamed of exchanging confidences behind light cretonne curtains or between pitch-pine partitions, resonant as a musical instrument in that they carried from room to room, at night, the news that one of the inmates of the villa had switched off a light, or coughed, or dropped a key. There was enough of the primitive savage in both these Paris-born children to make them shun the pitfalls of human habitation and seek out some nook—in the middle of an open field, the edge of a rocky fastness, the hollow of a wave—and there conduct their lovers' tiffs and idylls in security.

"It's four o'clock," said Phil, consulting the sun. "Wouldn't you like me to fetch you your tea before we settle down?"

"I'm not hungry," Vinca answered. "But wouldn't you like something?"

"No thanks. My little dizzy spell has taken away my appetite. You sit down there in the middle, it's better for me to be near the edge."

They spoke simply, each knowing they were about to embark on a serious conversation, or on an equally revealing period of silence.

Vinca's smooth brown legs, crossed under the hem of her white frock, gleamed in the rays of the September sun. Far below them, a harmless ground-swell, soothed and smoothed by the passing of the heavy fog patch, was beginning to dance and by degrees be decked out in its clear weather finery. Gulls cried overhead, and a string of fishing-smacks hove into sight, sail following sail from behind the shadow of the Meinga to gain the open sea. A shrill, tremulous, childish lilt was borne down past them on the breeze; Philippe turned round, shivered, and a kind of querulous moan escaped him. At the tip-top of the highest cliff, in faded blue crowned with red hair a little boy. . . .

"Yes," Vinca said, following his gaze, "that's the little boy."

Phil recovered himself in time to say, "You're referring, I suppose, to the fisherwoman's little boy?"

Vinca shook her head. "The little boy," she said, correcting him, "who came to speak to you just now."

"Who came to . . ."

"The little boy who came to tell you the lady has has gone away."

Philippe was seized with a sudden loathing for the dazzling sun, the hard sand so uncomfortable under his body, the breeze burning his cheeks.

"Who . . . what are you talking about, Vinca?"

She disdained to answer, and went on, "The little boy was looking for you and gave me the message first. So you see . . ."

She let the sentence peter out on a fatalistic gesture. With something approaching a feeling of comfort, Phil took a deep breath.

"Oh, so you knew, then. . . . What did you know?"

"Certain things about you. . . . Not for very long, though. What I knew I learnt all at once, about . . . about three or four days ago, but I can't be sure. . . ."

She broke off and Philippe noticed, where the curve of her fresh childish cheeks began, immediately under the blue of her eyes, the mother-of-pearl traces of sleepless nights spent in tears, the satiny moonshine shadow that is seen only on the eyelids of women constrained to suffer in silence.

"Right," he said. "Now we can talk, unless you'd rather not talk. I'll do whatever you wish."

She repressed a tiny quiver at the corners of her mouth, but no tears flowed.

"No, let's talk. I think it's best."

From the very first words of their conversation, they both felt an identical bitter satisfaction at having overridden the common ground of altercation and fib-telling. Only heroes, actors, and children can perform the feat of feeling at ease on an exalted plane. These two children fondly believed that a noble grief could be born of their love.

"Listen, Vinca, the day I first met her . . ."

"No, no," she broke in precipitately, "not that!

I beg of you, not that! I know all about it. Down there, on the sea-wrack road. Do you imagine I've forgotten it?"

"But," Philippe protested, "there was nothing that day either to remember or forget, since . . ."

"Stop! Stop, can't you! Do you think I brought you here so that you could talk about her?"

From the sharp simplicity of Vinca's tone, he knew his own accents of a moment since must have lacked all semblance of contrition.

"To tell me the whole story of your love affair, that's what you want, isn't it? Don't bother. When you came back to the house last Wednesday, I was out of bed, but hadn't switched on my lamp. . . . I saw you . . . like a thief. . . . It was almost daylight. And what a look you had on your face! I got all the information I wanted then, I can tell you! Do you suppose what goes on along the coast isn't known to everyone? It's only parents who know nothing."

Philippe was shocked, and showed it in a frown. He was offended by the fundamental feminine brutality roused in Vinca by jealousy. He had felt ready, when climbing up to their hanging refuge, for a few half-confidences, a few tears, more than ready, indeed, for a lengthy confession. But he would not support this wanton flaying alive, this expeditious savagery which was destroying his idea of picturesquely flattering slow stages, and was leading to . . . to what, in fact? 'I can only suppose she wants to do away with herself,' he said to himself. 'She wanted to die here at this very

spot one day not so long ago. . . . She's going to wish
to die now. . . .'

"Vinca, you must promise me . . ."

She turned to listen without looking at him, and in
this slight movement the whole of her body expressed
a wealth of ironic independence.

"Yes, Vinca. You must promise me that you'll
never try, either here on this rock or anywhere else in
the world . . . never try to . . . do away with yourself."

She dazzled him with a flash of blue, staring at him
with wide-open eyes.

"What's that you said? Do away with myself?"

He put his hands on her shoulders and gave her a
nod heavy with experience.

"I know you, darling. Six weeks ago, at this very
spot, for no known reason you wanted to let yourself
slide down over the edge, and now . . ."

All the while he was speaking, her eyebrows rose
in a heightened arc of utter stupefaction. With a twist
of her shoulders she jerked off Philippe's hands.

"Now? . . . Kill myself? . . . Why?"

The last word had made him blush, and she took his
blush for an answer.

"Because of her?" she shouted. "You must be mad!"

Phil tore scraps of the meagre grass in his frustration, and quite suddenly looked four or five years
younger.

"One would have to be a raving lunatic to try to
find what a woman wants, or to imagine that she knows
herself!"

"But I do know, Phil. I know very well. And I also know what I don't want. You may rest assured I shan't kill myself on that woman's account. Six weeks ago . . . Yes, I did let myself slip over the edge there, and I dragged you with me. But that time it was for your sake I wanted to die, and for my own . . . for my own. . . ."

She shut her eyes and threw back her head, letting her voice linger on the last phrase, and, thus, she bore a strange resemblance to all women who throw back their heads and close their eyes in an excess of felicity. For the first time Philippe recognised in Vinca a close kinship to her who, with eyes shut and head relaxed, appeared to separate herself from him at the very moments he was holding her closest.

"Vinca! Stop that at once! Vinca!"

She opened her eyes again and sat bolt upright.

"What?"

"Why, don't carry on like that! You look as if you're going to faint."

"No, I'm not going to faint. You're the one that needs smelling-salts and eau-de-Cologne and all the rest of the bag of tricks!"

From time to time, mercifully, a childish ferocity crept between them. They drew fresh strength from it, becoming steeped once more in anachronistic clearsightedness, before plunging headlong back into the follies of their elders.

"I'm off," Philippe said. "You're making me feel wretched."

Vinca gave a laugh, the unpleasant staccato laugh of almost any woman wounded in her pride.

"That's rich! So now you're the one who's made to feel wretched, are you?"

"You bet I am!"

She uttered a piercing cry like an irritated bird, so unexpected that Philippe was startled.

"What's wrong?"

She was supporting her body on her outspread hands, crouching like an animal, almost on all fours. He saw that she had suddenly become purple with rage, frantic. The two flaps of her hair were almost touching as she leaned forward, leaving a clear glimpse only of parched red lips, a short nose dilated by the fury of her breathing, and eyes burning with the blue of a flame.

"Shut up, Phil! Shut up, or I shall hurt you! You dare to say that you are to be pitied, to say that you are wretched, when it's you who deceived me, you, a liar, who deserted me for another woman! You've no shame, no sense, no pity! You brought me here to tell me what you've been doing with another woman. Deny it! Deny it! Deny it if you can!"

She was shrieking on the full flood of her feminine fury, in her element, like a petrel in the teeth of a storm. She collapsed in a heap, but her groping hands happened upon a fragment rock and this she hurled far out to sea with a strength that astounded Philippe.

"Now be quiet, Vinca!"

"No! I won't! First, we're all by ourselves, and

then I want to scream! I've got something to scream
about, too, I can tell you! You've brought me up here
because you want to tell me, to go back over the whole
story of what you did with her, for the pleasure of
listening to yourself, of hearing your own words . . .
of speaking of her, and saying her name, eh! her
name, perhaps . . ."

Suddenly she struck his face a blow so unexpected
and so tomboyish, that he only just stopped himself
setting about her and giving her a sound hiding. What
held him back were the words she had shouted at the
pitch of her voice, while his innate sense of masculine
decency recoiled before the extent of her knowledge
and her brazen use of it.

'She thinks, she really believes it would give me
pleasure to tell her. . . . Oh! . . . and it's Vinca, Vinca
who's got these ideas in her head!'

She did stop for a moment, speechless and coughing,
scarlet from face to bosom. Two small tears brimmed
and fell from her eyes, but she had not yet reached the
soothing stage of silent crying. 'So I've never known
what thoughts were in her mind,' Philippe mused.
'Every word she's said is as great a surprise to me as
the strength I've so often noticed when swimming or
jumping or when she throws a stone!'

He kept a wary eye on Vinca's movements, feeling
none too sure of her. The bright colour of her skin and
eyes, the precise outline of her slender figure, the hem
of her white frock stretched over her long legs, helped
to relegate to some remote sphere the almost sweet

suffering that had stretched him, prone, on the grass.

Profiting by the momentary lull, he wished to show proof of his superior self-control.

"I didn't strike you, Vinca. But your words asked for it even more than what you did. But I had no wish to hit you. It would have been the first time I'd ever let myself go to that extent."

"Of course," she broke in hoarsely. "You'd hit anyone rather than me. I never come first in anything."

He felt reassured by her all-devouring jealousy and able to smile, but her vindictive expression warned him that it was no time for joking. They both remained silent, watching the sun set beyond the Meinga and the splashes of rosy pink, like in-curving petals, that danced on the crest of every wave.

From the cliff-top came the tinkling of cow-bells, and at the point where the ill-omened urchin had passed singing out of sight, a black goat showed its horned head and bleated.

"Vinca, darling," Philippe sighed.

She looked at him indignantly.

"Do you dare to call me that?"

He bent his head. "Vinca, darling," he sighed.

She bit her lip, rallying her strength against the assault of tears she knew to be on their way, since they brought a lump to her throat and swelled her eyes, and did not dare to risk a word. Philippe's neck was supported by the rock patched with a short-napped purple moss, and he was staring out to sea, without, perhaps, seeing it. Because he was tired, because the weather was lovely, because the evening hour, its scents and melancholy, made it imperative, he sighed "Vinca, darling," as he would have sighed "Oh, how happy I am!" or else "How miserable I feel!" In his present despondent mood, he found utterance in the oldest words of all, the first that came to his lips; just as the war-scarred veteran, grievously wounded, moans in his agony the name of a mother long since forgotten.

"Shut up, you fiend, shut up! What have you done to me, oh, what have you done to me!"

She showed him her face streaming with tears that left no trace on the velvety cheeks. The sunlight played on her brimming eyes and enhanced the deeper blue of their pupils. The upper part of her face shone with all the attributes of a woman in love, hurt past endurance, yet magnificent enough to forgive everything; while her trembling mouth and chin, not uncomic in their quaint grimace, were those of a desperately unhappy little girl.

Without lifting his head from its stony pillow, Philippe turned to look at Vinca, his dark eyes softened by their languishing appeal. Anger had brought out from her overheated body the smell peculiar to all fair-haired women, so curiously akin to that of the pink flower of the restharrow or to crushed green corn, acrid and pungent, and it completed the impression of vigour imposed on Philippe by every gesture she made. Yet there she sat in tears, stammering "What have you done to me?", and gnawing a hand on which he could see the mauve semicircular mark left by her young teeth.

"Little savage!" he whispered, with the caressing inflection he might have used to a woman he did not know.

"More so than you'd think," she answered in similar vein.

"Don't say such things!" Philippe shouted. "Your least word sounds like a threat."

"Before, you would have said 'like a promise'."

"They're one and the same," he protested vehemently.

"Why?"

"Because they are."

He nibbled a blade of grass, determined on prudence, incapable, as it happened, of putting into precise words his cloudy claim to think what he liked, his right to speak the polite and refreshing lie, which his youth and the expansive excitement of his first affair made him long to assert.

"I'm wondering how you're going to treat me, Phil, later on?"

She seemed dismayed, bereft of argument; but Philippe knew her powers of recovery and how speedily, as if by magic, she rallied her strength.

"Then stop wondering," he begged, shortly.

'Later on . . . later on. . . . Even the future is under distraint. She's got a nerve; fancy being able to think how the future's going to pan out, at a moment such as this! It's her mania for tying things up that makes her talk like this. She's miles away from any idea of wanting to die!'

In his peevishness, he misinterpreted the will-to-survive vested in the female of every species, and the imperious instinct to wallow in calamity while at the same time working it like a mine rich in precious ore. Abetted by the evening hour and his own fatigue, he felt exasperated by this combative chit, battling as she was in her primitive way for the preservation of their united future. He tore his thoughts forcibly away from her presence, and let them rush off in pursuit of a car as it disappeared behind its cloud of dust and, catching up with it, he gazed like a roadside beggar through the window behind which lolled a head turbaned in white veils. . . . Once more he looked closely at every detail—the darkened lashes, the small black mole close to the lip, the close-set, sensitive nostrils—traits that he had observed only at close range, oh, so very close! Distraught, terrified, he leapt to his feet, filled with the fear of suffering and with surprise at his discovery that while talking with Vinca he had ceased to suffer. . . .

"Vinca!"

"What's the matter?"

"I . . . I think I'm going to faint!"

An irresistible arm seized hold of his and forced him down on to the safest spot, for he had been swaying on the edge of their perilous escarpment. Knocked out, he had no fight left in him, and said only "Perhaps it would be the easiest way out after all. . "

"Hush, hush, oh hush!"

She sought for no further words after this trite cry. She cradled his enfeebled body against her own and cuddled his dark head against breasts newly rounding out with fuller softer flesh. Philippe relapsed into his recently formed habit of passive lack of resistance acquired in the embrace of another, whose readily accessible bosom and clinging scent he sought in vain; yet in his almost unbearable frustration he still was able to murmur "Vinca darling . . . Vinca darling. . . ."

She took to rocking him to and fro, knees pressed together and arms folded, swaying with the motion known to every female creature the world over. She cursed him for being so wretched and so spoilt. She longed for him to lose consciousness and forget, in his delirium, a certain woman's name.   Inwardly she murmured "There, there now . . . you'll learn to understand me . . . I'll see that you do," while outwardly she removed from his forehead a stray black hair, the vein in the marble. She enjoyed testing the weight and the new feel of a young man's body which the day before, running and laughing, she had carried pick-a-back. When Philippe opened his eyes and sought hers, begging her to give him back all that he had lost, she struck the sand beside her with her free hand and cried out in her heart of hearts "Why, oh why were you born!" like the heroine in an eternal triangle.

And all the while she kept an eagle eye on the house and its immediate surroundings; like a mariner she gauged the time by the setting sun, "It's after six,";

her roving glance lit on Lisette, like a white pigeon in her fluttering frock, as she made her way back from beach to villa. And she thought 'We mustn't stay here longer than another quarter of an hour or they'll be coming to look for us. Then I must bathe my eyes properly . . .', before she started to re-assemble body and soul, love, jealousy, slow-cooling anger, sorting them out in the inner recesses a mind as primordial and rugged as their nest among the rocks.

"Get up," she said in a low voice.

Philippe mumbled a protest and his body grew heavier. She guessed he was grumbling, and making the most of his inertia, to stave off her questions and reproaches. She shook his neck and supine warm body with arms that had been dandling him with a mother's care, and her charge, once freed of her embrace, turned back into the youth who had lied to her, the unknown stranger, capable of betraying her now that he had been smoothed and polished by a woman's hands.

'If I could only tether him, like that black goat, at the end of a couple of yards of rope . . . or shut him up in a room somewhere, my room . . . or live in a land where I was the only woman. Or better, if I were only beautiful, really beautiful . . . or else, that he were just ill enough for me to have to look after him!' The drifting shadows of her thoughts flitted across her face.

"What are you going to do?" Philippe asked.

Snatched back from her day-dreaming, she gazed at features which one day, doubtless, would be those of a handsome enough dark-haired man, but would remain, for his seventeenth year and a little time after, just this side of manhood. She was amazed that no terrifying or revealing mark disfigured the smooth chin or the nose so quick to show anger. . . . 'Oh, but his eyes. His too gentle brown eyes, with their whites a pale blue! Now I know that a woman has admired herself in them!' and she tossed her head.

"What am I going to do! Get myself ready for dinner. And so are you."

"And is that all?"

Now on her feet, she pulled down her frock under the silk elastic belt, keeping a wary eye on Philippe, the villa, and the sea, that lay grey and cold, ready for sleep, refusing to participate in the glory of the sunset.

"That's all . . . unless you go and do something. . . ."

"Depends on what you mean by something."

"Oh well . . . disappear, dash off to find that woman again . . . make up your mind that she's the one you love. And announce the fact to your parents."

She spoke in chilling childlike tones, tugging at her dress as if she wished to eliminate her breasts.

'She's got breasts like clinging limpets, or like those little conical hills in Japanese prints,' and he blushed because, in his thoughts, he had enunciated so distinctly the word 'breasts', and accused himself of lack of respect.

"I shall do nothing of the sort, Vinca!" he blurted out. "But I'd very much like to know how you'd take it, if I were capable of doing even the half of what you suggest!"

She looked at him open-eyed, but there was no

answer he could read in eyes that were all the bluer for the tears they had shed.

"Me! It wouldn't make me change my way of life in the slightest."

She flung the lie in his teeth, but behind the glaring falsehood in her eyes he came upon the tenacious, restless, unscrupulous constancy that upholds a woman in love and binds her fast to life and her lover, when once she discovers that she has a rival.

"You're making yourself out to be more level-headed than you really are, Vinca."

"And you're making too much of yourself. Weren't you saying just now that you thought I'd wanted to do away with myself? Die, because my lord has had an affair?"

She pointed at him with her open hand as children do after a squabble.

"An affair!" Philippe repeated, hurt and at the same time flattered. "Good Lord, all the boys of my age . . ."

"Then I suppose I must get used to the fact," she interrupted him, "that you differ in no way from 'all the boys' of your age."

"Vinca darling, I swear that a girl like you can't speak . . . oughtn't to listen to . . ." He lowered his eyes priggishly and bit his lip before adding, "You must believe me."

He held out a hand to help Vinca leap across the bench-long schistous slabs outside the entrance to their shelter and then over the low whin bushes before they reached the coast guard's path. Three hundred yards

ahead they could see Lisette, twirling like a white
convolvulus on the links as her midget brown arms
signalled to them, semaphoring "Come on quick,
you're late!" Vinca waved back in answer, but
again turned to Philippe before starting on her way
down.

"Phil, it's simply that I can't believe you. Otherwise
the whole of our life up to now has been simply one of
those mawkish little tales we've read in books we don't
much care for. You speak of 'A young man, a girl . . .',
when it's ourselves we're discussing. You said to me
'An affair like all the boys of my age . . .'; but, Phil,
you're making a big mistake, all the same. You see,
I'm talking quite quietly."

He listened to her, a little impatient and perplexed,
for at the moment he was finding it hard to recollect
all the whips and scorpions of his horrid torment, and
found it even harder when he noticed the look of
extreme embarrassment behind her bold exterior, and
when, to add to his difficulties, the evening breeze
sprang up with spiteful malevolence.

"Well! What else?"

"You're making a big mistake, all the same, Phil,
because it's me you ought to have asked. . . ."

He wanted no more, weary, longing to be alone,
yet full of apprehension at the thought of the
long night ahead. She had made allowances for his
crying out, or being indignant, or else being heartily
ashamed of his questionable behaviour: he measured
her up from toe to top through half-closed eyes

and said, "Poor little mite! It's all very well to say 'asked'; but what can you give in return?"

He saw that she was reduced to offended silence, and watched her quick blood mount in a dark flush to her cheeks and then spread down under the sun-burnt skin of her neck and throat. He put his arm round her shoulders and walked pressed close against her along the path.

"Vinca darling, you must see what nonsense you're talking. The nonsense of an ignorant girl, thank God!"

"Thank Him for something else, Phil. Don't you realise I know as much as the first woman He created?"

She did not draw away from him but, without turning her head, looked at him sideways, then down at the path ahead, and then again at Philippe, whose attention was riveted on the angle of her eye which, as the pupil shifted, showed alternate white and peri-winkle blue, like the nacreous lining of a shell.

"Tell me, Phil. Don't you believe I know as much as . . ."

"Hush, Vinca. You do not know. You don't know anything."

At the bend in the path they came to a halt. All the azure in the sea had drained into a solid grey metal almost without a ripple on it, while across the horizon the setting sun had left a lengthy streak of discouraging red and above it a pale green zone lighter than the dawn, where the moist evening star glimmered feebly. Philippe tightened his grasp round Vinca's shoulders and with his other arm pointed to the sea.

"Hush, Vinca. You know nothing. It's so . . . It's such a secret. So big!"

"I'm big."

"No. You don't understand what I'm trying to tell you."

"But I do, perfectly. You're behaving like that young Jallon boy who sings in the choir on Sundays. He tries to make himself sound important by saying, 'Oh, Latin! Well, you know, Latin's jolly difficult'; but he doesn't know a word of Latin."

She gave a sudden laugh, raising her head, and Philippe did not like the way, so quickly and so naturally, she shifted from tears to laughter, from dismay to irony. Perhaps because night was falling, he began to assert his claim to a calm haven fraught with smouldering sensual desires, and a silence during which the blood drumming in his ears was like torrential rain; he yearned for the latent fears, the speech-depriving, peril-infested period of subjugation, that made him crouch outside portals which other youths of his age entered reeling and blaspheming.

"Be quiet, do. Don't make it sound coarse and cheap. Once you do know . . ."

"But I'm only asking to be told."

She spoke the first words that came into her head and giggled like an inexpert actress trying to cover up 'the butterflies'; also because she felt as miserable as all children scorned, who are ready to risk untold hardships on the chance that by suffering a little more, then more still, then still a little more, they will get what they want in the end.

"Vinca, please! You're making me very uncomfortable. That sort of talk is so unlike you."

He removed his arm from her shoulder and continued on down the path at a faster pace. She kept up with him, avoiding, where the path narrowed, the spiky tufts already wet with dew by jumping over them; as she went along she moulded her features in readiness to face the Shades, all the while repeating in an undertone that Philippe could hear, "So unlike me? . . . So unlike me? . . . That's one thing that you, Phil, with all your knowledge, do not know."

Throughout dinner they both behaved in a manner that did credit to themselves and their secrets Philippe laughed off his "vapours", required fussing over, and drew attention to himself in his fear that remarks might be passed on Vinca's blazing eyes, red and bruised round the rims, which she did her best to shade under the silky thatch, cut in a thick fringe above her eyebrows. She, for her part, acted the child; she demanded champagne as soon as the soup was on the table— "to put Phil on his feet again, Maman"—and emptied her glass at one draft.

"Vinca!" scolded a Shade.

"Let her be," from another indulgent Shade, "What harm can it do her?"

As the meal drew to an end, Vinca noticed Philippe's

gaze wander out over the night sea in search of the invisible Meinga, the white road swallowed up by the darkness, the junipers petrified beneath the dust of that road.

"Lisette!" she cried. "Give Phil a hard pinch, he's falling asleep!"

"She's drawn blood!" Philippe groaned. "The little pest, she's brought tears to my eyes!"

"It's true, it's true," Vinca shrieked. "She's brought tears to your eyes."

She laughed as he began to rub his arm under his white flannel shirt; but on her cheeks and in her eyes he noticed the effect of the sparkling wine and a kind of controlled craziness that he found far from reassuring.

A few moments later a far away fog-horn bellowed across the pitch black swell, and one or other among the Shades stopped shuffling, on the games table, the star-incised surfaces of the dominoes.

"Fog at sea. . . ."

"The beam of the Granville lighthouse was sweeping over a sea of cotton-wool a few moments ago," said another Shade.

But to Philippe the blast of the fog-horn evoked the prolonged blare of a hooting car as it sped away along the coast road, and he leapt to his feet.

"It's coming on again," Vinca mocked.

Adept at self-concealment, she had turned her back to the Shades, and her gaze followed Philippe like a lamentation.

"Nothing of the sort," he said. "But I'm feeling dead tired, so if you'll excuse me, I think I'll go up to

bed. Good night, Maman, good night, Father. . . .
Good night, Madame Ferret. . . . Good night . . ."

"We'll let you off the rest of your litany for to-night,
my boy."

"Would you like a cup of weak camomile tea
brought up to you?"

"Don't forget to open your window wide."

"Vinca, did you take your bottle of salts to Phil's
room?"

The friendly voices of the Shades followed him as
far as the door, a rather faded tutelary wreath of faint-
scented dried herbs. He exchanged with Vinca the
customary good-night kiss, which as a rule glanced
off her proffered cheek toward the ear, and ended up
on her neck or the corner of her downy mouth. Then
the door closed behind him, the propitiating garland
was severed, and he found himself alone.

His room, agape to the moonless sky, accorded him
a cold welcome. Hostile and none too strong, he stood
beneath the bulb, bagged in yellow muslin, sniffing
the smell Vinca called "boy's smell": school books,
leather case packed and ready for the day after the
next, bitumen from rubber-soled shoes, cakes of
toilet soap and scented hair oil.

He was not suffering particularly; but he felt exiled
and utterly exhausted, for which the best remedy is
total oblivion. He hurried into bed, put out the lamp,
and snuggled down instinctively into the place against
the wall where, during nights of childhood illnesses
and the later fevers of youth, he had found better cover

and protection when the sheet was amply tucked in, and watched the action of his dreams, affected by the moon, high tides, or July thunderstorms, unfold across the flower-patterned paper. He went to sleep at once, only to be assailed by all the usual bad dreams and others most vividly revolting. In one, Camille Dalleray had Vinca's head and face; in another, a crudely improper Vinca held authoritative sway over him with all the cold aloofness of a magician. But in these dreams, Camille Dalleray and Vinca both refused to remember that Philippe was only a young and tender little boy, who longed for nothing better than to nestle his head against a shoulder—a little boy of ten years old. . . .

He woke to find by his watch that it was only a quarter to twelve, and so he would have to squander the remainder of his feverish night in the midst of a sleeping household; he slipped on his sandals, tied the cord of his bath gown tight round his waist, and went downstairs.

The moon, in the first quarter, was a burnished sickle rising over the top of the cliff. It shed no light over the landscape and appeared to be extinguished at every turn—now red, now green—of the revolving Granville lighthouse. Yet, because of its presence, the clumps of foliage were not totally submerged by the night and the white pebble-dashed walls looked faintly phosphorescent between the projecting wooden beams of the villa. Leaving the french windows open, Philippe stepped out into the mild night as into a melancholy but sure refuge. He sat down on the bare damp-resisting earth of the terrace, crammed with the accumulated refuse of sixteen summer holidays, from which Lisette's spade occasionally exhumed an oxidised fragment of some antique toy that had lain there buried for ten, twelve, or fifteen years. . . .

He felt disconsolate, worldly wise, outside the pale. 'Perhaps it's all part of becoming a man,' he thought. He was worried, and to no purpose, by the unconscious need to find someone to whom he could confide his sadness and his worldly wisdom, like all honest little atheists for whom a secular education provides no all-seeing God.

"Is that you, Phil?"

The voice came down to him like a leaf on the wind. He got up and walked noiselessly across to the window with a wooden balcony.

"Yes," he breathed. "Aren't you asleep?"

"Obviously not. I'm coming down."

Before he had heard a sound, she was standing close beside him. All he had seen of her approach was a whitish face suspended above a silhouette that seemed part and parcel of the night itself.

"Won't you feel cold?"

"No. I've put on my blue kimono. Besides it's mild enough. Don't let's stay here."

"Why weren't you asleep?"

"I didn't feel sleepy. I was thinking. Don't let's stay here. We shall wake someone up."

"I don't want to go down to the beach at this time of night, you'll catch cold."

"I'm not in the habit of catching cold. But it wasn't

my idea to go down to the beach, you know. I'd rather go for a short stroll up the hill."

She spoke in a voice that was hard to catch, yet Philippe never missed a single word. It's toneless quality afforded him infinite pleasure. It was no longer Vinca's voice, or any woman's for that matter, but simply a little presence, almost invisible, with something familiar about it; a little presence, devoid of all bitterness, suggestive of a stroll in the still watches of the night . . .

His foot struck against some object and she put out a hand to steady him.

"It's sure to be the geranium pots, didn't you see them?"

"No."

"Neither did I. But I see them as the blind do, I know that they are there. . . . Take care that there isn't a trowel lying somewhere beside them."

"How do you know that?"

"Oh, just an idea I've got it should be there. And it would make a noise like the clatter of a coal shovel. . . . There, what did I tell you!"

Philippe was entranced by this naughty little whispering. He could have wept with relief and pleasure at finding Vinca so sweet and, among the shadows, just like the Vinca of the old days when she was only twelve and used to whisper in the same way, bending over the wet sand, with the full moon dancing on the bellies of the fish during their midnight netting escapades.

"You remember, Vinca, the time we went fishing at midnight with the big square dipping-net?"

"And you caught bronchitis. That proved a splendid excuse for putting a stop to our fishing at night. . . . Listen! . . . Did you close the french windows?"

"No. . . ."

"The wind's freshening, don't you hear, and they're beginning to rattle? Oh, if I didn't think of everything . . ."

She disappeared and returned like a sylph on feet so light that Phil only guessed her approach from the scent wafted on the wind ahead of her.

"What on earth's that scent you've got on, Vinca? How strong you smell of it!"

"Don't speak so loud. I was feeling so hot that I gave myself a spirit rub before coming down."

He made no further comment, but now that his attention was awakened he did indeed register that she thought of everything.

"Go on through, Phil. I'm holding the gate open. Try not to tread on the salads."

The proximity of the sea could easily be forgotten among all the market garden aromas that rose from the cultivated soil. Philippe rasped his bare legs on a low wall of dense thyme and in passing let his fingers brush along the velvety muzzles of the snapdragons.

"You know, Vinca, that in the kitchen garden one can't hear a sound that may come from the house, because of this clump of bushes!"

"But no sound is coming from the house, Phil. And besides, we're doing no harm."

She had picked up a little windfall pear that had

ripened prematurely and smelt of musk from the insect inside it.

He heard her bite into it and then throw it away.

"What are you up to? You're eating something?"

"It's only one of those yellow pears. But it wasn't good enough to let you have it."

Philippe's vague resentment was not to be broken down altogether by her exceptional lack of restraint. He found Vinca a little too sweet, airy and serene as a sylph, and he suddenly thought of the laughter of nuns and how through its maddening genteel affectedness there rings a mirthless gaiety that might have escaped from the tomb. 'I'd very much like to see her face,' he said to himself. And he shivered to think that the toneless voice and the playful girlish words might have issued from the convulsed mask, its own colours heightened and shining with rage, when confronting his in their nest among the rocks.

"Vinca, listen! Let's go back in."

"If you wish. Just one moment more. Let me have one moment more. I'm so happy. What about you? We're both so happy. How easy life is at night! But not indoors. Oh, how I've come to loathe my room these last few days. Out here, I have no fears. . . . A glow-worm, look! So late in the season! No, don't try to catch it. . . . Silly, why are you trembling so? It's only a cat out on the prowl. At night they hunt field-mice."

He caught the sound of a little laugh, and Vinca's arm tightened round his waist. His ear was attuned to the slightest breath, the least snap of a twig, held

entranced, despite his uneasiness, by the variety of
unceasing whisperings. Far from being frightened of
the dark, Vinca threaded her way through it as through
a familiar and well-loved landscape, explaining it all to
Philippe as she guided him like a blind guest for whom
she was performing the midnight honours.

"Vinca darling, let's go back."

She gave a little toad-like croak.

"Oh, you've called me Vinca darling! Why can't it
always be night? At this particular moment you're no
longer the person who deceived me, and I'm not the
person who has suffered so much. Oh, Phil, don't let's
go back to the house just yet, let me be a little happy, a
little loving, as certain of you as I was in my dreams.
Phil . . . Phil, you don't know me."

"Perhaps I don't, Vinca darling."

They stumbled over some sort of coarse hay that
crackled under their footsteps.

"It's the threshed buckwheat," Vinca said. "They
were threshing it by flail to-day."

"How do you know?"

"All the time we were having our heated argument,
didn't you hear the thuds of the two flails? I heard
them. Sit down, Phil."

'She . . . she heard them. . . . She was frantic, she struck
my face, she never drew breath as the words kept pouring out—yet she heard the thudding of the two flails!'

He could not help comparing this awareness of all
her feminine senses with his memory of a certain other
feminine skill. . . .

"Don't go away and leave me, Phil! I've not been naughty; I've not cried, I've not scolded. . . ."

Her round head, with its evenly-cut silken hair, rolled on to his shoulder, and the warmth of her cheek brought warmth to his.

"Kiss me, Phil, please. Please. . . ."

He kissed her, blending with his own pleasure the inept clumsiness of extreme youth that looks no further than the gratification of its own desires, and the all too precise memory of a kiss that other lips had taken from his, but not for the asking. But pressed to his lips he felt the form and shape of Vinca's mouth, still tasting of the fruit she had just bitten into, felt the haste of her lips to open and discover their secret that they might squander its sweetness on his—and he swayed in the darkness. 'I really believe that we are lost,' he thought. 'Oh, that it may happen quickly, since it must, and since she now could never wish for it to be otherwise. Oh God, how wonderful and inevitable her mouth is, and so understanding since the first time our lips met! Oh, let it happen quickly, quickly. . . .'

But possession is a miracle not so speedily accomplished. His neck was held in a tight embrace by an arm that would not let go its hold. He tried to shake it free, but Vinca only tightened her grip, thinking Philippe must wish to end their kiss. At length he seized the stiffened wrist close to his ear and flung her backwards on to the bed of straw. She gave a little moan and did not move again; but when, half ashamed, he leaned over her body, she caught hold of him again and held him close. There they lay, like brother and sister, enjoying a pleasant interlude, each showing the other a little pity and affection with the discretion of experienced lovers. On one arm Philippe held Vinca, invisible, lying on her back, and with his free hand stroked her skin, already aware of its delicacy and of every mark scratched or incised upon it by the prick of a thorn or the sharp point of a rock. She tried to laugh as she begged him in a whisper, "Do leave my beautiful grazes alone.... What do you want with those, when we have this lovely soft straw to lie on. . . ."

But he could hear her breath trembling in her words, and trembled himself. Again and again he returned to her mouth, the one thing about her he knew least of all. He resolved, during a respite for breath, to spring to his feet and make a dash for the house. But as he drew away from Vinca, he was seized with horror at finding his arms empty and the air cold, as if his whole body had been suddenly denuded, and he went back to her body with an impulse she matched, so that their knees became interlaced. Then he summoned up the courage to call her "Vinca darling" in humble accents, beseeching her to grant him what he asked of her and at the same time to forget what it was he wanted of her. She understood, and thereafter revealed only a desperately stubborn silence, beyond words perhaps, and a haste in which she did herself violence. He heard a brief cry of remonstrance and felt an involuntary contortion, but the body he was handling so roughly did not flinch and demanded no mercy.

SEVENTEEN

HE slept little but soundly, and got out of bed convinced that the whole house was empty. But downstairs he saw the caretaker with his non-barking dog and all his fishing gear, and from the first floor came the sound of his father's early morning cough. He went and hid himself between the spindlewood hedge and the terrace wall to spy on Vinca's window. A fresh breeze was chivvying the clouds that melted at its breath; by turning his head he could see the sails of the Cancale fishing smacks cradled on a short steep sea. All the windows of the house were still shuttered.

'What about her, is she still asleep? They're always said to weep, after. Perhaps Vinca is crying now. Yet at this moment she ought to be lying in my arms as we used to lie on the sandy links. Then I should say to her "It isn't true. It never really happened. You're just my Vinca, as you always were. You never gave me that moment of happiness, which didn't amount to so very much, after all. None of it ever occurred, not even your sigh or your song that broke off almost as soon as begun, which made you suddenly grow heavy and stiff as a corpse in my arms. None of it is true. If, this evening, I disappeared along the road to *Ker-Anna* and to-morrow crept in by myself before dawn, I should manage it so skilfully that you'd never know. . . . Let's go for a walk along the shore and let's take Lisette with us." '

It never occurred to him that it might be possible to perfect the give-and-take of an act of pleasure so clumsily performed. He was driven by the idealism of his tender age to salvage only what he knew must not be allowed to perish: his fifteen enchanted years of single-minded affection, their fifteen years together as pure and loving twins.

'I should say to her, "You are wrong if you think that our love, the Phil-and-Vinca love, ends there, there on the bed of threshed buckwheat, prickly with straw. It leads elsewhere than to the bed in your room, or in mine. It only goes to show, believe me! Since the love given me by a woman I never knew is a joy so lasting that it makes me quiver, even when she is far away, like the heart of an eel that goes on quivering after it has been cut from the living body, what do you suppose our love couldn't do to us? It only goes to show. . . . But if I do happen to be wrong, then you must never know that I'm wrong. . . ." '

'I should say to her, "It is a dream come true before it's time, a delirious dream, a torture you had to endure while biting your hand, you poor brave little pal playing opposite me in my cruel dilemma. For you it was a dream, and perhaps a frightful one; for me the humiliation was worse, the pleasure less entrancing than the surprising delights of solitude. But nothing will be lost, if you can forget all about it, and I myself can expunge the memory of something that was mercifully veiled by the shades of night. . . . No, I never gripped your flexible body between my knees— Now take me on your back, and let's ride-a-cock-horse across the sands. . . ." '

When he heard the jingle of her curtains being drawn, it required all his courage for him not to turn away his head.

Vinca appeared between the flaps of the shutters as she folded them back against the outside wall. She stood blinking her eyes deliberately and staring fixedly in front of her. Then she plunged both her hands into her thick hair and from her tousled head drew out a wisp of straw. Blushing and laughing simultaneously, she leaned forward and peered out from her dishevelled mop, no doubt looking for Philippe himself. Wide awake by now, she fetched from the room behind her a varnished earthenware pitcher, and carefully watered the purple-flowering fuchsia on her wooden balcony. She looked up at the clear blue sky that gave promise of fine weather, and began to sing the little song she sang every morning. Hidden among the spindlewood, Philippe kept watch, like a man who had come there to make an attempt on her life.

'She's singing. . . . I suppose I must believe my eyes and ears, she's actually singing. And she's just watered the fuchsia.'

It never for an instant crossed his mind that such an apparition ought to bring joy to his heart, so exactly did it fit the recent vows he had made to himself. His thoughts dwelt solely on his own disappointment and, too young and inexperienced for self-analysis, he pigheadedly persisted in drawing comparisons.

'I came here one night, under this window, to knock my brains out, because, in a revealing flash, a thunderbolt had just fallen between my childhood and the present. And here she is singing . . . singing. . . .'

Vinca's eyes vied with the bright blue of the morning sea. She was combing her hair, and once again started to num through pursed lips, over which played a vague smile.

'She's singing. She'll look lovely at breakfast. She'll shout "Lisette, pinch him till it hurts!" No great good and no great harm will have come of it, I dare say, for there she stands unaffected. . . .'

He saw that Vinca was leaning out over the balcony, crushing her breasts against the wooden support, gazing in the direction of his room.

'If only I could appear at the window opposite and leap across the balcony to join her, she would throw her arms round my neck. . . .'

'O you that I called "my master", why did you sometimes seem to me to be more full of wonder than this fresh young girl with her simple ways! You went away without telling me the whole story. If it was only the pride of those who derive their pleasure from giving that made you care for me, then to-day,

SIX NOVELS

for the first time, you should take pity on me. . . .'

From the window came a faint, happy little tune that passed over his head. Nor did the thought strike him that in a few weeks' time the child who was singing might well be standing in tears, doomed and frantic, at the same window. He hid his face in the hollow of the arm on which he was leaning and pondered his own insignificance, his downfall, his kindliness. 'Neither a hero, nor yet an executioner. . . . A little pain, a little pleasure. . . . That's all I shall have given her, that and nothing else . . . nothing . . .'

THE CAT

Translated by
Antonia White

ONE

TOWARDS ten o'clock, the family poker-players began to show signs of weariness. Camille was fighting against sleepiness as one does at nineteen. By starts she would become fresh and clear-eyed again; then she would yawn behind her clasped hands and reappear pale, her chin white and her cheeks a little black under their ochre-tinted powder, with two tiny tears in the corners of her eyes.

"Camille, you ought to go to bed!"

"At ten o'clock, Mummy, at ten o'clock! Who on earth goes to bed at ten o'clock?"

Her eyes appealed to her fiancé, who lay back, overcome, in the depths of an armchair.

"Leave them alone," said another maternal voice. "They've still seven days to wait for each other. They're a bit dazed at the moment. It's very natural."

"Exactly. One hour more or less . . . Camille, you ought to go home to bed. So ought we."

"Seven days!" cried Camille. "But it's Monday today! And I hadn't given it a thought! Alain! Wake up, Alain!"

She threw her cigarette into the garden and lit a fresh one. Then she sorted out the scattered cards, shuffled them and laid them out as fortune tellers do.

"To know whether we'll get the car, that marvellous baby roadster, before the ceremony! Look, Alain! I'm not cheating! It's coming out with a journey and an important piece of news!"

"What's that?"

"The roadster, of course!"

Without raising the nape of his neck from the chair, Alain turned his head towards the open french window, through which came the sweet smell of fresh spinach and new-mown hay. The grass had been shorn during the day, and the honeysuckle, which draped a tall dead tree, added the nectar of its first flowers to the scent of the cut grass. A crystalline tinkle announced the entrance of the ten o'clock tray of soft drinks and iced water, carried by old Émile's tremulous hands, and Camille got up to fill the glasses.

She served her fiancé last, offering him the misted tumbler with a smile of secret understanding. She watched him drink and felt a sudden pang of desire at the sight of his mouth pressing against the rim of the glass. But he felt so weary that he refused to share that pang and merely touched the white fingers with the red nails as they removed his empty tumbler.

"Are you coming to lunch tomorrow?" she asked him under her breath.

"Ask the cards."

Camille drew back quickly, and began to act the clown a little over her fortune-telling.

"Never, never joke about Twenty-four-hours! Doesn't matter so much about crossed knives, or pennies with holes in them, or the talkies, or God the Father . . ."

"Camille!"

"Sorry, Mummy. But one mustn't joke about Twenty-four-hours! He's a good little chap, the knave of spades. A nice black express messenger, always in a hurry."

"In a hurry to do what?"

"Why, to talk, of course! Just think, he brings the news of the next twenty-four hours, even of the next two days. If you put two more cards on his right and left, he foretells the coming week."

She was talking fast, scratching at two little smudges of lipstick at the corners of her mouth with a pointed nail. Alain listened to her, not bored, but not indulgent either. He had known her for several years and classified her as a typical modern girl. He knew the way she drove a car, a little too fast and a little too well; her eye alert and her scarlet mouth always ready to swear violently at a taxi-driver. He knew that she lied unblushingly, as children and adolescents do; that she was capable of deceiving her parents so as to get out after dinner and meet him at a night-club. There they danced together, but they drank only orange-juice because Alain disliked alcohol.

Before their official engagement, she had yielded her discreetly-wiped lips to him both by daylight and in the dark. She has also yielded her impersonal breasts, always imprisoned in a lace brassière, and her very lovely legs in the flawless stockings she bought in secret; stockings "like Mistinguett's, you know. Mind my stockings, Alain!" Her stockings and her legs were the best things about her.

'She's pretty,' Alain thought dispassionately, 'because not one of her features is ugly, because she's an out-and-out brunette. Those lustrous eyes perfectly match that sleek, glossy, frequently-washed hair that's the colour of a new piano.' He was also perfectly aware that she could be as violent and capricious as a mountain stream.

She was still talking about the roadster.

"No, Daddy, *no*! Absolutely no question of my letting Alain take the wheel while we're driving through Switzerland! He's too absent-minded. And besides, he doesn't really like driving. I know him!"

'She knows me,' Alain echoed in his own mind. 'Perhaps she really thinks she does. Over and over again, I've said to her too: "I know you, my girl." Saha knows her too. Where is that Saha?'

His eyes searched round for the cat. Then, starting limb by limb, first one shoulder, then the other, he unglued himself from the armchair and went lazily down the five steps into the garden.

The garden was very large and surrounded by other gardens. It breathed out into the night the heavy smell of well-manured earth given over to producing flowers and constantly forced into fertility. Since Alain's birth, the house had hardly changed at all. "An only son's house," Camille said jeeringly. She did not hide her contempt for the high-pitched roof with the top-storey windows set in the slates and for certain modest mouldings which framed the french windows on the ground floor.

The garden, like Camille, also seemed to despise the house. Huge trees, which showered down the black, calcined twigs which fall from elms in their old age, protected it from neighbours and passers-by. A little further on, in a property for sale and in the playground of a school, stood isolated pairs of similar old elms, relics of a princely avenue which had formed part of a park which the new Neuilly was fast destroying.

"Where are you, Alain?"

Camille was calling him from the top of the steps but, on an impulse, he refused to answer. Deliberately, he made for the safer refuge of the shadows, feeling his way along the edge of the shaven lawn with his foot. High in the sky a hazy moon held court, looking larger than usual through the mist of the first warm days. A single tree—a poplar with newly-opened glossy leaves—caught the moonlight and trickled with as many sparkles as a waterfall. A silver shadow leapt out of a clump of bushes and glided like a fish against Alain's ankles.

"Ah! There you are, Saha! I was looking for you. Why didn't you appear at table tonight?"

"Me—rrou—wa," answered the cat, "me-rrou-wa."

"What, me-rrou-wa? And why me-rrou-wa? Do you really mean it?"

"Me-rrou-wa," insisted the cat, "me-rrou-wa."

He stroked her, tenderly groping his way down the long spine that was softer than a hare's fur. Then he felt under his hand the small, cold nostrils dilated by her violent purring. 'She's my cat. My very own cat.'

"Me-rrou-wa," said the cat very softly. "R . . . rrou-wa."

Camille called once more from the house and Saha vanished under a clipped euonymus hedge, black-green like the night.

"Alain! We're going!"

He ran to the steps, while Camille watched him with a welcoming smile.

"I can see your hair running," she called out. "It's crazy to be as fair as all that!"

He ran quicker still, strode up the five steps in one bound, and found Camille alone in the drawing-room.

"Where are the others?" he asked under his breath.

"Cloakroom," she whispered back. "Cloakroom and visit to 'work in progress'. General gloom. 'It's not getting on! It'll never be finished.' What the hell do we care! If one was smart, one could hold on to Patrick's studio for keeps. Patrick could find himself another. I'll fix it, if you like."

"But Patrick would only leave the 'Wedge' as a special favour to please *you*."

"Of course. One will take advantage of that."

Her face sparkled with that peculiarly feminine unscrupulousness which Alain could not bring himself to accept as a matter of course. But he remonstrated only on her habit of saying 'one' for 'we', and she took this as a reproach.

"I'll soon get into the way of saying 'we'."

So that he should want to kiss her, she turned out the ceiling light as if by accident. The one lamp left alight on a table threw a tall, sharply defined shadow behind the girl.

With her arms raised and her hands clasped on the nape of her neck, Camille gave him an inviting look. But he had eyes only for the shadow. 'How beautiful she is on the wall! Just fine-drawn enough, just as I should like her to be.'

He sat down to compare the one with the other. Flattered, Camille arched herself, thrusting out her breasts and her hips like a nautch-girl, but the shadow was better at that game than she was. Unclasping her hands, the girl walked across the room, preceded by the ideal shadow. Arrived at the open french window, the shadow leapt to one side and fled out into the garden along the pink gravel of a path, embracing the moon-spangled poplar between its two long arms as it went. "What a pity!" sighed Alain. Then he feebly reproached himself for his inclination to love in Camille herself some perfected or motionless image of Camille. This shadow, for example, or a portrait or the vivid memory she left him of certain moments, certain dresses.

"What's the matter with you tonight? Come and help me put on my cape, at least."

He was shocked at what that "at least" secretly implied and also because Camille, as she passed before him through the door leading to the cloakroom and pantry, had almost imperceptibly shrugged her shoulders. 'She doesn't need to shrug her shoulders. Nature and habit do that for her anyway. When she's not careful, her neck makes her look dumpy. Ever, ever so slightly dumpy.'

In the cloakroom they found Alain's mother and Camille's parents stamping as if with cold and leaving footmarks the colour of dirty snow on the matting. The cat, seated on the window-sill outside, watched them inhospitably but with no animosity. Alain imitated her patience and endured the ritual of pessimistic lamentations.

"It's the same old thing."

"It's hardly any further on than it was a week ago."

"My dear, if you want to know what I think, it won't be a fortnight, it'll be a month. What am I talking about, a month? More likely *two* months before their nest . . ."

At the word "nest", Camille flung herself into the peaceful fray so shrilly that Alain and Saha closed their eyes.

"But since we've already decided what to do! And since we're actually frightfully *pleased* at having Patrick's place! And since it suits Patrick down to the ground because he hasn't a bean—hasn't any money—sorry, Mummy. We'll just take our suitcases and—Alley Oop! —straight up to heaven on the ninth floor! Won't we, Alain?"

He opened his eyes again, smiled into the void, and put her light cape round her shoulders. In the mirror opposite them he met Camille's black, reproachful look but it did not soften his heart. 'I didn't kiss her on the lips when we were alone. All right, very well then, I didn't kiss her on the lips. She hasn't had her full ration of kisses-on-the-lips today. She had the quarter-to-twelve one in the Bois, she had the two o'clock one after coffee, she had the half-past-six one in the garden, but she's missed tonight's. Well, if she's not satisfied, she's only got to put it down on the account . . . What's the matter with me? I'm so sleepy, I'm going mad. This life's idiotic: we're seeing far too much of each other and yet we never see each other properly. On Monday I'll definitely go down to the shop and . . .'

In imagination, the chemical acidity of the bales of new silk assailed his nostrils. But the inscrutable smile of M. Veuillet appeared to him as in a dream and, as in a dream, he heard words which, at twenty-four, he had still not learnt to hear without dread. "No, no, my young friend. Will a new adding-machine that costs seventeen thousand francs pay back its initial outlay within the year? It all depends on that. Allow your poor father's oldest partner . . ." Catching sight again in the looking-glass of the vindictive image and handsome dark eyes which were watching him, he folded Camille in both his arms.

"Well, Alain?"

"Oh, my dear, let him alone! These poor infants . . ."

Camille blushed and disengaged herself. Then she held up her cheek to Alain with such a boyish brotherly grace that he nearly put his head on her shoulder. 'Oh, to lie down and go to sleep! Oh, good Lord! Just to lie down and sleep!'

From the garden came the voice of the cat.

"Me-rrou-wa . . . Rrr-rrouwa."

"Hark at the cat! She must be hunting," said Camille calmly. "Saha! Saha!"

The cat was silent.

"Hunting?" protested Alain. "Whatever makes you think that? To begin with, we're in May. And then she's saying: 'Me-rrou-wa!' "

"So what?"

"She wouldn't be saying 'Me-rrou-wa' if she were hunting! What she's saying there—and it's really rather strange—means a warning. It's almost the cry calling her little ones together."

"Good Lord!" cried Camille, flinging up her arms. "If Alain's going to start interpreting the cat, we shall be here all night!"

She ran down the steps and, at the touch of old Émile's

shaking hand, two old-fashioned gas-globes, like huge mauve planets, illuminated the garden.

Alain walked ahead with Camille. At the entrance gate, he kissed her under her ear, breathed in, under a perfume too old for her, a good smell of bread and dark hair, and squeezed the girl's bare elbows under her cape. When she seated herself at the steering-wheel, with her parents in the back, he felt suddenly wide awake and gay.

"Saha! Saha!"

The cat sprang out of the shadow, almost under his feet. When he began to run, she ran too, leaping ahead of him with long bounds. He guessed she was there without seeing her; she burst before him into the hall and came back to wait for him at the top of the steps. With her frill standing out and her ears low, she watched him running towards her, urging him on with her yellow eyes. Those deep-set eyes were proud and suspicious, completely masters of themselves.

"Saha! Saha!"

Pronounced in a certain way, under his breath, with the "h" strongly aspirated, her name sent her crazy. She lashed her tail, bounded into the middle of the poker-table and, with her two cat's hands spread wide open, she scattered the playing-cards.

"That cat, that cat!" said his mother's voice. "She hasn't the faintest notion of hospitality. Look how delighted she is that our friends have gone!"

Alain let out a spurt of childish laughter, the laugh he kept for home and the close intimacy which did not extend beyond the screen of elms or the black, wrought-iron gate. Then he gave a frantic yawn.

"Good heavens, how tired you look! Is it possible to look as tired as that when one's happy? There's still some orangeade. No? We can go up then. Don't bother, Émile will turn out the lights."

'Mother's talking to me as if I were getting over an illness or as if I were starting up paratyphoid again.'

"Saha! Saha! What a demon! Alain, you couldn't persuade that cat? . . ."

By a vertical path known to herself, marked on the worn brocade, the cat had almost reached the ceiling. One moment she imitated a grey lizard, flattening against the wall with her paws spread out; then she pretended to be giddy and tried an affected little cry of appeal. Alain obediently came and stood below and Saha slid down, glued to the wall like a raindrop sliding down a pane. She came to rest on Alain's shoulder and the two of them went up together to their bedroom.

A long hanging cluster of laburnum, black outside the open window, became a long pale yellow cluster when Alain turned on the ceiling light and the bedside lamp. He poured the cat off on to the bed by inclining his shoulder, then wandered aimlessly to and fro between his room and the bathroom like a man who is too tired to go to bed.

He leaned out over the garden, looked with a hostile eye for the white mass of the "alterations". Then he opened and shut several drawers and boxes in which reposed his real secrets: a gold dollar, a signet ring, an agate charm attached to his father's watch chain, some red and black seeds from an exotic canna plant, a First Communicant's mother-of-pearl rosary and a thin broken bracelet, the souvenir of a tempestuous young mistress who had passed swiftly and noisily out of his life. The rest of his worldly goods consisted merely of some paper-covered books he had had rebound and some letters and photographs.

Dreamily he turned over these little scraps of wreckage, bright and worthless as the coloured stones one finds in the nests of pilfering birds. 'Should I throw all this away . . . or leave it here? It means nothing to me. Or does it mean something?' Being an only child, he was attached to everything which he had never shared with anyone else and for whose possession he had never had to fight.

He saw his face in the glass and became suddenly irritated with himself. 'Why can't you go to bed? You look a wreck. Positively disgraceful!' he said to the handsome fair young man. 'People only think me handsome because I'm fair. If I were dark, I'd be hideous.' For the hundredth time, he criticised his long cheeks and his slightly equine nose. But, for the hundredth time, he smiled so as to display his teeth to himself and admiringly touched the natural wave in his fair, over-thick hair. Once again he was pleased with the colour of his eyes, greenish-grey between dark lashes. Two dints hollowed his cheeks on either side of the smile, the eyes receded, circled with mauve shadows. He had shaved that morning but already a pale, stubbly bristle coarsened his upper lip. 'What a mug! I pity myself. No, I repel myself. Is *that* a face for a wedding night?' In the depths of the mirror, Saha gravely watched him from the distance.

"I'm coming, I'm coming."

He flung himself on the cool expanse of the sheets, humouring the cat. Rapidly, he went through certain ritual litanies dedicated to the particular graces and virtues of a small, perfect, pure-bred Russian Blue.

"My little bear with the big cheeks. Exquisite, exquisite, exquisite cat. My blue pigeon. Pearl-coloured demon."

As soon as he turned out the light, the cat began to trample delicately on her friend's chest. Each time she pressed down her feet, one single claw pierced the silk of the pyjamas, catching the skin just enough for Alain to feel an uneasy pleasure.

"Seven more days, Saha," he sighed.

In seven days and seven nights he would begin a new life in new surroundings with an amorous and untamed young woman. He stroked the cat's fur, warm and cool at the same time and smelling of clipped box, thuya and lush grass. She was purring full-throatedly and, in the darkness, she gave him a cat's kiss, laying her damp nose for a second under Alain's nose between his nostrils and his lip. A swift, immaterial kiss which she rarely accorded him.

"Ah! Saha. Our nights . . ."

The headlights of a car in the nearest avenue pierced the leaves with two revolving white beams. Over the wall of the room passed the enlarged shadow of the laburnum and of a tulip-tree which stood alone in the middle of a lawn. Above his own face Alain saw Saha's face illuminated for a moment. Before it was eclipsed again, he had seen that her eyes were hard.

"Don't frighten me!" he implored.

For, when Alain was sleepy, he became once more weak and fanciful, caught in the mesh of a sweet and interminable adolescence.

He shut his eyes while Saha kept vigil, watching all the invisible signs which hover over sleeping human beings when the light is put out.

He always dreamed a great deal and descended into his dreams by definite stages. When he woke up, he did not talk about his adventures of the night. He was jealous of a realm which had been enlarged by a delicate and ill-governed childhood; by long sojourns in bed during his swift growth into a tall frail slender boy.

He loved his dreams and cultivated them. Not for anything in the world would he have revealed the successive stages which awaited him. At the first stopping-place, while he could still hear the motor-horns in the avenue, he met an eddy of faces, familiar yet distorted, which he passed through as he might have passed through a friendly crowd, greeting one here and there. Eddying, bulbous, the faces approached Alain, growing larger and larger. Light against a dark background, they became lighter still as if they received their illumination from the sleeper himself. Each was furnished with one great eye and they circled round in an effortless gyration. But a submerged electric current shot them far away as soon as they touched an invisible barrier. In the humid gaze of a circular monster, in the eye of a plump moon or that of a wild archangel with rays of light for hair, Alain could recognise the same expression, the same intention which none of them had put into words and which the Alain of the dream noted with a sense of security: "They'll tell it me tomorrow."

Sometimes they disappeared by exploding into scattered, faintly luminous fragments. At other times, they only continued as a hand, an arm, a forehead, an eyeball full of thoughts or as a starry dust of chins and noses. But always there remained that prominent, convex eye which, just at the moment of making itself clear, turned round and exposed only its other, black surface.

The sleeping Alain pursued, under Saha's watchful care, his nightly shipwreck. He passed beyond the world of convex faces and eyes and descended through a zone of darkness where he was conscious of nothing but a powerful, positive blackness, indescribably varied and, as it were, composed of submerged colours. On the confines of this, he launched into the real, complete, fully-formed dream.

He came up violently against a barrier which gave a great clang like the prolonged, splintering clash of a cymbal. And then he found himself in the dream city, among the passers-by, the inhabitants standing in their doorways, the gold-crowned guardians of the square and the stage crowd posted along the path of an Alain who was completely naked and armed with a walking-stick. This Alain was extremely lucid and sagacious: "If I walk rather fast, after tying my tie in a special way, and parricularly if I whistle, there's every chance that no one will notice I am naked." So he tied his tie in a heart-shaped knot and whistled. "That's not whistling, what I'm doing. It's purring. Whistling's like this . . ." But he still continued to purr. "I'm not at the end of my tether yet. All I've got to do . . . it's perfectly simple . . . is to cross this sun-drenched open space and go round the bandstand where the military band is playing. Child's play. I run, making perilous jumps to distract attention, and I come out in the zone of shadow . . ."

But he was paralysed by the warm, dangerous look of a dark man in the stage-crowd; a young man with a Greek profile perforated by a great eye like a carp's. "The zone of shadow . . . the zone of *the* shadow . . ." Two long shadowy arms, graceful and rustling with poplar leaves appeared at the word "shadow" and carried Alain away. During the most ambiguous hour of the short night, he rested in that provisional tomb where the living exile sighs, weeps, fights and succumbs, and from which he rises, unremembering, with the day.

TWO

THE high sun was edging the window when Alain awoke. The newly-opened cluster of laburnum hung, translucid, above the head of Saha: a blue, diurnal Saha, innocently engaged in washing herself.

"Saha!"

"Me-rrang!" answered the cat aggressively.

"Is it my fault if you're hungry? You only had to go downstairs and ask for your milk if you're in a hurry."

She softened at her friend's voice and repeated the same word less emphatically, showing her red mouth planted with white teeth. That look of loyal and exclusive love alarmed Alain: 'Oh heavens, this cat! What to do with this cat? I'd forgotten I was getting married. And that we've got to live in Patrick's place.'

He turned towards the photograph in the chromium frame where Camille gleamed as if covered in oil; a great splash of reflected light on her hair, her painted mouth vitrified in inky black, her eyes enormous between two palisades of eyelashes.

"Fine piece of studio portraiture," muttered Alain.

He had quite forgotten that he himself had chosen this photograph for his room; a photograph which bore no resemblance to Camille or to anyone at all. 'That eye . . . I've seen that eye.'

He took a pencil and lightly retouched the eye, toning down the excess of white. All he succeeded in doing was to spoil the print.

"Mouek, mouek, mouek. Ma-a-a-a . . . Ma-a-a-a,"
said Saha, addressing a little moth imprisoned between
the window-pane and the net curtain.

Her leonine chin was trembling; she coveted it so much
that she stammered. Alain caught the moth with two
fingers and offered it to the cat.

"*Hors-d'œuvre*, Saha!"

In the garden, a rake was lazily combing the gravel.
Alain could see in his mind the hand that guided the
rake; the hand of an ageing woman; a mechanical,
obstinate hand in a huge white glove like a policeman's.

"Good morning, Mother!" he called.

A distant voice answered him, a voice whose words he
did not try to catch; the affectionate, insignificant murmur was all that he needed. He ran downstairs, the cat at
his heels. In broad daylight, she knew how to change
herself into a kind of blustering dog. She would hurtle
noisily down the stairs and rush into the garden with
tomboyish jumps that had no magic about them. She
seated herself on the little breakfast table, among the
medallions of sunlight, beside Alain's plate. The rake,
which had stopped, slowly resumed its task.

Alain poured out Saha's milk, stirred a pinch of salt
and a pinch of sugar into it, then gravely helped himself.
When he breakfasted alone, he did not have to blush for
certain gestures elaborated by the unconscious wishes of
the maniac age between six and seven. He was free to
blind all the "eyes" in the bread with butter and to frown
when the coffee in his cup rose above the water-line
marked by a certain gilt arabesque. A second thin slice
had to follow the first thick slice, whereas the second

cup demanded an extra lump of sugar. In fact a very small Alain, hidden in the depths of a tall, fair, handsome young man, was impatiently waiting for breakfast to be over so that he could lick both sides of the honey spoon; an old ivory spoon, blackened and flexible with age.

'Camille, at this moment, is eating her breakfast standing up. She's biting at one and the same time into a slice of lean ham squeezed between two rusks and into an American apple. And she keeps putting down a cup of tea without sugar in it on various bits of furniture and forgetting it.'

He raised his eyes and contemplated his domain; the domain of a privileged child which he cherished and whose every inch he knew. Over his head the old, severely pollarded elms stirred only the tips of their young leaves. A cushiony mass of pink silene, fringed with forget-me-nots, dominated one lawn. Dangling like a scarf from the dead tree's scraggy elbow, a trail of polygonum intertwined with the four-petalled purple clematis fluttered in every breath of wind. One of the standard sprinklers spread a white peacock tail shot with a shifting rainbow as it revolved over the turf.

'Such a beautiful garden . . . such a beautiful garden,' said Alain under his breath. He stared disgustedly at the silent heaps of rubbish, timber and bags of plaster which defaced the west side of the house. 'Ah! It's Sunday, so they're not working. It's been Sunday all the week for me.' Though young and capricious, and pampered, he now lived according to the commercial rhythm of a six-day week and felt Sunday in his bones.

A white pigeon moved furtively behind the weigela

and the pink clusters of the deutzias. 'It's not a pigeon;
it's mother's hand in her gardening glove.' The big white
glove moved just above ground, raising a drooping stalk,
weeding out the blades of grass that sprang up overnight.
Two green finches came hopping along the gravel path
to pick up the breakfast crumbs, and Saha followed them
with her eye without getting excited. But a tomtit,
hanging upside down in an elm above the table, chirped
at the cat out of bravado. Sitting there with her paws
folded, her head thrown back, and the frill of fur under
her chin displayed like a pretty woman's jabot, Saha tried
hard to restrain herself; but her cheeks swelled with fury
and her little nostrils moistened.

"As beautiful as a fiend! More beautiful than a fiend!"
Alain told her.

He wanted to stroke the broad skull in which lodged
ferocious thoughts, and the cat bit him sharply to relieve
her anger. He looked at the two little beads of blood on
his palm with the irascibility of a man whose woman has
bitten him at the height of her pleasure.

"Bad girl! Bad girl! Look what you've done to me!"

She lowered her head, sniffed the blood and timidly
questioned her friend's face. She knew how to amuse him
and charm him back to good humour. She scooped up a
rusk from the table and held it between her paws like a
squirrel.

The May breeze passed over them, bending a yellow
rosebush which smelt of flowering reeds. Between the
cat, the rose-bush, the pairs of tomtits and the last cock-
chafers, Alain had one of those moments when he slipped
out of time and felt the anguished illusion of being once

more back in his childhood. The elms suddenly became enormous, the path grew wider and longer and vanished under the arches of a pergola that no longer existed. Like the hag-ridden dreamer who falls off a tower, Alain returned violently to the consciousness of being nearly twenty-four.

'I ought to have slept another hour. It's only half-past nine. It's Sunday. Yesterday was Sunday for me too. Too many Sundays. But tomorrow . . .'

He smiled at Saha as though she were an accomplice. "Tomorrow, Saha, there's the final trying-on of the white dress. Without me. It's a surprise. Camille's dark enough to look her best in white. During that time, I'll go and look at the car. It's a bit cheese-paring, a bit mingy, as Camille would say, a roadster. That's what you get for being 'such a young married couple'."

With a vertical bound, rising in the air like a fish leaping to the surface of the water, the cat caught a black-veined cabbage-white. She ate it, coughed, spat out one wing and licked herself affectedly. The sun played on her fur, mauve and bluish like the breast of a woodpigeon.

"Saha!"

She turned her head and smiled at him.

"My little puma! Beloved cat! Creature of the tree-tops! How will you live if we're separated? Would you like us to enter an Order? Would you like? . . . oh, I don't know what . . ."

She listened to him, watching him with a tender, absent expression. But when the friendly voice began to tremble, she looked away.

"To begin with, you'll come with us. You don't hate

cars. If we take the saloon instead of the roadster, behind the seats there's a ledge . . ."

He broke off and became gloomy at the recent memory of a girl's vigorous voice, ideally pitched for shouting in the open air, trumpeting the numerous merits of the roadster. "And then, when you put down the windscreen, Alain, its *mar*vellous. When she's all out, you can feel the skin of your cheeks shrinking right back to your *ears*."

"Shrinking right back to your ears. Can you imagine anything more frightful, Saha?"

He compressed his lips and made a long face like an obstinate child planning to get its own way by guile.

'It's not settled yet. Suppose *I* prefer the saloon? I suppose I've got *some* say in the matter?'

He glared at the yellow rose-bush as if it were the young girl with the resonant voice. Promptly the path widened, the elms grew taller and the non-existent pergola re-appeared. Cowering among the skirts of two or three female relatives, a childish Alain surveyed another compact family among whose opaque block gleamed a very dark little girl whose big eyes and black ringlets rivalled each other in a hostile, jetty brilliance. "Say 'How d'you do. . . .' Why don't you want to say 'How d'you do'? " It was a faint voice from other days, preserved through years of childhood, adolescence, college, the boredom of military service, false seriousness, false business competence. Camille did not want to say, 'How d'you do?'. She sucked the inside of her cheek and stiffly sketched the brief curtsy expected of little girls. 'Now she calls that a "twist-your-ankle" curtsy. But when she's in a temper, she still bites the inside of her cheek. It's a funny thing, but at those moments she doesn't look ugly.'

He smiled and felt an honest glow of warmth for his fiancée. After all, he was quite glad that she should be healthy and slightly commonplace in her sensuality. Defying the innocent morning, he called up images designed now to excite her vanity and impatience, now to engender anxiety, even confusion. Emerging from these disturbing fancies, he found the sun too white and the wind dry. The cat had disappeared but, as soon as he stood up, she was at his side and accompanied him, walking with a long, deerlike step and avoiding the round pebbles in the pinkish gravel. They went together as far as the "alterations" and inspected with equal hostility the pile of rubbish, a new french window, devoid of panes, inserted in a wall, various bathroom appliances and some porcelain tiles.

Equally offended, they calculated the damage done to their past and their present. An old yew had been torn up and was very slowly dying upside down, with its roots in the air. "I ought never, never to have allowed that," muttered Alain. "It's a disgrace. You've only known it for three years, Saha, that yew. But I . . ."

At the bottom of the hole left by the yew, Saha sensed a mole whose image, or rather whose smell went to her head. For a minute she forgot herself to the point of frenzy, scratching like a fox-terrier and rolling over like a lizard. She jumped on all four paws like a frog, clutched a ball of earth between her thighs as a fieldmouse does with the egg it has stolen; escaped from the hole by a series of miracles, and found herself sitting on the grass, cold and prudish and recovering her breath.

Alain stood gravely by, not moving. He knew how to keep a straight face when Saha's demons possessed her beyond her control. The admiration and understanding of cats was innate in him. Those inborn rudiments made it easy for him, later on, to read Saha's thoughts. He had read her like some masterpiece from the day, when on his return from a cat-show, Alain had put down a little five-months old she-cat on the smooth lawn at Neuilly. He had bought her because of her perfect face, her precocious dignity and her modesty that hoped for nothing behind the bars of a cage.

"Why didn't you buy a Persian instead?" asked Camille.

'That was long before we were engaged,' thought Alain. 'It wasn't only a little she-cat I bought. It was the nobility of all cats, their infinite disinterestedness, their knowledge of how to live, their affinities with the highest type of humans.' He blushed and mentally excused himself. 'The highest, Saha, is the one that understands *you* best.'

He had not yet got to the point of thinking "likeness" instead of "understanding" because he belonged to that class of human beings which refuses to recognise or even to imagine its animal affinities. But at the age when he might have coveted a car, a journey abroad, a rare binding, a pair of skis, Alain nevertheless remained the young-man-who-has-bought-a-little-cat. His narrow world resounded with it. The staff of Amparat et Fils in the Rue des Petits Champs were astonished and M. Veuillet inquired after the "little beastie".

"Before I chose you, Saha, I don't believe I'd ever

realised that one *could* choose. As for all the rest . . . My marriage pleases everyone, including Camille. There are moments when it pleases me to, but . . ."

He got up from the green bench and assumed the important smile of the heir of Amparat Silks who is condescendingly marrying the daughter of Malmert Mangles, "a girl who's not *quite* our type," as Mme. Amparat said. But Alain was well aware that, when Malmert Mangles spoke about Amparat Silks among themselves, they did not forget to mention, sticking up their chins: "The Amparats aren't in silk any more. The mother and son have only kept their shares in the business and the son's not the real director, only a figurehead."

Cured of her madness, her eyes gentle and golden, the cat seemed to be waiting for the return of mental trust, of that telepathic murmur for which her silver-fringed ears were straining.

"You're not just a pure and sparkling spirit of a cat either," went on Alain. "What about your first seducer, the white tom without a tail? Do you remember that, my ugly one, my trollop in the rain, my shameless one?"

"What a bad mother your cat is!" exclaimed Camille indignantly. "She doesn't even give a thought to her kittens, now they've been taken away from her."

'But that was just what a young girl would say,' Alain went on defiantly. 'Young girls are always admirable mothers before they're married.'

The full, deep note of a bell sounded on the tranquil air. Alain leapt up with a guilty start at the sound of wheels crushing the gravel.

'Camille! It's half-past eleven . . . Good Heavens!'

He pulled his pyjama jacket together and retied the cord so hastily and nervously that he scolded himself. 'Come, come, what's the matter with me? I shall be seeing plenty more of them in a week. Saha, are you coming to meet them?'

But Saha had vanished and Camille was already stamping across the lawn with reckless heels. 'Ah! She really does look attractive.' His blood pulsed pleasurably in his throat and flushed his cheeks. He was entirely absorbed in the spectacle of Camille in white, with a little lock of well-tapered hair on either temple and a tiny red scarf which matched her lipstick. Made-up with skill and restraint, her youth was not obvious at the first glance. Then it revealed itself in the cheek that was white under the ochre powder; in the smooth, unwrinkled eyelids under the light dusting of beige powder round the great eyes that were almost black. The brand-new diamond on her left hand broke the light into a thousand coloured splinters.

"Oh!" she cried. "You're not ready! On a lovely day like this!"

But she stopped at the sight of the rough, dishevelled fair hair, of the naked chest under the pyjamas and Alain's flushed confusion. Her young girl's face so clearly expressed a woman's warm indulgence that Alain no longer dared to give her the quarter-to-twelve kiss of the Bois.

"Kiss me," she implored, very low, as if she were asking him for help.

Gauche, uneasy and ill-protected by his thin pyjamas,

he made a gesture towards the pink flowering shrubs from whence came the sound of the shears and the rake. Camille did not dare throw herself on his neck. She lowered her eyes, plucked a leaf, and pulled her shining locks of hair forward on her cheeks. But, from the movement of her nostrils, Alain saw that she was searching in the air, with a certain primitive wildness, for the fragrance of a fair-skinned, barely-covered body. In his heart he secretly condemned her for not being sufficiently afraid of it.

THREE

WHEN he woke up, he did not sit up in bed at one bound. Haunted in his sleep by the unfamiliar room, he half-opened his eyes and realised that cunning and constraint had not entirely left him during his sleep, for his left arm, flung out across a desert of linen sheet, lay ready to recognise, but ready, also, to repel. . . . But all the wide expanse of bed to his left was empty and cool once more. If there had been nothing in front of the bed but the barely rounded corner of the triangular room and the unaccustomed green gloom, split by a rod of bright yellow light which separated two curtains of solid shadow, Alain would have gone to sleep again lulled by the sound of someone humming a little Negro song.

He turned his head cautiously and opened his eyes a trifle wider. He saw someone moving about, now white, now pale blue according to whether she was in the narrow strip of sunlight or in the shadow. It was a naked young woman with a comb in her hand and a cigarette between her lips, wandering about the room and humming. 'What impudence,' he thought. 'Completely naked! Where does she think she is?'

He recognised the lovely legs with which he had long been familiar, but the stomach, shortened by a navel placed rather low, surprised him. An impersonal youthfulness justified the muscular buttocks and the breasts were small above the visible ribs. 'Has she got thinner, then?' The solidity of her back, which was as wide as her

chest, shocked Alain. 'She's got a common back.' At
that moment, Camille leaned her elbow on one of the
window-sills arched her back and hunched up her
shoulders. 'She's got a back like a charwoman.' But
suddenly she stood upright again, took a couple of
dancing steps and made a charming gesture of embracing
the empty air. 'No, I'm wrong. She's beautiful. But what
a . . . what brazenness! Does she think I'm dead? Or does
it seem perfectly natural to her to wander about stark
naked? Oh, but that will change!'

As she turned towards the bed, he closed his eyes again.
When he opened them, Camille had seated herself at the
dressing-table they called the "invisible dressing-table",
a transparent sheet of beautiful thick glass laid on a black
metal frame. She powdered her face, touched her cheeks
and chin with the tips of her fingers and suddenly smiled,
turning her eyes from the glass with a gravity and a
weariness which disarmed Alain. 'Is she happy, then?
Happy about what? *I* certainly don't deserve it. But why
is she naked?'

"Camille!" he called out.

He thought she would rush towards the bathroom,
hastily covering herself with some hastily snatched-up
undergarment. Instead, she ran to the bed and bent over
the young man who lay there, overwhelming him with
her strong brunette's smell.

"Darling! Have you slept well?"

"Stark naked!" he scolded.

She opened her big eyes comically.

"What about you?"

Bare to his waist, he did not know what to reply. She

paraded for him, so proudly and so completely devoid of modesty that he rather rudely flung her the crumpled pyjama-jacket which lay on the bed.

"Quick, put that on. Personally, I'm hungry!"

"Old mother Buque's at her post. Everything's in working order and functioning."

She disappeared and Alain wanted to get up and dress and smooth his rumpled hair. But Camille returned, girded in a big bathrobe that was new and too long for her, and gaily carrying a loaded tray.

"What a mess, my dears! There's a kitchen bowl and a pyrex cup and the sugar's in the lid of a tin. I'll get it all straightened out in a day or two. My ham's dry. These anaemic peaches are left-overs from lunch. Mother Buque's a bit lost in her electric kitchen. I'll teach her how to manage the various switches. Then I've put some water in the ice compartments of the 'fridge. It's a good thing I'm here! Monsieur has his coffee very hot and his milk boiling and his butter hard. No, that's my tea, don't touch! What are you looking for?"

"No, nothing."

Because of the smell of coffee, he was looking for Saha.

"What's the time?"

"At last a tender word!" cried Camille. "Very early, my husband. It was a quarter-past eight by the kitchen alarm-clock."

As they ate, they laughed a good deal and spoke little. By the increasing smell of the green oilcloth curtains, Alain could guess the strength of the sun which warmed them. He could not take his mind off that sun outside, the unfamiliar horizon, the nine vertiginous storeys and the bizarre architecture of the 'Wedge' which was their temporary home.

He listened to Camille as attentively as he could, touched at her pretending to have forgotten what had passed between them in the night. He was touched, too, by her pretending to be perfectly at home in their haphazard lodging and by her unselfconsciousness, as if she had been married at least a week. Now that she had something on, he tried to find a way of showing his gratitude. 'She doesn't resent either what I've done to her or what I haven't, poor child. After all, the most tiresome part is over. Is it always like this the first night? This bruised, unsatisfactory feeling? This half-success, half-disaster?'

He threw his arm cordially round her neck and kissed her.

"Oh! You're nice!"

She had said it so loud and with so much feeling that she blushed and he saw her eyes fill with tears. But she bravely fought down her emotion and jumped off the bed on the pretext of removing the tray. She ran towards the windows, tripped over her long bathrobe, let out a great oath and hauled on a ship's rope. The oilcloth curtains slid back. Paris, with its suburbs, bluish and unbounded like the desert, dotted with still-fresh verdure and flashes of shining panes, entered at one bound into the triangular room which had only one cement wall, the other two being half-glass.

"It's beautiful," said Alain softly.

But he was half-lying and his head sought the support of a young shoulder from which the bathrobe had slipped. 'It's not a place for human beings to live. All this horizon right on top of one, right in one's bed. And what about stormy days? Abandoned on the top of a lighthouse among the albatrosses.'

Camille was lying beside him on the bed now. Her arm was round his neck and she looked fearlessly, now at the giddy horizons of Paris, now at the fair, dishevelled head. This new pride of hers which seemed to draw strength ahead from the coming night and the days that would follow, was no doubt satisfied with her newly-acquired rights. She was licensed to share his bed, to prop up a young man's naked body against her thigh and shoulder, to become acquainted with its colour and curves and defects. She was free to contemplate boldly and at length the small dry nipples, the loins she envied and the strange design of the capricious sex.

They bit into the same tasteless peach and laughed, showing each other their splendid, glistening teeth and the gums which were a little pale, like tired children's.

"That day yesterday!" sighed Camille. "When you think that there are people who get married so often!"

Her vanity returned and she added: "All the same, it went off very well. Not a single hitch. It did go off well, didn't it?"

"Yes," said Alain feebly.

"Oh, *you* . . . You're just like your mother. I mean, as long as your lawn isn't ruined and people don't throw cigarette-ends on your gravel, you think everything's fine. Isn't that a fact? All the same, our wedding would have been prettier at Neuilly. Only that would have disturbed the sacred cat! Tell me, you bad boy, what do you keep looking at all round you?"

"Nothing," he said sincerely, "because there's nothing to look at. I've seen the dressing-table, I've seen the chair,—we've seen the bed . . ."

"Couldn't you live here? I'd love to. Just think . . . three rooms and three balconies! If only one could stay here!"

"Doesn't one say: 'If only *we* could stay here'?"

"Then why do *you* say: 'One says'? Yes, if only one could stay here, as *we* say."

"But Patrick will be back from his cruise in three months."

"Who cares? He'll come back. And we'll explain that we want to stay on. And we'll chuck him out."

"Oh! You'd actually do that?"

She shook her black mop affirmatively with a radiant, feminine assurance in dishonesty. Alain wanted to give her a severe look but, under his eyes, Camille changed and became as nervous as he felt himself. Hastily he kissed her on the mouth.

Silent and eager, she returned his kiss, feeling for the hollow of the bed with a movement of her loins. At the same time her free hand, which was holding a peach-stone, groped in the air for an empty cup or an ashtray.

Leaning over her, he caressed her lightly, waiting for her to open her eyes again.

She was pressing her eyelashes down over two small, glittering tears which she was trying to stop from flowing. He respected this restraint and this pride. They had done their best, the two of them, aided by the morning warmth and their two odorous, facile bodies.

Alain remembered Camille's quickened breathing and

her warm docility. She had shown an untimely eagerness which was very charming. She reminded him of no other woman; in possessing her for the second time, he had thought only of the careful handling she deserved. She lay against him, her legs and arms relaxed, her hands half-closed, catlike for the first time. 'Where is Saha?'

Mechanically he gave Camille the ghost of a caress "for Saha", drawing his nails slowly and delicately all the way down her stomach. She cried out with shock and stiffened her arms. One of them hit Alain who nearly hit her back. She sat up, with her hair on end and her eyes hostile and threatening.

"Are you vicious, by any chance?"

He had expected nothing like this and burst out laughing.

"There's nothing to laugh about!" cried Camille. "I've always been told that men who tickle women are vicious. They may even be sadists!"

He got off the bed so as to be able to laugh more freely, quite forgetting he was naked. Camille stopped talking so suddenly that he turned round and surprised her lit-up, dazed face staring at the body of the young man whom one night of marriage had made hers.

"D'you mind if I steal the bathroom for ten minutes?"

He opened the glass door let into one end of the longest wall which they called the hypotenuse.

"And then I'll go over to my mother's for a moment."

"Yes . . . Don't you want me to come with you?"

He looked shocked and she blushed for the first time that day.

"I'll see if the alterations . . ."

"Oh! the alterations! Don't tell me you're interested in those alterations! Admit"—she folded her arms like a tragic actress—"admit that you're going to see my rival!"

"Saha's not your rival," said Alain simply.

'How could she be your rival?' he went on to himself. 'You can only have rivals in what's impure.'

"I didn't need *such* a serious protestation, darling. Hurry up! You haven't forgotten that we're lunching together on our own at Père Léopold's? On our own at last, just the two of us! You'll come back soon? You haven't forgotten we're going for a drive? Are you taking in what I'm saying?"

What he took in very clearly was that the words "come back" had acquired a new and preposterous significance and he looked at Camille askance. She was flaunting her newly-married bride's tiredness, drawing his attention to the faint swelling of her lower lids under the corners of her great eyes. 'Will you always have such enormous eyes the moment you wake up, whatever time of day or night? Don't you know how to keep your eyes half-closed? It gives me a headache to see eyes as wide open as all that.'

He felt a dishonest pleasure, an evasive comfort in calling her to account in his mind. 'After all, it's less ungracious than being frank.' He hurried to reach the square bathroom, the hot water and a solitude propitious to thought. But, as the glass door inserted in the hypotenuse reflected him from head to foot, Alain opened it with complacent slowness and was in no haste to shut it again.

When he was leaving the flat an hour later, he opened

the wrong door on to one of the balconies which ran along every side of the Wedge. Like the sharp down-stroke of a fan, the east wind which was turning Paris blue, blowing away the smoke and scouring the distant Sacré Cœur, caught him full in the face. On the cement parapet, five or six pots, put there by well-meaning hands, contained white roses and hydrangeas and lilies sullied by their pollen. 'Last night's dessert is never attractive.' Nevertheless, before he went down, he sheltered the ill-treated flowers from the wind.

FOUR

HE stole into the garden like a boy in his teens who has stayed out all night. The air was full of the heady scent of beds being watered, of the secret exhalation of the filth which nourishes fleshy, expensive flowers and of spray blown on the breeze. In the very act of drawing a deep breath to inhale it all, he suddenly discovered he needed comforting.

"Saha! Saha!"

She did not come for a moment or two, and at first he did not recognise that bewildered, incredulous face which seemed clouded by a bad dream.

"Saha darling!"

He took her on his chest, smoothing the soft flanks which seemed to him a trifle hollow, and removed cobwebs, pine needles and elm twigs from the neglected fur. She pulled herself together quickly and resumed her familiar expression and her cat's dignity. Her face, her pure golden eyes looked again as he had known them. Under his thumb, Alain could feel the palpitations of a hard, irregular little heart and also the beginnings of a faint, uncertain purr. He put her down on an iron table and stroked her. But at the moment of thrusting her head into Alain's hand, wildly and as if for life in the way she had, she sniffed that hand and stepped back a pace.

His eyes sought the white pigeon, the gloved hand behind the pink flowering shrubs, behind the flaming rhododendrons. He rejoiced that yesterday's "ceremony" had respected the beautiful garden and only ravaged Camille's home.

'Imagine those people here! And those four brides-maids in pink paper! And the flowers they'd have picked, and the deutzias sacrificed to adorn fat women's bosoms! And Saha!'

He called in the direction of the house: "Has Saha had anything to eat or drink? She looks awfully queer. I'm here, Mother."

A heavy white shape appeared in the doorway of the hall and answered from the distance: "No. Just fancy, she had no supper and wouldn't drink her milk this morning. I think she was waiting for you. Are you all right, dear?"

He stood at the foot of the steps, deferential in his mother's presence. He noticed that she did not offer him her cheek as usual and that she kept her hands clasped together at her waist. He understood and shared this motherly sense of decency with a mixture of embarrass-ment and gratitude. 'Saha hasn't kissed me either.'

"After all, the cat's often seen you go away. She made allowances for your going off sometimes."

'But I didn't go so far,' he thought.

Near him, on the iron table, Saha drank her milk avidly like an animal that has walked far and slept little.

"Alain, wouldn't you like a cup of warm milk too? Some bread and butter?"

"I've had breakfast, Mother. *We've* had breakfast."

"Not much of a breakfast, I imagine. In such a glory-hole!"

With the eye of an exile, Alain contemplated the cup with the gilt arabesque beside Saha's saucer; then his mother's heavy face, amiable under the mass of wavy, prematurely white hair.

"I haven't asked you whether my new daughter is satisfied." She was frightened he would misunderstand her and added hurriedly: "I mean, whether she's in good health."

"Excellent, Mother. We're going out to Rambouillet for lunch in the forest. I've got to run the car in." He corrected himself: "*We've* got to run the car in, I mean."

They remained alone together in the garden, he and Saha, both torpid with silence and weariness and overcome with longing to sleep.

The cat fell asleep suddenly on her side, her chin up and her teeth bared like a dead wild animal. Feathery panicles from the Venetian sumach and clematis petals rained down on her without her so much as twitching in the depths of the dream in which, no doubt, she was enjoying the security of her friend's inalienable presence. Her defeated attitude, the pale, drawn corners of her periwinkle-grey lips gave evidence of a night of miserable watching.

Above the withered stump draped with climbing plants, a flight of bees over the ivy-flowers gave out a solemn cymbal note, the identical note of so many summers. 'To go to sleep out here, on the grass, between the yellow rosebush and the cat. Camille won't come till dinner-time, that will be very pleasant. And the cat, good heavens, the cat . . .' Over by the 'alterations' could be heard the rasp of a plane shaving a beam, the clang of an iron hammer on a metal girder, and Alain promptly embarked on a dream about a village peopled with mysterious blacksmiths. As eleven sounded from the belfry of the school nearby, he got up and fled without daring to wake the cat.

FIVE

JUNE came with its longer days, its night skies devoid of mystery which the late glow of the sunset and the early glimmer of dawn over the east of Paris kept from being wholly dark. But June is cruel only to city-dwellers who have no car and are caged up in hot stone and forced to live elbow to elbow. A never-still breeze played round the Wedge, rippling the yellow awnings. It blew through the triangular room and the studio, broke against the prow of the building and dried up the little hedges of privet that stood in boxes on the balconies. With the help of their daily drives, Alain and Camille lived pleasantly enough. The warm weather and their sensual life combined to make them drowsy and less exacting with each other.

'Why did I call her an untamed girl?' Alain asked himself in surprise. Camille swore less when she was driving the car and had lost certain crudities of speech. She had also lost her passion for night-clubs with female gipsy singers who had nostrils like horses.

She spent much time eating and sleeping, opened her now much gentler eyes very wide, gave up a dozen summer projects and became interested in the 'alterations' which she visited daily. Often she lingered long in the garden at Neuilly, where Alain, when he came back from the dark offices of Amparat Fils in the Rue des Petits-Champs, would find her idle, ready to prolong the afternoon and drive along the hot roads.

Then his mood would darken. He would listen to her giving orders to the singing painters and the distant electricians. She would question him in a general, peremptory way as if, as soon as he was there, it was her duty to renounce her new gentleness.

"Business going all right? Crisis still expected? Have you managed to put over the spotted foulard on the big dress-houses?"

She did not even respect old Émile, whom she shook until he let fall certain formulas pregnant with oracular imbecility.

"What do you think of our shanty, Émile? Have you ever seen the house looking so nice?"

Between his whiskers, the old butler muttered answers as shallow and colourless as himself.

"You wouldn't know the place any more. Had anyone told me, in the old days, that this house would be divided up into little compartments . . . There's certainly a difference. It will be very nice being so near each other, very gay."

Or else, drop by drop, he poured a stream of blessings over Alain, blessings in which there was an undercurrent of hostility.

"Monsieur Alain's young lady is beginning to look ever so well. What a fine voice she has. When she's speaking loud, the neighbours can hear every word. You can't deny she has a splendid voice but . . . The young lady speaks her mind all right. She told the gardener that the bed of pink silene and forget-me-not looked cuckoo. I still have to laugh when I think of it."

And he raised his pale, oyster-coloured eyes, which

had never laughed in their life, to the pure sky. Alain did not laugh either. He was worried about Saha. She was getting thinner and seemed to have given up a hope; undoubtedly the hope of seeing Alain every day again— and alone. She no longer ran away when Camille arrived. But she did not escort Alain to the gate and, when he sat by her, she looked at him with a profound and bitter wisdom. 'Her look when she was a little cat behind the bars. The same, same look.' He called her very softly: "Saha . . . Saha . . ." strongly aspirating the "h"s. But she did not jump or flatten her ears and it was days since she had given her insistent: "Me-rrang!" or the "Mouek-mouek-mouek" of good humour and greed.

One day, when he and Camille had been summoned to Neuilly to be informed that the enormous, heavy, new sunk bath would cave in the tiled platform supporting it, he heard his wife sigh: "It'll never be finished!"

"But," he said, surprised, "I thought you really much preferred the Wedge with its petrels and cormorants."

"Yes. But all the same . . . And after all it's your house here, your real house. *Our* house."

She leaned on his arm, rather limp and unusually hesitant. The bluish whites of her eyes, almost as blue as her light summer dress; the unnecessary but admirable make-up of her cheeks and mouth and eyelids did not move him in the least.

Nevertheless, it seemed to him that, for the first time, she was asking his advice without speaking. 'Camille here with me. So soon! Camille in pyjamas under the rose trellis.' One of the oldest climbing roses carried its load of flowers, which faded as soon as they opened, as high as his head and their oriental scent dominated the garden in the evening; he could smell it where they stood by the steps. 'Camille in a bathrobe under the screen of elms. Wouldn't it be better, all things considered, to keep her shut away in the little gazebo of the Wedge? Not here, not here . . . not yet.'

The June evening, drenched with light, was reluctant to give way to darkness. Some empty glasses on a wicker table were still attracting the big orange bumble-bees but, under all the trees except the pines, an area of impalpable damp was growing, bringing a promise of coolness. Neither the rose geraniums, so prodigal of their southern scent upon the air, nor the fiery poppies suffered from the fierce onslaught of summer. 'Not here, not here,' Alain repeated to the rhythm of his own footsteps. He was looking for Saha and did not want to call her out loud. He found her lying on the little low wall which buttressed a blue knoll covered with lobelias. She was asleep, or appeared to be asleep, curled up in a ball. 'Curled up in a ball? At this time and in this weather? Sleeping curled up like that is a winter position!'

"Saha darling!"

She did not quiver as he picked her up and held her in the air. She only opened two hollow eyes, very beautiful and almost indifferent.

"Heavens, how light you are! But you're ill, my little puma!"

He carried her off and ran back to his mother and Camille.

"But, Mother, Saha's ill! Her coat's shocking—she weighs next to nothing—and you never told me!"

"It's because she eats nothing," said Mme. Amparat. "She refuses to eat."

"She doesn't eat? And what else?"

He cradled the cat against his chest and Saha abandoned herself to him. Her breathing was shallow and her nostrils dry. Mme. Amparat's eyes, under the thick white waves, glanced intelligently at Camille.

"Nothing else," she said.

"She's bored without you," said Camille. "After all, she's your cat, isn't she?"

He thought she was laughing at him and raised his head defiantly. But Camille's face had not changed and she was curiously examining Saha, who shut her eyes again as soon as touched by her.

"Feel her ears," said Alain sharply. "They're burning."

In an instant, his mind was made up.

"Right. I'm taking her with me. Mother, get them to fetch me her basket, will you? And a sack of sand for the tray. We've got everything else she needs. You understand I simply couldn't bear . . . This cat believes . . ."

He broke off and turned belatedly to his wife.

"It won't worry you, Camille, if I take Saha while we're waiting to come back here?"

"What a question! But where do you propose to put her at night?" she added so naïvely that Alain blushed because of his mother's presence and answered acridly: "That's for her to decide."

They left in a little procession; Alain carrying Saha, mute in her travelling-basket. Old Émile was bowed under the sack full of sand and Camille brought up the rear, bearing an old frayed kasha travelling-rug which Alain called the Kashasaha.

SIX

"No, I never thought a cat would get acclimatised so quickly."

"A cat's merely a cat. But Saha's Saha."

Alain was proudly doing the honours of Saha. He himself had never kept her so close at hand, imprisoned in twenty-five square metres and visible at all hours. For her feline meditation, for her craving for solitude and shadow, she was reduced to withdrawing under the giant armchairs scattered about the studio or into the miniature hall or into one of the built-in wardrobes camouflaged with mirrors.

But Saha was determined to triumph over all obstacles. She accepted the uncertain times of meals and of getting up and going to bed. She chose the bathroom with its cork-topped stool to sleep in and she explored the Wedge with no affectation of wildness or disgust. In the kitchen, she condescended to listen to the lazy voice of Mme. Buque summoning "the pussy" to raw liver. When Alain and Camille went out, she installed herself on the giddy parapet and gazed into the abysses of air, following the flying backs of swallows and sparrows below her with a calm, untroubled eye. Her impassiveness on the edge of a sheer drop of nine storeys and the habit she had of washing herself at length on the parapet, terrified Camille.

"Stop her," she yelled to Alain. "She makes my heart turn over and gives me cramp in my calves."

Alain gave an unperturbed smile and admired his cat who had recovered her taste for food and life.

It was not that she was blooming or particularly gay. She did not recover the iridescence of her fur that had gleamed like a pigeon's mauve plumage. But she was more alive; she waited for the dull "poum" of the lift which brought up Alain and accepted extra attentions from Camille, such as a tiny saucer of milk at five o'clock or a small chicken bone offered high up, as if to a dog who was expected to jump for it.

"Not like that! Not like that!" scolded Alain.

And he would lay the bone on a bathmat or simply on the thick-piled beige carpet.

"Really . . . on Patrick's carpet!" Camille scolded in turn.

"But a cat can't eat a bone or any solid food on a polished surface. When a cat takes a bone off a plate and puts it down on the carpet before eating it, she's told she's dirty. But the cat needs to hold it down with her paw while she crunches and tears it and she can only do it on bare earth or on a carpet. People don't know that."

Amazed, Camille broke in: "And how do *you* know?"

He had never asked himself that and got out of it by a joke: "Hush! It's because I'm extremely intelligent. Don't tell a soul! M. Veuillet hasn't a notion of it."

He taught her all the ways and habits of the cat, like a foreign language over-rich in subtle shades of meaning. In spite of himself, he spoke with emphatic authority as he taught. Camille observed him narrowly and asked him any number of questions which he answered unreservedly.

"Why does the cat play with a piece of string when she's frightened of the big ship's rope?"

"Because the ship's rope is the snake. It's the thickness of a snake. She's afraid of snakes."

"Has she ever seen a snake?"

Alain looked at his wife with the grey-green, black-lashed eyes she found so beautiful . . . "so treacherous" she said.

"No . . . certainly not. Where could she have seen one?"

"Well, then?"

"Well, then she invents one. She creates one. You'd be frightened of snakes too, even if you'd never seen one."

"Yes, but I've been told about them. I've seen them in pictures. I know they exist."

"So does Saha."

"But how?"

He gave her a haughty smile.

"How? But by her birth, like persons of quality."

"So I'm not a person of quality?"

He softened, but only out of compassion.

"Good Heavens, no. Console yourself: I'm not either. Don't you believe what I tell you?"

Camille, sitting at her husband's feet, contemplated him with her widest eyes; the eyes of the little girl of other days who did not want to say 'How d'you do?'

"I'd better believe it," she said gravely.

They took to dining at home nearly every night, because of the heat, said Alain, "and because of Saha" insinuated Camille. One evening after dinner, Saha was sitting on her friend's knee.

"What about me?" said Camille.

"I've two knees," Alain retorted.

Nevertheless, the cat did not use her privilege for long. Some mysterious warning made her return to the polished ebony table where she seated herself on her own bluish reflection immersed in a dusky pool. There was nothing unusual about her behaviour except the fixed attention she gave to the invisible things straight in front of her in the air.

"What's she looking at?" asked Camille.

She was pretty every evening at that particular hour; wearing white pyjamas, her hair half loosened on her forehead and her cheeks very brown under the layers of powder she had been superimposing since the morning. Alain sometimes kept on his summer suit, without a waistcoat, but Camille laid impatient hands on him, taking off his jacket and tie, opening his collar and rolling up his shirt-sleeves, seeking and displaying the bare skin. He treated her as a hussy, letting her do as she wished. She laughed a little unhappily as she contained her feelings. And it was he who lowered his eyes with an anxiety that was not entirely voluptuous: 'What ravages of desire on that face! Her mouth is quite distorted with it. A young wife who's so *very* young. Who taught her to forestall me like that?'

The round table, flanked by a little trolley on rubber wheels, gathered the three of them together at the entrance to the studio, near the open bay window. Three tall old poplars, relics of a beautiful garden that had been

destroyed, waved their tops at the height of the balcony
and the great setting sun of Paris, dark red and smothered
in mists, was going down behind their lean heads from
which the sap was retreating.

Mme. Buque's dinner—she cooked food well and
served it badly—enlivened the hour. Refreshed, Alain
forgot his day and the Amparat office and the tutelage
of M. Veuillet. His two captives in the glass tower made
a fuss of him. "Were you waiting for me?" he murmured
in Saha's ear.

"I heard you coming!" cried Camille. "One can hear
every sound from here!"

"Have you been bored?" he asked her one evening,
fearing that she was going to complain. But she shook
her black mop in denial.

"Not the least bit in the world. I went over to
Mummy's. She's presented me with the treasure."

"What treasure?"

"The little woman who'll be my maid over there.
Provided old Émile doesn't give her a baby. She's quite
attractive."

She laughed as she rolled up her white crêpe sleeves
over her bare arms before she cut open the red-fleshed
melon round which Saha was tiptoeing. But Alain did
not laugh: he was too taken up with the horror of
imagining a new maid in his house.

"Yes? But do remember," he brought out, "my
mother's never changed her servants since I was a
child."

"That's obvious," said Camille trenchantly. "What a
museum of old crocks!"

She was biting into a crescent of melon as she spoke and laughing, with her face to the setting sun. Alain admired, in a detached way, how vivid a certain cannibal radiance could be in those glittering eyes and on the glittering teeth in the narrow mouth. There was something Italian about her regular features. He made one more effort to be considerate.

"You never see your girl friends nowadays, it seems to me. Mightn't you perhaps . . ."

She took him up fiercely.

"And what girl friends, may I ask? Is this your way of telling me I'm a burden on you? So that I shall give you a little breathing space. That's it, isn't it?"

He raised his eyebrows and clicked his tongue "tst . . . tst". She yielded at once with a plebeian respect for the man's disdain.

"It's quite true. I never had any friends when I was a little girl. And now . . . can you see me with a girl who's not married? Either I'd have to treat her as a child or I'd have to answer all her dirty questions: 'And what does one do *here* and how does he do *that* to you!' Girls," she explained with some bitterness, "girls don't stick together decently. There's no solidarity. It's not like all you men."

"Forgive me! I'm not one of 'all-you-men'!"

"Oh, I know that all right," she said sadly. "Sometimes I wonder if I wouldn't rather . . ."

She was very rarely sad and, when she was, it was because of some secret reticence or some doubt that she did not express.

"*You* haven't any friends either," she went on.

"Except Patrick and he's away. And even Patrick, you don't really care a damn about him."

She broke off at a gesture from Alain.

"Don't let's talk about these things," she said intelligently. "There'll only be a quarrel."

The long-drawn-out cries of children rose from the ground level and blended with the airy whistling of the swallows. Saha's beautiful yellow eyes, in which the great nocturnal pupil was slowly invading the iris, stared into space picking out moving, floating, invisible points.

"Tell me, whatever's the cat looking at? Are you sure there's nothing, over there where she's staring?"

"Nothing . . . for us."

Alain evoked with regret the faint shiver, the seductive fear that his cat friend used to communicate to him in the days when she slept on his chest at night.

"She doesn't make you frightened, I hope?" he said condescendingly.

Camille burst out laughing, as if the insulting word were just what she had been waiting for.

"Frightened? There aren't many things that frighten *me*, you know!"

"That's the statement of a silly little fool," said Alain angrily.

"Let's say you're feeling the storm coming, shall we?" said Camille, shrugging her shoulders.

She pointed to the wall, purpled with clouds which were coming up with the night.

"And you're like Saha," she added. "You don't like storms."

"No one likes storms."

"I don't hate them," said Camille judicially. "Anyway, I'm not the slightest bit afraid of them."

"The whole world is afraid of storms," said Alain, hostile.

"All right, I'm not the whole world, that's all."

"You are for me," he said with a sudden, artificial grace which did not deceive her.

"Oh!" she scolded under her breath. "I shall hit you."

He bent his fair head towards her over the table and showed his white teeth.

"All right, hit me!"

But she deprived herself of the pleasure of rumpling that golden hair and offering her bare arm to those shining teeth.

"You've got a crooked nose," she flung at him fiercely.

"It's the storm," he said, laughing.

This subtlety was not at all to Camille's taste, but the first low rumblings of the thunder distracted her attention. She threw down her napkin to run out on the balcony.

"Come along! There'll be some marvellous lightning."

"No," said Alain, without moving. "Come along, yourself."

"Where to?"

He jerked his chin in the direction of their room. Camille's face assumed the obstinate expression, the dull-witted greed he knew so well. Nevertheless, she hesitated.

"But couldn't we look at the lightning first?"

He made a sign of refusal.

"Why not, horrid?"

"Because *I'm* frightened of storms. Choose. The storm or . . . me."

"What do you think!"

She ran to their room with an eagerness which flattered Alain's vanity. But, when he joined her there, he found she had deliberately lighted a luminous glass cube near the vast bed. He deliberately turned it out.

The rain came in through the open bay-windows as they lay calm again, warm and tingling, breathing in the ozone that filled the room with freshness. Lying in Alain's arms, Camille made him understand that, while the storm raged, she would have liked him once again to forget his terror of it with her. But he was nervously counting the great sheets of lightning and the tall dazzling trees silhouetted against the cloud and he moved away from Camille. She resigned herself, raised herself on her elbow and combed her husband's crackling hair with one hand. In the pulsations of the lightning-flashes their two blue plaster faces rose out of the night and were swallowed up in it again.

"We'll wait till the storm's over," she consented.

'And *that*,' said Alain to himself, '*that*'s what she finds to say after an encounter that really meant something. She might at least have kept quiet. As Émile says, the young lady speaks her mind straight out.'

A flickering flash, long as a dream, was reflected in a blade of fire in the thick slab of glass on the invisible dressing-table. Camille clutched Alain against her bare leg.

"Is that to reassure me? We know you're not frightened of lightning."

He raised his voice so as to be heard above the hollow rumbling and the rain cascading on the flat roof. He felt tired and on edge, tempted to be unjust yet frightened to say openly that nowadays he was never alone. In his mind he returned violently to his old room with its white wallpaper patterned with stiff conventional flowers, a room which no one had ever tried to make prettier or uglier. His longing for it was so fierce that the murmur of the inefficient old radiator came back with the memory of the pale flowers on the wallpaper. The wheezy mutter that came from the hollow space below its copper pipes seemed to be part of the murmurs of the whole house; of the whispering of the worn old servants, half-buried in their basement, who no longer cared to go out even into the garden . . . 'They used to say "She" when they talked about my mother but I've been "Monsieur Alain" since I first went into knickerbockers.'

A dry crackle of thunder roused him from the brief doze into which he had fallen. His young wife, leaning over him, propped on her elbow, had not stirred.

"I like you so much when you're asleep," she said. "The storm's going off."

He took this as a demand and sat up.

"I'm following its example," he said. "How hot and sticky it is! I'm going to sleep on the waiting-room bench."

The 'waiting-room bench' was their name for the narrow divan which was the solitary piece of furniture in a tiny room, a mere strip of glass-walled passage which Patrick used for sunbathing.

"Oh, no! Oh, no!" implored Camille. "Do stay."

But he had already slipped out of the bed. The great flashes in the clouds revealed Camille's hard, offended face.

"Pooh! Baby boy!"

At this, which he was not expecting, she pulled his nose. With an instinctive reflex of his arm, which he could not control and did not regret, he beat down the disrespectful hand. A sudden lull in the wind and rain left them alone in the silence, as if struck dumb. Camille massaged her hand.

"But . . ." she said at last, "But . . . you're a brute."

"Possibly," said Alain. "I don't like having my face touched. Isn't the rest of me enough for you? Never touch my face."

"But you *are* . . . you really *are* a brute," Camille repeated slowly.

"Don't keep on saying it. Apart from that, I've nothing against you. Just mind you don't do it again."

He lifted his bare leg back on to the bed.

"You see that big grey square on the carpet? It's nearly daybreak. Shall we go to sleep?"

"Yes . . . let's . . ." said the same, hesitant voice.

"Come on, then!"

He stretched out his left arm so that she could rest her head on it. She did so submissively and with a circumspect politeness. Pleased with himself, Alain gave her a friendly jostle and pulled her towards him by her shoulder. But he bent his knees a little to keep her at a safe distance and fell asleep almost at once. Camille lay awake, breathing carefully and watched the grey patch on the carpet growing lighter. She listened to the sparrows celebrating the end of the storm in the three poplars whose rustling sounded like the faint continuation of the rain. When Alain, changing his position, withdrew his arm, he gave her an unconscious caress. Three times his hand slid lightly over her head as if accustomed to stroking fur that was even softer than her soft black hair.

SEVEN

It was towards the end of June that incompatibility became established between them like a new season of the year. Like a season, it had its surprises and even its pleasures. To Alain, it was like a harsh, chilly spring inserted in the heart of summer. He was incessantly and increasingly aware of his repugnance at the idea of making a place for this young woman, this outsider, in his own home. He nursed this resentment and fed it with secret soliloquies and the sullen contemplation of their new dwelling. Camille, exhausted with the heat, called out from the high and now windless balcony: "Oh, let's chuck everything. Let's take the old scooter and go somewhere where we can bathe. Shall we, Alain?"

"All right by me," he answered with wily promptitude. "Where shall we go?"

There was a peaceful interlude while Camille enumerated beaches and names of hotels. With his eye on Saha who lay flat and prostrated, Alain had the leisure to think and to conclude: 'I don't want to go away with her I . . . I daren't. I'm quite willing to go for a drive, as we used to, and come back in the evening or late at night. But that's all. I don't want evenings in hotels and nights in a casino, evenings of . . .' He shuddered: 'I need time. I realise that I take a long time to get used to things, that I'm a difficult character, that . . . But I don't want to go off with *her*.' He felt a pang of shame as he realised that he had mentally said '*her*' just like Émile and Adèle when they were discussing 'Madame' in undertones.

Camille bought road-maps and they played at travelling through a France spread in quarters over the polished ebony table which reflected their two blurred, inverted faces.

They added up the mileage, ran down their car, cursed each other affably and felt revived, even rehabilitated by a comradeship they had forgotten. But tropical showers, unaccompanied by gales, drowned the last days of June and the balconies of the Wedge. Sheltering behind the closed panes, Saha watched the level rivulets, which Camille mopped up by stamping on table-napkins, winding across the inlaid tiles. The horizon; the city; the shower itself; all took on the colour of clouds loaded with inexhaustible rain.

"Would you rather we took the train?" suggested Alain suavely.

He had foreseen that Camille would fly out at the detested word. Fly out she did indeed—and blasphemously.

"I'm afraid," he went on, "that you're getting bored. All those trips we'd promised ourselves."

"All those summer hotels. All those restaurants full of flies. All those seas full of people bathing," she railed plaintively. "Look here, you and I are quite used to driving around. But what we're good at is just going for drives. We're quite lost when it comes to a real journey."

He saw she was slightly depressed and gave her a brotherly kiss. But she turned round and bit him on his mouth and under his ear. Once again, they fell into the diversion which shortens the hours and makes the body attain its pleasure easily. It was beginning to make Alain tired. When he dined at his mother's with Camille and had to stifle his yawns, Mme. Amparat lowered her eyes and Camille invariably gave a little, swaggering laugh. For she was proudly conscious of the habit Alain had acquired of making love to her hurriedly and almost peevishly, flinging her away the moment it was over to return to the cool side of the uncovered bed.

Ingenuously, she would rejoin him there and he did not forgive her for that although, silently, he would yield again. After that he felt at liberty to probe at leisure into the sources of what he called their incompatibility. He was wise enough to put these outside their frequent lovemaking. Clear-headed, helped by the very fact of his sexual exhaustion, he returned to those retreats where the hostility of man to woman keeps its unageing freshness. Sometimes she revealed herself to him in some commonplace realm where she slept in broad sunshine, like an innocent creature. Sometimes he was astonished, even scandalised, that she should be so dark. Lying in bed behind her, he surveyed the short hairs on her shaved neck, ranged like the prickles of a sea-urchin and drawn on the skin like the hatching on a map. The shortest of them were blue and visible under the fine skin before each one emerged through a small blackened pore.

'Have I never really had a dark woman?' he wondered. 'Two or three little black-haired things haven't left me any impression of *such* darkness.' And he held his own arm up to the light. It was yellowish-white; a typical fair man's arm with green-gold down and jade-coloured veins. His own hair seemed to him like a forest with violet shadows, whereas Camille's showed the strange whiteness of the skin between the exotic abundance of those ranks of black, slightly crinkled stalks.

The sight of a fine, very black hair stuck to the side of a basin made him feel sick. Then the little neurosis changed and, abandoning the detail, he concentrated on her whole body. Holding that young, appeased body in his arms in the night which hid its contours he began to be annoyed that a creative spirit, in moulding Camille, had shown a strict reasonableness like that of his English nurse. "Not more prunes than rice, my boy," she used to say. "Not more rice than chicken." That spirit had modelled Camille adequately but with no concessions to lavishness or fantasy. He carried his annoyances and regrets into the ante-chamber of his dreams during that incalculable moment reserved for the black landscape peopled with bulbous eyes, fish with Greek noses, moons and chins. There he desired a big-hipped charmer of the 1900 type, liberally developed above a tiny waist, to compensate for the acid smallness of Camille's breasts. At other times, half-asleep, he compromised and preferred a top-heavy bosom; two quivering, monstrous hillocks of flesh with sensitive tips. Such feverish desires, which were born of the sexual act and survived it, never affronted the light of day nor even complete wakefulness. They merely peopled a narrow isthmus between nightmare and voluptuous dream.

When her flesh was warm, the 'foreigner' smelt of wood licked by tongues of flame; birch, violets . . . a whole bouquet of sweet, dark tenacious scents which clung long to the palms. These fragrances produced in

Alain a kind of perverse excitement but did not always arouse his desire.

"You're like the smell of roses," he said one day to Camille, "you take away one's appetite."

She looked at him dubiously and assumed the slightly gauche, downcast expression with which she received double-edged compliments.

"How awfully eighteen-thirty you are," she murmured.

"You're much more so," replied Alain. "Oh, ever so much more so. I know who you're like."

"Marie Dubas, the actress. I've been told that before."

"Hopelessly wrong, my girl! Minus the bandeaux, you're like all those girls who weep on the tops of towers in the works of Loïsa Puget. You can see them weeping on the cover of his romantic songs, with *your* great, prominent Greek eyes and those thick rims to the lower lid that makes the tears jump down on to the cheeks . . ."

One after another, Alain's senses took advantage of him to condemn Camille. He had to admit, at least, that she stood up admirably to certain remarks he fired at her point-blank. They were provocative rather than grateful remarks that burst out of him at the times when, lying on the floor, he measured her with narrowed eyes and appraised her new merits without indulgence or regard for her feelings. He judged her particular aptitudes; he noted how that sensual ardour of hers, that slightly monotonous passion, had already developed an en-lightened self-interest remarkable in so young a married woman. Those were moments of frankness and certainty and Camille did all she could to prolong their half-silent atmosphere of conflict; their tension like that of a tight-rope on which balance was precarious and dangerous.

Having no deep-seated malice in herself, Camille never suspected that Alain was only half taken in by deliberate challenges, pathetic appeals and even by a cool Polynesian cynicism, and that each time he possessed his wife, he meant it to be the last. He mastered her as he might have put a hand on her mouth to stop her from screaming or as he might have murdered her.

When she was dressed again and sitting upright beside him in their roadster, he could look at her closely without rediscovering what it was that had made her his worst enemy. As soon as he regained his breath, listening to his decreasing heartbeats, he ceased to be the dramatic young man who stripped himself naked before wrestling with his companion and overthrowing her. The brief routine of pleasure; the controlled expert movements, the real or simulated gratitude were regulated to the ranks of what is over, of what will probably never happen again. Then his greatest preoccupation would return, the one which he accepted as natural and honourable, the question which reassumed the first place it had so long deserved: 'How to stop Camille from living in MY house?'

Once his period of hostility towards the 'alterations' had passed, he had genuinely put his faith in the return to the home of his childhood, in the tranquillising influence of a life on ground level; a life in contact with the earth and everything the earth brings forth. 'Here, I'm suffering from living up in the air. Oh, to see branches and birds from *underneath* again!' he sighed. But he concluded severely 'Pastoral life is no solution,' and once more had recourse to his indispensable ally, the lie.

On a blazing afternoon which melted the asphalt he went to his domain. All about it, Neuilly was a desert of the empty roads and empty tramways of July; the gardens were abandoned except for a few yawning dogs. Before leaving Camille, he had installed Saha on the coolest balcony of the Wedge. He was vaguely worried every time he left his two females alone together.

The garden and the house were asleep and the little iron gate did not creak as he opened it. Overblown roses, red poppies, the first ruby-throated Canna lilies and dark snapdragons burned in isolated clumps on the lawns. At the side of the house gaped the new doorway and two new windows in a freshly-painted little one-storeyed building. 'It's all finished,' Alain realised. He walked carefully, as he did in his dreams, and trod only on the grass.

Hearing the murmur of a voice rising from the basement, he stopped and absent-mindedly listened. It was only the old well-known voices of servility and ritual grumbling, the old voices which used to say "She" and "Monsieur Alain". Once upon a time they had flattered the fragile, fair-haired little boy and his childish pride . . . 'I was a king, once,' Alain said to himself, smiling sadly.

"Well, so *she'll* soon be coming to sleep here, I suppose?" one of the old voices asked audibly.

'That's Adèle,' thought Alain. Leaning against the wall, he listened without the least scruple.

"Of course she will," bleated Émile. "That flat's shockingly badly built."

The housemaid, a greying Basque woman with a hairy face, broke in: "You're right there. From their bathroom you can hear everything that goes on in the water-closet. Monsieur Alain won't like *that*."

"*She* said, the last time *she* came that *she* didn't need curtains in her little drawing-room because there are no neighbours on the garden side."

"No neighbours? What about us when we go to the wash-house? What's one going to see when *she's* with Monsieur Alain?"

Alain could guess the smothered laughter and the ancient Émile continued: "Oh, perhaps one won't see as much as all *that*. *She'll* be put in her place, all right. Monsieur Alain's not the sort to let himself go on a sofa at any time of day or night."

There was a silence during which Alain could hear nothing but the sound of a knife on the grindstone. But he stayed listening, with his back against the hot wall and his eyes vaguely searching between a flaming geranium and the acid green of the turf as if he half-expected to see Saha's moonstone-coloured fur.

"As for me," said Adèle. "I think it's oppressive, that scent *she* puts on."

"And her frocks," supplemented Juliette, the Basque woman. "The way she dresses isn't really good style. *She* looks more like an actress. Behaves like one too, with that brazen way of hers. And now what's she going to land us with in the way of a lady's maid? Some creature out of an orphanage, I believe, or worse."

A fanlight slammed and the voices were cut off. Alain felt weak and trembling. He breathed like a man who has just been spared by a gang of murderers. He was neither surprised nor indignant. There was not much difference between his own opinion of Camille and that of the harsh judges in the basement. But his heart was beating fast because he had meanly eavesdropped without being punished for it and because he had been listening to prejudiced witnesses and unsought accomplices. He wiped his face and took a deep breath as if inhaling this gust of misogyny, this pagan incense offered exclusively to the male principle, had anaesthetised him. His mother, who had just wakened from her siesta and was putting back the shutters of her room, saw him standing there, with his cheek still leant against the wall.

She called softly, like a wise mother.

"Ah! my boy . . . Is anything the matter?"

He took her hands over the window-sill, like a lover.

"Nothing at all. I was out for a walk and just thought I'd look in."

"A very good idea."

She did not believe him but they smiled at each other, perfectly aware that neither was telling the truth.

"Mother, could I ask you to do me a little favour?"

"A little favour in the way of money, isn't that it? I know you're none too well off this year, my poor children."

"No, Mother. Please, would you mind not telling Camille that I came here today? As I didn't come here for any special reason, I mean with no special reason except just to look in and give you a kiss, I'd rather . . . Actually, that's not all. I want you to give me some advice. Strictly between the two of us, you know."

Mme. Amparat lowered her eyes, ran her hand through her wavy white hair and tried to avert the confidence.

"I'm not much of a talker, as you know. You've caught me all untidy. I look like an old gipsy. Won't you come inside into the cool?"

"No, Mother. Do you think there's any way . . . it's an idea I can't get out of my head . . . a polite way, of course . . . something that wouldn't offend anyone . . . but some way of stopping Camille from living here?"

He seized his mother's hands, expecting them to tremble or to draw away. But they stayed, cold and soft, between his own.

"These are just a young husband's ideas," she said, embarrassed.

"What do you mean?"

"With young married couples, things go too well or they go too badly. I don't know which works out best in the end. But they never go straightforwardly, just of their own accord."

"But, Mother, that's not what I'm asking you. I'm asking you whether there isn't any way . . ."

For the first time, he was unable to look his mother in the face. She gave him no help and he turned away irritably.

"You're talking like a child. You run about the streets in this frightful heat and you come to me after a quarrel and ask me impossible questions. I don't know. Questions whose only answer is divorce. Or moving house. Or heaven knows what."

She got breathless whenever she talked and Alain only reproached himself for making her flush and pant even at saying so little. 'That's enough for today,' he thought prudently.

"We haven't had a quarrel, Mother. It's only I who can't get used to the idea . . . who doesn't want to see . . ."

With a wide, embarrassed gesture, he indicated the garden that surrounded them: the green lake of the lawn; the bed of fallen petals under the rose-arches; a swarm of bees over the flowering ivy; the ugly, revered house.

The hand he had kept in one of his clenched and hardened into a little fist and he suddenly kissed that sensitive hand: 'Enough, that's enough for today.'

"I'm off now, Mother. Monsieur Veuillet's telephoning you at eight tomorrow about this business of the shares going down. Do I look better now, Mother?"

He raised his eyes that looked greener in the shade of the tulip-tree and threw back his face which from habit, affection and diplomacy he had forced into his old childish expression. A flutter of the lids to brighten the eye, the seductive smile, a little pout of the lips. His mother's hand unclenched again and reached over the sill to feel Alain's well-known weak spots; his shoulder-blades, his Adam's apple, the top of his arm. She did all this before replying.

"A little better. Yes, really, quite a lot better."

'I've pleased her by asking her to keep something secret from Camille.' At the remembrance of his mother's last caress, he tightened his belt under his jacket. 'I've got thinner, I'm getting thinner. No more physical culture— no physical culture other than making love.'

He went off with a light step, in his summer clothes, and the cooling breeze dried his sweat and blew the acrid smell of it ahead of him. He left his native castle inviolate, his subterranean cohort intact, and the rest of the day would pass easily enough. Until midnight, no doubt, sitting in the car beside an inoffensive Camille, he would drink in the evening air, now sylvan as they drove between oak plantations edged with muddy ditches, now dry and smelling of wheatstraw. 'And I'll bring back some fresh couch-grass for Saha.'

Vehemently, he reproached himself for the lot of his cat who lived so soundlessly at the top of their glass tower. 'She's like her own chrysalis, and it's my fault.' At the hour of their conjugal games she banished herself so rigorously that Alain had never seen her in the triangular room. She ate just sufficient to keep alive; she had lost her varied language and given up all her demands, seeming to prefer her long waiting to everything else. 'Once again, she's waiting behind bars. She's waiting for me.'

Camille's shattering voice came through the closed door as he reached the landing.

"It's that filthy bloody swine of an animal! I wish it were dead! What? No, Madame Buque, I don't care what you say. To hell with it! To hell with it!"

He made out a few more violent expressions. Very softly he turned the key in the lock but, once over his own threshold, he could not consent to listen without being seen. 'A filthy bloody swine of an animal? But what animal? An animal in the house?'

In the studio Camille, wearing a little sleeveless pullover and a knitted béret miraculously balanced on her skull, was furiously pulling a pair of gauntlet gloves over her bare hands. She seemed stupefied at the sight of her husband.

"It's you! Where have you sprung from?"

"I haven't sprung from anywhere. I've simply arrived home. Who are you so furious with?"

She avoided the trap and neatly turned the attack on Alain.

"You're very cutting, the first time you get home punctually. *I'm* ready. I've been waiting for you."

"You haven't been waiting for me since I'm punctual to the minute. Who were you so angry with? I heard 'filthy bloody swine of an animal?' What animal?"

She squinted very slightly but sustained Alain's look.

"The dog!" she cried. "That damned dog downstairs, the dog that barks morning, noon and night. It's started again! Can't you hear it barking? Listen!"

She raised her finger to make him keep quiet and Alain had time to notice that the gloved finger was shaking. He yielded to a naïve need to make sure.

"Just fancy, I thought you were talking about Saha."

"Me?" cried Camille. "Me speak about Saha in that tone? Why I wouldn't dare! The heavens would fall if I did! For goodness sake, are you coming?"

"Go and get the car out, I'll join you down below. I've just got to get a handkerchief and a pullover."

His first thought was to find the cat. On the coolest balcony, near the deck-chair in which Camille occasionally slept in the afternoon, he could see nothing but some fragments of broken glass. He stared at them blankly.

"The cat's with me, Monsieur," came the fluting voice of Mme. Buque. "She's very fond of my wicker stool. She sharpens her claws on it."

'In the kitchen,' thought Alain painfully. 'My little puma, my cat of the garden, my cat of the lilacs and the butterflies, in the kitchen! Ah! All that's going to change!'

He kissed Saha on the forehead and chanted some ritual praises, very low. He promised her couch-grass and sweet acacia flowers. But he found both the cat and Mme. Buque artificial and constrained; Mme. Buque in particular.

"We may be back to dinner and we may not, Madame Buque. Has the cat everything she needs?"

"Yes, Monsieur. Oh yes, indeed Monsieur," said Mme. Buque hurriedly. "I do everything I possibly can, really I do, Monsieur!"

The big, fat woman was red in the face and seemed on the verge of tears. She ran a friendly, clumsy hand over the cat's back. Saha arched her back and proffered a little "m'hain", the mew of a poor timid cat which made her friend's heart swell with sadness.

The drive was more peaceful than he had hoped. Sitting at the wheel, her eyes alert, her feet and hands perfectly synchronised, Camille drove him as far as the slope of Montfort-l'Amaurey.

"Shall we have dinner out-of-doors, Alain? Shall we, Alain darling?"

She smiled at him in profile, beautiful as she always was in the twilight; her cheek brown and transparent, her teeth and the corner of her eye the same glittering white.

In the forest of Rambouillet, she put down the wind-screen and the wind filled Alain's ears with a sound of leaves and running water.

"A little rabbit! . . ." cried Camille. "A pheasant!"

"It's still a rabbit . . . One moment more and . . ."

"He doesn't know his luck, that chap!"

"You've got a dimple in your cheek like you have in your photos as a child," said Alain, beginning to come to life.

"Don't talk about it! I'm getting enormous!" she said, shaking her shoulders.

He watched for the return of the laugh and the dimple, and his eyes wandered down to the robust neck, free of any trace of the "girdle of Venus", the round, inflexible neck of a handsome white Negress. 'Yes, she really has got fatter. And in the most seductive way. For her breasts, those too . . ." He withdrew into himself once more and came up, morosely, against the age-old male grievance. 'She's getting fat from making love. She's battening on *me*.' He slipped a jealous hand under his jacket, felt his ribs and ceased to admire the childish dimple in her cheeks.

But he felt a certain gratified vanity when they sat down a little later at a famous inn and the neighbouring diners stopped talking and eating to stare at Camille. And he exchanged with his wife the smiles, the movements of the chin and all the rituals of coquetry suitable to a "handsome couple".

However, it was only for him that Camille lowered her voice and displayed a certain languor and certain charming attentions which were not in the least for show. In revenge, Alain snatched out of her hand the dish of raw tomatoes and the basket of strawberries, insisted that she ate chicken with a cream sauce and poured her out a wine which she did not care for but which she drank fast.

"You know perfectly well I don't like wine," she repeated each time she emptied her glass.

The sun had set but the sky was still almost white, dappled with small deep-pink clouds. But night and coolness seemed to be rising as one from the forest which loomed, massive, beyond the tables of the inn. Camille laid her hand on Alain's.

"What is it? What is it? What's the matter?" he said in terror.

Astonished, she withdrew her hand. The little wine she had drunk gleamed gaily in her eyes in which shone the tiny, quivering image of the pink balloons hung from the pergola.

"Nothing's the matter, silly. You're as nervous as a cat! Is it forbidden for me to put my hand on yours?"

"I thought," he admitted weakly, "I thought you wanted to tell me something . . . something serious . . . I thought," he burst out with it, "you were going to tell me you were pregnant."

Camille's shrill little laugh attracted the attention of the men at the nearby tables.

"And you were as overcome as all that? With joy or . . . fed-up-ness?"

"I don't exactly know. What about you? Would you be pleased or not pleased? We've hardly thought about it . . . at least, I haven't. But what are you laughing at?"

"Your face! All of a sudden, a face as if you were just going to be hanged. It's too funny. You'll make my eye-black come unstuck."

With her two forefingers, she lifted up either eyelid.

"It isn't funny, it's serious," said Alain, glad to put her in the wrong. 'But why was I so terrified?' he thought.

"It's only serious," said Camille, "for people who've got nowhere to live or who've only got two rooms. But people like us . . ."

Serene, lulled into optimism by the treacherous wine, she smoked and talked as if she were by herself, her thigh against the table and her legs crossed.

"Pull down your skirt, Camille."

She did not hear him and went on: "We've got all the essentials a child needs. A garden—and what a garden! And a dream of a room with its own bathroom."

"A room?"

"Your old room. We'd have it repainted. And it would be very nice of you not to insist on a frieze of little ducks and fir trees on a sky-blue background. That would ruin the taste of our offspring."

He restrained himself from stopping her. She was talking at random, her cheeks flushed, as she stared into the distance, seeing all she was building up. He had never seen her so beautiful. He was fascinated by the base of her neck, like the smooth unwrinkled bole of a tree, and by the nostrils which were blowing out smoke. 'When I give her pleasure and she tightens her lips, she opens her nostrils like a little horse as she breathes.'

He heard such crazy predictions fall from the reddened, scornful lips that they ceased to alarm him: Camille was calmly proceeding with her woman's life among the wreckage of Alain's past. 'Good Lord,' he thought. 'How she's got it all organised. I'm certainly learning something!' A tennis-court was to replace the great, useless lawn. The kitchen and the pantries . . .

"Haven't you ever realised how inconvenient they are? And think of all that wasted space. It's like the garage. I'm only saying all this, darling, so as you should know I think a lot about our real setting up house. Above all, we must be tactful with your mother. She's so awfully sweet . . . we mustn't do anything she wouldn't approve of. Must we?"

He put in haphazard "Yeses" and "Noes" as he picked up some wild strawberries scattered on the cloth. After hearing her say "your old room", he had been immunised by a provisional calm, a foretaste of indifference.

"Only one thing may make things awkward for us," Camille went on. "Patrick's last postcard's dated from the Balearic Isles. Do pay attention! It'll take less time for Patrick to get back from the Balearics than for our decorator to get everything finished. I hope he comes to a violent end, that son of Penelope by a male tortoise! But I shall put on my siren voice: 'Patrick, my pet . . .' You know my siren voice makes a tremendous impression on Patrick."

"From the Balearic Isles . . ." broke in Alain thoughtfully. "From the Balearic Isles."

"Otherwise practically from next door. Where are you off to? Do you want us to go? It was so nice here."

Her brief intoxication was over. She stood up shivering and yawning with sleepiness.

"I'll drive," said Alain. "Put on the old coat that's under the cushion. And go to sleep."

A flak of flying insects, bright silver moths and stag-beetles hard as pebbles, whirled in front of the headlights and the car drove back the wing-laden air like a wave. Camille did indeed go to sleep, sitting perfectly upright. She was trained not to encumber the driver's arm and shoulder, even in her sleep. She merely gave a little forward jerk of her head at every jolt in the road.

'From the Balearic Isles,' Alain kept repeating to himself. The dark air, the white fires which caught and repulsed and decimated the flying creatures took him back to the populous threshold of his dreams; the sky with its stardust of exploded faces, the great hostile eyes which put off till tomorrow a reckoning, a password or a significant figure. He was so deep in that world that he forgot to take the short cut between Pontchartrain and the Versailles toll-gate and Camille scolded him in her sleep. 'Bravo!' applauded Alain. 'Good reflex action! Good little faithful, vigilant senses. Ah, how much I like you, how well we get on, when you're asleep and I'm awake.'

Their sleeves and their unprotected hair were wet with dew when they set foot in their newly-built street, empty in the moonlight. Alain looked up: nine storeys up, in the middle of the almost round moon, the little horned shadow of a cat was leaning forward, waiting.

"Look! Look how she's waiting!"

"You've got good eyes," said Camille, yawning.

"If she were to fall! Whatever you do, don't call her!"

"You needn't worry," said Camille. "If I did call her, she wouldn't come."

"For good reason," said Alain unpleasantly.

As soon as he had said it, he was angry with himself. 'Too soon, too soon! And what a bad moment to choose!' Camille dropped the hand that was just about to push the bell.

"For good reason? For what good reason? Come on, out with it. I've been lacking in respect to the sacred animal again? The cat's complained of me?"

'I've gone too far,' thought Alain, as he closed the garage door. He crossed the street again and rejoined his wife who was waiting for him in battle order. 'Either I give in for the sake of a quiet night, or I stop the discussion by giving her a good, hard slap . . . or . . . It's too soon.'

"Well! I'm talking to you!"

"Let's go up first," said Alain.

They did not speak as they went up, squeezed side by side in the narrow lift. As soon as they reached the studio, Camille tore off her béret and gloves and threw them across the room as if to show she had not given up the quarrel. Alain busied himself with Saha, inviting her to quit her perilous post. Patient, determined not to displease him, the cat followed him into the bathroom.

"If it's because of what you heard before dinner, when you came in," began Camille shrilly the moment he reappeared.

Alain had decided on his line and interrupted her wearily: "My dear, what are we going to say to each other? Nothing that we don't know already. That you can't bear the cat, that you blew up Mother Buque because the cat broke a vase—or a glass—I saw the pieces. I shall answer that I'm extremely fond of Saha and that you'd be just as jealous if I'd kept a warm affection for some friend of my childhood. And so it'll go on all night. I'd prefer to sleep, thanks very much. Look here, the next time, I advise you to take the initiative and have a little dog."

Startled, embarrassed by having nothing for her temper to fasten on, Camille stared at him with raised eyebrows.

"The next time? What next time? What do you mean? What initiative?"

As Alain merely shrugged his shoulders, she flushed, her face suddenly became very young again and the extreme brightness of her eyes presaged tears. 'Oh, how bored I am!' groaned Alain inwardly. 'She's going to admit it. She's going to tell me I was right. How boring!'

"Listen, Alain."

With an effort, he feigned anger and assumed a false air of authority.

"No, my dear. No, no, no! You're not going to force me to finish off this charming evening with a barren discussion. You're not going to make a drama out of a piece of childish nonsense any more than you're going to stop me being fond of animals."

A kind of bitter gaiety came into Camille's eyes but she said nothing. 'Perhaps I was a little harsh. "Childish nonsense," was unnecessary. And as to being fond of animals, what do I know about that?' A small, shadowy blue shape, outlined like a cloud with a hem of silver, sitting on the dizzy edge of night, absorbed his thoughts and removed him from that soulless place where, inch by inch, he was defending his chance of solitude, his egotism, his poetry . . .

"Come along, my little enemy," he said with disloyal charm, "let's go and rest."

She opened the door of the bathroom where Saha, installed for the night on the cork-seated stool, appeared to take only the faintest notice of her.

"But why, but why? Why did you say 'the next time'?"

The noise of running water drowned Camille's voice. Alain did not attempt to answer. When he rejoined her in the huge bed, he wished her good-night and kissed her carelessly on her unpowdered nose, while Camille's mouth clung to his chin with a small greedy sound.

Waking early, he went off quietly to lie down on the 'waiting-room bench', the narrow divan squeezed between two walls of glass panes.

It was there that, during the following nights, he finished off his sleep. He closed the opaque oilcloth curtains on either side; they were almost new but already half destroyed by the sun. He breathed on his body the very perfume of his solitude, the sharp feline smell of rest-harrow and flowering box. One arm extended, the other folded on his chest, he resumed the relaxed, lordly attitude of his childhood sleep. Suspended from the narrow top of the three-cornered house, he encouraged with all his might the return of his old dreams which the lover's exhaustion had dispersed.

He escaped more easily than Camille could have wished, constrained as he was to fly on the very spot. Escape no longer meant a staircase descended on tiptoe, the slamming of a taxi door, a brief farewell note. None of his mistresses had prepared him for Camille and her young girl's eagerness; Camille and her reckless desire. Neither had they prepared him for Camille's stoical behaviour as an offended partner. She made it a point of honour not to complain.

Having escaped and lain down again on the waiting-room bench, Alain strained an uneasy ear towards the room he had just left, as his head felt for the hard little cushion he preferred to all the others. But Camille never reopened the door. Left alone, she pulled the crumpled sheet and the silk eiderdown over her, gnawed her bent finger in resentful regret and snapped off the chromium strip-light which threw a narrow white beam across the bed. Alain never knew whether she had slept in the empty bed or whether she was learning so young that a solitary night imposes an armed vigil. It was impossible to tell, since she reappeared fresh and rather carefully dressed instead of in the bathrobe and pyjamas of the night before. But she could not understand that a man's sensuality is brief and seasonal and that its unpredictable return is never a new beginning.

Lying alone, bathed in the night air, measuring the height and the silence of his tower-top by the faintness of the hoots from the boats on the nearby Seine, the unfaithful husband delayed going to sleep till the apparition of Saha. She came to him, a shadow bluer than the shadows, along the ledge outside the open glass pane.

There she stayed on the watch and would not come down on to Alain's chest although he implored her with the words that she knew: "Come, my little puma, come along. . . . My cat of the tree-tops, my cat of the lilacs, Saha, Saha, Saha."

She resisted, sitting there above him on the window sill. He could see nothing of her but her cat's shape against the sky, her chin down and her ears passionately orientated towards him. He could never catch the expression of her look.

Sometimes the dry dawn, the dawn before the wind got up, found the two of them sitting on the east side balcony. Cheek by cheek they watched the sky pale and the flight of white pigeons leaving the beautiful cedar of the Folie-Saint-James one by one. Together they felt the same surprise at being so high above the earth, so alone and so far from being happy. With the ardent, sinuous movement of a huntress, Saha followed the pigeons' flight and uttered an occasional "ek . . . ek . . ." the faint echo of the "mouek . . . mouek . . ." of excitement, greed and violent games.

"Our room," Alain said in her ear. "Our garden, our house."

She was getting thin again and Alain found her light and enchanting. But he suffered at seeing her so gentle and patient. Her patience was that of all those who are wearied out and sustained by a promise.

Sleep overcame Alain again as soon as daylight had begun to shorten the shadows. Rayless at first and looming larger through the mist of Paris, the sun swiftly shrank and lightened. As it rose, already burning hot, it awoke a twittering of sparrows in the gardens. The growing light revealed all the untidiness of a hot night on balconies and window-sills and in little yards where captive shrubs languished—a garment forgotten on a deck-chair, empty glasses on a metal table, a pair of sandals. Alain hated the indecency of small dwellings oppressed by summer and regained his bed with one bound through a yawning panel in the glass. At the foot of the nine-storeyed building, a gardener lifted his head and saw this white young man leap through the transparent wall like a burglar.

Saha did not follow him. Sometimes she strained her ears in the direction of the triangular room; sometimes she dispassionately watched the awakening of the distant world on ground level. Someone let out a dog from a small decrepit house. The dog leapt forward without a bark, rushed round and round the tiny garden, and did not recover its voice until it had finished its aimless run. Women appeared at the windows; a maid furiously slammed doors and shook out orange cushions on a flat roof; men, waking regretfully, lit the first bitter cigarette. At last, in the fireless kitchen of the Wedge, the automatic, whistling coffee-pot and the electric teapot clashed against each other; through the porthole window of the bathroom there emerged Camille's perfume and her noisy yawning. Saha resignedly folded her paws beneath her and pretended to sleep.

EIGHT

ONE evening in July, when the two of them were waiting for Alain's return, Camille and the cat were resting on the same parapet; the cat crouched on all four paws, Camille leaning on her folded arms. Camille did not like this balcony-terrace, reserved for the cat and shut in by two cement partitions which cut off both the wind and all communication with the balcony on the prow.

They exchanged a glance of sheer mutual investigation and Camille did not say a word to Saha. Propped on her elbows, she leant over as if to count the storeys by the orange awnings that flapped from top to bottom of the dizzy façade, she brushed against the cat who got up to make room for her, stretched, and lay down a little further off.

When Camille was alone, she looked very much like the little girl who did not want to say 'how d'you do?' Her face returned to childhood because it wore that expression of inhuman innocence, of angelic hardness which ennobles children's faces. Her gaze wandered over Paris, over the sky from which the light drained a little earlier each day, with an impartial severity which possibly condemned nothing. She yawned nervously, stood upright and took a few absent-minded steps. Then she leant over again, forcing the cat to jump down. Saha stalked away with dignity and would have preferred to go back into the room. But the door in the hypotenuse had been shut and Saha patiently sat down. The next moment she had to get out of Camille's way for she was pacing from one partition to the other with long, jerky strides. The cat jumped back on to the parapet. As if in play, Camille dislodged her as she leant on her elbows and once again Saha took refuge against the closed door.

Motionless, her eyes far away, Camille stood with her back to her. Nevertheless the cat was looking at Camille's back and her breath came faster. She got up, turned two or three times on her own axis and looked questioningly at the closed door. Camille had not moved. Saha inflated her nostrils and showed a distress which was almost like nausea. A long, desolate mew escaped from her, the wretched reply to a silent, imminent threat. Camille faced round abruptly.

She was a trifle pale; that is to say, her rouge stood out in two oval moons on her cheeks. She affected an air of absent-mindedness as she would if a human eye had been staring at her. She even began to sing under her breath and resumed her pacing from one partition to the other, pacing to the rhythm of her song, but her voice failed her. She forced the cat, whom her foot was about to kick, to regain her narrow observation post with one bound, then to flatten herself against the door.

Saha had regained her self-control and would have died rather than utter a second cry. Tracking the cat down, without appearing to see her, Camille paced to and fro in silence. Saha did not jump on the parapet till Camille's feet were right on top of her and she only leapt down again on to the floor of the balcony to avoid the outstretched arm which would have hurled her from the height of the nine storeys.

She fled methodically and jumped carefully, keeping her eyes fixed on her adversary and condescending neither to fury nor to supplication. The most violent emotion of all, the terror of dying, soaked the sensitive soles of her paws with sweat so that they left flower-like prints on the stucco balcony.

Camille seemed the first to weaken and to lose her criminal strength. She made the mistake of noticing that the sun was going down, gave a glance at her wrist watch, and was aware of the clink of glasses inside. A moment or two more and her resolution would have deserted her as sleep deserts the somnambulist, leaving her guiltless and exhausted. Saha felt her enemy's firmness waver, hesitated on the parapet and Camille, stretching out both arms, pushed her into space.

She had time to hear the grating of claws on the rough-cast wall, to see Saha's blue body, twisted into an S, clutching the air with the force of a rising trout; then she shrank away, with her back to the wall.

She felt no temptation to look down into the little kitchen garden edged with new rubble. Back in the room, she put her hands over her ears, withdrew them and shook her head as if she could hear the hum of a mosquito. Then she sat down and nearly fell asleep. But the on-coming night brought her to her feet again. She drove away the twilight by lighting up glass bricks, luminous tubes and blinding mushrooms of lamps. She also lit up the long chromium eye which poured the opaline beam of its glance across the bed.

She walked about with supple movements, handling objects with light, adroit, dreaming hands.

"It's as if I'd got thinner," she said out loud.

She changed her clothes and dressed herself in white.

"My fly in the milk," she said, imitating Alain's voice. Her cheeks regained their colour at a sudden, sensual memory which brought her back to reality and she waited for Alain's arrival.

She bent her head in the direction of the buzzing lift and shivered at every noise; those dull knockings, those metallic clangs, those sounds as of a boat grinding at anchor, those muffled bursts of music which echo the discordant life of a new block of flats. But she was not surprised when the hollow tinkle of the bell in the hall replaced the fumbling of a key in the lock. She ran and opened the door herself.

"Shut the door," Alain ordered. "I must see first of all whether she hasn't hurt herself. Come and hold the lamp for me."

He carried Saha alive in his arms. He went straight to the bedroom, pushed aside the things on the invisible dressing-table and gently put the cat on the slab of glass She held herself upright and firm on her paws but her deep-set eyes wandered all about her as they would have done in a strange house.

"Saha!" called Alain in a whisper. "If there's nothing the matter with her, it's a miracle. Saha!"

She raised her head, as if to reassure her friend, and leant her cheek against his hand.

"Walk a little, Saha. Look, she's walking! Good Lord! Falling six storeys! It was the awning of the chap on the second floor that broke the fall. From there she bounced off on to the concierges' little lawn—the concierge saw her pass in the air. He said: 'I thought it was an umbrella falling,' What's she got on her ear? No, it's some white off the wall. Wait till I listen to her heart."

He laid the cat on her side and listened to the beating ribs, the tiny disordered mechanism. With his fair hair spread out and his eyes closed, he seemed to be sleeping on Saha's flank and to wake with a sign only to see Camille standing there silent and apart, watching the close-knit group they made.

"Can you believe it? There's nothing wrong. At least I can't find anything wrong with her except a terribly agitated heart. But a cat's heart is usually agitated. But however could it have happened! I'm asking you as if you could possibly know, my poor pet! She fell from this side," he said, looking at the open french window. Jump down on the ground, Saha, if you can."

After hesitating, she jumped but lay down again on the carpet. She was breathing fast and went on looking all round the room with the same uncertain look.

"I think I'll 'phone Chéron. Still, look, she's washing herself. She wouldn't wash herself if she'd been injured internally. Oh. good Lord!"

He stretched, threw his jacket on the bed and came over to Camille.

"What a fright. How pretty you look, all in white. Kiss me, my fly in the milk!"

She let herself fall into the arms which had remembered her at last and could not hold back some broken sobs.

"No? You're actually crying?"

He was upset himself and hid his forehead in the soft, black hair.

"I . . . I didn't know that you were kind."

She had the courage not to draw away from him at that. However, Alain quickly returned to Saha whom he wanted to take out on the balcony because of the heat. But the cat resisted and contented herself with lying near the open door, turned towards the evening blue, as herself. From time to time, she gave a brief shudder and looked anxiously into the triangular room behind her.

"It's the shock," explained Alain. "I wanted her to go and sit outside."

"Leave her alone," said Camille faintly, "since she doesn't want to."

"Her wishes are orders. Today, of all days! Is there likely to be anything eatable left over at this hour? It's half-past nine!"

Mother Buque wheeled the table out on to the balcony and they dined looking over the east side of Paris where the most lights glimmered. Alain talked a lot, drank water with a little wine in it and accused Saha of clumsiness, imprudence and "cat's sins".

" 'Cat's sins' are the kind of playful mistakes and lapses of judgment which can be put down to their having been civilised and domesticated. They've nothing in common with the clumsiness and carelessness that are almost deliberate."

But Camille no longer asked him: "How do you know that?" After dinner, he carried Saha and drew Camille into the studio where the cat consented to drink the milk she had refused. As she drank, she shivered all over as cats do when they are given something too cold to drink.

"It's the shock," Alain repeated. "All the same, I shall ask Chéron to look in and see her tomorrow morning. Oh, I'm forgetting everything!" he cried gaily. "Will you 'phone the concierge? I've left that roll of plans down in his lodge. The one that Massart, our precious furnishing chap, deposited there."

Camille obeyed while Alain, tired and relaxed after the strain, dropped into one of the scattered armchairs and closed his eyes.

"Hallo!" said Camille at the telephone. "Yes . . . That must be it. A big roll . . . Thanks so much."

He laughed with his eyes still closed. She had returned to his side and stood there, watching him laugh.

"That asburd little voice you put on! What is this new little voice? 'A big roll . . . Thanks so much'," he mimicked. "Do you keep that extremely small voice for the concierge? Come here, it needs the two of us to face Massart's latest creations."

He unrolled a sheet of thick drawing-paper, on the ebony table. Saha, who loved all kinds of paper, promptly leapt on the tinted drawing.

"Isn't she sweet!" exclaimed Alain. "It's to show me she's not in the least hurt. O my miraculously escaped one! Hasn't she a bump on her head? Camille, feel her head. No, she hasn't a bump. Feel her head all the same, Camille."

A poor little murderess meekly tried to emerge from her banishment, stretched out her hand and touched the cat's head with humble hatred.

Her gesture was received with the most savage snarl, a scream and an epileptic leap. Camille shrieked "Ha!" as

if she had been burned. Standing on the unrolled drawing
the cat covered the young woman with a flaming stare
of accusation; the fur on her back erect, her teeth bared
and the dry red of her open jaw showing.

Alain had sprung up, ready to protect Saha and
Camille from each other.

"Take care! She's . . . perhaps she's mad . . . Saha!"

She stared at him angrily but with a lucidity that
proved she had not lost her reason.

"What happened? Where did you touch her?"

"I didn't touch her at all."

They were both speaking low, hardly moving their
lips.

"Then, why this?" said Alain. "I don't understand.
Put your hand out again."

"No, I don't want to!" protested Camille. "Perhaps
she's gone wild," she added.

Alain took the risk of stroking Saha. She flattened her
erect fur and yielded to the friendly palm but glared once
more at Camille with brilliant, accusing eyes.

"Why *this*?" Alain repeated slowly. "Look, she's got
a scratch on her nose. I hadn't seen it. It's dried blood.
Saha, Saha, good now," he said, seeing the fury growing
in the yellow eyes.

Because her cheeks were swelled out and her whiskers
stiffly thrust forward as if she were hunting, the furious
cat seemed to be laughing. The joy of battle stretched
the mauve corners of her mouth and tautened the mobile,
muscular chin. The whole of her feline face was striving
towards a universal language, towards a word forgotten
by men.

"Whatever's *that*?" said Alain suddenly.

"Whatever's *what*?"

Under the cat's stare Camille was recovering her courage and the instinct of self-defence. Leaning over the drawing, Alain could make out damp prints in groups of four little spots round a central, irregular patch.

"Her paws . . . wet?" muttered Alain.

"She must have walked in some water," said Camille. "You're making a fuss about nothing."

Alain raised her head towards the dry blue night.

"In water? What water?"

He turned again to his wife. He looked at her with round eyes which made him look suddenly extraordinarily ugly.

"Don't you know what those footprints mean?" he said harshly. "No, *you* wouldn't know. Fear, d'you understand, *fear*. The sweat of fear. Cat's sweat, the only time cats *do* sweat. So she was frightened."

Delicately, he lifted one of Saha's front paws and dried the sweat on the fleshy pad. Then he pulled back the living white sheath into which the claws had been drawn back.

"She's got all her claws broken," he said, talking to himself. "She must have held on . . . clutching. She scratched the stone trying to save herself. She . . ."

He broke off his monologue and, without another word, took the cat under his arm and carried her off to the bathroom.

Alone, unmoving, Camille strained her ears. She kept her hands knotted together; free as she was, she seemed to be loaded with fetters.

"Madame Buque," said Alain's voice, "have you any milk?"

"Yes, Monsieur. In the 'fridge."

"Then it's ice-cold?"

"But I can warm it on the stove. It won't take a second. Is it for the cat? She's not ill, is she?"

"No, she's . . ."

Alain's voice stopped short and changed its tone: "She's a little off meat in this heat. Thank you, Madame Buque. Yes, you can go now. See you in the morning."

Camille heard her husband moving to and fro and turning on a tap. She knew that he was giving the cat food and fresh water. A diffused shadow, above the metal lampshade, came up as high as her face which was as still as a mask except for the slow movement of the great eyes.

Alain returned, carelessly tightening his leather belt, and sat down again at the ebony table. But he did not summon Camille back to sit beside him and she was forced to speak first.

"You've sent old Mother Buque off?"

"Yes. Shouldn't I have?"

He lit a cigarette and squinted at the flame of the lighter.

"I wanted her to bring something tomorrow morning. Oh, it doesn't matter a bit . . . don't apologise."

"But I'm not apologising. Though, actually, I ought to."

He went over to the open bay window, drawn by the blue of the night. He was studying a certain tremor in himself, a tremor which did not come from his recent emotion, but which was more like the tremolo of an orchestra, muffled and foreboding. From the Folie-Saint-James a rocket shot up, burst into luminous petals that withered one by one as they fell and the blue of the night recovered its peace and its powdery depth. In the amusement park, a grotto, a colonnade and a waterfall were suddenly lit up with incandescent white; Camille came nearer to him.

"Are they having a gala night? Let's wait for the fire-works. Do you hear the guitars?"

Absorbed in his inner tremor, he did not answer her. His wrists and hands were tingling, his loins were weak and felt as if a thousand insects were crawling over them. His state reminded him of the hateful lassitude, the fatigue he used to feel after the school sports. After running and rowing he would emerge vindictive; throbbing and exhausted and equally contemptuous of his victory or defeat. Now, he was at peace only in that part of himself which was no longer anxious about Saha. For several minutes—or perhaps for very few—ever since the discovery of the broken claws, ever since Saha's furious terror, he had lost all sense of time.

"It's not fireworks," he said. "Probably just some dances."

From the movement Camille made beside him in the shadow, he realised that she had given up expecting him to answer her. He felt her come closer without appre-hension. He saw the outline of the white dress; a bare arm; a half-face lit by the yellow light from the lamps indoors and a half-face that showed blue in the clear night. The two halves were divided by the small straight nose and each was provided with a large, almost unblinking eye.

"Yes, of course, it's dances," she agreed. "They're mandolines, not guitars. Listen . . . "*Les donneurs . . . de sé-é-réna . . . des, Et les bel-les é-écou-teu . . .*"

Her voice cracked on the highest note and she coughed to excuse her failure.

'But what a tiny voice . . .' thought Alain, astonished. 'What has she done with her voice that's as big and open as her eyes? She's singing in a little girl's voice. Hoarse, too.'

The mandolines stopped and the breeze brought a faint human noise of clapping and applause. A moment later, a rocket shot up, burst into an umbrella of mauve rays in which hung tears of living fire.

"Oh!" cried Camille.

Both of them had emerged from the darkness like two statues; Camille in lilac marble; Alain whiter, with his hair greenish and his eyes almost colourless. When the rocket had gone out, Camille sighed.

"It never lasts long enough," she said plaintively.

The distant music started again. But the capricious wind deadened the sound of the stringed instruments into a vague shrill buzzing and carried the blasts of the accompanying brass, on two notes, loudly and insistently right into their ears.

"What a shame," said Camille. "They've probably got a frightfully good jazz band. That's '*Love in the Night*' they're playing."

She hummed the tune in a high, shaky, almost in-audible voice, as if she had just been crying. This new voice of hers acutely increased Alain's disquiet. It induced in him a need for revelation, a desire to break down whatever it was that—a long time ago or only a moment ago?—had risen between himself and Camille. It was something to which he could not yet give a name but which was growing fast; something which prevented him from putting his arm round her neck like a boy; something which kept him motionless at her side, alert and expectant, against the wall still warm from the heat of the day. Turning impatient, he said: "Go on singing."

A long red, white and blue shower, falling like the branches of a weeping willow, streaked the sky over the park and showed Alain a Camille, startled and already defiant: "Singing what?"

"*Love in the Night* or anything else. It doesn't matter what."

She hesitated, then refused.

"Let me listen to the jazz . . . even from here you can hear it's simply marvellous."

He did not insist. He restrained his impatience and mastered the tingling which had now spread over his entire body.

A swarm of gay little suns, revolving brightly against the darkness, took flight. Alain secretly confronted them with the constellations of his favourite dreams.

'Those are the ones to remember. I'll try and take them with me down there,' he noted gravely. 'I've neglected my dreams too much.' At last, in the sky over the Folie, there rose and expanded a kind of straying pink and yellow dawn which burst into vermilion discs and fiery ferns and ribbons of blinding metal.

The shouts of children on the lower balconies greeted this miraculous display. By its light, Alain saw a Camille absent and remote, absorbed in other lights in her own mind.

As soon as the night closed in again, his hesitation vanished and he slipped his own bare arm under Camille's. As he touched that bare arm, he fancied he could see it; its whiteness hardly tinged by the summer and clothed in a fine down that lay flat on the skin, reddish-brown on the forearm, paler near the shoulder.

"You're cold," he murmured. "You're not feeling ill?"

She began to cry very quietly and so promptly that Alain suspected she had been preparing her tears.

"No. It's you. It's you who . . . who don't love me."

He leant back against the wall and drew Camille against his hip. He could feel her trembling, and cold from her shoulders to her knees, bare above her rolled stockings. She clung to him faithfully, leaning all her weight on him.

"Aha, so I don't love you. Right! Is this another jealousy scene on account of Saha."

He felt a muscular tremor run through the whole of the body he was supporting, a renewal of energy and self-defence. Encouraged by the moment, by a kind of indescribable opportunism, he insisted: "Instead of adopting this charming animal, like me. Are we the only young couple who have a cat or a dog? Would you like a parrot or a marmoset—a pair of doves—a dog, to make me very jealous in my turn?"

She shook her shoulders, protesting with annoyance

through closed lips. With his head high, Alain carefully controlled his own voice and egged himself on. 'Go on, a few more bits of nonsense; fill her up and we'll get somewhere. She's like a jar that I've got to turn upside down to empty. Go on. Go on.'

"Would you like a little lion . . . or a baby crocodile of barely fifty? No? Come on, you'd much better adopt Saha. If you'd just take the least bit of trouble, you'd soon see. . . ."

Camille wrenched herself out of his arms so violently that he staggered.

"No!" she cried. "*That*, never! Do you hear me? *Never!*"

"Ah, now we've got it!' Alain said to himself with delight. He pushed Camille into the room, pulled down the outer blind, lit up the rectangle of glass in the ceiling and shut the window. With an animal movement, Camille rushed over to the window and Alain opened it again.

"On condition you don't scream," he said.

He wheeled the only armchair up to Camille and sat astride on the solitary chair at the foot of the wide, turned-down bed with its new, clean sheets. The oilcloth curtains, drawn for the night, gave a greenish cast to Camille's pale face and her creased white dress.

"Well?" began Alain. "No compromise possible? Appalling story? Either her or me?"

She answered with a brief nod and Alain realised that he must drop his bantering tone.

"What do you want me to say?" he went on, after a silence. "The only thing I don't want to say to you? You know very well I'll never give up this cat. I should be ashamed to. Ashamed in myself and ashamed before her."

"I know," said Camille.

"And before you," Alain finished.

"Oh, *me*!" said Camille, raising her hand.

"You count too," said Alain hardly. "Tell me. Is it only me you've anything against? You've no reproach against Saha except her affection for me?"

She answered only with a troubled, hesitant look and he was irritated at having to go on questioning her. He had thought that a short, violent scene would force all the issues; he had relied on this easy way out. But, after her one cry, Camille had stiffened defensively and was furnishing no fuel for a quarrel. He resorted to patience: "Tell me, my dear. What is it? Mustn't I call you my dear? Tell me, if it were a question of another cat and not Saha, would you be so intolerant?"

"Of course I wouldn't," she said very quickly. "You wouldn't love it as much as that one."

"Quite true," said Alain with loyal accuracy.

"Even a woman," went on Camille, beginning to get heated, "you probably wouldn't love a *woman* as much as that."

"Quite true," said Alain.

"You're not like most people who are fond of animals. No, you're *not*. Patrick's fond of animals. He takes big dogs by the scruff of their necks and rolls them over. He imitates cats to see the faces they make—he whistles to the birds."

"Quite. In other words, he's not difficult," said Alain.

"But you're quite different. You *love* Saha."

"I've never pretended not to. But I wasn't lying to

you, either, when I said to you: 'Saha's not your rival.' "

He broke off and lowered his eyelids over his secret which was a secret of purity.

"There are rivals *and* rivals," said Camille sarcastically.

Suddenly she reddened. Flushed with sudden intoxication, she advanced to Alain.

"I saw the two of you!" she almost shrieked. "In the morning, when you spend the night on your little divan. Before daybreak, I've seen you, both of you."

She pointed a shaking hand towards the balcony.

"Sitting there, the two of you . . . you didn't ever hear me! You were like that, cheek to cheek."

She went over to the window, recovered her breath and marched down on Alain again.

"It's for you to say honestly whether I'm wrong in being jealous of this cat and wrong in suffering."

He kept silence so long that she became angry again.

"Do speak! Do *say* something! At the point we've got to . . . What are you waiting for?"

"The sequel," said Alain. "The rest."

He stood up quietly, bent over his wife and lowered his voice as he indicated the french window: "It was you, wasn't it? You threw her over?"

With a swift movement she put the bed between herself and him but she did not deny it. He watched her escape with a kind of smile: "You threw her over," he said dreamily. "I felt very definitely that you'd changed everything between us. You threw her over . . . she broke her claws trying to clutch on to the wall."

He lowered his head, imagining the attempted murder.

"But *how* did you throw her over? By holding her by

the skin of her neck? By taking advantage of her being asleep on the parapet? Had you been planning this for a long time? You hadn't had a fight with each other first?"

He raised his head and stared at Camille's hands and arms.

"No, you've no marks. She accused you well and truly, didn't she, when I made you touch her? She was magnificent."

His eyes left Camille and embraced the night, the dust of stars, the tops of the three poplars which the lights in the room lit up.

"Very well," he said simply, "I'm going away."

"Oh listen . . . do *listen* . . ." Camille implored wildly, almost in a whisper.

Nevertheless, she let him go out of the room. He opened cupboards, talked to the cat in the bathroom. The sound of his footsteps warned Camille that he had changed into his outdoor shoes and she looked, automatically, at the time. He came in again, carrying Saha in a bulging basket which Mme. Buque used for shopping. Hurriedly dressed, with his hair dishevelled and a scarf round his neck, his untidiness so much suggested that of a lover that Camille's eyelids pricked. But she heard Saha moving in the basket and tightened her lips.

"As you see, I'm going away," repeated Alain. He lowered his eyes, lifted the basket a trifle and corrected himself with calculated cruelty. "*We're* going away."

He secured the wicker lid, explaining as he did so: "This was all I could find in the kitchen."

"You're going to your home?" inquired Camille, forcing herself to imitate Alain's calm.

"But of course."

"Are you . . . can I count on seeing you during the next few days?"

"Why, certainly."

Surprise made her weaken again. She had to make an immense effort not to plead, not to weep.

"What about you?" said Alain. "Will you stay here alone tonight? You won't be frightened? If you insisted, I'd stay, but . . ."

He turned his head towards the balcony.

"But, frankly, I'm not keen on it. What do you propose to say to your family?"

Hurt at his sending her, by implication, home to her people, Camille pulled herself together.

"I've nothing to say to them. These are things which only concern *me*, I presume. I've no inclination for family councils."

"I entirely agree with you . . . provisionally."

"Anyway, we can decide as from tomorrow."

He raised his free hand to ward off this threat of a future.

"No. Not tomorrow. Today there isn't any tomorrow."

In the doorway, he turned back.

"In the bathroom, you'll find my key and all the money we've got here."

She interrupted with irony: "Why not a hamper of provisions and a compass?"

She was putting on a brave act and surveyed him with one hand on her hip and her head erect on her handsome neck. 'She's building up my exit,' thought Alain. He wanted to reply with some similar last-minute coquetry, to

toss his hair over his forehead and give her that narrowed
look between his lashes which seemed to disdain what it
rested on. But he renounced a pantomime which would
look absurd when he was carrying a shopping-basket and
confined himself to a vague bow in Camille's direction.

She kept up her expression of bravado and her
theatrical stance. But before he went out, he could see
more clearly, at a distance, the dark circles round her
eyes and the moisture which covered her temples and her
smooth, unlined neck.

Downstairs, he crossed the street automatically, the
key of the garage in his hand. 'I can't do that,' he thought
and he retraced his steps towards the avenue some way
off where cruising taxis could be picked up at night.
Saha mewed two or three times and he calmed her with
his voice. 'I can't do that. But it really would be much
pleasanter to take the car. Neuilly is impossible at night.'
He was surprised, having counted on a blessed sense of
release, to find himself losing his composure as soon as
he was alone. Walking did not restore his calm. When,
at last, he found a stray taxi, the five-minute drive seemed
almost interminable.

He shivered in the warm night under the gas-jet,
waiting for the gate to be opened. Saha, who had recognised the smell of the garden, was giving short sharp
mews in the basket which he had put down on the
pavement.

The scent of the wistarias in their second flowering
came across the air and Alain shivered more violently,

stamping from one foot to the other as if it were bitterly cold. He rang again but the house gave no sign of life in spite of the solemn, scandalous clamour of the big bell. At last a light appeared in the little buildings by the garage and he heard old Émile's dragging feet on the gravel.

"It's me, Émile," he said when the colourless face of the old valet peered through the bars.

"Monsieur Alain?" said Émile, exaggerating his quavering voice. "Monsieur Alain's young lady isn't indisposed? The summer is so treacherous. Monsieur Alain has some luggage, I see."

"No, it's Saha. Leave her, I'll carry her. No, don't turn up the gas-lamps, the light might wake Madame. Just open the front door for me and go back to bed."

"Madame is awake—it was she who rang for me. I hadn't heard the big bell. In my first sleep, you see."

Alain hurried ahead to escape Émile's chatter and the sound of his shaky footsteps following him. He did not stumble at the turnings of the paths though there was no moon that night. The great lawn, paler than the flower-beds, guided him. The dead, draped tree in the middle of the grass looked like a huge standing man with his coat over his arm. The smell of watered geraniums made Alain's throat tighten and he stopped. He bent down, opened the basket with groping fingers and released the cat.

"Saha, our garden."

He felt her glide out of the basket and, from pure

tenderness, took no more notice of her. Like an offering, he gave her back the night, her liberty, the soft spongy earth, the wakeful insects and the sleeping birds.

Behind the shutters on the ground floor, a lighted lamp was waiting and Alain's spirits fell again. 'To have to talk again, to have to explain to my mother . . . explain what? It's so simple. It's so difficult."

All he longed for was silence, the room with the faded flowers on the wallpaper, his bed and, above all, for vehement tears; great sobs as raucous as coughs that would be his secret, guilty compensation.

"Come in, darling, come in."

He seldom went into his mother's room. His selfish aversion to medicine bottles and droppers, boxes of digitalis pills and homœopathic remedies dated from childhood and was as acute as ever. But he could not resist the sight of the narrow, unadorned bed and of the woman with the thick white hair who was heaving herself up on her wrists.

"You know, Mother, there's nothing extraordinary about all this."

He accompanied this idiotic statement with a smile of which he was promptly ashamed; a horizontal, stiff-cheeked smile. His tiredness had overwhelmed him in a sudden rush, making him do and say the exact opposite of what he meant to. He sat down by his mother's bedside and loosened his scarf.

"Forgive my appearance. I came just as I was. I arrive at preposterous times without giving you warning."

"But you did give me warning," said Mme. Amparat. She glanced at Alain's dusty shoes.

"Your shoes look like a tramp's."

"I've only come from my place, Mother. But it was a long time before I could find a taxi. I was carrying the cat."

"Ah," said Mme. Amparat, with an understanding look. "You've brought back the cat?"

"Yes, of course. If you knew . . ."

He stopped, restrained by an odd discretion. 'These are things one doesn't tell. These stories aren't for parents.'

"Camille's not very fond of Saha, Mother."

"I know," said Mme. Amparat.

She forced herself to smile and shook her wavy hair.

"That's extremely serious!"

"Yes. For Camille," said Alain spitefully.

He got up and paced about among the furniture. It had white covers on it for the summer like the furniture in houses in the provinces. Having made up his mind not to denounce Camille, he could find nothing more to say.

"You know, Mother, there haven't been any screams or smashing of crockery. The glass dressing-table's still intact and the neighbours haven't come rushing up. Only I just need a little . . . a little time to be by myself . . . to rest. I won't hide it from you. I'm at the end of my tether," he said, seating himself on the bed.

"No. You don't hide it from me," said Mme. Amparat. She laid a hand on Alain's forehead, turning up the young face, on which the pale stubble was beginning to show, towards the light. He complained, turning his changeable eyes away, and succeeded in holding off a little longer the storm of tears he had promised himself.

"If there aren't any sheets on my old bed, Mother, I'll wrap myself up in any old thing."

"There are sheets on your bed," said Mme. Amparat.

At that, he threw his arms round his mother and kissed her blindly on her eyes and cheeks and hair. He thrust his face into her neck, stammered "Good-night" and went out of the room, sniffing.

In the hall, he pulled himself together and did not go upstairs at once. The night which was ending called to him and so did Saha. But he did not go far. The steps down into the garden were far enough. He sat down on one of them in the darkness and his outstretched hand encountered the fur, the sensitive antennae-like whiskers and the cool nostrils of Saha.

She turned round and round on one spot according to the ritual of wild creatures when they caress. She seemed very small to him and light as a kitten. Because he was hungry himself, he thought she must be needing food.

"We'll eat tomorrow . . . quite soon now . . . it's almost daylight."

Already she smelt of mint and geranium and box. He held her there, trusting and perishable, promised, perhaps ten years of life. And he suffered at the thought of the briefness of so great a love.

'After you, probably anyone can have me who wants me. A woman, many women. But never another cat.'

A blackbird whistled four notes that rang through the whole garden. But the sparrows had heard it and answered. On the lawn and the massed flowerbeds, faint ghosts of colour began to appear. Alain could make out a sickly white, a dull red more melancholy than black itself, a yellow smeared on the surrounding green, a round yellow flower which began to revolve and become more yellow and was followed by eyes and moons. Staggering, dropping with sleep, Alain reached his room, threw off his clothes, uncovered the bed and was unconscious almost as soon as he had slipped between the cool sheets.

Lying on his back with one arm flung out and the cat, silent and concentrated, kneading his shoulder, he was falling straight like a plummet into the very depths of sleep when a start brought him back to the daylight, the swaying of the awakened trees and the blessed clanging of the distant trams.

'What's the matter with me? I wanted . . . Ah, yes! I wanted to cry.' He smiled and fell asleep again.

His sleep was feverish and crowded with dreams. Two or three times he thought he had woken up and was becoming conscious of where he was, but each time he was undeceived by the expression of the walls of his room. They were angrily watching the fluttering of a winged eye.

'But I'm asleep . . . of course, I'm asleep.'

'I'm asleep . . .' he answered again to the crunching gravel. 'I'm asleep, I tell you,' he called to two dragging feet that brushed against the door. The feet went away and the sleeper congratulated himself in his dream. But the dream had come to a head under the repeated solicitings and Alain opened his eyes.

The sun he had left on the window-sill in May had become an August sun and reached no further than the satiny trunk of the tulip-tree opposite the house. 'How the summer has aged,' Alain said to himself. He got up, naked, looked for something to wear and found some pyjamas, too short and too tight in the sleeves and a faded dressing-gown which he joyfully pulled on. The window summoned him but he was stopped by Camille's photograph which he had left, forgotten, by his bed. Curiously, he examined the inaccurate, retouched little portrait; whitened here, blackened there. 'It's more like her than I supposed,' he thought. 'How was it I didn't notice it? Four months ago I used to say "Oh, she's entirely different from that. Much more subtle, not nearly so hard." But I was wrong.'

The long, steady breeze ran through the trees with a murmur like a river's. Dazed and quite painfully hungry, Alain lay back on his pillows. 'How delightful it is, a convalescence.' To complete the illusion a knuckle tapped on the door and the bearded Basque woman entered, carrying a tray.

"But I'd have had breakfast in the garden, Juliette!"

A kind of smile appeared among the grey hairs on her face.

"I thought as much. Would Monsieur Alain like me to take the tray down?"

"No, no, I'm too hungry. Leave that there. Saha'll come in by the window."

He called the cat who rose from some invisible retreat as if she had come into existence at his call. She bounded up the vertical path of climbing plants and fell back again —she had forgotten her broken claws.

"Wait, I'm coming!"

He brought her back in his arms and they gorged themselves, she on milk and rusks, he on slices of bread and butter and scalding hot coffee. On one corner of the tray, a little rose adorned the lid of the honey-pot.

'It's not one of my mother's roses,' Alain decided. It was an ill-made, stunted little rose, picked from a low branch, that gave out the queer smell of a yellow rose. 'It's a little homage from the Basque.'

Saha, radiant, seemed to have grown plumper overnight. Her shirt-frill erect, her four darker stripes well marked between her ears, she stared at the garden with the eyes of a happy despot.

"How simple it all is, isn't it, Saha? For you, at any rate.'

Old Émile entered in his turn and insisted on removing Alain's shoes.

"There's one of the laces got very worn. Monsieur Alain hasn't another? It doesn't matter, I'll put one of my own laces in," he bleated with emotion.

'Decidedly, it's my gala-day,' said Alain to himself. The word drove him back by contrast to all the things that only yesterday had been daily bothers; time to get up and dress, time to go to the Amparat office, time to come back to lunch with Camille.

"But I've nothing on earth to put on!" he cried.

In the bathroom, he recognised the slightly rusty razor, the worn cake of pink soap and the old toothbrush and used them with the delight of a man who has got shipwrecked for fun. But he had to come down in the outgrown pyjamas as the Basque woman had carried off his clothes.

"Come Saha, Saha."

She went ahead and he ran after her uncertainly in a pair of frayed raffia sandals that kept threatening to slip off. He stretched out his shoulders to feel the cape of the mild sun fall on them and half-closed his eyes that had grown unaccustomed to the green reverberations of the lawns and the hot colours which blazed above a serried block of crimson love-lies-bleeding and a tuft of red salvias bordered with heliotrope.

'Oh, the same, the very same salvias!'

Alain had always known that little heart-shaped bed as red and invariably bordered with heliotropes. It was shaded by a lean, ancient cherry-tree which occasionally produced a few cherries in September.

"I can see six . . . seven. Seven green cherries!"

He was talking to the cat who, with empty, golden eyes, had her mouth half-open, almost overcome by the excessive scent of the heliotropes. Her face had the look of almost sickened ecstasy animals assume when confronted with an overpowering smell.

She ate a blade of grass to recover herself, listened to various voices and rubbed her nose against the hard twigs of the privet hedge. But she did not display any exuberance, any irresponsible gaiety and she walked nobly, surrounded by the tiny silver halo which outlined all her body.

'Thrown, from a height of nine storeys, Alain thought as he watched her. 'Grabbed . . . or pushed. Perhaps she defended herself . . . perhaps she escaped to be caught again and thrown over. Assassinated.'

He tried by such conjectures to arouse his just anger,

but he did not succeed. 'If I truly, deeply loved Camille, how furious I should be.' Around him shone his kingdom, threatened like all kingdoms. 'My mother assures me that in less than twenty years no one will be able to keep on houses and gardens like this. She's probably right. I'm quite willing to lose them. I don't want to let *them* come into them.'

He was shaken by the sound of a telephone ringing in the house. 'Come, come now! I'm not frightened, am I? Camille's not so stupid as to telephone me. To do her justice, I've never known a young woman so restrained in using that instrument.'

But he could not stop himself from running awkwardly towards the house, losing his sandals and tripping over pebbles, and calling out: "Mother! Who's that on the 'phone?"

The thick white dressing-gown appeared on the steps and Alain felt ashamed of having called out.

"How I love your big white dressing-gown, Mother! Always the same, always the same."

"Thank you very much on behalf of my dressing-gown," said Mme. Amparat.

She kept Alain waiting a moment before she said: "It was Monsieur Veuillet. It's half-past nine. Have you forgotten the ways of the house?"

She combed her son's hair with her fingers and buttoned up the too-tight pyjamas jacket.

"You're a pretty sight! I suppose you don't intend to spend the rest of your life as a ragamuffin?"

Alain was grateful to her for questioning him so adroitly.

"No question of that, Mother. In a moment, I'll get busy about all that."

Mme. Amparat tenderly interrupted his vague, wide gesture.

"Tonight . . . where will you be?"

"Here!" he cried, and the tears welled up in his eyes.

"Good gracious, what a child!" said Mme. Amparat and he took up the word with the earnestness of a boy-scout.

"Perhaps I am a child, Mother. That's why I want to think over what I ought to do to get out of this childishness."

"Get out of it how? By a divorce? That's a door that makes a lot of noise."

"But which lets in some air," he dared to retort sharply.

"Wouldn't a separation . . . a temporary one, give just as good results? What about a thorough rest or a little travel, perhaps?"

He threw up his arms indignantly.

"My poor dear Mother, you've no idea. You're a thousand miles from imagining."

He was going to bring it all out and tell her about the attempted murder.

"Very well then, leave me a thousand miles! Such things don't concern me. Have a little . . . a little reserve," said Mme. Amparat hastily and Alain took advantage of a misunderstanding which was due to her innate modesty.

"Now, Mother, there's still all the tiresome side to be thought of. I mean the family point of view which is all mixed up with the business side. From the Malmerts' point of view, my divorce will be quite indefensible, no matter how much Camille may be partly responsible. A bride of three and a half months! I can hear it all."

"Where do you get the idea that there's a business side involved? You and the little Malmert girl aren't running a firm together. A married couple is not a pair of business partners."

"I know, Mother. But if things turn out as I expect, there's bound to be a horrible period of formalities and interviews and so on. It's never as simple as everyone says, a divorce."

She listened to her son with gentle forbearance. She knew that certain causes produce unexpected results and that, all through his life, a man has to be born many times with no other assistance than that of chance, of bruises, of mistakes.

"It's never simple to leave anything we've wanted to attach to ourselves," said Mme. Amparat. "She's not so bad, that little Malmert. A little . . . coarse, a little lacking in manners. No, not so bad. At least, that's my way of seeing it. I don't want to impose it on you. We've plenty of time to think it over."

"I've taken care of that," said Alain with harsh politeness. "And, at the moment, I prefer to keep a certain story to myself."

His face suddenly lit up in a laugh that restored it to childhood. Standing up on her hindlegs, Saha, using her paw as a spoon, was fishing drowned ants out of a brimming watering-can.

"Look at her, Mother! Isn't she a miraculous cat?"

"Yes," sighed Mme. Amparat. "She's your chimera."

He was always surprised when his mother employed

an unusual word. He greeted this one with a kiss on her prematurely aged hand with its swollen veins and the little brown flecks which Juliette lugubriously called "earth-stains".

At the sound of the bell ringing at the gate, he jerked himself upright.

"Run and hide," said Mme. Amparat. "We're right in the way of the tradesmen. Go and dress yourself. Do you want the butcher's little boy to catch you in that extra-ordinary get-up?"

But they both knew perfectly well that it was not the butcher's little boy ringing at the visitor's gate. Mme. Amparat had already turned her back and was hurrying up the steps, holding up her dressing-gown in both hands. Behind the clipped hedge Alain could see the Basque woman retreating in disorder, her black silk apron flying in the wind, while a slither of slippers on the gravel announced the flight of old Émile. Alain cut off his escape.

"You have at least opened the gate?"

"Yes, Monsieur Alain. The young lady's behind her car."

He lifted terrified eyes to the sky, hunched up his shoulders, as if he were in a hailstorm, and vanished.

'Well, that's certainly something like a panic! I wish I'd had time to get dressed. Gracious, she's got a new suit!'

Camille had seen him and came straight up to him without overmuch haste. In one of those moments of almost hilarious anxiety that crop up on dramatic occasions, he thought confusedly: 'Perhaps she's come to lunch.'

Carefully and lightly made-up as she was, armed with black lashes and beautiful parted lips and shining teeth, she seemed all the same to lose her self-assurance when Alain came forward to meet her. For he was approaching without breaking away from the shelter of his protective atmosphere. He was treading his native lawn under the rich patronage of the trees, and Camille looked at him with the eyes of a poor person.

"Forgive me, I look like a schoolboy who's suddenly shot up out of all knowledge. We didn't arrange to meet this morning, did we?"

"No. I've brought you your big suitcase. It's packed full."

"But you shouldn't have done that!" he expostulated. "I'd have sent Émile round to-day to fetch it."

"Don't talk to me about Émile. I wanted to give him your case but the old idiot rushed off as if I'd got the plague. The case is down there by the gate."

She flushed with humiliation, biting the inside of her cheek. 'It's beginning well,' said Alain to himself.

"I'm terribly sorry. You know what Émile's like. Listen," he decided, "let's go on the lawn inside the yew-hedges. We'll be quieter there than in the house."

He promptly repented his choice for that clearing, enclosed in clipped yews and furnished with wicker chairs, had been the scene of their secret kisses in the old days.

"Wait while I dust the twigs off. You mustn't spoil the pretty suit. Incidentally, I don't know it, do I?"

"It's new," said Camille in a tone of profound sadness, as if she had said: "It's dead."

She sat sideways, looking about her. Two arched

arcades, one opposite the other, broke the circle of greenery. Alain remembered something Camille had once confided to him: "You've no idea how your beautiful garden used to frighten me. I used to come here like the little girl from the village who comes to play with the son of the grand people at the château, in their park. And yet, when you come to think of it . . ." She had spoilt everything by that last remark. That "when you come to think of it" implied the prosperity of Malmert Mangles compared with the declining house of Amparat.

He observed that Camille kept her gloves on. 'That's a precaution that defeats its own ends. Without those gloves it's possible I mightn't have thought about her hands, about what they've done. Ah, at last a little . . . just a little anger,' he said to himself, listening to his heartbeats. 'I've taken enough time about it.'

"Well," said Camille sadly, "well, what are you going to do? Perhaps you haven't decided yet."

"Oh yes. I've decided," said Alain.

"Ah!"

"Yes. I can't come back."

"I quite understand that there's no question of your coming back today."

"I don't want to come back."

"Not at all? Ever?"

He shrugged his shoulders:

"What does that mean, ever? I don't want to come back. Not now. I don't want to."

She watched him closely, trying to distinguish the false from the true, the deliberate irritation from the authentic shudder. He returned her suspicion for suspicion. 'She's small, this morning. She looks rather like a pretty shop-girl. She's lost in all this green. We've already exchanged a fair number of useless remarks.'

In the distance, through one of the arched arcades, Camille caught sight of traces of the 'alterations' on one side of the face of the house; a new window, some freshly-painted shutters. Bravely she threw herself into the path of danger: "Suppose I'd said nothing yester-day?" she suggested abruptly. "Suppose you'd known nothing?"

"What a superb woman's idea," he sneered. "It does you honour."

"Oh," said Camille, shaking her head. "Honour, honour. It wouldn't be the first time that the happiness of two married people depended on something that couldn't be owned up to . . . or wasn't owned up to. But I've got the idea that by *not* telling you, I'd only have made things worse than ever for myself. I didn't feel you were . . . I don't know how to put it."

Hunting for the word, she mimed it by clenching her hands together. 'She's wrong to draw attention to her hands,' thought Alain vindictively. 'Those hands that have sent someone to their death.'

"After all, you're so awfully little on my side," said Camille. "That's true, isn't it?"

That struck him. He had to admit, mentally, that she was right. He said nothing and Camille insisted plaintively in a voice he knew all too well.

"Isn't it true, you hateful man?"

"But, good God!" he burst out. "That's not the question. The only thing that can possibly interest me—

interest me in *you*—is to know whether you regret what you've done, whether you can't stop thinking about it, whether it makes you sick to think of it. Remorse, good heavens, remorse! There does exist such a thing as remorse!"

Carried away, he got up and strode round the circular lawn, wiping his brow on his sleeve.

"Ah!" said Camille with a contrite, affected expression. "Naturally, of course. I'd a million times rather *not* have done it. I must have lost my head."

"You're lying!" he cried, trying not to shout. "All you regret is that you didn't bring it off! One's only got to listen to you, to look at you with your little hat on one side and your gloves and your new suit—everything you've so carefully arranged to charm me. If you really had any regret, I'd see it in your face. I'd feel it!"

He was shouting now, in a low grating voice and was no longer quite master of the rage he had fostered. The worn stuff of his pyjamas burst at the elbow and he tore off nearly the whole of his sleeve and flung it on a bush.

At first Camille had eyes only for the gesticulating arm, extraordinarily white against the dark block of the yew hedge.

He put his hands over his eyes and forced himself to speak lower.

"A little blameless creature, blue as the loveliest dreams. A little soul. Faithful, capable of quietly, delicately dying if what she has chosen fails her. You held *that* in your hands, over empty space . . . and you opened your hands. You're a monster. I don't wish to live with a monster."

He uncovered his damp face and came nearer to Camille, trying to find words which would overwhelm her. Her breath came short and her eyes went from the white naked arm to the bloodless face which was no less white.

"An animal!" she cried indignantly. "You're sacrificing me to an animal. I'm your wife, all the same! You're leaving me for an animal!"

"An animal? Yes. An animal."

Apparently calm now, he hid behind a mysteriously informed smile. 'I'm perfectly willing to admit that Saha's an animal. If she's really one, what is there higher than this animal and how can I make Camille understand that? She makes me laugh, this barefaced little criminal, all virtue and indignation, who pretends to know what an animal is.' He was prevented from going further by the sound of Camille's voice.

"*You're* the monster?"

"Pardon?"

"Yes, *you*. Unfortunately I can't exactly explain why. But I assure you I'm right. *I* wanted to get rid of Saha. That wasn't at all admirable. But to kill something that gets in her way, that makes her suffer—it's the first idea that comes into a woman's head, especially a jealous woman's. It's perfectly normal. What's abnormal, what's monstrous, is you. It's . . ."

She was struggling to make herself understood and, at the same time, pointing to certain accidental things about Alain which did indeed suggest a kind of delirium: the torn-off sleeve; the trembling, insulting mouth; the cheek from which all the blood had retreated; the wild crest of dishevelled fair hair. He made no protest and did not deign to defend himself. He seemed lost in some exploration from which there was no return.

"If I'd killed . . . or wanted to kill . . . a woman out of jealousy, you'd probably forgive me. But since I raised my hand against the cat, you're through with me. And yet you don't want me to treat you as a monster."

"Have I said I didn't want you to?" he broke in haughtily.

She looked at him with terrified eyes and made a gesture of impotence. Sombre and detached, he watched the young, execrable gloved hand every time it moved.

"Now for the future, what are we going to do? What's going to happen to us, Alain?"

He was so brimming over with intolerance that he nearly groaned. He wanted to cry out: 'We separate, we keep silent, we sleep, we breathe without the other always there! I'll withdraw far, far away—under this cherry-tree for example, under the wing of that magpie. Or into the peacock's tail of the hose-jet. Or into my cold room under the protection of a little golden dollar, a handful of relics and a Russian Blue cat.'

He mastered himself and deliberately lied:

"But nothing, at the moment. It's too soon to make a . . . a decision. Later on, we'll see."

This final effort to be reasonable and sociable exhausted him. He tottered as soon as he took the first steps when he got up to accompany Camille. She accepted this vague conciliation with hungry hope.

"Yes, of course. It's much too soon. A little later on. Stay where you are, don't bother to come with me to the gate. With your sleeve, people will think we've been fighting. Listen, perhaps I'll go and get a little swimming at Ploumanach with Patrick's brother and sister-in-law. Because the mere idea of living with my family at this moment . . ."

"Yes, do that. Take the roadster," proposed Alain.

She flushed and thanked him too effusively.

"I'll give it you back, you know, the minute I get back to Paris. You may need it. Don't hesitate to ask me for it back. Anyway, I'll let you know when I'm going and when I get back."

'Already she's organising it all. Already she's throwing out the strands of her web, throwing out bridges. Already she's picking up the fabric, darning it, weaving the threads together again. It's horrifying. Is that what my mother admires in her? Perhaps, after all, it's very fine. I don't feel any more capable of understanding her than of making things up with her. How completely at ease she is in everything I find insupportable. If she'd only go now, if she'd only go away!'

She was going away, carefully avoiding holding out her hand to him. But, under the arcade of clipped trees, she dared vainly to brush against him with her ripening breasts. Left alone, he collapsed into a chair and near him, on the wicker table, suddenly, like a miracle, appeared the cat.

A bend in the path and a gap in the leaves allowed Camille to see Alain and the cat once more from the distance. She stopped short and made a movement as if to retrace her steps. But she swayed only for an instant and then walked away faster than ever. For while Saha, on guard, was following Camille's departure as intently as a human being, Alain was half-lying on his side, ignoring it. With one hand hollowed into a paw, he was playing deftly with the first green, prickly August chestnuts.

GIGI

Translated by
Roger Senhouse

"Don't forget you are going to Aunt Alicia's. Do you hear me, Gilberte? Come here and let me do your curls. Gilberte, do you hear me?"

"Couldn't I go there without having my hair curled, Grandmamma?"

"I don't think so!" said Madame Alvarez, quietly. She took an old pair of curling-irons, with prongs that ended in little round metal knobs, and put them to heat over the blue flame of a spirit-lamp while she prepared the tissue-papers.

"Grandmamma, couldn't you crimp my hair in waves down the side of my head for a change?"

"Out of the question. Ringlets at the very ends—that's as far as a girl of your age can possibly go. Now sit down on the footstool."

To do so, Gilberte folded up under her the heron-like legs of a girl of fifteen. Below her tartan skirt, she revealed ribbed cotton stockings to just above the knees, unconscious of the perfect oval shape of her knee-caps. Slender calf and high-arched instep—Madame Alvarez never let her eyes run over these fine points without regretting that her granddaughter had not studied dancing professionally. At the moment, she was thinking only of the girl's hair. She had corkscrewed the ends and fixed them in tissue-paper, and was now compressing the ash-blonde ringlets between the heated knobs. With patient, soft-fingered skill, she gathered up the full magnificent weight of finely kept hair into sleek ripples which fell to just below Gilberte's shoulders. The girl sat quite still. The smell of the heated tongs, and the whiff of vanilla in the curling-papers, made her feel drowsy. Besides, Gilberte knew that resistance would be useless. She hardly ever tried to elude the authority exercised by her family.

"Is Mamma singing Frasquita today?"

"Yes. And this evening in *Si j'étais Roi*. I have told you before, when you're sitting on a low seat you must keep your knees close to each other, and lean both of them together, either to the right or to the left, for the sake of decorum."

"But, Grandmamma, I've got on my drawers and my petticoat."

"Drawers are one thing, decorum is another," said Madame Alvarez. "Everything depends on the attitude."

"Yes. I know. Aunt Alicia has told me often enough," Gilberte murmured from under her tent of hair.

"I do not require the help of my sister," said Madame Alvarez testily, "to instruct you in the elements of propriety. On that subject, thank goodness, I know rather more than she does."

"Supposing you let me stay here with you today, Grandmamma, couldn't I go and see Aunt Alicia next Sunday?"

"What next!" said Madame Alvarez haughtily. "Have you any other *purposal* to make to me?"

"Yes, I have," said Gilberte. "Have my skirts made a little longer, so I don't have to fold myself up in a Z every time I sit down. . . . You see, Grandmamma, with my skirts too short, I have to keep thinking of my you-know-what."

"Silence! Aren't you ashamed to call it your you-know-what?"

"I don't mind calling it by any other name, only . . ."

Madame Alvarez blew out the spirit-lamp, looked at the reflection of her heavy Spanish face in the looking-glass above the mantelpiece, and then laid down the law.

"There is no other name."

A sceptical look passed across the girl's eyes. Beneath the cockle-shells of fair hair they showed a lovely dark blue, the colour of glistening slate. Gilberte unfolded with a bound.

"But, Grandmamma, all the same, do look! If only my skirts were just that much longer! Or if a small frill could be added!"

"That *would* be nice for your mother, to be seen about with a great gawk looking at least eighteen! In her profession! Where are your brains?"

"In my head," said Gilberte. "Since I hardly ever go out with Mamma, what would it matter?"

She pulled down her skirt, which had rucked up towards her slim waist, and asked, "Can I go in my everyday coat? It's quite good enough."

"That wouldn't show that it's Sunday! Put on your serge coat and blue sailor-hat. When will you learn what's what?"

When on her feet, Gilberte was as tall as her grandmother. Madame Alvarez had taken the name of a Spanish lover now dead, and accordingly had acquired a creamy complexion, an ample bust, and hair lustrous with brilliantine. She used too white a powder, her heavy cheeks had begun to draw down her lower eyelids a little, and so eventually she took to calling herself Inez. Her unchartered family pursued their fixed orbit around her. Her unmarried daughter Andrée, forsaken by Gilberte's father, now preferred the sober life of a second-lead singer in a State-controlled theatre to the fitful opulence of a life of gallantry. Aunt Alicia—none of her admirers, it seemed, had ever mentioned marriage—lived alone, on an income she pretended was modest. The family had a high opinion of Alicia's judgment, and of her jewels.

Madame Alvarez looked her granddaughter up and down, from the felt sailor-hat trimmed with a quill to the ready-made Cavalier shoes.

"Can't you ever manage to keep your legs together? When you stand like that, the Seine could flow between them. You haven't the shadow of a stomach, and yet you somehow contrive to stick it out. And don't forget your gloves, I beg of you."

Gilberte's every posture was still governed by the unconcern of childish innocence. At times she looked like Robin Hood, at others like a carved angel, or again like a boy in skirts; but she seldom resembled a nearly grown up girl. "How can you expect to be put into long skirts, when you haven't the sense of a child of eight?" Madame Alvarez asked. And Andrée sighed, "I find Gilberte so discouraging." To which Gilberte answered quietly, "If you didn't find *me* discouraging, then you'd find something else." For she was sweet and gentle, resigned to a stay-at-home life and seeing few people outside the family. As for her features, no one could yet predict their final mould. A large mouth, which showed beautiful strong white teeth when she laughed, no chin to speak of, and, between high cheekbones, a nose— "Heavens, where did she get that button?" whispered her mother under her breath. "If you can't answer that question, my girl, who can?" retorted Madame Alvarez. Whereupon Andrée, who had become prudish too late in life and disgruntled too soon, relapsed into silence, automatically stroking her sensitive larynx. "Gigi is just a bundle of raw material," Aunt Alicia affirmed. "It may turn out very well—and, just as easily, all wrong."

"Grandmamma, there's the bell! I'll open the door on my way out."

"Grandmamma," she shouted from the passage, "it's Uncle Gaston!"

She came back into the room with a tall, youngish-looking man, her arm linked through his, chattering to him with the childish pomposity of a schoolgirl out of class.

"What a pity it is, Tonton, that I've got to desert you so soon! Grandmamma wishes me to pay a call on Aunt Alicia. Which motor-car are you out in today? Did you come in the new four-seater de Dion-Bouton with the collapsible hood? I hear it can be driven simply with one hand! Goodness, Tonton, those are smart gloves, and no mistake! So you've had a row with Liane, Tonton?"

"Gilberte!" scolded Madame Alvarez. "What business of yours can that be?"

"But, Grandmamma, everybody knows about it. The whole story came out in *Gil Blas*. It began: *A secret bitterness is seeping into the sweet product of the sugar-beet.* . . .

At school, all the girls were asking me about it, for of course they know I know you. And I can tell you, Tonton, there's not a soul at school who takes Liane's side! They all agree that she's behaved disgracefully!"

"Gilberte!" repeated Madame Alvarez. "Say goodbye to Monsieur Lachaille, and run along!"

"Leave her alone, poor child," Gaston Lachaille sighed. "She, at any rate, intends no harm. And it's perfectly true that all's over between Liane and me. You're off to Aunt Alicia's, Gigi? Take my motor-car and send it back for me."

Gilberte gave a little cry, a jump of joy, and hugged Lachaille.

"Thank you, Tonton! Just think of Aunt Alicia's face! The concierge's eyes will be popping from her head!"

Off she went, with the clatter of a young filly not yet shod.

"You spoil her, Gaston," said Madame Alvarez.

But in this she was not altogether speaking the truth. Gaston Lachaille did not know how to "spoil" anyone—even himself. His luxuries were cut and dried: motor-cars, a dreary mansion on the Parc Monceau, Liane's monthly allowance and birthday jewels, champagne and baccarat at Deauville in the summer, at Monte Carlo in the winter. From time to time he would drop a fat cheque into some charity fund, or finance a new daily paper, or buy a yacht only to resell it almost at once to some Central European monarch: yet from none of this did he get any fun. He would say, as he looked at himself in the glass, "That's the face of a man who is branded." Because of his rather long nose and large dark eyes he was regarded on all sides as easy game. His commercial instinct and rich man's caution stood him in good stead, however; no one had succeeded in robbing him of his pearl studs, of his massive gold or silver cigarette-cases encrusted with precious stones, of his dark sable-lined top coat.

From the window he watched his motor-car start up. That year, fashionable automobiles were being built with a slightly higher body and a rather wider top, to accommodate the exaggerated hats affected by Caroline Otero, Liane de Pougy, and other conspicuous figures of 1899: and, in consequence, they would sway gently at every turn of the wheel.

"Mamita," said Gaston Lachaille, "you wouldn't make me a cup of camomile?"

"Two rather than one," answered Madame Alvarez. "Sit down, my poor Gaston."

From the depths of a dilapidated armchair she removed some crumpled illustrated papers, a stocking waiting to be darned, and a box of liquorice allsorts, known as *agents de change*. The jilted man settled down into it luxuriously, while his hostess put out the tray and two cups.

"Why does the camomile they brew at home always smell of faded chrysanthemums?" sighed Gaston.

"It's simply a matter of taking pains. You may not believe it, Gaston, but I often pick my best camomile flowers in Paris, on waste ground, insignificant little flowers you would hardly notice. But they have a taste that is *unesteemable*. My goodness, what beautiful cloth your suit is made of! That deep-woven stripe is as smart as can be. Just the sort of material your father liked! But, I must confess, he would never have carried it with such distinction."

Never more than once during the course of a conversation did Madame Alvarez evoke the memory of an elder Lachaille, whom she claimed to have known intimately. From her former relationship, real or invented, she drew no advantage other than the close friendship of Gaston Lachaille, and the pleasure to be derived from watching a rich man enjoying the comforts of the poor when he made himself at home in her old armchair. Under their gas-blackened ceiling, these three feminine creatures never asked him for pearls, chinchillas, or solitaire diamonds, and they knew how to converse with tact and due solemnity on scandalous topics traditional and recondite. From the age of twelve, Gigi had known that Madame Otero's string of large black pearls were "dipped"—that is to say, artificially tinted—while the three strings of her matchlessly graded pearl necklace were worth "a king's ransom"; that Madame de Pougy's seven rows lacked "life"; that Eugénie Fougère's famous diamond bolero was quite worthless; and that no self-respecting woman gadded about, like Madame Antokolski, in a coupé upholstered in mauve satin. She had obediently broken her friendship with a school friend, Lydia Poret, after the girl had shown her a solitaire, set as a ring, the gift of Baron Ephraim.

"A solitaire!" Madame Alvarez had exclaimed. "For a girl of fifteen! Her mother must be mad!"

"But Grandmamma," pleaded Gigi, "it's not Lydia's fault if the Baron gave it to her!"

"Silence! I'm not blaming the Baron. The Baron knows what is expected of him. But plain common-sense should have told the mother to put the ring in a safe at the Bank, while waiting."

"While waiting for what, Grandmamma?"

"To see how things turn out."

"Why not in her jewel-case?"

"Because one never knows. Especially as the Baron is the sort of man who might change his mind. If, on the other hand, he has declared himself openly, Madame Poret has only to withdraw her daughter from her studies. Until the matter has been properly cleared up, you will oblige me by not walking home with that little Poret. Whoever heard of such a thing!"

"But supposing she marries, Grandmamma?"

"Marries? Marries whom, pray?"

"Why, the Baron!"

Madame Alvarez and her daughter exchanged glances of stupefaction. "I find the child so discouraging," Andrée had murmured. "She comes from another planet."

"My poor Gaston," said Madame Alvarez, "is it really true, then, that you have broken with her? In some ways it may be the best thing for you; but in others I'm sure you must find it most upsetting. Whom can one trust, I ask you!"

Poor Gaston listened while he drank the scalding camomile. The taste of it gave him as much comfort as the sight of the plaster rose on the ceiling, still black from the hanging lamp now "converted to electricity", and still faithfully retaining its shade—a vast frilly bell of palest green. Half the contents of a work-basket lay strewn over the dining-room table, from which Gilberte had forgotten to remove her copy-book. Above the upright piano hung an enlarged photograph of Gilberte at eight months, as a pendant to a portrait in oils of Andrée, dressed for her part in *Si j'étais Roi*. The perfectly inoffensive untidiness, the ray of spring sunshine coming through the point-lace curtains, the warmth given out by a little stove kept at a low heat—all these homely things were like so many soothing potions to the nerves of a jilted and lonely millionaire.

"Are you positively in torment, my poor Gaston?"

"To be exact, I'm not in torment. I'm just very upset, as you say."

"I have no wish to appear inquisitive," said Madame Alvarez, "but how did it all happen? I've read the papers, of course; but can one believe what they say?"

Lachaille tugged at his small waxed moustache, and ran his fingers over his thick, cropped hair.

"Oh, much the same as on previous occasions. She waited for her birthday present, then off she trotted. And, into the bargain, she must needs go and bury herself in such a wretched little hole in Normandy—so stupid of her! Any fool could have discovered that there were only two rooms at the inn, one occupied by Liane, the other by Sandomir, a skating-instructor from the *Palais de Glace*."

"He's Polaire's tea-time waltzing-partner, isn't he? Oh, women don't know where to draw the line' nowadays! And just after her birthday, too! Oh, it's so tactless! What could be more unladylike!"

Madame Alvarez stirred the tea-spoon round and round in her cup, her little finger in the air. When she lowered her gaze, her lids did not quite cover her protuberant eyeballs, and her resemblance to George Sand became marked.

"I'd given her a rope," said Gaston Lachaille. "What you might call a rope—thirty-seven pearls. The middle one as big as the ball of my thumb."

He held out his white, beautifully manicured thumb, to which Madame Alvarez accorded the admiration due to a middle pearl.

"You certainly know how to do things in style," she said. "You come out of it extremely well, Gaston."

"I came out of it with a pair of horns, certainly."

Madame Alvarez did not seem to have heard him.

"If I were you, Gaston, I should try to get your own back on her. I should take up with some society lady."

"That's a nice pill to offer me," said Lachaille, who was absent-mindedly helping himself to the *agents de change*.

"Yes indeed, I might even say that sometimes the cure may prove worse than the disease," Madame Alvarez continued, tactfully agreeing with him. "Out of the frying-pan into the fire." After which she respected Gaston Lachaille's silence.

The muffled sounds of a piano penetrated through the ceiling. Without a word, the visitor held out his empty cup, and Madame Alvarez refilled it.

"Is the family all right? What news of Aunt Alicia?"

"Oh, my sister, you know, is always the same. She's smart enough to keep herself to herself. She says she would rather live in a splendid past than an ugly present. Her King of Spain, her Milan of Serbia, her Khedive, her rajahs by the half-dozen—or so she would have you believe! She is very considerate to Gigi. She finds her a trifle backward for her age, as indeed she is, and puts her through her paces. Last week, for instance, she taught her how to eat *homard à l'Américaine* in faultless style."

"Whatever for?"

"Alicia says it will be extremely useful. The three great stumbling-blocks in a girl's education, she says, are *homard à l'Américaine*, a boiled egg, and asparagus. Shoddy table manners, she says, have broken up many a happy home."

"That has been known," said Lachaille dreamily.

"Oh, Alicia is no fool! And it's just what Gigi requires —she is so greedy! If only her brain worked as well as her jaws! But she might well be a child of ten. And what breathtaking scheme have you got for the Battle of Flowers? Are you going to dazzle us again this year?"

"Oh Lord, no!" groaned Gaston. "I shall take advantage of my misfortune, and save on the red roses this year."

Madame Alvarez wrung her hands.

"Oh, Gaston, you mustn't do that! If you're not there, the procession will look like a funeral!"

"I don't care what it looks like," said Gaston gloomily.

"You're never going to leave the prize banner to people like Valérie Cheniaguine? Oh, Gaston, we can't allow that!"

"You will have to. Valérie can very well afford it."

"Especially since she does it on the cheap. Gaston, do

you know where she went for the ten thousand bunches thrown last year? She had three women tying them up for two days and two nights, and the flowers were bought in the market! In the market! Only the four wheels, and the coachman's whip, and the harness trappings bore the hall-mark of Lachaume."

"That's a dodge to remember!" said Lachaille, cheering up. "Good Lord! I've finished the liquorice!"

The tap-tap of Gilberte's marching footsteps could be heard crossing the outer room.

"Back already!" said Madame Alvarez. "What's the meaning of this?"

"The meaning," said the girl, "is that Aunt Alicia wasn't in good form. But I've been out in Tonton's 'tuf-tuf'."

Her lips parted in a bright smile.

"You know, Tonton, all the time I was in your automobile, I put on a martyred expression—like this— as if I was bored to death with every luxury under the sun. I had the time of my life."

She sent her hat flying across the room, and her hair fell tumbling over her forehead and cheeks. She perched herself on a rather high stool, and tucked her knees up under her chin.

"Well, Tonton? You look as if you were dying of boredom. What about a game of piquet? It's Sunday, and Mamma doesn't come back between the two performances. Who's been eating all my liquorice? Oh, Tonton, you can't get away with that! The least you can do is to send me some more to make up for it."

"Gilberte, your manners!" scolded Madame Alvarez.

"Your knees! Gaston hasn't the time to bother about your liquorice. Pull down your skirts! Gaston, would you like me to send her to her room?"

Young Lachaille, with one eye on the dirty pack of cards in Gilberte's hand, was longing simultaneously to give way to tears, to confide his sorrows, to go to sleep in the old armchair, and to play piquet.

"Let the child stay! In this room I can relax. It's restful. Gigi, I'll play you for twenty pounds of sugar."

"Your sugar's not very tempting. I much prefer sweets."

"It's the same thing. And sugar is better for you than sweets."

"You only say that because you make it."

"Gilberte, you forget yourself!"

A smile enlivened the mournful eyes of Gaston Lachaille.

"Let her say what she likes, Mamita. And if I lose, Gigi, what would you like? A pair of silk stockings?"

The corners of Gilberte's big, childish mouth fell.

"Silk stockings make my legs itch. I would rather . . ."

She raised the snub-nosed face of an angel towards the ceiling, put her head on one side, and tossed her curls from one cheek to the other.

"I would rather have an eau-de-nil Persephone corset, with rococo roses embroidered on the suspenders. No. I'd rather have a music-case."

"Are you studying music now?"

"No, but my older friends at school carry their copy-books in music-cases, because it makes them look like students at the Conservatoire."

"Gilberte, you are making too free!" said Madame Alvarez.

"You shall have your case, and your liquorice. Cut, Gigi."

The next moment, the heir of Lachaille-Sugar was deep in the game. His prominent nose, large enough to appear false, and his slightly negroid eyes did not in the least intimidate his opponent. With her elbows on the table, her shoulders on a level with her ears, and her blue eyes and red cheeks at their most vivid, she looked like a tipsy page. They both played passionately, almost in silence, exchanging occasional insults under their breath. "You spindly spider! You sorrel run to seed!" Lachaille muttered. "You old crow's beak!" the girl countered. The March twilight deepened over the narrow street.

"Please don't think I want you to go, Gaston," said Madame Alvarez, "but it's half-past seven. Will you excuse me while I just see about our dinner?"

"Half-past seven!" cried Lachaille, "and I'm supposed to be dining at Larue with de Dion, Feydeau, and one of the Barthous! This must be the last hand, Gigi."

"Why one of the Barthous?" asked Gilberte. "Are there several of them?"

"Two. One handsome and the other less so. The best known is the least handsome."

"That's not fair," said Gilberte. "And Feydeau, who's he?"

Lachaille plopped down his cards in amazement.

"Well, I declare! She doesn't know who Feydeau is! Don't you ever go to a play?"

"Hardly ever, Tonton."

"Don't you like the theatre?"

"I'm not mad about it. And Grandmamma and Aunt Alicia both say that going to plays prevents one from thinking about the serious side of life. Don't tell Grandmamma I told you."

She lifted the weight of her hair away from her ears, and let it fall forward again. "Phew!" she sighed. "This mane does make me hot!"

"And what do they mean by the serious side of life?"

"Oh, I don't know it all off by heart, Uncle Gaston. And, what's more, they don't always agree about it. Grandmamma says: 'Don't read novels, they only depress you. Don't put on powder, it ruins the complexion. Don't wear stays, they spoil the figure. Don't dawdle and gaze at shop windows when you're by yourself. Don't get to know the families of your school friends, especially not the fathers who wait at the gates to fetch their daughters home from school.' "

She spoke very rapidly, panting between words like a child who has been running.

"And on top of that Aunt Alicia goes off on another tack! I've reached the age when I can wear stays, and I should take lessons in dancing and deportment, and I should be aware of what's going on, and know the meaning of 'carat', and not be taken in by the clothes that actresses wear. 'It's quite simple,' she tells me. 'Of all the dresses you see on the stage, nineteen out of twenty would look ridiculous in the paddock.' In fact, my head is fit to split with it all! What shall you be eating at Larue this evening, Tonton?"

"How should I know! *Filets de sole aux moules*, for a

change. And of course, saddle of lamb with truffles. Do get on with the game, Gigi! I've got a point of five."

"That won't get you anywhere. I've got all the cards in the pack. Here, at home, we're having the warmed-up remains of the *cassoulet*. I'm very fond of *cassoulet*."

"A plain dish of *cassoulet* with bacon rind," said Inez Alvarez modestly, as she came in. "Goose was exorbitant this week."

"I'll have one sent to you from Bon-Abri," said Gaston.

"Thank you very much, Gaston. Gigi, help Monsieur Lachaille on with his overcoat. Fetch him his hat and stick!"

When Lachaille had gone, rather sulky after a regretful sniff at the warmed up *cassoulet*, Madame Alvarez turned to her granddaughter.

"Will you please inform me, Gilberte, why it was you returned so early from Aunt Alicia's? I didn't ask you in front of Gaston. Family matters must never be discussed in front of a third person, remember that!"

"There's no mystery about it, Grandmamma. Aunt Alicia was wearing her little lace cap to show me she had a headache. She said to me, 'I'm not very well.' I said to her, 'Oh! Then I mustn't tire you out. I'll go home again.' She said to me, 'Sit down and rest for five minutes.' 'Oh!' I said to her, 'I'm not tired. I drove here.' 'You drove here!' she said to me, raising her hands like this. As you may imagine, I had kept the motor-car waiting a few minutes, to show Aunt Alicia. 'Yes,' I said to her. 'The four-seater de-Dion-Bouton-with-the-collapsible-hood, which Tonton lent me while he was paying a call on us. He has had a rumpus with Liane.' 'Who do you think you're talking to?' she says to me. 'I've not yet got one foot in the grave! I'm still kept informed about public events when they're important. I know that he has had a rumpus with that great lamp-post of a woman. Well, you'd better run along home, and not bother about a poor ill old creature like me.' She waved to me from the window as I got into the motor-car."

Madame Alvarez pursed her lips.

"A poor ill old creature! She has never suffered so much as a cold in her life! I like that! What . . .?"

"Grandmamma, do you think he'll remember my liquorice and the music-case?"

Madame Alvarez slowly lifted her heavy eyes towards the ceiling.

"Perhaps, my child, perhaps."

"But, as he lost, he owes them to me, doesn't he?"

"Yes, yes, he owes them to you. Perhaps you'll get them after all. Slip on your pinafore, and set the table. Put away your cards."

"Yes, Grandmamma. Grandmamma, what did he tell you about Madame Liane? Is it true she hopped it with Sandomir and the rope of pearls?"

"In the first place, one doesn't say 'hopped it'. In the second, come here and let me tighten your ribbon, so that your curls won't get soaked in the soup. And finally, the sayings and doings of a person who has broken the rules of etiquette are not for your ears. These happen to be Gaston's private affairs."

"But, Grandmamma, they are no longer private, since everyone's talking about them, and the whole thing came out in *Gil Blas*."

"Silence! All you need to know is that the conduct of Madame Liane d'Exelmans has been the reverse of sensible. The ham for your mother is between two plates: you will put it in the larder."

Gilberte was asleep when her mother—Andrée Alvar, in small type on the Opéra-Comique play-bills—returned home. Madame Alvarez, the elder, seated at a game of patience, enquired from force of habit whether she was not too tired. Following polite family custom, Andrée reproached her mother for having waited up, and Madame Alvarez made her ritual reply.

"I shouldn't sleep in peace unless I knew you were in. There is some ham, and a little bowl of warm *cassoulet*. And some stewed prunes. The beer is on the window-sill."

"The child is in bed?"

"Of course."

Andrée Alvar made a solid meal—pessimists have good appetites. She still looked pretty in theatrical make-up. Without it, the rims of her eyes were pink and her lips colourless. For this reason, Aunt Alicia declared Andrée never met with the admiration in real life that she gained on the stage.

"Did you sing well, my child?"

"Yes, I sang well. But where does it get me? All the applause goes to Tiphaine, as you may well imagine. Oh dear, oh dear, I really don't think I can bear to go on with this sort of life."

"It was your own choice. But you would bear it much

better," said Madame Alvarez sententiously, "if you had someone! It's your loneliness that gets on your nerves, and you take such black views. You're behaving contrary to nature."

"Oh, Mother, don't start that all over again. I'm tired enough as it is. What news is there?"

"None. Everyone's talking of Gaston's break with Liane."

"That's certainly the case: even in the green-room at the Opéra-Comique, which can hardly be called up-to-date."

"It's an event of world-wide interest," said Madame Alvarez.

"Is there any idea of who's in the running?"

"I should think not! It's far too recent. He is in full mourning, so to speak. Can you believe it, at a quarter to eight he was sitting exactly where you are now, playing a game of piquet with Gigi? He says he has no wish to attend the Battle of Flowers."

"Not really!"

"Yes. If he doesn't go, it will cause a great deal of talk. I advised him to think twice before taking such a decision."

"They were saying at the Théâtre that a certain music-hall artiste might stand a chance," said Andrée. "The one billed as the Cobra at the Olympia. It seems she does an acrobatic turn, and is brought on in a basket hardly big enough for a fox-terrier, and from this she uncurls like a snake."

Madame Alvarez protruded her heavy lower lip in contempt.

"What an idea! Gaston Lachaille has not sunk to that level! A music-hall performer! Do him the justice to admit that, as befits a bachelor of his standing, he has always confined himself to the great ladies of the profession."

"A fine pack of bitches!" murmured Andrée.

"Be more careful how you express yourself, my child. Calling people and things by their names has never done anyone any good. Gaston's mistresses have all had an air about them. A liaison with a great professional lady is the only suitable way for him to wait for a great marriage, always supposing that some day he does marry. Whatever may happen, we're in the front row when anything fresh turns up. Gaston has such confidence in me! I wish you had seen him asking me for camomile! A boy, a regular boy! Indeed, he is only thirty-three. And all that wealth weighs so heavily on his shoulders."

Andrée's pink eyelids blinked ironically.

"Pity him, Mother, if you like. I'm not complaining, but all the time we've known Gaston, he has never given you anything except his confidence."

"He owes us nothing. And thanks to him we've always had sugar for our jams, and, from time to time, for my *curaçao*; and birds from his farm, and odds and ends for the child."

"If you're satisfied with that!"

Madame Alvarez held high her majestic head.

"Perfectly satisfied. And even if I was not, what difference would it make?"

"In fact, as far as we're concerned, Gaston Lachaille, rich as he is, behaves as if he wasn't rich at all. Supposing we were in real straits! Would he come to our rescue, do you suppose?"

Madame Alvarez placed her hand on her heart.

"I'm convinced that he would," she said. And after a pause, she added, "But I would rather not have to ask him."

Andrée picked up the *Journal* again, in which there was a photograph of Liane the ex-mistress. "When you take a good look at her, she's not so extraordinary."

"You're wrong," retorted Madame Alvarez. "She is extraordinary. Otherwise she would not be so famous. Successes and celebrity are not a matter of luck. You talk like those scatterbrains who say, 'Seven rows of pearls would look every bit as well on me as on Madame de Pougy. She certainly cuts a dash—but so could I.' Such nonsense makes me laugh. Take what's left of the camomile to bathe your eyes."

"Thank you, Mother. Did the child go to Aunt Alicia's?"

"She did indeed, and in Gaston's motor-car, what's more! He lent it to her. It can go at forty miles an hour, I believe! She was in the seventh heaven."

"Poor lamb, I wonder what she'll make of her life. She's quite capable of ending up as a mannequin or a saleswoman. She's so backward. At her age, I——"

There was no indulgence in the glance Madame Alvarez bestowed on her daughter.

"Don't boast too much about what you were doing when you were her age. If I remember rightly, at her age you were snapping your fingers at Monsieur Mennesson and all his flour-mills, though he was perfectly

ready to make you your fortune. Instead, you must needs
bolt with a wretched music-master."

Andrée Alvar kissed her mother's lustrous plaits.

"My darling Mother, don't curse me at this hour.
I'm so sleepy. Good night, Mother. I've a rehearsal
tomorrow at a quarter to one. I'll eat at the tea-shop
during the interval; don't bother about me."

She yawned and walked in the dark through the little
room where her daughter was asleep. All she could see
of Gilberte in the obscurity was a bush of hair and the
Russian braid of her nightdress. She locked herself into
the exiguous bathroom and, late though it was, lit the
gas under a kettle. Madame Alvarez had instilled into
her progeny, among other virtues, a respect for certain
rites. One of her maxims was, "You can, at a pinch, leave
the face till the morning, when travelling or pressed for
time. For a woman, attention to the lower parts is the
first law of self-respect."

The last to go to bed, Madame Alvarez was the first to
rise, and allowed the daily woman no hand in preparing
the breakfast coffee. She slept in the dining-sitting-room,
on a divan-bed, and, at the stroke of half-past seven, she
opened the door to the papers, the quart of milk, and the
daily woman—who was carrying the others. By eight
o'clock she had taken out her curling-pins, and her
beautiful coils were dressed and smooth. At ten minutes
to nine Gilberte left for school, clean and tidy, her hair
well-brushed. At ten o'clock Madame Alvarez was

"thinking about" the midday meal, that is, she got into her mackintosh, slipped her arm through the handle of her shopping net, and set off to market.

On that day, as on all other days, she made sure that her granddaughter would not be late; she placed the coffee-pot and the jug of milk piping hot on the table, and unfolded the newspaper while waiting for her. Gilberte came in fresh as a flower, smelling of lavender-water, with some vestiges of sleep still clinging to her. A cry from Madame Alvarez made her fully wide awake.

"Call your mother, Gigi! Liane d'Exelmans has committed suicide."

The child replied with a long drawn-out "Oooh!" and asked, "Is she dead?"

"Of course not. She knows what she's about."

"How did she do it, Grandmamma? A revolver?"

Madame Alvarez looked pityingly at her granddaughter.

"The idea! Laudanum, as usual. *'Doctors Morèze and Pelledoux, who have never left the heart-broken beauty's bedside, cannot yet answer for her life, but their diagnosis is reassuring. . . .'* My own diagnosis is that if Madame d'Exelmans goes on playing that game, she'll end by ruining her stomach."

"The last time she killed herself, Grandmamma, was for the sake of Prince Georgevitch, wasn't it?"

"Where are your brains, my darling? It was for Count Berthou de Sauveterre."

"Oh, so it was. And what will Tonton do now, do you think?"

A dreamy look passed across the huge eyes of Madame Alvarez.

"It's a toss-up, my child. We shall know everything in good time, even if he starts by refusing to give an interview to anybody. You must always start by refusing to give an interview to anybody. Then later you can fill the front page. Tell the concierge, by the way, to get us the evening papers. Have you had enough to eat? Did you have your second cup of milk, and your two pieces of bread and butter? Put on your gloves before you go out. Don't dawdle on the way. I'n going to call your mother. What a story! Andrée, are you asleep? Oh, so you're out of bed! Andrée, Liane has committed suicide!"

"That's a nice change!" muttered Andrée. "She's only the one idea in her head, that woman, but she sticks to it."

"You've not taken out your curlers yet, Andrée?"

"And have my hair go limp in the middle of rehearsal? No thank you!"

Madame Alvarez ran her eyes over her daughter, from the spiky tips of her curlers to the felt slippers. "It's plain that there's no man here for you to bother about, my child! A man in the house soon cures a woman of traipsing about in dressing-gown and slippers. What an excitement, this suicide! Unsuccessful, of course."

Andrée's pallid lips parted in a contemptuous smile: "It's getting too boring—the way she takes laudanum as if it was castor oil!"

"Anyhow, who cares about her? It's the Lachaille heir who matters. This is the first time such a thing has happened to him. He's already had, let me see. He's had Gentiane, who stole certain papers; then that foreigner, who tried to force him into marriage; but Liane is his first suicide. In such circumstances, a man so much in the public eye has to be extremely careful about what line he takes."

"Him! He'll be bursting with pride, you may be sure."

"And with good reason, too," said Madame Alvarez. "We shall be seeing great things before very long. I wonder what Alicia will have to say about the situation."

"She'll do her best to make a mountain of a molehill."

"Alicia is no angel. But I must confess that she is far-sighted. And that without ever leaving her room!"

"She's no need to, since she has the telephone. Mother, won't you have one put in here?"

"It's expensive," said Madame Alvarez, thoughtfully. "We only just manage to make both ends meet, as it is. The telephone is of real use only to important business-men, or to women who have something to hide. Now, if you were to change your mode of life—and I'm only putting it forward as a supposition—and if Gigi were to start on a life of her own, I should be the first to say, 'We'll have the telephone put in.' But we haven't reached that point yet, unfortunately."

She allowed herself a single sigh, pulled on her rubber gloves, and coolly set about her household chores. Thanks to her care, the modest flat was growing old without too many signs of deterioration. She retained, from her past life, the honourable habits of women who have lost their honour, and these she taught to her daughter and her daughter's daughter. Sheets never stayed on the beds longer than ten days, and the char-cum-washerwoman told everyone that the chemises and drawers of the ladies of Madame Alvarez' household were changed more often than she could count, and so were the table napkins. At any moment, at the cry of "Gigi, take off your shoes!" Gilberte had to remove shoes and stockings, exhibit white feet to the closest inspection, and announce the least suspicion of a corn.

During the week following Madame d'Exelmans' suicide, Lachaille's reactions were somewhat incoherent. He engaged the stars of the National Musical Academy to dance at a midnight fête held at his own house, and, wishing to give a supper party at the Pré-Catalan, he arranged for that restaurant to open a fortnight earlier than was their custom. The clowns, Footit et Chocolat, did a turn: Rita del Erido caracoled on horseback between the supper tables, wearing a divided skirt of white lace flounces, a white hat on her black hair with white ostrich feathers frothing round the relentless beauty of her face. Indeed, Paris mistakenly proclaimed, such was her beauty, that Gaston Lachaille was about to hoist her (astride) upon a throne of sugar. Twenty-four hours later, Paris remedied the mistake. For, owing to the false prophecies it had published, *Gil Blas* nearly lost the subsidy it received from Gaston Lachaille. A specialised weekly, *Paris en amour*, provided another red herring, under the headline: "*Young Yankee millionairess makes no secret of weakness for French sugar.*"

Madame Alvarez' ample bust shook with incredulous laughter when she read the daily papers: she had received

her information from none other than Gaston Lachaille
in person. Twice in ten days, he had found time to drop
in for a cup of camomile, to sink into the depths of the
now sagging conch-shaped armchair, and there forget
his business worries and his dislike of being unattached.
He even brought Gigi an absurd Russian leather music-
case with a silver-gilt clasp, and twenty boxes of liquorice. Madame Alvarez was given a *pâté de foie gras* and
six bottles of champagne, and of these bounties Tonton
Lachaille partook by inviting himself to dinner. Throughout the meal, Gilberte regaled them rather tipsily with
tittle-tattle about her school, and later won Gaston's
gold pencil at piquet. He lost with good grace, recovered
his spirits, laughed and, pointing to the child, said to
Madame Alvarez, "There's my best pal!" Madame
Alvarez' Spanish eyes moved with slow watchfulness
from Gigi's reddened cheeks and white teeth to Lachaille,
who was pulling her hair by the fistful. "You little devil,
you'd the fourth king up your sleeve all the time!"

It was at this moment that Andrée, returning from the
Opéra-Comique, looked at Gigi's dishevelled head rolling
against Lachaille's sleeve and saw the tears of excited
laughter in her lovely slate-blue eyes. She said nothing,
and accepted a glass of champagne, then another, and
yet another. After her third glass, Gaston Lachaille was
threatened with the Bell Song from *Lakmé*, at which point
her mother led her away to bed.

The following day, no one spoke of this family party
except Gilberte, who exclaimed, "Never, never in all my
life, have I laughed so much! And the pencil-case is real
gold!" Her unreserved chatter met with a strange silence,

or rather with "Now then, Gigi, try to be a little more serious!" thrown out almost absent-mindedly.

After that, Gaston Lachaille let a fortnight go by without giving a sign of life, and the Alvarez family gathered its information from the papers only.

"Did you see, Andrée? In the Gossip Column it says that Monsieur Gaston Lachaille has left for Monte Carlo. *The reason for this seems to be of a sentimental nature—a secret that we respect.* What next!"

"Would you believe it, Grandmamma, Lydia Poret was saying at the dancing class that Liane travelled on the same train as Tonton, but in another compartment! Grandmamma, do you think it can be true?"

Madame Alvarez shrugged her shoulders.

"If it was true, how on earth would those Porets know? Have they become friends with Monsieur Lachaille all of a sudden?"

"No, but Lydia Poret heard the story in her aunt's dressing-room at the Comédie Française."

Madame Alvarez exchanged looks with her daughter.

"In her dressing-room! That explains everything!" she exclaimed, for she held the theatrical profession in contempt, although Andrée worked so hard. When Madame Emilienne d'Alençon had decided to present performing rabbits, and Madame de Pougy—shyer on the stage than any young girl—had amused herself by miming the part of Columbine in spangled black tulle, Madame Alvarez had stigmatised them both in a single phrase, "What! have they sunk to that?"

"Grandmamma, tell me, Grandmamma, do you know him, this Prince Radziwill?" Gilberte went on again.

"What's come over the child today? Has she been bitten by a flea? Which Prince Radziwill, to begin with? There's more than one."

"I don't know," said Gigi. "The one who's getting married. Among the list of presents, it says here, *are three writing-sets in malachite.*' What is malachite?"

"Oh, you're being tiresome, child. If he's getting married, he's no longer interesting."

"But if Tonton got married, wouldn't he be interesting either?"

"It all depends. It would be interesting if he were to marry his mistress. When Prince Cheniaguine married Valérie d'Aigreville, it was obvious that the life she had led for him for the past fifteen years was all he wanted; scenes, plates flung across the room, and reconciliations in the middle of the Restaurant Durand, Place de la Madeleine. Clearly, she was a woman who knew how to make herself valued. But all that is too complicated for you, my poor Gigi."

"And do you think it's to marry Liane that they've gone away together?"

Madame Alvarez pressed her forehead against the window-pane, and seemed to be consulting the spring sunshine, which bestowed upon the street a bright side and shady one.

"No," she said, "not if I know anything about anything. I must have a word with Alicia. Gigi, come with me as far as her house; you can leave me there and find your way back along the quais. It will give you some fresh air, since, it would seem, one must have fresh air nowadays. I have never been in the habit of taking the air more than twice a year, myself, at Cabourg and at Monte Carlo. And I am none the worse for that."

That evening Madame Alvarez came in so late that the family dined off tepid soup, cold meat, and some cakes sent round by Aunt Alicia. To Gilberte's "Well, what did she have to say?" she presented an icy front, and replied in clarion tones:

"She says that she is going to teach you how to eat ortolans."

"Scrumptious!" cried Gilberte. "And what did she say about the summer frock she promised me?"

"She said she would see. And that there's no reason why you should be displeased with the result."

"Oh!" said Gilberte gloomily.

"She also wants you to go to luncheon with her on Thursday, sharp at twelve."

"With you, too, Grandmamma?"

Madame Alvarez looked at the willowy slip of a girl facing her across the table, at her high, rosy cheekbones beneath eyes as blue as an evening sky, at her strong even teeth biting a fresh-coloured but slightly chapped lip, and at the primitive splendour of her ash-gold hair.

"No," she said at last. "Without me."

Gilberte got up and wound an arm about her grandmother's neck.

"The way you said that, Grandmamma, surely doesn't mean that you're going to send me to live with Aunt Alicia? I don't want to leave here, Grandmamma!"

Madame Alvarez cleared her throat, gave a little cough, and smiled.

"Goodness gracious, what a foolish creature you are!

Leave here! Why, my poor Gigi, I'm not scolding you, but you've not reached the first stage towards leaving."

For a bell-pull, Aunt Alicia had hung from her front door a length of bead-embroidered braid on a background of twining green vine-leaves and purple grapes. The door itself, varnished and revarnished till it glistened, shone with the glow of a dark brown caramel. From the very threshold, where she was admitted by a "man-servant", Gilberte enjoyed in her undescriminating way an atmosphere of discreet luxury. The carpet, spread with Persian rugs, seemed to lend her wings. After hearing Madame Alvarez pronounce her sister's Louis XV little drawing-room to be "boredom itself", Gilberte echoed her words by saying: "Aunt Alicia's drawing-room is very pretty, but it's boredom itself!" reserving her admiration for the dining-room, furnished in pale almost golden lemon wood dating from the Directoire, quite plain but for the grain of a wood as transparent as wax. "I shall buy myself a set like that one day," Gigi had once said in all innocence.

"In the Faubourg Antoine, I dare say," Aunt Alicia had answered teasingly, with a smile of her cupid's bow mouth and a flash of small teeth.

She was seventy years old. Her fastidious taste was everywhere apparent: in her silver-grey bedroom with its red Chinese vases, in her narrow white bathroom as warm as a hot-house, and in her robust health, concealed by a pretence of delicacy. The men of her generation, when trying to describe Alicia de Saint-Efflam, fumbled for words and could only exclaim, "Ah, my deah fellow!" or "Nothing could give you the faintest ideah!" Those who had known her intimately produced photographs which younger men found ordinary enough. "Was she really so lovely? You wouldn't think so from her photographs!" Looking at portraits of her, old admirers would pause for an instant, recollecting the turn of a wrist like a swan's neck, the tiny ear, the profile revealing a delicious kinship between the heart-shaped mouth and the wide-cut eyelids with their long lashes.

Gilberte kissed the pretty old lady, who was wearing a peak of black Chantilly lace on her white hair, and, on her slightly dumpy figure, a tea-gown of shot taffeta.

"You have one of your headaches, Aunt Alicia?"

"I'm not sure yet," replied Aunt Alicia; "it depends on the luncheon. Come quickly; the eggs are ready! Take off your coat! What on earth is that dress?"

"One of Mamma's, altered to fit me. Are they difficult eggs today?"

"Not at all. *Œufs brouillés aux croutons*. The ortolans are not difficult, either. And you shall have chocolate cream. So shall I."

With her young voice, a touch of pink on her amiable wrinkles, and lace on her white hair, Aunt Alicia was the perfect stage marquise. Gilberte had the greatest reverence for her aunt. In sitting down to table in her presence, she would pull her skirt up behind, join her knees, hold her elbows close to her sides, straighten her shoulder-blades, and to all appearances become the perfect young lady. She would remember what she had been taught, break her bread quietly, eat with her mouth shut, and take care, when cutting her meat, not to let her forefinger reach the blade of her knife.

Today her hair, severely tied back in a heavy knot at the nape of her neck, disclosed the fresh line of her forehead and ears, and a very powerful throat, rising from the rather ill-cut opening of her altered dress. This was a dingy blue, the bodice pleated about a let-in piece and, to cheer up this patchwork, three rows of mohair braid had been sewn round the hem of the skirt, and three times three rows of mohair braid round the sleeves, between the wrist and the elbow.

Aunt Alicia, sitting opposite her niece and examining her through fine dark eyes, could find no fault.

"How old are you?" she asked suddenly.

"The same as I was the other day, Aunt. Fifteen and a half. Aunt, what do you really think of this business of Tonton Gaston?"

"Why? Does it interest you?"

"Of course, Aunt. It worries me. If Tonton takes up with another lady, he won't come and play piquet with us any more or drink camomile tea—at least not for some time. That would be a shame."

"That's one way of looking at it, certainly."

Aunt Alicia examined her niece critically, through narrowed eyelids.

"Do you work hard, in class? Who are your friends? Ortolans should be cut in two, with one quick stroke of the knife, and no grating of the blade on the plate. Bite up each half. The bones don't matter. Go on eating while you answer my question, but don't talk with your mouth full. You must manage it. If I can, you can. What friends have you made?"

"None, Aunt. Grandmamma won't even let me have tea with the families of my school friends."

"She is quite right. Apart from that, there is no one who follows you, no little clerk hanging round your skirts? No schoolboy? No older man? I warn you, I shall know at once if you lie to me."

Gilberte gazed at the bright face of the imperious old lady who was questioning her so sharply.

"Why, no, Aunt, no one. Has somebody been telling you tales about me? I am always on my own. And why does Grandmamma stop me from accepting invitations?"

"She is right, for once. You would only be invited by ordinary people—that is to say, useless people."

"And what about us? Aren't we ordinary people ourselves?"

"No."

"What makes these ordinary people inferior to us?"

"They have weak heads and dissolute bodies. Besides, they are married. But I don't think you understand."

"Yes, Aunt, I understand that we don't marry."

"Marriage is not forbidden to us. Instead of marrying 'at once', it sometimes happens that we marry 'at last'."

"But does that prevent me from seeing girls of my own age?"

"Yes. Are you bored at home? Well, be a little bored. It's not a bad thing. Boredom helps one to make decisions. What is the matter? Tears? The tears of a silly child who is backward for her age. Have another ortolan."

Aunt Alicia, with three glittering fingers, grasped the stem of her glass and raised it in a toast.

"To you and me, Gigi! You shall have an Egyptian cigarette with your coffee. On condition that you do not make the end of it wet, and that you don't spit out specks of tobacco—going *ptu, ptu.* I shall also give you a note to the *première vendeuse* at Béchoff-David, an old friend of mine who was not a success. Your wardrobe is going to be changed. Nothing venture, nothing have."

The dark blue eyes gleamed. Gilberte stammered with joy.

"Aunt! Aunt! I'm going to . . . to Bé——"

"—choff-David. But I thought you weren't interested in clothes?"

Gilberte blushed.

"Aunt, I'm not interested in home-made clothes."

"I sympathise with you. Can it be that you have taste? When you think of looking your best, how do you see yourself dressed?"

"Oh, but I know just what would suit me, Aunt! I've seen——"

"Explain yourself without gestures. The moment you gesticulate you look common."

"I've seen a dress . . . oh, a dress created for Madame Lucy Gérard! Myriads of tiny ruffles of pearl-grey silk muslin from top to bottom. And then a dress of lavender-blue cloth cut out on a black velvet foundation, the cut-out design making a sort of peacock's tail on the train."

The small hand with its precious stones flashed through the air.

"Enough! Enough! I see your fancy is to be dressed

like a leading *comédienne* at the Théâtre Français—and
don't take that as a compliment! Come and pour out the
coffee. And without jerking up the lip of the coffee-pot
to prevent the drop from falling. I'd rather have a footbath in my saucer than see you juggling like a waiter
in a café."

The next hour passed very quickly for Gilberte: Aunt
Alicia had unlocked a casket of jewels to use for a lesson
that dazzled her.

"What is that, Gigi?"

"A marquise diamond."

"We say, a marquise-shaped brilliant. And that?"

"A topaz."

Aunt Alicia threw up her hands and the sunlight,
glancing off her rings, set off a myriad scintillations.

"A topaz! I have suffered many humiliations, but this
surpasses them all. A topaz among my jewels! Why not
an aquamarine or a chrysolite? It's a jonquil diamond,
little goose, and you won't often see its like. And
this?"

Gilberte half-opened her mouth, as though in a dream.

"Oh! That's an emerald. Oh, how beautiful it is!"

Aunt Alicia slipped the large square-cut emerald on
one of her thin fingers and was lost in silence.

"Do you see," she said in a hushed voice, "that almost
blue flame darting about in the depths of the green light?
Only the most beautiful emeralds contain that miracle of
elusive blue."

"Who gave it to you, Aunt?" Gilberte dared to ask.

"A king," said Aunt Alicia simply.

"A great king?"

"No. A little one. Great kings do not give very fine stones."

"Why not?"

For a fleeting moment, Aunt Alicia proffered a glimpse of her tiny white teeth.

"If you want my opinion, it's because they don't want to. Between ourselves, the little ones don't either."

"Then who does give great big stones?"

"Who? The shy. The proud, too. And the bounders, because they think that to give a monster jewel is a sign of good breeding. Sometimes a woman does, to humiliate a man. Never wear seond-rate jewels; wait till the really good ones come to you."

"And if they don't?"

"Well, then it can't be helped. Rather than a wretched hundred-guinea diamond, wear a half-crown ring. In that case you can say, 'It's a memento. I never part with it, day or night.' Don't ever wear artistic jewellery; it wrecks a woman's reputation."

"What is an artistic jewel?"

"It all depends. A mermaid in gold, with eyes of chrysoprase. An Egyptian scarab. A large engraved amethyst. A not very heavy bracelet said to have been chased by a master-hand. A lyre or star, mounted as a brooch. A studded tortoise. In a word, all of them fright-ful. Never wear baroque pearls, not even as hat-pins. Beware, above all things, of family jewels!"

"But Grandmamma has a beautiful cameo, set as a medallion."

"There are no beautiful cameos," said Alicia with a toss of the head. "There are precious stones and pearls.

There are white, yellow, blue, blue-white or pink diamonds. We won't speak of black diamonds, they're not worth mentioning. Then there are rubies—when you can be sure of them; sapphires, when they come from Kashmir; emeralds, provided they have no fatal flaw, or are not too light in colour, or have a yellowish tint."

"Aunt, I'm very fond of opals, too."

"I am very sorry, but you are not to wear them. I won't allow it."

Dumbfounded, Gilberte remained for a moment open-mouthed.

"Oh! Do you too, Aunt, really believe that they bring bad luck?"

"Why in the world not? You silly little creature," Alicia went bubbling on, "you must pretend to believe in such things. Believe in opals, believe—let's see, what can I suggest—in turquoises that die, in the evil eye . . ."

"But," said Gigi, haltingly, "those are . . . are superstitions!"

"Of course they are, child. They also go by the name of weaknesses. A pretty little collection of weaknesses and a terror of spiders are our indispensable stock-in-trade with the men."

"Why, Aunt?"

The old lady closed the casket, and kept Gilberte kneeling before her.

"Because nine men out of ten are superstitious, nineteen out of twenty believe in the evil eye, and ninety-eight out of a hundred are afraid of spiders. They forgive us—oh! for many things, but not for the absence in us of their own feelings. What makes you sigh?"

"I shall never remember all that!"

"The important thing is not for you to remember, but for me to know it."

"Aunt, what is a writing-set in . . . in malachite?"

"Always a calamity. But where on earth did you pick up such terms?"

"From the list of presents at grand weddings, Aunt, printed in the papers."

"Nice reading! But, at least you can gather from it what kind of presents you should never give or accept."

While speaking, she began to touch here and there the young face on a level with her own, with the sharp-pointed nail of her index finger. She lifted one slightly chapped lip, inspected the spotless enamel of the teeth.

"A fine jaw, my girl! With such teeth, I should have gobbled up Paris, and the rest of the world into the bargain. As it was, I had a good bite out of it. What's this you've got here? A small pimple? You shouldn't have a small pimple near your nose. And this? You've squeezed a blackhead. You've no business to have such things, or to squeeze them. I'll give you some of my astringent lotion. You mustn't eat anything from the pork-butchers' except cooked ham. You don't put on powder?"

"Grandmamma won't let me."

"I should hope not. . . . Let me smell your breath. Not that it means anything at this hour, you've just had luncheon."

She laid her hands on Gigi's shoulders.

"Pay attention to what I'm going to say. You have it in your power to please. You have an impossible little nose, a nondescript mouth, cheeks rather like the wife of a *moujik*——"

"Oh, Aunt!" sighed Gilberte.

"But, with your eyes and eyelashes, your teeth, and your hair, you can get away with it, if you're not a perfect fool. As for the rest——"

She cupped her hands like conch-shells over Gigi's bosom and smiled.

"A promise, but a pretty promise, neatly moulded. Don't eat too many almonds; they add weight to the breasts. Ah! remind me to teach you how to choose cigars."

Gilberte opened her eyes so wide that the tips of her lashes touched her eyebrows.

"Why?"

She received a little tap on the cheek.

"Because—because I do nothing without good reason. If I take you in hand at all, I must do it thoroughly. Once a woman understands the tastes of a man, cigars included, and once a man knows what pleases a woman, they may be said to be well matched."

"And then they fight," concluded Gigi with a knowing air.

"What do you mean, they fight?"

The old lady looked at Gigi in consternation.

"Ah!" she added, "you certainly never invented the triple mirror! Come, you little psychologist! Let me give you a note for Madame Henriette at Béchoff."

While her aunt was writing at a miniature rose-pink escritoire, Gilberte breathed in the scent of the fastidiously furnished room. Without wanting them for herself, she examined the objects she knew so well but hardly appreciated: Cupid, the Archer, pointing to the hours on the mantelpiece; two rather daring pictures; a bed like the basin of a fountain and its chinchilla coverlet; a rosary of small seed pearls and the New Testament on the bedside table; two red Chinese vases fitted as lamps— a happy note against the grey of the walls.

"Run along, my little one. I shall send for you again quite soon. Don't forget to ask Victor for the cake you're to take home. Gently, don't disarrange my hair! And remember, I shall have my eye on you as you leave the house. Woe betide you if you march like a guardsman, or drag your feet behind you!"

The month of May fetched Gaston Lachaille back to Paris, and brought to Gilberte two well-cut dresses and a light-weight coat—"a sack-coat like Cléo de Mérode's" she called it—as well as hats and boots and shoes. To these she added, on her own account, a few curls over the forehead, which cheapened her appearance. She paraded in front of Gaston in a blue-and-white dress reaching almost to the ground. "A full seven and a half yards round, Tonton, my skirt measures!" She was more than proud of her slender waist, held in by a grosgrain sash with a silver buckle; but she tried every dodge to free her lovely strong neck from its whale-bone collar of "imitation Venetian point" which matched the tucks of the bodice. The full sleeves and wide-flounced skirt of blue-and-white striped silk rustled deliciously, and

Gilberte delighted in pecking at the sleeves, to puff them out just below the shoulder.

"You remind me of a performing monkey," Lachaille said to her. "I liked you much better in your old tartan dress. In that uncomfortable collar you look just like a hen with a full crop. Take a peep at yourself!"

Feeling a little ruffled, Gilberte turned round to face the looking-glass. She had a lump in one of her cheeks caused by a large caramel, out of a box sent all the way from Nice at Gaston's order.

"I've heard a good deal about you, Tonton," she retorted, "but I've never heard it said that you had any taste in clothes."

He stared, almost choking, at this newly-fledged young woman, then turned to Madame Alvarez.

"Charming manners you've taught her! I congratulate you!"

Whereupon he left the house without drinking his camomile tea, and Madame Alvarez wrung her hands.

"Look what you've done to us now, my poor Gigi!"

"I know," said Gigi, "but then why does he go for me? He must know by now, I should think, that I can give as good as I get!"

Her grandmother shook her by the arm.

"But think what you've done, you wretched child! Good heavens! when will you learn to think? You've mortally offended the man, as likely as not. Just when we are doing our utmost to——"

"To do what, Grandmamma?"

"Why! to do everything to make an elegant young lady of you, to show you off to advantage."

"For whose benefit, Grandmamma? You must admit that one doesn't have to turn oneself inside out for an old friend like Tonton!"

But Madame Alvarez admitted nothing: not even to her astonishment, when, the following day, Gaston Lachaille arrived in the best of spirits, wearing a light-coloured suit.

"Put on your hat, Gigi! I'm taking you out to tea."

"Where?" cried Gigi.

"To the *Réservoirs*, at Versailles!"

"Hurrah! Hurrah! Hurrah!" chanted Gilberte.

She turned towards the kitchen.

"Grandmamma, I'm having tea at the *Réservoirs*, with Tonton!"

Madame Alvarez appeared, and without stopping to untie the flowered satinette apron across her stomach, interposed her soft hand between Gilberte's arm and that of Gaston Lachaille.

"No, Gaston," she said simply.

"What do you mean, No?"

"Oh! Grandmamma!" wailed Gigi.

Madame Alvarez seemed not to hear her.

"Go to your room a minute, Gigi. I should like to talk to Monsieur Lachaille in private."

She watched Gilberte leave the room and close the door behind her; then, returning to Gaston, she met his dark, rather brutal stare without flinching.

"What is the meaning of all this, Mamita? Ever since yesterday, I find quite a change here. What's going on?"

"I shall be glad if you will sit down, Gaston. I'm tired," said Madame Alvarez. "Oh, my poor legs!"

She sighed, waited for a response that did not come, and then untied her apron, under which she was wearing a black dress with a large cameo pinned upon it. She motioned her guest to a high-backed chair, keeping the armchair for herself. Then she sat down heavily, smoothed her greying black coils, and folded her hands on her lap. The unhurried movement of her large, dark, lambent eyes, and the ease with which she remained motionless, were sure signs of her self-control.

"Gaston, you cannot doubt my friendship for you." Lachaille emitted a short, businesslike laugh, and tugged at his moustache. "My friendship and my gratitude. Nevertheless, I must never forget that I have a soul entrusted to my care. Andrée, as you know, has neither the time nor the inclination to look after the girl. Our Gilberte has not got the gumption to make her own way in the world, like so many. She is just a child."

"Of sixteen," said Lachaille.

"Of nearly sixteen," consented Madame Alvarez. "For years you have been giving her sweets and playthings. She swears by Tonton, and by him alone. And now you want to take her out to tea, in your automobile, to the *Réservoirs*!"

Madame Alvarez placed a hand on her heart.

"Upon my soul and conscience, Gaston, if there were only you and me, I should say to you, 'Take Gilberte anywhere you like. I entrust her to you blindly.' But there are always the others. The eyes of the world are on you. To be seen *tête-à-tête* with you, is, for a woman——"

Gaston Lachaille lost patience.

"All right, all right. I understand. You want me to

believe that once she is seen having tea with me, Gilberte is compromised! A slip of a girl, a flapper, a chit whom no one notices!"

"Let us say, rather," interrupted Madame Alvarez gently, "that she will be labelled. No matter where you put in an appearance, Gaston, your presence is remarked upon. A young girl who goes out alone with you is no longer an ordinary girl, or even—to put it bluntly—a respectable girl. Now our little Gilberte must not, above all things, cease to be an ordinary young girl, at least not by that method. So far as it concerns you, it will simply end in one more story to be added to the long list already in existence, but personally, when I read of it in *Gil Blas*, I shall not be amused."

Gaston Lachaille rose, paced from the table to the door, then from the door to the window, before replying.

"Very good, Mamita. I have no wish to vex you. I shan't argue," he said coldly. "Keep your precious child."

He turned round again to face Madame Alvarez, his chin held high.

"I can't help wondering, as a matter of interest, whom you are keeping her for! A clerk earning a hundred a year, who'll marry her and give her four children in three years?"

"I know the duty of a mother better than that," said Madame Alvarez composedly. "I shall do my best to entrust Gigi only to the care of a man capable of saying, 'I take charge of her and answer for her future.' May I have the pleasure of brewing you some camomile tea, Gaston?"

"No, thank you. I'm late already."

"Would you like Gigi to come and say goodbye?"

"Don't bother. I'll see her another time. I can't say when, I'm sure. I'm very much taken up these days."

"Never mind, Gaston; don't worry about her. Have a good time, Gaston."

Once alone, Madame Alvarez mopped her forehead, and went to open the door of Gilberte's room.

"You were listening at the door, Gigi!"

"No, Grandmamma."

"Yes, you had your ear to the key-hole. You must never listen at key-holes. You don't hear properly and so you get things all wrong. Monsieur Lachaille has gone."

"So I can see," said Gilberte.

"Now you must rub the new potatoes in a cloth; I'll sauté them when I come in."

"Are you going out, Grandmamma?"

"I'm going round to see Alicia."

"Again?"

"Is it your place to object?" said Madame Alvarez severely. "You had better bathe your eyes in cold water, since you have been silly enough to cry."

"Grandmamma!"

"What?"

"What difference could it make to you, if you'd let me go out with Tonton Gaston in my new dress?"

"Silence! If you can't understand anything about anything, at least let those who are capable of using their reason do so for you. And put on my rubber gloves before you touch the potatoes!"

Throughout the whole of the following week, silence reigned over the Alvarez household, except for a surprise visit, one day, from Aunt Alicia. She arrived in a hired brougham, all black lace and dull silk with a rose at her shoulder, and carried on an anxious conversation, strictly between themselves, with her younger sister. As she was leaving, she bestowed only a moment's attention on Gilberte, pecked at her cheek with a fleeting kiss, and was gone.

"What did she want?" Gilberte asked Madame Alvarez.

"Oh, nothing . . . the address of the heart specialist who treated Madame Buffetery."

Gilberte reflected for a moment.

"It was a lengthy one," she said.

"What was lengthy?"

"The address of the heart specialist. Grandmamma, I should like a *cachet*. I have a headache."

"But you had one yesterday. A headache doesn't last forty-eight hours!"

"Presumably my headaches are different from other people's," said Gilberte, offended.

She was losing some of her sweetness, and, on her return from school, would make some such remark as "My teacher has got his knife into me!" or complain of not being able to sleep. She was gradually slipping into a state of idleness, which her grandmother noticed, but did nothing to overcome.

One day Gigi was busy applying liquid chalk to her white canvas button boots, when Gaston Lachaille put in an appearance without ringing the bell. His hair was

too long, his complexion sun-tanned, and he was wearing
a broad check summer suit. He stopped short in front of
Gilberte, who was perched high on a kitchen stool, her
left hand shod with a boot.

"Oh! Grandmamma left the key in the door. That's just
like her!"

As Gaston Lachaille looked at her without saying a
word, she began to blush, put down the boot on the table
and pulled her skirt down over her knees.

"So, Tonton, you slip in like a burglar! I believe you're
thinner. Aren't you fed properly by that famous chef of
yours who used to be with the Prince of Wales? Being
thinner makes your eyes look larger, and at the same time
makes your nose longer, and——"

"I have something to say to your grandmother,"
interrupted Gaston Lachaille. "Run into your room,
Gigi!"

For a moment she remained open-mouthed; then she
jumped off her stool. The strong column of her neck, like
an archangel's, swelled with anger as she advanced upon
Lachaille.

"Run into your room! Run into your room! And
suppose I said the same to you? Who do you think you
are here, ordering me to run into my room? All right,
I'm going to my room! And I can tell you one thing; so
long as you're in the house, I shan't come out of it!"

She slammed the door behind her, and there was a
dramatic click of the bolt.

"Gaston," breathed Madame Alvarez, "I shall insist
on the child apologising. Yes, I shall insist. If necessary,
I'll..."

Gaston was not listening to her, and stood staring at the closed door.

"Now, Mamita," said he, "let us talk briefly and to the point."

"Let us go over it all once again," said Aunt Alicia. "To begin with, you are quite sure he said, 'She shall be spoiled, more than——' "

"Than any woman before her!"

"Yes, but that's the sort of vague phrase that every man comes out with. I like things cut and dried."

"Just what they were, Alicia, for he said that he would guarantee Gigi against every imaginable mishap, even against himself, by an insurance policy; and that he regarded himself more or less as her godfather."

"Yes, yes. Not bad, not bad. But vague, vague as ever."

She was still in bed, her white hair arranged in curls against the pink pillow. She was absent-mindedly tying and untying the ribbon of her nightdress. Madame Alvarez, pale, and as wan under her morning hat as the moon behind passing clouds, was leaning cross-armed against the bedside.

"And he added, 'I don't wish to rush anything. Above all, I am Gigi's best pal. I shall give her all the time she wants to get used to me.' There were tears in his eyes. And he also said, 'After all, she won't have to deal with a savage.' A gentleman, in fact. A perfect gentleman."

"Yes, yes. Rather a vague gentleman. And the child, have you spoken frankly to her?"

"As was my duty, Alicia. This is no time for us to be

treating her like a child from whom the cakes have to be
hidden. Yes, I spoke frankly. I referred to Gaston as a
miracle, as a god, as——"

"Tut, tut, tut," criticised Alicia. "I should have
stressed the difficulties rather: the cards to be played, the
fury of all those ladies, the conquest represented by so
conspicuous a man."

Madame Alvarez wrung her hands.

"The difficulties! The cards to be played! Do you
imagine she's like you? Don't you know her at all? She's
very far from calculating; she's——"

"Thank you."

"I mean she has no ambition. I was even struck by the
fact that she did not react either one way or the other. No
cries of joy, no tears of emotion! All I got from her was,
'Oh, yes! Oh, it's very considerate of him.' Then, only
at the very end, did she lay down as her conditions——"

"Conditions, indeed!" murmured Alicia.

"——that she would answer Monsieur Lachaille's
proposals herself, and discuss the matter alone with him.
In other words, it was her business, and hers only."

"Let us be prepared for the worst! You've brought a
half-wit into the world. She will ask for the moon and, if
I know him, she won't get it. He is coming at four
o'clock?"

"Yes."

"Hasn't he sent anything? No flowers? No little
present?"

"Nothing. Do you think that's a bad sign?"

"No. It's what one would expect. See that the child is
nicely dressed. How is she looking?"

"Not too well today. Poor little lamb——"

"Come, come!" said Alicia heartlessly. "You'll have time for tears another day—when she's succeeded in wrecking the whole affair."

"You've eaten scarcely anything, Gigi."

"I wasn't too hungry, Grandmamma. May I have a little more coffee?"

"Of course."

"And a drop of Combier?"

"Why, yes. There's nothing in the world better than Combier for settling the stomach."

Through the open window rose the noise and heat from the street below. Gigi let the tip of her tongue lick round the bottom of her liqueur glass.

"If Aunt Alicia could see you, Gigi!" said Madame Alvarez lightheartedly.

Gigi's only reply was a disillusioned little smile. Her old plaid dress was too tight across the breast, and under the table she stretched out her long legs well beyond the limits of her skirt.

"What can Mamma be rehearsing today that's kept her from coming back to eat with us, Grandmamma? Do you think there really is a rehearsal going on at her Opéra-Comique?"

"She said so, didn't she?"

"Personally, I don't think she wanted to eat here."

"What makes you think that?"

Without taking her eyes off the sunny window, Gigi simply shrugged her shoulders.

"Oh, nothing, Grandmamma."

When she had drained the last drop of her Combier, she rose and began to clear the table.

"Leave all that, Gigi. I'll do it."

"Why, Grandmamma? I do it as a rule."

She looked Madame Alvarez straight in the face, with an expression the old lady could not meet.

"We began our meal late, it's almost three o'clock and you're not dressed yet. Do pull yourself together, Gigi."

"It's never before taken me a whole hour to change my clothes."

"Won't you need my help? Are you satisfied your hair's all right?"

"It will do, Grandmamma. When the door-bell rings, don't bother, I'll go and open it."

On the stroke of four, Gaston Lachaille rang three times. A childish, wistful face looked out from the bedroom door, listening. After three more impatient rings, Gilberte advanced as far as the middle of the hall. She still had on her old plaid dress and cotton stockings. She rubbed her cheeks with both fists, then ran to open the door.

"Good afternoon, Uncle Gaston."

"Didn't you want to let me in, you bad girl?"

They bumped shoulders in passing through the door, said, "Oh, sorry!" a little too self-consciously, then laughed awkwardly.

"Please sit down, Tonton. D'you know, I didn't have time to change. Not like you! That navy blue serge couldn't look better!"

"You don't know what you're talking about! It's tweed."

"Of course. How silly of me!"

She sat down facing him, pulled her skirt over her knees, and they stared at each other. Gilberte's tomboy assurance deserted her; a strange woebegone look made her blue eyes seem twice their natural size.

"What's the matter with you, Gigi?" asked Lachaille softly. "Tell me something! Do you know why I'm here?"

She assented with an exaggerated nod.

"Do you want to, or don't you?" he asked, lowering his voice.

She pushed a curl behind her ear, and swallowed bravely.

"I don't want to."

Lachaille twirled the tips of his moustache between two fingers, and for a moment looked away from a pair of darkened blue eyes, a pink cheek with a single freckle, curved lashes, a mouth unaware of its power, a heavy mass of ash-gold hair, and a neck as straight as a column, strong, hardly feminine, all of a piece, innocent of jewellery.

"I don't want what you want," Gilberte began again. "You said to Grandmamma . . ."

He put out his hand to stop her. His mouth was slightly twisted to one side, as if he had the toothache.

"I know what I said to your grandmother. It's not worth repeating. Just tell me what it is you don't want. You can then tell me what you do want. I shall give it to you."

"You mean that?" cried Gilberte.

He nodded, letting his shoulders droop, as if tired out. She watched, with surprise, these signs of exhaustion and torment.

"Tonton, you told Grandmamma you wanted to make me my fortune."

"A very fine one," said Lachaille firmly.

"It will be fine if I like it," said Gilberte, no less firmly. "They've drummed into my ears that I am backward for my age, but all the same I know the meaning of words. 'Make me my fortune': that means I should go away from here with you, and that I should sleep in your bed."

"Gigi, I beg of you!"

She stopped, because of the strong note of appeal in his voice.

"But, Tonton, why should I mind speaking of it to you? You didn't mind speaking of it to Grandmamma. Neither did Grandmamma mind speaking of it to me. Grandmamma wanted me to see nothing but the bright side. But I know more than she told me. I know very well that if you make me my fortune, then I must have my photograph in the papers, go to the Battle of Flowers and to the races at Deauville. When we quarrel, *Gil Blas* and *Paris en amour* will tell the whole story. When you throw me over once and for all, as you did Gentiane des Cevennes when you'd had enough of her——"

"What! You've heard about that? They've bothered your head with all those old stories?"

She gave a solemn little nod.

"Grandmamma and Aunt Alicia. They've taught me that you're world-famous. I know too that Maryse

Chuquet stole your letters, and you brought an action against her. I know that Countess Pariewsky was angry with you, because you didn't want to marry a *divorcée*, and she tried to shoot you. I know what all the world knows."

Lachaille put his hand on Gilberte's knee.

"Those are not the things we have to talk about together, Gigi. All that's in the past. All that's over and done with."

"Of course, Tonton, until it begins again. It's not your fault if you're world-famous. But I haven't got a world-famous sort of nature. So it won't do for me."

In pulling at the hem of her skirt, she caused Lachaille's hand to slip off her knee.

"Aunt Alicia and Grandmamma are on your side. But as it concerns me a little, after all, I think you must allow me to say a word on the subject. And my word is, that it won't do for me."

She got up and walked about the room. Gaston Lachaille's silence seemed to embarrass her. She punctuated her wanderings with "After all, it's true, I suppose! No, it really won't do!"

"I should like to know," said Gaston at last, "whether you're not just trying to hide from me the fact that you dislike me. If you dislike me, you had better say so at once."

"Oh no, Tonton, I don't dislike you at all! I'm always delighted to see you! I'll prove it by making a suggestion in my turn. You could go on coming here as usual, even more often. No one would see any harm in it, since you're a friend of the family. You could go on bringing me liquorice, champagne on my birthdays, and on Sunday we should have an extra special game of piquet. Wouldn't that be a pleasant little life? A life without all this business of sleeping in your bed and everybody knowing about it, losing strings of pearls, being photographed all the time and having to be so careful."

She was absent-mindedly twisting a strand of her hair round her nose, and pulled it so tight that she snuffled and the tip of her nose turned purple.

"A very pretty little life, as you say," interrupted Gaston Lachaille. "You're forgetting one thing only, Gigi, and that is, I'm in love with you."

"Oh!" she cried. "You never told me that."

"Well," he answered uneasily. "I'm telling you now."

She remained standing before him, silent and breathing fast. There was no concealing her embarrassment; the rise and fall of her bosom under the tight bodice, the high colour on her cheeks, and the quivering of her close-pressed lips—albeit ready to open again and taste of life.

"That's quite another thing!" she cried at last. "But then you are a terrible man! You're in love with me, and you want to drag me into a life where I'll have nothing but worries, where everyone gossips about everyone else, where the papers print nasty stories. You're in love with me, and you don't care a fig if you let me in for all sorts of horrible adventures, ending in separations, quarrels, Sandomirs, revolvers, and lau . . . and laudanum."

She burst into violent sobs, which made as much noise as a fit of coughing. Gaston put his arms round her to bend her towards him like a branch, but she escaped and took refuge between the wall and the piano.

"But listen, Gigi! Listen to me!"

"Never! I never want to see you again! I should never have believed it of you. You're not in love with me, you're a wicked man! Go away from here!"

She shut him out from sight by rubbing her eyes with closed fists. Gaston had moved over to her and was trying to discover some place on her well-guarded face where he could kiss her. But his lips found only the point of a small chin wet with tears. At the sound of sobbing, Madame Alvarez had hurried in. Pale and circumspect, she had stopped in hesitation at the door to the kitchen.

"Good gracious, Gaston!" she said. "What on earth's the matter with her?"

"The matter!" said Lachaille. "The matter is that she doesn't want to."

"She doesn't want to!" repeated Madame Alvarez. "What do you mean, she doesn't want to?"

"No, she doesn't want to. I speak plainly enough, don't I?"

"No. I don't want to," whimpered Gigi.

Madame Alvarez looked at her granddaughter in a sort of terror.

"Gigi! It's enough to drive one raving mad! But I told you, Gigi. Gaston, as God is my witness, I told her——"

"You have told her too much!" cried Lachaille.

He turned his face towards the child, looking just a poor, sad, lovesick creature, but all he saw of her was a slim back shaken by sobs and a dishevelled head of hair.

"Oh!" he exclaimed hoarsely. "I've had enough of this!" And he went out, banging the door.

The next day, at three o'clock, Aunt Alicia, summoned by *pneumatique*, stepped out from her hired brougham. She climbed the stairs up to the Alvarez' floor—pretending to the shortness of breath proper to someone with a weak heart—and noiselessly pushed open the door, which her sister had left on the latch.

"Where's the child?"

"In her room. Do you want to see her?"

"There's plenty of time. How is she?"

"Very calm."

Alicia shook two angry little fists.

"Very calm! She has pulled the roof down about our heads, and she is very calm! These young people of today!"

Once again she raised her spotted veil and withered her sister with a single glance.

"And you, standing there, what do you propose doing?"

With a face like a crumpled rose, she sternly confronted the large pallid face of her sister, whose retort was mild in the extreme.

"What do I propose doing? How do you mean? I can't, after all, tie the child up!" Her burdened shoulders rose on a long sigh. "I surely have not deserved such children as these!"

"While you stand there wringing your hands, Lachaille has rushed away from here and in such a state that he may do something idiotic!"

"And even without his straw hat," said Madame Alvarez. "He got into his motor bare-headed! The whole street might have seen him!"

"If I were to be told that by this time he's already

become engaged, or is busy making it up with Liane, it would not surprise me in the least!"

"It is a moment fraught with destiny," said Madame Alvarez lugubriously.

"And afterwards, how did you speak to that little chit?" Madame Alvarez pursed her lips.

"Gigi may be a bit scatter-brained in certain things and backward for her age, but she's not what you say. A young girl who has held the attention of Monsieur Lachaille is not a little chit."

A furious shrug of the shoulders set Alicia's black lace quivering.

"All right, all right! With all due respect, then, how did you handle your precious princess?"

"I talked sense to her. I spoke to her of the family. I tried to make her understand that we sink or swim together. I enumerated all the things she could do for herself and for us."

"And what about nonsense? Did you talk nonsense to her? Didn't you talk to her of love, travel, moonlight, Italy? You must know how to harp on every string. Didn't you tell her that on the other side of the world the sea is phosphorescent, that there are humming-birds in all the flowers, and that you make love under gardenias in full bloom beside a moonlit fountain?"

Madame Alvarez looked at her spirited elder sister with sadness in her eyes.

"I couldn't tell her all that, Alicia, because I know nothing about it. I've never been further afield than Cabourg and Monte Carlo."

"Aren't you capable of inventing it?"

"No, Alicia."

Both fell silent. Alicia, with a gesture, made up her mind.

"Call the chit in to me. We shall see."

When Gilberte came in, Aunt Alicia had resumed all the airs and graces of a frivolous old lady and was smelling the tea-rose pinned near her chin.

"Good afternoon, my little Gigi."

"Good afternoon, Aunt Alicia."

"What is this Inez has been telling me? You have an admirer? And what an admirer! For your first attempt, it's a master-stroke!"

Gilberte acquiesced with a guarded, resigned little smile. She offered to Alicia's darting curiosity a fresh young face, to which the violet-blue shadow in her eyelids and the high colour of her mouth gave an almost artificial effect. For coolness' sake, she had dragged back the hair off her temples with the help of two combs, and this had drawn up the corners of her eyes.

"And it seems you have been playing the naughty girl, and tried your claws on Monsieur Lachaille! Bravo, my brave little girl!"

Gilberte raised incredulous eyes to her aunt.

"Yes, indeed! Bravo! It will only make him all the happier when you are nice to him again."

"But I am nice to him, Aunt. Only, I don't want to, that's all."

"Yes, yes, we know. You've sent him packing to his sugar refinery; that's perfect. But don't send him to the Devil; he's quite capable of going. The fact is, you don't love him."

Gilberte gave a little childish shrug.

"Yes, Aunt, I'm very fond of him."

"Just what I said, you don't love him. Mind you, there's no harm in that, it leaves you free to act as you please. Ah, if you'd been head over heels in love with him, then I should have been a little anxious. Lachaille is a fine figure of a man. Well built—you've only to look at the photographs of him taken at Deauville in bathing costume. He's famous for that. Yes, I should feel sorry for you, my poor Gigi. To start by having a passionate love-affair—to go away all by your two selves to the other side of the world, forgetting everything in the arms of the man who adores you, listening to the song of love in an eternal spring—surely things of that sort must touch your heart! What does all that say to you?"

"It says to me that when the eternal spring is over Monsieur Lachaille will go off with another lady. Or else that the lady—me if you like—will leave Monsieur Lachaille, and Monsieur Lachaille will hurry off to blab the whole story. And then the lady, still me if you like, will have nothing else to do but get into another gentleman's bed. I don't want that. I'm not changeable by nature, indeed I'm not."

She crossed her arms over her breasts and shivered slightly.

"Grandmamma, may I have a *cachet Faivre*? I want to go to bed. I feel cold."

"You great goose!" burst out Aunt Alicia, "a tuppenny-ha'penny milliner's shop is all you deserve! Be off! Go and marry a bank clerk!"

"If you wish it, Aunt. But I want to go to bed."

Madame Alvarez put her hand on Gigi's forehead.

"Don't you feel well?"

"I'm all right, Grandmamma. Only I'm sad."

She leaned her head on Madame Alvarez' shoulder, and, for the first time in her life, closed her eyes pathetically like a grown woman. The two sisters exchanged glances.

"You must know, my Gigi," said Madame Alvarez, "that we won't torment you to that extent. If you say you really don't want to——"

"A failure is a failure," said Alicia caustically. "We can't go on discussing it for ever."

"You'll never be able to say you didn't have good advice, and the very best at that," said Madame Alvarez.

"I know, Grandmamma, but I'm sad, all the same."

"Why?"

A tear trickled over Gilberte's downy cheek without wetting it, but she did not answer. A brisk peel of the door bell made her jump where she stood.

"Oh, it must be him," she said. "It is him! Grandmamma, I don't want to see him! Hide me, Grandmamma!"

At the low, passionate tone of her voice, Aunt Alicia raised an attentive head, and pricked an expert ear. Then she ran to open the door and came back a moment later. Gaston Lachaille, haggard, his eyes bloodshot, followed close behind her.

"Good afternoon, Mamita. Good afternoon, Gigi!" he said airily. "Please don't move, I've come to retrieve my straw hat."

None of the three women replied, and his assurance left him.

"Well, you might at least say a word to me, even if it's only How-d'you-do?"

Gilberte took a step towards him.

"No," she said. "You've not come to retrieve your straw hat. You have another one in your hand. And you would never bother about a hat. You've come to make me more miserable than ever."

"Really!" burst out Madame Alvarez. "This is more than I can stomach. How can you, Gigi! Here is a man who, out of the goodness of his generous heart——"

"If you please, Grandmamma, just a moment, and I shall have finished."

Instinctively she straightened her dress, adjusted the buckle of her sash, and marched up to Gaston.

"I've been thinking, Gaston. In fact, I've been thinking a great deal——"

He interrupted her, to stop her saying what he was afraid to hear.

"I swear to you, my darling——"

"No, don't swear to me. I've been thinking I would rather be miserable with you than without you. So . . ."

She tried twice to go on.

"So . . . There you are. How d'you do, Gaston, how d'you do?"

She offered him her cheek, in her usual way. He held her, a little longer than usual, until he felt her relax, and become calm and gentle in his arms. Madame Alvarez seemed about to hurry forward, but Alicia's impatient little hand restrained her.

"Leave well alone. Don't meddle any more. Can't you see she is far beyond us?"

She pointed to Gigi, who was resting a trusting head and the rich abundance of her hair on Lachaille's shoulder.

The happy man turned to Madame Alvarez.

"Mamita," he said, "will you do me the honour, the favour, give me the infinite joy of bestowing on me the hand . . ."

FINIS